OXFORD WORLD'S CLASSICS

PARZIVAL AND TITUREL

WOLFRAM VON ESCHENBACH's *Parzival* is a Middle High German verse adaptation and continuation of Chrétien de Troyes' Old French Grail romance, *Perceval* or *Le Conte del Graal*, which was left incomplete when Chrétien, the founder of the Arthurian romance, died around 1190. Wolfram is not recorded in any contemporary historical documents; by his own admission he was a Bavarian knight in reduced circumstances, married and with a daughter. Allusions to the siege of Erfurt in 1203 and the sack of Constantinople in 1204 suggest that *Parzival* was composed in the first decade of the thirteenth century. The elegiac *Titurel* fragments, which take up the story of two of the characters in *Parzival*, Schionatulander and Sigune, were probably composed later, in a strophic form unique to Wolfram. One strophe refers to the death of Landgrave Hermann of Thuringia in 1217; he was probably Wolfram's patron, or one of them. Hermann's death is also referred to in Wolfram's final work, the anti-crusading epic *Willehalm*. Nine love lyrics, including five highly erotic dawn songs or *albas*, are also attributed to Wolfram. Wolfram probably died before completing *Willehalm*, at some point in the 1220s.

Parzival has inspired and influenced works as diverse as Wagner's *Parsifal* and *Lohengrin*, Franz Kafka's *The Castle*, and Umberto Eco's *Baudolino*.

CYRIL EDWARDS is a Lecturer in German at St Peter's College, Oxford, and a Research Fellow of Oxford's Faculty of Medieval and Modern Languages. He is the author of *The Beginnings of German Literature*, and numerous articles on the medieval lyric, Old High German, and the role of the supernatural in European literature. He has previously translated many German lyrics, including Hans Sachs's 'Song of the Nose' for the King's Singers. The books he has translated include Bernhard Maier's *Dictionary of Celtic Religion and Culture*, and a volume of essays on *The Medieval Housebook*. He is currently working on translations of the Arthurian romances of Hartmann von Aue, *Erec* and *Iwein*.

RICHARD BARBER's reputation as a medievalist is based on long familiarity with a wide range of medieval sources, literary and historical, which he has explored to illuminate both the lives and the culture of the middle ages. His most recent book is *The Holy Grail: Imagination and Belief*; he has also written *The Knight and Chivalry*, which won a Somerset Maugham Award, and *Tournaments* (with Juliet Barker). Biographies include lives of *Henry II* and *Edward Prince of Wales and Aquitaine* (the Black Prince), and among his other books are an edition of John Aubrey's *Brief Lives* and anthologies of medieval literature (*Epics of the Middle Ages*, *Myths and Legends of the British Isles*, *Legends of Arthur*).

OXFORD WORLD'S CLASSICS

*For over 100 years Oxford World's Classics have brought
readers closer to the world's great literature. Now with over 700
titles—from the 4,000-year-old myths of Mesopotamia to the
twentieth century's greatest novels—the series makes available
lesser-known as well as celebrated writing.*

*The pocket-sized hardbacks of the early years contained
introductions by Virginia Woolf, T. S. Eliot, Graham Greene,
and other literary figures which enriched the experience of reading.
Today the series is recognized for its fine scholarship and
reliability in texts that span world literature, drama and poetry,
religion, philosophy and politics. Each edition includes perceptive
commentary and essential background information to meet the
changing needs of readers.*

OXFORD WORLD'S CLASSICS

WOLFRAM VON ESCHENBACH

Parzival

and Titurel

Translated with Notes by
CYRIL EDWARDS

With an Introduction by
RICHARD BARBER

OXFORD
UNIVERSITY PRESS

OXFORD
UNIVERSITY PRESS

Great Clarendon Street, Oxford OX2 6DP

Oxford University Press is a department of the University of Oxford.
It furthers the University's objective of excellence in research, scholarship,
and education by publishing worldwide in

Oxford New York

Auckland Cape Town Dar es Salaam Hong Kong Karachi
Kuala Lumpur Madrid Melbourne Mexico City Nairobi
New Delhi Shanghai Taipei Toronto

With offices in

Argentina Austria Brazil Chile Czech Republic France Greece
Guatemala Hungary Italy Japan Poland Portugal Singapore
South Korea Switzerland Thailand Turkey Ukraine Vietnam

Oxford is a registered trade mark of Oxford University Press
in the UK and in certain other countries

Published in the United States
by Oxford University Press Inc., New York

British Library Cataloguing in Publication Data

Data available

Library of Congress Cataloging in Publication

Data available

ISBN 978-0-19-953920-8

17

Typeset in Ehrhardt
by RefineCatch Limited, Bungay, Suffolk
Printed in Great Britain by
Clays Ltd, Elcograf S.p.A.

CONTENTS

PARZIVAL

TITUREL

INTRODUCTION

WOLFRAM VON ESCHENBACH wrote *Parzival*, a romance about the quest for the Grail set against the background of the court of King Arthur, in the early thirteenth century. Everything about it was relatively unfamiliar and novel: his subject matter, the Arthurian stories, was less than a century old, the idea of knightly romances barely fifty years old, and the Grail had first been imagined some twenty-five years earlier. Arthurian legend is so familiar to us today that it is hard to recapture the excitement and enthusiasm that it aroused in these early years. In order to understand *Parzival* and Wolfram's approach to his subject, we need to look back at how this extraordinary phenomenon came about.

The origins of the Arthurian romances

Arthur himself is a figure so obscure that we cannot even be sure that he existed, a shadow of a shadow in the fragments of history and poetry that survive concerning sixth-century Wales. The deeds ascribed to him have often, if not always, been those of other men; even the twelve great battles which the Welsh chronicler Nennius tells us about in the eighth century may be borrowed from other heroes, and the only contemporary record of his last victory over the Saxons at Mount Badon, centre of so much speculation and invention, does not mention his name. What inspired the Welsh poets, however, was not the hero himself, whoever he may have been, but an idea, an idea which was a rallying-call to a people in retreat, driven by the Saxons into the western extremities of the land that had once been theirs: 'Their land they shall lose, except wild Wales.' They hoped and believed that Arthur, who had once held the Saxons at bay, would one day return to conquer them.

And, in a manner of speaking, he has done so. Later medieval stories about him make him emperor of much of Europe; and his story was called 'the matter of Britain'. Arthur came to play a leading part in the literature of France and Germany, and later of England, conquering minds and imaginations if not bodies and lands. It is he, obscure and perhaps fictional, who is the archetypal medieval heroic figure, not the real and imperial Charlemagne, around whom a series of rival, but less inspiring, romances evolved.

Much of the credit for the creation of the figure of Arthur must go to Geoffrey of Monmouth, probably of Welsh blood, but trained in the courts of the Norman kings and the schools of Paris, who produced his *History of the Kings of Britain* around 1135. Seeking to record what scraps he could find of the Welsh past, he shaped a history of the British people which created an empire to rival those of Rome and of Charlemagne, in which Arthur almost conquers Rome. Geoffrey may have drawn on the historical careers of the emperors of the later Roman period who began as British generals to create a fiction which was far from implausible, and it caught the imagination of his contemporaries. A few historians grumbled that there was no trace of Arthur in reliable books, but for the most part Geoffrey's work was taken up with enthusiasm, and incorporated into historical chronicles, where it filled an awkward blank in the past.

From chronicles in Latin, the transition into literature was easy. Much literature was about history, ranging from sober versions of the past of great dynasties, such as the poems written for the Norman dukes, to more fantastic recreations of the exploits of French barons against the Saracens or against their fellow lords in the *chansons de geste*, literally 'songs about deeds'. Arthur's exploits fitted into this pattern, and took their place in this genre, whose parallels as poems for fighting men are the Norse sagas and *Beowulf*. But with the coming of a more leisured and sophisticated society, and with the advent of new ideas about the relationship between the sexes, these heroic and violent works were supplanted by an entirely new genre, which gathered up in its wake whatever was new and exciting: the idea of courtly love, the new enthusiasm for chivalry, the sport of tournaments, even the spiritual teachings of the Cistercian order and the debate about the real presence of Christ's body in the Mass.

One of the earliest of the romances—it is difficult to date them precisely—was the love story of Tristan and Iseult, which first appears around the middle of the twelfth century. We think of this now as part of the legends of Arthur, but like many of the elements in these legends, it was originally an independent tale. Its characters seem to have been based on historical figures from seventh-century

Cornwall, and the substance of the story is the love triangle between Mark, lord of Cornwall; Tristan, who owes him allegiance; and Iseult, Mark's wife, whom Tristan has wooed and won for him. It introduces the concept of what we might call today romantic love as a theme for a major literary work into western literature. (In fact, the theme had always been present from classical times, but had been relegated to scraps of lyrics in the margins of manuscripts.) At the same time, poets in the south of France, the troubadours, were developing a sophisticated variation of romantic love, which we today call courtly love, where the outright passion of the Tristan story is sublimated and diverted into an elaborate code of conduct. Their chosen mode of expression was, however, short intense lyrics rather than the telling of stories in verse.

Chrétien de Troyes

If morals and manners were becoming more sophisticated, so were the ideas about knighthood. It is at the same time that we find the concept of chivalry emerging, as a code of conduct for knights which extends beyond their purely military function, and makes of them a social caste with their own customs and beliefs. This transition coincides with the emergence of the Arthurian romances, whose first master was the poet Chrétien de Troyes. Working in the cultured circle of the court of Champagne, whose countess, Marie, Eleanor of Aquitaine's daughter, was an enthusiastic follower of the southern poets, he draws together the different strands we have outlined: love, chivalry, Arthur. Drawing on the love of action of the knights and the longing for love stories of the ladies, and blending both with the newly current 'Breton tales' of Celtic marvels and enchantments, he created a new world and cast a spell over medieval literature from which it never quite awoke.

Chrétien's earliest 'story of adventure', as he himself calls it, was written about 1160. The story of *Erec et Enide* is known to English readers from Tennyson's 'Enid': the hero is a knight 'forgetful of the tilt and tournament' for love of the fair maiden he has married. The greater part of the action takes place after Erec's marriage, and the crux is how Enide can prove her faith to him in the series of adventures that befall them. Here for the first time we meet the unequal heroic combats, the magical adversaries, and the enchanted castles that are the stock in trade of the romances; here too tournaments and knight-errantry come into their own. For it is essential to the style of the romances that the knight should wander forth in search of adventures; the duels and marvels that befall him are rarely hindrances to his journey, but are usually its very purpose. Erec sets out to retrieve his reputation and to test his wife's love for him, and in the course of his adventures achieves both his objectives. It is in the picture Chrétien paints of Enide and Erec's adoration of each other, Erec's forgetfulness of knighthood in her arms, and her unswerving loyalty in face of his trials, that his skill is apparent. It is a new window on the ways of men's hearts. Chrétien is concerned with what actually happens, not with the stylized courtships and literary games of the troubadours. Even the troubadour idea that a lover gains moral worth through his love is transmuted into practical terms. Erec, at a pause in the battle for the sparrowhawk, looks towards his lady 'as she utters heartfelt prayers for him. No sooner has he seen her than great strength has surged back into him. Her love and beauty have restored his great fighting spirit.' The lover wins physical prowess from his lady's eyes; and the power of love becomes a charm to give might to his sword.

Yet Chrétien was uncomfortable with one of the central stories of Arthurian romance, the love of Lancelot for Guinevere, because it lay outside the bounds of his moral code. He tells us that *Le Chevalier de la Charrette*, or *Knight of the Cart*, was written because 'my Lady of Champagne wishes me to undertake a romance'. Chrétien insists that 'the material and the treatment of it are given and furnished to him by the Countess, and he is simply trying to carry out her concern and intention'. He focuses on the relationship between the two rather than the ethics of the affair. The romance deals with Meleagant's kidnapping of Guinevere and Lancelot's efforts to rescue her. Lancelot's complete subservience to Guinevere as his lady is the most remarkable feature of the story. He rides in shame in the hangman's cart (from which he earns the nickname of the title) purely to reach Guinevere more quickly when his horse has been killed. Even after Guinevere has surrendered herself to him, she still commands his every movement; whether her whim is for her lover to play the coward or the hero in a tournament, Lancelot obeys with equal alacrity. It seems that Chrétien could not finish the story, which was completed by another hand.

With *Yvain*, Chrétien's masterpiece, we return to the old ground of the wooing and winning of a bride within the knightly conventions, and of the history of the marriage. It tells how Yvain wins the hand of Laudine through a magical adventure; how he forgets knighthood, but when he is recalled to Arthur's court, forgets his promise to Laudine to return to her within a year. She rejects him, and he falls into madness; but he rescues a lion, and in its company his adventures lead him back to reconciliation with Laudine. From the beginning, when Calogrenant starts his tale of the spring in the forest of Broceliande, the atmosphere is magical. Here, if water is poured from the spring on to a stone, a tempest arises and a knight appears to overthrow the challenger. Against this background, however, Chrétien draws his characters in bold strokes: Yvain, generous, noble, impulsive; Laudine, haughty, clever, yet truly loving; and Lunete (her confidante) shrewd and devoted. Only once does he fail to convince us that he knows exactly how their minds work, and that is in Yvain's desertion of Laudine after a mere fortnight of marriage, and his forgetfulness of his pledge. Chrétien merely says 'as the year passed by my lord Yvain had such success that my lord Gawain strove to honour him and caused him to delay so long that the whole year slipped by'. Though this is the hinge on which his plot turns, it perhaps demands no greater suspension of disbelief than the marvels which precede and follow it. *Yvain* remains a highly moral work. Punishment is meted out for Yvain's forgetfulness, and Laudine's determination not to forgive him is only softened by Yvain's great deeds in his disguise as the Knight of the Lion; he has to earn forgiveness through the quality of his knighthood. Chrétien's message is that knighthood practised aright brings its own salvation with it. The cycle of sin and redemption is closed within an earthly limit.

Chrétien and the Grail

We have looked in some detail at Chrétien's romances because Wolfram inherits so much from them in terms of the genre in which he is working and the conventions that it uses. Wolfram also inherits and develops Chrétien's greatest invention, the grail.

The grail has become such a familiar symbol today, as the Holy Grail, that it is difficult to grasp the fact that in the twelfth century it was totally unknown. A *graal* was an unusual word for a large serving dish, and it seems to be this that lies at the back of Chrétien's use of the name in his last romance, *Perceval* or *Le Conte del Graal* (*The Story of the Grail*). But it is used in the context of a story which takes us beyond the secular boundaries of chivalry to which Chrétien has so far kept. *Perceval* is the moral tale of a knight's education, both worldly and spiritual. The hero does not begin as an accomplished warrior but as a raw simpleton, who has to be taught everything about the world of chivalry. In the process Chrétien's view of the real purpose of knighthood emerges, as Perceval comes first to maturity in physical skills, and then grows to his full moral and spiritual stature. Chrétien treats both the physical and moral qualities of knighthood as though they could only find fulfilment in the spiritual end. Charity and faith supersede the thirst for glory, prowess, and love as the ultimate goal.

Religious and secular chivalry are not exclusive in *Perceval*. From the very first, however, Perceval's chivalry has a religious aura, which is totally foreign to Gawain: Gornemans knights him thus: 'Next the worthy man took the sword, girt it on him and kissed him, saying to him that he had conferred on him with this sword the highest order created and ordained by God, namely the order of chivalry, which must be free of all baseness.' When he parts from his mother, her advice is largely religious in tone: succour the weak and helpless, and always turn aside to pray and hear Mass. Such advice as she does give him on courtly ways he later misinterprets completely. Gornemans likewise tells him to avoid killing other knights, and to succour the helpless. Again, Perceval misinterprets Gornemans's worldly advice, which is simply not to talk too much. His uncle the hermit, much later in the story, repeats this religious advice, and adds the virtue of humility.

The grail appears in a scene which is the crux of the story. Perceval comes to the castle of a lame king, who welcomes him generously, and treats him as an honoured guest. Before supper is served that evening, a mysterious procession enters the hall: a boy comes in with a white lance, from the head of which blood flows, running down the shaft. He is followed by two boys with golden candlesticks, and then a girl, 'holding a grail between her hands. When she entered holding the grail, so brilliant a light appeared that the candles lost their brightness like the stars or the moon when the sun rises.' The grail, made of gold and the richest of jewels, is borne into an inner chamber and vanishes from sight. Perceval suppresses his natural curiosity for fear of being thought rude. The next day he learns that, if he had asked whom the grail served, his host would have been cured of his lameness, and he finds that the castle is deserted. He rides out, and the castle vanishes. The remainder of the romance is concerned with his quest for the castle and its maimed lord; but the story was not finished by Chrétien, who seems to have died before completing it. We do learn, however, in a later scene, that the grail is 'a very holy thing'; it contains a single wafer from the mass which sustains the king's aged father; and Perceval could not ask the question because of the sins he had committed before he became a knight.

This enigmatic grail was an instant success. Three continuations of Chrétien's unfinished poem were produced. And within twenty years of the point at which Chrétien himself stopped work, no less than four very different versions of the grail story had been created. From being a mysterious 'very holy object', it had been identified as the cup used at the Last Supper in which Christ's blood had been collected at the taking down of his body from the Cross by Joseph of Arimathea. It had caught the imagination of writers, and was to become a central feature of the story of Arthur and his court.

Arthur in Germany

The German poets of the late twelfth and early thirteenth century were the closest heirs of Chrétien. Chrétien's work was not the first to find its way across the Rhine from France: there were already versions of the Tristan story and of the Trojan legends taken from the French, and troubadour poetry won followers among German poets. Hartmann von Aue's adaptation of Chrétien's *Erec* is the first German romance of chivalry to survive. Hartmann came from the borders of southern Germany and Switzerland, and probably wrote his *Erec* in the last decade of the twelfth century, some thirty years after Chrétien. He is more interested in the knight's place in society, and the ethical values this implies, than in the analysis of character and emotion in which Chrétien specialized, though he develops this theme as well. He followed this some years later with a version of *Yvain* (transcribed as *Iwein*) in which the same traits appear, though the details are less lavish and more acutely observed. The other great

Arthurian writer in Germany at this time was Gottfried von Strassburg, who took the Anglo-Norman poems about Tristan and Iseult and reshaped them radically, infusing ideas about courtly love which are a world apart from the original fatalistic story of lovers united by a magic potion.

Wolfram von Eschenbach

Medieval authors are more often than not anonymous, and if not anonymous, merely a name on the parchment. Wolfram von Eschenbach, whose authorship of *Parzival* is attested not only by the manuscripts but by comments from his fellow poets, is only a little more than such a name. We have no legal documents that name him, and we can only deduce, with some hesitation, that he came from a little village called Eschenbach in Franconia; the village has renamed itself Wolframs-Eschenbach to make the connection more persuasive, but Wolfram describes himself as a Bavarian, and Eschenbach only became part of Bavaria in the nineteenth century. But none of the other Eschenbachs in the region can put forward a better claim.

Effectively, everything we know about Wolfram comes from what he himself tells us. By the time we have read his poem, we know a good deal about him: or we think we do. For a start, he claims that 'I don't know a single letter of the alphabet. There are plenty of people who take such as a starting-point—this adventure makes its way without books' guidance.' He tells us that he was so poor at home that even the mice were hard put to it to find something to eat. And he can be scathing about his fellow courtiers, telling his patron Hermann of Thuringia that he should employ someone like Keie, Arthur's notoriously bad-tempered seneschal, 'since true generosity has imposed upon you such a varied entourage—now an ignominious throng, now a noble press of people'. And elsewhere he says that he would never bring his wife to Arthur's court, because someone would soon be whispering sweet nothings in her ear, telling her that he was dying of love for her and if she would end his sufferings, he would serve her for evermore.

We can deduce that he may have been a knight, and was almost certainly experienced in warfare and knightly ways. He was also a career poet, writing for patrons, and therefore a member of a lord's court. Beyond that, we can only point to his character as revealed in his writing: but he is not a reliable witness. He is imaginative, outspoken, and quite prepared to play sophisticated games with his listeners or readers, so his declaration that he is illiterate is not to be taken at face value, and, while he was almost certainly not wealthy, he is unlikely to have been as poor as he claimed to be. Even his education and range of knowledge and culture is unclear, though the enormous range of references in his poetry means that he must have been well versed in Latin learning, and indeed in some surprising and rather obscure fields of knowledge as well. He shows particular interest in natural sciences, geography, astronomy, and medicine, and knows a good deal about Arab science as well as affairs in the Near East. He is prepared to make bold theological speculations, though in the case of his account of the 'neutral angels' and the grail, he later retracted what he had said, because it could have been taken for heresy. And he certainly knew the latest French romances as well as the *chansons de geste*, the heroic forerunners of the romances. Further evidence of his learned approach is to be found in the language he uses: his style is deliberately convoluted, and he is happy to invent new words, often coining them from the French. Even his contemporaries found his poem difficult: Gottfried von Strassburg attacks an unnamed poet whom he calls 'friend of the hare', and Wolfram is clearly intended. His hostile characterization of Wolfram's work does nonetheless give us some clues as to what we are in for: 'Inventors of wild tales, hired hunters after stories, who cheat with chains and dupe dull minds, who turn rubbish into gold for children, and from magic boxes pour pearls of dust . . . These same story-hunters have to send commentaries with their tales: one cannot understand them as one hears and sees them. But we for our part have not the leisure to seek the gloss in books of the black art.'

Wolfram's sources and the structure of Parzival

And there is indeed an air of the black art about Wolfram's poem. In broad terms, Wolfram's story is on the same lines as that of Chrétien, and his objective is similar, but, as we shall see, far from identical. In the first two books, Wolfram tells the story of Parzival's father, Gahmuret, a subject on which Chrétien offers only a few paragraphs. Wolfram's inspiration may well have been a romance similar to the Anglo-Norman dynastic poems such as *Beves of Hampton* and *Guy of Warwick*, which centre on the 'founding father' of a great noble family. In particular, Beves, the hero of the former, has eastern adventures which are not dissimilar in tone to those of Gahmuret. This addition to Chrétien's account of Perceval was, however, not a mere prologue, but an essential part of Wolfram's plan. Wolfram puts a different emphasis on Chrétien's theme of the development of the character of the hero. In Chrétien, the chivalric element is sub-servient to the spiritual journey. In Wolfram the spiritual element is only part of the chivalric whole, but because Parzival's destiny is to guard the Grail, it is an essential part.

From Book III onwards, the story follows the French original quite closely, though Wolfram handles the details very freely, reinventing them to his own taste. The French poet prefers sim-plicity and an almost reticent narration; Wolfram is picturesque and full of vivid images, and the story is told as if to an audience which is reacting to events as they are unfolded by the poet: he teases the listeners and jokes with them. *Le Conte del Graal* is, if you like, Romanesque, clean-lined, and restrained, while Wolfram is exuber-ant and Gothic. Wolfram follows Chrétien's poem up to the begin-ning of Book XIII, the point at which it was left unfinished. He does not seem to have known the continuations written by other hands, except perhaps the first of these; so from Book XIII to the end of the story his tale is original, and very different from the later French versions. In these pages he completes the account of Parzival's des-tiny, by bringing him to his rightful inheritance, the kingship of the Grail, and he concludes by glancing into the future at the exploits of Parzival's descendants.

Wolfram and 'Meister Kyot'

Within the pages where Wolfram is following Chrétien, there is one major deviation; and it is perhaps of this that Gottfried was thinking when he talked of the 'black art'. For Wolfram makes of the Grail something totally novel and startling. He is completely silent about the nature of the Grail when it first appears, but when Parzival's uncle Trevrizent explains the significance of what his nephew has seen, Wolfram declares that Parzival is about to 'learn the hidden tidings concerning the Grail', and offers as his excuse for the delay in revealing these secrets an assertion that such matters should not be related 'until the adventure took it, through words, to meet the stories' greeting'. What Wolfram tells us, however, is far from clear; indeed, there is an air of deliberate obfuscation. He tells us that 'Meister Kyot' found the tale 'in heathen script', yet 'it helped that baptism dwelt with him, or this tale would still be unheard. No heathen cunning could avail us to tell about the Grail's nature—how its mysteries were perceived.' Yet it is precisely the heathen Flegetanis who 'wrote about the Grail's adventure', while Kyot's own contribution was to 'seek for those tidings in Latin books, of where there had been a people fitting to tend the Grail and embrace such chastity'. What he found enabled him to tell the history of the Grail dynasty, Parzival's kin, and of their guardianship of the Grail.

Is this all in Wolfram's imagination, or did Kyot really exist? If we answer the latter question in the affirmative, we accept the existence of a lost Grail tradition of great importance; if we deny Kyot's existence, we have to be able to show that Wolfram could have imagined *Parzival* on the basis of existing French tradition. Medieval authors are usually vague about their fictitious sources. Wolfram tells us a good deal more about Kyot than is usual with such a source: he says that he came from Provence, wrote in French, and that he had lived in Toledo and could read Latin and Arabic. The connection with Toledo, the great centre of intellectual contact between Christian and Moslem scholars, ties in with Wolfram's keen interest in astronomical lore and abstruse natural history, but not with the actual story of Parzival as Wolfram tells it. Wolfram first invokes the name of Kyot quite suddenly, in the eighth book, as assurance that he has named a minor character correctly: Kyot found Parzival's adventures written in the heathen tongue, and translated them into French. He is cited in the same way at the end of Book VIII, but it is only in the account of the Grail we have just quoted that his full story emerges. The implication is that he translated Flegetanis's work, but found it unsatisfactory or incomplete, and searched elsewhere for the story of the Grail dynasty. Wolfram briefly cites him once more as an authority before the conclusion of the tale; but as he ends, he insists that Chrétien has told the story wrongly, and that Kyot's version is the correct one: 'If master Chrestien of Troyes has done this tale an injustice, Kyot, who sent us the true tidings, has good reason to wax wroth. Definitively, the Provençal tells how Herzeloyde's son won the Grail, as was decreed for him, when Anfortas forfeited it. From Provence into German lands the true tidings have been sent to us . . .' This is the only time that Wolfram names Chrétien, showing that he knows of the French poet's work; and he immediately conjures up Kyot in order to deny that he is dependent on the famous master of Arthurian romance. This relationship, of French original and German reworking, would have been the norm for German romances on Arthur at this time. Wolfram has to be different: *he* has found the original that lies behind the French story, and knows better than to follow the French slavishly. Furthermore, the ending of the story is not to be found in the romances which he has followed so far, and he therefore needs a new 'authority' to authenticate his tale, even though he increasingly puts himself forward as the creator of the work in the later books.

This scenario seems to offer a plausible sub-text to Wolfram's protestations. We can support it by pointing to his dependence on the French poems, and by showing the inconsistencies in his description of Kyot: a Provençal writer of the time would have written in Occitan, not French. This points to what may be a solution: knowing Wolfram's delight in playing with names, he has taken the name of the perfectly respectable Guiot de Provins, a real contemporary author, and has turned him into a Provençal rather than a native of Provins, to the south-east of Paris. The real Kyot never existed; the Kyot in the poem is in effect another of Wolfram's characters, and as such has to be provided with a history of his own; his role is a familiar one, and just as the medieval versions of the story of Troy were ascribed to the fictitious Dictys the Cretan, who took the side of the Greeks, and Dares the Phrygian, who favoured the Trojans, so Kyot is the 'authority' for Wolfram's reworkings of Chrétien.

Wolfram is writing in the light of an interest in or knowledge of the kind of scientific learning that had come from Arabic Spain in the twelfth century. This reintroduced the thinking of the Greek philosophers to the west, but also provided access to the Arabs' own discoveries. In this field, the figures of Flegetanis, the learned heathen, and Kyot, the Christian interpreter, have many parallels: but in order to attribute this interest to Wolfram himself, and not to an unknown source, we have to refuse to believe Wolfram's own declaration that he was not a learned man. There are many reasons for thinking that this declaration is an example of Wolfram's ironical playfulness; he is evidently knowledgeable about astronomy, the lore of precious stones, and he is prepared to venture into obscure corners of theology. But the Grail itself does not stem from this lore, or represent some hidden tradition of necromancy; Wolfram uses his arcane lore to add to the mystery of the Grail, not to define the object itself.

Wolfram's inventiveness

As with everything about this extraordinary writer, the argument over the nature of his text and its meaning continues to rage; there is not space to rehearse the complex arguments here, but we shall proceed on the assumption that we are dealing with a formidable intellect and imagination, widely read but ultimately eclectic—we come back yet again to Gottfried von Strassburg's description of him as 'friend of the hare'. Just as a hare will jink and circle when hunted, unlike the fox or deer, which will run in a straight line, so with Wolfram nothing is straightforward, and his train of thought is often unexpected. He will pick up a name from an earlier poem and subtly change it, or he will make a dramatic alteration: Blancheflor becomes 'Condwiramurs', the bringer of love (*conduire amours*), and the Proud Knight of the Heath, *Orgueilleus de la Lande*, is transformed in the opposite direction, pride becoming the proper name Orilus. Wolfram's name-play has been extensively studied; the problem is that we cannot tell how far the changes are due to oral misunderstandings, or to visual misreadings, or to sheer exuberant invention. Compared to other poets, his work is full of names, a total of over six hundred; they are evidently a kind of extension to his poetic vocabulary, adding to the qualities of richness and mystery which characterize his style. He loves lists of names, whether of countries and people as when Parzival and Feirefiz describe their exploits and followers to Arthur when Feirefiz first comes to the king's court; or of the exotic gems to be found decorating Anfortas's sickbed. The first and last lists occupy exactly one section of thirty lines each, as if to underline their importance in the poem. Such lists are not unknown in epic poetry, from Homer's list of the ships in the *Iliad* onwards, and Wolfram's contemporary Hartmann von Aue has a similar list of Arthurian knights in his *Erec*.

But nothing in all this can prepare us for Wolfram's concept of the

Grail itself when it is finally revealed. Parzival, when Trevrizent has calmed his rage against God, asks to be told about the Grail. In response, Trevrizent seems to answer obliquely, for he describes Munsalvæsche and its warriors, who continually ride out in search of adventure, and then says, 'I will tell you of their food'. The source of their sustenance is 'a stone whose nature is most pure', named '*lapsit exillis*', by virtue of which the phoenix is able to die and be born again. It has the power to prolong youth, and to delay death. Only at the end of the description does Trevrizent add, 'That stone is also called the Grail'. He goes on to explain that 'today a message will appear upon it [the Grail], for therein lies its highest power': each Good Friday a dove brings a small white wafer from heaven and places it on the stone, 'by this the stone receives everything good that bears scent on this earth by way of drink and food, as if it were the perfection of Paradise'. The method of selection of the members of the company at Munsalvæsche is revealed: an inscription appears on the Grail, naming the chosen child and their lineage, for all members of the Grail company go as children, and to be named is regarded as the highest honour. And finally, Trevrizent associates the Grail with the neutral angels, those who sided with neither God nor Lucifer after the rebellion of the latter and his fall from heaven; they were forced to descend to earth to the Grail. Thereafter the Grail had been in the keeping of the dynasty to whom it had been entrusted. It is housed in a temple, and its keepers are called 'templeise'; this word has often been translated as 'Templars' and it has been argued that Wolfram had the Order of the Knights Templar in mind. But there are also reasons why the Templar identification does not work, particularly in the light of evidence that in the late Middle Ages German nobles did not think that the *templeise* had any connection with the Templars.

Wolfram's Grail and the Grail kingdom

All this raises a host of difficult questions. We can only begin to see something of Wolfram's vision of the Grail if we read him slowly and cautiously; as one critic has said, he 'writes in symbols'. First, the Grail is unequivocally a stone; there is no ambiguity in the German text. It has magical powers, and can provide food, but these powers are conferred on it by a divine providence. The symbol of the Grail knights is the turtle-dove, and this was an accepted symbol for the Holy Ghost, taken from the biblical account of Christ's baptism when 'he saw the Spirit of God descending like a dove'. The Grail's own powers derive ultimately from the Holy Ghost, which descends to the Grail each Good Friday in the form of a dove; and the white wafer which it bears can only be intended as the mass wafer. It is therefore the medium through which the Eucharist acts on the anniversary of Christ's crucifixion.

But Wolfram's chief concern is not with the theology of the Grail; its function in his tale is to represent a mysterious, supernatural power whose guardianship is the highest of earthly honours. This guardianship is in turn Parzival's destiny, and it is his struggle to achieve his destiny which is the central topic of the poem. Hence the Grail need not be fully explained to fulfil Wolfram's purpose, and we should not see it as the key to understanding the poem: Wolfram's work has rightly become known as *Parzival*, and the Grail has never been part of its title, unlike the French romances.

The conditions which bind the guardians of the Grail owe much more to Wolfram's imagination than to any actual military order of knighthood. The most obvious objection to such an identification is the presence of the women who serve the Grail, and who seem to be the most important figures at Munsalvæsche, saving only the king himself. There is also the question of the marriage of the Grail knights and ladies, which, while it does not happen at the Grail castle itself, is a frequent occurrence when they are sent out into the world. To use the word 'utopia' is an anachronism; but the imagined structure of the Grail society is a daring stroke, to say the least. It is a society subject to a rule, dictated by the Grail itself. Yet it is not a monastic society as such, and there is only one mention of a priest; its purpose is both religious—if the service of the Grail can indeed be counted as such—and secular. Because the members of the society are both chosen by the Grail and directed by it, the Grail company is a means by which God can intervene directly in human affairs.

When Wolfram first describes the Grail, he lays emphasis on its powers as a source of nourishment, and this is reiterated in Trevrizent's dialogue with Parzival, and its power to feed the brotherhood who serve it is ascribed to the mass wafer which the dove lays on it each year. Here Wolfram is echoing the idea that the Eucharist is

by itself sufficient to sustain life, but linking it back to his earlier
portrayal of the Grail feast. In Chrétien, the Grail nourishes the
father of the lame king; here it is the entire company of Grail knights
whom it supports, and it has moved from providing sumptuous
feasts to being the source of their everyday sustenance, though it still
only appears at solemn occasions. Wolfram goes on to describe how
this company is chosen from noble families outside the Grail king-
dom by messages which appear on the Grail itself. The emphasis is
on the idea of a dedicated community, membership of which is a
high honour and a cause for rejoicing: 'They are fetched from many
lands. Against sinful disgrace they are guarded for evermore, and
their reward will be good in Heaven.' The function of this chivalric
brotherhood was not only to guard the Grail, but to maintain order
in lands where the succession was in doubt because there was no
male heir: knights were sent secretly from the Grail to marry the
heiresses of the lands and restore peace. Girls chosen to serve the
Grail were given openly in marriage, and Herzeloyde, Parzival's
mother, had been one of the servants of the Grail before she married
her first husband. The Grail company acts as a stabilizing influence
in an unstable world; Wolfram himself was only too aware of the
troubles that could result from weak rule, having lived through a
decade of civil war in the Holy Roman Empire, when Otto IV and
Philip of Swabia vied for the imperial crown. *Parzival* was probably
written in exactly this period of turmoil, from 1198 to 1208. Like Sir
Thomas Malory writing his Arthurian epic during the Wars of the
Roses, Wolfram used *Parzival* to appeal from his present woes to an
image of ideal society.

Parzival's progress

As in Chrétien, the central theme of the poem is Parzival's spiritual
development from almost total ignorance of both the society he lives
in and of Christian belief. We can only guess that in the French
original the romance would have concluded with the healing of the
maimed king when Perceval was at last able to ask the question
which he had failed to put on his first visit to the Grail castle, 'Whom
does the Grail serve?' Wolfram takes an altogether bolder approach.
Parzival's rightful place in society is as a member of the Grail dyn-
asty; hence the lengthy prologue describing the history of his father

and mother. It is through Herzeloyde, his mother, that he inherits his right to the kingship of the Grail. By his heartless treatment of her, which leads to her death, and by killing his kinsman Ither, also from the Grail dynasty, he has sinned not only against ordinary morality but against the Grail itself. He begins to learn to mend his ways at the castle of Gurnemanz, who instructs him in chivalry; and this enables him to woo and win Condwiramurs, whom he rescues from her besieging enemies. But he does not yet understand the nature of sympathy and how human relationships work, and he has not expiated his sins, so he cannot ask the right question when he first sees the maimed king, Anfortas, at the Grail castle. He is condemned to wander alone, abandoning his beloved Condwiramurs, trying to return to the Grail.

But the Grail is not to be won by physical force, by simple knightly achievements, but by a spiritual struggle. Wolfram uses the word *strîten*, which means both physical fighting and debate or argument. The latter best describes the process by which Parzival attains his goal, for although he undertakes three great contests, against Gawan, Gramoflanz, and Feirefiz, his real struggle is against despair, *zwîvel*; this is the great enemy, and leads Parzival to question God's purposes, and even to deny him. The scene with Trevrizent is hence crucial, for before he reveals the secrets of the Grail, Trevrizent shows him the error of his ways. Parzival cannot succeed until he resolves his quarrel with God, and diverts his energy into making himself worthy of being summoned to the Grail. Trevrizent confirms this in the final scene: he tells Parzival that 'it has ever been uncustomary that anyone, at any time, might gain the Grail by fighting. I would gladly have deflected you from that purpose.' It is also in the first scene with Trevrizent that Parzival learns the story of his family, the dynasty whose task he is destined to take up. Only when Parzival has truly understood the nature of this task can he return to the castle and heal Anfortas by asking the question 'Uncle, what troubles you?'

Other heroes

The romance does not focus exclusively on Parzival. For many pages, there are other heroes: we have already seen how the exploits of Gahmuret occupy the first two books, and provide the crucial background to the central story. Gahmuret is an idealized fighter, uncomplicated in his heroism. In the central section of the romance, Parzival's exploits are intertwined with those of Gawan, Arthur's nephew, the central figure among Arthur's knights in the early romances. Gawan acts as a kind of foil to Parzival: his quest is not for the Grail, but for earthly love, sometimes physical, sometimes more idealized, as in his pursuit of a scornful *belle dame sans merci*. This is in sharp contrast to Parzival's steadfast devotion to Condwiramurs. Gawan represents the natural man; he is not a spiritual being, but is courtly and chivalrous nonetheless, though his devotion to love leads him into a variety of situations which almost seem to illustrate the range of meanings that can be attached to love: his 'love-service' of the 10-year-old Obilot, for whom he fights, his attempted seduction of Antikonie, and finally his trials at the hands of Orgeluse, duchess of Logroys, who mocks Gawan and tries to dissuade him from his courtship of her; but in the end apparent hatred turns to love as she gradually recognizes his true worth. Even Gawan's sister, Itonje, who falls in love with a man she has never seen, echoes the troubadour theme of *amor de lonh*, distant love. It is an alternative view of the chivalric world, but like Parzival, Gawan has to be tried and tested before he comes to marriage.

Another important figure is Feirefiz, Parzival's half-brother, son of Gahmuret and the eastern princess Belacane. His appearance declares his descent, for he is spotted black and white. He represents the virtuous pagan, the natural goodness of man despite his lack of the Christian faith. It is he who provides Parzival with his greatest physical challenge when they fight towards the end of the romance; the contest perhaps symbolizes Parzival's need to overcome the natural man in himself. Feirefiz is converted and marries the bearer of the Grail, and is thus made part of the Grail society.

In one sense, Wolfram is therefore completing and bringing together the themes set out by Chrétien; but he does so with a free hand, and creates both a different world, a different Grail, and a higher set of values. For Wolfram's central concern is not with the spiritual alone, but with the place of the spiritual within the chivalric world, as the guiding light of the truly chivalrous. The Grail functions as the link between the spiritual and the physical worlds, for through it God makes his wishes known to the Grail company, and is thus able to intervene directly in human affairs. This is an altogether bolder concept of the chivalric world than anything that has gone before: Arthur's court, the nearest equivalent to the Grail company in French romance, is the background for the exploits of individual knights, and Chrétien and his continuators are concerned with the fortunes of Perceval as an individual, not as part of a divine scheme of things. The authors of the great prose version of the Arthurian legends, the *Lancelot-Grail*, move away from the chivalrous world until the ethos of the Grail and that of the knights who seek it are in opposition, and the resulting conflict is only resolved with difficulty. Wolfram, on the other hand, gives a picture of the development of the individual within society: Parzival's rebellion against God is also an unconscious rebellion against his destiny as Grail king, and a betrayal of the society to which he and his family belong. For Wolfram is deeply conscious of dynasty and heredity: Parzival can only find himself by achieving the task which has been laid upon him from birth. If he can recognize his own true nature and be reconciled to God through confession and penance, he will come again to the Grail, find Condwiramurs again, and heaven and earth will move once more in harmony. It is a rich vision, told in ambitious if eclectic style, and ultimately perhaps the greatest of all the Grail poems.

Wolfram's legacy

Wolfram himself began another romance on the Grail company; it is usually known as *Titurel*, because the surviving fragments tell how Titurel came to be keeper of the Grail, before moving on to the tale of Schionatulander and Sigune, which seems to have been a more conventional romance. *Titurel* was completed by another poet a century or so later, and his work was long attributed to Wolfram himself. At the end of the Middle Ages, Wolfram's reputation remained high, but although a printed version appeared as early as 1477, his fame soon faded. His work was rediscovered in the mid-eighteenth century, and quickly acquired a high reputation again; when Richard Wagner discovered it and began to plan an opera based on it, there was an excellent scholarly edition and translations as well. Wagner's version of the story owes much to Wolfram, but he treats it very freely, drawing on many other sources as well. It remains one of the key works of medieval German literature, but its influence has been less than that of the French romances and Malory in terms of inspiring new writers to take up its themes, perhaps simply because Wolfram's vision is too individual and too complete to leave much room for reworking. One striking modern attempt to do so is Adolf Muschg's baroque version, _Der rote Ritter_ (_The Red Knight_) which weaves an extensive set of variations on the original, not always respectful, and ends with a much darker vision of the future of the Grail kingdom than Wolfram's. In the end, we return gratefully to Wolfram's original; it is difficult to rewrite a masterpiece, and the present translation gives us the opportunity to see why this should be the case.

NOTE ON THE TEXT AND TRANSLATION

KARL LACHMANN's edition of *Parzival* appeared in 1833. This translation is based upon the sixth revised edition (1926); manuscript variants have been consulted and sometimes preferred, and other editions have been adduced. Lachmann based his edition on seven complete manuscripts, nine fragments, and the print of 1477. There are now approaching ninety manuscripts and fragments of *Parzival*. No other German courtly romance proved as popular. For the *Titurel*, Lachmann's sixth edition again served as a base; I have drawn also upon the editions by Marion E. Gibbs and Sidney M. Johnson (1988), and Helmut Brackert and Stephan Fuchs-Jolie (2002), and consulted facsimiles of the manuscripts. The hardback version of this translation appeared with D. S. Brewer in 2004; I have taken the opportunity to make a few minor changes to the text.

Parzival is written in the customary form of the courtly romance, the rhyming couplet. Generally, the lines have three or four trochaic feet, but five-feet lines sometimes serve to emphasize the content, or to mark finality at the end of a 'book'.

The division into sixteen 'books' derives from the poem's editor, Karl Lachmann, who based it on the use of majuscule initials in one of the earliest manuscripts (St Gall, Stiftsbibliothek, 587). The division works well, not least in that it assigns pivotal importance to the central Book IX. Up to and including Book X the books begin with a prologue-like introduction; Book VIII has a staggered prologue, constantly warning of the dangers that are apparently to befall Gawan. Books XI–XIII, the final Gawan books, are less clearly demarcated at their outset.

A further subdivision is into sections of thirty lines (here marked in the margin). From Book V onwards, Wolfram seems to have composed in thirty-line units, which come to a clear syntactic halt. These probably corresponded to the ruled lines of the parchment page before him.

Titurel has an entirely different form. Its elegiac note is emphasized by its long lines and falling cadences. The strophic form, not found elsewhere in the courtly romance, resembles and was probably influenced by that of the Middle High German (MHG) heroic epic, the *Nibelungenlied*, in its employment of long lines subdivided by caesuras. The literary allusions in Book VIII of *Parzival* show that Wolfram was well acquainted with the *Nibelungenlied*.

Syntax and style

Wolfram's style was, if anything, more admired than his content. 'No layman's mouth ever spoke better' was the verdict of his contemporary Wirnt von Grafenberg, and this was echoed by many subsequent poets. Yet Wolfram also found a hostile critic. Gottfried's *Tristan* contains a literary excursus, an analysis of the contemporary literary scene, which launches a seemingly unprovoked attack upon an unnamed author who is the 'friend of the hare', reminding the reader of the 'startled hare' in Wolfram's prologue to *Parzival*. This unnamed author 'desires to be present upon the word-heath, high-leaping and wide-hunting with dice-words, aspiring to the laurel wreathlet without following'. Gottfried's words are uncharacteristically obscure here, and the unique compounds and syntax he employs are reminiscent of Wolfram's own style. It seems probable that he is indulging in parody. His critique continues, again attacking an anonymous target, this time in the plural: 'inventors of wild tales, wildmen of tales, who lie in ambush with chains and deceive dim minds, who know how to make gold out of inferior matter for children and how to pour forth pearls of dust from the pouch'. Here the attack is upon obscurity of both substance and style, and the allusions to Wolfram's prologue to *Parzival*, that essay in obscurity, are unmistakable.

Rudolf von Ems's *Alexander*, written about the middle of the thirteenth century, has an excursus largely derivative of Gottfried. German literature is seen as a branching tree, an image perhaps derived ultimately from the Tree of Jesse. Rudolf, however, has a more positive attitude to Wolfram than Gottfried: 'the second branch was trained onto it, robust, twisted in many ways, wild, good and cunning, ornamented by strange sayings. It was grafted onto the trunk by Sir Wolfram von Eschenbach. With wild adventures he was well capable of steering his art, so that his adventure promoted our entertainment.' Ulrich von Türheim, in his *Rennewart*, a continuation of

Wolfram's *Willehalm*, is more succinct in his praise: 'his poem . . . was sweet and masterly'. Praise for Wolfram's diction is to be found in many German authors of the thirteenth and fourteenth centuries. Imitations of and sequels to his works continued to appear until the early sixteenth century.

The richness of Wolfram's imagery is unparalleled in medieval German narrative. It draws upon many spheres of life: recurrent fields are the mercantile imagery of profit and loss, weights and measures, the favourite pastimes of falconry and gaming, and wildlife. Mixed metaphors, despite the strictures of the schools of rhetoric, are regarded by Wolfram as integral to his poetry.

Gottfried von Strassburg's attack on his anonymous antagonist's use of 'dice-words' (*bickelwort*) probably refers not merely to Wolfram's preference for gambling imagery, but also to his constant creation of neologisms, nonce-words. Generally, this translation has attempted to render these by employing unusual English words, sometimes risking a neologism for a neologism. For instance, as the prologue turns to the hero, Wolfram describes Parzival as *træclîche wîs*, 'laggardly wise', and *mæreshalp noch ungeborn*, 'storywise, yet unborn'. *Træclîche* is a rare word, first attested here; *mæreshalp* is unique to Wolfram.

From the very first line, where the heart is neighbour to doubt, personification is central to Wolfram's style. Abstract qualities, such as courage or loyalty are personified, but so also are the sun, which in Plippalinot the ferryman's words 'knows how to stand so low', or, lower still, Gawan's new boots, which 'indulged in no great narrowness'. This literary device is lacking in Chrétien's *Conte du Graal*, as are the similes and metaphors in which Wolfram's text abounds.

A more difficult aspect of Wolfram's style for the modern reader is his syntax, which indulges in frequent grammatical leaps and bounds. This translation attempts to convey something of the texture of Wolfram's syntax by remaining closer to his word order than previous translations into English. There are many points in *Parzival* when Wolfram's sentences defy grammatical logic, sometimes losing their way altogether.

Wolfram himself is well aware that his syntax and imagery do not make for an easy read. In the prologue to *Parzival*, which has no parallel in Chrétien, he revels in the difficulties posed by his imagery: 'This flying image is far too fleet for fools. They can't think it through, for it knows how to dart from side to side before them, just like a startled hare.' In *Willehalm*, he addresses himself specifically to the problem of translating a work from French: 'Behold what revenge I wreak upon those for whom I am to translate this tale: the German language would suit them well—*my* German, however, is so crooked on occasion that a man may readily prove too stupid for me if I do not convey the meaning to him hastily—then we are both delaying matters!' (*Willehalm*, 237, 8–14). It is typical of Wolfram in his playful arrogance that his syntax should be so elliptical in a passage in which he is addressing the problem of stylistic clarity.

Wolfram's syntax sometimes brings about what might be called the 'hand-held camera' effect, emphasizing visual detail at the expense of normal word order. In Book XIII, for example, Gawan and Arnive observe the arrival of Arthur's army at Joflanze: 'Tents and many banners Arnive and Gawan saw being borne onto the plain—amongst them all only one shield whose arms had a device Arnive could recognize.' In MHG syntax, as in Modern German, the accusative may be placed first for emphasis. Here the initial position of the 'tents and many banners' lets us follow the immediate visual impact of Arthur's cavalcade, so that we are only secondarily informed that Arnive and Gawan are the observers.

In the first encounter between Condwiramurs and Parzival, the jerky syntax has an almost stream-of-consciousness effect, singularly appropriate for the tentative thoughts of the young princess: 'The queen's first thoughts were: "I think this man despises me because my body is wasted away. No, it's a ruse on his part—he's a guest, I'm the hostess—the first speech ought to be mine. He must have looked kindly upon me, since we come to be sitting here. He has shown courtesy to me—my words have been all too long spared—let there be no more silence here!"' Here, as elsewhere, this translation supplies dashes to indicate parenthesis (whereas Lachmann's edition employs colons).

In the later books of *Parzival*, Wolfram occasionally employs the device of *apo koinu*, where two clauses are linked by the same subject: 'Gawan at that moment saw in the pillar riding a knight and a lady could he there both see.' Peter Knecht's translation into Modern German boldly attempts to reproduce this device, but this seems beyond the possibilities of contemporary English. The frequent switches of tense from past to present, sometimes but by no means always brought about by rhyme-compulsion, have an approximate equivalent in the English use of the Historic Present, so they have been retained, as has the frequent use of litotes and euphemism. When Orgeluse says to Gawan: 'In iron-clad arms I have seldom grown warm', she obviously means 'never'.

Another of Wolfram's stylistic traits is his predilection for the preposed genitive, or double, or even triple genitive. The 'Saxon' preposed genitive, 'the man's hat', is quite common in MHG, but the more condensed grammatical formulations are very rare outside Wolfram and his imitators. Kenning-like constructions like *herzen ougen regen*, 'heart's eyes' rain' should not, however, prove beyond the reader's mind's grasp. Such genitive constructions are deliberately economical, helping to knit a dense poetic fabric.

Wolfram is the boldest and most innovative of the medieval German narrative poets, but also the most dense. If Wolfram's meaning were immediately apparent, he would forfeit his greatness. In some ways his style anticipates in its opacity the language of the German mystics of the late thirteenth and fourteenth centuries. One of these, from the anonymous circle surrounding the Franciscan David von Augsburg, wrote: 'Whoever reads or hears this should act like the squirrel: it chews the husk of the nut until it comes to the kernel; thus one must chew the words with the teeth of intelligence until one enters the enjoyment of the Divine Mystery. Whoever wants to eat the honey must take it out of the comb, and thus one must draw the divine sweetness and the divine, honeysweet grace forth from the words.' Wolfram would certainly have appreciated the dictum of the most poetic of the mystics, Mechthild von Magdeburg: 'all who desire to understand this book must read it nine times'. Wolfram's audience, as is clear from the manuscript reception, much enjoyed the tussle with meaning that is central to the reading experience.

How, then, can the poor translator set about his task? There clearly has to be a compromise between the endeavour to capture the flavour of the author's style, and the limits of what is possible in modern English. Here it is instructive to observe that two previous translators of *Parzival* into English say strikingly similar things in their introductions. Helen Mustard and Charles Passage state: 'The ellipses we have not reproduced, for fear of merely confusing the reader.'[1] Arthur Hatto remarks that 'the reader must imagine Wolfram to be in one sense rougher and less tidy than he appears in these pages'.[2] This translation, in the interest of trying to convey something of Wolfram's stylistic originality, will give the reader a rougher ride than its predecessors.

Sometimes this translation—like all its predecessors—cheats, ducking the problems posed by Wolfram's obscurantism. The intention, however, is to supply a translation which is so close to the original that the student may read it in conjunction with the MHG, while the translator retains the hope that it may be possible for the non-specialist not merely to enjoy the thread of the narrative, but also to sample something of the zest of Wolfram's style.

[1] Wolfram von Eschenbach, *Parzival*, trans. Helen Meredith Mustard and Charles E. Passage (New York: Vintage Books, 1961), p. liii.

[2] Wolfram von Eschenbach, *Parzival*, trans. A. T. Hatto, Penguin Classics (Harmondsworth: Penguin, 1980), 12.

SELECT BIBLIOGRAPHY

THE original hardback edition of the present volume (Woodbridge, 2004) contains a more technical presentation of the text, with an introduction concentrating on the place of Wolfram in the literary world of the thirteenth century and notes which discuss both the syntax and language of the original and the problems of translation. A. T. Hatto's edition in Penguin Classics (1980) has a valuable introduction and afterword, though the translation itself is high-flown and somewhat dated. Hugh Sacker's *An Introduction to Wolfram's 'Parzival'* (Cambridge 1963) is still the best general introduction. *A Companion to Wolfram's Parzival*, edited by Will Hasty (Rochester, NY and Woodbridge, 1999), is a useful scholarly collection on aspects of the poem. On the Grail legend, see Richard Barber, *The Holy Grail: Imagination and Belief* (London and Cambridge, Mass., 2004). Lucy Beckett's Cambridge opera handbook on Wagner's *Parsifal* (Cambridge 1981) has a good discussion of the relationship between Wagner's libretto and Wolfram's original.

The standard German edition of the text is still that of Karl Lachmann, first published in 1833 and republished frequently since then. There is a huge literature in German on Wolfram, but this is largely at a highly specialist level.

On the Arthurian legend in general, there is a vast literature: the best place to start is probably Sir Thomas Malory's *Morte Darthur*, of which there are many editions and modernizations. *The New Arthurian Encyclopedia*, edited by Norris Lacy (Chicago and London 1991), is an excellent reference work; for a general introduction, see Richard Barber, *King Arthur: Hero and Legend* (Woodbridge and New York, 1986).

Further reading in Oxford World's Classics

Beowulf, trans. Kevin Crossley-Holland, ed. Heather O'Donoghue.
Lancelot of the Lake, trans. Corin Corley, ed. Elspeth Kennedy.
Langland, William, *Piers Plowman*, trans. A. V. C. Schmidt.
Lorris, Guillaume de, and Meun, Jean de, *The Romance of the Rose*, trans. Frances Horgan.
Malory, Thomas, *Le Morte Darthur*, trans. Helen Cooper.
The Poetic Edda, ed. Caroline Larrington.

A CHRONOLOGY OF *PARZIVAL* AND *TITUREL* IN THE ARTHURIAN CONTEXT (TO *c.*1300)

All dates are necessarily speculative.

?late fifth–early sixth century   The period of the 'historical' Arthur.

*c.*545 — Gildas's account of British history refers to some possibly Arthurian events.

*c.*600 — The Old Welsh poem *Gododdin* refers to Arthur as a legendary hero.

*c.*800 — Nennius's chronicle lists twelve battles fought by Arthur against the Saxons.

*c.*960 — The *Annales Cambriae* (Welsh Annals) record the deaths of Arthur and Medraut at Camlann.

*c.*1000 — Origins of the earliest Welsh Arthurian story, *Culhwch and Olwen*.

*c.*1135 — Geoffrey of Monmouth's *Historia Regum Britanniae* (*History of the Kings of Britain*) places Arthur in a quasi-historical context.

*c.*1160–90 — Chrétien de Troyes' Old French romances; *Perceval* or *Le Conte del Graal*, the first romance with Perceval as its hero, left uncompleted at the time of Chrétien's death.

*c.*1180–1200 — Hartmann von Aue's Middle High German adaptations of Chrétien's romances, *Erec* and *Iwein*.

*c.*1200–10 — Wolfram von Eschenbach's *Parzival*.

*c.*1200–30 — Four Old French continuations of Chrétien's *Conte del Graal*

*c.*1210 — The Old French *Perlesvaus* or *The High Book of the Grail*

*c.*1215 — The Old French *Perceval*, attributed to Robert de Boron

*c.*1220 — Wolfram's *Titurel* fragments

*c.*1275–1300 — *Der jüngere Titurel*, attributed to Albrecht von Scharfenberg, a continuation of Wolfram's fragmentary poem.

*c.*1300 — *Peredur*, a Middle Welsh romance now included in the *Mabinogion*.

PARZIVAL

BOOK I

Prologue

IF doubt is near neighbour to the heart, that may turn sour on the 1
soul. There is both scorning and adorning when a man's undaunted
mind turns pied like the magpie's hue. Yet he may still enjoy bliss,
for both have a share in him, Heaven and Hell. Inconstancy's com-
panion holds entirely to the black colour and will, indeed, take on
darkness's hue, while he who is constant in his thoughts will hold to
the white.

This flying image is far too fleet for fools. They can't think it
through, for it knows how to dart from side to side before them, just
like a startled hare. Tin coated with glass on the other side, and the
blind man's dream—these yield a countenance's shimmer, but that
dull light's sheen cannot keep company with constancy. It makes for
brief joy, in all truth. Who pulls my hair where none ever grew, in my
hand's palm? That man has learned close grips indeed!

If I say 'ouch!' because of such fears as these, that reflects my wit,
does it not?—if I seek to find loyalty where it knows how to vanish 2
like fire in the well, and the dew before the sun? Nor did I ever know
a man so wise that he wouldn't gladly gain acquaintance with what
guidance these tales crave, and what good doctrine they confer. They
are never daunted, but they both flee and give chase, retreat and turn
back, disgrace and honour. He who can cope with all these turns of
the dice has been well blessed with wit, if he does not sit too long nor
go astray, and keeps a clear mind in other respects. A mind that keeps
company with falsity is destined for Hell's fire, and is a hailstorm
falling down upon high honour. Its loyalty has such a short tail that it
would not pay back the third horsefly's bite, if it fled into the forest.

These diverse distinctions do not apply, however, merely to men.
To women I set the following goals: if any of them will mark my
counsel, she must know which way to guide her fame and her hon-
our, and to whom, accordingly, she is ready to accord love and her
virtue, so that her chastity and her loyalty are no source of regret to 3
her. Before God I pray that true moderation may reside with good
women. Modesty is a lock upon all morality. I can wish them no

higher blessing. She who is false wins false fame. How constant is thin ice when August-hot sun strikes it? Such a woman's reputation dissolves just as speedily.

Many a woman's beauty is widely praised. If such a woman's heart is counterfeit, then I praise her as I ought to praise the blue bead set in gold. I think it no trifling matter if a man works a noble ruby into base brass—and the whole of his adventure*—to that I liken a true woman's mind. If if a woman does justice to her womanliness, then it is not for me to scrutinize her complexion, nor her heart's covering—what is outwardly visible. Provided she is intact within her breast, then noble fame will remain unimpaired there.

If I were now to scrutinize both women and men as I am well capable of doing, it would bring with it a long tale. Hear now *this* adventure's ways. It will acquaint you with both joy and sorrow. Joy and peril ride by its side. Now, even if there were three of me, each individually practising skills counterweighing mine, it would require wild invention if they were willing to acquaint you with what I alone shall make known to you—all three would have their work cut out!

A story I will now renew for you, which tells of great loyalty, womanly woman's ways, and man's manliness so steadfast that it never bent before hardship. His heart never betrayed him there— steel he was, whenever he entered battle. His hand seized victoriously full many a praiseworthy prize. Bold was he, laggardly wise—it is the hero I so greet, woman's eyes' sweetness alongside woman's heart's desire, a true refuge from misdeed. He whom I have chosen for this purpose is, storywise, yet unborn—he of whom this adventure tells, in which many marvels will befall him.

They still practise the custom, as they did then, where Gallic law rules and then ruled—the practice obtains on one part of German soil—you have heard this without needing me to tell you: whoever ruled over those lands gave order, incurring no disgrace thereby— this is undeniably true—that the eldest brother should have his father's entire inheritance. This was a curse upon the younger ones—that death caused a breach with such duties as their father's life had vouchsafed them. Before all had been shared—now the elder possesses it alone. It was a wise man, however, who saw to it that old age should have property. Youth possesses great honour, old age sighing and sorrow. Never was there anything as wretched as old age coupled with poverty. Kings, counts, dukes—this I tell you, it is no lie—that they should be disinherited of possessions with the exception of the eldest child—it is a curious institution. The chaste* and bold warrior Gahmuret thus lost castles and lands, where his father had in splendour borne sceptre and crown, with great kingly power, until he lay dead by knightly deeds.

Then they mourned grievously for him. He had taken unimpaired 6 loyalty and honour with him to the very point of death. His elder son commanded to his presence the princes of the kingdom. They came in knightly fashion, for it was only right and proper that they should accept great fiefs from him. When they had come to court and their lawful claims had been heard, and they had all received their fiefs, hear now what they initiated. They desired, as their loyalty advised, rich and poor alike, the entire company, one single, small, earnest request: that the king should magnify brotherly loyalty by Gahmuret and do himself honour, by not expelling his brother entirely, but according him some portion of his land, by which token it might be seen that that lord might lay claim to his name and his liberty. That did not displease the king. He said: 'You know how to ask in moderation! I shall grant you this and more besides. Why do you not call my brother Gahmuret Angevin? Anjou is my country. Let us both take our names from it.'

The noble king then said: 'My brother may be confident of more 7 constant help from me than I would promise here in haste. He is to be part of my household. Truly, I shall show you all that one mother bore us both. He has little, and I ample. My hand shall so share that with him that my bliss shall not be forfeit before Him who gives and takes away—as both justly beseem Him.'

When the mighty princes heard, all alike, that their lord practised loyalty, that was a dear day for them. Each and every one of them bowed before him. Gahmuret was silent no longer, but spoke in accordance with what his heart averred. To the king he said, graciously: 'Lord and brother mine, if I wished to be of your or any man's retinue, then my bed would be made. But now have an eye to my honour—you are loyal and wise—and advise as is now fitting. Lend me a helpful hand. All I have is my armour. If I had done more in it, to bring me praise from far afield, I would be better thought of elsewhere.'

Gahmuret continued: 'Sixteen squires I have, six of whom are 8 iron-clad. Give me four youths in addition, of good breeding, of high lineage. They will never be denied anything that my hand may win. I intend to head for those lands where I have travelled to some extent before. If Fortune favours me, then I shall gain a goodly woman's greeting. If I am to serve her to this end, and if I prove worthy, then my best inclination advises me to follow this course with true loyalty. May God guide me along Fortune's path. We journeyed companionably—in those days our father Gandin still possessed your kingdom—we both suffered many a grievous pang for love's sake. You were knight and thief at once—you knew how to serve and dissimulate. If only I, too, could now steal love! Alas, if only I possessed your skill and might find true favour in that field!'

The king sighed and said: 'Alas that I ever beheld you, now that
9 with your merry ways you have lacerated my whole heart, and now you act as if we are to part! My father has bequeathed to us both property in great plenty. I'll give to you equal measure. I am bound by my heart to you. Bright gems, red gold, people, weapons, chargers, clothing—take as much from my hands as will enable you to travel as you will, and uphold your generosity. Your valour is peerless. Even if you were born of Gylstram or hailed from Ranculat* I would still hold you in that place where I now most gladly hold you. You are my brother, beyond doubt.'

'Sir, you praise me by necessity, as your good breeding commands. Make your help manifest in accordance. If you and my mother wish to share your chattels with me, then I shall rise and never fall. Yet my heart still strives towards the heights. I don't know why it lives like this, why my left breast so swells. Oh, whither is my desire hunting me? I must make the endeavour, if I prove capable. Now my leave-taking's day nears.'

The king granted him all, more than Gahmuret himself requested:
10 five chargers of excellent repute, the best in all his land, bold, strong, far from sluggish—many a precious vessel of gold and many a golden ingot. The king was far from reluctant to fill four saddlebags for him. Many precious stones had to be packed into the bags, too. When these lay there, filled, pages to see to them were well clad and mounted. Then sorrow was not avoided when he walked into his mother's presence, and she embraced him so closely: '*Fil li roy* Gandin,* do you no longer wish to stay with me?' said the womanly woman. 'Alas, it was my own body bore you, and you are also Gandin's son. Is God

blind in his help, or is he deafened, that he does not believe me? Am I to have new grief now? I have buried my heart's strength, the sweetness of my eyes. If He is to rob me of still more, even though He is a judge, then the tale they tell me of His help is a lie, since He has thus failed me.'

Then the young Angevin said: 'God console you, lady, for the loss 11 of my father. We must both willingly bemoan his death. No-one can give you cause to lament on my account. For my honour's sake I am now setting off for foreign lands, in search of knightly deeds. Lady, that is my purpose.'

Then the queen said: 'Since it is to lofty love that you are turning your service and mind, dear son, do not disdain my possessions as you embark on your journey. Bid your chamberlains receive from me four heavy saddle-bags—in them lie broad phellel-silks, whole, never yet cut, and many a costly samite.* Sweet son, let me hear the time when you return—you will add to my joys.'

'Lady, I do not know in what country I shall be seen, but wherever I am headed when I leave you, you have acted nobly by me in accordance with knights' honour. The king, too, has released me in such fashion that my service must thank him. I sincerely trust that you 12 will respect him the more for it, however my affairs turn out for me.'

As the adventure tells us, the undaunted warrior had then received, by love's power and womanly companionship, love-tokens worth a thousand marks. If a Jew were nowadays to demand a pledge, he'd gladly accept that amount for them—there'd be no need for him to turn it down. This had been sent him by a beloved of his. Profit resided with his service—the love of women and their greeting. Yet seldom was he free of sorrow.

The warrior took his leave. His eyes never again beheld his mother, his brother, nor his land. By that many a man lost much. All those who had treated him in friendly fashion before he departed, and who had shown him any mark of favour, were thanked by him profusely. Their treatment seemed more than adequate to him— well-bred as he was, it never occurred to him that they were giving him his due. His disposition was straighter than a die. If a man himself says how worthy he is, incredulity may obtain. Such matters should be spoken of by bystanders, and by those who have observed his deeds in places where he is a stranger. Then the tidings might be 13 believed.

Gahmuret had such ways as kept balance with true moderation, not throwing any other dice. He boasted little, suffering great honour passively. Loose desires shunned him entirely. Yet that compliant man believed that there was no-one who wore a crown—king, emperor, empress—whose household he would join, except that one whose highest hand held sway over all lands on earth. That was the desire that lay in his heart. He was told that in Baldac* there was a man so mighty that two thirds of the earth or more were subject to him. His name was held so high that in the heathen tongue he was called the Baruch.* So great was his grip on power that many kings were his subjects, crowned but subordinate to him. The office of the Baruch still exists today. Behold, just as Christian rule obtains in Rome, as baptism tells us, there heathen order is seen to prevail— from Baldac they obtain their papal law. They believe that to be
14 unwaveringly straight. The Baruch gives them absolution's proof for their sins.

From two brothers of Babylon, Pompey and Ipomidon, the Baruch took Nineveh—it had belonged to all their ancestors before—they showed powerful resistance. To that city came the young Angevin. The Baruch became very fond of him. There noble Gahmuret accepted remuneration for his service. Permit him now to have different arms than those that Gandin, his father, had given him before. It was Lord Gahmuret's aspiring custom to have embroidered on his caparison* anchors of bright ermine. The rest of his equipment had to be of the same kind—on his shield and his clothing. Greener even than an emerald all his saddle-gear was made, and of the hue of achmardi.* That is a silken fabric. Of this he had himself made a tabard and surcoat—it is better than samite—ermine anchors sewn upon it, golden ropes coiling from it.

15 His anchors had tested neither mainland nor headland. Nowhere had they struck ground. The lord was obliged to carry further this heraldic burden—these marks of the anchor—into many lands, that noble stranger, for he had nowhere to stay nor anywhere to tarry. How many lands did he ride through, and skirt round in ships? If I were to swear to that, then my knightly pledge would say to you, on my oath, what the adventure tells me—I've no other witness now. It tells that his valiant prowess won the prize in heathendom, in Morocco and in Persia. His hand took such toll elsewhere, too—in Damascus and in Aleppo, and wherever knightly deeds were proffered, in

Arabia and before Araby—that he was proof against counter-charge, against any other man in single combat. That was the reputation he won there. His heart's desire grasped after fame. All other men's deeds were razed to the ground before him, all but annihilated. That was the lesson he taught to any man who ever jousted against him. In Baldac it was said of him: his courage strove onwards without waver- 16 ing. From there he travelled towards the kingdom of Zazamanc. There they were all alike lamenting Isenhart, who had lost his life in service of a woman. He was compelled to it by Belacane, that gentle lady free of falsity. Because she never offered him her love, he lay dead for love for her. His kinsmen avenged him both openly and in ambush. They oppressed the lady with their army. She was defending herself valiantly when Gahmuret came into her land, to which Fridebrant of Scotland, with his ship's army, had set fire before he departed.

Now hear how our knight fares: the sea threw him there with such a storm that he scarcely survived. Heading for the queen's great hall, he came sailing into the harbour—there he was gazed at by many eyes looking down. Then he looked out over the plain, where many a tent was pitched all around the city, except facing the sea. There two mighty armies lay encamped. Then he ordered that information be asked as to whose was the castle, as he had no knowledge of it; nor 17 had any of his seamen. They informed his messengers that it was Patelamunt. The message was phrased in friendly terms. They implored him by their gods to help them—they were in dire need of it, fighting for nothing less than their lives.

When the young Angevin heard about their sorrowful plight he offered his services for hire, as very often a knight still does—or else they should tell him why he should suffer their foes' hostility. Then, with one voice the sick and the hale said that their gold and their jewels were all at his disposal—he was to be lord of it all, and it would be well worth his while to stay amongst them. He had little need, however, of such reward, having brought many an ingot of the gold from Arabia with him. People dark as night were all those of Zazamanc—in their company time seemed to him to pass slowly. Nevertheless, he gave orders for lodgings to be taken, and it obvi- ously suited them very well to give him the best. The ladies were still reclining at the windows, looking down at what was happening. They 18 observed closely his squires and his armour, and how it was adorned.

The magnanimous warrior was wearing on an ermine shield I don't know how many pelts of sable. The queen's marshal thought it was a huge anchor. To see that by no means disconcerted him. His eyes then did not fail to attest that he had seen this knight or his like before. It must have been in Alexandria, when the Baruch lay encamped there. No-one equalled his fame there.

Thus the noble-minded knight made his leisurely way into the city: he ordered that ten pack-horses be loaded; these walked through the lanes. Twenty squires rode after them. Ahead of these his household staff were to be seen: pages, cooks and their scullions had set off in advance. Proud was his retinue—twelve well-born youths rode in the rear behind the squires, of good breeding, gentle of demeanour, several of them Saracens. Following these, there were also to be led
19 eight chargers, all draped in sendal-silk. The ninth carried his saddle. The shield I mentioned before was carried alongside by a most merry squire. After these rode trumpeters, who are also essential. A drummer beat his tabor, tossing it high up in the air. The lord would have thought very little of all this unless flautists rode in the entourage, and good fiddlers three. None of these was in too much of a hurry. He himself rode at the rear, along with his wise and famed ship's captain.

All the people in the city, both women and men, were Moors and Mooresses. The lord observed many a shattered shield, pierced right through by spears. Many were hung outside on the walls and the doors. Sorrow and wailing they had there. At the windows, facing the air, beds had been made for many a wounded man who, even if he were
20 to find a doctor, could not recover—he had been among foes. Such has ever been the fate of that man unwilling to flee. Lots of chargers were led towards him, pierced through and hacked. Many dark ladies he saw on both sides of him—of the raven's hue was their complexion.

His host gave him a gracious welcome, which afterwards turned out happily for the former. He was a man rich in courage. With his hands he had delivered many a thrust and cut, for he had charge of one of the gates. Gahmuret found with him many a knight whose hands hung in slings and whose heads were bandaged. These had wounds that were such that they were still capable of deeds of chivalry—their strength had not deserted them.

The burgrave* of the city then graciously requested his guest not to forbear to press whatever claim he wished upon his property and person. He led him to where he found his wife, who kissed Gahmuret, though he took little pleasure in that. After that he went to have breakfast. When this was over the marshal left him at once to find the queen, where he asked for a costly messenger's reward:* he 21 said: 'Lady, our danger has disappeared amid joys. The man we have welcomed here is a knight of such a nature that we must always pray thanks to our gods who have brought him to us, for ever thinking to do so.'

'Now tell me, by your loyalty, who this knight may be.'

'Lady, he is a proud warrior, the Baruch's paid soldier, an Angevin of high lineage. Ah, how little does he spare himself when he is unleashed into the attack! How skilfully he dodges and twists, this way and that! To his foes he teaches affliction. I saw him fight splendidly where the Babylonians sought to free Alexandria, and when they wanted to drive the Baruch away by force. How many of them were felled there in that defeat! There that comely knight performed such deeds with his own hands that they had no choice but to flee. Moreover, I have heard it pronounced of him that he must be acknowledged to have sole claim to fame over many lands.' 22

'Now look for some occasion or other, and arrange for him to speak with me here. We have a truce, after all, for the whole of today, so the warrior can easily ride up here to me. Or should I go down? He is of a different colour to us—oh, I do hope that does not displease him! I would like to find out first whether my people advise that I should offer him hospitality. If he deigns to approach me, how am I to receive him? Is he sufficiently well-born that my kiss of greeting would not be wasted?'

'Lady, he's known to be of a king's kin—let my life be the pledge for that! Lady, I will say to your princes that they should put on rich clothing and wait upon you, until we ride up to you. Tell all your ladies about it, for when I go down now, I will bring to you the noble stranger, who was never lacking in sweet virtue.'

Very little of this fell by the wayside. With all speed the marshal carried out his lady's request. Soon rich garments were then brought 23 to Gahmuret—these he put on. I heard tell that they were costly. Anchors, heavy with Arab gold, were upon them as he desired. Then Love's Requitement's Reward was mounted upon a charger which a Babylonian had ridden towards him in a joust—Gahmuret had thrust him off it, much to his grief.

Did his host perhaps ride with him? Indeed he did, and all his
knights. Truly they are delighted to do so. They rode up the hill
together then and dismounted before the great hall, up in which
many a knight was present—all elegantly dressed, of necessity. His
pages ran in before him in pairs, each couple holding each other by
the hand. Their lord found there many a lady, splendidly dressed.
The mighty queen's eyes caused her great pain when she beheld the
Angevin. He was of such delightful appearance that he opened up
her heart entirely, whether joy or sorrow might befall her—till then
her womanliness had kept her heart enlocked.

She stepped a little towards him then, and asked her guest to kiss
24 her. She, and no other, took him by the hand. Facing the foes, they
sat down by the wall in the broad window-seats, on a cushion piled
with samite, which had soft bedding lying beneath. If anything is
brighter than the day, the queen bears it no resemblance. She had,
however, womanly feelings and was in other respects of courtly dis-
position. Unlike the dewy rose, her sheen was black in hue, her
crown a single bright ruby, through which her head could clearly be
seen. The hostess said to her guest that she was glad of his coming:
'Sir, I have heard much of your knightly fame. By your courtesy, do
not be aggrieved if I bemoan my troubles to you, which I bear close
to my heart.'

'My help, Lady, will not fail you. Whatever has troubled or
troubles you, if my hand is to avert it, it is at your service. I am but
one man alone, but whoever harms or has harmed you, I offer my
shield against him—little though it may trouble the enemies.'

At this one of the princes spoke up courteously: 'If we had a
25 captain, we should spare few of our enemies, now that Fridebrant
has departed. He is freeing his own land yonder from a siege. A king
called Hernant, whom he slew for Herlinde's sake—his kin are caus-
ing Fridebrant harm enough, they won't readily relent. He has left
warriors behind here—Duke Hiuteger, whose knightly deeds cause
us many injuries, and his company. They are skilled and mighty in
battle. And then Gaschier of Normandy, that wise and noble warrior,
has many a paid soldier here. Kaylet of Hoskurast has even more
knights at his command, many a hostile foreigner. All these
Fridebrant, King of the Scots, brought into this country, together
with four of his peers, with many a paid soldier. To the west there, by
the sea, lies Isenhart's army, their eyes flowing. Since their lord died

by the joust, no man has ever beheld them, be it in public or in private, without their expressing wondrous sorrow—their hearts' rain has brought about these showers.'

The guest said, chivalrously, to his hostess: 'Tell me, if you will, 26 for what reason you are being attacked with such hostile force. You have so many bold warriors. It troubles me that they are burdened with the hatred of foes seeking to harm them.'

'I'll tell you, lord, since you wish it. A knight served me, who was noble. He was a blossoming branch of knightly virtue. That warrior was bold and wise, a well-rooted fruit of loyalty. His courtesy outweighed all others'. He was more chaste than a woman. He possessed boldness and courage. No knight ever grew to be more generous than he in any land (I don't know what will happen after our time—let other people talk of that!). He was a fool when it came to false conduct—of black colour, like myself, a Moor. His father was called Tankanis, a king—he too was of high repute. My beloved was called Isenhart. My womanhood was unguarded when I accepted his love-service. That it did not lead to happiness for him is something I must always regret. They believe it was I who caused him to be slain, but I 27 am little versed in treachery, although his subjects accuse me of it. He was dearer to me than to them. I am not without witnesses for this, by whom I'll yet prove it. My gods, and his gods, too, know the real truth. He caused me many a pang. Now my bashful womanhood has protracted his reward and my suffering.

'My maidenhood won for that warrior much fame for his deeds of chivalry. I was testing him then, to see if he could be a true lover. That became clear very soon. He abandoned, for my sake, his equipment and armour, which stands there like a palace—that lofty tent was brought by Scots onto this plain. Once the warrior had rid himself of this, his body was little spared. He grew weary of life then, seeking many an adventure unarmed. This being so, a prince—Prothizilas he was called, one of my household, free of cowardice—rode out in search of adventure, to where great harm did not shun him. In the greenwood of Azagouc a joust did not deny him death, which he delivered at a bold man, who also met his end there. It was 28 my beloved, Isenhart. Each of them felt the thrust of a spear through his shield and his body. This I still lament today, most wretched woman that I am. Both their deaths will trouble me forever. Grief blooms upon my loyalty. I never became wife to any man.'

Gahmuret's immediate thought was that, although she was a heathen, a more womanly and loyal disposition had never glided into a woman's heart. Her chastity was a pure baptism, as was the rain which poured upon her, the flood that flowed from her eyes down upon her sable and her breast. Contrition's cult was her delight, and true grief's doctrine. She told him more:

'Then, from across the sea, the King of the Scots attacked me with his army. He was Isenhart's uncle's son. They could not do me any more harm than had befallen me on Isenhart's account, I must admit.'

The lady sighed time and again. Through her tears she cast many
29 bashful glances, in stranger-like fashion, at Gahmuret; then her eyes at once informed her heart that he was handsome. She knew how to judge pale complexions, for she had seen many a fair-skinned heathen before. Between the two of them there great mutual desire grew—she looked at him, and he looked at her.

Then she ordered the parting-cup to be poured at once; if she had dared, that would have been neglected. It troubled her that it was not postponed, for it has always driven away those knights who would willingly converse with women. Yet she was already his own, and he had also inspired in her such feelings that his life was the lady's own.

Then he stood up, saying: 'Lady, I am imposing upon you. I tend to sit too long—it's not a clever habit of mine. I am truly sorry, speaking as your humble servant, that your sorrow is so great. Lady, I am at your disposal: I'll wreak vengeance wherever you wish. I'll serve you in any way I can.'

She said: 'Sir, I've every confidence in you.'

His host, the burgrave, neglects very little now in whiling
30 Gahmuret's time away. He asked whether he wanted to ride out for exercise—'and see where we do battle, and how our gates are guarded.' Gahmuret the worthy warrior said that he would gladly see where knightly combat had taken place there.

Down with the warrior rode many a high-spirited knight, some of them seasoned, some inexperienced. They led him right round sixteen gates, and assured him that none of these had been spared, since vengeance for Isenhart had been directed—'at us in anger. Night and day our battle has been almost evenly balanced. None of the gates has been closed since. At eight gates Isenhart's loyal subjects are offering us battle; they have inflicted great losses upon us. They fight in anger, those well-born princes, the King of Azagouc's men.'

Before each gate a bright banner fluttered above a bold company, portraying a pierced knight, in the manner in which Isenhart lost his life—his people had chosen the device for that reason.

'We, for our part, hold to a custom whereby we assuage her grief. Our banners can be recognised by two fingers of one hand, offering 31 an oath that she has never suffered so much as since Isenhart's death—he causes my lady heart's distress. Thus the queen's image, Lady Belacane's, has stood cut in black against white samite from that moment when we saw that device of theirs—her loyalty profits by grief—those banners stick out high above the gates. Before the other eight gates proud Fridebrant's army still attacks us—the baptized ones from across the sea.

'Every gate is guarded by a prince, who advances into battle with his banner. We have captured from Gaschier, one of his counts—he is offering us a great deal of his possessions as ransom. He is Kaylet's sister's son. Whatever Kaylet may now inflict upon us, this count must pay for. Such luck seldom befalls us. Little green meadow, but perhaps thirty horse-charge lengths of sandy ground stretch from the moat to their tents—there a lot of jousts are fought.'

His host told him all these tidings: 'There is one knight who never 32 fails to advance for a joust. If his service for the lady who sent him here were to prove in vain, what help to him then would his bold desire for battle be? That is proud Hiuteger. I may as well say more of him: ever since we have been besieged here, that rash warrior has always been at the ready in the morning, at the gate before the great hall. And from that bold man many tokens* have been taken, he thrusting them through our shields—they were reckoned to be of high value when the heralds broke them off the shields. He has felled many of our knights. He likes to let himself be seen. Our ladies praise him, too. When women praise a man, he is acknowledged, he holds fame in his hands, and his heart's delight, as well.'

By then the weary sun had gathered to herself her bright glance. It was time for their exercises to be at an end. The guest rode home with his host—he found his food all ready for him. I must tell you of their meal: it was placed before them with all due courtesy. They 33 were served in noble fashion. The mighty queen advanced proudly to his table. Here stood the heron,* there the fish. The reason she had ridden down to him was that she wanted to see for herself that he was being properly entertained; she had come with her damsels. She knelt down*—he was sorry to see it—and with her own hand she cut part of the knight's food. The lady was delighted with her guest. Next she offered him drink, and tended him well. He, for his part, took heed of her bearing and her words. At one end of his table sat his minstrels, and at the other his chaplain. Bashfully he looked at the lady; with much embarrassment he said:

'I've never in my life been honoured by such hospitality as you offer me, lady! If you had been ruled by me, then only such treatment as I might merit would have been requested of you tonight— you would not have ridden down here. If I may make so bold, lady, as to ask, then let me live in proper moderation. You have shown me too much honour.'

34   Nor did she refrain from pressing food on his pages sitting there. That she did to honour her guest. All those young lordlings took a liking to the queen. After that the lady did not neglect to go over, also, to where the host sat, and his wife, the burgravine. The queen raised her goblet, saying: 'Let our guest be commended to your care. The honour is yours. I urge you both to be mindful of it.' She took her leave, and then went back again to her guest. His heart bore her love's burden. The same had befallen her on his account, as her heart and her eyes affirmed—they were obliged to make common cause with her. Courteously, the lady then said: 'Command me, lord. Whatever you wish I'll arrange, for you are worthy of it. And let me have your leave to depart. If you are comfortably tended here, we shall all be delighted.' Her candle-holders were of gold; four lights were carried on them before her, and she was riding to a place where she found plenty more.

    Then they ate no longer there. The warrior was both sad and 35 happy. He was pleased that great honour had been offered him, yet distress of a different kind oppressed him. That was harsh love, which lowers high spirits.

    His hostess had gone to her chamber; that happened in all haste. The warrior's bed was made ready for him at once; no trouble was spared. The host said to his guest: 'Now you must sleep deeply and rest tonight—you will have need of it!' The host ordered his men to depart. The beds of the guest's pages lay in a circle around his own, with their heads next to it, as was Gahmuret's custom. Tall candles stood there, burning brightly. It irked the warrior that the night lasted so long. The black Mooress, that country's queen, caused him to swoon again and again. He twisted and turned, time and again, like a bundle of willow twigs, his joints cracking. Battle and love were his desire—now wish that he be granted them! His heart resounded with blows, for it swelled with chivalry, stretching both the warrior's breasts, as the crossbow does the cord—all too 36 rash was his desire.

The lord lay there, not sleeping at all, until he espied the grey dawn—it yielded as yet no bright sheen. The man who was his chaplain was duty-bound to be at the ready for the mass. He sang it at once, for God and for Gahmuret. His armour was immediately brought to him; he rode off to where he could find jousting.

On this occasion he was mounted upon a charger well versed both in charging forward and leaping rapidly aside, turnable whenever its reins were tugged. His anchor, high upon the helmet, could be seen being borne towards the gate. Women and men alike declared there that never had they seen such a splendid warrior—their gods, so they thought, resembled him. Sturdy spears were also carried alongside him. How is he accoutred? His charger wore a covering of iron—that was its comfort against blows. On top of this lay a second cover, light, of no great weight—it was of green samite. His tabard and his surcoat were also green, of achmardi. They had been wrought over in Araby. I am not lying to anyone in this: his shield- 37 straps and all that belonged to them were of unbleached braid, studded with most precious stones. His shield-boss of red gold had been refined in fire. His service took love's reward—a fierce battle weighed little with him.

The queen reclined in the window—other ladies sat by her. Now see, there Hiuteger was halting, too, in the very place where fame had befallen him before. When he saw this knight come galloping towards him, he thought: 'When or how did this Frenchman come to this land? Who sent this haughty fellow here? If I took him for a Moor I'd be an idiot at best!'

Though their chargers were not slow to prance they both drove them on with spurs, from the gallop into the full tilt. They showed knightly courage, neither denying the other the joust. The splinters flew high into the air from bold Hiuteger's spear, but his defence felled him on the grass behind his charger. He was most unaccustomed to such usage. Gahmuret rode over to him and trampled him down. 38 Hiuteger picked himself up time and again, making a good show of his desire to defend himself, but Gahmuret's lance was stuck fast in his arm. He asked him to yield—Hiuteger had found his master. 'Who has vanquished me?' asked the bold man. The conqueror told him directly: 'I am Gahmuret Angevin.' Hiuteger said: 'Let my surrender be yours.' That Gahmuret accepted, and he sent him back into the castle. He was, inevitably, much praised for this by the the watching ladies.

Then there came hastening towards him Gaschier of Normandy, that proud knight rich in courage, that mighty jouster. Handsome Gahmuret, for his part, halted there, poised for the second joust. His spearhead's iron was broad, and the shaft firm. There the two foreigners opposed one another—the balance proved uneven. Gaschier lay on the ground, charger and all, felled by the joust, and was forced

39 to yield, whether he liked it or not. Gahmuret the warrior said: 'Your hand surrenders to me—it defended you valiantly. Now ride to the Scots' army and entreat them to refrain from battle against us, if they will be so kind, and follow me then into the city.'* Whatever he commanded or entreated was carried out to the letter—the Scots had to abandon battle.

Then Kaylet came riding up. Gahmuret turned away from him, as he was his aunt's son.* Why, then, should he harm him? The Spaniard shouted out after him long enough. He wore an ostrich upon his helmet. He was accoutred—so I am instructed—in phellel-silk, wide and long. The field resounded with the noise made by the warrior— his bells made music.* A flower of manly beauty he was! His complexion won the battle in beauty, with the exception of two who grew up after his time, Beacurs,* Lot's son, and Parzival, not present there—they were still unborn, but their beauty was acknowledged in time to come.

Gaschier took Kaylet by the bridle: 'Your wildness will be well

40 tamed, I tell you by my loyalty, if you take on that Angevin who has accepted my oath of surrender. You must heed my advice, and my request, too, lord. I have promised Gahmuret to turn you all back. I swore it, we clasped hands on it. For my sake, cease your struggle— or he will show you what strength in combat means!' King Kaylet replied: 'If it is my kinsman Gahmuret, *fil li roy* Gandin, then I will abandon battle against him. Let go of my bridle.' 'I won't let it go until my eyes see your head bared. Mine is all bedazed.' Kaylet then unbuckled his helmet.

Gahmuret found more fighting. It was by then about mid-morning. Those from the city who had beheld those jousts were delighted. They all hurried to their defensive outposts. Gahmuret was a net spread before them—whatever came under it was caught. The noble knight mounted a second charger, so I hear tell. It flew, and swept the ground, adroit on both sides, bold when battle was to be done, read- 41 ily restrainable, and yet swift. What did he do on this mount? This, I must aver, was courageous on his part: he rode to where the Moors could see him, where they lay encamped with their army, on the western side, there by the sea.*

There was a prince there called Razalic. Not for a single day did he desist, that mightiest man of Azagouc—his heritage did not betray him, his lineage was of kingly fruit—but he always headed off to joust before the city. There the warrior of Anjou dealt check-mate to his might. This a black lady lamented who had sent him there—that anyone should overpower him there. A squire, without even being asked, proffered his lord Gahmuret a spear, whose shaft was of bam- boo. With that he thrust the Moor onto the gravel, behind his char- ger—he left him lying there no longer—there his hand forced him to surrender. Then the battle itself was grounded, and great fame had fallen to Gahmuret. He saw eight banners fluttering, moving towards 42 the city—these he asked the bold, vanquished man to avert quickly, and then he ordered him to follow him at once back into the castle. That he did, for so it had to be.

Gaschier did not fail to arrive, either. Only then did Gahmuret's host realise that his guest had already gone forth into battle. That he did not devour iron like an ostrich,* nor mighty rocks, was only because he found none to hand. His anger fell to growling and roaring like a lion. He tore out his own hair, saying: 'Now my years are turning senile on me. The gods have sent me a bold, noble guest. If he is overladen with battle's burden, then my honour is lost forever. What use to me are shield and sword? Any man can curse me, who reminds me of this!' Then he turned away from his men, moving fast towards the gate. A page met him, carrying a shield, the inside and the outside painted with the image of a pierced man, fashioned in Isenhart's land. He also carried a helmet in his hand, and a sword that Razalic had courageously brought into battle. He 43 had been parted from it, that bold, black heathen, whose reputation ranged far and wide. If he afterwards died without being baptized, may He who holds sway over all wonders recognize the worth of that bold warrior!

When the burgrave saw that, such true happpiness had never befallen him before! He recognized the arms. Out of the gate he ran. He saw his guest halting there, that young man—not old by any means—still desiring a warlike joust. Then Lachfilirost,* his host, took hold of his reins, and drew him back by force. He thrust down no more men there.

Lachfilirost *Schahtelacunt** said: 'Lord, you must tell me, has your hand vanquished Razalic? Our land is safe from battle forever. He is lord over all the Moors, loyal Isenhart's men, who have done us this harm. Our peril is at an end. It was an angry god that commanded them to attack us here with their army—now their forces are defeated.'

44 He led him in, much to his regret. The queen rode to meet him. She took his bridle by her hand; she untied the fastenings of his ventail.* His host was obliged to leave him then. His pages did not neglect to follow hard after their lord. Through the city the wise queen was seen to lead her guest, who had won the prize there. She dismounted when the time seemed right to her: 'Alas, how loyal you squires are! You believe you are going to lose this man—his comfort will be seen to without your aid. Take his charger and lead it away— *I* am his companion here.'

Many ladies he found up there in the hall. He was disarmed by the queen's black hand. Upon a sable coverlet and a well-adorned bed intimate hospitality was granted him in increased measure. No-one else was present there. The damsels went out and locked the door behind them. Then the queen practised noble, sweet love, as did Gahmuret, her heart's beloved. Yet their skins were unalike.

45 They made many offerings to their gods, the people of the city. What commands were issued to bold Razalic, when he left the battlefield? He executed them them out of loyalty, but his grief on account of his lord, Isenhart, was renewed. The burgrave was alerted to his arrival. A great din arose then. The princes from all over the Queen of Zazamanc's land had arrived there. They thanked Gahmuret for the fame he had won there. In formal joust he had felled twenty-four knights, and had led most of their chargers back into the castle. Three princes had been taken captive there; many a knight rode with them to court, up to the great hall. He slept and ate,

and was splendidly arrayed in well-tailored clothes, the highest lord of that land. She who was called a maiden before was now a woman. She led him forth by her hand, saying: 'My person and my land are subject to this knight, if our enemies will concede it to him.'

Then Gahmuret was granted a courteous request: 'Come closer, 46 my lord Razalic: you are to kiss my wife. And do you the same, lord Gaschier.' He asked Hiuteger, the proud Scot, to kiss her on the mouth—he had been wounded by his joust.

He asked them all to be seated. Still on his feet, quick-wittedly he said: 'I would also gladly see my kinsman, if permission be granted by him who holds him captive here.* For kinship's sake I have no choice but to set him free.' The queen smiled at that, ordering a messenger to leap to fetch him. The charming *bêâ kunt** began to press his way through the crowd. He was wounded as a result of his knightly deeds, and had acquitted himself very well in the field. Gaschier the Norman brought him there—he was courteous, his father was a Frenchman. He was Kaylet's sister's son; he'd travelled in a woman's service. Killirjacac was his name, a counterweight to all men's beauty.

When Gahmuret beheld him—their countenances attested their kinship, they resembled one another greatly—he asked the mighty queen to kiss and embrace him. He said: 'Now come over here to 47 me.' The host then kissed him himself—they were delighted to see one another. Gahmuret then said: 'Alas, gentle youth, what were you doing here, being of such tender years? Tell me, did a woman command it of you?'

'They rarely command me, lord. It was my kinsman Gaschier brought me here, he himself knows well how. I have a thousand knights here for him and am in his service. In Rouen, in Normandy, I came to the muster, bringing him young warriors. I departed from Champagne for his sake. Now misfortune desires to ply her art and skill against him, unless you do honour to yourself. If it be your command, let him benefit by me, relieve his distress.'

'Take the solution entirely into your hands. Go now, and you, my lord Gaschier, and bring Kaylet here to me.' They did as the warrior desired, and fetched him at his request. Then he, too, was lovingly welcomed by Gahmuret, and often embraced by the mighty queen. 48 She kissed the charming warrior. It was entirely fitting that she should do so, he being her husband's aunt's son, and by lineage a noble king.

The lord then smilingly continued: 'God knows, Sir Kaylet, if I were to take Toledo from you, and your land of Spain, for the benefit of the King of Gascony, who often attacks you in his anger, that would be disloyal on my part, for you are my aunt's son. The best of men are all with you here, the hard core of chivalry. Who forced this journey upon you?'

Then the bold young warrior said: 'My kinsman Schiltunc, whose daughter Fridebrant has in marriage, commanded me to serve him; it was his counsel. On his wife's account he has—from me alone— six thousand renowned knights here. They are valiant fighters. I brought even more knights here on his behalf; some of them have since departed. These valiant bands were here to support the Scots.

49 Warriors bold came to him from Greenland, two kings commanding great forces—they brought with them a deluge of chivalry, and many a keel. Their band pleased me greatly. Morholt, too, was here for Fridebrant's sake—he fights with strength and cunning.* They have left now. Whatever my lady instructs me, I shall do, as will my men. My service shall be made manifest to her—there is no need for you to thank me for my service, for our kinship commands it. These bold warriors are now yours. If they were baptized like mine, and of the same skin-colour, then no man who was ever crowned might have his fill of fighting from them. I wonder what brought you here. Tell me the full story of how that came about.'

[Gahmuret:] 'I arrived yesterday, and today I have become lord over this land. The queen captured me with her hand—then I fought back with love, as my senses counselled.' [Kaylet:] 'I believe your sweet defence vanquished the armies on both sides.' [Gahmuret:] 'You mean because I ran away from you. You shouted at me loud enough! What did you want to gain from me by force? Let me deal 50 with you differently now.'* [Kaylet:] 'I didn't recognize your anchor then. My aunt's husband Gandin seldom bore it into battle.' [Gahmuret:] 'Yet I recognized your ostrich well enough, and the *sarapandratest** on your shield. Your ostrich stood erect, without a nest. I saw by your attitude that you were very angry that two men had surrendered to me. They'd fought very well there.' [Kaylet:] 'The same would probably have happened to me. I have to admit, even if the victor were a devil whose ways I could never rejoice in—if he had won such fame from bold warriors as you have, the women would gobble him up, rather than sugar!' [Gahmuret:] 'Your mouth grants me too much praise.' [Kaylet:] 'No, I'm no flatterer. Count on my help in other ways.'

They called Razalic over to them. Courteously Kaylet then said: 'My kinsman Gahmuret has captured you with his own hands.'

'Sir, that is what has happened. I have acknowledged to this warrior that the land of Azagouc will never stint to serve him, since our lord Isenhart is not to wear the crown here. He was slain in the service of her who is now your kinsman's wife. For her love he gave his life. My kiss on her lips has settled that dispute. I have lost my lord and kinsman. If your aunt's son will now act chivalrously and compensate us for the loss of him, then I will fold my hands in his.* Thus he has gained wealth and fame, and all that Tankanis bequeathed to Isenhart—he who lies embalmed among the army there. Every day since this spearhead broke his heart I have gazed upon his wounds.' He drew the spearhead out of his bosom, where it hung by a silk thread. Then the bold warrior hung it back on his chest, next to his bare skin. 'It is still broad daylight. If my lord Killirjacac will take a message to the army, at my request, then the princes will ride with him.' He sent a ring there. Those who were of Hell's colour rode, all those that were princes there, through the city up to the great hall.

Then Gahmuret's hand conferred lands upon the princes of Azagouc, banners marking the ceremony. Each was delighted with his portion, yet the greater part remained with Gahmuret their lord. Those princes were the first. Closer, then, pressed those of Zazamanc, with full ceremony, none too shabby. They accepted from him, as their lady commanded, their land and its usufruct, as befitted each and every one of them. Poverty had fled their lord. Protyzilas, who was a prince by lineage, had left behind him a duchy; this Gahmuret bestowed upon him who had won much fame by his hand—never was he daunted in the face of battle—Lahfilirost *Schahtelacunt* accepted it at once, with the banner.

The noble princes of Azagouc then led forward the Scot Hiuteger and Gaschier the Norman. Next they walked up to their lord. He set them free at their request, for which they then thanked Gahmuret. The princes entreated Hiuteger the Scot, in all sincerity: 'Leave my lord the tent here, as his adventure's reward. It plucked Isenhart's life from us when Fridebrant was given this jewel of our country. His joy was pledged away. Here he now lies on the funeral bier. Unrequited service brought him too much sorrow.'

There was nothing so precious on earth as that helmet, made out of adamant, thick and strong, a good companion in battle. Then Hiuteger's hand vowed that, when he arrived back in his lord's land, he would gather all the armour together and send it back in perfect condition. That Hiuteger did unprompted. All the princes there present pressed forward to the king to take their leave. Then they left the hall. Although his land was laid waste, Gahmuret's hand could still lavish such gifts by way of reward that it seemed as if all the trees bore gold. He distributed great gifts. His subjects and his kinsmen accepted from him the warrior's wealth—that was the queen's intention.

The bridal ceremony had been preceded by many a great battle; thus they were now reconciled. I didn't think this up myself—they told me that Isenhart was buried in kingly fashion. It was carried out
54 by those who knew his worth. The tax on his lands, what it might amount to over a year, all that they left behind them there. That they did of their own volition. Gahmuret ordered Isenhart's people to keep his great wealth—they should dispose of it themselves.

The next morning, outside the fortress, all the foreigners decamped. Those there parted from one another, carrying many a bier with them. The field stood bare of all lodgings, except for one tent, of great size. That the king ordered to be taken on board ship. He then went about telling the people that he wanted to take it to Azagouc—with these words he was deceiving them.

There the proud, bold man remained until he began to pine a great deal. That he found no deeds of knighthood caused his joy to be sorrow's forfeit. Yet the black woman was dearer to him than his own life. Never was a woman better shaped. That lady's heart never neglected to give him good company—womanly bearing alongside true chastity.

Of Seville, from that city, was born that man whom he asked to take him away, some time soon. He had transported him many a mile
55 in the past—he had brought him there. He was not like a Moor in colour. The wise mariner said: 'You must quietly conceal this from all those who have black skins here. My cogs are so quick that they cannot get near us. We must leave here in haste!'

Gahmuret ordered his gold to be carried on board ship. Now I must tell you of a parting: that night the noble king set off—it was done in secret. When he deserted his wife, she had already been bearing a child in her womb for some twelve weeks, alive. Speedily the wind led him away.

The lady found in her purse a letter in her husband's writing, in French—which she knew. The writing told her: 'Here one sweetheart sends a message to another sweetheart. I am, by dint of this journey, a thief. I had to steal it from you, because it causes such grief. Lady, I cannot conceal from you that if your religion were within my law, then I would always long for you—and as it is, I shall always feel pangs for you. If the little child born to us both takes on a man's countenance, truly he will be rich in courage. He's born of 56 Anjou. Love will be his lady, but he will be a storm in battle, a harsh neighbour to his foes. My son should know that his grandfather was called Gandin—he died in knightly combat. His father suffered the same fate—he was called Addanz—his shield seldom remained intact. He was by lineage a Briton. He and Uther Pendragon were the sons of two brothers, whose names are both written here: one of them was Lazaliez; Brickus the other was called. The father of these two was called Mazadan. A fairy took him into Famurgan—she was called Terdelaschoye*—he was her heart's fetter. From these two comes my line, which will forever shed a bright sheen. Each of them afterwards wore a crown, and enjoyed ample honour. Lady, if you'll be baptized, you may yet win me for your own.'

She wished for no other outcome: 'Oh, how soon that will happen! If he will only return, I will quickly put an end to the matter! To 57 whom has his manly courtesy here abandoned his love's fruit? Alas for loving companionship, if grief's power is now forever to oppress me! For the honour of his god,' said the woman, 'I would gladly be baptized and live as he would wish.' Distress waged war upon her heart. Her joy found the dry twig, as the turtle-dove* still does. She is always of one mind: when she has lost her love, her loyalty has always chosen the dry branch.

When her time was due the lady gave birth to a son, who was of two colours. By him God devised a miracle—both black and white was his appearance. The queen kissed him incessantly, very often on his white marks. The mother called her baby Feirefiz Angevin. He became a wood-waster—the jousts of his hands shattered many a spear, riddling shields with holes. His hair and his entire skin, too, became, in hue, like that of a magpie.

Now over a year had passed since Gahmuret had been much

58 praised, there at Zazamanc; his hand had won the victory there. He was still sailing the sea, the harsh winds causing him distress. A silk sail he saw, red—it was borne by a cog, as were the messengers which Fridebrant of the Scots had sent to Lady Belacane. He asked her to pardon him, although he had lost a kinsman by her, for having attacked her. They carried with them the adamant, a sword, a hauberk, and a pair of leg-guards.* Here you may hear a great wonder, that the cog met Gahmuret's ship, as the adventure swore to me. They gave the equipment to him. Then he vowed, for his part, that his mouth would be a guarantor of that message, when he returned to her. They parted. I am told that the sea bore him into a harbour; from there he headed for Seville. With gold bold Gahmuret then rewarded his mariner well for his toil. They parted—to the latter's grief.

BOOK II

THERE in that land of Spain he knew the king: it was his cousin
59 Kaylet. In search of him, he headed for Toledo. Kaylet had already departed in pursuit of chivalry, where shields were not to be spared. Then Gahmuret ordered that he, too, should be equipped for battle—so the adventure assures me—with spears well-painted, with green pennants of sendal-silk. Each spear had a banner proudly displaying three ermine anchors, of such splendour that their costliness was acclaimed far and wide. They were long and broad, reaching down almost to the hand, when tied a span below the spearhead. For bold Gahmuret a hundred of these were prepared and proudly carried after him by his cousin's people. They knew how to show him due honour and affection—that by no means displeased Kaylet, their lord.

Gahmuret had travelled, I don't know how long, in search of Kaylet, when he spotted strangers' tents in the country of Waleis.* Before the city of Kanvoleis many a pavilion had been pitched upon the plain. This isn't guesswork I'm reporting to you—by your leave, this is the truth. He ordered his people to come to a full halt. The
60 lord sent ahead into the city his clever master squire; he intended, at his master's request, to take up lodgings there. He didn't waste any

time—the packhorses were already being led after him. His eyes
saw not a single house there that did not have a second roof, made of
shields, and the walls were hung with spears all around. The Queen
of Waleis had proclaimed a tournament at Kanvoleis, organized
along such lines that many a coward would be daunted these days if
he saw the like—he'd take no part in it! She was a maiden, unmar-
ried, and offered two countries as well as her person to whoever won
the prize there. These tidings felled many a man behind his charger,
down upon the turf. Those who took such a fall were declared losers
at the game—it was played by undaunted warriors, who made show
of knightly valour. Many a charger was spurred to the headlong
gallop there, lots of swords made to ring out.

A pontoon above a plain crossed a stream's flow; it was closed by a
gate. Knowing no fear, the squire opened it, being so inclined. High 61
above stood the great hall. Within sat the queen at the windows,
together with many a noble lady. They were watching what those
squires were doing. After consultation they had decided to pitch a
tent. Out of unrequited love a king had been deprived of it, driven to
it by Belacane.

Laboriously it was erected, that tent. It had taken thirty pack-
horses to carry it. What a display of luxury! The plain was, I believe,
quite wide enough for the tent-ropes to be stretched out. Meanwhile
noble Gahmuret was having breakfast outside the city; after that he
applied himself diligently to how he might ride in and make a courtly
entrance. Then there was no further delay—his squires at once tied
his spears together in bundles of five. Each carried a sixth lance in
his hand, with a banner. Thus the proud knight came riding up.

Those near the queen heard that a stranger from a far-off land was 62
to arrive, not known to anyone there: 'His retinue is courtly, both
heathen and French—some of them may indeed be Angevins, to
judge by their speech. Their disposition is proud, their garments are
radiant, well-tailored, for sure. I was close to his pages—they are
beyond reproach. They say that if anyone is minded to seek out their
lord, he will part him from distress by his generosity. I asked for
information about him. Then they told me straight out that it is
the king of Zazamanc'—a squire told her these tidings—'Oh what a
pavilion! Your crown and your country couldn't be pawned for half
its price.'

'There's no need for you to sing its praises to me. I can tell you

with my own lips that it probably belongs to a nobleman who knows
nothing of poverty!'—the queen said. 'Oh, why doesn't he come into
the city himself?' She asked the squire to make enquiry.

In courtly fashion, through the city the warrior commenced his
63 ride, waking those still slumbering. He saw the glint of many shields.
The bright trumpets sounded out ahead of him, making a loud
clamour. Two tabors were thrown up into the air and thumped
loudly; all over the city the din resounded. The melody was, how-
ever, varied by flutes, playing a march to accompany the procession.
Let us not lose sight, now, of how their lord has made his entry!
Fiddlers were riding at his side.

Then the noble warrior cocked one leg in front of him on his horse,
a pair of light summer boots drawn over his bare legs. His mouth
shone like a ruby, red as if it were ablaze; his lips were thick—by no
means too thin. His appearance was radiant in every detail. Bright and
curly was his hair, where it could be seen beneath his hat—that was a
costly piece of headgear! His cloak was of green samite; a sable at the
front shone black over a tunic, which was white. The crowd jostled
one another, eager to catch a glimpse. Again and again they asked who
the beardless knight was who brought such luxury with him. Rapidly
64 the news spread—his retinue gave them a straight answer. They were
advancing towards the bridge—both Gahmuret's men, and other
companies, too. At the sight of the bright sheen cast by the queen he
quickly brought his leg down to the side. The noble knight sat up,
erect, like a falcon desiring its prey. That lodging looked attractive,
the warrior thought. Nor, I imagine, did she have any objection to
him—the lady of the land, the Queen of Waleis.

Then the King of Spain heard that on the Leoplan* a tent had been
pitched which, at bold Razalic's request, had fallen to Gahmuret's
lot, on the field of Patelamunt, so a knight informed him. At this he
leapt like a deer—he was a soldier in joy's pay. The same knight
continued: 'Your aunt's son I saw, making as proud an entrance as
ever. There are a hundred banners, together with a single shield,
planted in the green grass before his tall tent. The banners, too, are
all green, and the bold warrior has three ermine anchors, brightly
painted, on each sendal silk.'

65   'Is Gahmuret arrayed for battle here? Oh, then they'll see how he
turns the charge aside, how his onrush confounds the attacker!
Proud King Hardiz has directed his anger long and hard against

me—Gahmuret's hand shall now cow him by his joust. It is not my fate to be doomed, after all!'

Kaylet sent his messengers immediately to where Gaschier the Norman was encamped with a great retinue, along with the resplendent Killirjakac—they were there at his entreaty. In company with Kaylet they walked to the pavilion. There they welcomed, with warm affection, the noble King of Zazamanc. It seemed to them too long a wait by far since they had last seen him—as, indeed, they loyally averred. Then Gahmuret asked them for news of what knights were present there.

His aunt's son replied: 'Here from far-off lands are knights pursued by Love—many bold, undaunted warriors. *Roys* Uther Pendragon has many a Briton with him here. One matter pierces him 66 like a thorn—that he has lost his wife, who was Arthur's mother. A cleric, well read in magic—with him the lady has gone off—Arthur has gone in pursuit of him. It is getting on for three years now, indeed, since he lost his son and wife. Here, too, is his daughter's husband, well-versed in chivalry, Lot of Norway,* slow to falsehood and quick to fame, a bold and wise warrior. Here too is Gawan, his son, too frail as yet to engage in any kind of chivalry. He was over here with me, the little one. He says that if he could break a shaft, if he could be confident in his strength, he would gladly do a knight's deeds. How early his desire for it has begun! The king of Patrigalt has brought a whole forest of spears here. His proud ways count for nothing, though, because the men of Portugal are also here. These we call bold knights indeed—they want to thrust lances through shields! Here the Provençals have brought their well-painted shields. Here are the men of Waleis, bent on pressing home their lances 67 wherever they will, backed by their numbers here in their homeland. Here, for women's sake, is many a knight I cannot identify. All these I have named, we are encamped in great splendour—no doubt about that—inside the city, at the queen's request.

'I'll tell you now who are quartered out in the field*—they think but little of our defence: the noble King of Ascalun, and the proud King of Aragon, Cidegast of Logrois, and the King of Punturtoys— he is called Brandelidelin. Here too is bold Lähelin. Then there is Morholt of Ireland,* who plucks precious pledges from us. There on the plain the proud Alemans are encamped. The Duke of Brabant has travelled to this land on King Hardiz's behalf. To him the

King of Gascony gave his sister Alice. His service has won reward
in the past.

'These are my angry opponents here. Now I trust I can count on
68   you. Think of our kinship. By the true affection that you bear me,
come to my aid!'

Then the King of Zazamanc replied: 'You have no need to thank
me for any service I perform in your honour here. We must be of one
single purpose. Has your ostrich found no nest yet? You must carry
your *sarapandratest* against Hardiz's half-griffin. My anchor will be
firmly struck to land in his tilt's charge—he'll have to find his own
ford, behind his charger, down on the gravel. If they let us at one
another, I'll fell him, or he'll fell me—I'll guarantee you that much,
by my loyalty.'

Kaylet rode back to his lodgings, full of joy, free of sorrow. There
arose heralds' cries, announcing two proud warriors: Schyolarz of
Poitou and Gurnemanz *de* Graharz,* who were jousting on the plain.
At once the vesper tournament* began. Six rode here, another three
or so there, another troop, perhaps, accompanying them. They set
about performing true knightly deeds—there was simply no choice
in the matter then!

69   It was as yet no later than midday. The lord lay in his tent. Then
the King of Zazamanc heard that the mounted charges, wide and
long, had begun on the field, all according to chivalric rules. He, too,
headed in that direction, with many a brightly-coloured banner. He
had no interest in hasty charges. At his leisure he intended to see
what deeds were being done on both sides there. His carpet they
spread out on the meadow, where the charges were criss-crossing,
and the horses whinnying as they were spurred onward. A ring of
pages formed about him, amid the clash and clang of swords—how
they strove for fame, how their blades rang out! Spears splintered
with a great crack. He had no need to ask anyone for directions.
Charges were his tent-walls—they were wrought by knights' hands!

The knightly deeds were so close by that the ladies, looking down
from the great hall, could clearly see the warriors' labours. The
queen, however, was sorry that the King of Zazamanc did not enter
the press with the others. She said: 'Oh, where is he of whom I have
heard such wonders?'

Now it happened that the *rois de Franze* had died, he whose wife
had often brought great distress upon Gahmuret because of his love

for her. The noble queen had sent messengers to him there, inquir- 70
ing whether he had yet returned to the country from heathen lands.
Great affection's power compelled her to this.

Great deeds were done there by many a poor man of courage, who
had, however, no aspiration to the heights promised by the queen,
her person and her lands—they desired other pledges.*

Now Gahmuret, too, was clad in armour, whereby his wife was
reminded of a reconciliation. It had been sent by Fridebrant of
Scotland as a gift to compensate her for her losses—he had over-
burdened her with battle. Nothing was so precious on this earth.
Gahmuret gazed at the adamant—some helmet that was! On top
of it they tied an anchor, in which precious stones were found set,
huge, none too small—that was, however, a heavy burden. Thus the
stranger was accoutred.

How was his shield embellished? A precious boss had been beaten
upon it, of gold of Araby, heavy, but he had to carry it. It gave off 71
such a red glare that you could see yourself reflected in it. A sable
anchor was beneath. I myself would have no objection to what he
asked them to put on him, for it was worth many a mark.

His surcoat was very wide. I doubt if any as good was ever borne
into battle since. It was so long it reached right down to the carpet.
Let me try to describe it: it shone as if a bright flame was burning in
the night. Faded colours were scarce there—its brilliance did not shun
glances. A weak eye would have cut itself on it. It was figured with
gold, which gryphons' claws had torn from a rock in the Caucasus
mountain.* Gryphons guarded it then, and still guard gold there
today. From Araby people make their way there, to acquire it by
cunning—there is nothing as precious anywhere else—and they take
it back to Araby, where the green achmardi are worked, and the rich
brocades. Other clothing bears little resemblance to this.

Next he slung the shield around his neck. A charger stood at the
ready, of great beauty, armed right down to the hoof. Here, heralds, 72
call out, cry out! He leapt upon the horse—because it was there.
Many stout spears were splintered by the warrior's hand in the tilt,
scattering his opponents' charges, always thrusting through, and out
the other side. The anchor was followed by the ostrich.

Gahmuret thrust Poytwin *de* Prienlascors down, behind his char-
ger, and many another noble man, from whom he won surrender.
Where knights rode who wore the cross,* they profited from the

warrior's labour. He gave them the chargers he had won—great was their gain by him.

Four identical banners were led towards him—bold squadrons rode under them—their lord knew how to do battle—each of them sporting a gryphon's tail. This hind part was a hailstorm of chivalry—such were its bearers! The front part of the gryphon was worn by the King of Gascony on his shield—an astute knight. He was so arrayed as to please women's scrutiny. He advanced in front of the others when he saw the ostrich on top of the helmet, but it was the anchor which met him first. He was thrust to the ground behind his charger by the noble King of Zazamanc, who took him prisoner. Then a great crowd pressed close, deep furrows were threshed even, much combed by swords. There a whole forest of lances was laid waste, and many a knight felled. These retreated—so I heard tell—to the rear, where cowards halted.

The battle was, I believe, so close by that all the ladies could see who was likely to win the prize there. The ardent Riwalin*—from his spear a fresh path of splinters snowed down. He was the King of Lohneis*—his charges sounded out with a loud crack! Morholt stole a knight from them,* hoisting him out of his saddle—that was a monstrously improper practice! Killirjacac was the knight's name. From him King Lac* had previously reaped such reward that he had fallen to the ground—he had done many a good deed there. But then mighty Morholt was seized by the desire to grapple with Killirjacac, without swords, and so he captured the noble warrior.

Kaylet's hand thrust down the Duke of Brabant* behind his charger—that prince was called Lambekin. What did his men do then? They shielded him with their swords—those warriors were eager for battle.

Then the King of Aragon thrust the aged Uther Pendragon, the King of Britain,* down behind his charger onto the meadow, where flowers grew in profusion about him. Alas, how uncouth am I, to land the noble Briton low in such a pretty setting before Kanvoleis, where no peasant's foot ever trod, if I am to tell you the truth of the matter—nor, in all likelihood, ever will. He had no need of a mount, sitting where he now sat. He was not, however, forgotten for long— he was shielded by those fighting above him there. Great charges were not spared there.

Along then came the King of Punturteis.* On that spot, before

73

74

Kanvoleis, he was felled in his charger's tracks, so that he lay behind
it there. That was proud Gahmuret's doing. Charge on, lord, charge
on! Locked in battle they found his aunt's son Kaylet—the men of
Punturteis captured him. Then the road became really rough! When 75
King Brandelidelin had been seized and separated from his men,
they took another king captive in their turn. There was a toing and
froing of many noble men in armour. Their hides were tanned by
horses' hooves and by cudgels. Their skins wore black swellings—
those handsome heroes won bruises for their pains there.

It's not a pretty tale I tell: rest was held in low regard there. Love
had driven noble warriors there; many a splendid shield, many a
decorated helmet acquired a covering of dust. Here the field blos-
somed with flowers, there short green grass grew in plenty—on
that those noble fighters fell to whom that honour was assigned.
My desire is capable of putting up with such aspirations, always
provided I stay seated on my foal.

Then the King of Zazamanc rode off to a place where no-one
crowded him, looking for a rested charger. They unbuckled the
adamant from his head—only to let him have a breath of air, not
because of any idle boast. They drew back his coif—his mouth was
red and proud.

A woman I have mentioned before—here now came one of her 76
chaplains, and three young lordlings. Sturdy squires rode at their
side, leading two packhorses. These messengers had been sent here
by Queen Ampflise. Her chaplain was a wise man. He immediately
recognized Gahmuret. At once he greeted him in French as follows:
'*Bien sei venûs, bêâs sir*** from my lady and myself. She is *rêgín de
Franze*,* she is touched by the lance of your love.' A letter he placed
in his hands, in which the lord found greetings, and an elegant ring.
This was intended as a token of good faith, as his lady had herself
received it from the Angevin. He bowed on recognizing the writing.
Would you like to hear what it said?

'To you I send love and greeting, I who have known no cure for
sorrow since I first felt love for you. Your love is the lock and fetter of
my heart and its joy. Your love puts me to death. If your love is to
estrange itself from me, then love may well confound me. Return, 77
and accept at my hand crown, sceptre and a land. These death has
bequeathed to me—now your love has won them. Take also as your
reward the rich gifts in these four panniers. You are, moreover, to be

my knight in the land of Waleis, before the capital of Kanvoleis. I care not whether the queen sees it. It cannot do me much harm. I am more beautiful and more powerful, and know better how, with greater charm, to receive love and to give love. If you would live in accord with noble love, then take my crown as love's reward.'

In this letter he found no more. A page's hand drew his coif back over his head. Sorrow fled Gahmuret. They buckled the adamant, which was thick and hard, upon his head—he was in the mood for arduous toil. The messengers he ordered to be led, for their repose, into the pavilion. Where the crowd pressed, he made room.

One man lost, another won. A man could readily make amends
78 there, if he had failed in deeds before—there was opportunity enough. Some were to joust, others to attack in teams. They abandoned those sneaking touches that are called friendly taps—close kinship was wrenched apart by anger's power. Crookedness is seldom straightened there. There was not much talk there of knightly law—whoever won anything, kept it, not caring if another objected. They had come from many different lands, those who plied the shield's office there with their hands, little fearing the cost.

There Gahmuret granted Ampflise's request that he should be her knight—a letter had brought him the tidings. Ah, now he was loosed into battle! Did love and courage spur him on? Great affection and strong fidelity replenished all his powers. Now he saw where King Lot was fending off hardship with his shield, almost forced to turn in flight—Gahmuret's hand prevented that. With his charge he broke
79 the enemy's onset. The King of Aragon he thrust behind his charger with a spear of cane—Schafillor that king was called. The spear with which he felled that proud warrior had no banner; he had brought it with him from heathendom. Schafillor's men defended him in numbers, yet Gahmuret took the noble knight captive. The inner army then forced the outer to ride hard across the plain. Their vesper tournament reaped battle's reward—it could easily have been called a tourney proper, for many a spear lay on the ground, broken in two.

Then Lähelin grew angry: 'Are we to be thus dishonoured? This is the doing of the knight who bears the anchor. One of us two will lay the other low before the day is out, in some place where he will lie uneasily. They have almost vanquished us!' Their charge created a wide space about them—now child's play was at an end! Their hands wrought such deeds that the wood began to be laid waste. Both shared a single desire: 'A spear here, lord, a spear, a spear!' Yet Lähelin was doomed to suffer shameful torment. The King of Zazamanc thrust him behind his charger, a good spear's length—it had a cane shaft. Gahmuret gathered his surrender. For my part, I'd rather pick up 80 sweet pears, fast though the knights dropped down before him.

The cry in many an opponent's mouth, facing his joust, was: 'Here comes the anchor, beware! Beware!' A prince of Anjou came charging towards him—grief was his mistress—with an inverted shield. Sorrow had taught him that lesson. Gahmuret recognized the device. Why did he turn away from him? If you wish, I shall inform you: the arms had been assigned by proud Galoes, *fil li roi* Gandin, his most loyal brother, before Love brought about his death in a joust.

Then Gahmuret unbuckled his helmet. Neither the grass nor the dust were trodden any more that day by his combat. Great sorrow rebuked him. He cursed himself for not questioning Kaylet, his aunt's son, more closely as to what his brother's intentions were, and why he was not tourneying here. He didn't know, unfortunately, that Galoes had died before Muntori. And another sorrow already troubled him more, forced upon him by the noble love of a mighty 81 queen. She, for her part, afterwards suffered for his sake—she lay dead of lamenting loyalty.

Although Gahmuret was so sad, he had, nevertheless, in that half day, split so many spears in two that if the tournament proper had taken place, the whole wood would have been laid waste. A hundred coloured spears were accounted to him, all broken by that proud knight. His bright banners had fallen to the heralds, which was well within their rights.

Then he rode towards the pavilion. The Queen of Waleis's page followed in his tracks; to him was given the costly surcoat, pierced through and hewn to pieces—he carried it into the lady's presence. Its gold still retained its mettle, glistening like a glowing coal, its wealth apparent to all. Then the queen, in merry mood, said: 'A noble woman has sent you, along with this knight, into this land.* Now, my discretion admonishes me that the others whom adventure has brought here should not be belittled. Let all of them heed my wish, for they are all kin to me, by Adam's rib. Yet I believe 82 Gahmuret's deeds have won the highest prize here.'

The others were still engaged in knightly deeds, inspired by such aggression that they hewed away almost till nightfall. The inner army had by their combat forced the outer back to their pavilions. Were it not for the King of Ascalun and Morholt of Ireland, they would have run through their ropes.

There were both wins and losses there—a good few had met with disgrace, others with fame and honour. Now it is time for them to be parted from one another. No-one can see anything here now. If the stake-holder didn't lay on light for them, who would play blackjack in the dark? That would be asking too much of weary men.

They were oblivious to darkness where my lord Gahmuret sat, as if it were bright day. It was nothing of the kind, but there were a tremendous number of lights, many a cluster of little candles; placed upon olive-tree leaves were many costly quilts, spread out with care, with many a broad carpet before them. The queen rode up to the

83 tent-ropes with many noble ladies in attendance; she was keen to see the noble King of Zazamanc. A crowd of weary knights pressed after her.

The tablecloths had been taken away* before she entered the pavilion. The host leapt quickly to his feet, as did four captured kings, who had several princes in their train. He welcomed her as good manners demanded. He pleased her well, now that she had a good look at him. The Queen of Waleis said joyfully: 'You are host here where I have found you, yet I am queen over this country. If it's your will that I should kiss you, then I will willingly do so.'

He replied: 'Your kiss shall be mine, provided these lords are kissed, too. If any king or prince is to be deprived of it, then I, for my part, daren't desire a kiss of you.'

'Indeed, that too shall happen. I hadn't noticed any of them till now.' She kissed those who were worthy of it there, as Gahmuret requested.

He asked the queen to be seated. My lord Brandelidelin sat down courteously next to the lady. Green rushes, wet with dew, thinly

84 spread over the carpets—upon these, delighted, the noble Queen of Waleis sat down. Love of Gahmuret, though, oppressed her. He sat down in front of her, so close that she could take hold of him and draw him back, to the other side, close to her person. She was a maiden and not a woman, she who had him sit so close. Would you like to hear her name now?—Queen Herzeloyde, and her paternal

aunt was Rischoyde, wife to King Kaylet, whose aunt's son on his mother's side was Gahmuret. Lady Herzeloyde cast such radiance that even if all the candles had been extinguished, she alone would have supplied light enough. Were it not for the fact that great grief undercut the height of his joy, his love would have been entirely at her disposal.

They exchanged greetings as decorum chose. After a while cup-bearers came up with jewels from Azagouc, whose great luxury deceived no-one—young lords carried them in. Those must have been costly goblets, made of noble gems, broad, none too small. Each and every one of them was of gold. It was that land's taxes' payment which Isenhart had offered time and again to Belacane, to obtain relief from his great duress. Drinks were offered to them there in 85 many a beautiful precious stone—emeralds and sardines—there was the odd ruby amongst them.

Up to the pavilion there then rode two knights under oath of surrender. They had been captured out in the field, and now came walking in. One of these was Kaylet. He saw King Gahmuret sitting in an unhappy pose. He said: 'Why are you acting like this? Your fame is openly acknowledged—you have won Lady Herzeloyde and her lands. All tongues tell of this here, be they Britons or Irishmen, or all those who can speak the Romance tongue here, Frenchmen or Flemish, they all acknowledge your prowess and follow your lead. In a game of this kind no-one can match you here. I read the true letter of this here—your courageous strength was not slumbering when these lords were endangered, hands which had never before offered surrender: my lord Brandelidelin, and bold Lähelin, Hardiz and Schafillor. Alas for Razalic the Moor, whom you also acquainted with 86 surrender before Patelamunt! Your fame in battle aspires to new heights, far and wide.'

'My lady may imagine that you are raving, since you praise me so excessively. You can't sell me at this price, though, because some-body or other will see a flaw in me. Your mouth has let too much praise be heard. Tell me now, how did you find your way back?'

'The noble people of Punturtoys have set me and this Champenois entirely at liberty. Morholt, who stole my nephew—Killirjacac is to be set free by him, provided my lord Brandelidelin may be freed by your hand. Otherwise we'll both still be hostages, I and my sister's son. You must show us mercy. Such a vesper tournament has been

endured here that all further tourneying will be renounced before
Kanvoleiz at this time. I know that for a fact, because the outer
army's hard core is sitting here. Now just tell me, how could they
possibly make a stand against us now? You have a lot of fame at your
disposal!'

87   The queen addressed to Gahmuret a gentle request, which came
from her heart: 'Whatever my legal claim upon you may be, you
must grant me. Moreover, my service desires your favour. If I am
granted both these here, if that should be to the detriment of your
fame, then let me withdraw.'

But the chaplain to Ampflise, that chaste and wise queen, immedi-
ately leapt to his feet, saying: 'No! By rights he belongs to my lady,
who has sent me to this country in pursuit of his love. She lives
consumed by love for him. Her love has a vested claim upon him.
She has a right to keep her hold on him, for she cherishes him more
than all other women. Here are her messengers, princes three,
youths free of reproach. One is called Lanzidant, of high lineage,
from Greenland. He has come to Carolingia* and has learned the
language. The second is called Liedarz, *fil li cuns* Schiolarz.'

Now who might the third be? Hear a tale of this, too: his mother
was called Beaflurs, and his father Pansamurs—they were of fairy
88 stock. Their son was called Liahturteltart. They all three ran up to
him: 'Lord, if you're sensible, *regin de Franze* will pay the cost of
noble Love's dice-throws for you—that way you can play without
any pledge. Your joy will at once be free of sorrow.'

As this embassy was being heard, Kaylet, who had arrived before
the messengers, was sitting under the edge of the queen's robe.* To
him she spoke these words: 'Tell me, has anything else happened to
you? I see the mark of blows upon you.' Then the lovely lady
touched his bruises with her gentle white hands—these were the
work of God's diligence. His cheeks, chin and nose were crushed and
sorely bruised. His wife was the aunt of that queen who showed him
this honour, drawing him to her with her hands.

She said, as courtesy taught her, further words to Gahmuret: 'The
noble Frenchwoman urges her love upon you. Now honour all
women by me and let me have my rights. Remain here until I have
89 my verdict—otherwise you will put me to shame.' That noble
Gahmuret promised her. She took her leave, then departed. Kaylet,
the noble warrior, lifted her onto her horse without the assistance of

any footstool, and then walked back inside, to meet the looks of his friends.

He said to Hardiz: 'Your sister Alize offered me love, which I accepted. She is now placed elsewhere, and more worthily than with me. By your courtesy, abandon your anger. She is now the wife of Prince Lambekin. Even though she is not crowned, she has recognized true worth. Hainaut and Brabant serve her, and many a good knight. Greet me as a friend now, let me be in your good graces, and accept in return my service.'

The King of Gascony replied, as his manly courage prompted him: 'Your words were always gentle. If a man upon whom you had inflicted much disgrace were to greet you on that count, he would be overlooking the injury out of fear.* It was your aunt's son captured me—he is incapable of maltreating anyone.'

'You may easily be freed by Gahmuret. That shall be my first request. When you are no longer captive, my service may yet live to see the day when you accept me as a friend. By now you might easily have got over your disgrace. Whatever harm you may do me, your sister would not have slain me!'

They all laughed at this speech. Then a cloud was cast over their merriment. His loyalty led the host to be troubled by his longing to return home, for sorrow is a sharp goad. Each of them perceived that he was wrestling with troubles and that all his joy was but slight. Then his aunt's son grew angry, saying: 'You're acting in unseemly fashion!'

'No, I have no choice but to grieve. I long for the queen. I left behind in Patelamunt one for whom my heart is wounded, in her pure nature a sweet woman. Her noble chastity calls to my mind sorrow for love of her. She gave me her people and lands. Lady Belacane deprives me of manly joys—yet it is very manly, if a man is ashamed of inconstancy in love. The lady's restrictions so tethered me down,* that I could find no knightly deeds. Then I thought that chivalry would free me from discontent's power—such as I have in some part enacted here. Now many an ignorant man believes it was her blackness drove me away—that I would look on rather than the sun! Her womanly honour causes me sorrow. She is the boss on nobility's shield. This is one cause for lament, but there is another, too: I saw my brother's arms being carried with the point inverted. Alas that I must speak such words!'

The tale then took a wretched turn. The eyes of the noble Spaniard grew rich with water: 'Alas, *fole** Queen, for love of you Galoes gave his life, he over whom all women ought to grieve from their hearts, loyally, if they desire their behaviour to bring them praise wherever they are in men's thoughts. Queen of Navarre, little as it troubles you, it was my kinsman I lost through you. He chose a knightly end by a joust which slew him, when he was wearing your token. Princes,

92 his companions, are manifesting their heartfelt lament. They have turned the broad part of their shield, as sorrow's escort, to the ground. Deep sadness so instructs them. Thus they now do knightly deeds. They are overburdened by grief's load since Galoes, my aunt's son, is no longer to serve in love's cause.'

When Gahmuret heard of his brother's death, that was his second heart's extremity. Wretchedly, he spoke these words: 'How my anchor's point has now gripped land's harbour in grief!' He then discarded his armour. His grief accorded him harsh sorrow. The warrior said, in true loyalty: 'Galoes of Anjou! No-one ever needs to ask further—never was more manly courtesy born. True generosity's fruit blossomed from your heart. Now I grieve for your goodness.'

He said to Kaylet: 'How fares Schoette, my mother poor in joy?'

'So that may God have mercy on her! When Gandin died, and Galoes your brother, and when she no longer saw you at her side, death broke her heart, too.'

93 Then King Hardiz said: 'Apply yourself to manly courage now. If you can bear up in manly fashion, then you must grieve in moderation.'

His troubles, sadly, were too great. A shower flowed from his eyes. He saw to the comfort of the knights, then went to where he found his bedchamber, a small tent of samite. That night he suffered sorrow's season.

When the next day dawned they all agreed, the inner and the outer army, all those equipped for combative defiance there, young or old, timid or bold, that they should not joust. Then the bright mid-morning sun appeared. They were rubbed so raw from fighting, and the chargers were so sore from the prick of spurs that the bold company of knights was as yet oppressed by weariness. The queen herself then rode out to the field to meet the noble knights, and took them back with her into the city. Once inside, she asked the best of them to ride with her to the Leoplan. Her request was not ignored. They came to where mass was being sung for the sad King of Zazamanc.

As the benediction was being given, Lady Herzeloyde approached. 94
She spoke to Gahmuret, requesting that which common consent accorded her. He replied: 'Lady, I have a wife—she is dearer to me than my life. Even if I did not have her, I would still have good reason to renounce you altogether, if anyone were to respect my rights.'

'You must abandon the Mooress for the sake of my love. Baptism's blessing has the better power. Now, relinquish heathendom and love me in accordance with our religion, for I long for your love. Or am I to lose you to the Queen of the French? Her messengers spoke sweet words—they played their game right down to the last move.'

'Indeed, she is my true lady. I brought back to Anjou her counsel and my good breeding.* Her help still guides me today, for it was my lady who educated me—she whom womanly misconduct always shunned. We were both children then, but we were happy to see one another. Queen Ampflise dwells in womanly repute. That lovely 95
lady gave me the best support in the country—I was poorer then than now—I helped myself with a will. Number me still among the poor! You ought, lady, to have pity on me. My noble brother is dead. By your courtesy, do not distress me further. Turn love to where happiness may be, for nothing but sorrow lives in my company.'

Herzeloyde: 'Let me not waste away any longer. Tell me, how will you defend yourself?' Gahmuret: 'I shall reply to your question's bent. A tournament was proclaimed here. No such tourney has taken place. Many a witness will bear me out on that.' Herzeloyde: 'The vesper tournament crippled it. The bold have been so tamed here that the tourney has fallen into abeyance.' Gahmuret: 'I strove in your city's defence alongside those who have done good deeds here. You ought to spare me speeches in my defence. Many a knight did better here. Your claim upon me is void—apart from your common greeting, if I may have that of you.'

As the adventure tells me, the knight and the maiden then resorted to an arbitrator concerning the lady's case. It was by then nearing midday. The verdict was spoken at once: 'Whichever knight 96
has here buckled on his helmet, having come here in pursuit of chivalry, if he has won the prize here, the queen shall have him.' That verdict was accepted. Then she said: 'Sir, now you are mine. I

shall show you service to win your favour, and make you party to
such joys that you shall be merry after your grief.'

Yet grief still caused him pain. April's sheen had then passed by;
thereafter had come short, slender, green grass. The fields were all
covered in green—that emboldens timid hearts and gives them
high spirits. Many trees stood in blossom because of the sweet air
of May. His faërie lineage* compelled him to love or desire love.
His lady-love wished to grant it him there. He then looked at
Herzeloyde. His sweet mouth spoke with courtesy: 'Lady, if I am to
live with you, then let me be free of surveillance. For, if grief's power
ever deserts me, I would gladly do knightly deeds. If you do not
97 allow me to go tourneying, then I am still capable of that old trick, as
when I ran away from my wife, whom I also won by chivalry. When
she tied me down, keeping me from battle, I abandoned her people
and lands to her.'

She said: 'Sir, set your own mark. I will let you have your own way
in plenty.'

'I still want to split many spears—every month a tournament,
permit me so much, lady, that I may seek one out.' That she vowed,
so I was told. He accepted the lands and the maiden, too.

Those three young lordlings of Ampflise the Queen were standing
there, as was her chaplain, when the agreement and verdict were
pronounced, in the hearing and sight of the latter. In private he
spoke to Gahmuret: 'My lady has been informed that before Patela-
munt you won the highest prize and ruled over two crowns there.
She too has lands and inclination, and will give you her person and
property.'

'When she conferred knighthood upon me, I was obliged, by that
order's power, as the shield's office tells me, to remain undaunted.
Were it not that I obtained my shield from her, none of this would
98 ever have been accomplished. Whether I am sorry for it or glad, the
verdict of knights keeps me here. Return, tell her of my homage—I
shall be her knight in spite of all. Even if all crowns were at my
disposal, it is on her account I suffer most.' He offered them much
from his possessions—they declined his gifts. The messengers
returned to their country, incurring no discredit whatever upon their
lady. They asked no permission to take leave, as readily happens in
anger still. Her princely squires, those youths, were very nearly
blinded by their tears.

Those who had carried inverted shields there—to them their friends in the field said: 'Lady Herzeloyde the Queen has won the Angevin!' 'Why, who was there from Anjou? Our lord is, sadly, else-where, gone to gain knightly fame among the Saracens. That is now our greatest grief.' 'He who has won the prize here and felled so many a knight, who so thrust and struck, and who wore the costly anchor on his brightly bejewelled helmet—that is the very person you have in mind! King Kaylet himself tells me that the Angevin is Gahmuret!—he has done well here!' They then leapt to their char- 99 gers. Their clothes were wetted by their eyes, as they came to where their lord was sitting. They welcomed him; he welcomed them too. Joy and sorrow were both present there.

Then he kissed those loyal men, saying: 'You must not grieve immoderately over my brother—I can readily compensate you for his loss. Turn the shield the right way up, as is fitting. Keep to joy's path. I must now bear my father's arms. My anchor has struck his land. The anchor is a wandering knight's mark. Let him now wear it and take it upon himself who will. I must now live the life of the living. I am powerful. Why should I not be a people's lord? They would be grieved by my sorrow. Lady Herzeloyde, help me, that we may ask, I and you, the kings and princes present here to remain for the sake of my service, until you grant me what Love's deeds desire of Love.' This request was put by both their mouths. The nobles present promised immediate assent.

Everyone went to his rest. The queen said to her beloved: 'Now 100 give yourself over to my care.' She led him along private paths. His guests were well attended to, no matter where their host had gone. Their retinues made common cause, but he departed entirely alone, except for two little lords. Damsels and the queen took him to where he found joy, and all his sadness disappeared entirely. His grief was vanquished and his high spirits all renewed. Such, indeed, had to be the effects of Love's company. Lady Herzeloyde the Queen was there deprived of her maidenhood. Mouths were unspared—they exerted them to the full with kisses and warded grief away from joys.

After that he behaved courteously, freeing those whom he had taken captive there. Hardiz and Kaylet—behold!—those Gahmuret reconciled. There such a festivity was held that if anyone has done likewise since, his hand must indeed have been mighty. Gahmuret determined to be most unsparing of his possessions. Arabian gold

was given out to poor knights, no exceptions being made, and to the
101 kings precious stones were distributed by Gahmuret's hand, as to all
the princes he found there. The travelling people* were made most
merry—they received a share of the rich gifts.

Let them ride, all those who were strangers there—to those the
Angevin gave leave. The panther that his father had worn, of sable,
they hammered onto his shield. All of delicate white silk, a shift of
the queen, as it touched her bare body—she who now had become
his wife—that was now his hauberk's cover. Eighteen of them were
seen thrust through and slashed all to pieces by swords before he
parted from the lady. She, for her part, placed that same shift next to
her bare skin, when her beloved returned from chivalry—he who
riddled many a shield with holes. That pair's love spoke of loyalty.

He had honour in plenty, when his manly courage bore him away
towards hardship. I grieve over his journey. Reliable report came to
him that his lord, the Baruch, had been overridden by cavalry from
Babylon. One of those was called Ipomidon, the other Pompey—so
102 the adventure names him. He was a proud, noble man (not he who
ran away from Rome, from Julius, in ancient time). King Nebuchad-
nezzar was his mother's brother, he who read in deceitful books that
he himself was destined to be a god. People would now hold that in
ridicule. They were unsparing of themselves, and of their posses-
sions. Those brothers were of high lineage, descended from Ninus
who reigned before Baldac was founded. That same Ninus also
founded Nineveh. Disgrace and shame had afflicted them—the
Baruch claimed both cities were subject to him. Wins and losses
accrued on both sides in plenty—warriors were seen in battle there.
Then Gahmuret took ship, crossing the sea, and found the Baruch
under arms. He was welcomed with joy, greatly though his journey
grieves me.

What is happening here, what befalls there, wins and losses, how it
stands—of all that Lady Herzeloyde knows nothing. She was bright
as the sun and lovely of person. That woman enjoyed both wealth
and youth, and joys in superabundance; she was high above perfec-
103 tion's mark. She turned her heart to gracious skills, winning thereby
the world's favour. Lady Herzeloyde the Queen—her bearing found
profit in praise, her chastity knew fame—queen over three lands,
Waleis and Anjou—over these she was lady. She also wore the crown
in Norgals, in the capital, Kingrivals. Moreover, her husband was, I

believe, so dear to her that if any other lady ever won such a noble lover, how could it harm her? She could have let that pass without bearing any grudge.

When he had stayed away for six months, she was truly anxious for his return—that was the hope of her whole being. Then her joy's blade burst in two, in the middle of the hilt. Alas and alack, that goodness carries such grief with it, that loyalty always stirs sorrow! This is the race that mankind runs—today joy, tomorrow sorrow.

The lady, around noon one day, slept an anxious sleep. A dreadful shock came upon her. It seemed to her that a shooting star bore her up into the skies, where she was violently assailed by many a fiery 104 thunderbolt. These flew at her, all at once—then her long plaits sizzled and hissed with sparks. With a loud crack the thunder gave voice—burning tears were what it shed.

She came to herself again—then a gryphon seized her right hand. At that everything changed for her. It seemed to her, weirdly, as if she were wet-nurse to a worm, which afterwards tore apart her womb, and as if a dragon sucked at her breasts, and flew fast from her, so that she never beheld it again. It tore her heart out of her body. Such horrors her eyes were forced to see that seldom has a woman ever seen greater anguish in her sleep. Till then she had been of knightly bearing. Alas and alack, now all this will be changed! She takes on grief's hue now. Her losses will be long and broad—future heart's sorrows now near her.

The lady now began to behave in a manner of which she had been incapable before, both writhing and wailing, crying out loud in her sleep. Many damsels sat in attendance—they leapt over and woke her.

Then Tampanis came riding up, her husband's wise master- 105 squire, with many young lordlings. There joy's path ended. Lamenting, they told her of their lord's death. At that Lady Herzeloyde was sorely afflicted, falling down unconscious.

The knights said: 'How is it my lord's been conquered, in his armour—so well armed as he was?'

Although grief pursued the squire, he replied to the warriors: 'Life's length fled my lord. He had pulled off his coif, extreme heat compelling him to do so. Cursed heathen's guile stole the goodly warrior from us. A knight had poured he-goat's blood* into a tall glass; he broke that upon the adamant. Then it became softer than a sponge. He who is still painted as the Lamb, and with the Cross in His hooves—may He have mercy on what was done there!

'When they rode towards one another in bands, *âvoy** how they fought there! The Baruch's company of knights defended themselves valiantly. In the field before Baldac many shields were pierced
106 through, as they rushed at one another. The charges intertwined themselves there, the banners entangled themselves—many a proud warrior fell there. There my lord's hand wrought such deeds that all others' fame vanished. Then Ipomidon came riding up—with death he gave my lord his reward, thrusting him down in the sight of many thousand knights, there before Alexandria. My lord, free of falsity, had turned to face the king whose joust taught him death's lesson. Ipomidon's spear-tip cut through his helmet, drilling through his head, so that a splinter was afterwards found inside. The warrior still retained his seat—all dying, he rode away from the battle to a plain, which was broad. His chaplain came, and as he stood above him, Gahmuret spoke his confession, in brief words, and sent here this shift and this same spear, which has parted him from us. He died free of all misdeed, commending his squires and pages to the queen.

'He was buried in Baldac. The expense counted for little with the
107 Baruch. Gold was lavished upon it, great wealth applied in the form of precious stones, to the tomb in which immaculate Gahmuret lies. His young corpse was embalmed. Many people were afflicted by grief. The stone above his grave is a precious ruby, through which he shone.* Our counsel was followed in this matter: a cross, according to the Passion's custom, as when Christ's death redeemed us, was erected for his solace, to shelter his soul, above the grave. The Baruch bore the cost—it was a costly emerald. We did this without the heathens' counsel. Their order knows nothing of the care of that Cross by which Christ's death bequeathed us benediction. Heathens worship Gahmuret, in all sincerity, as their honoured god, not because of the Cross's honour, nor because of baptism's doctrine, which will, at the Judgemental end, redeem us from our bonds. His manly loyalty will give him bright sheen in Heaven, as will his contrite confession. Falsity was shallow in him.

108 'Upon his helmet, the adamant, an epitaph was engraved, sealed upon the cross, above the grave. The letters read thus: "Through this helmet a joust slew this noble man, bearer of valour. Gahmuret he was named, mighty king over three lands, each of which acknowledged

his crown. Powerful princes walked in his train. He was born of Anjou, and before Baldac he lost his life, in the Baruch's cause. His fame shot so high that no-one can match its mark, no matter where knights are tried today. That man is unborn of mother to whom his valour swore surrender—I mean those who have the shield's office. Help and manly counsel he gave with constancy to his friends. For women's sake he suffered most sharp pangs. He bore baptism and Christian faith. His death grieved Saracens—that is no lie, but the truth. All the reasoning years of his times, his valour so strove for fame that it was with knightly fame that he died. He had won the victory over falsity. Now wish salvation to him who lies here." ' This was what the squire averred.

Many Waleis were seen to weep. They had, indeed, good reason to 109 grieve. The lady had been carrying a child that pushed within her body, but she had been left lying without help. For eighteen weeks* it had been alive, that child whose mother—Lady Herzeloyde the Queen—was struggling against death. Those others were foolish not to help the woman, for she bore in her body one who will be the flower of all knights, if death passes him by here. Then a man, old and wise, came to condole with his lady, as she wrestled with death. He prised her clenched teeth apart—they poured water into her mouth—at once consciousness made her acquaintance.

She said: 'Alas, where has my beloved gone?' The lady grieved for him, louder than loud: 'My heart's joy, far and wide, was Gahmuret's honour. His bold aspiration has taken him from me. I was much younger than he, yet am his mother and his wife, for I carry here his body and his life's seed, given and taken by our mutual love. If God is of loyal mind, then let him bear fruit by me, for I have gained too 110 much affliction by my proud, noble husband. How death has injured me! Gahmuret never partook of a woman's love without delighting in all her joy. He was troubled by a woman's grief. To that he was counselled by his manly loyalty, for he was free of falsity.'

Now hear new tidings, hear what the lady did next. Child and womb she embraced to herself with her arms and hands, saying: 'May God send to me the noble fruit of Gahmuret. This is my heart's prayer. May God avert me from such foolish anguish—it would be a second death for Gahmuret, if I were to slay myself, while I still carry with me what I received from his love—he who showed me man's loyalty.'

The lady did not care who saw it: she tore the shift from her breast. Her little breasts, soft and white—to those she turned her diligence, pressing them to her red mouth. She avowed womanly bearing. This is what that wise woman said: 'You are the hoard of a child's nourishment, sent on ahead by the child itself, since I first found it living in my body.'

The lady saw her wish fulfilled, in that this nourishment was her heart's covering, the milk in her litttle tits. The queen pressed it out of them, saying: 'You have come from loyalty. If I had not accepted baptism, you would be my baptism's true mark. I must pour upon myself in plenty from you, and from my eyes, in public and in private, for I will mourn Gahmuret.'

The lady commanded a shift of bloody appearance to be brought closer there—that in which, in the Baruch's company, Gahmuret had lost his life—he who had chosen a valiant end, with true manly aspiration. The lady also asked after the spear which had given death to Gahmuret. Ipomidon of Nineveh had granted such warlike reward—that proud, noble Babylonian—that the shift was a rag, because of his blows. The lady wanted to put it on, as she had done before when her husband returned from knightly deeds. Then they took it out of her hands. Those who were worthiest in the land buried the spear, and with it the blood, in the minster, as is due to the dead. In Gahmuret's land grief was then well-known.

Fourteen days from then, the lady gave birth to a baby, a son, who was of such limbs that she scarcely survived. Here the adventure's dice are thrown and its beginning marked, for now at last he is born on whose account this tale was chosen. His father's joy and his anguish, both his life and his death—of these you have, I believe, heard some account. Know, now, whence has come to you this tale's protagonist, and how he was preserved from harm. Chivalry was concealed from him until he had his wits about him.

When the queen had recovered consciousness and taken her baby back to her, she and other ladies all stared, between his legs, at his pizzle.* He had to put up with many caresses, for he had manly limbs. He became a smith of swords thereafter, striking much fire from helmets—his heart bore manly valour. The queen delighted in kissing him over and over again, saying to him, assiduously: '*Bon fîz, scher fîz, bêâ fîz.*'*

The queen then took, without delay, those red, fallow tips—I mean her tits' beaklets—these she pressed into his little gob. She herself was his wet-nurse who had borne him in her womb. To her breasts she drew him, she whom womanly misconduct shunned. It seemed to her as if she had called Gahmuret back into her arms. She had no thought of haughtiness. Humility came readily to her.

Lady Herzeloyde said in her wisdom: 'The Highest Queen offered her breasts to Jesus, who afterwards, for our sake, accepted in human form the cruellest death on the Cross, manifesting His loyalty to us. If anyone belittles His wrath, his soul risks ungentle judgement, no matter how chaste he be or was. Of that I know the true tidings.'

That land's lady wetted herself with her heart's sorrow's dew; her eyes rained down upon the boy. She knew how to hold to a woman's loyalty. Her mouth knew full well how to form both sighs and smiles. 114 She rejoiced in her son's birth. Her mirth drowned at grief's ford.

Wolfram's Self-Defence*

If anyone now speaks better of women, then truly I have no objection. I would be glad to hear their joy bruited wide. There is only one to whom I am unwilling to offer loyal servitude. My anger is always new against her, ever since I detected her in deviance.

I am Wolfram von Eschenbach and know a little of singing, and I am a pair of tongs holding my anger against one woman in particular: she has inflicted such wrong upon me that I have no choice but to hate her. That is why I bear the brunt of other women's enmity. Alas, why do they act in this way!

Although their enmity grieves me, it stems from their womanliness, after all, because I have spoken out of turn and done myself wrong— the chances are it will never happen again! Yet they should not be overhasty in storming my bastion—they will find valorous battle. I have not forgotten how to be a good judge of both their bearing and 115 their ways. If chastity keeps company with a woman, I will be her reputation's champion. Her sorrow grieves me from the heart.

That man's praise hobbles with a spavin* if he says check-mate to all other ladies for the sake of his own lady alone.* If any lady wishes to assess my order—both see and hear it—I shall not make a fool of her: the shield's office is my lineage. If my courage is ever stinted, if any woman then loves me for the sake of my song, then I think her weak of wit. If I desire a good woman's love, if I cannot earn her

love's reward by shield and also by spear, let nothing else be the basis
for her favour, for the stakes a man plays for are most high indeed, if
he strives for love by chivalry.

If women didn't think it flattery, I would advance further
unfamiliar words to you by this tale—I would continue telling you
this adventure. If anyone desires this of me, let him not attribute it to
any book. I don't know a single letter of the alphabet.* There are
plenty who take such as a starting-point—this adventure goes its way
116 without books' guidance. Rather than have people think it a book, I
would be naked without a towel, as if sitting in the bath—provided I
didn't forget the bundle of twigs.*

BOOK III

IT makes me sad that so many are called 'woman'. Their voices are
all equally high of pitch—plenty are quick towards falsehood, some
few are devoid of falsity—there are two sides to this coin. My heart
has felt shame that they are all named the same. Womankind, your
true order keeps and always has kept company with loyalty.

Plenty of people say poverty serves no useful function.* If anyone
suffers it out of loyalty, hell-fire shuns that person's soul. Such
poverty one woman endured out of loyalty; because of that the gift
she gave was renewed in Heaven with endless return. I believe there
are very few now alive who, at a young age, would abandon the
earth's wealth for the sake of Heaven's fame. I know of none. Men
and women are all alike, it seems to me, in this—they would all alike
avoid it. Mighty Lady Herzeloyde became a stranger to her three
117 lands; she bore joy's dearth's burden. Falsity disappeared from her
so entirely that neither eye nor ear could ever find any in her. The
sun was a mist to her—she fled this world's delight. Night and day
were all alike to her. Her heart fostered nothing but sorrow.

This lady quick to sorrow withdrew from her land to a forest, to
the Waste of Soltane*—not looking for flowers on the meadow.* Her
heart's sorrow was so entire that she had no interest in any garland,*
whether red or faded. To that place she took, seeking refuge, noble
Gahmuret's son. The people with her there have to cultivate and
clear the ground. She knew well how to cherish her son. Before he

reached the age of reason, she gathered all her people about her, both
men and women, ordering them all, on pain of death, never to voice
the word 'knight'—'for if my heart's beloved ever heard what a
knight's life is, that would oppress me sorely. Now keep your wits
about you, and conceal all chivalry from him.'

That practice ran a risky road. The boy was hidden thus, brought 118
up in the Waste of Soltane, cheated of kingly ways, were it not for
one sport—a bow and little bolts. Those he cut with his own hand
and shot down many birds he found there. Yet whenever he shot a
bird whose noise had been so loud with song before, he would weep
and tear at himself, wreaking vengeance on his hair. His person was
radiant and proud. On the meadow by the riverbank he would wash
himself every morning. He was ignorant of anxiety, except for the
birdsong above him—that sweetness pressed into his heart, stretch-
ing his little breasts. All in tears he ran to the queen. She said: 'Who
has done you harm? You were out there on the plain.' He could not
tell her about it, as still may happen to children today.

This was a matter she long pursued. One day she saw him gazing
up into the trees, following the birds' sound. She observed that her
child's breast swelled at the sound of their voices, compelled to it by
lineage and his desire. Lady Herzeloyde turned her hostility against
the birds, although she knew no reason for it. She intended to silence 119
their sound. She commanded her ploughmen and farmhands to
make haste to choke and catch the birds. The birds were better
mounted—the death of a good few was avoided. A number remained
alive there, afterwards making merry with song.

The boy said to the queen: 'What grudge do they bear the birdlets?'
He asked for an immediate truce for them. His mother kissed him
on the mouth, saying: 'Why do I contravene His commandment—
He who is, after all, the Highest God? Shall birds for my sake
abandon joy?'

The boy at once said to his mother: 'Alas, mother, what is God?'

'Son, I'll tell you, in all earnest. He is even brighter than the day,
He who took upon himself a countenance fashioned after man's
countenance. Son, take one piece of advice to heart, and call upon
Him in your hour of need. His loyalty has always offered help to the
world. But then there is one who is called Hell's lord—he is black,
disloyalty does not avoid him. Turn your thoughts away from him,
and also from doubt's deviation.'*

His mother taught him in full the distinction between darkness
120 and light. Thereafter his boldness leapt and bounded. He learned the
javelin's* throw, shooting down by it many a stag, to the profit of his
mother and her people. Whether there were thaw or snow, his hunt-
ing gave grief to the game. Now hear strange tales: when he'd shot
such a weight as a mule would have found a heavy enough load, all
uncut-up* he'd carry it home.

One day he was following a hunting track, along a mountain
slope—a long one. He broke off a twig, for the sake of the leaf's
voice. Close by him there ran a path—there he heard the sound of
hoofbeats. He weighed his javelin in his hand, saying: 'What have I
heard? Oh, if only the Devil would come now, in his fearful wrath!
I would take him on, for sure! My mother talks of his terrors—I
believe her courage is daunted.'

Thus he stood, avid for battle. Now see, towards him there came
galloping three knights, of perfect form, fully armed from the foot
upwards. The boy thought in all sincerity that each of these was a
god. Then he stood there no longer, but threw himself into the path,
121 down upon his knees. Loudly the boy then cried: 'Help, God! You
surely have help in your power!'

The foremost knight grew angry at the boy lying in his path: 'This
foolish Waleis is barring us from swift passage.'

One thing for which we Bavarians are famed I may also apply to
the Waleis: they are more foolish than Bavarian folk, and yet valorous
in combat. If any man grows up in both those lands, propriety will
work wonders by him.

Then there came galloping up, well accoutred, a knight who was
in great haste. He was riding in warlike pursuit of some who had by
now got far away from him; two knights had abducted a lady from
him in his land. The warrior thought it a disgrace—he was grieved
by the distress of the damsel who rode, wretched, ahead of them.
The other three were his subjects. He rode a handsome Castilian.
Very little of his shield was intact. His name was Karnahkarnanz, *leh
cons Ulterlec*.* He said: 'Who is blocking our way?' With these words
he rode up to the boy. Parzival thought he was shaped like a god.
122 He'd never seen anything so bright. His surcoat swept the dew. By
little golden bells, before each leg, his stirrups were made to ring out,
and were adjusted in correct proportion. His right arm rang with the
sound of bells whenever he thrust or swung it. It sounded so loud as

his sword-blows struck—that warrior was bold in pursuit of fame!
Thus rode that mighty prince, magnificently accoutred.

Karnahkarnanz asked Parzival, that garland of all manly beauty:
'Young lord, did you see two knights ride past you, who are incapable
of adhering to the knightly code? They wrestle with rape and are
daunted when it comes to honour. They have with them a maiden
they have abducted.' The boy believed, no matter what Karnahkar-
nanz said, that it was God, as Lady Herzeloyde the Queen had
described to him, when she defined bright radiance for him. He
called out loudly and in all sincerity: 'Now help me, helpful God!'
Again and again *fil li roy* Gahmuret fell to his knees in prayer. The
prince said: 'I am not God, though I willingly carry out His
command. You can see four knights here—if you could see aright.' 123

The boy asked on: 'You name knights—what does that mean? If
you don't have divine power, then tell me, who gives knighthood?'

'King Arthur does that. Young lord, if you enter his castle, he will
confer upon you a knight's name, so that you will never have need to
feel ashamed of it. You may well be of knightly lineage.'

The warriors eyed him closely. God's skill lay in his creation, they
saw. From the adventure I learn—which imparted to me the truth of
the matter—that no man's appearance had ever turned out better
since Adam's time. Because of this his praise ranged far and wide in
women's mouths.

Again the boy spoke, giving rise to laughter: 'Oh, knight God,*
what may you be? You have so many rings tied to your body, up there
and down here.' At this place and that the boy's hand clutched at all
the iron he found on the prince. He scrutinized his armour closely:
'My mother's damsels wear their rings on strings—they don't fit
into one another like this.' The boy then asked the prince, following 124
his instinct: 'What is the purpose of this that can suit you so well? I
can't pick it apart!'

At that the prince showed him his sword: 'Look now, if anyone
desires battle of me, I defend myself against him with blows. To
protect myself against his, I have to put armour on, and to defend
myself against bowshot and the thrust of spears I must arm myself
like this.' To that the bold boy replied: 'If the stags wore hides like
this, then my javelin wouldn't wound any of them—many a one falls
dead before me!'

The knights grew angry that Karnahkarnanz was lingering with

the boy, who wielded great folly. The prince said: 'God keep you!
Oh, if only your beauty were mine! God would have granted you
perfection, if you but had your wits about you. May God's power
keep sorrow far from you!'

His men and he himself rode on in great haste, until they came to
a glade in the forest. There that courtly man found Lady Herzeloyde's
ploughs. Greater sorrow had never befallen her people. He saw them
hastening to the plough, then sowing, and afterwards harrowing,
plying their goads over sturdy oxen.

125　　The prince offered them good morning and asked them if they
had seen a damsel in distress. They could no other than answer what
he asked: 'Two knights and a maiden rode by that way this morning.
The lady rode in sorrow. They used their spurs hard, those who took
the damsel with them.' (It was Meljahkanz.* Karnahkarnanz caught
up with him, taking the lady from him by battle—she who was lame
of joy before. She was called Imane of the Beafontane.)*

The farm-folk were in despair, as the warriors sped by them. They
said: 'How did this happen to us? If our young lord has seen the
slashed helmets on these knights, then we haven't taken proper care.
We shall hear the queen's anger because of this, and rightly so, for he
was running alongside us this morning, while she was still asleep.'

The boy cared little then who shot stags, small or great. He
headed back to his mother and told her the news. At that she col-
126　lapsed; she was so greatly shocked by his words that she lay
unconscious before him.

When the queen returned to her senses, although she had been
daunted before, she said: 'Son, who has told you of knighthood's
order? Where did you learn of this?'

'Mother, I saw four men, even brighter than God in appearance—
they told me about chivalry. Arthur's kingly might, in accordance
with knightly honour, must conduct me to the shield's office.'

Now new wretchedness arose. The lady did not rightly know how
to devise a plan to divert him from this intention. The boy, foolish
yet worthy, repeatedly asked his mother for a horse. It grieved her to
the heart. She thought: 'I don't want to deny him anything, but it'll
have to be a most miserable nag!' Then the queen thought: 'Lots of
people are prone to scorn. My child shall wear fool's clothes over his
fair body. If he is torn and trounced, he may well come back home to
127　me.' Alas for such wretched suffering! The lady took a length of

sackcloth. She cut him a shirt and breeches, both visibly of one piece, reaching down to the middle of his white legs. This was acknowledged as fool's garb. A hood was to be found above. All of fresh, rough calfskin, from a single hide, two boots were cut to fit his legs. There great sorrow was not shunned.

It was the queen's intention to entreat him to remain there that night. 'You mustn't leave here before I have given you some advice: on untrodden roads you must avoid dark fords—those which are shallow and clear, there you must ride in boldly. You must cultivate courteous ways, offer to all the world a greeting. If a grey, wise man is willing to teach you courtesy, as he well knows how, you must follow his instructions willingly, and not be angry with him. Son, let this be commended to you: wherever you may win a good woman's ring and her greeting, take them—they will cure you of sorrow. You must hasten towards her kiss and grasp her firmly in your embrace— that will bring good fortune and high spirits,* provided she is chaste 128 and worthy.

'You must also know, son of mine, that the proud, bold Lähelin has won in battle from your princes two lands, which ought to serve your hand: Waleis and Norgals.* One of your princes, Turkentals, met his death at his hand—he slew and took captive your people.'

'That I'll avenge, mother, God willing. My javelin will wound him yet.'

Next morning, when day appeared, the boy quickly formed his decision—he was in a hurry to find Arthur. Lady Herzeloyde kissed him and ran after him. Sorrow befell the whole world there! When she could no longer see her son, he having ridden off—who's any the better for this?—then that lady slow to falsity fell down upon the ground, where grief gave her such a cut that death did not shun her.

The lady's most loyal death warded off Hell's anguish from her. Praise be to her that she ever became a mother! Thus that root of goodness and trunk of humility went upon the reward-bearing road. Alas that we do not now possess her descendants down to the eleventh branch! In their absence, many a person turns to treachery. Yet 129 loyal women ought now to wish good fortune upon this boy, who has departed from her here.

Then the handsome boy headed towards the woodland in Broceliande.* He came riding to a brook. A cock could have easily stepped across it. Although flowers and grass grew there, because its current was so dark the boy avoided fording it. That whole day he rode alongside it, as befitted his wits. He passed the night as best he might, until bright day shone before him. Then the boy made his way, all alone, to a ford, clear and beautiful. On the other side of it the plain was graced by a tent, in which great wealth had been invested. Of samite of three colours, it was high and wide; on its seams lay noble brocade. A leather top hung from it, to be drawn over it whenever rain threatened.

Duc Orilus *de* Lalander's wife he found there beneath it, lying in
130 her loveliness, that mighty duchess, most like a knight's beloved. Jeschute was her name. The lady had fallen asleep. She bore Love's arms: a mouth translucently red, an ardent knight's heart's anguish. Whilst the lady slept, her lips slipped apart—her mouth bore Love's heat's fire. Thus she lay, perfection's venture. Of snow-white bone, close to one another, delicate, were her bright teeth. I doubt if anyone could ever make me accustomed to kissing such a well-praised mouth—I have seldom known the like.

Her sable coverlet was turned back at her slender hips—she had thrust it from her because of the heat, after her lord had left her alone. She was fashioned and formed, no skill neglected in her shaping. God himself wrought her sweet person. Moreover, this lovely lady had long arms and white hands. The boy found a ring there which compelled him towards the bed, where he wrestled with the duchess. His thoughts then turned to his mother, who had advised
131 him to aim at a woman's ring, and so the handsome boy leapt at once from the carpet to the bed.

That sweet, chaste lady was ungently startled to find the boy lying in her arms. She had no choice but to wake up. Embarrassed, not smiling at all, the lady schooled in courtesy said: 'Who has dishonoured me? Young lord, you take too great a liberty—you might have chosen a different mark.'

The lady lamented loudly. He didn't care what she said, but pressed her mouth to his. Then it was not too long before he pressed the duchess to himself, and also took from her a ring. Pinned on her shift he saw a brooch—clumsily he broke it off. The lady had only a woman's weapons—to her his strength was that of a whole army— yet much wrestling took place there. Next the boy complained of hunger. The lady was radiant of person. She said: 'You are not to eat me! For your own good, you'd be wise to choose different food.

There's bread and wine there, and two partridges as well, which a damsel brought, little thinking they'd be yours!'

He didn't care where his hostess sat.* He ate a good cropful, and 132 afterwards downed heavy draughts. The lady thought he had dwelt far too long in the pavilion. She thought he was a page who had taken leave of his wits. Her shame started to sweat.* Nevertheless the duchess said: 'Young lord, you must leave my ring here, and my brooch. Be off now, for if my husband arrives, you may suffer such anger as you might prefer to avoid.'

Then the well-born boy replied: 'Hah, what do I fear your husband's anger! But if it harms your honour, then I will depart.' Then he went up to the bed—a second kiss took place there, to the distress of the duchess. The boy rode off without taking leave, although he did say: 'God keep you! So my mother advised me.'

The boy was well pleased with his spoils. When he had ridden away from there for a while, perhaps almost a mile in distance, along came he of whom I will speak. He traced in the dew that his lady had been visited. Some of the ropes had been trodden down—there 133 some squire had waded through the grass. The prince, noble and renowned, found his wife there, full of sadness. Then proud Orilus said: 'Alas, lady, why have I so directed my service to you? Much knightly fame which I have earned has ended in disgrace—you have another *amîs*.'* The lady proffered her denial with water-rich eyes, claiming that she was innocent. He did not believe her tale.

She, however, said fearfully: 'A fool came riding up to me here. Of all the people I have known, I never saw such a handsome person. My brooch and a ring he took, against my will.'

'Ho! His person pleases you well! You have made him your lover!'

She replied: 'Now God forbid! His boots, his javelin were too close to me by far! You ought to be ashamed of such talk! It would ill become a princess to accept love from such a quarter!'

The prince immediately replied: 'Lady, I have done you no wrong, unless you choose to be ashamed for one reason: you abandoned a 134 queen's name, and for my sake are called duchess. That purchase has brought me poor profit. Yet my valour is so bold that your brother Erec, my brother-in-law, *fil li roy* Lac,* may well bear you a grudge on that account. That discerning king, however, knows me to be possessed of such fame as is proof against dishonour anywhere— were it not for the fact that, before Prurin,* he felled me by his joust.

Afterwards I earned high fame from him before Karnant. In formal joust my hand thrust him behind his horse, forcing his surrender. Through his shield my lance delivered your token. Little did I then think, my lady Jeschute, that your love would favour another lover.

'Lady, believe me when I say that proud Galoes, *fil li roy* Gandin, lay dead by my joust. You were also halting close by when Plihopliheri* rode towards me to joust, and his combat did not evade me. 135 My joust swept him off behind his charger, so that his saddle no longer pinched him anywhere. I have often won fame, and felled many a knight, but this has brought no profit to me now—so my deep disgrace informs me.

'They hold me in especial enmity, those of the Table Round,* eight of whom I thrust down where many a noble damsel saw it, in the cause of the sparrowhawk at Kanedic.* I won you fame and myself the victory. This you saw, as did Arthur, who keeps my sister in his castle, sweet Cunneware.* Her mouth can shape no smile until she sees that man to whom the highest fame is accorded. If only that same man were to encounter me! Then there would be a battle waged here as this morning, when I fought and wrought suffering upon a prince who offered me his jousting—by my joust he lay dead.*

'I will not speak to you of such anger as has brought many a man to beat his wife because of lesser guilt on her part. If there were any service or homage I ought to offer you, you will have to make do 136 without it. No more shall I warm myself in your white arms, where I sometimes lay, for love's sake, many a delightful day. I must make your red mouth pale and acquaint your eyes with redness. I must dishonour you of joy and teach your heart to sigh.'

The princess looked at the prince. Wretchedly her mouth replied: 'Now honour knight's fame by me. You are faithful and wise, and have, I suppose, such power over me that you can cause me great pain. You must first hear my case—for the sake of all women deign to do so. You can still cause me distress thereafter. If I were to lie dead at others' hands, without causing your high fame to be lowered, how quickly I would then die! That would be a sweet time for me, now that your enmity is directed against me.'

Then the prince spoke again: 'Lady, you defend yourself against me far too haughtily—I must teach you moderation. No more will company be kept in drinking and in eating. Lying together shall be forgotten. You will receive no further clothing than that in which I

found you sitting. Your bridle must be a rope of bast, your horse shall 137
win its share of hunger, your well-adorned saddle—that shall be
despoiled.' In all haste he tore and broke the samite from it. When
that had been done, he broke into pieces the saddle on which she
rode. Her chastity and her womanliness had no choice but to suffer
his enmity. With bast cords he bound it back together again. To her
his hatred came all too soon.

Thereupon he said: 'Lady, now let us ride. If I were to catch up
with him, I'd be delighted—he who partook here of your love. I
would venture to attack him even if his breath gave off fire, like a
wild dragon's.'

All in tears, unsmiling, the lady rich in wretchedness departed
sadly. She did not care about what happened to her, but only about
her husband's distress. His sadness caused her such great grief that
she would have found death far gentler. Now you must pity her out
of loyalty. She begins to bear great sorrow now. Even if all women's
enmity were my lot, I would still be troubled by Lady Jeschute's
suffering.

Thus they rode in pursuit of his tracks. The boy ahead of them 138
was in great haste, too, but the undaunted youth did not know that
he was being pursued, for everyone whom his eyes saw, as he drew
near him, the good boy greeted, saying: 'So my mother advised me.'

And so our foolish boy came riding down a mountain slope. A
woman's voice he heard, by a rock's edge. A lady was crying out, for
pure sorrow—true joy had been torn in two for her. Quickly the
boy rode up to her. Now hear what this lady is doing—Lady
Sigune,* in her wretchedness, was tearing her long brown plaits out
from her scalp. The boy looked about him—Schionatulander* the
prince he found dead there in the damsel's lap. She was weary of all
mirth.

'Whether they be sad or of joy's hue, my mother asked me to greet
them all. God keep you!' said the boy's mouth. 'I have found here a
wretched find in your lap. Who gave you this wounded knight?'
Undeterred, the boy spoke on: 'Who shot him? Did it happen with a 139
javelin? It seems to me, lady, that he lies dead. Will you tell me
something about who slew your knight? If I can catch him up on my
horse, I will gladly do battle with him!'

Then the renowned boy reached for his quiver—many sharp
javelins he found there. He also still carried both the tokens he had

torn from Jeschute, when an act of folly had happened. If he had
learned his father's ways, which kept noble company with him, the
boss would have suffered a more pointed charge, when the duchess
sat there all alone—she who afterwards suffered much sorrow on his
account. For more than a whole year her husband's greeting shunned
her person. Injustice befell that woman.

Now hear tell of Sigune, too: she knew how to lament her sorrow
with grief. She said to the boy: 'You have noble qualities. Honoured
be your sweet youth and your charming countenance. Truly, you will
come to be blessed by fortune. This knight was shunned by the
140 javelin. He lay dead by jousting. You are born of loyalty, to feel such
pity for him.' Before she let the boy ride on, she first asked him what
he was called, saying he bore the mark of God's industry.

'*Bon fîz, scher fîz, bêâ fîz**—so I was named by those who knew me
back home.'

When these words had been spoken she knew him at once by the
name. Now hear him named more correctly, so that you may recognise
who is this adventure's lord—there he was, halting by that maiden.

Her red mouth said without delay: 'In truth, you are called Parzival.
That name means: "straight down the middle."* Great love ploughed
such a heart's furrow through your mother's loyalty—your father
bequeathed her grief. I don't tell you this so you can boast about it:
your mother is my aunt,* and I'll tell you now, without any false
tricks, the real truth about who you are: your father was an Angevin;
on your mother's side you are a Waleis, born in Kanvoleiz. I know
the real truth of it—you are also king in Norgals. In that land's
141 capital, at Kingrivals, your head shall wear the crown. This prince
was slain for your sake, for he always defended your land. No notch
was ever cut in his loyalty. Young fair sweet man, those brothers have
done you great wrong. Two lands Lähelin took from you. Orilus slew
in jousting this knight and your father's brother.* He it was who also
left me in such sorrow. This prince of your land served me, without
any disgrace—at that time your mother was bringing me up. Dear,
good cousin, hear now how these events came about—a bercelet's*
leash brought this grief upon him. Serving us both, he hunted down
death, and won me misery's extremity for love of him. I was foolish
in my mind not to give him love, and consequently sorrow's source
has cut my joy to pieces. Now I love him, dead though he is.'

Then he said: 'Cousin, I am grieved by your sorrow and by the

great offence to my honour. If ever I can avenge it, I will gladly settle
the score.' He was in a hurry to do battle. She pointed him in the
wrong direction, fearing he might lose his life, and that she would   142
incur greater loss. He then took a road which led towards the
Britons—it was paved and broad. Whoever walked or rode towards
him, whether it was a knight or merchant, he immediately greeted
them all, saying it was his mother's advice. Nor did she do wrong in
giving him that counsel.

The evening began to draw near, great weariness hurrying
towards him. Then folly's companion caught sight of a house, of a
fair size. Its inhabitant was an ill-tempered host, such as still spring
up from base birth. He was a fisherman, devoid of all kindness.
Hunger taught the boy to head that way and complain to the host of
hunger's need. He said: 'I wouldn't give you half a loaf, not these
thirty years. Anybody on the look-out for generosity from me, for no
return, is wasting his time. I care nothing for anybody except myself,
and, after that, my little children. You'll not come inside, not this
long day. If you had pennies or anything to pawn, I'd put you up on
the spot.'

Then the boy at once offered him Lady Jeschute's brooch. When   143
the peasant saw that, his mouth smiled and said: 'If you'd like to stay
here, gentle boy, all who live inside will honour you.'

'If you'll feed me well tonight and show me the right way towards
Arthur tomorrow—he is dear to me—then you can keep this gold.'

'That I'll do,' said the peasant. 'I never saw such a well-favoured
person! I'll take you—for curiosity's sake—as far as the King's Table
Round.'

That night the boy stayed there—next morning he was seen else-
where. He could scarcely wait for daybreak. His host also made
himself ready and ran ahead of him, the boy riding after—both of
them were in a hurry.

My lord Hartmann von Aue,* a guest of mine is coming to Lady
Guinevere your mistress and to your lord, King Arthur, to their
castle. Pray protect him from scorn. He's neither fiddle nor rote—let
them take another plaything! Let them, out of courtesy, rest content
with that. Otherwise your Lady Enite and her mother Karsnafite,
will be dragged through the mill and their reputation crushed. If I   144
am to wear out my mouth with mockery, with mockery I will defend
my friend.

Then the fisherman, and the famed boy too, came so close to a
great city that they could see Nantes before them. Then the fisher-
man said: 'Child, God keep you! See now, there you must ride in.'
Then the feeble-witted boy said: 'You must lead me further.' 'Far be
it from me to do anything of the kind! That household's of such a
kind that if ever a peasant approached them, that would be a most
grave offence!'

The boy rode on alone, coming to a meadow, none too broad,
brightly coloured by flowers. No Curvenal* had reared him; he knew
nothing of courtesy, as still befalls a man of no experience. His bridle
was of bast and his pony was very frail. Stumbling caused it to
take many a fall. Moreover, his saddle was entirely unnailed by new
leather. Samite, ermine down—precious little of that was to be seen
145 on it. He had no need of fastenings for his cloak. To surcoats and
tabards he preferred his javelin. He whose demeanour was matched
against fame, his father, was better clad upon the carpet before
Kanvoleiz—he never exuded fearful sweat.

A knight came riding towards him. Parzival greeted him in his
customary way: 'God keep you, so my mother advised me!' 'Young
lord, God reward you and her!' said Arthur's aunt's son. He had
been brought up by Uther Pendragon. This same warrior also laid
hereditary claim to the land of Britain. He was Ither of Gaheviez.
The Red Knight they called him.

His equipment was all so red that it brought redness to the eyes.
His charger was red and speedy. All red was its hood-piece; of red
samite was its caparison. His shield was even redder than fire. All
red was his gambeson, wide, well-tailored to him. Red was his shaft,
red was his spear. All red, as the warrior wished, was his sword,
reddened, yet leaded* for sharpness. The King of Kukumerlant held
146 in his hand a goblet, all of red gold, most finely engraved, lifted up
from the Table Round. White was his skin, red was his hair. He
spoke to the boy without deceit:

'Honoured be your gentle person! It was a pure woman brought
you into this world. Hail to the mother that bore you! I never saw
such a well-favoured person! You are true Love's radiance, her defeat
and her victory. Much womanly joy will conquer you; thereafter
sorrow will weigh heavy with you. Dear friend, if you desire to enter
there, then say for me, if you would serve me, to Arthur and his men:
I have no wish to appear to have taken flight. I will willingly wait here

for anyone to ready himself for the joust. Let none of them be amazed at this—I rode up to the Table Round, I laid claim to my land. This goblet my clumsy hand snatched up, so that the wine spilled into Lady Guinevere's lap. It was my claim that instructed me to act in this way. If I had upturned torches,* then my skin would have turned sooty. That I avoided,' said the bold warrior. 'Nor did I do it with any intent to steal—my crown spares me such deeds. Friend, now tell the Queen I poured wine upon her unintentionally, 147 there where the nobles sat, neglecting proper defence. Whether they be kings or princes, why do they let their lord go thirsty? Why don't they fetch him back his gold goblet? Otherwise their quick fame will be found lagging.'

The boy said: 'I'll take your message, all you have told me.' He rode away from him, into Nantes. There the little pages followed him into the courtyard, in front of the great hall, where various kinds of activity were taking place. Quickly a crowd pressed about him. Iwanet leapt towards him—that squire free of falsity offered him company.

The boy said: 'God keep you, my mother asked me to say, before I left her castle. I see many an Arthur here. Who is to make me a knight?'

Iwanet started to laugh, saying: 'You can't see the right one, but it'll happen soon enough now!'

He led him into the hall where the noble household was assembled. Despite the din, Parzival managed this much—he said: 'God save all you lords, especially the King and his wife. My mother commanded 148 me on pain of death to greet them in particular, and those who have places at the Table Round by virtue of their true fame. Those she requested me to greet. To do this, knowledge of one thing eludes me: I don't know which one is lord in here. To him a knight has sent a message—I saw him, red all over—he wants to wait out there for him. I think he wants to do battle. He is also sorry that he spilled the wine over the Queen. Oh, if only I had received his clothing from the King's hand! Then I would be rich in joy, for it looks so knight-like!'

The impetuous boy was jostled hard, pushed in this direction and that. They marked his complexion. That indeed was self-evident— never was lovelier fruit sired nor ladied. God was in a sweet mood for breeding when he wrought Parzival, who feared few terrors.

Thus he was taken before Arthur, he for whom God had devised

149 perfection. No-one could possibly be hostile to him. Then the Queen inspected him, too, before she left the great hall, where wine had been spilled over her earlier. Arthur looked at the boy. To the foolish youth he then said: 'Young lord, God reward you for your greeting, which I must most willingly serve to merit, with my person and my property. That is, indeed, my full intent.'

'Would God that were true! It seems to me as if a whole year has passed without my becoming a knight! That causes me more pain than pleasure. Now do not hold me back any longer, but treat me as befits knights' honour.'

'That I will willingly do,' said his host, 'if honour does not fail me. You are, indeed, so comely that my gifts, rich in wealth's guidance, will be at your disposal. Truly, I would be unwilling to leave it undone. You must wait until tomorrow. I wish to equip you well.'

The well-born boy halted there, stamping his feet like a bustard.* He said: 'I don't want to beg for anything here. A knight came riding towards me—if his armour is not to be mine, I care nothing for what 150 they say of a king's gifts. My mother will give me the like, anyway—I believe she's a queen, after all.'

Arthur replied to the boy: 'That armour such a man has on him that I daren't give it you. As it is, I must live in constant sorrow through no fault of mine, since I have forfeited his favour. It is Ither of Gaheviez who has thrust sadness through my joy.'

'You would be an ungenerous king to hesitate over such a gift! Give it to him,' said Kay at once, 'and let him at him, out onto the plain! If anyone is to bring us the goblet—here halts the whip, there the top! Let the boy spin it around—then he'll be praised before women! He may have to face quarrels often enough in years to come, and risk such throws of the dice. I care nothing about either of their lives—hounds have to be sacrificed for the boar's head!'

'I would be unwilling to refuse him, but I fear he'll be slain—he whom I am to help to knighthood,' said Arthur from the depths of his loyalty.

The boy obtained the gift, nevertheless. Grief came of it afterwards. Then he was in a hurry to leave the king. Young and old 151 pressed after him. Iwanet took him by the hand, leading him past a gallery, none too high. He looked along it and back. Moreover, the gallery was so low that he was able to hear and see something up there which caused him sadness.

The Queen, meanwhile, had decided to be at the window herself, with knights and ladies. They were all watching Parzival. There sat Lady Cunneware, proud and radiant. She would never laugh on any account, unless she were to see that man who had won or was to win the highest prize. She would rather die first. All laughter she had shunned until that boy came riding by her. Then her lovely mouth began to laugh—to the ill-health of her back. Then Kay the Seneschal took Lady Cunneware *de* Lalant by her wavy hair. Her long, lustrous plaits he twisted about his hand, bolting them without a bar.* No oath was taken on her back, yet a staff* was so applied to it that, by the time its swishing had all died away, it had cut through her clothing and her skin.

Then the unwise seneschal said: 'Your noble repute has been 152 given a shameful end—I am its captive net.* I must forge it back into you, so that you feel it in your limbs. Into King Arthur's courtyard and his castle so many a worthy man has ridden on whose account you have avoided laughter, and now you laugh for a man who knows nothing of knightly bearing!'

In anger many marvels befall: none of his blows would have been dealt, before royalty, upon that maiden who was greatly pitied by her friends, if she had only carried a shield. Uncouthness struck its blows there, for she was by lineage a princess. Orilus and Lähelin, her brothers—if they'd seen this, fewer blows would have fallen.

The silent Antanor,* who was accounted a fool because of his silence—his speech and her laughter were conditioned by one cause: he would never say a word, unless she who had been beaten there laughed. When her laughter took place, his mouth said at once to Kay: 'God knows, Sir Seneschal, your delight in Cunneware *de* 153 Lalant having been thrashed because of this boy will yet come to be dispersed by his hand, however far he be from home.'

'Since your first speech threatens me, I think you'll have little pleasure from it.' Antanor's hide was tanned, blows from fists whispering hard in the wit-bearing fool's ears. Kay brooked no delay. The young Parzival had no choice then but to watch these troubles befall Antanor and the lady. Their distress touched him to the heart. Time and again he reached for his javelin—there was such a crowd before the Queen that he refrained from the throw.

Then Iwanet took his leave of *fil li roy* Gahmuret, who set out alone to meet Ither on the plain. To him he told the following tidings: that there was no-one in there who desired to joust. 'The King conferred a gift upon me. I said, as you told me, how it happened unintention-154 ally that you spilled the wine, that your uncouthness annoyed you. None of them desires combat. Give me what you ride upon, and all your equipment as well—I was granted that in the great hall, where I am to become a knight. My greeting shall be refused you* if you're unwilling to grant it me. Grant my desire, if you have your wits about you!'

The King of Kukumerlant said: 'If Arthur's hand has given you my armour, truly he's granted you my life as well—provided you can win it from me. So he favours his friends! Did you enjoy his favour before at all? Your service has so swiftly deserved this reward!'

'I dare, I think, to earn whatever I will by my service! And he has rewarded me most well. Hand it over, and abandon your claim to the land! I won't be a squire any longer—I shall have the shield's office!' At that he grasped for Ither's bridle: 'You may well be Lähelin, of whom my mother complains to me!'

The knight turned his shaft round,* and thrust at the boy with so much force that he and his little horse had no choice but to tumble 155 down upon the flowers. Ither the warrior was quick to wrath, so striking him that from the shaft's impact blood gushed out of his scalp. Parzival, the worthy boy, stood full of rage upon the plain. He immediately seized his javelin. Where Ither's helmet and his face-guard left a hole above the coif, through his eye the javelin pierced him, and through the nape of his neck, so that he fell dead, falsity's foe. Ither of Gaheviez's death brought women sighs, heart's sorrow's laceration, bequeathing women wet eyes. If any woman had felt his love, through her joy the charge had run, vanquishing her mirth, escorting it towards grief.

Foolish Parzival turned him over and over. He could pull nothing off him. It was an odd business: neither the helmet-ties nor the knee-plates could he untie with his fair white hands, nor could he twist them off, often as he tried, he whom wisdom ignored.

The charger and the little horse started whinnying so loudly that 156 Iwanet—Lady Guinevere's squire and kinsman—heard it outside the city, at the edge of the moat. When he heard the charger's bray, and when he saw no-one mounted upon it, because of the loyalty he bore Parzival the discerning squire hurried over to him.

He found Ither dead, and Parzival in foolish extremity. Quickly he leapt over to them both. He spoke his thanks to Parzival for the fame his hand had won by the King of Kukumerlant.

'God reward you! Now advise me what I am to do. I know very little of these matters—how do I get it off him and onto me?'

'That I can easily teach you,' said proud Iwanet to *fil li roy* Gahmuret. The dead man was disarmed, there before Nantes upon the plain, and his armour laid upon the living, whom great folly still moves.

Iwanet said: 'These boots ought not to be under the iron—you must wear knight's clothing now.'

These words displeased Parzival. The good boy replied: 'Of anything my mother gave me precious little shall come off me, whether 157 it hinders or helps.' This seemed strange enough to Iwanet (he being wise), yet he had to give in to him—he was not angry with him. Two bright hose of iron he shod over his boots. Without any leather, fastened by two silk ties, two spurs belonged to the gear—he fastened the gold handiwork upon him. Before he offered him his hauberk, he tied about him the knee-pieces. With no delay, with all speed, from the foot up Parzival was well armed, though he endured it impatiently.

Then the famed boy asked for his quiver. 'I will not hand you any javelin—knighthood has forbidden you that,' said Iwanet the noble squire. He buckled about him a sharp sword, teaching him how to draw it forth, and advising him against fleeing. Then he led over to him the dead man's Castilian—it bore legs that were high and long. Armoured, he leapt into the saddle. He had no wish for stirrups, he whose boldness is still acknowledged.

Iwanet was far from reluctant to teach him how to act skilfully 158 behind the shield, and aim at his enemies' disadvantage. He offered him a spear—Parzival had no wish whatever for it, but he asked him: 'What's this for?'

'If anyone comes jousting against you, you must break it at once, thrusting it through his shield. If you indulge in this often, you'll be praised before the women.'

As the adventure tells us, no artist of Cologne or Maastricht could have painted a better picture than of Parzival sitting upon the charger. Then he said to Iwanet: 'Dear friend, my companion, I've gained here what I asked for. You must announce my homage to King Arthur in the city, and complain to him also of my great disgrace. Take him

back his gold goblet. A knight so far forgot himself by me that he
beat the damsel because she was moved to laugh on my account. Her
woeful words still trouble me. They don't touch any outer edge of
my heart, but that lady's pain resides by rights in its very midst.
159 Now do this out of companionship, and take my disgrace to heart.
God keep you!—I will leave you now—He has the power to protect
us both.'

Ither of Gaheviez he left lying there in piteous state. Even in death
he was so fair—in life he was favoured by fortune. If chivalry had
been his end's guarantor, in the joust through the shield with a spear,
who would then grieve at so wondrous a calamity? It was by a javelin
he died.

Then Iwanet plucked bright flowers to make him a covering. He
thrust the javelin's shaft into the ground next to him, in the manner
of Christ's passion. That chaste and proud squire pressed a stick
crosswise through the javelin's blade. Nor would he then omit to take
the tidings into the city, at which many a woman was daunted and
many a knight wept, showing his grieving loyalty. There much sor-
row was suffered. The corpse was carried in in splendour. The
Queen rode out of the city to meet it, asking for the monstrance* to be
carried in procession.

Over the King of Kukumerlant, whom Parzival's hand had killed,
160 Lady Guinevere the Queen spoke words of wretched import: 'Alas
and alack! Arthur's honour will yet be broken in two by this won-
der—that he who at the Table Round ought by rights to bear the
highest fame lies slain before Nantes. It was his inheritance he
sought when death was granted to him. Yet he was one of our house-
hold here, such a man that no ear ever heard any misdeed spoken of
him. Against wild treachery he was tame—that had been scraped
from his parchment* entirely. Now I must bury, all too early, this lock
upon fame. His heart, wise in courtesy, a seal upon that lock,
prompted him to nothing but the best, wherever a man in pursuit of
a woman's love was to show man's loyalty with courageous intent.
An ever-bearing fruit of new sadness has been sown upon women.
From your wound sorrow gushes forth. Yet so splendidly red was
your hair that your blood had no need to make the radiant flowers
redder. You lay waste womanly smiles.'

161 Ither, rich in fame, was buried in kingly fashion. His death thrust
sighing upon women. It was his armour lost him his life—on that

account foolish Parzival's desire was his end's guarantor. Later, when Parzival had learned better, he would have been unwilling to do it.

The charger cultivated one habit: great hardship it weighed lightly. Whether it was cold or hot, it exuded no sweat because of the journey, whether it stepped upon stone or fallen tree-trunk. There was no need for a man to get it used to having its girth tightened, not even by a single notch, though he was mounted on it for two days. In armour, the foolish man rode it so far that day that a wise man, unarmoured, would have desisted—even if he had had to ride it for two days, he would have shunned the task. Parzival just let it gallop, rarely trot—he had little skill in reining it in.

Towards evening he espied a tower's pinnacle and its roof. The foolish boy was convinced that these towers were growing in number—so many stood there on a single castle. Then it occurred to him that Arthur was sowing them. He ascribed it to Arthur's holiness, and thought his blessings ranged far and wide.

The foolish man said: 'My mother's folk don't know how to till. 162 Their seed simply can't grow so high, no matter how much of it they have in the forest. Heavy rain seldom avoids them there.'

Gurnemanz *de* Graharz* was the name of the lord of the castle towards which he was riding. Before it stood a broad lime-tree on a green meadow, which was neither too broad nor too tall, but in proper proportion. The horse, and the road, too, carried him to where he found, sitting, that man to whom the castle, and also the land, belonged.

Great weariness so oppressed Parzival that he hung his shield wrongly, too far to the rear or to the fore, by no means in the customary manner regarded as laudable there. Gurnemanz the prince was sitting alone; moreover, the lime-tree's crown gave its shade, as it ought, to that captain of true courtesy. His ways were a refuge from falsity. He welcomed the stranger, as he was duty-bound. Neither knight nor squire was near him.

This was the answer Parzival gave him, dull of wit, without delay: 'My mother urged me to take advice from him who has grey locks. I'll willingly serve you to that end, since my mother told me to.' 163

'Since you have come here in search of advice, you must grant me your good will in return for advising you, if you would have the benefit of advice.'

Then the renowned prince cast a yearling sparrowhawk from his hand. Into the castle it soared, its golden bell tinkling. This was a messenger—immediately there came towards him many handsome squires. Gurnemanz requested that the stranger he saw before him should be led in and his comfort provided for. Parzival said: 'My mother says nothing but the truth—no malice lurks in an old man's words.'

At once they led him inside, where he found many a noble knight. At a place in the courtyard all of them asked him to dismount. Then he in whom folly was apparent said: 'It was a king commanded me to be a knight.* No matter what happens to me upon it, I'll not dismount from this charger. My mother advised me to give you greeting.'

They thanked both him and her. After these greetings were over—the charger being tired, as was the man—they had to think up 164 many entreaties before they could get him off the charger, and into a chamber. Then they all advised him: 'Let the armour be taken off you and lighten the load on your limbs.'

He was left no choice but to be quickly disarmed. When they beheld the rawhide boots and the fool's clothes, those tending to him were aghast. With great embarrassment the tale was told at court. The host was almost overcome with shame. One knight said, in his courtesy: 'Truly, never did my eyes' scrutiny behold such noble fruit. Upon him lies Fortune's glance, along with pure, gentle, high lineage. How is it that Love's radiance is kept in such custody? It will grieve me forever that I found such garb upon this world's joy. Hail, nonetheless, to the mother who bore him in whom such ample perfection lies. His helmet is richly adorned. His armour became him in knightly fashion before it came off the comely man. He has bloody bruising, caused by a collision, I at once observed.'

At this the host said to the knight: 'This has been done at women's bidding.'

'No, lord. The way he behaves, he couldn't ever persuade a woman 165 to accept his service. His complexion, though, would befit love.'

The host said: 'Now let's see this man whose clothes have proved such a wonder.'

They walked to where they found Parzival, wounded by a spear; it had, however, remained intact. Gurnemanz tended to him. He took such care of him that no father versed in loyalty could ever have tended his children better. With his own hands the host washed his wounds and dressed them.

By then bread had been laid upon the table. The young guest stood in need of that, for great hunger had not eluded him. Without breaking his fast at all, he had ridden away that morning from the fisherman. His wound and heavy armour, which he had won outside Nantes, spoke of weariness and hunger to him, as did the long day's journey away from Arthur the Briton—everywhere he'd been left to fast. The host told him to eat alongside him. The guest refreshed himself there, dipping so deep into the trough that he laid waste much of the food. The lord took all this as a joke. Gurnemanz, rich 166 in loyalty, implored him to eat his fill and forget his weariness.

They took the table away, when the time came. 'I believe you are tired,' said the host. 'Were you up early, perhaps?'

'God knows, my mother was still asleep then—she can't stay awake so long.'

The host burst out laughing. He led him to his sleeping-place. He asked him to take off his clothes. Reluctantly he did so; it had to be. An ermine bed-covering was laid over his bare body. Never did woman give birth to such noble fruit.

Great weariness and sleep taught him seldom to toss from side to side. In this fashion he waited for daybreak to come. The famed prince had ordered that a bath be ready, promptly for the middle of the morning, at one end of the carpet where he lay. This was duly carried out that morning. Roses were thrown onto the water's surface. Little though they called out in his presence, the guest awoke from his sleep there. The young, noble, gentle man went at once to sit in the tub.

I don't know who asked them to do so—damsels in rich clothing 167 and lovely of person arrived, as befitted courtesy's ways. They washed and quickly smoothed away his bruising with white, soft hands. Indeed, there was no need for him to feel he was in foreign parts, orphaned though he was of wit. Thus he endured pleasure and ease, paying little for his folly with them. Chaste and bold damsels thus curried him down. Whatever the subject of their parley, he knew well how to keep his silence. He had no need to think it too early in the day, except that a second dawn shone from them. Radiance thus did battle there—his complexion extinguished both lights—his person was not found wanting.

He was offered a bath-robe. He took very little notice of that. Such was his modesty before ladies that he didn't want to wrap it

about him in their presence. The damsels were obliged to go—they
dared stand there no longer. I believe they would willingly have
looked to see whether anything had happened to him down below.
Womankind keeps company with loyalty; it knows how to grieve over
a beloved's sorrow.

168 The guest walked over to the bed. Clothing all in white had been
prepared for him. It had been threaded with a girdle of gold and silk.
They drew scarlet hose over him whose courage never failed him.
Avoy! How splendid his legs looked! True elegance shone from
them. Of violet scarlet,* well-cut—fur linings not neglected—both
with white ermine on the inside, his tunic and cloak were long—broad
black and grey sable could be seen at the front. This the comely youth
put on. By a costly belt it was secured, and well adorned by a costly
brooch. His mouth burned with redness to match it.

Then the host, replete with loyalty, came in; a proud company of
knights followed him. He welcomed the stranger. When that had
taken place, each of the knights said he had never seen such a hand-
some person. In all sincerity they praised the woman who had given
the world such fruit. In all truth, and as their courtesy commanded,
they said: 'He will be well rewarded wherever his service desires
169 favour. Love and women's greeting will fall to his share, if he can
profit by his worth.' All there averred the same, as did whoever
beheld him thereafter.

The lord took him by the hand, walking companionably away with
him. The renowned prince asked him how he had rested there that
night.

'Sir, I would not be alive still, if my mother had not advised me to
come here on the day when I parted from her.'

'May God reward you and her.'

'Lord, you show me kindness.'

Then that warrior weak of wit walked to where they sang to God
and his host. At the mass the host taught him that which even today
would enhance bliss: how to make his offering and bless himself,
wreaking vengeance upon the Devil.

Then they walked up into the great hall, where the table was laid.
The guest sat down by his host, not scorning the food. The host said
out of politeness: 'Sir, you must not be offended if I ask you tidings
of where you have travelled from.' Parzival told him in all detail
170 how he'd ridden away from his mother, about the ring and about

the brooch, and how he had won the armour. The host recognized
the Red Knight. He sighed, pitying his downfall. He insisted upon
giving his guest the same name—he called him the Red Knight.

After the table had been taken away, a wild spirit then grew most
tame. The host said to his guest: 'You talk like a little child! Why not
be silent concerning your mother altogether, and pay heed to other
matters? Hold fast to my counsel—it will part you from wrongdoing.

'I'll begin as follows, may it please you: never must you lose your
sense of shame. A person past all shame, what further use is he?
He lives in moulting plumage, honour's feathers falling from him,
pointing him towards Hell.

'You are fair of figure and looks, you may well be a people's lord. If
your lineage is high and rises higher, then bear this in mind: you
must take pity on people in need; guard against their troubles with
generosity and kindness. Practise humility. He who is noble but
needy knows how to struggle with shame—that is no sweet labour— 171
your help should be at his disposal. Whenever you free him of his
trouble, then God's greeting will near you. He is even worse off than
those who go in search of a door but find windows.

'You should, with discretion, be both poor and rich, for if a lord
squanders all he owns, that is no lordly disposition, but if he grabs
treasure too greedily, that, too, is dishonourable. Give true moder-
ation its degree. I have perceived that you are well and truly in need
of advice—now leave unseemly ways to their own quarrel!

'You must not ask many questions. Nor should you hold back
from considered counter-speech, meeting a man's questioning head-
on if he wants to sound you out with words. You can hear and see,
taste and smell—that must bring you near to knowledge.

'Let mercy keep company with courage. Follow my advice in this:
if in battle you win a man's surrender, then unless he has done you
such grievance as amounts to heart's sorrow, accept his oath, and let
him live.

'You may often have occasion to bear arms. Once they are off you, 172
be sure that your face and hands are washed afterwards—that is
timely after iron's rust. Then you will be lovely of appearance—
women's eyes will mark it well.

'Be manly and in good spirits—that will further your noble fame.
And let women be dear to you—that enhances a young man's
esteem. Never waver in relation to women, not for a single day. That

is true manly disposition. If you like lying to them, you may deceive many—false cunning aimed at noble love enjoys short-lived fame. There the prowlers are prosecuted by the dry wood in the thicket—it snaps and cracks—the watchman awakes. Unpathed lands and fenced enclosures—there many a quarrel thrives. Measure Love by this standard. Noble Love possesses understanding, knows cunning ruses to oppose falsity. If you incur her displeasure, then you may be dishonoured, forever enduring shameful hurt.

173   'This teaching you must take to heart. I shall tell you more of woman's order. Man and woman are all one, just like the sun that shone today and the name that denotes day—neither of these may be separated from the other. They blossom from a single seed. Mark this with discernment.'

The guest bowed to the host for his advice. Concerning his mother he was now silent—in speech, but not in his heart, as still befalls a loyal man.

The lord said more that did him honour: 'You must still learn more skill in knightly ways. The way you came riding towards me! I have observed many a wall on which I found the shield hanging better than it did about your neck! It is not too late for us—let us hurry to the field. There you must draw near knightly skills. Bring him his charger, and me mine, and each knight his own! Squires are to come, too—let each take a stout shaft and bring it with him—let it be freshly painted!'

Thus the prince came onto the plain—there skill was shown in riding. He gave his guest advice as to how to change the charger's 174 gait from the gallop, with spurs' greeting's prick, thighs beating as if in flight, to the full tilt; how to lower the shaft correctly and hold the shield before him in the joust. He said: 'Take this to heart!'

Thus Gurnemanz fended uncouthness from him, better than the pliant switch that cuts into naughty children's skin. He then ordered bold knights to come and joust against him. He escorted him towards an opponent in the rink.* Then the youth delivered his first joust through a shield, surprising them all by knocking off, back behind his charger, a strong knight, no weakling.

A second jouster had arrived. Then Parzival, for his part, had taken a stout new shaft. His youth possessed courage and strength. That young, gentle, beardless man—Gahmuret's lineage and his innate valour compelled him to ride the charger at full career, head-on into

the charge, aiming at the four nails.* The host's knight did not keep
his seat—falling headlong, he took full measure of the turf. Then 175
lances could do no other than splinter into tiny fragments. In this
fashion he thrust five of them down. The host took him and led him
back. There in play he had won the prize; in battle he afterwards
grew wise.

Those who had seen his riding—all the wise folk said of him that
skill and courage kept him company: 'Now my lord will be free of
sorrow—his life may well now be rejuvenated. He ought to give
him his daughter, our lady, for a wife. If we see him act with wisdom,
then his sorrow's extremity will be quenched. For his three sons'
death, recompense has ridden into his castle. Fortune has not
shunned him now.'

So things stood when the prince came home that evening. The
table was laid, as a matter of course. He asked his daughter to come
to table, so I have heard. When he saw the maiden come in, hear now
what the host said to the beautiful Liaze: 'You must let him kiss you,
this knight, offer him honour—he journeys with Fortune's doctrine.
And, Parzival, for your part of the bargain, you must let the maiden
keep her ring—if she should have one, that is! Mind you, she hasn't 176
any, nor a brooch. Who should give her such wealth as that lady in
the greenwood had? She had someone from whom she obtained that
which you afterwards chanced to obtain. You may take nothing from
Liaze!' The stranger felt ashamed, but he kissed her on the mouth,
which was well acquainted, I believe, with fire's colour. Liaze was
lovely of person, moreover rich in true chastity.

The table was low and long. The host jostled with no-one there.
He sat alone at the head. He commanded his guest to sit there,
between himself and his child. Her white, gentle hands had to cut, as
the host ordered, food for the man they there called the Red
Knight—whatever he wished to eat. No-one was to prevent them
entering into intimacy. The maiden, rich in courtesy, carried out all
her father's wishes. She and the guest were both well-favoured.

Soon afterwards the maiden withdrew. Thus the warrior was
entertained for the next fortnight. Sorrow lay with his heart, for no 177
reason other than that he desired to fight further before growing
warm in such limbs as they call ladies' arms. He held noble hopes to
be a high aspiration in this life and the next. These words are still no
lie today.

One morning he asked for leave. Then he left that city of Graharz. The host rode out with him to the open fields. New heart's sorrow then arose. The prince, peerless in loyalty, said: 'You are my fourth lost son. Indeed, I thought I had been compensated for three sorrowful causes. There were only three then. If anyone were now to cut my heart in four with his hand and carry away each part, I would think it great profit: one part for you—you are riding away—the other three for my noble sons, who died valiantly. Such, however, is chivalry's reward—its tail is knotted with sorrow's snares.

'One death cripples me of joy entirely—that of my well-favoured son, who was called Schenteflurs.* There where Condwiramurs* would not yield her person and land, in her aid he lost his life, at the hands of Clamide and Kingrun. Because of this my heart is like a fence full of holes, lacerated by sorrow's cuts. Now you are riding all too soon away from me, inconsolable man that I am. Alas that I cannot die, since neither Liaze, the beautiful maiden, nor my land is to your liking.

'My second son was called *cons* Lascoyt. He was killed by Ider *fil* Noyt in the cause of a sparrowhawk—so it is that I stand devoid of joy. My third son was called Gurzgri. Mahaute rode with him, lovely of person, for she had been given to him as a wife by her proud brother, Ehkunat.* To Brandigan, the capital, he came riding, to Schoydelakurt,* where death was not denied him. There Mabonagrin slew him, upon which Mahaute lost her bright looks, and my wife, his mother, lay dead. Great grief for him commanded it of her.'

The guest marked his host's distress, for he had explained it to him so fully. He replied: 'Lord, I'm not wise. Yet if I ever win knight's fame, so that I may perhaps be capable of desiring love, you shall bestow upon me Liaze, your daughter, that beautiful maiden. You have told me all too much of sorrow—if I can then relieve you of grief, I shall not let you bear so heavy a burden.'

The young man then took his leave of the faithful prince and all his household. The prince's sorrow's three had fallen sadly on the four;* it was the fourth loss he had won.

BOOK IV

THUS Parzival departed. He took with him, together with courtesy, a knight's ways and a knight's looks, but, alas, much ungentle harshness moved him. To him width was too narrow, and breadth too confined by far. All greenness seemed faded to him, his red armour he thought white—his heart imposed this upon his eyes. Now that he was bereft of folly, Gahmuret's lineage would not spare him from thinking of the beautiful Liaze, that maiden rich in blessings who had, companionably, offered him, without love, honour. Whichever way his charger now heads, he cannot check it, so great is his grief, 180 whether it wants to prance or trot.

Wayside crosses and wattle fences, waggon wheels' ruts, too, all shunned his way through the woods. He rode then through much unpathed land, where little plantain grew. Dale and hill were unknown to him. There is a common saying that if a man rides astray, he will find the hammer. Signs of the hammer lay there in quantity beyond measure, if huge fallen tree-trunks may be taken as the hammer's mark.

Yet he did not go much astray, but riding only as the crow flies, he made his way that day from Graharz to the kingdom of Brobarz, through wild, lofty peaks. Day was drawing close to evening, when he came to a rapidly-flowing river, loud with its own roaring, tossed by one rock to the other. He rode downstream, and there he found the city of Pelrapeire. King Tampenteire had bequeathed it to his daughter, in whose company many are now in distress.

The river hurtled like bolts, well feathered and cut, when the 181 crossbow's stretch propels them forth by the cord's hurl. Across it went a drawbridge, on top of which lay many a hurdle. It flowed direct into the sea there. Pelrapeire stood well-defended. See how children ride on swings—those who are not begrudged swings—thus that bridge rode, but without a rope. Youth did not make it so merry!

There on the other side stood sixty knights or more, with helmets buckled. They all shouted out: 'Turn back! Turn!' Brandishing their swords, those enfeebled knights desired to do battle. Because they had often seen him there before, they thought that it was Clamide,

for he rode in such kingly fashion across the broad plain towards the
bridge.

When they shouted so loudly at this young man, no matter how
hard he cut into the charger with his spurs, out of fear it ducked the
drawbridge. He whom true timidity ever fled dismounted and led his
charger onto the bridge's sway. A coward's mind would have been far
too feeble to ride towards such strife. Moreover, Parzival had to keep
182 one thing in particular in mind, for he was afraid of the charger
falling. Then the din on the other side died away. The knights carried
back into the castle their helmets, shields, their swords' sheen, and
closed their gate. It was a bigger army that they feared.

Parzival then made his way across and came riding to a rampart,
where many a man had met with his death, losing his life in pursuit
of knightly fame, outside the gate before the great hall, which was
lofty and well adorned. He found a ring in the gate—he tugged at it
hard with his hand. No-one there took any notice of his shouting,
except for one well-favoured damsel. Looking out of a window that
maiden saw the hero halting there, undaunted. The beautiful maiden,
rich in courtesy, said: 'If it is as an enemy that you have come here,
lord, there's no need for that. Even without you, much enmity has
been proferred us, by land and by sea—a hostile, courageous army.'
He replied: 'Lady, here halts a man who will serve you, if I can. Let
your greeting be my reward. I will gladly serve you.' Then the
183 maiden prudently went to the queen, and so helped him to make his
way in. That afterwards averted great grief from him.

Thus he was admitted. To either side of the road there stood a
great crowd of folk. They had come there carrying arms, slingers
and foot-soldiers—of those there was a long line—and a great num-
ber of vile archers.* He also marked the presence of many bold men-
at-arms, the best of that land, with long, sturdy lances, sharp and
unbroken. As I heard the story tell, many a merchant stood there,
too, with axe and with javelin, as his guild commanded him. They
were all slack of skin. The queen's marshal had to lead him through
them, with some difficulty, to the courtyard. That was well equipped
for defence: towers above the chambers, barbicans, keeps, half-
turrets—there were more of these, for certain, than he had ever seen
before. From all directions knights then came up to welcome him, on
184 horseback and on foot. That wretched company was all ashen in
appearance, or like wan lime. My lord the Count of Wertheim

wouldn't have liked to have been a paid soldier there—he couldn't
have lived on *their* pay!

Want had brought hunger's need upon them. They had no cheese,
meat, nor bread. They had no truck with toothpicks, nor did they
grease the wine with their lips when they drank. Their bellies were
sunken, their hips high and thin; the skin about their ribs was shriv-
elled like a Hungarian's leather. Hunger had driven their flesh away;
deprivation forced them to suffer it. Very little fat dripped into their
coals.

This had been imposed upon them by a noble knight, the proud
King of Brandigan—they were reaping the harvest of Clamide's
suit. Rarely did the tankard or the jug spill over with mead there; a
Trühendingen frying-pan seldom shrieked with doughnuts*—for
them that note was out of key!

If I were to reproach them for this now, that would be very mean-
spirited of me, for where I have often dismounted and where they
call me master, back home in my own house, a mouse has seldom 185
cause to rejoice, for it would have to steal its food. No-one would
need to hide food from me—I can't find any lying around in the
open. All too often it befalls me, Wolfram von Eschenbach, that I
have to put up with such comfort as this.

Of my troubles much has been heard—now this tale must return to
how Pelrapeire stood full of woe. There the people paid toll on joys.
The warriors, rich in loyalty, lived a wretched life. Their true valour
commanded it. Now their distress must move you to pity! Their lives
are pledged away now, unless the Highest Hand redeems them.

Hear more, now, about these poor people—you must take pity on
them! They welcomed their guest, rich in courage, with some
embarrassment. He seemed to them so noble that in other circum-
stances he would have no requirement of such hospitality as they
could offer. Their great need was unknown to him.

They laid a carpet upon the grass, where a lime tree was walled-in
and pruned, to give shade. Then the retinue disarmed him. He was 186
unlike them in appearance, once he had washed all the rust off him
with water from a well. Then he would almost have put the sun's
bright glow to shame. Because of this he seemed a noble guest to
them. They offered him a cloak at once, similar to the tunic the
warrior had worn before; its sable smelt wild and fresh.

They said: 'Would you care to see the queen, our lady?' The

constant warrior replied that he would gladly do so. They walked over to the great hall, where steps led steeply upward. A lovely countenance's radiance, and his eyes' sweetness—from the queen shone a bright glow, even before she received him.

Kyot of Katelangen,* and the noble Manpfilyot—both these were dukes—were escorting their brother's daughter, that land's queen. For God's love they had given up their swords. Together these noble princes walked, grey and well-favoured, escorting the lady with great 187 courtesy to the middle of the steps. There she kissed the noble warrior—their mouths were both red. The queen offered him her hand. She led Parzival back up the steps, where they both sat down.

The ladies and the company of knights were all weak in strength, those standing and sitting there. They had abandoned joy, both the household and the lady of the castle. Condwiramurs' radiance set her apart, however, from competition with Jeschute, Enite,* and Cunneware *de* Lalant—and wherever the best in repute were to be found, where ladies' beauty was weighed, her radiance's sheen undercut them entirely, as it did both Isaldes.* Condwiramurs would have to take the prize—she who had the true *bêâ curs*. In German that means: 'beautiful person'. They were serviceable women, indeed, who gave birth to those two sitting together there. Neither woman nor man did anything but gaze at the two of them, next to one another. Parzival found good friends there.

188   As for the stranger's thoughts, I'll tell you them: 'Liaze is there, Liaze is here. God desires to moderate my sorrow. Now I see Liaze, noble Gurnemanz's daughter.'

Liaze's beauty was but a breath of air compared with the maiden who sat here. God forgot no degree of perfection in creating her— she was that land's lady—as when, because of the sweet dew, the rose peeps out of its bud, showing new, noble radiance, which is both white and red. That brought great pain to her guest. His manly good breeding was so complete, now that noble Gurnemanz had parted him from his folly and advised him against asking questions, unless it were discreetly—next to the mighty queen his mouth sat, entirely wordless—close by her there, not far apart. Many a man is still sparing of speech who has had more traffic with ladies.

The queen's first thoughts were: 'I think this man despises me because my body is wasted away. No, it's a ruse on his part—he's a 189 guest, I'm the hostess—the first speech ought to be mine. He must have looked kindly upon me, since we come to be sitting here. He has shown courtesy to me—my words have been all too long spared—let there be no more silence here!'

To her guest the queen said: 'Lord, a hostess must speak. A kiss won me your greeting. And you have offered service to us here in the castle, so one of my damsels said. We are not used to such behaviour from strangers—it is something my heart has longed for. Sir, may I ask you from where you have travelled here?'

'Lady, I rode away this day from a man whom I left lamenting, a man of loyalty without limit. That prince is called Gurnemanz; he is named after Graharz. It was from there I rode today into this land.'

The noble maiden replied: 'If anyone else had told me that, he wouldn't have been granted credence—that it happened in a single day—for any of my messengers, even riding at his fastest, would not have managed that journey in a good two days. His sister—that is, your host's—was my mother. His daughter's radiance has good reason, too, to fade for sorrow. We have lamented away many a bitter day, with wet eyes, I and the maiden Liaze. If you hold your host 190 dear, then accept tonight such fare as we've put up with for a long time here, women and men. By so doing you will serve Gurnemanz a little. I shall tell you the tale of our troubles. We have to suffer harsh deprivation.'

Then her kinsman Kyot said: 'Lady, I shall send you twelve loaves, shoulders and three hams, along with eight cheeses and two butts of wine. My brother shall assist you too, this very night—the need is great!'

Then Manpfilyot said: 'Lady, I'll send you the same amount!' Now the maiden sat at joy's journey's end—her great gratitude was not spared. The dukes took leave and rode off to their nearby hunting-lodge. By the wild alp's gorge the old men dwelt, defenceless. They had even been granted a truce by the hostile army.

Their messenger came trotting back, to the relief of the enfeebled company. The townsfolk's diet was much enhanced by this food. Many of them had died of hunger before that bread came to them. The queen ordered it to be shared out, together with the cheese, the 191 meat, the wine, among those people lacking in strength. Parzival, her guest, advised her in this. There remained scarcely a slice for the two of them. They shared it without squabbling.

Those supplies were soon consumed, averting many a man's death

among those whom hunger had left alive. Then they ordered the
guest's bed to be made ready—soft, or so I should imagine. If the
townsfolk had been falcons, their crops wouldn't have been over-
stuffed,* as the courses placed on their table testify. They all bore
hunger's marks, except for young Parzival.

He took sleep's leave. Were his candles stubs of tallow? No, they
were better by far. The well-favoured youth then walked over to a
sumptuous bed, adorned in kingly fashion, not of poverty's choice.
A carpet was spread before it. He asked the knights to retire; he did
not leave them standing there any longer. Pages drew off his shoes.
Straight away he slept, until true grief called out to him and bright
eyes' heart's rain—these soon awoke the noble warrior.

192   This came about as I will tell you—it did not break with womanly
boundaries—along with constancy she bore chastity, the maiden of
whom some account will be told here. War's exigencies and dear
helpers' deaths had pressed her heart to such a breaking-point that
her eyes had no choice but to keep awake. Then the queen—not in
pursuit of such love as provokes such a name as calls maidens
women—went in search of help and a friend's advice. She wore war-
like clothing—a shift of white silk. What could be more bellicose than
a woman thus approaching a man? In lieu of a shield she swung about
her a long cloak of samite. She walked like one oppressed by troubles.

Damsels, chamberlains—all those about her there—she left sleep-
ing everywhere, creeping quietly, not making a sound, into a separate
chamber. Those in charge there had arranged for Parzival to lie
alone. It was bright as day because of the candles beside his bedding-
193   place. Her path led towards his bed. On the carpet she knelt down
before him. Neither of them had much idea—neither he nor the
queen—about such love as involves lying together. Here is what
wooing ensued: the maiden's joy was ruined, shame so oppressed
her. Did he take her to him at all? Sadly, he knows nothing of such
matters—and yet, despite his lack of skill, it does happen, with such
conditions of truce that they did not combine their conciliatory
limbs—that was far from their thoughts.

The maiden's grief was so great that tear upon tear flowed from
her eyes down upon young Parzival. He heard such loud weeping
that he awoke and stared at her. At that both sorrow and joy befell
him. The young man rose to his feet, saying to the queen: 'Lady,
are you mocking me? It is before God that you should thus kneel. Be

so kind as to sit down beside me,'—that was his request and his desire—'or lie down right here where I have been lying. Let me lie where I can.'

She said: 'Provided you behave honourably and show such restraint towards me that you do not wrestle with me, then my lying 194 by you there will come to pass.' He agreed to a truce on those terms. She snuggled into the bed at once.

It was as yet so late that no cock crowed anywhere. The perches stood bare; hunger had shot the hens down from them. The lady rich in sorrow asked him courteously if he would like to hear her grievance, saying: 'I fear, if I tell you about it, it will deprive you of sleep—that will cause you pain. King Clamide and Kingrun, his seneschal, have laid waste to my castles and land, all except Pelrapeire. My father, Tampenteire, left me, poor orphan that I am, in fearful peril. Kinsmen, princes and subjects, rich and poor, a great courageous army was at my command. They have died in my defence, half of them or the greater part. What reason have I to be merry, poor me? Now it has come to the point that I will kill myself rather than surrender my maidenhead and person, and become Clamide's wife, for it was his hand slew my Schenteflurs, whose heart bore great 195 knightly fame. He was a blossoming branch of manly beauty; he knew how to rein in falsity, Liaze's brother.'

When Liaze was named, Parzival, her servitor, was reminded of much trouble on her account. His high spirits fell into a valley—love for Liaze prompted that. He said to the queen: 'Lady, can anyone's solace help you?'

'Yes, lord, if I were freed from Kingrun the Seneschal. In formal joust his hand has felled many of my knights. He will come back here tomorrow, and believes that his lord shall lie in my arms. You saw, I suppose, my great hall—however high its elevation, I'd rather fall down into the moat than have Clamide take my maidenhead by force. Thus I would fend off his fame!'

Then he said: 'Lady, whether Kingrun be a Frenchman or a Briton, or whatever land he has travelled from, you shall be defended by my hand, as far as I prove capable.' The night came to an end and 196 day arrived. The lady rose and bowed, not concealing her great gratitude. Then she crept quietly back. No-one there was astute enough to have marked her coming and going—except for Parzival of the bright complexion.

After that he slept no longer. The sun was hastening towards the heights, its beams thrusting through the clouds. Then he heard the sound of many bells: churches and minster were being visited by that people whom Clamide had parted from joy.

The young man arose. The queen's chaplain sang to God and his lady. Her guest could not help gazing at her until the benediction had been spoken. Then he asked for his armour—he was buckled into it with skill. He displayed, indeed, knightly courage, along with true manly defiance. Next Clamide's army arrived with many a banner. Kingrun rode rapidly, far ahead of the others, on a charger from 197 Iserterre,* as I have heard the story tell. By then *fil li roy* Gahmuret had also emerged from the gate. He had with him the townsfolk's prayers.

This was his first battle with the sword. He charged, I imagine, from such a distance that by his joust's force both steeds were ungirthed. Their saddle-belts broke in consequence, each horse sitting back on its haunches. Those who up to then had been mounted upon them did not forget their swords—they found them in their scabbards! Kingrun was carrying wounds, through his arm and into his chest. This joust taught him the loss of such fame as he had enjoyed up to this, his pride's-disappearing day. Such courage was attributed to him—he was said to have felled six knights who attacked him together on a plain. Parzival paid him back by his valorous hand, in such coin that Kingrun the Seneschal imagined strange things were happening—as if a catapult was hurling blows down upon him. It was battle of a different kind that felled him—a sword resounded through his helmet. Parzival hewed him down. He placed one knee on his chest. Kingrun offered what had never 198 been offered to any man before, his surrender. His antagonist would have none of that. He asked him to take his vow of surrender to Gurnemanz.

'No, sir, you might more willingly put me to death. I slew his son, I took Schenteflurs' life. God has granted you great honour. Wherever they talk about how your strength has been manifested by defeating me, you will have gained your purpose.'

Then young Parzival replied: 'I will give you another choice. Now offer your surrender to the queen, to whom your lord has caused great grief by his aggression.'

'Then I would be doomed. By swords my body would be cut into pieces small as float in sunbeams, for I have caused heart's sorrow to many a bold man inside that castle.'

'Then take your knightly oath of surrender from this plain to the land of Brittany, to a maiden who for my sake suffered what she should not have suffered, if justice were acknowledged. And tell her, whatever happens to me, she will never see me happy until I avenge 199 her by piercing shields. Say to Arthur and his wife, to both of them, that I serve them, and the whole household, and that I shall never return until I have renounced that disgrace I bear in companionship with the lady who offered me laughter. She suffered greatly on that account. Tell her I am her servitor, subject to her in subservient service.' These words found agreement there. The warriors were seen to part.

Back walked, to where his charger been caught, the townsfolk's battle's hope. They were afterwards freed by him. The outer army was in despair, now that Kingrun had been defeated in battle. Now Parzival was conducted to the queen. She embraced him openly, pressing him close to her, saying: 'I'll never become the wife of any man on this earth except him whom I hold in my arms.' She helped disarm him, her service far from being spared.

After his great labours poor hospitality awaited. The townsfolk 200 behaved as follows: they all swore allegiance to him and said that he must be their lord. Then the queen, too, said that he was to be her *âmis*, since he had won such high fame by Kingrun. Two brown sails were espied by those who looked down from the ramparts, a strong wind driving them direct into the harbour. The keels were laden in such fashion that the townsfolk rejoiced—they carried nothing but food. Wise God had so decreed it.

Down from the turrets they tumbled, scurrying towards the keels, the hungry people, bent on plunder. They might have floated like leaves, thin and shrivelled, light of flesh as they were—their skins were far from being stuffed. The queen's marshal ordered a truce for the ships, forbidding, at risk of the rope, any man to touch them. He took the merchants into the town, bringing them before his lord. Parzival urged that they be paid the price of their wares twice over. 201 The merchants were overwhelmed. What they had invested in purchases was thus fully repaid. Fat dripped into the townsfolk's coals.

I'd be glad to be a paid soldier there now, I daresay, because nobody is drinking beer there—they have wine and food in plenty!

Then flawless Parzival acted as I will tell you: first of all he divided the food into small portions with his own hands. He gave seats to the noble people he found there. He did not wish their empty bellies to suffer from overcropping. He gave them a due and proper share. They were delighted at his counsel. Come nightfall he supplied them with more. He was a straightforward man, far from being haughty.

The question was put as to whether they would lie together. He and the queen said yes. He lay with such skills as will not suffice nowadays for many women, if a man treats them in such fashion. Oh, how they mottle their manners in tormenting mood, putting on airs! In the presence of strangers they behave chastely, but all this 202 behaviour is undermined by the desires of their hearts. To their lovers they cause secret pain by their caresses. A man whose moderation has always proved true, a faithful, constant man, knows well how to spare his lady-love. He thinks, as may well be true: I have served all my years to win the reward of this woman who has offered me solace—now here I lie. It would have always sufficed for me if, with my bare hand, I might have touched her dress. If I were now to be greedy in my desire, disloyalty would be acting in my stead. Am I now to cause her strife, to bring disgrace upon us both? Before sleep sweet discourse is a better match for ladies' ways. Thus lay the Waleis, posing little threat.

He they called the Red Knight left the queen a maiden, but she believed she was his wife. For her handsome husband's sake next morning she put up her hair.* Then that maidenly bride gave him her castles and land, for he was her heart's beloved.

They passed the time together in this fashion, happy in their love, 203 for two days and the third night. Often it occurred to him to embrace her, as his mother had advised. Gurnemanz, too, had explained to him that man and woman are all one. They intertwined arms and legs. If I may make so bold as to tell you, he found that which was close and sweet. That way which is both old and new dwelt with them both there. They were happy, far from sad.

Now hear how Clamide, for his part, attacking in force, met with tidings that disconsoled him. A squire, whose charger was slashed through at the sides, told him: 'Before Pelrapeire, upon the plain, noble chivalry has been enacted, fierce enough, by a knight's hands. The seneschal has been overcome—the army's captain, Kingrun, is on his way to Arthur the Briton. The paid soldiers are still encamped

outside the city, as he requested them when he departed. You and
your two armies will find Pelrapeire well defended. Inside the city
there is a noble knight who desires nothing but battle. Your paid
soldiers say, each and every one of them, that the queen has sent to 204
the Table Round for Ither of Kukumerlant. It was his arms advanced
to the joust and were worn as befits fame.'

The king replied to the squire: 'Condwiramurs shall have me, and
I her person and her land. Kingrun, my seneschal, sent me true
word that they would surrender the city, compelled by starvation's
extremity, and that the queen would offer me her noble love.'

The squire won nothing there but hostility. The king rode on,
with his army. A knight came riding towards him, not sparing *his*
charger either—he told the same tidings. For Clamide happiness and
knightly intent became a heavy burden—these seemed to him great
losses.

One of the king's men, a prince, spoke up: 'No-one saw Kingrun
do battle on behalf of our forces—he fought there only for himself
alone. Even if he has been slain, are two armies to be intimidated on
that account, this here, and that outside the city? He entreated his
lord to abandon despondency: 'Let's make another attempt. If they're
resolved to resist, we'll give them plenty of battle yet, and put an end 205
to their joy. You must urge your subjects and kinsmen on, and attack
the town under two banners. We can easily ride at them along the
slope—the gates we'll attack on foot. We'll cure them of merriment,
for sure!'

It was Galogandres, the Duke of Gippones,* who gave that advice.
He inflicted distress upon the townsfolk, but also fetched death at
their outworks, as did Count Narant, a prince from Ukerlant,* and
many a poor nobleman who was carried away from there, dead.

Now hear a different story!—how the townsfolk attended to their
outworks. They took long tree-trunks and hammered stout spikes
into them—that gave the attackers grief. They hung them by ropes,
rolling the logs by wheels. All this had been prepared before Clamide
launched his attack against them, after Kingrun's defeat. Moreover,
along with their provisions, heathen wild fire* had come into the land.
The outer army's siege-engines were burned down. Their scaling- 206
towers and their mangonels, all that had rolled there on wheels, their
hedgehogs, their cats* aimed into the moat—all these the fire knew
well how to erase from the page.

Kingrun the Seneschal had arrived in the land of Britain, and found King Arthur in Broceliande, at the hunting-lodge—it was called Karminal. There he acted as Parzival, on taking him captive, had commanded him. He took to Lady Cunneware de Lalant his oath of surrender. The damsel was delighted that her distress was loyally lamented by him whom they there called the Red Knight.

These tidings were heard everywhere. By then the defeated, noble knight had entered the King's presence. He at once told Arthur and his household the message he had been commanded to take them. Kay, startled, began to blush, saying: 'Is it you, Kingrun? Oh, how many a Briton your hand has vanquished, Clamide's seneschal! Even if I never find favour with your master, you must, nevertheless, benefit by your office. The cauldron is subject to both of us, to me
207 here and to you in Brandigan. Help me, noble as you are, to win Cunneware's favour by means of thick doughnuts.' He offered her no other compensation.

Let such matters be—hear what is happening where we left the tale before. Clamide came before Pelrapeire. There was no avoiding fierce attacks there: those within fought against those without. The former had hope and strength, their warriors were found valiant, and so they held the rampart. Their land's lord, Parzival, fought far in advance of his men. The gates stood wide open there. With flailing arms he struck his blows, his sword clanging through hard helmets. Any knights he struck down there found trouble enough through the lesson they learned at their hauberks' gussets,* the townsfolk exacting their revenge by stabbing them through the slits. Parzival forbade them that practice. When they heard of his anger at this, they took twenty of them captive, alive, before they walked away from the battle.

Parzival observed that Clamide, along with his host, was avoiding knightly combat at the gates, and doing battle on the other side of
208 the city. Hardy of heart, the youth headed for the unpathed land. He hastened round towards the king's banner. Behold, then Clamide's pay was earned at last, but at a loss! The townsfolk knew how to fight till their stout shields disappeared entirely before their hands. Parzival's own shield was reduced to nothing by blows and shots. Not that they profited much by it, the attackers who saw this happening—they all admitted he won the day. Galograndres carried the banner—he knew well how to spur on the army—he lay dead at the king's side. Clamide himself came into danger—harm befell him

there, and his men. Then Clamide called a halt to the attack. The townsfolk, wise in valour, had won the advantage and the prize.

Parzival the noble warrior ordered that the prisoners be treated well until a third morning had dawned. The outer army was in some anxiety. The young, proud lord, well-contented, accepted the captives' oath of surrender, saying: 'When I send for you, return, good people!' He asked for their armour to be retained; they headed back to rejoin the army outside the city. Although the returning captives were flushed with drink, the outer army said to them: 'You have suffered hunger's pangs, poor things!' 209

'Do not pity us!' said the captive knights. 'There is such abundance of food in there that if you wanted to lie encamped here for another year, they could keep both you and themselves in food, for sure. The queen has the handsomest husband who ever gained shield's office. He may well be of high lineage—all knights' honour is safe with him.'

When Clamide heard this, his troubles grew afresh. He sent envoys back into the castle with a message to the effect that, whoever it was lying there with the queen, 'if he is battleworthy, and if it be the case that she judges him capable of daring to defend her person and her land in combat against me, then let there be a truce between the two armies.'

Parzival was delighted that the embassy thus promised him single combat. Undaunted, the young knight said: 'Let my loyalty be the pledge that no hand of the inner army will come to my defence if I am endangered!' Between the moat and the outer army this truce was established. Then those battle-smiths armed themselves. 210

The King of Brandigan then mounted an armoured Castilian. It was called Guverjorz. From his kinsman Grigorz,* the King of Ipotente, along with rich gifts, it had come to Clamide, from the north, across the Ukersee. It had been brought by *cuns* Narant, along with a thousand men-at-arms, in armour, but all without shields. They had been paid to serve for a full two years, if the adventure tells the entire truth. Grigorz sent him elegant knights, five hundred, each wearing a helmet buckled to his head, well versed in battle. Then Clamide's army had laid such siege, by land and sea, to Pelrapeire that the townsfolk had no choice but to foster grief.

Out Parzival rode to the field of ordeal, where God was to show whether He would let him keep King Tampenteire's child. Proudly he came riding, his charger immediately falling into the gallop before 211

the full career. It was well-armoured against danger—a red covering
of samite lay over the iron caparison. As for himself, he displayed a
red shield and red surcoat. Clamide began the battle. To fell his
opponent in the joust he had brought a short, uncut* spear, with
which he took aim for the long charge. Guverjorz bounded to the
attack. They jousted well there, those two young, beardless men, not
missing their mark. Neither man nor beast ever fought a harder
battle. Both their chargers steamed with exhaustion.

Thus they had fought until the chargers were incapable of
anything more. Then they collapsed beneath them, in unison, not
separately. Each was intent on finding fire in the other's helmet.
They could take no holiday—they were given work to do there!
Their shields disintegrated into dust, as if someone were playing at
212 throwing feathers into the wind for sport. As yet Gahmuret's son
was not weary in any limb, but Clamide thought that the truce pro-
mised by the city had been broken. He asked his battle-companion to
do himself honour and stop the mangonels from hurling stones.
Great blows were descending upon him—they were a good match
for mangonels' rocks. That land's lord made the following reply: 'I
believe no mangonel's hurling has harmed you, for my word of hon-
our is pledge against that. If you only had a truce from my hands, no
mangonel's hurl would break your chest, head or thigh.'

Weariness pressed upon Clamide. It had come far too early for
him. Victory won, victory lost—the battle went its separate ways
there. King Clamide, however, was seen to be defeated first. Jerked
to the ground by Parzival's grip, blood flowed out of his ears and
nose, rendering the green turf red. Quickly he freed his head from
the helmet and the coif. Clamide, vanquished, sat awaiting the blow.
213 The victorious Parzival said: 'My wife can now remain free of you!
Learn now what death is!'

'Oh, no, noble, bold warrior! Your honour will be multiplied thirty
times by my defeat, now you have been seen to lay me low. Where
could higher fame befall you? Condwiramurs may well say that I am
accursed, and that your bliss has won profit. Your land is redeemed
like a baled-out ship—it is all the lighter for it. My power is the
shallower; true manly delight has grown thin by me. Why should
you put me to death? As it is, I must bequeath disgrace to all my
heirs. You have won fame and the advantage. There's no need for
you to inflict more upon me. I bear the burden of living death, now

that I am parted from her who, by her power, held my heart and
mind forever enlocked—and never did I profit by it with regard to
her. And so, wretched man that I am, I must yield to you her person
and her land.'

Then he who had won the victory at once remembered
Gurnemanz's counsel—that courageous valour ought to be quick to 214
show mercy. Following that advice, he said to Clamide: 'I'll not
exempt you from taking to her father—Liaze's—your oath of
surrender.'

'No, sir, I have caused him heart's grief, I slew his son—you mustn't
deal with me like this! It was, indeed, because of Condwiramurs that
Schenteflurs fought with me, and I would have been killed by his
hand, if my seneschal had not helped me. Schenteflurs was sent into
the land of Brobarz by Gurnemanz de Graharz, along with a noble
armed force. Good knightly deeds were done there by nine hundred
knights, who battled well—they all rode armoured chargers—and
fifteen hundred men-at-arms—I found them armed in battle, lack-
ing nothing but shields. I feared his army would overwhelm me, but
of that harvest scarcely a seed returned. I have lost more warriors
since. Now I am bereft of joy and honour. What more do you desire
of me?'

'I will alleviate your peril. Take the road to the Britons—Kingrun, 215
indeed, is preceding you—to Arthur the Briton. You must offer him
my homage. Ask him to help me bring the case against the disgrace I
took away from his court. A damsel laughed on seeing me. That she
was beaten on my account—never did I regret anything as much.
Say to the lady herself, it grieves me, and take to her your oath of
surrender, vowing to carry out her command—or accept death here,
on this very spot!'

'If that is to be the choice, then I won't complain.' Those were the
King of Brandigan's words. 'I choose the journey that takes me from
here.' Having sworn his vow, he whom his arrogance had betrayed
before departed. Parzival the warrior walked to where he found his
charger, exhausted. His foot never groped for a mount, but he leapt
up, without any stirrup, scattering all around his hewn shield's
splinters.

The townsfolk were well pleased at this. The outer army saw
heart's sorrow. They were aching in flesh and limb. They led King
Clamide to where his helpers were. The dead, along with their biers,

216 he sent to their rest. Then the foreigners left that land. Noble Clamide
rode towards the land of Löver.*

Assembled together—not apart—those of the Table Round were
at Dianazdrun* with Arthur the Briton. If I have not lied to you, the
plain of Dianazdrun must be more used to tent-poles than Spessart*
is to tree-trunks, such was the household that lay encamped there
with Arthur for the Whitsun festivity, with many a lady. Also to be
seen there were many banners and shields marked by special devices,*
and many a well-adorned tent-ring. These would be thought very
great affairs nowadays. Who could make the travelling-clothes for
such an army of women? Moreover, a lady then would have immedi-
ately thought she had lost her repute unless she had her *âmîs* with
her there. There is absolutely no way I would do it—there was many
a young man there—I'd not like to take my wife into such a great
217 mêlée now—I'd be afraid of strangers jostling her! Someone or other
might say to her that her love had pierced him and blinded his joy—
if she were to avert his distress, he would serve her before and after
in return. I would rather get her out of there in a hurry!

I've been talking of my affairs. Hear now how Arthur's tent-ring
stood distinctly apart, surpassing the others, rich in many a delight.
The household ate in his presence, many a noble man slow to falsity,
and many a damsel so proud that her crossbow-bolt was nothing but
the joust—she shot her lover against the enemy. If battle taught him
great troubles there, then perhaps she was of a mind to repay his
labours kindly.

Clamide the youth rode into the middle of the ring. A caparisoned
horse, an armed body Arthur's wife observed, his helmet, his shield
hewn to pieces—all the ladies marked this. Thus he had come to
court. You have heard clearly before how he had been compelled to
this. He dismounted. He was much jostled before he found his way
218 to where Lady Cunneware de Lalant was sitting. Then he said:
'Lady, is it you I am to serve without enmity? It is in part duress that
compels me to this. The Red Knight sent you his homage, wanting
to take entire responsibility for any disgrace that has been inflicted
upon you. He also asks that the case be brought before Arthur. I
believe you were beaten for his sake. Lady, I bring you my oath of
surrender, as he who fought with me commanded. Now I'll willingly
carry this out, whenever you wish. My life was forfeit to death!'

Lady Cunneware de Lalant grasped the iron-clad hand, there

where Lady Guinevere sat eating with her, though the King was not
present. Kay was also standing at the table. When he heard these
tidings, he was somewhat taken aback, much to the amusement of
Lady Cunneware. Then he said: 'Lady, this man—all he has done
before you—he has been forced into it. Yet I believe he's been misled
by lies. What I did was for the sake of courtly custom, and I wished
to improve you by it—and for that I suffer your hostility! However,
my advice to you is: have this captive disarmed—he may weary of
standing here!'

The proud damsel requested him to take off helmet and coif. 219
When they had pulled off the latter and unbuckled the former,
Clamide was soon recognized. Kingrun cast frequent knowing
glances in his direction. Next his hands were wrung so hard that they
started crackling like dry faggots. Clamide's seneschal kicked the
table away from him at once. He asked his lord for tidings—he found
him devoid of joys. Clamide said: 'I am a born loser. I have lost such
a noble army that no mother ever offered her breast to one who knew
greater loss. My army's death does not grieve me so much in com-
parison—it is love's deprivation's distress loads such a heavy burden
upon me that joy is a lady strange to me, high spirits a stranger.
Condwiramurs is making me grey. Pilate of Poncia,* and the wretched
Judas, who kept kissing company on that faithless road where Jesus
was betrayed—no matter how their Creator might avenge it, I would
not renounce such duress, if only Brobarz's lady were my wife and 220
her favour mine, so that I might take her into my arms, whatever
might become of me thereafter. Sadly, her love is far distant from the
King of Iserterre. My land and the people of Brandigan must ever be
sorry for it. My paternal cousin, Mabonagrin,* also suffered overlong
sorrow there. Now I have ridden here, King Arthur, to your castle,
compelled by a knight's hand. You are well aware that in my country
many an injury has been done to you. Forget that now, noble King,
for as long as I am captive here; let me be spared such enmity. Lady
Cunneware, too, must part me from danger on that count, having
accepted my oath of surrender when I came as a captive before her.'
Arthur's most loyal mouth at once pardoned those offences.

Woman and man alike then heard that the King of Brandigan
had ridden up to the ring. How they now hustled and jostled!
Quickly the news spread. Courteously, Clamide, devoid of joy, asked 221
for company: 'You must commend me to Gawan, lady, if I am worthy

of it. Indeed I know well that he also desires it. If he carries out your command in this, he will honour you and the Red Knight.' Arthur asked his sister's son to act as companion to the king. It would have happened in any case. Then the prisoner, free of falsity, was made welcome by the noble household.

Kingrun said to Clamide: 'Alas that ever any Briton saw you captive in his castle! You were even richer than Arthur in allegiance and revenues, and your youth put you at an advantage over him. Is Arthur now to bear fame because Kay, in his anger, has beaten a noble princess, who, following her heart's inclination, chose by her laughter one to whom, undeniably, the greatest fame is truly accorded? The Britons now think they have raised their fame's garland high. It was no labour of theirs that caused the King of 222 Kukumerlant to be sent back here dead, and my lord to yield the victory to him who was seen in battle against him. That same knight defeated me, entirely without devious tricks. Fire was seen to waft from helmets then, and swords to twist about in hands!'

Then they all said, poor and rich alike, that Kay had done wrong. Let us leave this story here and return to the right road. The desolate land was cultivated again where Parzival wore the crown—there joy and clamour were beheld. His father-in-law, Tampenteire, had bequeathed to him in Pelrapeire bright jewels and red gold. These he shared out, winning favour by his generosity. Many banners and new shields adorned his land, and much tourneying was done by him and his men. He showed his courage time and again at the boundary that marked his land's limit, that young, fearless warrior. His deeds against strangers were accounted better than the best.

Now hear, too, of the queen—how could she ever be better off? 223 The young, sweet, noble lady possessed perfection on this earth. Her love was so great in strength that it was entirely unimpinged upon by wavering. She knew her husband's worth—each found the same in the other—he was dear to her, as she was to him. If I now take up the story to the effect that they must part, harm will grow out of it for them both. And I grieve for that noble woman. Her people, her land, her person, too, his hand had parted from great peril. In return she had offered him her love. One morning he spoke to her courteously—many a knight heard and saw it—'If you will permit me, Lady, by your leave I shall go and see how things stand with my mother, whether she is well or ill—of that I am most ignorant. I wish

to go there for a short time, and also in search of adventure. If I can
serve you greatly, that will reward you for your noble love.' Thus he
asked for leave. He was dear to her, so the story says—she had no
wish to refuse him anything. From all his men he parted, setting off
alone.

BOOK V

WHOEVER deigns to hear where he goes now, he whom Adventure 224
has sent forth, may mark great marvels, one after the other. Let
Gahmuret's son ride! Wherever loyal people are to be found now-
adays, may they wish him well! For it must be that he will now
endure great torment, yet sometimes joy and honour, too. One thing
troubled him sorely—that he had parted from such a woman that no
mouth ever read, or told the tale in this fashion either,* of any more
beautiful and better. Thoughts of the queen began to weaken his
wits. He would have lost them entirely, if he'd not been a man of
great heart.

Forcibly, the horse dragged the reins over fallen tree-trunks and
through the marsh, for no man's hand guided it. The adventure
makes known to us that in the course of that day he rode so far that a
bird would have been hard put to fly all that distance. Unless the
adventure has deceived me, his journey was not nearly so great on
that day when he speared Ither, and afterwards, when he made his
way from Graharz to the land of Brobarz.

Would you like to hear now how things stand with him? He came 225
that evening to a lake. There huntsmen had moored—to them those
waters were subject. When they saw him riding up, they were so
close to the shore that they could hear clearly all he said. There was
one man he saw in the boat who wore such clothing that even if all
lands served him, it could be no better. His hat was trimmed with
peacock feathers. This same fisherman he asked for information—
that he might advise him, by God's favour and his courtesy's com-
mand, where he might find lodging. The sad man replied as follows:

'Sir, to my knowledge neither water nor land within these thirty
miles is inhabited, except for one castle that lies nearby. By my
loyalty, I advise you to go there. Where else could you go before the

day is out? There, at the cliff's edge, take a right turn. When you come
up to the moat, I expect you'll have to halt there. Ask for the draw-
bridge to be let down for you and for the road to be opened to you.'

226   He did as the fisherman advised him, took his leave and departed.
The fisherman said: 'If you find your way there, I'll attend to you
tonight myself. Then thank me according to how you are treated. Be
on your guard—unfamiliar paths run there. You may well ride astray
along the slope. I would not wish that upon you by any means.'

Parzival set off, trotting watchfully along the right path up to the
moat. There the drawbridge was raised, the stronghold not deceived
of defence. It stood just as if it had been turned on a lathe. Unless it
flew or were blown by the wind, no attack might harm the castle.
Many towers, several great halls stood there, wondrously defended.
If all armies on earth were to attack them, they wouldn't yield a
single loaf under such pressure, not in thirty years.

A squire deigned to ask him what he sought, or where he had
travelled from. He said: 'The fisherman has sent me here. I bowed to
his hand,* only in the hope of finding lodgings. He asked for the
227   bridge to be lowered, and told me to ride in to you.'

'Lord, you are welcome. Since it was the fisherman who promised
it, honour and comfort will be offered you, for the sake of him who
sent you here,' said the squire, and let the bridge down.

Into the castle the bold youth rode, entering a courtyard wide and
broad. It had not been trampled down by merry sports. Short, green
grass grew everywhere. There bohorts* were shunned. Seldom was it
ridden over with banners like the meadow at Abenberg.* Rarely had
joyous deeds been done there, not for a long time now. They were
well versed in heart's sorrow.

That did not cost Parzival dear. Knights young and old welcomed
him. Many elegant young lordlings leapt towards his bridle, each
vying with the other to grasp it. They held onto his stirrup; thus he
had to dismount. Knights asked him to walk on—they led him to his
chamber. With all alacrity it followed that he was courteously dis-
armed. When they saw that the beardless youth was so winning in
appearance, they said that he was rich in blessings.

228   The young man asked for some water; he at once washed the rust
off him, from his face and off his hands. Old and young alike thought
that a new day shone from him as he sat there, that charming wooer.
Entirely free of reproach, a cloak with phellel-silk from Araby was

brought to him there. The well-favoured youth put it on. With open ties, it fetched him praise.

Then the discerning chamberlain said: 'Repanse de Schoye wore this cloak, my Lady the Queen. It is to be lent you by her, for no clothes have yet been cut for you. It was, I think, an honourable request for me to put to her, for you are noble, if I have judged right.'

'God reward you, lord, for saying so! If you assess me rightly, then I have won good fortune. It is God's power grants such reward.'

They poured him wine, treating him in such fashion that those sad people were happy in his company. They offered him honour and hospitality, for there was greater supply there than he found at Pelrapeire, when his hand had parted it from sorrow.

His equipment was carried away from him. This he later regret-   229
ted, not expecting to be the butt of any jest. Too haughtily a wag summoned the stranger, rich in courage, to come to court and meet the host, as if he were angry. In consequence he almost lost his life at young Parzival's hands. When he found that his beautifully coloured sword lay nowhere near him, he clenched his hand into a fist, so that the blood shot out of his nails and spilled itself all over his sleeve. 'No, lord!' said the knightly company. 'This is a man who retains the power of jesting, however sad we otherwise are. Show your courtesy towards him. All you need to have heard is that the fisherman has arrived. Go to him—you are his worthy guest—and shake from you anger's burden!'

They walked up into a great hall. A hundred chandeliers hung there, many candles pressed into them, high above the castle-dwellers—small candles all around the walls. A hundred couches he found lying there, as arranged by those in charge—a hundred quilts lying on top of them.

For every four companions there was a separate seat, with spaces   230
in between, and a circular carpet spread out before. *Fil li roy* Frimutel could well afford the like. One thing was not neglected there: they had spared no expense, but had walled in three square fire-frames with marble. In them was that fire's name, the wood called *lignum aloe*.* Such great fires no man has seen, neither since nor before, here at Wildenberg.* Those were costly constructions! The host asked that he himself be seated facing the middle fireplace, upon a camp-bed. Quits had been called between him and happiness—he lived only for dying.

Into the hall came walking one who was warmly welcomed—
Parzival the bright-hued—by him who had sent him there. He did
not permit him to remain standing there. The host asked him to
come closer and sit down, 'by me here. If I seated you at a distance,
over there, that would be far too inhospitable towards you,' said the
host, rich in woe.

231   Because of his sickness the lord had great fires lit, and wore warm
clothes. Of broad and long sable-skin—such, both outside and
inside, his fur jacket and the cloak over it had to be. The least of
those skins was well worthy of praise, being black and grey. Of the
same material was the hood on his head, doubly lined with sable
dearly bought. A braid of Arab silk ran round the top of it, with a
little button in the middle, a translucent ruby.

There sat many an elegant knight, when sorrow was carried before
them. A squire leapt in at the door, carrying a lance—a custom that
furthered grief. From its blade blood gushed forth, running down
the shaft to his hand, stopping at his sleeve. Then there was weeping
and wailing all over the wide hall. The populace of thirty lands
would be hard put to exact so much from their eyes! He carried the
lance in his hands round to all four walls, and back again to the door.
The squire leapt out through it.

232   Soothed was the company's distress, which grief had commanded
of them before, reminded of it by the lance which the squire had
carried in his hand.

If you will not weary of it now, I shall pick the tale up here and
take you to the point where they served with courtesy there. At one
end of the great hall a steel door was opened, from which two noble
maidens emerged. Now hear how they are arrayed—in such fashion
that they would reward love well if a man had earned it by his service
there! Those were lustrous damsels—two garlands over loose-
flowing hair, flowers forming their headdress.* Each carried in her
hand a candlestick of gold. Their hair was wavy, long and fair. They
carried burning lights. Nor should we forget here the damsels'
garments, in which they were seen to enter. The Countess of
Tenabroc—her dress was of brown scarlet; her playmate wore one of
the same; the dresses were both drawn in tight by two belts about
their figures, above the hip, at the waist.

233   After them came a duchess and her playmate, carrying two little
trestles of ivory. Their mouths shone as if with fire's redness. They

bowed, all four. Two quickly placed the trestles before the host. There service was carried out to perfection. They stood together in a group, all of them well-favoured.

Those four wore identical clothing. See now where other ladies have brooked no delay, four-times-two* of them, acting to order. Four carried huge candles. The other four, without reluctance, carried a precious stone, through which by day the sun shone brightly. Its name was renowned: it was a garnet hyacinth, both long and broad. To make it light of weight, it had been cut thinly by whoever measured it for a table-top. At its head the host dined, displaying his opulence. They walked in correct procession straight up to the lord, all eight of them, inclining their heads in a bow. Four placed the table-top upon ivory, white as snow—the trestles that had arrived there before. They knew how to withdraw decorously, to stand by the 234 first four.

On those eight ladies were dresses greener than grass, samite of Azagouc, well-cut, long and wide. About the middle they were squeezed together by belts, precious, slender and long. These eight discerning damsels all wore over their hair an elegant, flowery garland. Count Iwan of Nonel and Jernis of Ril—many a mile, indeed, their daughters had been brought to serve there. The two princesses were seen to approach in most lovely garments. Two knives, sharpedged as fish-spines, they carried, to proclaim their rarity, on two towels, one apiece. They were of silver, hard and gleaming. Wondrous skill lay therein, such sharpening not spared that they could readily have sliced through steel. Before the silver came noble ladies, called upon to serve there, carrying lights to accompany the silver, four maidens free of reproach. Thus they all six approached. Hear now what each does: they bowed. Two of them then carried the silver 235 forward to the beautiful table, and laid it down. Then they decorously withdrew, immediately rejoining the first twelve. If I've checked the numbers right, there should be eighteen ladies standing here. *Avoy!* Now six are seen to walk in clothing that had been dearly bought—half cloth-of-gold, the other half phellel-silk of Nineveh. These and the first six before them wore twelve dresses, of mixed material, bought at high price.

After them came the queen. Her countenance gave off such sheen that they all thought day wished to break. This maiden, they saw, wore phellel-silk of Araby. Upon a green achmardi she carried the

perfection of Paradise, both root and branch. This was a thing that
was called the Grail, earth's perfection's transcendence. Repanse
de Schoye was her name, she by whom the Grail permitted itself
to be carried. The Grail was of such a nature that her chastity had
to be well guarded, she who ought by rights to tend it. She had to
renounce falseness.

236   Before the Grail came lights. Those were of no small expense, six
glasses, long, clear, beautiful, in which balsam burned brightly.
When they had advanced from the door in fitting fashion, the queen
bowed decorously, as did all the little damsels carrying balsam-
vessels there. The queen, devoid of falsity, placed the Grail before
the host. The story tells that Parzival often looked at her and
thought: she who was carrying the Grail there—he was wearing her
cloak! Courteously, the seven went back to the first eighteen. Then
they admitted the most noble amongst them—twelve on either side
of her, they told me. The maiden with the crown stood there in great
beauty.

All the knights seated throughout the great hall had chamberlains
assigned to them, with heavy golden basins, one for every four knights,
and also a well-favoured page, carrying a white towel. Opulence was
237 seen there in plenty. There must have been a hundred tables carried
in through the door. One was placed with alacrity before each group
of four noble knights. Tablecloths, white in colour, were diligently
laid upon them.

Then the host himself took water.* He was lame of high spirits.
Together with him, Parzival washed himself. A silken towel, brightly-
coloured, was then proffered by a count's son, who hastened to kneel
before them.

Wherever any of the tables stood, four squires were instructed not
to be forgetful in serving those who sat at them. Two kneeled and cut
the food; the other two did not neglect to bring in drink and food,
and attended to them by their service.

Hear now more of opulence! Four trolleys had to carry many a
precious gold vessel to each knight sitting there. Those were drawn
to all four walls. Four knights were seen to place them on the tables
with their own hands. Each vessel was followed by a clerk who also
238 took it upon himself to collect them afterwards, after the meal had
been served there.

Now hear a new tale: a hundred squires had been given their

orders. Courteously they took bread in white towels from before the
Grail. They walked over in unison and apportioned themselves to
the tables. They told me—and this I tell upon the oath of each and
every one of you!—that before the Grail there was in good supply—
if I am deceiving anyone in this, then you must be lying along with
me!—whatever anyone stretched out his hand for, he found it all in
readiness—hot food, cold food, new food and old too, tame and wild.
'Never did anyone see the like!'—someone or other is about to say,
but he'll have to eat his words, for the Grail was bliss's fruit, such
sufficiency of this world's sweetness that it almost counterweighed
what is spoken of the Heavenly Kingdom.

From elegant golden vessels they partook, as befitted each course,
of sauces, pepper, verjuice.* There the abstinent and the glutton both
had plenty. With great decorum it was brought before them: mul- 239
berry juice, wine, red sinople.* Whatever anyone reached out his
goblet for, whatever drink he could name, he could find it in his cup,
all from the Grail's plenty. The noble company was entertained at
the Grail's expense. Parzival marked well the opulence and this great
mystery, yet out of courtesy he refrained from asking questions,
thinking: 'Gurnemanz advised me, in his great and limitless loyalty,
that I ought not to ask many questions. What if my stay here turns
out like that with him there? Without asking any questions, I'll learn
how it stands with this household.'

As these thoughts passed through his mind, a squire approached,
carrying a sword. Its scabbard was worth a thousand marks; its hilt
was a ruby, and its blade, too, might well be the cause of great
wonder. The host gave it to his guest, saying: 'Lord, I took this into
extremity in many a place, before God afflicted my body. Now let
this be your compensation, if you are not well treated here. You're
well capable of carrying it along all roads. Whenever you test its 240
mettle, you will be protected by it in battle.'

Alas that he did not ask then! I am still unhappy for him on that
account, for when he took the sword into his hand, he was admon-
ished to ask the question. I also grieve for his gentle host, whom
misfortune does not spare, but from which he would then have been
absolved by questioning. Enough has been dispensed there. Those in
charge laid to and took the tables away again. Four trolleys were then
loaded. Each and every lady did her duty, first those that had arrived
last, then the first. Then they led the most noble amongst them back

to the Grail. To the host and to Parzival the queen bowed courte-
ously, as did all the little damsels. They took back through the door
what they had decorously carried out before.

Parzival gazed after them. Lying on a camp-bed, he saw, in a
chamber, before they closed the door behind them, the most hand-
some old man of whom he ever gained knowledge. I may indeed say,
without exaggeration, that he was even greyer than the mist.

241   Who that man was—hear tidings of that later, and of the host, his
castle, his land. These shall be named to you by me later, when the
time comes, as is fitting, uncontentiously, and with no delay what-
soever. I tell the string without the bow. The string is an image. Now,
you think the bow is quick, but what the string dispatches is faster
still, if I have told you true. The string is like straightforward tales, as
indeed meet with people's approval. Whoever tells you of crooked-
ness desires to lead you astray. If anyone sees the bow strung, he
concedes straightness to the string, unless someone wishes to stretch
it to the curve, as when it must propel the shot. If someone, however,
shoots his tale at a man who is perforce disgruntled by it—for it has
no staying-place there, and a very roomy path—in one ear, out the
other—I'd be altogether wasting my toil, if my tale were to press
itself upon him. Whatever I said or sang, it would be better received
by a billy-goat—or a rotting tree-trunk.

242   I will tell you more, however, of these sorrow-laden people. There
where Parzival had come riding, seldom was joy's clamour seen, be it
a bohort or a dance. Their lamenting constancy was so entire that
they cared nothing for mirth. Wherever, these days, lesser gatherings
are seen, joy cheers them from time to time. There every nook and
cranny was well supplied, and at court, too, where they were now to
be seen.

The host said to his guest: 'I believe your bed has been prepared.
If you are weary, then my advice is that you go and lie down to sleep.'

Now I ought to raise the hue and cry because of this parting they
are enacting! Great harm will make itself known to them both.

From the camp-bed Parzival, that youth of high lineage, stepped
back onto the carpet. The host wished him goodnight. The company
of knights then leapt up in their entirety, some of them pressing
closer to him. Next they led the young man into a chamber, which
was so splendidly adorned, embellished by such a bed that my poverty
pains me forever, seeing that the earth flourishes with such luxury.

To that bed poverty was a stranger. As if glowing in a fire, a phellel- 243
silk lay upon it, of bright hue. Parzival then asked the knights to go
back to their chamber, as he saw no other beds there. With his
permission they departed.

Now service of a different kind will begin. The many candles and
Parzival's complexion vied in sheen—how might the day be any
brighter? Before his bed lay another bed, upon it a quilt, on which he
sat down. Pages quick—none too slow—many a one leapt nearer to
him. They drew the boots off his legs, which were white. More
clothing, too, was taken off him by many a well-born boy. They were
comely, those little youths. After that there then entered by the door
four lustrous damsels. They had the task of checking how the war-
rior was being tended and whether he lay comfortably. As the adven-
ture mentioned to me, before each of these a squire carried a candle,
burning brightly. Bold Parzival leapt beneath the bed-cover. They
said: 'You must stay awake for our sake, for a while yet.' He had 244
played a game with haste, to the limit. A fair match for bright hue*
refreshed their eyes before they received his greeting. Moreover,
their thoughts were troubled at his mouth being so red, and that he
was so young that no-one could see half a beard-hair on it.

Those four discerning damsels—hear what each of them car-
ried—mulberry juice, wine and clary* three bore in white hands. The
fourth wise damsel carried fruit of Paradise's kind,* upon a napkin,
white in colour. This damsel went so far as to kneel before him there.
He asked the lady to be seated. She said: 'Leave my head unturned—
otherwise you would not be granted the service required of me in
your presence here.' He was not forgetful of gentle discourse with
them. The lord drank; he ate a little. Taking their leave, they with-
drew. Parzival lay down. Young lordlings placed his candles on the
carpet, when they saw that he was sleeping. Then they hastened away.

Parzival did not lie alone. Keeping him company until daybreak, 245
harsh toil lay with him. Future sufferings sent their harbingers to
him in his sleep, so that the well-favoured youth fully counter-
weighed his mother's dream, when she yearned for Gahmuret. Thus
his dream was stitched with sword-blows about the seam, trimmed
with many a splendid joust. From head-on charges he suffered great
duress in his sleep. Even if he'd died thirty times over, he'd rather
have endured that awake—such payment did discomfort dole out
to him.

Because of these fearful matters he had no choice but to wake up in his extremity, his veins and bones sweating. Day, by then, was shining through the windows. He said: 'Alas, where are the youths, why are they not here before me? Who is to hand me my clothes?' The warrior lay waiting for them to come, until he fell asleep again. No-one talked or called out there—they were all hidden. About mid-morning the young man woke up again. Immediately the bold knight rose.

246 On the carpet the noble warrior saw his armour and two swords lying. One his host had ordered he be given; the other was from Gaheviez. Then he said to himself at once: 'Alas, what is the meaning of this? In truth, I must put on this armour. I suffered such torture in my sleep that waking peril most likely lies ahead of me before the day is out. If this host is pressed by war, then I will gladly carry out his command, and, loyally, the command of her who lent me this new cloak in her kindness. If only her mind were so inclined that she were willing to accept service! It would be fitting for me to undertake it on her behalf, yet not out of love for her, for my wife the queen is just as lustrous of person—or even more so, truly!'

He did as he had to do. From the foot up he armed himself well to meet battle, buckling two swords about him. Through the door the noble warrior went out. There was his charger, tethered to the steps, shield and spear propped next to it, as he would have wished.

247 Before Parzival the warrior attended to the charger, he ran through many of the chambers, calling out for the people. He neither heard nor saw anyone. Distress out of all proportion befell him at this, incited by his anger. He ran to where he had dismounted the previous evening, when he had arrived. There the ground and grass were disturbed by treading, and the dew all dispersed.

Yelling at the top of his voice, the young man ran back at once to his charger. Scolding loudly, he mounted it. The gate he found standing wide open, great tracks leading out through it. No longer did he halt there, but trotted briskly onto the bridge. A hidden squire pulled the rope, so that part of the drawbridge very nearly felled the charger. Parzival looked back—he'd gladly have questioned further then.

'Go, and take the sun's hatred with you!' said the squire: 'You are a goose! If only you'd opened your gob and questioned the host! It has cost you much fame.'

248 The stranger shouted back, asking for tidings. No reply met him

at all. No matter how much he called out, the squire acted just as if he were sleep-walking, and slammed the gate shut. Then his departure had come too soon, at that loss-laden time, for him who now pays interest on joy. Happiness is hidden from him. Sorrow's throw counted double when he found the Grail with his eyes,* without a hand, and without the die's edge. If troubles wake him now, that was something he was unused to before. He had not suffered much till then.

Parzival set off after them, hard on the tracks he saw there, thinking: 'Those who have ridden ahead of me will, I believe, do battle today, valorously, in my host's cause. If they were so inclined, then their ranks would not be weakened by including me. There would be no wavering then—I would help them in their need and earn my bread, and also this wondrous sword which their noble lord has given to me. Undeservedly I carry it. They perhaps believe that I am a coward!' Falsity's foe headed off along the hoofmarks' track. 249 His departure grieves me. Now for the first time adventure will be ventured!

Their tracks began to grow faint. Those riding ahead of him there separated, their trail becoming narrow, broad though it had been before. He lost it entirely, to his regret. Then the young man heard tidings by which he won heart's distress.

The warrior rich in courage heard a lady's woeful voice. It was as yet still wet with dew. Ahead of him, up in a lime-tree,* sat a maiden whose loyalty caused her distress. An embalmed knight, dead, leaned between her arms. If anyone were not to take pity on her, seeing her sitting in this state, I would accuse him of disloyalty.

He turned his charger towards her then, little knowing who she was. She was in fact his aunt's daughter. All earthly loyalty was but a breath of air, compared with what was seen in her. Parzival greeted her, saying: 'Lady, I am deeply sorry for your languishing distress. If you need my service at all, in your service I shall be seen.'

She thanked him out of the depths of her grief, and asked him 250 from where he had ridden, saying: 'It is not fit that anyone should take on himself a journey into this waste land. To a stranger, unacquainted with it, great harm may well happen here. I've heard and seen how many people have lost their lives here, finding death in battle. Turn back, if you would remain alive! But tell me first where you were last night?'

'It is a mile back or more—never did I see such a noble castle, with all kinds of opulence. It is only a short while since I rode away from there.'

She said: 'If anyone places any trust in you, you ought not to delight in deceiving him. You carry, after all, a stranger's shield. This forest might have proved too much for you, riding here from inhabited land. In a compass of thirty miles neither wood nor stone was ever carved for a building, except for one fortress, which stands alone. That castle is rich in earth's perfection. If anyone seeks it assiduously, he will, unfortunately, not find it. Yet many people are seen to seek it. It must happen unwittingly, if anyone is ever to see

251 that castle. I believe, sir, it's not known to you. Munsalvæsche* it is called. The castle's lord's *royâm** has the name *Terre de Salvæsche*. The aged Titurel* bequeathed it to his son, *rois* Frimutel—thus that noble warrior was called. Many a prize was won by his hand. He lay dead of a joust, to which Love had compelled him. He left behind him four noble children. Three, despite their wealth, are in sorrow. The fourth possesses poverty; for the sake of God he does so to atone for sin. He is called Trevrizent. Anfortas, his brother, leans. He can neither ride nor walk,* nor lie nor stand. He is lord over Munsalvæsche. Misfortune does not spare him.' She said: 'Sir, if you had arrived there, among that wretched company, then the host would have been redeemed from the great trouble he has long borne.'

The Waleis said to the maiden: 'Great wonders I saw there, and many a fair lady.'

By his voice she recognized the man. She said: 'You are Parzival!

252 Now just tell me if you saw the Grail, and the lord bereft of joy? Let joyful tidings be heard—is his peril averted? A blessing on you for this blissful journey, for you shall have sovereign power over all that the air has touched! Tame and wild will serve you. Along with wealth, perfection is allotted to you.'

Parzival the warrior said: 'How did you recognize me?'

She said: 'I am she, that maiden who lamented her troubles to you before, and who told you your name. You need not be ashamed of that kinship, of your mother being my aunt. A flower of womanly chastity she is, washed pure without any dew. God reward you that you then so grieved for my beloved, who lay dead of a joust on my behalf. I hold him here. Now judge the duress God has given me on his account—that he should live no longer! He fostered manly kindness. His dying pained me then, and ever since, from day to day, I have known new and further sorrow.'

'Alas, where has your red mouth gone? Is it you, Sigune, who told me who I was, without any deception? Your head has been bared of 253 your wavy, long, brown hair. In the forest of Broceliande I saw you then, most lovely, though you were rich in wretchedness. You have lost colour and strength. I would weary of such harsh company as you keep, if it were mine. We must bury this dead man.'

Then her eyes wetted her clothes. Nor did Lady Lunete's counsel* find any place in her heart. She advised her lady: 'Let this man live who slew your husband—he can compensate you amply.' Sigune desired no compensation, unlike those women who are seen to be inconstant, many a one, of whom I will be silent. Hear more told of Sigune's faithfulness.

She said: 'If anything were to make me happy, there is one thing would—if his dying were to leave him, that most sad man. If you departed from there helpfully, then you are well worthy of praise. You wear his sword about you, too. If you know that sword's charm, you may engage in fighting without peril. Its edges run true. Of noble lineage, Trebuchet's* hand wrought it. There is a spring near Karnant, from which King Lac* takes his name. The sword will 254 withstand one blow intact; at the second it will shatter entirely. If you then take it back to that spring, it will be made whole by the flowing water. You must take water from the source, beneath the rock, before daylight shines upon it. That spring is called Lac. If the pieces are not dispersed and a man fits them together properly, once the spring wets them, its weld and blade will be whole and even stronger, and its ornament will not lose its sheen. The sword requires, I believe, a charm's words. I fear you have left those behind there. If, however, your mouth has once learned them, then Fortune's power will grow and seed with you forever. Dear kinsman, believe me, whatever you found there by way of wonders must serve your hand entirely, and you may wear in splendour Fortune's crown forever, high above the noble. You'll have in your possession absolute perfection upon this earth. No-one is so rich he may vie with your wealth, if you have given the question its due.'

He said: 'I did not ask the question.' 255

'Alas that my eyes see you,' said the grief-laden maiden, 'since you were too daunted to ask the question! But you saw such great marvels there—to think that you should have refrained from asking then! There you were in the presence of the Grail—many ladies free of falsity, noble Garschiloye, and Repanse de Schoye, and cutting silver and bloody spear. Alas, what do you want here with me? Dishonoured, accursed man! You bore the venomous wolf's fangs when gall took so young a root in your loyalty! You should have taken pity on your host, by whom God has wrought a marvel, and should have asked about his anguish. You live, yet you are dead to bliss!'

Then he said: 'My dear cousin, show me more kindness. I shall atone, if I have done wrong.'

'There shall be no atonement for you!' said the maiden. 'I know full well that at Munsalvæsche honour and knightly fame vanished from you. You'll find no further converse of any kind now from me!' With that Parzival parted from her.

256   That he had been so slow to question when he sat by the sad host now greatly grieved the warrior rich in courage. Because of his distress and because the day was so hot, sweat began to bathe him. To get some air, he unbuckled his helmet and carried it in his hand. He untied his ventail. Through the iron's rust his sheen shone bright.

He came upon a fresh trail, for ahead of him there rode a charger that was well shod, and an unshod horse obliged to carry a lady, whom he espied. It befell him to ride after her. Her horse was forfeit to misery. You could easily have counted every single one of its ribs through its hide. It was the colour of an ermine. A halter of bast lay upon it. Its mane hung down as low as its hoof, its eyes deep, the sockets wide. Moreover, this lady's nag was neglected and jaded, often woken by hunger. It was dry as tinder. That it could even walk was a wonder, for it was ridden by a noble lady who seldom curried down a horse.

257   On it lay a saddle, narrow, lacking all width, bells and saddle-bow shed, great deprivation heaped upon it. That sad (none too merry) lady's saddle-girth was a rope, yet she was too well-born for that! Moreover, the branches and a thorn or two had torn her shift to pieces. Wherever it was touched by tearing, he saw many strings—bright glimpses between of her skin, whiter even than a swan. She wore nothing but knots. Wherever those were her skin's cover, he could see its white colour—the rest suffered distress from the sun's harshness. However this had come about, her mouth was red. It must have had such colour that fire could readily have been struck from it.

No matter from what direction you chose to charge at her, it was her exposed side.* If anyone had called her *common*, he would have been doing her an injustice, for most of her clothing had *come off*!* By your courtesy, believe me: she endured unmerited enmity. Never was she forgetful of womanly grace. I have spoken to you of great poverty, but what of it? This here is a match for wealth. Indeed, I would prefer such a bare body as this to quite a few well-clad women!

When Parzival spoke a greeting to her, she looked at him, recog- 258 nizingly. He was the fairest in all the lands, which was why she had soon recognized him. She said: 'I have seen you before. Sorrow befell me because of it! Yet may God ever grant you more joy and honour than you have deserved by me! Because of you, my clothing is poorer now than when you last saw it. If you had not approached me at that time, my honour would still be undisputed.'

He replied: 'Lady, be more discerning as towards whom you direct your enmity! Never, indeed, was disgrace heaped upon you, nor upon any woman, by me—then I would have dishonoured myself!— not since I first gained the shield and turned my thoughts to a knight's ways. That apart, I am sorry for your troubles.'

All in tears the lady rode, soaking her breastlets.* As if they had been turned upon a lathe, they stood out—white, high, round. Indeed, never was there a lathe so swift it could have turned them better. Lovely as the lady was as she sat there, he had no choice but to 259 take pity on her. With her hands and arms she started covering herself up before Parzival the warrior. Then he said: 'Lady, in God's name, put my surcoat over you, let me be of true service to you—I mean no insult!'

'Lord, even if it were indisputable that all my happiness depended upon it, I wouldn't dare touch it. If you would spare us from death, ride on, so that I'm far away from you! Not that I would greatly lament my own death, but I fear you would be endangered!'

'Lady, who would take our lives? It is God's might that has granted them to us. Even if a whole army desired it, I would be seen to defend us!'

She said: 'It is a noble knight who desires our deaths. He has so devoted himself to battle that six of you would be put to task. Your riding alongside me troubles me. There was a time when I was his wife. Now my neglected person would not be fit to be that warrior's whore, so great is the anger he shows me.'

Then he said to the lady: 'Who is here alongside your husband? For if I were to flee now, on your advice, you might perhaps think it a misdeed. If I were ever to learn to flee, I would as soon die!'

260

The naked duchess replied: 'He has no-one here, except myself. That offers little hope of victory in battle.'

Nothing but knots and the hem of the collar remained intact of the lady's shift. Womanly chastity's fame's garland she wore, along with poverty. She cultivated true grace, falseness vanishing from her.

He tied his ventail on, desiring to take into battle his helmet, which he adjusted to the correct position with the ties, so that he could see properly. As he did so, his charger leaned towards the mare, not failing to whinny at her. The man riding ahead of Parzival and the naked duchess there heard this and wanted to see who was riding alongside his wife. He wheeled his charger round angrily, forcing it from the path. Ready for warlike battle, Duke Orilus halted, prepared for a joust, with true valorous desire, armed with a spear from Gaheviez, which was amply coloured, just like the arms he bore.

261

His helmet had been wrought by Trebuchet. The warrior's shield had been wrought in Toledo, in Kaylet's land, its rim and boss sturdy. In Alexandria, in heathendom, a fine phellel-silk had been wrought, of which were made the surcoat and tabard that the haughty prince wore. His caparison had been wrought in Tenabroc, of hardy chain-mail. His pride taught him that the iron caparison's cover should be a phellel-silk, said to be costly. Sumptuous, and yet not heavy, were his hose, hauberk, coif, and this bold man was armed in iron knee-plates, wrought in Bealzenan,* in the capital of Anjou. That naked lady wore clothes unlike his, she who rode so sadly behind him—she'd little choice in the matter there. In Soissons his breast-plate had been beaten. His charger was from Brumbane *de Salvâsche ah muntâne.** In a joust *rois* Lähelin, his brother, had won it there.

262

Parzival was also at the ready. At the gallop he rode his charger at Orilus de Lalander. On his shield he found a dragon, live as life. Another dragon reared, buckled upon his helmet, and also many a little golden dragon, adorned to order by many a precious stone—their eyes were of ruby—on his caparison and surcoat. There the charge was aimed from a distance by the two undaunted warriors. On neither side were hostilities proclaimed—they were free of loyalty's claims.* Splinters, mighty, freshly hewn, flew up from them into the skies. I would be bragging if I had seen such a joust as that of which this tale has told me! At the full tilt they rode, not shirking such a joust.

Lady Jeschute's mind conceded that she had never seen a more splendid joust. She halted there, wringing her hands. Exiled from joy as she was, she wished neither warrior harm. The chargers had no choice but to bathe in sweat. Fame was what they both desired. 263 The flashes from their swords and the fire that sprang from their helmets, and many a courageous blow started to shine into the distance, for there the best in battle had met one another in the charge, whether it turns out ill or well for those bold, famed warriors. No matter how willing the chargers were on which they both were mounted, they did not forget their spurs, nor their brightly adorned swords. Parzival is earning fame here, proving himself capable of warding off some hundred dragons and one man!

One dragon was injured, wounds heaped upon it—that which lay on Orilus' helmet. So translucent that the day shone fully through it, many a precious stone was struck off it. This happened on horseback, not on foot.* Lady Jeschute's greeting* was won by merry sword-play there, by undaunted heroes' hands. In the charge they shoved at one another time and again, so that the chain-mail fell from their knees, ground to dust, though it was of iron. If you will, they made a fair show of battle!

I shall tell you of the one man's wrath: it was because his well- 264 born wife had been raped. He was, after all, her rightful guardian, so she ought to look to him for protection. He believed her womanly mind had turned against him, and that she had dishonoured her chastity and her reputation with another *amîs*. That disgrace he took upon himself as his responsibility. Indeed, the judgement that he passed upon her was such that no woman ever suffered greater distress, short of death—and without her being at all to blame. He could refuse her his favour, whenever he wished. None might hinder him in that, if a husband has mastery over his wife.

Parzival the bold warrior desired to win Orilus' favour for Lady Jeschute with the sword. That weapon, so I've heard, has always put its requests graciously. Here flattery's ways have been altogether abandoned! It seems to me that they both have right on their side. He who created both crooked and straight, if He can part them, let Him prevent death becoming the outcome for either of them there. They are hurting each other enough as it is!

265   A hard, fierce battle ensued there, each of them stoutly defending
his fame against the other. *Duc* Orilus de Lalander fought in his
trained way. I believe no man ever fought as much. He possessed skill
and strength. Consequently he was often victorious in many a place,
irrespective of what happened here. Confidently, he grasped towards
him the young, strong Parzival, who then immediately seized him, in
return, and wrested him out of his saddle. As if he were a sheaf of
oats, he grabbed him firmly between his arms, leaping with him
down from his charger, and thrusting him over a fallen tree-trunk.
There one unfamiliar with such calamity was obliged to familiarize
himself with defeat.

'You harvest the suffering this lady has endured by your anger.
Now you are lost, unless you let her have your favour.'

'It will not be done in such a hurry!' said Duke Orilus—'I have
not yet been forced to that!'

Parzival the noble warrior pressed him to himself, so that blood's
266 rain spurted through his visor. Then the prince was soon compelled
to do whatever was sought of him. He acted as one unwilling to die,
saying at once to Parzival: 'Alas, bold, strong man, how did I ever
deserve this duress, to lie dead before you?'

'Indeed I will most gladly let you live,' said Parzival, 'if you will
grant this lady your favour.' 'I shall not do so! Her guilt towards me
is too great. She was rich in honour—that she has altogether dimin-
ished, and sunk me into extremity. That apart, I will do whatever
you wish, if you will grant me my life. Once I held it by God's
grace—now your hand has become His emissary, so that I owe it to
your fame.' Those were the wise prince's words. 'I shall pay a pretty
price for my life. In two lands,* by his might, my brother wears a
crown—he is wealthy. Of those take whichever you will, in return for
not slaying me. I am dear to him; he will ransom me on the terms I
agree with you. Over and above that, I shall hold my duchy from you
267 as a fief. Your renowned fame has earned honour by me. Now spare
me, bold, courageous warrior, reconciliation with this woman, and
command of me anything else that may redound to your honour.
With the dishonoured duchess I cannot undertake reconciliation,
whatever else befalls me.'

Parzival the proud said: 'Neither people, lands, nor chattels, none
of these can help you, unless you surrender to me on condition that
you ride to Britain, putting off the journey no longer, to a maiden

who, for my sake, was beaten by a man upon whom my vengeance is unremitting, unless she requests otherwise. You must surrender to that well-born maiden and tell her of my service, or you shall be slain on this very spot. Say to Arthur and his wife, to them both, that I serve them, and that they may reward me for my service by making amends to the maiden for her blows. Moreover, I will see this lady in your favour, reconciled, in all sincerity, or you must ride dead on a bier from here, if you wish to defy me in this. Mark these words, and match them with your works! Give me your oath on that here and now!'

Then Duke Orilus said to King Parzival: 'If no-one can give anything to ransom me, then I'll do it, for I still desire to live.'

For fear of her husband, fair Lady Jeschute despaired altogether of battle-parting. She lamented her enemy's extremity. Parzival allowed him to rise, once he had promised reconciliation with Lady Jeschute. The vanquished prince said: 'Lady, since this has happened for your sake, my defeat in battle, come here, you must be kissed. I have lost much fame by you. What of it? It is pardoned now.' The lady with the naked skin was most quick to leap down from her horse onto the turf. Although the blood flowing from his nose had made his mouth red, she kissed him when he commanded a kiss.

Then they delayed there no longer. The two men, and the lady, too, rode up to a hermit's cell in a rocky wall. There Parzival found a reliquary. A painted spear leant against it. The hermit was called Trevrizent.

Parzival then acted with loyalty. He took the relic, swearing an oath upon it. He worded his oath himself, saying: 'If I have honour—whether I have it or not—whoever sees me with a shield will judge me by knighthood's mark. That name's rightful power, as prescribed to us by the shield's office, has often won high fame, and it remains a high name. May I be forever misdirected towards worldly disgrace and all my fame destroyed—may my fortune before the Highest Hand—which, as I believe, is God's—be pledge for these words, along with my deeds—may I now suffer damnable disgrace in both lives, forever, by His power, if this lady acted wrongly, when it befell that I tore her brooch from her! Indeed, I took more gold away with me, too. I was a fool and not a man, not yet full-grown in my wits. Much weeping and sweating for sorrow she suffered. She is, in all truth, an innocent woman. To that I will hold

270 firm forever—let my bliss and honour be the pledge for it. If you are
so inclined, she shall be acknowledged innocent. See here, give her
back her ring. Her brooch was given away in such a manner that my
folly must be held responsible.'

The goodly warrior accepted the gift. Then he wiped the blood
from his mouth and kissed his heart's beloved. Her naked skin was
also covered then. Orilus, the renowned prince, pressed the ring
back onto her finger and gave her his tabard to wear—it was of rich
phellel-silk, broad, cut to pieces by a hero's hand. Indeed, I have
seldom seen a lady wear a tabard so torn in battle. Nor was a tourney
ever assembled by her herald's cry,* nor a spear split in two, wherever
it might be. The good squire and Lämbekin* would have arranged a
better joust. Thus the lady was freed of sorrow.

Then Prince Orilus addressed Parzival again: 'Warrior, your
unforced oath gives me great joy, and little sorrow. I have endured a
defeat which has fetched me happiness. Indeed, with honour I can
271 now make amends to this noble woman for thrusting her from my
favour. When I left the gentle lady all alone, what could she do about
it, whatever befell her? Yet when she spoke of your beauty, I thought
some intimacy lay behind it. Now, God reward you, she's free of
falseness. I have treated her uncouthly. By the woodland in Broceli-
ande I then rode into *jûven poys*.'*

Parzival picked up that spear from Troyes* and took it away with
him. It had been forgotten there by the wild Taurian,* Dodines'*
brother. Now tell me, how or where did the warriors pass that night?
Their helmets and shields had suffered sorely—they were visibly all
hewn to pieces. Parzival took leave of the lady and her *âmîs*. Then the
wise prince invited him to go with him to his hearth. He had no
success, no matter how much he entreated him.

The warriors parted there and then, so the adventure vouches me
its tale. When Orilus, that renowned prince, arrived where he found
his pavilion and part of his household, the people all as one rejoiced
that reconciliation had been made manifest to the bliss-bearing
duchess.

272   Then no further time was lost. Orilus was disarmed; he washed
blood and rust off him. He took the discerning duchess by the hand
and led her to the place of reconciliation, ordering that two baths be
prepared for them. Then Lady Jeschute lay, all in tears, by her belov-
ed's side—tears of joy, and not of sorrow, however, as still befalls a

good woman today. And, as plenty of people know, weeping eyes own
a sweet mouth.

On this subject I will say still more: great love is the target of both
joy and grief. Whenever anyone lays love's tidings on the scales—
even if he were to weigh them forever—the dice* cannot fall out any
other way.

There a reconciliation took place, so I believe. Then the two took
their separate baths. Twelve lustrous damsels were to be seen at her
side. Those had tended to her, ever since, for no fault of her own, she
had born the brunt of her dear husband's anger. She had always had
clothes to cover her at night, naked though she rode by day. They
bathed her joyfully then.

Would you care now to hear—as Orilus was informed—the adven-
ture of Arthur's journey? A knight gave him the following account: 273
'I saw, pitched upon a plain, a thousand pavilions or more. Arthur,
the mighty, proud king, lord of the Britons, lies not far from us here,
with a host of comely ladies. It is a mile away, through unpathed
land. There great clamour of knights is also to be heard. By the
Plimizœl, in the valley, they lie encamped on both banks.'

Then Duke Orilus hurried from his bath. Jeschute and he acted as
follows: that gentle, sweet, lovely lady also went straight from her
bath to his bed. There sadness was helped away. Her limbs earned
better covering than she had worn for a long time past. With close
embrace their love—that of the princess and the wise prince—
retained joy's fame. Then damsels clothed their lady; his armour was
brought there for her husband. Jeschute's clothing demanded praise.
Birds, caught on the cleft-stick, they ate with joy, there where they
sat by their bed. Lady Jeschute received a kiss or two, given her by
Orilus.

Then they led to that noble lady—strong, well-paced—a hand- 274
some horse, saddled and well-bridled. They lifted her up onto it—
she who was to ride away with her bold husband. Next his charger
was armed, just as when he rode it into battle. His sword, with which
he had fought that day, was hung at the front of his saddle. Armed
from cap-à-pie, Orilus walked to his charger. He leapt upon it, in
front of the duchess. Jeschute and he rode off. All his household he
asked to head immediately for Lalant, except that one knight was to
instruct him what road he should ride towards Arthur. He asked his
people to await the knight's return.

They came so close to Arthur that they could see his pavilions, very near, a mile downstream. The prince sent back the knight who had guided him there. Lady Jeschute the well-favoured was his retinue, and no-one more.

Unhaughty Arthur, none too proud, had walked, after he had eaten that evening, to a plain. Around him sat the noble household

275 there. Orilus, free of falsity, came riding up to that tent-ring. His helmet and his shield were so cut to pieces that no-one could perceive any device on them. Those blows had been struck by Parzival. The bold man alighted from his charger, Lady Jeschute immediately taking hold of it. Many pages leapt over to them; a great crowd pressed about him and her. The pages said: 'It is for us to see to the horses!' Orilus the noble warrior laid the shield's splinters upon the grass. He enquired at once after her for whose sake he had gone there. Lady Cunneware de Lalant was pointed out to him, where she sat. Her ways were fame's yardstick.

In full armour, he walked up close. The King and the Queen welcomed him. He thanked them, offering his surrender immediately to his comely sister. By the dragons on his surcoat she recognized him, except for one cause of contention. She said: 'You are one of my brothers, Orilus or Lähelin. I'll take no oath of surrender from either of you. You were always ready, both of you, to serve me as I asked you. It would be check-mate to my loyalty if I were to war with you, and betray my own good breeding!'

276 The prince knelt before the maiden, saying: 'You have spoken nothing but the truth. It is I, your brother Orilus. The Red Knight compelled me to give you my oath of surrender in this fashion. By so doing I then purchased my life. Accept my oath. Then all will have been done here which I vowed to him.'

Then she received his true oath in her white hands, from him who wore the serpent, and set him free. When that had taken place, he stood up and said: 'I shall and must, by my loyalty, make complaint: alas, who has beaten you? Any blows that you have been dealt will never please me. If the time comes for me to avenge them, I'll show whoever's inclined to see it, that a great affront has befallen me. And the boldest man a mother ever brought into this world will help me lodge my complaint—he calls himself the Red Knight. Sir King, Lady Queen, he sent to both of you his homage, but especially to this sister of mine. He requests you to repay his service and make amends to this maiden for her blows. Indeed, I would have benefited more at that undaunted warrior's hands if he'd known how nearly she is related to me, and how her affront touches my heart.'

Kay then won new hostility from the knights, the ladies, from all 277 who sat there by the bank of the Plimizœl. Gawan and Jofreit *fiz* Idœl, and he whose distress you have heard of before, the captive King Clamide, and many another noble man—I can readily name their names, but I don't want to prolong the tale—began to gather round in a crowd. Their service was endured with courtesy. Lady Jeschute was brought by, upon her horse, where she sat. King Arthur did not neglect, nor did the Queen his wife, to welcome Jeschute. Many a kiss was exchanged by ladies there. Arthur said to Jeschute: 'Your father the King of Karnant, Lac, I knew to be so noble that I have lamented your distress ever since I was first told of it. And you yourself are so fair that a lover should have spared you the same, for your lovely radiance won the prize at Kanedic. Because of your famed beauty the sparrowhawk fell to you; on your hand it rode away. Although an affront befell me at Orilus's hands, I wished no 278 sadness upon you, nor shall do so, whatever happens. I'm glad that you have his favour now and that you wear lady-like clothing, after your great suffering.'

She said: 'Sir, God reward you for that. By this you heighten your fame.' Then Jeschute and her *âmîs* were led away by Lady Cunneware de Lalant.

On one side of the King's ring, above a spring's source, stood her pavilion on the plain, as if a dragon, above it, held half of the whole apple* in its claws. The dragon was pulled by four tent-ropes, just as if it were flying there, alive, and drawing the pavilion up into the air. Orilus recognized it by this, for his arms were the same. Inside the tent he was disarmed. His sweet sister knew how to offer him honour and comfort. Everywhere the household talked of how the Red Knight's courage had gained fame for a companion. That was spoken out loud, not whispered.

Kay asked Kingrun to serve Orilus in his stead. He was well capable of it, he whom Kay asked to do so there, for he had often 279 performed that service before Clamide at Brandigan. The reason why Kay relinquished his service was that misfortune had commanded him to tan the prince's sister overmuch with a stick. Out of good breeding he shirked his service. Nor had his guilt been forgiven by the well-born maiden. Yet he saw that they were amply provided with food there. Kingrun carried it before Orilus.

Cunneware, wise of fame, cut food for her brother with her white, gentle hands. Lady Jeschute of Karnant ate with womanly demeanour. Arthur the King did not neglect to come over to where the two sat eating in friendly fashion. Then he said: 'If you have eaten poorly here, that was far from ever being my intent. Never did you sit over a host's bread who offered it you with a better will, so entirely without deviation's malice. My lady Cunneware, you must take good care of your brother here. May God's blessing give you good night!' Arthur then went to his bed. Orilus was so bedded that his wife Jeschute tended him companionably until daybreak.

BOOK VI

280 WOULD you like now to hear how Arthur departed from his castle in Karidœl,* and from his land, as his household advised him? He rode with the nobles of his land and of other countries, this tale tells, for a full week, searching for the man who called himself the Red Knight and who had done him such honour, parting him from great grief when he speared King Ither, and who had also sent Clamide and Kingrun to the Britons, to his court, one after the other. He wished to invite him to sit at the Table Round, to make him one of that company. That was why he rode in pursuit of him, having decreed that both poor and rich who were subject to the shield's office should vow to Arthur's hand that, no matter where they saw knightly deeds, they would, by their vows' authority, do no joust unless they first asked him for permission to do battle. He said: 'We must ride into
281 many a land where knights' deeds may well oppose us. We may well see raised spears. If you want to go leaping ahead of one another, like impudent mastiffs slipped from the leash by their master's hand—that is by no means my desire. I must still such clamour. I'll help you if there's no choice in the matter—look to my courage for that!'

You have clearly heard vows. Would you like now to hear where Parzival the Waleis has gone? A fresh cover of snow had fallen thickly upon him that night. Not that it was snow's season, if what I've heard is true. Arthur, the Mayful man—all that was ever told of him happened at Whitsun, or in May's flower-time. What sweet air is ascribed to him! *This* tale, here, is of most mixed cloth. It is pied with snow's ways.

His falconers had ridden that evening from Karidœl to the Plimizœl, intent on hunting, but there they met with harm. They lost their best falcon—it hastened away from them and stood that night* in the forest. It was overcropping that made it hasten away from the lure.

That night the falcon stood close by Parzival, both of them 282 unacquainted with the forest and both feeling the frost hard there. When Parzival saw day appear, his path's track was snowed over. Through much unpathed land he rode, over fallen tree-trunks and many a rock. The day, as it lengthened, shone ever higher, and the forest began to thin out, although there was one tree-trunk which had been felled upon a meadow. Towards that he slowly made his way, Arthur's falcon keeping pace with him all the time. There a good thousand geese lay. A great gaggling arose. With a charge* it flew in amongst them, the falcon, striking one of them such a blow that it only escaped by the skin of its teeth, under the fallen tree-trunk's branch. Pain had put paid to its high flight. From its wounds, down onto the snow, fell three red tears of blood, which caused Parzival distress.

It was his loyalty brought this about. When he saw the drops of blood on the snow—which was entirely white—he thought: 'Who has turned his skill to these bright colours? Condwiramurs, truly, these colours resemble you! God desires to enrich me with blessings, since 283 I have found your likeness here. Blessed be God's hand and all His Creation! Condwiramurs, here lies your semblance, since the snow has offered whiteness to the blood, and that makes the snow so red. Condwiramurs, your *bêâ curs** resembles this—that you can't deny!'

The warrior's eyes matched—so it came to pass there—two drops with her cheeks, the third with her chin.* It was true love he felt for her, entirely without deviation. He so immersed himself in these thoughts that he halted there, unconscious. Mighty love held sway over him there, his wife causing him such distress. These colours bore a likeness to the Queen of Pelrapeire's person—she it was who plucked his wits from him.

Thus he halted there, as if asleep. Who ran towards him there? Cunneware's page had been sent forth—he was to go to Lalant. Now

he saw a helmet with many a wound, and a shield all hacked to pieces
284 in the service of his—that squire's—lady. There a warrior halted,
accoutred, looking as if he desired to indulge in jousting, with spear
raised high. The page turned back. If that squire had recognized
him in time, he wouldn't have raised any great hue and cry against
him, it being his own lady's knight. As if against an outlaw, he
hustled the people out at him, intent on doing him harm. He for-
feited his courtesy by this—let it be! His lady, too, was loose.* This
was the squire's cry: 'Fie! Fie! Fie! Fie upon you accursèd knights!
Do they reckon Gawan, and others of this knightly company, in the
lists of noble fame, and Arthur the Briton?'—so shouted the page—
'The Table Round is disgraced! Someone has run through your
tent-ropes here!'

Then great clamour arose among the knights, all of them asking
whether chivalry had been done there. Then they heard that a single
man halted there, ready for the joust. There were enough among
them who regretted the vow that Arthur had received from them. So
285 swiftly—not by any means at the walk!—Segramors both ran and
leapt, he who always strove for battle! Wherever he thought he might
find fighting, they had to tie him down, or else he would be in the
thick of it. No matter how wide the Rhine, if he saw fighting on the
opposite bank, there would be little testing as to whether the bath-
water were hot or cold—he would throw himself in, come what way,
that bold warrior!

Quickly the youth made his way to court, to Arthur's tent-ring.
The noble King was fast asleep. Segramors ran through his ropes,
pushing his way in through the pavilion's door. A bed-covering of
sable he tore off those who lay enjoying sweet sleep, giving them no
choice but to wake up and laugh at his uncouthness. Then he said to
his cousin: 'Guinevere, Lady Queen, our kinship is openly acknow-
ledged, so that across many lands it is well known that I look to you
for favour. Now help me, Lady, and speak with Arthur your hus-
band, and have him give me leave—an adventure is close at hand
here—to be the first to the joust!'

286   Arthur said to Segramors: 'Your oath assured me that you would
act as I wished and keep your indiscretion in check. If a joust is
delivered by you here, then many another man after you will want
me to let him ride and fight for fame, too—my defences would be
weakened by that. We are nearing Anfortas's army, which rides out

of Munsalvæsche and defends the woodland by battle. As we do not
know where that castle stands, it may easily cost us dear.'

Guinevere pleaded with Arthur to such effect that Segramors was
overjoyed. When she secured the adventure for him, short of his
dying of sheer joy, absolutely anything might have happened there!
Unwillingly would he then have conceded to anyone else his right to
future fame by that adventure.

That young, proud, beardless man—his charger and he were
armed. Forth rode Segramors *roys*, galloping *ulter juven poys*.* His
charger leapt over high bushes, many a golden bell jingling, dangling
from the horse's caparison and the man. A falconer would have had
no trouble throwing *him* from his hand to pursue a pheasant into the   287
thicket! If anyone were in a hurry to seek him out, he would find him
by the bells—they knew how to ring out loudly!

Thus that reckless warrior rode towards him who was forfeit to
love. He neither struck him nor thrust at him until he had spoken his
declaration of enmity. Lost in thought, Parzival halted there. It was
the blood's marks made him do so, and also harsh love, which often
deprives me of my senses and ungently stirs my heart. Oh, what
distress a woman imposes upon me! If she will thus oppress me and
seldom bring me help, I must lay the blame at her door and flee from
her solace!*

But hear now something of these two, of their meeting and their
parting. Segramors spoke as follows: 'You act, lord, as if you are
happy that a king lies encamped here with his people. Lightly
though you weigh this, you must make amends to him for it, or I
shall lose my life. You have ridden too near in search of battle. Yet
still I would ask you, out of courtesy, to surrender yourself into my
custody, or else you will receive quick payment from me—your   288
fall shall shift the snow! You'd be better advised to surrender, with
honour, before we fight.'

Parzival, faced with this threat, said nothing. Lady Love spoke to
him of other troubles. To deliver the joust, bold Segramors wheeled
his charger away. The Castilian also turned round—that upon which
comely Parzival sat, lost in thought—with the result that he looked
beyond the blood. His glance was turned away from it, which
increased his fame. When he no longer saw the drops, Lady Wit
conceded reason to him again.

Along came Segramors *roys*! Parzival lowered in his hand the

spear from Troyes, the sturdy and stout one, the brightly-dyed one, which he had found in front of the cell. He received a joust through his shield. His joust in return was so targeted that Segramors, the noble warrior, was obliged to practise saddle-vacating, and because Parzival's spear remained, despite this, intact, Segramors made acquaintance with falling. Parzival rode without questioning to where the blood-drops lay. When he found them with his eyes, Lady
289 Love tied him in her bonds. He didn't say a word, neither one way or the other, for he at once parted from his wits.

Segramors' Castilian set off at once for its stall. Its master had to stand up to obtain rest, if he wanted to walk anywhere. Plenty of people lie down to obtain rest—you have often heard tell of that since. What rest did he find in the snow? Lying there would bring me woe. The loser has always won scorn, while Fortune's party has been helped by God.

The company lay encamped so near, I imagine, that they could see Parzival halting, as he had before. He was obliged to yield victory to Love, she who also vanquished Solomon. After that it was not too long before Segramors walked in amongst them there. Whether a man was hostile towards him or gave him a hearty welcome, he met them all with equal favour, such were the great gifts of abuse he doled out. He said: 'You have heard much of how chivalry is dice-play, and if a man falls by the joust—well, a sea's keel may sink, too, in its time. Let me never contend that he would have dared await me, if he had recognized my shield. That is why he has got the better
290 of me—he who still desires a joust out there. He is well worthy of praise, I admit.'

Kay, that bold man, took the news to the King at once: that Segramors had been thrust down, and that out there a sturdy youth halted, desiring a joust, just as before. He said: 'Sir, I shall always regret it if he's to leave here and get off scot-free. If I am worthy enough in your eyes, let me attempt what he desires, since he halts there with raised spear, in your wife's presence. Never more will I remain in your service, the Table Round will be dishonoured, if he is not granted his wish in good time. His courage is eating away at our fame! Now give me leave to do battle! Even if we were all blind or deaf, you would have to grant it him—it is high time!' Arthur gave permission to Kay to do battle.

The seneschal was armed. Then he wanted to lay waste the wood by his joust at the newly arrived stranger. The latter bore Love's great burden, brought upon him by the snow and blood. It is a sin if anyone inflicts more upon him now. Love, too, has small fame by it—it was Love that had raised her might's sceptre against him.

Lady Love, why do you act thus, making a sad man happy with 291 short-lasting joy? You will soon be the death of him. How does it become you, Lady Love, that you thus vanquish a manly mind and hearty high spirits? The lowly and the noble, and all who ever take up arms against you on this earth—all these you have soon vanquished. We have no choice but to let your power prevail—in all truth, beyond doubt.

Lady Love, there is one honour you retain—and precious little more: Lady Affection keeps you company—otherwise your power would be riddled with holes.*

Lady Love, you practise disloyalty with ways old and new alike. You pluck fame from many a woman, advising her to take an *amîs* of close kin. And many a lord, because of your power, has acted badly by his man, and many a friend by his companion—your ways can take a Hellish turn!—and many a man by his lord. Lady Love, it ought to grieve you that you teach the body lustful habits, for which the soul suffers.

Lady Love, since you have power thus to make youth old, though it 292 only numbers a few short years, your deeds are ambush-like of aspect.

This discourse would befit no man, save one who never won solace from you. If you had helped me more, my praise would not be so slow to greet you. You have allotted me short rations, and so gambled away my eyes' edges* that I cannot trust you. My distress has always weighed very lightly with you. Yet you are too well-born for my feeble wrath ever to press a charge against you. Your pressure has so sharp a spear-point, you load a heavy burden upon the heart. Sir Heinrich von Veldeke* matched with skill his tree to your nature. If only he had then spelled out for us better how we might retain you! He split splinters from the trunk, telling us how you are to be wooed. Out of folly many a fool's lofty find must perish. Whatever I have learned of this or have still to learn, I lay the blame at your door, Lady Love. You are a lock upon the mind. Against you neither shield nor sword can help, nor swift charger, nor high citadel with noble towers—you prevail against all such defences. Whether on land or 293 out at sea, what can flee from your warfare, whether it floats or flies?

Lady Love, it was an act of violence on your part, too, when Parzival the bold warrior parted from his wits because of you, as his loyalty then advised him. His noble, sweet, lustrous wife sent you as a messenger to him—the Queen of Pelrapeire. Kardeiz* *fiz* Tampenteire, her brother—from him you also took his life. If you are to be paid such interest, good for me that I hold nothing from you on account, if you won't give me easier terms!

I have been talking about matters that concern us all—now hear, too, what befell there. Kay, rich in courage, emerged armed in knightly fashion, desirous of battle—and battle, I believe, he was granted by King Gahmuret's son! Wherever ladies still subjugate lovers, they must wish him good fortune now, for it was a woman brought to him this pass, Love lopping* his wits from him. Kay held back from his joust until he had first spoken to the Waleis: 'Lord, 294 since it has thus befallen you to offend the King, if you would be ruled by me, then my advice is—and it seems to me your best prospect of salvation—that you put a bercelet's leash* on yourself and let yourelf be led before him. You cannot flee from me so far that I will not take you back over there, come what may, vanquished. Then you will be treated ungently!'

Love's power imposed silence upon the Waleis. Kay raised his shaft and dealt him a swinging blow at the head, so that his helmet resounded. Then he said: 'You must wake up! No linen sheets will be appointed for your sleep here. My hand aims at an entirely different target—you will soon be laid upon the snow! He who carries the sack from the mill—if he were to be so beaten, he might regret his idleness.'*

Lady Love, look at this now! I believe this is done to disgrace you! Only a peasant would say outright that this has been done to my lord Parzival! He'd lodge a complaint himself, if only he could speak! Lady Love, let the noble Waleis avenge himself, for if your peril and your harsh, ungentle burden were to quit him, I believe this stranger would defend himself!

295 Kay charged hard at him, forcing his charger to turn right round, until the Waleis looked beyond his sweet, bitter distress, his wife's semblance, that of Pelrapeire's queen—I mean the pied snow. Then Lady Wit returned to him as before, giving him back his reason. Kay let his charger into the gallop—he had come there to joust! They lowered their lances for the full tilt.

Kay delivered his joust, as his eyes' measure intended, breaching a broad window through the Waleis's shield. He paid dearly for this combat. Kay, Arthur's seneschal, was felled by the counter-joust, thrown across the tree-trunk where the goose had escaped, so that horse and man alike suffered extremity—the man was wounded, the horse lay dead. Caught between the saddle-bow and a boulder, Kay's right arm and left leg were broken by that fall—saddle-girth, saddle, bells all shattered by the collision. Thus the stranger paid back two beatings—the one a maiden had suffered for his sake, the second he had had to put up with himself.*

Parzival, falsity's uprooter—his loyalty taught him to find three   296
drops of snowy blood, which deprived him of his wits. His pondering upon the Grail and the marks that resembled the queen—both were harsh extremities—Love's lead weighed the heavier with him. Sadness and Love break tough minds. Is this supposed to be adventure? Both might rightly be termed torment.

Bold folk ought to lament Kay's distress. His valour urged him bravely into many a battle. It is said in many lands, far and wide, that Kay, Arthur's seneschal, was a ruffian in his ways—from this reproach my tales free him. He was nobility's companion. Little though I may be believed, Kay was a loyal and courageous man—so my mouth avers. And I shall tell you more of him: Arthur's court was a destination to which many strangers came, both noble and ignominious. As for those who were of dapper manners, if any one of them practised trickery, he counted for little with Kay. If a man   297
possessed courtesy and noble sociability, he knew how to honour him and show him service.

The tale I tell of him is that he was a watcher.* He made much show of roughness to protect his lord, parting tricksters and false company from those who were truly noble. He was a harsh hailstorm falling upon their misdeeds, sharper even than the bee's tail. You see, it was such as these who distorted Kay's reputation. He was wise in manly loyalty, winning much enmity from these.

Prince Hermann of Thuringia,* some I saw inside your walls who would be better ranked outsiders. You, too, could do with a Kay, since true generosity has imposed upon you such a varied entourage—now an ignominious throng, now a noble press of people. This is why Sir Walther is obliged to sing: 'Good day, base and worthy alike!'* Wherever such song is heard today, the false are being honoured. Kay would not have taught them such manners, nor would Sir Heinrich of Rispach.*

298   Hear more marvels, hear what happened there on Plimizœl's plain. Kay was fetched back straight away, carried into Arthur's pavilion. His friends began to mourn for him there, lots of ladies, and many a man. Then my lord Gawan came, too, and stood over Kay as he lay there. He said: 'Alas for the accursed day on which this joust was delivered, by which I have lost a friend!' He pitied him grievously.

Kay, rich in anger, said: 'Lord, do you pity me? It is for old women to moan in such fashion! You are my lord's sister's son—if only I could serve you now, as your will desired when God still granted me limbs! Indeed, my hand did not hold back from fighting a great deal on your behalf. I'd do the same again, if it had to be. Now lament no longer, leave me in my pain. Your uncle, that proud King, will never get such a Kay again. You are too well-born to avenge me, yet if you'd lost a single finger out there, I'd have risked my head for it! Let's see if you believe me! Don't take any notice of my chiding. He
299 knows how to mete out ungentle rewards, he who still halts out there, unfleeing—he neither gallops nor trots away. Nor is there here any lady's hair, be it ever so fine or fair, that it would not be a firm enough fetter to hold *your* hand back from battle. If a man makes such a show of humility, that does honour to his mother, indeed. It is from his father's side that he ought to have courage. Take after your mother, Sir Gawan! Then you'll turn pale at the bright sword's flash and soft in manly rigour!'

Thus that well-praised man was charged at on his exposed side, by words. He could not pay them back, as still befalls a well-bred man whose mouth modesty closes, matters which are unknown to him who has lost all sense of shame.

Gawan said to Kay: 'Wherever blows have been struck or spears have thrust, whatever of that kind has befallen me, if anyone desired to assess my colour, never did it, I believe, grow pale at a blow or thrust. You are angry with me for no reason. I am one who has always offered you service.'

Out of the pavilion walked Sir Gawan, ordering his charger to be brought straight away. Without sword and without spurs, the well-
300 born warrior mounted upon it. He headed off to find the Waleis, whose wits were in pawn to love. He bore three jousts through his shield, targeted by heroes' hands—Orilus had cut through it, too.

Gawan came riding towards him thus—not at the gallop, nor at the charge. He intended to find out, with kindly intent, by whom battle had been done there.

He addressed Parzival greetingly, though he took little note of it. Thus it had to be: there Lady Love showed her mettle in him to whom Herzeloyde gave birth. Uncounted kinship,* and torment inherited from his father's and his mother's lineage parted him entirely from his wits. The Waleis took little note of what my lord Gawan's mouth made known to him there in words.

King Lot's son then said: 'Lord, you wish to wield force now, since you deny me greeting, but I am not so entirely daunted as to refrain from a further question: you have dishonoured man and kinsman, and the King himself, heaping disgrace upon us here. I 301 shall win for you such favour that the King will acquit you of blame, if you will live according to my advice and bear me company into his presence.'

To King Gahmuret's son threatening and pleading were but a breath of wind. The Table Round's highest fame, Gawan, was well versed in such pangs. He had met their ungentle acquaintance when he pierced his hand with the knife.* Love's power compelled him to that, and worthy womanly companionship. From death a queen parted him, when bold Lähelin overcame him so entirely by a powerful joust. That gentle, sweet, well-favoured lady placed her head as a pledge then, *roin* Inguse de Pahtarliez—so that loyal lady was called. Then my lord Gawan thought: 'What if Love is oppressing this man as she oppressed me then, and his faithful fancy is being forced to concede defeat to Love?'

He observed the Waleis' line of sight, where his eyes were directed. A head-scarf of Syrian cloth, lined with yellow sendal-silk—that he threw over the blood's marks. When the scarf became the drops' 302 cover, so that Parzival saw nothing of them, the Queen of Pelrapeire gave him back his wits—yet she still kept hold of his heart there. Now be so kind as to hear his words:

He said: 'Alas, my lady and my wife, who has taken your person away from me? Did my hand win by chivalry your noble love, crown and a land? Am I he who freed you from Clamide? I found "Alas!" and "Woe!" and many a bold, sighing heart among those who had come to help you. Eyes' mist has taken you from me in the bright sun here, I don't know how!'

He said: 'Alas, where has my spear gone, which I brought here with me?'

My lord Gawan replied: 'Lord, it has been shattered by jousting.'

'Against whom?' said the noble warrior. 'You have neither shield nor sword here. What fame might I win by you? Well, I suppose I must put up with your mockery. Perhaps you will treat me better later. There was a time when I, too, kept my seat against the joust. Even if I never do battle against you, the lands still, I suppose, range so far that I may win fame and hardship there, endure both joy and peril.'

303   My lord Gawan replied: 'All the words that met you here were sincere and amiable, not rich in false obscurity. I desire only what I would earn by my service. Here a king and many knights lie encamped, and many a well-favoured lady. I shall accompany you into their presence, if you will let me ride with you. I shall guard you against any attack there.'

'My thanks, lord. You speak well, and I shall most gladly seek to deserve it of you, since you offer me your company. Now who is your lord—or who are you?'

'I call a man lord from whom I hold many possessions. I shall name some of them now. He has always been well-disposed towards me, treating me in knightly fashion. His sister, who brought me into this world, was wife to King Lot. Whatever God has destined for me offers service to his hand. King Arthur is his name. My name, too, is far from hidden, in all places unconcealed. Those who know me call me Gawan. I and my name are at your service, provided you don't wish me dishonour.'

304   Then Parzival said: 'It's you,* is it, Gawan? What feeble fame I gain if you treat me kindly here! I always heard it said of you that you treat everyone well. Yet I shall accept your service, but only at counter-service's cost. Now tell me, whose are the tents, so many of which have been pitched there? If Arthur lies encamped there, then I can only regret that I cannot with honour see him, nor the Queen. I must first avenge a beating, because of which I have ever since ridden with regret. The cause was as follows: a noble maiden offered me laughter. The seneschal beat her because of me, so that the forest splintered* from her.'

'That has been ungently avenged,' said Gawan. 'His right arm's broken, and his left leg. Ride over here, look at the charger and the rock. Here, too, lie splinters on the snow from your spear, which you asked after before.'

When Parzival saw the truth of the matter, he asked further questions, saying: 'I shall depend on you in this, Gawan. If this is that same man who allotted disgrace to me before, then I shall ride with you wherever you wish.'

'I've no wish to deal in lies with you,' said Gawan. 'Here lay, felled 305 by the joust, Segramors, a hero in battle, whose deeds were always choice, directed towards fame. You did that before Kay was felled. By both of them you've won fame.'

They rode off with one another, the Waleis and Gawan. A crowd of people, on horseback and on foot, offered them a noble greeting inside the tent-ring, both to Gawan and to the Red Knight, as their courtesy commanded. Gawan headed away towards his own pavilion. Lady Cunneware *de* Lalant's tent-ropes ran right next to his. She was delighted; with joy the maiden welcomed her knight, who had avenged what she had suffered before at Kay's hands. She took her brother by the hand, and Lady Jeschute of Karnant. Parzival saw them all coming towards him. Through the iron's marks his face shone as though dewy roses had flown there. His armour had been drawn off him. He leapt to his feet when he saw the ladies.

Now hear what Cunneware said: 'First may God bid you welcome, and then I, since you have held true to manly ways. I had shunned all laughter until my heart recognized you, whereupon Kay 306 pawned my joy away, when he so beat me. That you have amply avenged. I would kiss you, if I were worthy of the kiss.'

'I would have requested the same today, at once,' said Parzival, 'if I'd dared, for I am delighted by your welcome!'

She kissed him and sat him down. She sent away a damsel, ordering her to bring rich clothes. These were ready cut, out of phellel-silk from Nineveh. They were to have been worn by King Clamide, her captive. The maid brought them, then cried out with dismay: the cloak had no cord! Cunneware acted as follows: from next to her white side she drew a little cord and threaded it through for him. With permission he then washed the rust from him—the youth bore a red mouth alongside a bright complexion. The bold warrior was dressed—then he was proud and radiant. Whoever saw him said, in all truth, that he flowered above all other men. This praise his complexion commanded.

Parzival's clothing became him well. She fastened a green emerald
307 at his collar. Cunneware gave him yet more: a costly, elegant belt.
Many animals carved in precious stones must needs be on the out-
side of the girdle—the clasp was a ruby. What figure did the beard-
less youth cut when he was belted? This story says: good enough!
The people looked kindly upon him. Whoever saw him, man or
woman, they held him in high esteem.

The King had heard mass. Arthur was seen to approach, with the
company of the Table Round, none of whom ever practised treach-
ery. They had all heard before that the Red Knight had arrived in
Gawan's pavilion. Arthur the Briton went there too.

The flogged Antanor* pranced ahead of the King the whole way,
until he espied the Waleis. He asked him: 'Is it you who avenged me,
and Cunneware *de* Lalant? Great praise is spoken of your hands.
Kay has paid his debt; his threats are in dry dock now. I have little
fear of his reach—his right arm is too weak!'

308 Then young Parzival bore the mark of an angel without wings,
blossoming here on earth. Arthur, along with his nobles, welcomed
him in friendly fashion. All who saw him there were rich in goodwill
towards him. Their hearts' accord gave assent, no-one saying no to
his praise, so truly winning was he of appearance.

Arthur then said to the Waleis: 'You have caused me pleasure and
pain. Yet you have brought and sent me more honour than I ever
received from any man. My service would have done but little in
return if you had achieved nothing more praiseworthy than that the
duchess, Lady Jeschute, should regain favour. Moreover, Kay's
wrongdoing would have been atoned for, unavenged, if I had spoken
to you before.' Arthur told him what he asked—why he had ridden
to that place and through more lands besides. They all then, one by
one, began to entreat him to swear knightly companionship to those
of the Table Round. Nor was their request repugnant to him.
309 Indeed, he had good reason to rejoice at it. Parzival then granted
them their wish.

Now advise, listen and aver whether the Table Round can observe
its custom this day! For it was in the custody of Arthur, who held to
one practice: no knight ever ate in his presence on a day when
Adventure so far forgot itself as to avoid his court. Now Adventure is
at his disposal. One claim to fame the Table Round must have:
although it had been left behind in Nantes, its law was spoken on the

flowers' field, unimpeded by bushes and tents. King Arthur ordered
that it should be so in honour of the Red Knight—thus his worth
was rewarded there. A phellel-silk from Acraton,* brought from far-
off heathendom, served a special purpose there—not wide, of circu-
lar cut, entirely in the manner of the Table Round, for their courtesy
vouchsafed that no-one should claim the seat of honour, facing
the host. All the seats were equal in rank. Moreover, King Arthur
commanded that noble knights and noble ladies were to be seen at
the ring. Those who were measured against praise there, maidens,
women and men, ate at court then.

Then Lady Guinevere arrived, with many a fair lady—with her 310
many a noble princess who cast a lovely glow. Moreover, the circle
was drawn so wide that, without jostling and without dispute, many
a lady sat next to her *âmîs*. Arthur, slow to falsity, led the Waleis by
his hand. Lady Cunneware *de* Lalant walked on the other side of
him—she was now freed from sorrow. Arthur looked at the Waleis.
Now you must hear what he said: 'I shall have my old wife* kiss your
radiant person. You have no need to ask for kisses from anyone here,
since you have ridden from Pelrapeire, for there is kissing's highest
goal. One thing I would ask of you: if ever I enter your castle, pay
back this kiss,' said Arthur.

'I shall do whatever you ask of me there,' said the Waleis, 'and
elsewhere, too.'

Then she took a little step towards him. The Queen welcomed
him with a kiss. 'Here and now I forgive you, by my loyalty,' she said,
'for abandoning me to grief—that was what you gave to me when
you took the life of *rois* Ither.'

At this reconciliation the Queen's eyes grew moist, for Ither's 311
death brought women woe. King Clamide was assigned a seat by the
bank of the Plimizœl. Next to him sat Jofreit *fiz* Idœl. Between
Clamide and Gawan the Waleis had to take his seat. As the adventure
meted out to me, no-one who ever sucked at mother's breast sat in
that circle whose nobility deceived so little, for the Waleis brought
with him strength and comely youth. If anyone were to assess him
rightly, then many a lady has looked at herself in a dimmer glass than
his mouth. I shall acquaint you with his complexion, about the chin
and the cheeks—his colour would make a good pair of tongs—it
could hold fast to such constancy as can readily scrape away* doubt. I
am thinking of women who vacillate and think twice about their

amours. His radiance was a bond to tie down women's constancy—
their doubt disappeared entirely in his presence. Their looking wel-
comed him with loyalty—through their eyes into their hearts he
went. He found favour with both men and women.

312   Thus he endured esteem—until the sigh-laden end. Along came
she of whom I would speak, a maiden well praised on account of
her loyalty, except that her courtesy was crazed by rage. Her tidings
brought grief to many people. Hear now how the damsel rode—a
mule tall as a Castilian, fallow, and otherwise of the following
appearance: nose-slit and branded,* in the recognized manner of
Hungarian war-horses. Her bridle and her saddle had been industri-
ously wrought, expensive and costly. Her mule walked impeccably.
She was not ladylike of appearance. Alas, why did she come before
them? Yet come she did—it had to be. To Arthur's company she
brought sorrow.

The maiden's learning vouchsafed that she spoke all languages
well: Latin, heathen,* French. She had a cultivated mind, encompass-
ing dialectic and geometry; known to her, too, were the skills of
astronomy.* She was called Cundrie; her byname was Surziere.* She
was not lame about the mouth, for that part of her had plenty to say.

313   She struck down high joy in abundance. That maiden rich in wit
bore little resemblance to those they call *bêâ schent*.* A bridal cloth
from Ghent, bluer even than lapis lazuli, that downpour on joy had
donned. It was a well-cut cape, all in the French style. Beneath, next
to her person, she wore fine furs. A peacock-feather hat from London,
lined with cloth-of-gold—the hat was new, its ribbon not old—hung
at her back. Her tidings were a bridge carrying grief over joy. She
plucked ample mirth from them there.

A plait crossed the hat and dangled down from her, as far as the
mule. It was so long, and black, tough, none too lustrous, soft as a
pig's back-hair. She was nosed like a dog. Two boar's teeth stuck out
from her mouth, a good span in length. Each eyebrow thrust,
plaited, past her hair-band. My courtesy has trespassed in the inter-
ests of truth, having to say such things of a lady! No other lady can
complain of me on that count!

Cundrie had ears like a bear's, no match for a suitor's love's desire.
314   Her countenance was hairy, as all acknowledged. She carried a whip
in her hand whose thongs were of silk, and whose stock was a ruby.
This comely sweetheart had hands the colour of an ape's skin. Her

nails were none too bright, for the adventure tells me they stuck out like a lion's claws. Seldom was a joust delivered for her love.

Thus she came riding into the ring, sorrow's occasion, joy's oppression. She headed for where she might find the host. Lady Cunneware *de* Lalant was eating with Arthur; the Queen of Janfuse was eating with Lady Guinevere. Arthur the King sat in splendour. Cundrie halted in front of the Briton, speaking to him *en franzoys*—if I must tell you them in German, her tidings bring me little pleasure.

'*Fil li roy* Uther Pendragon, your doings here have disgraced yourself and many a Briton. The best in all lands would be sitting here in honour, except that one gall has slashed through their fame's vintage. The Table Round is annihilated! Treachery has joined its ranks! King Arthur, your praise stood high above your peers—now your rising fame is sinking, your swift honour hobbling, your high praise bowing down, your fame manifesting falsity. The Table Round's fame's strength has been crippled by the companionship accorded it by Sir Parzival—he who, nevertheless, bears a knight's marks there! You call him the Red Knight, after him who lay dead before Nantes. Their two lives were unlike, for no mouth ever read of a knight who practised such entire nobility as Ither.'

Leaving the King, she rode up to the Waleis. She said: 'It is you who deprive me of my manners, so that I deny my greeting to Arthur and his household. Dishonoured be your bright sheen and your manly limbs! If I had reconciliation or truce at my disposal, neither would have any truck with you! I seem to you uncomely, yet I am comelier than you. Sir Parzival, just say to me, tell me one thing only—when the sad fisherman sat devoid of joy and without solace, why didn't you redeem him from his sighs? He bore before you sorrow's load, you most disloyal guest! His extremity ought to have moved you to pity! May your mouth come to be as empty—I mean of the tongue within it—as your heart is of true feeling! You are destined for Hell, as appointed in Heaven before the Highest Hand, as you are doomed upon this earth, if those who are noble come to their senses, you ban on salvation, you curse on bliss, true disregard of all fame! You are shy of manly honour, and so sick of nobility that no doctor can cure you. I shall swear by your head, if anyone will take my oath, that greater treachery never fell to the part of so handsome a man. You feather-hook, you adder's fang!

'Yet the host gave you a sword, though your worth never merited

315

316

it. There silence won you sin's mark. You are Hell's lords' plaything, you are accursed, Sir Parzival! You saw the Grail brought before you, too, and cutting silver and bloody spear—you outpost of joys, you breastwork of sorrows! If questioning had kept you company

317 there—in Heathendom, in Tabronit, a city holds earth's perfection's reward—yet there at Munsalvæsche your questioning would have fetched you more. That land's queen was won in fierce knightly combat by Feirefiz Angevin, in whom that valour did not fail which the father of you both bore. Your brother practises marvels in plenty—both black and white is the queen's son of Zazamanc.

'Now I think again of Gahmuret, from whose heart treachery was ever weeded out. Your father was called King of Anjou and bequeathed to you a different legacy from the way in which you have acted. Your fame has gone to ruin. If your mother had ever erred, then I would willingly believe you could not be his son. But no, her loyalty taught her torment. Believe good tidings of her, and that your father was wise in manly loyalty, and far-catching of high fame. He knew well how to make merry. Great heart and little gall—over these his breast was a cover. He was a fish-trap and cageing weir. His manly courage knew well how to entrap fame.

318 'Now *your* fame has come to falseness! Alas that it was ever heard from me that Herzeloyde's bairn has thus trespassed against fame!'

Cundrie herself was sorrow's pawn. All in tears, she wrung her hands, many a tear striking the next. She bore great grief forth from her eyes. Her loyalty taught the maiden to lament her heart's regret to the full.

Back to the host she then turned, adding to her tidings there. She said: 'Is there no worthy knight here whose courage has desired fame, and loftly love as well? I know of four queens and four hundred damsels well worth beholding. They are at Schastel Marveil. All adventure is but a breath of air compared with what may be won there, lofty love's noble booty. Hard as my journey may prove, I want to be there this night.'

That sad maiden—far from comely—rode from the ring, not taking leave. All in tears, she looked back again and again. Hear now her last words: 'Oh, Munsalvæsche, grief's goal! Alas that no-one will console you!'

319 Cundrie la Surziere, ungentle and yet proud, has brought woe upon the Waleis. What help to him was bold heart's counsel, and

true good breeding, along with valour? Still more was, indeed, at his disposal—a sense of shame, to crown all his ways. True treachery he had shunned, for shame brings fame as its reward and is, after all, the soul's crown. Shame is a practised practice above all ways.

Cunneware was the first to begin to weep when Cundrie la Surziere scolded Parzival the bold warrior thus—such a strange wight! Heart's grief's eyes' sap she gave to many a noble lady, who could be seen weeping. Cundrie was their sorrow's cause.

She rode away. Now up rode a knight of noble bearing. All his armour was so fine, from his feet to his head's covering, that it was averred to have been dearly bought. His accoutrements were costly; his charger and he himself were armed in knightly fashion. Here at the ring he found maiden, man and woman in sadness now. He rode up to it—hear now how: he was high-minded, yet full of grief. These 320 two dice-falls I must name. His valour counselled him pride; grief taught him heart's sorrow.

He rode out to the ring. Did they jostle him at all there? Many squires leapt closer at once to welcome the noble knight. His shield and he himself were unknown. He did not unbuckle his helmet. That exile from joy carried his sword in his hand, covered by the scabbard. Then he asked after two of those present: 'Where are Arthur and Gawan?' Young lords pointed them out to him at once.

Thus he walked through the wide ring: costly was his surcoat, well trimmed with bright fur. Before the lord of the ring's company he stood, saying: 'God keep King Arthur, and his ladies and men! To all those I have seen here I offer homage and greeting. To one alone my service is denied—to him my service will never be shown. I desire enmity of him. Whatever enmity he is capable of, my enmity offers him enmity, blow for blow.

'Yet I must name who he is. Ah, what a wretched man I am, and 321 alas that he ever thus lacerated my heart! The grief he has caused me is too great. I mean Sir Gawan here, who has often won fame and gained high honour. Infamy held sway over him when his desire misled him into slaying my lord in the act of greeting. It was the kiss that Judas gave that sold him such desire. It hurts many thousands of hearts that my lord has been put to harsh, murderous death. If Sir Gawan denies this, let him answer for it with combat's blow, forty days from today, before the King of Ascalun in the capital, Schanpfanzun. I summon him there, combatively, to meet me in combat's guise.

'If he is not daunted, but desires to bear shield's office there, then I admonish him, moreover, by the helmet's honour and by knights' orderly rule. That yields two rich revenues: true modesty and noble
322 loyalty, which grant fame old and new. Sir Gawan ought not to lose his sense of shame if he wishes to share the companionship of the Table Round, which stands there, apart. Its law would be broken immediately if a faithless man sat at it. I've not come here to scold. Believe me, since you have heard my words: I demand combat rather than scolding—combat whose only reward must be death, or life with honour, depending on whom Fortune favours.'

The King was silent, and unhappy. He did, however, reply to that speech, as follows: 'Sir, he's my sister's son. If Gawan were dead, I would take on the combat myself, rather than have his bones lie faithless and sullied. If Fortune wills, then Gawan's hand will make known to you clearly in combat that he keeps company with loyalty and has refrained from falseness. If anyone else has done you wrong, then do not thus broadcast his disgrace without due cause, for if he wins your favour, proving his innocence, you have, in this short space of time, said such things of him as will diminish your fame, if people are discerning.'

323 Proud Beacurs, who was Sir Gawan's brother, leapt up at once, saying: 'Lord, I must stand surety, wherever the combat against Gawan is appointed. This false accusation against him moves me ungently. If you won't release him from this, then trust to me—I am his pledge. I must stand in his stead in combat. Speeches alone cannot bring about the fall of that high fame which is Gawan's undisputed due.'

He turned to where his brother sat, not forgetting to fall at his feet there. Hear now how he pleaded with him: 'Remember, brother, that you have always helped me to great honour. Let me be a combative hostage against your hardship. If I live through the combat, the honour shall be yours forever.' He pleaded with him still further, for the sake of brotherly knight's fame.

Gawan said: 'I am so wise, brother, as not to grant you your brotherly desire. I don't know why I must fight, nor does fighting bring me so much pleasure. I'd be unwilling to refuse you, but it would bring disgrace upon me.'

324 Beacurs pleaded as hard as he could. The stranger stood his ground, saying: 'A man of whom I have no knowledge offers me

combat. I have no cause for complaint against him. Strong, bold, well-favoured, loyal and mighty—if he possesses all these qualities in full, he can stand surety all the better. I bear him no enmity.

'He on whose account I raise this quarrel was my lord and my kinsman. Our fathers were brothers; they never left each other in the lurch. No man was ever crowned whom I might not challenge to combat by right of equal lineage, to wreak revenge upon him. I am a prince of Ascalun, the landgrave of Schanpfanzun, and my name is Kingrimursel. If Sir Gawan is quick to fame he cannot refuse, but must do combat against me there. Moreover, I'll give him safe-conduct across the whole land, safe from any attacker except me. In good faith I promise him a truce, outside the combat's circle. May God protect all I leave behind here—except for one—he himself doubtless knows the reason!'

With that the well-praised knight departed from Plimizœl's plain. 325 When Kingrimursel had named himself—*ohteiz!**—he was quickly recognized. That wise prince enjoyed noble, far-reaching fame. They said that Sir Gawan had good reason to be anxious about the combat, given the true valour of the prince riding away from them there. Moreover, sadness's extremity had prevented many from offering him due honour there. Such tidings had arrived there—as you have indeed heard by now—as might well prevent a stranger from being accorded his host's greeting.

From Cundrie they had also learned Parzival's name and his lineage, that a queen had given birth to him, and how she'd been wooed by the Angevin. Many among them said: 'I know full well how his hurtling service earned her before Kanvoleiz, with many a splendid charge, and that his undaunted courage won the the bliss-laden maiden. It was the imperious Ampflise who instructed Gahmuret, teaching the warrior courtesy. Now every Briton must rejoice that 326 this warrior has come to us, fame being truthfully pronounced of him, as it was of Gahmuret—true nobility was *his* yoke-fellow.'

To Arthur's company both joy and lamentation had come that day, such a pied existence was granted to the warriors there. Everyone rose to his feet. Sadness beyond measure was present there. Those of noble mind went at once to where the Waleis and Gawan stood next to one another, consoling them as best they could.

The well-born Clamide thought he had lost more than anyone else who might be present there, and that his torment was too severe. He said to Parzival: 'If you were in the presence of the Grail, then I must say, in all earnest—Tribalibot in heathendom and the Caucasus mountains besides—all that any mouth has ever read of wealth—and the Grail's great worth—could not compensate for that heart's sorrow I won before Pelrapeire. Alas poor wretch that I am! It was your hand parted me from happiness. Here is Lady Cunneware *de* Lalant,

327 and that noble princess desires so greatly to be subject to your command that she will let no-one serve her, although her service's reward is great. Yet it may weary her that I have been her captive for so long here. If I am to live on in happiness, then help me to the end that she does herself such honour that her love may compensate me in part for what I lost through you, when joy's mark missed me. I'd have won out, but for you. Now help me win this maiden.'

'That I will do,' said the Waleis, 'if she is courteous enough to comply with the request. I shall willingly make amends to you, for after all, she's mine, she on whose account you claim to be in anguish. I mean she who bears the *bêâ curs*, Condwiramurs.'

The heathen Queen of Janfuse, Arthur and his wife, and Cunneware *de* Lalant, and Lady Jeschute of Karnant—these walked over to console them. What more would you have them do now? They gave Cunneware to Clamide, for he felt love's pangs for her. He gave himself to her as a reward, and to her head a crown.

328 When the Queen of Janfuse saw this, the heathen lady said to the Waleis: 'Cundrie named to us a man who, I grant, may well be your brother. His power ranges far and wide. Two crowns' wealth stands fearfully subject to him, upon the water's and the earth's ways, Azagouc and Zazamanc. Those lands are powerful, far from weak. Nothing can compare with his wealth, but for the Baruch—no matter where they talk of such matters—and except for Tribalibot. They worship him as a god. His skin has a most mysterious sheen; he is a stranger to all other men's hue. He is known to be white and black. I travelled through one of his lands on my way here. He would gladly have prevented the journey I have made to this place. He tried, but couldn't. I am his mother's aunt's daughter. He is a mighty king. I shall tell you more marvels of him: never did a man keep his seat against his joust. His fame holds a most high price. Never did such a generous person suck at the breast! His ways are falsity's loss—Feirefiz Angevin, whose deeds on women's behalf know how to suffer torment.

'However strange it may be for me here, I came here to learn new 329
tidings and to find out about adventure. Now the highest gift lies in
you, by which all baptized people might part by fame from disgrace,
if gracious demeanour is to help you at all, and the true words
spoken of your fair complexion and manly ways. Strength, and youth,
too, bear them company.'

That wealthy, wise heathen queen had acquired the ability to
speak French well. The Waleis replied to her in the following words:
'God reward you, lady, for giving me such kind comfort here. Yet I
am not redeemed from sadness, and will tell you why. I can't express
my sorrow in the way that sorrow proclaims itself to me, with many a
man now sinning against me who knows nothing of my lament,
though I have to put up with his scorn. I will say no word of joy until
I have first seen the Grail, whether the time till then be short or long.
That is the end to which my thoughts hunt me. Never in my life will
I part from this purpose.

'If I am now to hear the world's scorn because of my courtesy's 330
command, then it may be that his advice was incomplete—noble
Gurnemanz advised me to avoid arrogant questions and always strive
against uncouthness. I see many noble knights here. By your cour-
tesy advise me now how I may approach your good graces. Words
have wrought severe, sharp vengeance upon me here. If I have lost
any man's favour by this, I will bear him little reproach. If in time to
come I win fame, treat me then as I deserve. I am in haste to part
from you. You all gave me companionship as long as I stood in fame's
plenty. Be free of that now, until I have paid off the debt that causes
my green joy to fade. Great grief must tend me now, my heart grant
rain to my eyes, now that I have left behind in Munsalvæsche that
which has thrust me away from true joys. *Ohteiz*, how many lustrous
maidens! Whatever anyone has told of marvels, the Grail caps them
all! The host holds to a sigh-laden sojourn. Ah, helpless Anfortas!
How little it helped you that I was at your side!'

They can no longer remain standing here. Now a parting must 331
come about. Then the Waleis said to Arthur the Briton, and to the
knights and ladies, that he wished to see their leave-taking, and hear
it with their favour. No-one found it at all fitting that he should ride
away from them so sadly. I believe it grieved them all.

Taking him by the hand, Arthur vowed that if his land were ever
so endangered as it had been by Clamide, he would treat the disgrace

as his own. It grieved him, too, that Lähelin had taken his two wealthy crowns from him. Many there offered him much service. Grief's extremity drove the warrior from them.

Lady Cunneware the lustrous maiden took the undaunted hero by the hand and led him away. Then my lord Gawan kissed him. That valiant knight said to the warrior rich in courage: 'I know well, friend, that your journey will not be spared on battle's road. May God grant you good fortune there, and help me, also, that I may yet be of such service to you as I would wish. May His power grant me this!'

332   The Waleis said: 'Alas, what is God? If He were mighty, He would not have given us both such scorn—if God could live in power. I served Him as His subject, hoping for favour from Him. Now I'll refuse Him service. If He is capable of enmity, that I shall bear. Friend, when combat's time comes for you, let a woman fight for you. Let your hand be guided by her in whom you have recognized chastity and womanly kindness. Let her love guard you there. I don't know when I shall see you next. May my wishes for you be fulfilled!'

Their parting granted them both sadness as a harsh neighbour. Lady Cunneware *de* Lalant led him to her pavilion. She asked for his armour to be brought there. Her gentle, fair hands armed Gahmuret's son. She said: 'I ought by rights to do this, since the King of Brandigan desires to have me because of your doing. Great troubles on account of your nobility grant me sigh-laden sorrow. If you are not spared sadness, your grief will devour my joy.'

333   Now his charger was bedded in armour, his own extremity awakened. The handsome warrior also wore bright-shining iron armour, costly beyond any shadow of doubt. His tabard and surcoat were adorned by jewels. It was only his helmet that he had not yet buckled on—then he kissed Cunneware the lustrous maiden—so I was told of her. A sad parting there ensued between the two dear friends.

Away rode Gahmuret's son. Such adventures as have so far been narrated cannot be compared with what will follow here, not until you've heard what he will do now, where he will head and where he will ride. Any man who shirks from knightly deeds had better not think about him for the time being—if his proud mind so counsels him. Condwiramurs, your lovely *bêâ curs*—of that he will think often now. What adventure will be brought to you! The shield's office will now be much exercised in the cause of the Grail, without hesitation, by him whom Herzeloyde bore. He was, after all, co-heir to it.

Then many of the household journeyed towards the arduous goal, 334 to behold an adventure, where four hundred damsels and four queens were held captive in Schastel Marveil. Whatever befell them there, they're welcome to it! I don't begrudge it them. For my part, I'm laggardly in reaping ladies' reward.

Then Clias the Greek* said: 'I for one failed there.' Before them all he admitted it. 'The Turkoyt* thrust me behind my charger there, to my shame. He told me, however, the names of four ladies who are crown-bearers there. Two are old, two as yet only young. Of these one is called Itonje, the second is called Cundrie,* the third is called Arnive, the fourth Sangive.'*

Each and every one of them there wanted to see that. Their journey proved incapable of affording them a full view—they had no choice but to meet with losses there. That I must, however, lament in moderation, for if a man endures hardship for a woman's sake, it brings him joy, although sometimes sorrow weighs heavier in the final balance. Such is the reward that Love often offers.

Then Sir Gawan also arrayed himself like a battle-laden knight, to 335 meet the King of Ascalun. Many a Briton was sad at this, and many a woman and maiden. Heartily they lamented his combat's journey away from them. The Table Round was now orphaned of worth. Gawan inspected individually the weapons with which he thought to win victory. Old, hardy shields, well-tried—he did not care what colour they were—had been brought there by merchants on their packhorses, but not for sale—three of these he had obtained. Then that true battle-hero acquired seven chargers, chosen for combat. From his friends he then obtained twelve sharp spears from Angram, with strong reed shafts, from Oraste Gentesin,* from a heathen marsh. Gawan took his leave, departing with undaunted valour. Arthur's wealth was at his disposal; he gave him rich expense's reward, bright gems and red gold and many a sterling of silver. Towards sorrow his affairs now rolled.

Young Ekuba* travelled towards her embarkment—I mean the 336 wealthy heathen queen. The people headed away from the Plimizœl, in many different directions. Arthur rode towards Karidœl. Cunneware and Clamide also took leave of him before he left. Orilus the renowned prince and Lady Jeschute of Karnant also took their leave of him then, yet they remained on the plain with Clamide for three days, for he was celebrating his marriage—not the wedding proper—that took place later with greater celebration at his home. But his generosity counselled him to the following action: many knights and poor folk remained in Clamide's company, and all the travelling people in their entirety—these he took home to his own land. With honour, without disgrace, his possessions were doled out to them there—they were not falsely spurned.

Then Lady Jeschute, along with Orilus her beloved, travelled for Clamide's sake to Brandigan. This was done to honour Lady Cunneware the Queen. There his sister was crowned.

337   Now I know that any sensible woman, if she is true, seeing these tales written down, will admit to me sincerely that I am capable of speaking better of women than the song I once aimed at one woman in particular.* Queen Belacane was free of reproach, devoid of all treachery, when a dead king besieged her. Thereafter Lady Herzeloyde's dream granted her sigh-laden heart's mist! How great was Lady Guinevere's lament on Ither's death-day! Sadness grieved me, moreover, that the king's daughter of Karnant rode in such shameful fashion, Lady Jeschute, famed for chastity. How Lady Cunneware was held fast by her hair and tanned! They have both come out of this well. The disgrace that befell them both has won fame.

To make this tale, let some man take it up who knows how to assess adventure and can recite rhymes, both linking and breaking them.* I'd gladly tell you the tale further, if one mouth would command it of me—one borne by other feet, however, than those that venture into *my* stirrups!

BOOK VII

338   HE who never courted disgrace shall now, for a while, hold this adventure in his hands, noble, renowned Gawan. This adventure subjects many to scrutiny, without fear or favour, alongside or ahead of the story's lord, Parzival. He who hunts his friend with words, constantly praising him to the skies, will be slow to lavish praise elsewhere. People ought by rights to give assent to that man who often bestows praise with veracity, or else, whatever he says or has

said, such speech will remain without shelter. Who is to provide a home for reason's words, unless the wise prevail? A false, deceitful tale,* to my mind, would be better off without a host, out upon the snow, the mouth that broadcasts it as truth suffering woe. Then God would have dealt with such a man in accordance with good people's wishes, those whose loyalty incurs hardship. If a man is eager in pursuit of such deeds as bring disrepute in their train, if a noble person cultivates such gain as that, he must be instructed by a foolish mind. He'd do better to shun such behaviour, if he is capable of feeling shame. That is the custom he should make his master.

Gawan, that right-minded man—his courage kept such guard that 339 real cowardice never inflicted injury upon his fame. His heart was a fortress in the field, so very stout against fierce fighting—in battle's throng he was seen. Friend and foe alike averred of him that his war-cry rang out clearly in pursuit of fame, gladly though Kingrimursel would have deprived him of it by combat.

Now he had ridden away from Arthur—I don't know how many days—Gawan, he who practised valour. Thus the noble, bold warrior rode his right road out of a wood, with his retinue, through a hollow. Up on the hill he made acquaintance with a matter that taught him peril and magnified his mettle.

There the warrior saw—no mistake about it—retinues following many a banner, with great display of splendour—no small matter. He thought: 'It's too long a way for me to flee back into the wood.' Then he ordered a charger to be girthed quickly, one that Orilus had given him. This was its name: Gringuljete of the Red Ears. Orilus had obtained it without any kind of asking. It had come 340 from Munsalvæsche, and Lähelin had captured it by the lake of Brumbane. His joust had hurt a knight, whom he had thrust dead behind his horse, as Trevrizent later averred.

Gawan thought: 'If a man is so daunted that he flees before he is pursued, his fame's come to him too early by far. I'll walk my horse nearer to them, no matter what may happen to me in consequence. Most of them have seen me, anyway. There must be a way out of this, surely.'

Then he alighted to the ground, acting as if he were stabling his horse. The troops riding past there with their trains were beyond number. He saw plenty of well-cut clothes, and many shields of whose markings he knew nothing at all, nor did he recognize any of

the banners amongst them. 'To this army I am a stranger,'—so said
noble Gawan—'for I have no knowledge of them. If they decide to
take this amiss, I'll be sure to deliver them a joust by my own hand
before I have left them.'

341   By then Gringuljete had been girthed, a horse which in many a
perilous pass had been brought into battle to face the joust. The
same was expected of it here.

Gawan saw many helmets lavishly decorated and accoutred. To
their hostilities they had brought a wondrous number of white, new
spears, all painted in distinct colours, given to squires to carry, their
lords' arms clearly identified.

Gawan *fil li roy* Lot saw the great press of a throng, mules obliged
to carry battle equipment, and many a well-laden wagon. They were
in a hurry to find lodgings. Behind them followed the tradesmen,
with wondrous wares, as had to be the case. There were plenty of
ladies there, too. One or two of them wore a twelfth girdle as a love-
token. They were no queens—those camp-followers were called
soldieresses. Here the young, there the old, a lot of rabble were on
that road. Their march had made them weary of limb. One or two
belonged high up on the gallows, rather than adding to the army
there and dishonouring worthy folk.

342   The army whose arrival Gawan had awaited had marched and
ridden past. An error lay behind this: everyone who saw the warrior
halting there imagined he belonged to the same army. Neither this
side of the Sea* nor beyond it did prouder chivalry ever ride. They
had high spirits in abundance.

Now, soon after them there followed, hard on their trail—he was
in great haste—a squire free of all uncouthness. A riderless horse ran
alongside him. He carried a new shield. With both spurs he urged on
his palfrey, spurning tenderness. He was in a rush to enter the battle.
His cloak was well-cut.

Gawan rode up to the squire. After greeting him he asked for
tidings about whose the retinue was. The squire replied: 'You are
mocking me! Lord, if I have earned such affliction from you by
incivility—if I had suffered any other extremity, it would better
become my pursuit of fame. Pray mollify your hostility now. You
know one another better than I! How can it help if you ask me? The
army must be better known to you than to me, once and for all!'

343   Gawan offered many an oath: he knew nothing of whatever folk

had ridden past him there. He said: 'It is a disgrace to all my travels that, in truth, I have to admit I have never seen any of them anywhere before today, no matter where my service has ever been requested.'

The squire said to Gawan: 'Sir, then the fault is mine. I ought to have told you before. My better inclination was daunted. Now judge of my guilt as your own favour prompts you. I'll gladly tell you, afterwards. Let me first lament my incivility.'

'Young sir, now tell me who they are, if your decorous distress permits.'

'Sir, the name of him who rides ahead of you—for his journey permits no hindrance—is *roys* Poydiconjunz—along with *duc* Astor *de* Lanverunz. Together with them rides a reckless man, to whom no woman ever offered love. He wears incivility's garland and is called Meljacanz. Whether it were woman or maiden, all that he won by way of love from them he took by force. He ought to be put to death for it! He is Poydiconjunz's son, and also desires to do knightly deeds here. Rich in courage, he often practises the like, undauntedly. What help are his valorous ways to him? A sow, if her piglets ran by her side, would defend them, too. Never did I hear a man praised if his courage lacked civility. Enough agree with me in this. 344

'Sir, hear of a further wonder—let me tell you of it in full. A great army is being led behind you here by one whom his incivility urges on, King Meljanz of Liz. He has indulged, needlessly, in arrogant anger's practice. Wrongful love commanded it of him.'

The squire in his courtesy continued: 'Lord, I'll tell you more, for I saw it for myself: King Meljanz's father, on his deathbed, summoned to him the princes of his land. His courageous life stood unredeemedly pledged away—to death it had to yield. In this state of contrition he commended the radiant Meljanz to the loyalty of all those there present. He chose one in particular amongst them. That 345 prince was his highest man, so proven in loyalty, devoid of all falsity. He asked that man to rear his son, saying: "You can now seal by him your loyalty's document. Beseech him to treat in worthy fashion both strangers and intimates. Whenever a poor wretch desires charity, beseech him to share his possessions with him." With these words the boy was commended to his care.

'Then Prince Lyppaut carried out all that his lord, King Schaut, had sought of him on his deathbed. Very little of it was neglected; it was afterwards carried out to the letter. The prince took the boy back home with him. There at home he had children of his own, dear to him, as they deserve to be still. One daughter amongst them was lacking in nothing, except that people said that at her years she might well be an *âmîe*. She is called Obie; her sister is called Obilot. It is Obie has brought us to this pass.

'One day it came to the point that the young king asked her for
346 love in return for his service. She cursed his intentions, asking him what he was thinking of, why he was dispensing with his senses. She said to him: "If you were so old that your days numbered five years spent in noble hours beneath the shield, with helmet buckled to head, facing arduous perils—if you had won fame in such fashion, and were then to return at my command—if I were then at last to say 'yes', complying with your wishes, I would be granting you your will all too early! You are as dear to me—who would deny it?—as Galoes was to Annore, who afterwards met death for his sake when she lost him by a joust."*

'"Unwillingly, lady," said he, "do I behold such affection in you that your wrath turns against me. Favour, after all, stands side by side with service, if loyalty is rightly measured. Lady, you presume far too much in thus scorning my sentiments. You have acted far too hastily. I might, after all, have profited by the fact that your father is my man, and that he holds many a castle and all his land from my hands."

347 '"If you enfeof anyone, let him serve to earn it," she replied. "My sights are raised higher. I don't wish to hold a fief of anyone. My freedom is such that it is a high enough match for any crown that earthly head ever wore."

'He said: "You have been taught to magnify arrogance in this fashion! Since it was your father who gave this counsel, he will atone to me for this misdeed. I shall bear weapons here in such fashion that there will be thrusts and blows. Whether it be a battle or a tourney, many broken spears will be left behind here!"

'In anger he parted from the maiden. His wrath was greatly lamented by all the household. Obie lamented it, too. Faced with this mishap, Lyppaut, who was innocent, offered his oath to that effect, and ample further compensation. Whether he was in the wrong or right, he desired his peers' verdict, that court be held in the presence of princes, and asserted that he had come upon these matters

without any guilt on his part. He implored his lord to grant him his
gracious favour, but Meljanz's wrath had checkmated his joy.

'There could be no rushing on Lyppaut's part into taking his lord 348
prisoner there, for he was his king's host; even now a loyal man
forbears to act in such fashion. The king departed without taking
leave, as his weak mind advised him. His squires, princes' little sons,
made show of sorrow, all in tears, those who had been there with the
king. No harm will come to Lyppaut if they have anything to do with
it, for he has brought them up with loyalty, not deceived in noble
conduct—except for my own lord, though he too was shown the
prince's loyalty. My lord is a Frenchman, *li schahteliur* de* Beauvais;
his name is Lisavander. All of them, without exception, had to
declare hostilities against Prince Lyppaut when they were obliged to
bear the shield's office. Today many princes and other youths have
been knighted by King Meljanz.

'The advance army is in the care of a man who is well versed in
fierce fights, King Poydiconjunz of Gors. He brings with him many
a well-armoured charger. Meljanz is his brother's son. They are
both capable of arrogance, the young one and the old one, too. Let
uncouthness take its course! Now anger has spread, both kings desir- 349
ing to advance upon Bearosche, where women's greeting must be
won by hard-fought service. Many spears must be broken there,
both in the charge and in the thrust. Bearosche is so well defended
that even if we had twenty armies, each one bigger than we have,
we'd have to leave it undestroyed.

'My journey's kept secret from the rearguard. This shield I stole
from among the other pages, hoping my lord might find a joust
through his first opponent's shield, aimed at it with the charge's full
tilt.' The squire glanced backwards. His lord was following hard on
his heels. Three chargers and twelve white spears were hurrying
along with him. I believe his desire deceived no-one—he would
gladly, by fore-flight,* have won the first joust there. This is what the
adventure has told me.

The squire said to Gawan: 'Sir, permit me to take leave of you.'

He headed off towards his lord. What would you have Gawan do
now, other than look into these matters? Yet doubt* taught him harsh
torment. He thought: 'If I am to see fighting and not be involved 350
myself at all, then all my fame is entirely quenched. Yet if I go there
to do battle and I am delayed there, then truly all my worldly fame

will be unseated. I'll not do it, not on any account. I must first carry
out my own combat.'

His one extremity cramped the next. Faced with his duel's road, it
was all too hard to stay there, yet nor could he ride on by. He said:
'Now may God preserve my manly powers!' Gawan rode towards
Bearosche.

Fortress and town lay before him, such that no-one ever had a
better castle in his care. Towards him shone in splendour the crown
of all strongholds, well adorned with towers. The army now lay
encamped on the plain before it. My lord Gawan marked many a
splendid tent-ring. Pride was magnified there. He quickly perceived
many wondrous banners, and foreign mobs of many kinds. Doubt
351 was his heart's plane, great anxiety slicing through him. Gawan rode
through the midst of them. Although each tent-rope pressed against
the others, their army was broad and long. He observed how they
were encamped, what this and that group was about. If anyone said
to him '*Byen sey venûz!*' he would reply: '*Gramerzís!*'* A massive
troop was encamped at one end, men-at-arms from Semblidac.
Close by them, separately, lay turcoples,* from Kaheti. Little love is
lost among strangers. On rode King Lot's son, no-one's request
entreating him to remain. Gawan headed towards the town.

He thought: 'If I am to be a pillager,* I may be safer against losses
there in the town than among those here. I'm not looking for any
profit, only for how I can keep what's mine, if luck's on my side.'

Gawan rode towards one of the gates. The townsfolk's behaviour
bothered him. They had spared no pains in walling up all their
gates and defending all their wall-towers; moreover, an archer with
a crossbow manned every turret, motioning forth as if to shoot.
352 They were busying themselves with warcraft. Gawan rode on up
the hill.

Though he was little known there, he rode up to where he found
the castle. His eyes could not ignore many a noble lady there. The
lady of the castle herself had come up to the great hall to see what
was happening, together with her two beautiful daughters, from
whom much bright colour shone. Soon he heard the sound of their
voices talking:

'Who can have come to us here?' said the elderly duchess. 'What
retinue may this be?'

Her elder daughter replied at once: 'Mother, it is a merchant.'

'But they are carrying shields for him.'

'That is the way of many merchants.'

Her younger daughter then said: 'You are accusing him of something unheard-of! Sister, you ought to be ashamed of yourself! *He* never earned a merchant's name! He has such lovely looks, I want to have him for my knight. His service may desire reward here—I will grant him that out of affection.'

His squires then observed that a linden and some olive-trees stood beneath the wall. That seemed to them a welcome find. What more 353 would you have them do now? Indeed, King Lot's son did nothing other than dismount then, there where he found the best shade available. His chamberlain immediately brought over a cushion and a mattress, upon which the proud nobleman sat down. Up above him sat a deluge of womenfolk. His chamber robes and his battle equipment were unloaded from the packs. Apart, under other trees, the squires now arriving there took lodging.

Seeing this, the elderly duchess said: 'Daughter, what merchant could act thus? You oughn't to malign him so!'

Then young Obilot said: 'Uncouthness has commanded still more of her! She inflicted her arrogant behaviour upon King Meljanz of Liz when he asked her for her love. A curse upon such sentiments!'

Obie, not free of anger, replied: 'His bearing matters nothing to me. That *is* a hawker sitting there! His business may well prosper here. His packs are so guarded—your "knight's", I mean, foolish sister mine!—that he wants to be their watchman himself!'

All these words' hearing entered Gawan's ears. Let us leave this 354 matter as it now stands. Hear now how the town is faring. A shippable river flowed past it, through a great stone bridge, not in the direction of the enemies' bank; on the other side the land was unoccupied by armies. A marshal came riding up at that point. He took up large lodgings beyond the bridge, on the plain. His lord arrived punctually, and others who had been summoned there. I'll tell you, in case you haven't heard, who had ridden to the host's aid and who, out of loyalty, was fighting on his behalf. To him came from Brevigariez his brother, *duc* Marangliez. In his cause came two bold knights: the noble King Schirniel, who wore the crown at Lyrivoyn, as did his brother at Avendroyn.

When the townsfolk saw that help desired to draw near them, all they had previously counselled now seemed to them mistaken.

Prince Lyppaut then said: 'Alas that it ever befell Bearosche that her
355 gates should be walled up! For if I ever show shield's office against
my lord, my best courtesy is doomed. It would help me and would
indeed be more fitting if I had his favour, rather than his great
enmity. How becoming would it be if a joust should be directed
through my shield by his hand, or if my sword should cut through
his shield, my noble lord's! If any wise lady ever praises such action,
she would be too frivolous by far. Suppose, now, I were to hold my
lord prisoner in my tower—I would have to let him free, along with
his men. No matter what harm he wishes to cause me, I stand
entirely at his command. I ought, though, to thank God most will-
ingly that he does not hold me captive, since his anger is unrelenting
and he wants to besiege me here. Now give me wise counsel,' he said
to the townsfolk, 'in this dire situation.'

Then many a wise man there said: 'If your innocence had availed
you, it would not have come to this pass.' They advised him strongly
to open his gate and urge all the best knights to ride out to the joust.
356 They said: 'We may as well do battle thus, rather than defending
ourselves from the turrets against Meljanz's two armies. Most of
those who have come here with the king are, after all, only youths.
We may very easily win a pledge* there, by which great wrath has
always been dispersed. The king may perhaps be so minded, if he
has once done knightly deeds here, as to spare us duress and moder-
ate his wrath entirely. Field-fighting, after all, must suit us better
than that they should fetch us off the walls. We might, indeed, be
confident of carrying the battle into their tent-ropes there, were it
not for Poydiconjunz's might—he it is who leads the hard core of
their knights. Our greatest danger there is the captive Britons, led by
Duke Astor. He can be seen in the forefront of the battle here.
There, too, is his son, Meljacanz. If Gurnemanz had reared him, his
fame would have reached great heights. Yet here he is to be seen in
battle's band. To counter these great help has come to us.'

You have clearly marked their counsel. The prince did as they
advised him, removing the masonry from the gates. The townsfolk,
357 undeceived of courage, advanced out on to the field. Here one joust,
there another! The army also began to push towards the town,
prompted by their pride. Their vesper tournament worked out very
well—on both sides companies uncounted, heralds' cries of many
kinds. Both Scottish and Welsh* was called out there, undeniably.

The knights' deeds recognized no truce. The warriors gave full swing to their limbs there.

For the most part, however, they were all youths who had advanced there from the army. They enacted many worthy deeds there, but the townsfolk took ransom from them for trespassing on their sown fields.* He who had never earned a jewelled token from a woman* could never have worn better apparel on his person. As for Meljanz, I heard tell that his accoutrements were goodly. He himself was of high spirits and rode a handsome Castilian, which Meljacanz had won when he thrust Kay so high behind his horse that he was seen hanging from a branch.* Meljacanz having won it there, Meljanz of Liz rode it well here. His deeds so outshone all others that all his jousting found Obie's eyes, up there in the great hall, where she had gone to watch.

'Look now,' she said, 'sister mine! Truly, my knight and yours are 358 enacting unequal deeds here. Yours imagines we are to lose the hill and the castle. We must look to other defence.'

The young girl had no choice but to put up with her mockery. She said: 'He may well make amends. I'm still confident he has courage enough to redeem himself from your scorn. He shall render me service, and I will increase his joy. Since you say he is a merchant, he shall market my reward.'

Gawan heard and marked the pair's words of strife. As then befitted him, he sat it through as best he could. If a pure heart is not to feel shame, it is because death has forestalled it.

The great army led by Poydiconjunz lay all still there, except for one noble youth who was in the battle, together with all his tent-ring, the Duke of Lanverunz. Along came Poydiconjunz, and that aged, wise man took away with him those fighting here and there. The vesper tournament was over, and had been well fought for worthy women's sake.

Then Poydiconjunz said to the Duke of Lanverunz: 'Will you not 359 deign to wait for me when you go fighting out of sheer bravado? You imagine you have done fine deeds! Here is noble Laheduman, and Meljacanz, my son, too. As for what these two might have done, and I myself, then you might indeed have seen some fighting, if you could judge a battle! I won't leave this town until I've sated us all with battle, or both men and women have come out and surrendered themselves to me as captives.'

Duke Astor replied: 'Lord, your nephew, the king, was in the vanguard, and all his army from Liz. Ought your army to have indulged in sleeping practice in the meantime? Is that what you have taught us? In that case, I'll sleep when battle is to take place. I'm perfectly capable of sleeping in the middle of battle. Yet, believe me, if I hadn't arrived, the townsfolk would have won for themselves the advantage and fame there. I protected you from disgrace there. In God's name, temper now your anger! More has been won than lost by your company, as even Lady Obie may admit.'

360   All Poydiconjunz's anger was directed at his nephew Meljanz. Yet that noble young man brought many jousts through his shield away with him. His new fame had no cause to complain.

Now hear tell of Obie. She proffered hostility in plenty to Gawan, who bore it in all innocence. She desired to bring disgrace upon him. She sent a page over to where Gawan was sitting, saying: 'Now ask him for information as to whether the horses are for sale, and if there are any noble clothes to be bought, lying in his panniers. We ladies'll buy them on the spot!'

The page walked over; with wrath he was welcomed. Gawan's eyes' flashes taught him heart's tremors. The page was so daunted that he neither asked nor told him the whole message that his lady had commanded him to take. Gawan did not permit him to have his say, but said: 'On your way, riffraff! You'll feel my fist in your face here, time without number, if you choose to come any closer!' The page ran away—or walked.

361   Now hear what Obie did next. She requested a young nobleman to speak to the burgrave of the town; the latter was called Scherules. She said: 'You are to request him to do this for my sake, and take up the matter manfully. Under the olive-trees by the moat stand seven horses. These he is to have, and much other wealth besides. A merchant is intent on deceiving us here. Ask him to prevent this. I trust to his hand to seize the goods without payment, and they may be his without reproach!'

The squire repeated down below all his lady's complaint. 'It is for me to protect us against deception,' said Scherules. 'I will ride over there.'

He rode up to where Gawan sat, he who seldom neglected courage. In him Scherules found debility's absence, a bright countenance and broad chest, and a well-favoured knight. Scherules scrutinized him all over—his arms and both his hands, and what figure he found there. Then he said: 'Lord, you are a stranger. We have been wholly lacking in wit, since you have no lodging. Now, take that as a mistake on our part. I myself must now be your marshal. People and posses- 362 sions, all that is called mine, I devote to your service. Never did a guest come riding to a host who would so entirely be subject to him.'

'Sir, my thanks to you,' said Gawan. 'As yet I have not deserved this much, but I shall gladly act as you wish.'

Scherules, exalted of praise, spoke as his loyalty taught him: 'Since this has fallen to my lot, I am now your guarantor against loss—unless the outer army takes you prisoner. I'll stand alongside you to prevent that!' With a smiling mouth he said to all the pages he saw there: 'Load all your equipment onto the horses. We must go down into the valley.' Gawan rode with his host.

Now Obie does not forbear to send a minstrel-woman, well-known to her father, to take a message to him, saying a counterfeiter was passing that way, 'whose goods are costly and fine. Request of him, in true knightly spirit, since he has many paid soldiers serving to earn horses, silver and apparel, that this be their first reward. It will be enough to send a good seven onto the battlefield.'

The minstrel-woman told the prince all his daughter had averred. 363 Any man who has ever waged war has stood in great need of booty to defray high costs. Loyal Lyppaut was so overburdened by paid soldiers that his immediate thought was: 'I shall get hold of this property, by fair means or by foul.' Nor did he omit to set out in pursuit. Scherules rode towards him, asking him where he was riding in such a hurry. 'I am riding after a swindler. They tell me he is a counterfeiter.'

Sir Gawan was innocent. It was all the fault of the horses and the other belongings he'd brought with him. Scherules was moved to laughter, saying: 'Lord, you are mistaken. Whoever tells you so is lying, be it maiden, man or woman. My guest is innocent. You must accord him different praise. He never acquired a coining-stamp, if you'll hear the truth of the matter. He never carried a money-changer's bag. Look at his bearing, hear his words! In my own house I left him, back there. If you know how to judge a knight's demean- 364 our, then you must accord him his deserts. He was never quick to falsity. If, nevertheless, anyone does violence to him, even if it were my father or my child—anybody who acts in anger against him—

even my kinsman or my brother—they'll have to pull battle's oars against *me*! shall defend him, protect him against unjust assault, wherever I may, lord, by your leave. I would desert shield's office for a beggarman's scrip, flee so far from my lineage to where none might know me, rather than that you, lord, should disgrace yourself by your treatment of him. It would be more just if you were to give a gracious welcome to all who have come here and have heard about your troubles, rather than desiring to rob them, believe you me.'

The prince said: 'Well, let me have a look at him. That can't do any harm.' He rode to where he could see Gawan. The two eyes and the one heart that Lyppaut took there with him averred that the stranger was well-favoured, and that true manly ways lived alongside his bearing.

365   Any man whom true love has caused to suffer heart's love knows so much of heart's love that the heart is true love's pledge, so sold and surrendered that no mouth can ever tell to the full what wonders love can work. Be it woman or man, heart's love, time and again, lowers their high minds. Obie and Meljanz—the love of those two was so entire and embraced such loyalty that his anger ought to grieve you—that he rode away from her in anger. It followed that her sadness brought such suffering upon her that her chastity became quick to wrath. Innocently, Gawan paid for this, as did others who suffered along with her there. Often she departed from ladylike ways; thus her chastity intertwined itself with wrath. It was a thorn in the eyes of both of them. Whenever she espied that noble man, her heart averred that Meljanz had to be by far the highest. She thought: 'Even if he teaches me torment, I must bear with it gladly for his sake. I love that young, noble, gentle man before all the world.
366   That is where my heart's senses hunt me.' Love gives rise to much anger still, so don't reproach Obie for it.

Hear now what her father said when he saw noble Gawan and welcomed him into the land, how he then commenced the conversation. He said: 'Lord, your arrival may bring us profit in bliss. Many a journey I have travelled, but my eyes never beheld so sweet a countenance. In the face of this misfortune, your day's advent must console us, for it is capable of solace.'

He entreated him to do knight's deeds there: 'If you lack equipment, let yourself be supplied in full. If you will, lord, be in my company.'

Noble Gawan replied: 'I would be ready and willing to do so. I have the equipment and strong limbs, but my fighting is bound by a truce until an appointed hour. Whether you were to triumph or succumb, I would gladly suffer it for your sake, but for this reason I must avoid battle, lord, until this one combat of mine takes place, to which my loyalty stands so dearly pledged. To win the greeting of all who are worthy, I must redeem that pledge by combat—that is why I am on the road—or else I must abandon life there.' 367

This brought heart's sorrow upon Lyppaut. He said: 'Sir, by your honour, and by your courtesy's favour, hear of my innocence. I have two daughters who are dear to me, for they are my own children. Whatever God has given me in them, I will happily rest content with. Praise be that I ever acquired such troubles as I have on their account! One of the two bears this sorrow along with me, but the company we keep is unequal. My lord hurts her with love and me with unlove! The way I see it, my lord desires to do violence to me because I have no son.* Daughters ought in any case to be dearer to me. What of it if I now suffer torment because of them? I will count that among my blessings. Whoever has to choose together with his daughter—although the sword is forbidden her, her defence is as valuable in other respects—she will procure for him, chastely, a son most rich in courage. This is the hope I cherish.'

'Now may God grant you as much!' said Gawan.

Prince Lyppaut pleaded urgently with him. 368

'Sir, in God's name, cease such talk,' replied King Lot's son. 'By your courtesy, you must do so, and let me not dispense with loyalty. One thing I will grant you—this very night I will tell you what I have decided upon.'

Lyppaut thanked him and departed at once. At the court he found his daughter and the burgrave's little daughter. The two of them were tossing rings.* He said to Obilot: 'Daughter, where did you spring from?'

'Father, I'm on my way down there. I'm sure he'll grant me my wish—I want to ask the foreign knight to serve me in return for reward.'

'Daughter, I grieve to tell you that he's neither agreed nor refused *me*. Pursue my entreaty to its conclusion.' The maid hastened towards the stranger.

As she entered the chamber, Gawan leapt to his feet. After he'd

welcomed her, he sat down next to the sweet girl. He thanked her for
not ignoring him when he had met harsh treatment. He said: 'If ever
a knight suffered duress in the cause of such a dainty maidlet, I
ought to do so for your sake.'

369　　The young, sweet, lustrous girl said, in all sincerity: 'As God
knows full well, lord, you are the first man ever to be my companion
in converse. If my courtesy, and also my sense of modesty, remain
intact, then this will profit me in happiness, for my instructress
averred to me that speech is the mind's clothing.

'Sir, I plead with both you and me. It is veritable distress that
teaches me to do so. I shall name that to you, if you please. If you
think any the worse of me for it, it is, nevertheless, moderation's path
that I tread, for it was with myself I pleaded when I pleaded with
you. *You* are in truth *I*, although the names diverge. You must pos-
sess my person's name. Be now both maid and man. I have put my
request to you and to me. If you let me, lord, go away from you
shamefully unrewarded now, then your fame must be called to
account before your own courtesy, since my maidenly flight seeks
your favour. If you, lord, are so inclined, I will give you love with
370　heartfelt sentiment. If you possess manly ways, then I truly believe
that you will not refrain from serving me—I am worthy of service.
Since my father, too, desires help from friends and kinsmen, do not
refrain from service, though you serve us both for my reward alone.'

He said: 'Lady, your mouth's melody seeks to part me from loy-
alty. Disloyalty ought by rights to offend you. My loyalty suffers
such duress by a pledge that, if it is unredeemed, I am dead. Yet even
supposing I were to turn my service and sentiments to your love—
before you may give love in return you must live five further years.
That's the count of your love's season.'

Yet then he thought of how Parzival placed more faith in women
than in God. His commendation was this maid's messenger into
Gawan's heart. Then he vowed to the maidlet that he would bear
arms for her sake. He went on to say to her: 'Let my sword be in your
hands. If anyone desires to joust against me, you must ride that
charge, you must fight in my stead there. People may see me in battle
there, but it must fall to you to fight for me!'

371　　She said: 'I have very little fear on that account. I am your protec-
tion and your shield, and your heart and your solace, now that
you have redeemed me from doubt. I am your guide and your

companion, guarding you against mishap, a roof against misfortune's
storm, I am your easeful resting-place. My love shall bring you pro-
tection, grant you good fortune in the face of peril, so that your
courage will not fail, even though you have to defend yourself so
hard that only the host is left alive.* I am host and hostess and will be
by your side in battle. If you hold to this hope, fortune and courage
will not desert you.'

Noble Gawan replied: 'Lady, I will possess both, since I live at
your command, being your love and your solace's gift.'

All this while her handlet lay between his hands. Then she said:
'Sir, let me leave now. There are matters I must see to myself. How
would you fare without my reward? You're far too dear to me for
that. I must busy myself with preparing my token for you. When you
wear that, no other fame can ever in any way surpass yours.'

Away went the maid and her playmate, both offering great homage   372
to Gawan their guest. He bowed deeply in acknowledgement of their
favour, saying: 'If you grow to be old, if then the forest were to bear
nothing but spears—rather than the other wood it has—that would
be a scant seeding for you two.* If your youth can exert such compul-
sion, if you wish to carry this on into maturity, your love will yet
teach a knight's hand that whereby a shield has ever dwindled before
a spear!'

Away went the two maids, with joy, without sorrow. The bur-
grave's little daughter said: 'Now tell me, lady mine, what have you
in mind to give him? As we have nothing but dolls, if any of mine are
more beautiful, give them to him—I don't mind! There will be very
little quarrelling over that!'

Prince Lyppaut came riding along, halfway up the hill. He saw
Obilot and Clauditte walking up ahead of him—he asked them both
to stop. Young Obilot then said: 'Father, I was never in such need of
your help. Give me your advice, too! The knight has granted my
request!'

'Daughter, whatever your will desires, if I possess it, you are   373
granted it. Blessed be the fruit of your mother's womb! Your birth
was a day of blessings!'

'Father, I'll tell you then, in secret I'll lament my troubles to you.
By your good grace, speak your mind about them.'

He asked that she be lifted up onto his horse before him. She said:
'Where would my playmate go then?' Many knights were halting by

him there. They disputed as to who should take her. It would have well become any one of them. To one, in the end, she was offered. Clauditte, too, was well-favoured.

As he rode, her father said to her: 'Obilot, now tell me something of your needs.'

'Well, I promised a token to the foreign knight there. I think my mind was raving! If I have nothing to give him, what use am I alive, since he has offered me service? Indeed I must blush for shame if I have nothing to give him. Never was a man so dear to a maid!'

He replied: 'Daughter, leave it to me. I must see that you are well supplied. As you desire service from him, I shall give you what you
374 shall bestow upon him, if your mother leaves you in the lurch. God grant that I may profit by it! Oh, that proud, noble man, what hopes I have of him! I never yet spoken a single word to him, but I saw him in my sleep last night.'

Lyppaut went before the duchess, along with Obilot his daughter, saying: 'Lady, give both of us your aid. My heart cried out for joy when God supplied me with this maid and parted me from distress.'

The aged duchess replied: 'What would you have of my property?'

'Lady, if you are willing to help us, Obilot would like better clothes. She thinks she's worthy of them in her worthiness, since such a worthy man desires her love, offering her much service and also desiring her token.'

Then the maid's mother said: 'What a gentle man, a most goodly man—I believe you mean the stranger from foreign parts! His glance is truly like May's gleam!'

Then the discerning lady commanded samite from Ethnise* to be brought in. Together with this they carried uncut cloth, furs from Tabronit, from the land of Tribalibot. By the Caucasus the gold is
375 red, and the heathens work many garments from it, richly and most artfully ornamented on a silk base. Lyppaut gave orders that clothes should be cut, quickly, for his daughter. He gladly measured both for her—the coarse and the fine. A phellel-silk with stiff gold was cut for the maidlet. One of her arms had to be bared; from it a sleeve was taken, which was to go to Gawan.

This was her cadeau, phellel-silk from Noriente, brought from far-off heathendom. It had touched her right arm, but had not been sewn to the dress; no thread had yet been twisted to it. This Clauditte took to well-favoured Gawan. Then he was entirely free of anxiety. He had three shields; to one he nailed it at once. All his sadness vanished entirely. He did not conceal his great gratitude, bowing time and again towards the road walked by the damsel who had welcomed him so graciously, and so charmingly made him rich in joy.

The day took its end, and night came. On both sides there were 376 great forces, many a valiant, worthy knight. Even if there weren't such a deluge of men in the outer army, the inner would still have had a fight on its hands. Then they marked out their furthermost outposts by the bright moon. They had little truck with timid cowardice. Before daybreak they had prepared twelve broad breastworks, ditched against attack, each breastwork supplied with three barbicans for mounted sorties.

Kardefablet de Jamor's marshal took four gates there, where come morning his army could be clearly seen in brave defence. The mighty duke fought in knightly fashion there. The lady of the castle was his sister. He was stronger of purpose than many another fighting man who knows well how to hold out in battle; therefore, in battle, he often suffered strife. His army had filed in that night. He had come from far afield, for rarely had he retreated from warlike hardship. Four gates he well defended there.

All the army that lay encamped on the other side of the bridge had 377 marched across, before day came, into the town of Bearosche, at Prince Lyppaut's urging. Those of Jamor had ridden across the bridge ahead of them. Each of the gates had been so commanded that they were in a good state of defence when day appeared. Scherules chose one for himself, which he and my lord Gawan did not desire to leave unguarded.

Some of the strangers there were heard—I believe those were the best amongst them—to regret the fact that knightly deeds had happened there without them seeing them at all, and that the vesper tournament had taken place without any of them being on the receiving end of a joust. There was no need at all for such complaint. Fighting uncounted was on offer there to all who were so inclined, if they once sought it out in the field.

In the lanes deep hoof-tracks were perceived. Here and there many a banner was seen filing in, all by the moon's beam, and many a helmet of lavish expense—these they desired to take into the joust—and many a gaily painted spear. A Regensburg sendal-silk would 378 have counted for little there, on the ground before Bearosche. Many surcoats were to be seen there of greater value.

Night kept to its old custom, the new day marching in step with its close. It was not by larks' song that it was perceived—many a clash clanged loud and clear there—combat was the cause. Spears could be heard there, cracking like a cloudburst! There the young army from Liz had met with the men of Lirivoyn and the King of Avendroyn. There many a splendid joust resounded, like someone tossing whole chestnuts* into high flames. *Avoy!* How the strangers rode on the plain and how the townsfolk fought!

For Gawan and the burgrave, because of their souls' venture and in their heavenly bliss's cause, a priest gave mass. He sang it both for God and them. Now their honour's gain drew nigh, for that was the law by which they lived. Then they rode to their outpost. Their redoubt had been guarded, before their arrival, by many a noble, 379 worthy knight. Those were Scherules' men—they did well there.

What more can I say now? Except that Poydiconjunz was proud. He rode up with such forces that even if the Black Forest's every bush were a shaft, more wood might have been seen there, if a man wished to size up his army! He came riding up with six banners, before which battle began at an early hour. Trumpeters gave out clamour's crack like thunder, which has ever fostered much fearful dread. Many a drummer did his work there, alongside the trumpeters' din. If any blade of stubble remained untrod there, I could do nothing about it. Erfurt's vineyard* still bears witness to the same extremity, caused by trampling—many a charger's hoof dealt those blows.

Then Duke Astor arrived to do battle with the men of Jamor. There jousts were whetted, many a noble man unseated behind his charger upon the field. They were busy about their battle. Many strange heralds' cries were called there, many a charger ran loose without its master, leaving its lord standing on foot there—I believe falling made his acquaintance!

380   When my lord Gawan perceived that the plain was interwoven, with friends in the enemies' ranks, he too charged in there at full tilt. It was no easy matter to follow him, though Scherules and his men little spared their chargers. Gawan gave them grief! How many knights he thrust down there, and what stout spears he splintered, that noble Table Round's ambassador! If his strength had not derived from God, then fame might rightly have been craved for him

there! Then many a sword was clanged! Both armies against whom his hand fought were as one to him—those of Liz and those of Gors. From both sides he soon brought many a charger back, led to his host's banner. He asked if anyone there wanted them—there were many who said yes! They all alike grew rich by his companionship.

Then a knight came riding up who was also not sparing of spears. The burgrave of Beauvais and Gawan the courteous rode at one another, with the result that young Lisavander lay behind his charger 381 upon the flowers, for he had practised the joust's fall. This grieves me for the sake of that squire who, the other day, rode with courtesy, and told Gawan tidings of how these events had come about. He dismounted, bending over his lord. Gawan recognized him and returned to him the charger that had been won there. The squire bowed to him, I am told.

See now where Kardefablet himself is standing on the ground, because of a joust with famed impact, aimed by Meljacanz's hand. Then his men snatched him up. 'Jamor!' was often cried out there as fierce sword-blows were struck. It grew tight there, none too roomy, one collision pressing upon another. Many helmets sounded in their wearers' ears. Gawan assembled his company. Then his charge was carried out, with no little power! With his host's banner he came most speedily to the aid of the noble lord of Jamor. Then many knights were felled to the ground. Believe it, if you will—all my witnesses have left me in the lurch—only the adventure vouches for it.

*Leh kuns de Muntâne** rode towards Gawan. There a fine joust took 382 place, with the result that stout Laheduman lay behind his charger on the field. Thereupon he gave his oath of surrender, that proud, noble, renowned warrior; to Gawan's hand the oath was given.

Duke Astor was then fighting at the front, closest to the redoubts, where many a warlike charge took place. 'Nantes!' was shouted time and again, Arthur's war-cry. Those hardy men, no weaklings, were there—many an exiled Briton, and the paid soldiers from Destrigleis, from Erec's land. Their deeds were acknowledged there. They were led by the *duc de* Lanverunz. Poydiconjunz might indeed have let the Britons have their freedom, such deeds were performed by them there. They had been captured from Arthur at the Muntâne Cluse,* where fighting had been seen. It had happened in a skirmish. They shouted 'Nantes!' as was their custom, here or wherever they bided

383 for battle—that was their war-cry and their way. Several among them had very grey beards. Moreover, each and every Briton had as a device a gampilun* either on his helmet or on his shield, derived from the device of Ilinot, he who was Arthur's noble son. What could Gawan then do but sigh, seeing those arms, for his heart spoke to him of sorrow! His uncle's son's death brought Gawan to grief's extremity. He knew the arms' sheen well. His eyes ran over with tears then. He left the men of Britain to hold out upon the plain. He had no desire to fight with them, as is still the case where friendship is acknowledged.

He rode towards Meljanz's army. There the townsfolk were defending their posts in a manner that merited gratitude, but they had no chance, nevertheless, of holding the field against superior forces—they had retreated towards a moat. One knight, all in red, offered many a joust there to the townsfolk. He was called 'the Unnamed', for no-one there knew him. I'm telling the tale to you as I heard it. He had joined Meljanz three days before. That brought grief to the townsfolk.

384 He had set about helping Meljanz. The latter, moreover, had supplied him with twelve squires from Semblidac, who attended to him in the joust and in the massed charge. No matter how many spears their hands could offer him, he reduced them all to splinters. His jousts rang out loud with clashes, for he took King Schirniel and his brother prisoner there. Yet more happened there at his hands. He did not spare Duke Marangliez surrender. They were the army's spearhead. Their men defended themselves still.

Meljanz the king himself fought there. All those to whom his deeds had brought pleasure or heart's sorrow had to admit that rarely had more been achieved by so young a man as he did there. His hand cleaved many sturdy shields asunder. What strong spears splintered into dust before him, where tilt interlocked with tilt! His young heart was so great that he could do no other but be avid for battle. No-one could grant it him in sufficient measure there—that was extremity indeed!—until he offered Gawan a joust.

Gawan took from his squires one of the twelve spears from 385 Angram, which he had acquired by the Plimizœl. Meljanz's war-cry was 'Barbigœl!'—the noble capital of Liz. Gawan concentrated upon his joust with diligence. Then that stout cane shaft from Oraste Gentesin taught Meljanz pain, piercing his shield and sticking fast in

his arm. A splendid joust took place there! Gawan thrust him into
flight, breaking in two his rear saddle-bow, so that both warriors
ended up—no deception!—behind their chargers. Then they acted
as they well knew how, making shift with their swords. Two peasants
would have found more than ample threshing there—each carried
the other's sheaf—they were both flailed to bits. Meljanz was
obliged, moreover, to carry a spear which had stuck fast in that
warrior's arm. Bloody sweat made him hot. Then my lord Gawan
tugged him away into Brevigariez's* barbican and forced him to
surrender; he was willing to do so. If that young man had not been
wounded, no-one there would have learned so quickly that he
had surrendered to Gawan—he would certainly have been spared
surrender longer.

Lyppaut the prince, that land's lord, did not refrain from manly 386
courage. Against him fought the King of Gors. Both people and
chargers there had to suffer torment from arrowfire, the Kahetine
and the men-at-arms from Semblidac all applying their arts. The
turcopoles knew how to twist and turn. The townsfolk had to con-
sider what might deter the enemies from their outposts. They had
sarjande ad piet.* Their redoubts were as well guarded as is exemplary
practice even now. All the worthy men who lost their lives there paid
ungently for Obie's anger, for her foolish arrogance brought hard-
ship to many. How was Prince Lyppaut to blame in this? His lord,
old King Schaut, would have spared him such punishment entirely.
Then even those bands began to tire.

Still Meljacanz fought on with vigour. Was his shield intact?
There was not a hand's breadth of it left. Duke Kardefablet had
driven him far afield. The tourney has come to a complete halt
upon a flowery plain. Then my lord Gawan also arrived, causing 387
Meljacanz such distress that noble Lancelot never attacked him so
fiercely, when he had come down from the Sword Bridge* path, and
afterwards did battle with him. Lancelot was angry at the imprison-
ment suffered by Lady Guinevere, whom he rescued by his fighting
there.

Lot's son then rode into the charge. What choice had Meljacanz
now but to spur his charger on in turn? That joust was watched by
many spectators. Who was left lying there behind his charger? He
whom the man of Norway felled upon the meadow. Many a knight
and lady who observed this joust accorded fame to Gawan. It was a

goodly sight to behold for the ladies, looking down from the great hall. Meljacanz was trampled upon, many a charger that never again nibbled verdure wading through his surcoat. The bloody sweat gushed down upon him. Then befell the chargers' plague-day, followed by the vultures' booty. Then Duke Astor rescued Meljacanz from the men of Jamor—he had very nearly been taken prisoner. The tourney was over.

388   So who had ridden in search of fame there and fought for women's reward? I couldn't identify them if I had to name all of them to you—I would have my hands full! As regards the inner army, goodly deeds were done for the sake of young Obilot, and as regards the outer army, a Red Knight—those two won the prize there, no-one else excelling them, not by any means.

When the outer army's guest realized that he lacked service-thanks from his captain, the latter having been taken captive inside the city, he rode over to his squires. To his captives he then said: 'You lords gave me your surrender. Sorrow has befallen me here. The King of Liz has been taken prisoner. Now make whatever efforts you can to see if he may be set free, if he may so profit by my prowess,'— he said to the King of Avendroyn, and to Schirniel of Lyrivoyn, and to Duke Marangliez. With a cunningly worded vow he permitted them to ride away from him into the city. He urged them to ransom Meljanz, or that they should procure for him the Grail. They could
389   not tell him anything at all about where that was, except that it was in the custody of a king called Anfortas. When they spoke those words, the Red Knight replied: 'If my request is not fulfilled, then make your way to where Pelrapeire stands. Take to the queen your oath of surrender and tell her that he who fought on her behalf there against Kingrun, and against Clamide, now suffers on account of the Grail, and yet also for love of her. Both are always in my thoughts. Now give her this message, tell her I sent you there. You warriors, may God preserve you!'

Taking their leave, they rode into the city. Then the Red Knight said to his squires: 'We are undaunted of profit. Take whatever chargers have been won here. Leave me just one now. As you can see, mine is sorely wounded.'

The worthy squires replied: 'Sir, our thanks to you for bestowing such generous help upon us. We'll be rich forever now!'

He chose for himself one charger for his road, Ingliart of the

Short Ears,* which had gone astray from Gawan while he was taking Meljanz captive. There the Red Knight's hand had taken it, causing several rims* to be riddled with holes.

Taking his leave, he made his departure. Fifteen chargers or more 390 he left to them, unwounded. The squires were well capable of thanking him. They pressed him to stay, but a further goal stood before him. Then the comely knight headed for where great ease was rare, seeking nothing but battle. I believe that in his times no man ever fought as much.

The outer army all rode in file to their lodgings, to take their rest. Inside the walls Prince Lyppaut spoke, asking what had happened on the field, for he had heard that Meljanz had been captured. That was good news to him, serving to console him later. Gawan loosed the sleeve from his shield, without tearing it—he set higher store by his prize. He gave it to Clauditte. At the edge and in the middle, too, it was pierced and hewn through. He ordered that it be taken to Obilot. At that the maiden's joy grew great. Her arm was white and bare. She immediately pinned it on, saying: 'Who has injured me there?' 391 whenever she came before her sister, who received that jest with anger.

The knights there were in need of rest, for great weariness commanded it of them. Scherules took Gawan and Count Laheduman. He found yet more knights there, whom Gawan that day, with his own hands, had captured in the field, where many a great charge had taken place. Then the mighty burgrave seated them in knightly fashion. He and all his weary company remained standing in their entirety before the king, until Meljanz had eaten. Scherules busied himself with goodly hospitality there.

This seemed too much to Gawan. 'If the king will permit, Sir Host, you ought to be seated,' said Gawan, sensibly—his courtesy hunted him to those words.

The host refused the request, saying: 'My lord* is the king's man. He would have performed this service himself, if it befitted the king to accept his service. My lord, out of courtesy, sees nothing of him now, for he does not enjoy his favour. If God ever unites them in friendship, then we'll all obey His command.'

Then the young Meljanz said: 'Your courtesy was always so entire 392 for as long as I lived here that your counsel never deserted me. If I had followed your advice better then, I would be seen to be happy today. Now help me, Count Scherules, for I have full trust in you, in this matter of my lord who holds me captive here—they will both* listen, I expect, to your counsel—and Lyppaut, my second father— let him show his courtesy towards me now. I would not have lost his favour at all if his daughter had refrained from making mock of me as if I were a fool! That was unladylike demeanour!'

Then noble Gawan said: 'A truce shall be made here which only death shall part.' Then those arrived whom the Red Knight had captured out in the field, and came walking towards the king. They told him how that had come about. When Gawan had heard about the device of the knight who had fought with them there and to whom they had given surrender, and when they told him about the Grail, he thought that Parzival lay behind this story. He bowed to

393 Heaven in thanks that God had parted their battle's antagonism from one another that day. Their concealing courtesy had guaranteed that neither of them was named there. Nor did anyone recognize them, though they did so elsewhere.

Scherules said to Meljanz: 'Lord, if I may ask it of you, be so kind as to see my lord. To what friends say on both sides you ought to give willing assent, and do not be angry with him.' That seemed good to all present there. Then they went up from the town to the king's hall,* the inner army, at the request of Lyppaut's marshal. My lord Gawan took with him Count Laheduman and others he had captured—they too walked up. He asked them to give their oath of surrender, which he had won from them that day by fighting, to Scherules, his host. Many now have no choice but to go, as had been vowed there, up to the great hall of Bearosche. The burgrave's wife gave to Meljanz rich clothes and a little veil, in which he hung his wounded arm, which Gawan's joust had pierced.

394 Gawan sent a message by Scherules to his lady Obilot, that he would dearly like to see her, and also truly acknowledge that he was her subject, and, moreover, desired to take his leave of her—'and say, I leave the king at her disposal here. Entreat her to consider how she may so keep him here that fame may hold sway over her conduct.'

These words were heard by Meljanz, who said: 'Obilot will be the garland of all womanly grace. It eases my mind if it is to her I must give surrender—that I must live here under her conditions of truce.'

'You must acknowledge that none but her hand took you captive here,' said noble Gawan. 'My fame she alone must possess.'

Scherules came riding up. Now, at court, nothing was neglected to ensure that maiden, man and woman all wore such garments that inferior, poor people's clothing was readily dispensed with there that day. Together with Meljanz there rode to court all those who had pledged their oath of surrender out there in the field. There all four sat: Lyppaut, his wife and his daughters. Those newly arrived came walking up to them. The host leapt towards his lord. There was a great press in the hall as he welcomed foe and friends alike. Meljanz walked alongside Gawan.

'If you were not to disdain the offer, your old lady-friend would welcome you with a kiss—I mean my wife, the duchess.'

Meljanz immediately answered the host: 'I shall gladly have their kiss of greeting—that of two ladies I see here—but to the third I shall grant no reconciliation!'

The parents wept at that. Obilot was delighted. The king was welcomed with a kiss, as were two other beardless kings,* and Duke Marangliez also. Gawan too was not spared a kiss, nor taking his lady to him. He pressed the well-favoured child like a doll to his breast, as loving inclination obliged him. He said to Meljanz: 'Your hand has granted me surrender. Be free of that oath now, and grant it here instead. All my joys' guarantor sits in my arms. It is her prisoner you must be!'

Meljanz, with that purpose in mind, walked nearer. The maiden clasped Gawan to her, but surrender was granted to Obilot there, in the sight of many a noble knight.

'Sir King, you have acted badly now by granting him surrender, if my knight is indeed a merchant, as my sister has so fiercely contended'—so said the maiden Obilot. Next she commanded Meljanz to transfer the oath of surrender he had made to her hand to her sister Obie. 'You must have her as your *âmîe*, to win knight's fame. She must have you always, willingly, as her lord and her *âmîs*. I'll not let either of you off!'

God spoke out of her young mouth. Her entreaty prevailed on both counts. There Lady Love crafted by her mighty mastery, together with heartfelt loyalty, the love of those two all anew. Obie's hand slipped out of her cloak, grasping Meljanze's arm. All in tears, her red mouth kissed the place where he had been wounded by the joust. Many a tear soaked his arm, flowing from her bright eyes. Who made her be so bold before that company? It was Love that did so, at

once young and old. Lyppaut saw his heart's desire fulfilled then, for
never had such happiness befallen him. Since God had not spared
him that honour, he then called his daughter 'Lady'.

How the wedding went—ask that of him who obtained a gift*
there!—and whither many a man then rode, whether he took his ease
or did battle—to that I have no solution. They tell me that Gawan
took his leave in the great hall, where he had gone to take his leave.
Obilot wept copiously at that, saying: 'Take me away with you, now!'
But Gawan denied the young, sweet maid that request. Her mother
could barely tear her away from him. Then he said his farewells to all
of them. Lyppaut offered him ample homage, for he was dear to his
heart. Scherules, his proud host, together with all his men, did not
refrain from riding out with the bold warrior. Gawan's road led into
a forest. Scherules sent huntsmen and food ahead for a long distance,
to accompany him. The noble warrior took his leave. Gawan's fate
was forfeit to sorrow.

BOOK VIII

398 OF all who had gone to Bearosche, Gawan would have won the prize
there, none but he of both sides, were it not that one knight appeared
in the field, in red armour, unrecognized, one whose fame was tied to
the top of the flagstaff.

Gawan enjoyed honour and good fortune, each in its full share.
Now, however, his duel's time draws nigh. The wood through which
he had to make his way was long and wide, if he would not shirk the
combat. Though guiltless, he had been summoned to it. Now
Ingliart, too, was lost, his charger of the Short Ears. No better char-
ger was ever spurred on by Moors in Tabronit. Now the forest
became mixed—here a copse, there a field, one or two so broad that a
tent might, with difficulty, have been pitched there. His eyes made
acquaintance with an inhabited land, called Ascalun. There he asked
his way to Schampfanzun of such people as encountered him. High
mountains and many a marsh—through much of this he had made
his way, when he espied a castle. *Avoy!* It shed a most noble gleam!
That stranger to the land headed towards it.

399   Now hear tell of adventure, and help me, as you do so, to lament

Gawan's great anguish. My sage and my fool, may they both do so
out of companionship and grieve for him as I do! Alas, I ought to be
silent now! But no, let him sink lower, he who erstwhile bowed his
thanks to Fortune, and now was sinking towards hardship.

So exalted was that castle that Aeneas never found Carthage* so
lordly, where Lady Dido's death was Love's forfeit. What halls did it
have, and how many towers stood there? Acraton would have found
them ample, that city which, Babylon apart, had the broadest cir-
cumference ever, according to heathens' words' contention. It was, I
imagine, so high all round, and where it bordered on the sea, that it
feared no attack, nor any great, violent hostility.

Before it lay a plain, some miles wide. Across that rode Sir Gawan.
Five hundred knights or more—over them all one alone was lord—
came riding towards him there, in brightly-coloured clothes,
well-tailored.

As the adventure told me, their falcons were hunting cranes there, 400
or whatever took to flight before them. King Vergulaht rode a tall
charger of Spanish breeding. His looks were, I imagine, like day next
to night. His kin had been sent forth by Mazadan,* from the moun-
tain of Famurgan. His lineage was of faërie stock. Anyone would
imagine he was looking at May, in the proper season with all its
flowers, if he beheld the king's complexion. To Gawan it seemed,
when the king so shone towards him, that he was a second Parzival,
and that he possessed Gahmuret's features—as this tale knows of—
when he rode into Kanvoleiz.

A heron, taking flight, had retreated to a marshy pond. Falcons'
charges* had pursued it thither. The king sought out the wrong ford;
coming to the falcons' aid* he was soaked. He lost his horse in the
effort, along with all his clothes, yet he parted the falcons from their
torment. The falconers took his clothes. Did they have any right to
do so? It was their right, they ought to have them. They too must be
allowed their rights! Then he was lent another horse. He gave up all 401
hope of his own. Other clothes, instead, were hung upon him. The
old ones were the falconers' gain.

Gawan came riding up. *Avoy!* Now there was no avoiding his
being better welcomed there than happened when Erec was received
at Karidœl, when he drew near Arthur, after his battle, and when
Lady Enite was the escort of his joy, after Maliclisier the dwarf had
ungently pierced his skin with his scourge, in the sight of Guinevere,

and when at Tulmeyn a battle took place in the broad circle, with the sparrowhawk as prize. Renowned Ider *fil* Noyt* offered him his surrender there. He was obliged to offer it, or else die.

Let that matter be and hear this instead. Never, I believe, did you hear of a more noble reception or greeting. Alas, noble Lot's son will have to pay dearly for it! If you so advise, I'll stop, and won't tell you
402 any more. Because it's such a sad tale, I'll back away—and yet, by your favour, hear how the treachery of strangers brought murk upon a pure mind. If I persevere with this tale and tell it you rightly, then you'll lament along with me!

Then King Vergulaht said: 'Lord, I have decided that you should ride into the castle there. If it meets with your approval, I shall break with your company now. Yet, if my riding on offends you, I shall abandon all I have to do here.'

Noble Gawan replied: 'Sir, whatever you command is within your rights, nor do I take any offence, but pardon you most willingly.'

Then the King of Ascalun said: 'Lord, you can see Schampfanzun clearly before you. Up there resides my sister, a maiden. Of all that mouths have spoken of beauty she has her full share. If you'll look on it as good fortune, then, truly, she must take it upon herself to attend to you until I arrive. I'll be with you more quickly than I ought— indeed, you won't mind waiting for me at all, once you've seen my sister! You wouldn't object if I were to take even longer!'

403 'I shall be glad to see you, as to see her, although grown-up ladies* have always spared me worthy hospitality,'—so spoke proud Gawan. The king sent ahead a knight with a message to the maiden that she should so attend to Gawan that a long time should seem to him a short spate. Gawan rode to where the king commanded. If you wish, I shall yet keep silent about the great extremity ahead!

No! I'll tell you more! The road and a horse bore Gawan towards the gate at the side of the great hall. Anyone who has ever set about building could speak better than I about that building's massive strength. There stood a fortress, the best ever named an edifice on this earth—immeasurably broad was its compass.

This castle's praise we must abandon here, for I have much to tell you of the king's sister, a maiden. Here much has been said about build—I will assess *her* as I rightly ought. If she was beautiful, that became her well, and if she was also of righteous mind, that counted towards her honour, so that her ways and her disposition resembled

the Margravine, who broadly beamed over all the borderland 404
from Haidstein.* Happy is he who can try out the resemblance to her
in private! Believe me, he'll find better pastime there than elsewhere!
I can only say of ladies what my eyes are capable of observing. Where
I turn my speech to good cause, it is in good need of courtesy's
guard. Now let this adventure be heard by the loyal and the comely! I
care nothing for the disloyal! By their hole-riddled contrition they
have forfeited all heavenly bliss—for that their souls must suffer
wrath.

Into the courtyard there, before the great hall, Gawan rode to
meet such society as the king had sent him towards—he who dis-
graced himself by his treatment of him. A knight who had brought
him there led him to where well-favoured Antikonie,* the queen, sat.
If womanly honour were to be profit, then she had made many such
purchases, and renounced all falsity; thereby her chastity had won
fame. Alas that the sage of Veldeke died so early!* He could have
praised her better.

When Gawan espied the maiden, the messenger went over and 405
told her all that the king had commanded him. The queen then did
not neglect to say: 'Sir, come closer to me. It is you who are my
courtesy's mentor: command, now, and instruct. If time is to pass
pleasantly for you, that must depend upon your command, since my
brother has commended you to me so warmly. I shall kiss you, if a
kiss is in order. Command, now, according to your standards, what I
am to do or omit to do.' With great courtesy she stood before him.

Gawan said: 'Lady, your mouth is so kissably shaped that I must
have your kiss in greeting!'

Her mouth was hot, full and red—to it Gawan proffered his own.
There an unstrangerly kiss ensued. Next to the maiden rich in cour-
tesy the well-born stranger sat down. Gentle discourse did not fail
them, both speaking with sincerity. They were well versed in
reiteration—he his request, she her denial. He took to lamenting this
from his heart, imploring her for favour. What the maiden said I'll
tell you:

'Sir, if you are discerning in other respects, this may seem to you 406
sufficient. I've offered you, at my brother's request, more than
Ampflise ever offered Gahmuret, my uncle—short of lying together.
My loyalty would ultimately weigh heavier in the balance by a good
lead, if anyone were to weigh us accurately—and I don't know,

after all, lord, who you are! Yet in such a short time you would have my love!'

Noble Gawan replied: 'My intelligence of my kin informs me, I tell you, lady, that I am my aunt's brother's son. If you would show me favour, do not desist on account of my lineage. It is so well vouched for, compared with yours, that they are both of entirely equal status and tread in proper measure.'

A maid made shift to pour them wine, then darted away from them. Other ladies still sitting there did not neglect to go about their business either. The knight who had brought Gawan there was also out of the way. Gawan thought, now that they had all gone out of the

407 room, that often the big ostrich is caught by the weakest eagle. He groped beneath her cloak—I believe he touched her hiplet.* At that his distress was magnified. Love brought such extremity upon both maid and man that *something* very nearly happened there—if evil eyes hadn't espied it! They were both ready and willing! See now, their hearts' sorrow nighs!

Through the door there then entered a white knight—for he was grey. 'To arms!' he cried, naming Gawan, as soon as he recognized him, shouting out loudly, time and again: 'Alas and alack for my lord whom you slew! And as if that were not enough, you're raping his daughter here as well!'

The call to arms has always been followed; that same custom held true there. Gawan said to the damsel: 'Lady, now give me your counsel. Neither of us has much by way of defence here. If only I had my sword!' he said.

The noble damsel replied: 'We must retreat to defend ourselves, flee up to that tower there, which stands close by my chamber! With luck we may get away!'

408 Knights here, merchants there—the damsel could already hear the rabble coming up from the town. Together with Gawan she stepped towards the tower. Her beloved had no choice but to suffer sorrow. She appealed to the people again and again to desist, but they were making such a hubbub and racket by now that none of them took any notice of her.

Intent on battle, they pressed towards the door. Gawan stood in defence before it, preventing their entry. A bolt barred the tower's door. He wrenched it out of the wall. His villainous neighbours retreated before him, again and again, with their company. The queen ran to and fro, to see if there were anything in the tower which might serve to defend them against that disloyal host. Then the pure maiden found a stone chess-set, and a board, beautifully inlaid, broad. This she brought to Gawan for the battle. It hung by an iron ring; Gawan took hold of that. Upon that square shield much chess was played—it was hewn to pieces!

Now hear of the lady, too! Heedless of whether it were king or rook, she hurled it against the enemy. The pieces were big and heavy. 409 The tale they tell of her relates that whoever was hit there by her throw's hurl tumbled down, willy-nilly. The mighty queen fought chivalrously there, putting up such a good show of defence at Gawan's side that the pedlar-women of Dollnstein never fought better at Shrovetide—for they act out of ribaldry, exerting themselves without it being forced upon them. If a woman becomes armour-rusty, she has forgotten her order, if chastity is to be accorded to her—unless she does so out of loyalty. Antikonie's grief was made manifest at Schampfanzun, and her high spirits lowered. In battle she wept sorely. She showed clearly that amorous affection is constant.

What did Gawan do then? Whenever such leisure fell to his lot that he could have a good look at the maiden—her mouth, her eyes, and her nose—you never saw a better-shaped hare on the spit, I believe, than she was in this place and that, between her hip and her breast—her person was well capable of inspiring amorous desire. You never saw an ant better graced by a waist than she was, where 410 her girdle lay. To her companion Gawan this gave manly courage. She held out with him in their extremity. The only hostage named to him was death, and no other conditions. Gawan weighed his enemies' hostility very lightly whenever he looked upon the maiden. In consequence many of them lost their lives.

Then King Vergulaht arrived. He saw the warlike force doing battle against Gawan. Unless I were to deceive you, I can't put a pretty face upon his behaviour, for he's intent upon disgracing himself by his treatment of his noble guest. The latter stood full firm in defence; his host, however, acted in such fashion that I grieve for Gandin, King of Anjou, that such a noble lady as his daughter ever gave birth to such a son, who now urged his people to do fierce battle alongside a faithless company. Gawan had to wait until the king was armed. Vergulaht himself set off on battle's journey.

Gawan was then obliged to retreat, yet unshamefully. He was 411 forced beneath the tower's door. Now see, then there arrived the very man who had challenged him to combat before. In Arthur's presence that had happened. Landgrave Kingrimursel clawed through his scalp and skin, wringing his hands at Gawan's extremity, for his loyalty was pledged to guarantee that he should have a truce there, unless it were that one man's limbs alone should oppress him in combat. He drove back old and young alike from the tower. The king ordered it be demolished.

Kingrimursel then called up to where he could see Gawan: 'Warrior, grant me safe conduct to join you in there! I desire to share companionable distress with you in this extremity. Either the king must strike me dead, or else I shall save your life!'

Gawan granted him safe conduct. The landgrave leapt in to join him there. At that the outer army began to falter, Kingrimursel being burgrave there. Whether they were youngsters or greybeards, 412 they wavered in their fighting. Gawan leapt into the open, as did Kingrimursel also. They were both quick to courage.

King Vergulaht admonished his people: 'How long are we to suffer torment at the hands of these two men? My uncle's son* has taken it upon himself to rescue this man, who has done me such damage that it would be more proper if Kingrimursel were to avenge it, if he were not lacking in courage!'

Plenty of them, prompted by their loyalty, chose one to speak to the king: 'Lord, if we may say as much to you, the landgrave will be unslain by many a hand here. May God direct you toward ways which might be better welcomed! Worldly fame will pour its scorn upon you if you slay your guest. You will heap shame's load upon yourself. Moreover, the other man is your own kinsman—he against whose safe-conduct you raise this quarrel. You must desist! You will be reviled for this! Now grant us a truce for as long as this day lasts. Let the truce hold for this night, too. What you then decide will still stand entirely in your hands, whether you be praised or disgraced.

413   'My lady Antikonie, free of falsity, stands there beside him, all in tears. If that does not move you to the heart, you both being born of one mother, then bear in mind, lord, if you are discerning, it was you who sent him to the maiden here. Even if no-one had guaranteed his safe-conduct, he ought to be spared for her sake alone.'

The king proclaimed a truce until he had consulted further about how he might avenge his father. Sir Gawan was innocent. Another

man had done the deed, for it was proud Ehkunat who had taught a
lance its path through him, when he was leading Jofreit *fiz* Idœl
towards Barbigœl; he had captured him when he was accompanying
Gawan.* It was because of Ehkunat that this calamity came about.

When the truce had been agreed, the people at once quitted the
battle, many a man returning to his quarters. Antikonie the queen
embraced her cousin warmly. Many a kiss met his mouth for having
saved Gawan and remained free of misdeed himself. She said:
'You are my father's brother's son—you could do no wrong, not on
anyone's behalf!'

If you will listen, I will tell you why my mouth spoke before of   414
a pure mind being muddied. Cursed be the battle's journey that
Vergulaht made to Schampfanzun! For it was not what he had
inherited, neither from his father nor his mother. The goodly young
man suffered very great distress because of the shame he felt when
his sister, the queen, started to pour scorn upon him. They heard
how she pleaded urgently with him.

Then the noble damsel said: 'Sir Vergulaht, if I bore the sword
and were, by God's command, a man possessing the shield's office,
you would have flinched from any fighting here. There I was, a
maiden without defence, except that I did, after all, bear one shield,
emblazoned with honour. I shall name its arms to you, if you care to
know them: gracious conduct and chaste ways—with those two
much constancy resides. These I offered to protect my knight, whom
you sent to me here. No other protection did I have. Whatever com-
pensation you are now seen to make, you have, nevertheless, acted
wrongly by me, if womanly fame is to be accorded its rights. I have   415
always heard that wherever it happened that a man took refuge in a
woman's protection, courageous pursuit ought to flinch from fight-
ing with him, if manly courtesy were present there. Sir Vergulaht,
your guest's refuge, which he sought with me in the face of death,
will yet teach your fame disgrace's extremity.'

Then Kingrimursel said: 'Lord, it was for your solace that I gave
to Sir Gawan, on Plimizœl's plain, safe-conduct into your country
here. Your oath was the pledge that, if his valour brought him here, I,
standing in for you, would guarantee he would not be attacked here,
except by one man alone. Sir, I am wronged by this. My peers are
looking on here. This disgrace has come upon us too early by far. If
you cannot protect princes, then we in turn will weaken the crown. If

you are to be seen in courtesy, then your courtesy must concede that kinship reaches down from you to me. Even if it were a concubinely trick on my side of the blanket, wherever that kinship of ours is acknowledged, you would have acted overhastily towards me, for

416 I am, after all, a knight in whom falsity was never yet found. And my fame must must procure for me death without falsity, I truly trust to God! May my salvation be messenger to Him for that! And wherever these tidings are heard—that Arthur's sister's son came in my safe-conduct to Schampfanzun—Frenchman or Briton, Provençal or Burgundian, Galicians and those of Punturtoys—if they hear of Gawan's extremity—if I have fame, then it is dead. His perilous battle will bring upon me most slender praise, make my disgrace broad. It will lay waste my joy and put in pawn my honour.'

When this speech was done, up stood one of the king's men, called Liddamus. Kyot* himself names him so. Kyot was called *la schanti-ure**—he whose art has not spared him from so singing and speak-ing* that plenty still rejoice at it. Kyot is a Provençal, he who saw this adventure of Parzival written down in heathen tongue. What he told of it *en franzoys*,* if I am not slow of wit, I shall pass on in German.

417 Then Prince Liddamus said: 'What is he doing in my lord's castle, he who slew his father and brought disgrace so close upon him? If my lord is acknowledged as noble, his own hand will avenge it here. Thus one death will pay for the other. I believe these extremities to be equal.'

Now you see how Gawan stood then. Only now did great peril make his acquaintance.

Then Kingrimursel said: 'Any man so quick with threats ought also to hasten into battle. Whether you are closely pressed, or in the open field, it is easy enough to defend oneself against *you*, Sir Liddamus. I have full confidence that I can protect this man against you. Whatever he might have done to you, you'd leave it unavenged. You have spoken entirely out of turn. It may be readily believed of you that never did man's eyes see you in the forefront where battle was waged. Fighting was always so averse to you, I believe, that you took to flight. You were capable of yet more: wherever men pressed forward into battle, you beat a woman's retreat. Any king who trusts in your counsel is wearing his crown

418 most crookedly. In the ring here, my hands were to have done battle against Gawan the valorous warrior. I had undertaken with him that

the duel was to take place here, if my lord had only permitted it. He bears, for his sins, my enmity. I hoped for better things of him. Sir Gawan, swear to me in truth that you, a year's time from today, will answer to me in combat, if it so happens that my lord spares your life here. There battle will be granted you by me—I challenged you by the Plimizœl—let the duel now be at Barbigœl, before King Meljanz. I'll wear sorrows for my garland until that day of trial comes when I meet you in the ring. There your valorous hand must make me acquainted with anxiety.'

Gawan, rich in courage, courteously offered his oath in compliance with this request. Then Duke Liddamus had words at the ready, beginning his speech as follows, cunningly worded, in the hearing of all present. He said, it being his turn to speak: 'Whenever I enter 419 battle, if I engage in fighting there, or in flight to my misfortune, whether I am a daunted coward, or if I win fame there, Sir Landgrave, thank me as you know how to take my measure. Even if I never receive your payment for it, I shall, nonetheless, enjoy my own favour.'

Mighty Liddamus spoke as follows: 'If you would be Sir Turnus, then let me be Sir Tranzes,* and scold me if you know a reason why, and do not be overhaughty. Even if you be, among my princely peers, the noblest and highest, I too am a lord and land's master. I possess many a castle in various parts of Galicia, as far as Vedrun.* For all the harm you and any Briton* might do me there, I'd never hide a single hen from you!

'He whom you have challenged to combat has come here from Britain. Now avenge your lord and kinsman. You must leave me out of your quarrel. Your father's brother—you were his subject— whoever took his life, avenge it upon him! I did him no harm. I 420 believe no-one accuses me of it, either. I shall overcome my grief for your uncle easily enough. His son is to wear the crown after him; he is sufficiently exalted to be my lord. Queen Flurdamurs gave birth to him; his father was Kingrisin, his grandfather King Gandin. I will tell you still more: Gahmuret and Galoes were his uncles. Rather than malign him, I would accept with due honours my lands, with banners, from his hand.

'Whoever desires to fight, let him do so. If I am slow to do battle, I still enjoy hearing tales about it.* If a man wins fame in battle, let proud women thank him for it. I have no desire to be led astray for anyone's sake into all too severe torment. What kind of Wolfhart* would I make? My road to battle is barred by ditches, my desire to fight hooded over.* Even if it never won your favour, I would rather act like Rumolt,* who gave King Gunther his advice when he left Worms to go to the Huns—he urged him to baste long cutlets and turn them round in the cauldron.'

421   The landgrave, rich in courage, replied: 'You talk like the man many have, in all truth, known you to be all your days and all your years. You advise me to go where I wanted to in any case, and yet you say you act like that cook who advised the bold Nibelungs, who set off, undeterred, for where vengeance was wrought upon them for what had happened to Siegfried in the past. Either Sir Gawan must slay me, or I shall teach him vengeance's extremity.'

'I'll go along with that,' said Liddamus, 'only, all that his uncle Arthur possesses, and those of India—if anyone were to give me here all that they have there, if anyone were to bring it to me, without ties, I'd give it all up rather than fight. Keep, now, whatever fame you are accorded. I'm no Segramors,* who has to be tied up to stop him fighting. I shall earn a king's greeting well enough in my own way. Sibeche never drew sword; he was always among those who fled. Still, people had to come to him cap in hand; he received great gifts and huge fiefs in plenty from Ermenrich,* although he never pierced helmet with sword. Never will my hide be harmed by you,
422   Sir Kingrimursel. That is my considered opinion of you.'

Then King Vergulaht said: 'Enough of this repartee! It burdens me that you are both so free with words. You are too near my presence by far for such banter. It becomes neither me nor you!'

This took place up in the great hall, where his sister had now arrived. Next to her stood Sir Gawan and many another noble knight. The king said to his sister: 'Now take away your companion, and the landgrave, too. Those who wish me well shall go with me and advise what it is most seemly for me to do.'

She replied: 'Add your good faith to that balance!'

Now the king goes to his counsel. The queen has taken with her her kinsman's son and her guest—and as a third her anxiety's burden. Without any misdemeanour she took Gawan by the hand and led him to where she wished to be. She said to him: 'If you had not survived, all lands would have lost by it!' Hand in hand with the queen walked noble Lot's son. He had good reason to be delighted to do so.

Then the queen and the two men walked into the chamber. It 423
remained empty of others—chamberlains saw to that—except that
lustrous little damsels must needs be there in abundance. Courte-
ously the queen attended to Gawan, who lay close to her heart. The
landgrave was present, but did not hinder her at all in this. Yet that
noble maiden was most anxious about Gawan, I was told. Thus the
two remained there in the chamber with the queen, until day yielded
its battle. Night came—then it was time to eat. Mulberry-juice, wine,
clary were brought by damsels slender about the waist, and other
good food: pheasant, partridges, good fish, and white rolls. Gawan
and Kingrimursel had emerged from great extremity. Since the
queen commanded it, they ate as they ought, as did others who so
desired. Antikonie cut their food for them herself. For courtesy's
sake that grieved them both. Of all the kneeling cup-bearers that
were to be seen there, not one's trouser-belt was split—they were 424
maidens, of such season as are still reckoned the best years. I would
not be discomposed if they had moulted,* like a falcon shedding its
plumage—to that I would raise no objection!

Now hear, before the council disbanded, what they advised that
country's king. He had gathered the wise about him—to his council
they had come. One or other of them spoke his mind, as his best
intelligence vouchsafed him. They turned things over this way and
that. The king asked that his own voice might also be heard. He said:
'I have met with battle. I came riding in search of adventure into the
woodland of Læhtamris.* A knight saw far too high renown this week
at my expense, for he thrust me in flight behind my charger, wasting
no time. He forced from me a vow to procure the Grail for him. Even
if I were to die in the cause, I must fulfil the oath his hand won from
me in battle. Now give counsel—there is need. My best shield against
death was for my hand to offer the vow, as my words have here made
known to you. He lords over valour and courage. That warrior gave 425
me further commands: that I, with no deception or duplicity, within
a year's time, if I should not obtain the Grail, should then go to
her who is accorded Pelrapeire's crown—her father was called
Tampenteire—and as soon as my eyes should see her, should offer
her surrender. He sent her this message: if she were to think of him,
that would be to the profit of his joys, and that it was he who had
freed her before from King Clamide.'

When they had heard this speech, Liddamus spoke up again:

'With these lords' leave I now speak—they advise to the same end: let Sir Gawan here be the pledge for all which that one man exacted of you—he is fluttering in your cleft stick.* Ask him to vow before us all that he will procure the Grail for you. Let him ride from you here in all amity and fight for the Grail. We would all have to lament the disgrace if he were slain in your castle. Now, forgive him his guilt, for

426 the sake of your sister's favour. He's suffered great extremity here and must now head for death. No matter what land the sea surrounds, never was a castle so well defended as Munsalvæsche. Wherever it stands, it is a rough path of battle that leads there. Let him rest in comfort tonight. Let him be told tomorrow of this counsel.' All the counsellors agreed to this. Thus Sir Gawan kept his life there.

They took such care of the undaunted warrior that night there, I was told, that his repose was of the very best. When mid-morning was seen and mass had been sung, there was a great press in the palace of rabble and of noble folk. The king did as he was advised. He commanded that Gawan be brought in. He desired to exact nothing of him other than what you yourselves have heard. See now where well-favoured Antikonie escorted him in; her uncle's son came in with her, and others of the king's subjects in plenty. The queen led Gawan by the hand before the king. A garland was her headdress. Her mouth took fame away from the flowers. None in the

427 garland grew anywhere near as red. If she graciously offered her kiss to anyone, the wood would have no choice but to be laid waste by many uncounted jousts! With praise we must now greet chaste and sweet Antikonie, free of falsity, for she lived according to such precepts that in no respect was her fame ridden down by false words. The mouths of all those who heard of her fame wished for her then that her fame might continue to be thus preserved against false mirky report. Pure, far-reaching as a falcon-gaze, was the balsam-like constancy she possessed.

As her noble desire advised, that sweet maiden, rich in blessings, spoke courteously: 'Brother, here I bring the warrior to whom you yourself ordered me to attend. Now let him profit by me—that ought not to offend you. Think on your brotherly loyalty and do this without regret. Manly loyalty befits you better than that you should suffer the world's hatred—and mine, if I could hate—teach me to moderate it towards you!'

428   Then the noble, gentle king replied: 'That I will do, sister, if I can.

Give me your own counsel in this matter. It seems to you that misdeed
has flown beneath* my honour, thrusting me away from fame. What
use would I then be to you as a brother? For even if all crowns served
me, I would renounce them at your command. Your enmity would be
my greatest extremity. Joy and honour are indifferent to me, except
as you instruct. Sir Gawan, I would put to you this request—you
came riding here in search of fame. Now do this for fame's favour:
help me to the end that my sister forgives my fault. Rather than lose
her, I renounce my heart's anger towards you, if you will give me
your oath that you will at once seek in good faith to win the Grail.'

There and then the truce was concluded, and Gawan sent at once
to strive for the Grail. Kingrimursel also forgave the king who had
before repudiated him by breaching his safe-conduct. In the pre-
sence of all the princes this took place. There their swords had been   429
hung—they had been seized from them, from Gawan's squires, in
fighting's hour, to prevent any of them being wounded.* An influen-
tial man from the town, who had asked for a truce for them against
the others, had taken them captive and put them in prison. Whether
they were Frenchmen or Britons, sturdy squires or slender pages,
from whatever countries they had come, they were then brought,
freed unconditionally, to Gawan, rich in courage. When the youths
espied him, great embracing took place there, each clinging, weep-
ing, to him. Those tears were, however, shed for joy. *Cons* Liaz *fîz*
Tinas of Cornwall was with him there. A noble page also accom-
panied him, *duk* Gandiluz *fîz* Gurzgri, who lost his life in the cause
of Schoydelacurt,* where many a lady met with misery. Liaze was that
youth's aunt. His mouth, his eyes and his nose were truly of Love's
grain—all the world beheld him gladly. There were six other little
pages, too. These eight young lords of his were of guaranteed high
birth, all of high, noble lineage. They were fond of him because of   430
kinship and served him for his pay. He gave them distinction as a
reward, and tended them well besides.

Gawan said to his little pages: 'Bless you, gentle kinsmen of mine!
It seems to me you would have mourned for me if I had been slain
here!' Indeed, grief might well have been expected of them. As it
was, they were in despond's slough. He said: 'I was most anxious
about you. Where were you when they fought with me?' They told
him, not one of them denying it: 'A moulted merlin* flew away from
us while you were sitting with the queen—we all ran off in pursuit.'

Those who stood and sat there, not neglecting observation, marked that Sir Gawan was a valorous, courtly man. He then asked for leave, which the king granted, and the people in general, with the sole exception of the landgrave. The queen took those two aside, along with Gawan's young lordlings. She led them to where they were tended by damsels, with no squabbling. They were well cared for there with courtesy by many a well-favoured damsel.

431   When Gawan had eaten—I tell you the story as Kyot read it—out of heartfelt loyalty great sorrow arose there. He said to the queen: 'Lady, if I am of sound wit and if God preserves me, then I must always devote to your service and to your womanly kindness, my servitor's travels and chivalrous mind. For Fortune has known how to teach you to conquer falsity—your fame outweighs all other fame. May Fortune grant you bliss! Lady, I desire to ask leave. Grant it me, and let me go. May your courtesy preserve your fame!'

His parting grieved her. Then there wept, to keep her company, many a lustrous damsel. The queen said in all sincerity: 'If you had profited more by me, my joy would have lorded it over my sorrows. As it is, there could be no better truce for you. Believe me, though, whenever you suffer torment, if chivalry leads you into grievous troubles' power, know then, my lord Gawan, you must be in my
432 heart's keeping, whether loss or profit ensue.' The noble queen kissed Gawan's mouth. He grew weak in joy at having to ride so hastily from her. I believe it grieved them both.

His squires had seen to it that his horses had been brought into the courtyard outside the great hall, where the lime-tree gave shade. The landgrave's companions had also arrived—so I heard tell—he rode with him out beyond the town. Gawan asked him courteously to take the trouble to escort his retinue to Bearosche: 'Scherules is there. They themselves must ask him for escort to Dianazdrun, where several Britons live who will take them to my lord, or to Guinevere the Queen.'

Kingrimursel promised him as much. The bold warrior took his leave. Gringuljete was armed at once then, the charger, as was my lord Gawan. He kissed his kinsmen, the little pages, and also his noble squires. His oath commanded him to pursue the Grail. He rode, all alone, towards wondrous peril.

BOOK IX

'OPEN up!'   433

To whom? Who are you?

'I want go into your heart.'

That's a narrow space you want to enter!

'What of it, even if I barely survive! You'll seldom have cause to complain of *my* jostling! I want to tell you of wonders now!'

Oh, it's you, is it, Lady Adventure? How fares the comely knight—I mean noble Parzival, whom Cundrie, with ungentle words, chased in pursuit of the Grail, when many a lady lamented that his journey was not averted? It was from Arthur the Briton that he then set off. How does he fare now? Take up those tales: is he daunted of joys, or has he won high fame? Is his unimpaired honour both long and broad, or is it short and narrow? Read us the reckoning, now, of what has happened at his hands. Has he seen Munsalvæsche since, and gentle Anfortas, whose heart was then full of sighs? By your kindness grant us hope that he may be redeemed from misery. Let us hear the tales! Has Parzival been there—your lord as well as   434 mine? Enlighten me now as to his progress—sweet Herzeloyde's child—how has Gahmuret's son fared since he rode away from Arthur? Has he won joy or heart's sorrow by battle since? Is he still roaming far and wide, or has he since fallen into sloth?* Tell me his ways and all he has done.

Now the adventure makes known to us that he had traversed many lands on horseback, and in ships upon the waves. Unless it were a fellow-countryman or kinsman who aimed the joust's charge at him, none ever retained his seat. Thus his weighted scale can sink, his own fame rising and teaching others to fall. In many fierce fights he has defied defeat, so spent himself in battle that anyone desirous of borrowing fame from him would have to do so with trepidation. His sword, which Anfortas had given him when he was in the presence of the Grail, broke afterwards, when he was attacked. Then the art of the spring near Karnant, which is called Lac, made it whole again. That sword has helped him in fame's pursuit. Anyone who doesn't   435 believe this is a sinner.

The adventure tells us that Parzival, the bold warrior, came riding to a forest—I don't know at what hour. There his eyes found a hermit's cell standing, of recent build, through which a quick spring flowed. On the one side the cell had been built over the brook. The young warrior, unafraid, rode in pursuit of adventure. God then deigned to take his part. He found a hermitess, who for the love of God had renounced her maidenhood and her joy. Womanly sorrows' source blossomed ever anew from her heart, although old loyalty was the cause.

Schionatulander and Sigune he found there. The warrior lay dead, buried within. Her life suffered anguish, bent over his coffin. *Doschesse* Sigune rarely heard mass, yet her whole life was a genuflection. Her full lips, hot, red-hued, had by now become pallid and pale, for worldly joy had entirely deserted her. Never did maiden suffer such great torment. In order to mourn she must be all alone.

436   Because of the love that died with him, the prince not having won her hand, she loved his dead body. If she *had* become his wife, Lady Lunete* would have hesitated to voice such a rash entreaty as when she counselled her mistress. You can still see Lady Lunetes often, riding headlong into some overhasty counsel or other. If any woman now, out of loving companionship and good breeding, refrains from cultivating love elsewhere—as I understand it—if she desists from this in her husband's lifetime, he has been granted perfection in her. No waiting becomes her as well. I shall prove that if I must. After his death, let her do as she may be instructed. If, nonetheless, she preserves her honour, then she will wear no garland as bright if she goes dancing in pursuit of joy.*

Why do I measure joy against such anguish as Sigune's loyalty commanded of her? I ought rather to refrain. Over fallen tree-trunks, taking no roads, Parzival rode past the window, much too close—to his regret.* Then he thought to ask about the forest, or which way his
437   journey was leading him. He requested converse there: 'Is anyone within?'

She said: 'Yes.'

When he heard that it was a lady's voice, he wheeled his charger away in all haste, onto untrodden grass. It seemed far too late to him! He smarted for very shame that he had not dismounted earlier.

He tied the charger securely to a fallen tree-trunk's branch, hanging his hole-riddled shield on it, too. When that chaste, bold man had, out of courtesy, unbuckled his sword, he walked up to the window, by the wall; there he wished to ask for tidings. The cell was devoid of joy and bare of all mirth. He found nothing there but great grief. He asked her to come to the window. The damsel, pale of complexion, courteously rose from her genuflection. As yet he had no idea who she was or might be. She wore a hair shirt next to her skin, beneath a grey dress. Great sorrow was her confidante. That had laid her high spirits low, raising much sighing from her heart. Courteously the maiden went to the window. With gentle words she welcomed him. She carried a psalter in her hand. Parzival the war- 438 rior espied a little ring there, which, intent on hardship, she had never lost, preserving it as true love counselled her. Its little stone was a garnet; its gleam shone out of the darkness just like a little fiery spark. Her headdress* was sorrowful. 'Out there by the wall, sir,' she said, 'there stands a bench. Be so kind as to sit down, if your thoughts so instruct you and your affairs permit. That I have come to meet with your greeting here—may God reward you for it! He repays loyal usage.'

The warrior did not neglect her counsel, but sat down outside the window. He asked her to take a seat, too, inside. She said: 'Well, I've seldom sat next to any man here.'

The warrior began to ask her about her ways and sustenance: 'Residing as you do so far away from the track in this wilderness, it is beyond my imagining, lady, how you live, as no habitation stands nearby.'

She said: 'My meals come here from the Grail, with no delay whatever. Cundrie la Surziere brings me my food promptly from 439 there, every Saturday night—she has taken it upon herself—all I need for the whole week.' She went on: 'If I were happy in other respects, I would care little about my nourishment. I am provided with that in plenty.'

Then Parzival thought she might be lying, and inclined to deceive him in other respects. He said in jest to her, through the window: 'For whose sake do you wear that ring? I have always heard tell that hermitesses and hermits ought to avoid amours.'

She said: 'If your speech had the power, you would gladly prove me false. If I ever do learn falseness, then reproach me for it, if you are present. God willing, I am free of falsity. I am incapable of imposture.' She went on: 'This betrothal-ring I wear for the sake of a dear man whose love I never embraced by human deed. A maidenly heart's counsels counsel me love for him.'

She said: 'I keep him here within—he whose token I have worn
440 ever since Orilus's joust slew him. All my wretched years' seasons I will truly grant him love. I am his true love's guarantor, for he wooed with a knight's hands, both with shield and spear, to that end, until he died in my service. My maidenhood I retain, unmarried. He is, however, my husband before God. If thoughts are to bring about deeds, then I bear no hiding-place anywhere that might fly between* my marriage. His death brought affliction upon my life. This ring of true wedlock must be my escort into God's presence. It is a seal upon my loyalty, my eyes' flood from my heart. There are two of us inside here—Schionatulander is the one, I the other.'

Parzival then realized that it was Sigune. Her troubles weighed heavy with him. The warrior then hesitated little, but bared his head from his coif before he spoke to her. The damsel perceived, through the iron's rust, his very fair skin; then she recognized the bold warrior. She said: 'It's you, Sir Parzival! Tell me, how stands it with you
441 as regards the Grail? Have you determined its nature yet? Or where is your journey directed?'

He said to the well-born maiden: 'There I lost much joy. The Grail gives me ample sorrow. I abandoned a land where I wore the crown, and the most lovely woman. Never on this earth was such beauty born of human fruit. I long for her chaste courtesy. For love of her I am deeply sorrowful, and still more so because of the high goal—how I may come to see Munsalvæsche and the Grail. That is as yet unfulfilled. Cousin Sigune, you act cruelly in scolding me, knowing as you do my troubles to be manifold.'

The maiden said: 'Let all my vengeance upon you, cousin, be renounced! You did, indeed, lose much joy when you permitted yourself to delay with the noble question, and when gentle Anfortas was your host and your fortune. Questioning there would have won you bliss. Now your joy must needs be daunted and all your high spirits lamed. Your heart has tamed sorrow, which would be most wild and estranged from you, had you asked for tidings then.'

442 'I acted like a born loser,' he said. 'Dear cousin, give me counsel, consider the true kinship between us, and tell me also, how do things stand with you? I ought to bemoan your grief, except that I bear loftier troubles than any man ever bore before. My anguish is too out of joint.'

She said: 'Now may His hand help you, to whom all troubles are known. Perhaps you may so far succeed that a trail may take you to where you will see Munsalvæsche, where you tell me your happiness lies. Cundrie la Surziere rode away from here very recently. I am sorry that I did not ask whether she was headed there or elsewhere. Whenever she comes, her mule stands there, where the spring emerges from the rock. I advise that you ride after her. Perhaps she is not in such a hurry ahead of you that you may quickly catch up with her.'

Then there was no further waiting. The warrior immediately took his leave, heading after the fresh trail. Cundrie's mule had taken such a route that unpathed land cut him off from the trail he had chosen. Thus the Grail was lost again. All his joy he then forgot. I believe he would have questioned further, if he had arrived at Munsalvæsche, than he did as you heard before. 443

Now let him ride. Where is he to go? A man came riding towards him there. His head was bare, his surcoat of great expense, the armour beneath white in colour. Except for his head he was fully armed. He rode towards Parzival at speed. Then he said: 'Lord, I am aggrieved that you thus make your passage through my lord's forest! You will be quickly issued with such a rebuke that your spirits will repine. Munsalvæsche is not accustomed to have anyone ride so near it, unless it be one who fights perilously, or offers such atonement as they call death outside this forest.'

He carried a helmet in his hand whose ties were strings of silk, and a sharp spearhead, its shaft quite new. The warrior, urged on by anger, tied his helmet squarely on his head. His threatening and fighting were to cost him dear on this occasion. Nonetheless, he readied himself for the joust. Parzival had also used up many shields at similar cost. He thought: 'I would not go unpunished if I rode over this man's seed.* How could his anger then be avoided? But here I am treading on the wild bracken! Unless my hands and both my arms fail me, I shall give such a pledge for my journey that his hand shall not bind me at all!' 444

On both sides they did the same, letting their chargers loose into the gallop, driving them on with their spurs, leading them firmly into the tilt's charge. Neither's joust missed the mark there. Parzival's high chest was a counterpin to many a joust. His skill and impulse taught him to direct his joust evenly, straight in at the knot of the helmet-cords. He hit him where the shield is hung high when chivalry's game is played, so that the templar* of Munsalvæsche tumbled from his charger into a gully, so far down—it was so deep—that his bed slept little there.

Parzival followed on in the direction of the joust. His charger was 445 overhasty. It plunged down, shattering every bone. Parzival grasped a cedar branch with his hands. Now don't count it a disgrace on his part that he hung himself without a hangman! With his feet he found a foothold on the rock's firm ground beneath him. In the great pathless land below his charger lay dead. The templar hastened away from the calamity, up the other side of the gully. If he'd wanted to share the profit he'd won by Parzival, then the Grail back home would have given him a better deal!

Parzival climbed back up. The reins had sunk to the ground. The charger had trampled through them, as if it had been asked to wait there—the charger forgotten by that knight there. Once Parzival had mounted it, nothing but his spear was lost—that loss was cancelled out by the find. In my belief, neither mighty Lähelin, nor proud Kingrisin, nor *roys* Gramoflanz, nor *cons* Lascoyt *fiz* Gurnemanz ever rode a better joust than when that charger was won in battle. Parzival rode on then—he didn't know where, but the Munsalvæsche company avoided all further battle with him. The Grail's remoteness grieved him.

446   If anyone is inclined to hear it, I'll tell him how things stood with him subsequently. I can't count the number of weeks during which Parzival afterwards rode in pursuit of adventure as before. One morning there was thin snow, it having snowed, however, so thickly, I suppose, as still gives people the feel of frost. It had fallen upon a huge forest. Towards him came walking an aged knight, whose beard was entirely grey, although his skin was bright and radiant. His wife had the same hue. Both wore, over bare bodies, grey, coarse cloaks, on their confession's path. His daughters, two damsels, a sight to gladden the eye, walked in the same garb there, as chaste heart's counsel advised them. They all walked barefoot. Parzival offered his greeting to the grey knight walking there. By his counsel he afterwards won good fortune. He might well gave been a lord. Ladies' little bercelets ran alongside there. With gentle demeanour, not overhaughty, other knights and squires were walking there, decorously, on God's journey, enough of them so young as to be entirely beardless.

Parzival, the noble warrior, had so attended to his person that his 447
rich accoutrements were of wholly knightly aspect. He rode in
armour that bore little resemblance to the clothes worn by the grey
man coming towards him. By the bridle he at once wheeled the
charger away from the path. Then his questioning took scrutiny of
those good people's journey. By gentle speech he learned their pur-
pose. Then the grey knight lamented that those hallowed days did
not help him to embrace the custom of riding unarmed, or walking
barefoot and observing that day's season.

Parzival replied to him: 'Sir, I do not know one way or the other
how the year's juncture stands, nor how the weeks' count advances.
How the days are named is all unknown to me. I used to serve one
who is called God, before His favour imposed such scornful disgrace
upon me—never did my mind waver from Him of whose help I had
been told. Now His help has failed me.'

Then the grey-hued knight said: 'Do you mean God, whom the 448
Virgin bore? If you believe in His humanity, what He on this very
day suffered for our sake, as is commemorated on this day's occasion,
then your armour ill becomes you. Today is Good Friday, because of
which all the world may rejoice, and at the same time sigh in
anguish. Where was greater loyalty ever shown than that which God
manifested for our sake—He whom they hung on the Cross for us?
Sir, if you practise baptism's faith, then grieve for that purchase. He
gave His noble life, by His death, for our guilt, by which mankind
had been doomed, allotted to Hell because of guilt. If you are no
heathen, then think, lord, upon this season. Ride on, on our trail. Not
too far ahead of you resides a holy man. He will give you counsel,
penance for your misdeed. If you wish to tell him of your contrition,
he will part you from sins.'

His daughters started to speak: 'What wrong do you wish to
avenge, father? Such evil weather as we now have—what counsel do
you presume to offer him? Why don't you take him to where he can 449
get warm? His iron-clad arms, however knightly they are shaped, it
seems to us, nevertheless, that they are cold. He would freeze, even if
there were three of him! You have standing close by here your pavil-
ion and slavin's* store. Even if King Arthur himself were to come to
you, you would keep him well supplied with food. Now do as a host
ought, take this knight along with you!'

Then the grey knight said: 'Sir, my daughters speak nothing but the truth. Near here, every year, I journey to this wild wood, whether it be hot or cold, always about His Martyrdom's time—He who gives constant reward for service. What food I have brought from home with me, in God's name, I will certainly share with you.'

With a will the damsels pressed him to stay—and it would have been to his honour to remain there—each of them said as much, sincerely. Parzival observed, looking at them, that no matter how rare, because of the frost, sweat was there, their mouths were red, full, hot—they were in no languishing state, unlike that day's season. 450 If I were to avenge some small matter there, I would unwillingly forgo fetching a kiss of reconciliation from them—provided they were to assent to such a truce. Women are, let's face it, always women. They are quick to conquer a valiant man's person. Such success has often befallen them.

Parzival, turning this way and that, listened to their gentle words of entreaty—the father's, mother's, and the daughters'. He thought: 'Even if I stop here, I'm unwilling to walk in this company. These maidens are so well-favoured that my riding alongside them would be unfitting, since man and woman are on foot* here. My parting from them is more seemly, since I bear enmity towards Him whom they love from their hearts, and they hope for help from Him who has barred His help from me, and not spared me sorrows.'

Parzival then said to them: 'Lord and lady, let me have your leave. May Fortune grant you salvation, and joy's full portion. You sweet damsels, may your courtesy thank you for wishing me good comfort. 451 I must have your leave to depart.' He bowed, and the others bowed. Their lament was not suppressed there.

Away rides Herzeloyde's fruit. His manly courtesy counselled him chastity and pity. Because the young Herzeloyde had bequeathed loyalty to him, his heart's contrition arose. For the first time he then thought about who had perfected all the world, about his Creator, how potent He was. He said: 'What if God has at His disposal such help as may vanquish my sadness? If He ever grew well-disposed towards a knight—if a knight ever earned His reward—or if shield and sword may prove so worthy of His help, and true manly valour, that His help may protect me from sorrows—if today is His helpful day, then let Him help, if help He may!'

He turned back in the direction from which he had ridden. They were still standing there, grieving that he had headed away from them. It was their loyalty taught them that lesson. The damsels were still following him with their eyes. His heart also averred that he was glad to look upon them, for their radiance spoke of their beauty.

He said: 'If God's power is so sublime that it can guide both   452
horses and beasts, and people, too, I will praise His power. If God's skill possesses such help, let it direct this Castilian of mine along the best road for my journey. Then His goodness will indeed make help manifest. Now go as God chooses!'

He laid the reins over the charger's ears, pricking it hard with the spurs. It walked towards Fontane la Salvatsche,* where Orilus had taken the oath. Chaste Trevrizent resided there, he who ate ill on many a Monday, as he did the whole week long. He had renounced entirely mulberry juice, wine, and bread, too. His chastity commanded still more of him: he had no inclination for such food—neither fish nor meat—as might bear blood. Such was his hallowed way of life. God had given him that intent. That lord was making all possible preparations to join the heavenly host. By fasting, he suffered great distress. His chastity strove against the Devil.

From him Parzival will now learn the hidden tidings concerning the Grail. Whoever asked me about this before and squabbled with   453
me for not telling him about it has won infamy by it. It was Kyot who asked me to conceal it, for the adventure commanded him that no-one should ever think of it until the adventure took it, through words, to meet the stories' greeting—so that now it *has*, after all, to be spoken of.

Kyot, the renowned scholar, found in Toledo,* lying neglected, in heathen script, this adventure's fundament. The a b c of those characters he must have learned beforehand, without the art of necromancy. It helped that baptism dwelt with him, or else this tale would still be unheard. No heathen cunning could avail us to tell about the Grail's nature—how its mysteries were perceived.

A heathen, Flegetanis, had won high fame by his skills. That same visionary was born of Solomon's line, begotten of age-old Israelite stock, before baptism became our shield against hell-fire. He wrote about the Grail's adventure. He was a heathen on his father's side,   454
Flegetanis, worshipping a calf as if it were his god. How can the Devil inflict such mockery upon such wise people, without Him who bears the Highest Hand parting them, or having parted them from such practice—He to whom all marvels are known?

Flegetanis the heathen knew well how to impart to us each star's departure and its arrival's return—how long each revolves before it stands back at its station. By the stars' circuit's journey all human nature is determined. Flegetanis the heathen saw with his own eyes—modestly though he spoke of this—occult mysteries in the constellation. He said there was a thing called the Grail, whose name he read immediately in the constellation—what it was called: 'A host abandoned it upon the earth, flying up, high above the stars. Was it their innocence drew them back? Ever since, baptized fruit has had to tend it with such chaste courtesy—those human beings are always worthy whose presence is requested by the Grail.'

455   Thus Flegetanis wrote of it. Kyot, that wise scholar, began to seek for those tidings in Latin books, of where there had been a people fitting to tend the Grail and embrace such chastity. He read the chronicles of the lands, those of Britain and elsewhere, of France and Ireland. In Anjou he found the tidings. He read there the whole, undoubted truth concerning Mazadan. A true account of all his lineage was written there, and how, on the other side, Titurel and his son, Frimutel, bequeathed the Grail to Anfortas, whose sister was Herzeloyde, by whom Gahmuret gained that son of whom these tales tell.

He is riding, now, along the fresh trail made by the grey knight who had walked towards him. He recognized one particular place, although snow lay where bright flowers had grown before. It was by that mountain's wall where his valorous hand had won favour for
456   Lady Jeschute, and where Orilus's anger perished. The trail did not permit him to halt there. Fontane la Salvatsche was the name of the dwelling to which his journey led. He found the host, who welcomed him.

The hermit said to him: 'Alas, sir, that such things have befallen you at this hallowed time! Was it perilous battle forced you into this armour? Or have you remained without battle? In that case, different garb would become you better, if arrogance's counsel were to abandon you. Now be so good as to dismount, lord—I doubt if that will trouble you at all—and warm yourself by a fire. If adventure has sent you forth in pursuit of love's reward—if true love is dear to you— then love such Love as is now in season, as becomes this day's Love. Serve afterwards for women's greeting. Be so kind as to dismount, if I may ask as much.'

Parzival the warrior dismounted at once, standing before him with great courtesy. He told him of the people who had directed him there—how they had praised his counsel. Then he said: 'Sir, now give me counsel. I am a man who possesses sin.'

When these words had been spoken, the good man replied: 'I am 457 your guarantor of counsel. Now tell me, who directed you here?'

'Sir, in the forest a grey man walked towards me, who welcomed me warmly, as did his household. That same man, free of falsity, has sent me to you here. I rode along his trail until I found you.'

His host said: 'That was Kahenis. He is most wise in worthy conduct. That prince is a Punturteis. The mighty King of Kareis has married his sister. Never was more chaste fruit born of mankind than his daughters, who walked towards you there. The prince is of a king's lineage. Every year he makes his journey to me here.'

Parzival said to his host: 'When I saw you standing before me, were you at all afraid when I rode up to you? Did my approach not trouble you at all?'

The hermit replied: 'Lord, believe me, the bear, and the stag too, have startled me more often than man. One thing I can truly tell you: I don't fear anything that is human. I too possess human cunning. If 458 you won't think it boasting, I am still a virgin when it comes to fleeing. My heart never felt such weakness that I ducked defence. In my combative time I was a knight as you are, also striving for lofty love. There was a time when I pied sinful thoughts with chastity. I adorned* my life in the hope that a woman would grant me her favour. That I have now forgotten.

'Hand me your bridle. There under that rock's wall your charger shall stand, to take its ease. After a while we'll both go and pick fir-twigs and bracken for it. For other fodder I am poorly off, but we'll feed it pretty well, I imagine.'

Parzival was reluctant to let him take hold of the bridle.

'Your courtesy will not permit you to contend against any host, if uncouthness shuns your good breeding,' said the good man. The bridle was yielded to the host. He led the horse below the rock, where the sun seldom shone in. That was a wild stable. Through it passed a spring's fall.

Parzival stood in the snow. A weakling would have felt it hard, 459 wearing armour with the frost so assailing him. The host led him into a cave, where the wind's gust seldom entered. There glowing coals lay. The guest had little objection to those! The host's hand lit a candle. Then the warrior disarmed himself. Beneath him lay purple moorgrass and bracken. All his limbs grew warm, his skin giving off a bright sheen. He had good cause to be wood-weary, for he had ridden few roads, waiting without shelter that night for day to come, as he had many another night. A faithful host he found there.

A cloak lay there, which his host lent him to put on, and then he led him off into a second cave, in which were the books which the chaste hermit read. According to that day's custom an altar-stone stood there, quite bare.* Upon it a reliquary was to be seen. That was soon recognized. Upon it Parzival's hand had sworn an unfalsified oath, by which Lady Jeschute's suffering had been converted to joy, and her happiness magnified.

460 Parzival said to his host: 'Lord, this reliquary's appearance I recognize, for I swore an oath upon it once, when I rode past it here. A painted spear I found next to it. Sir, it was my hand took it on this very spot. With it I won fame, as I was afterwards told. I was so deep in thoughts of my own wife that I lost my wits. Two splendid jousts I rode with that lance. Unwittingly I fought them both. Then I still had honour. Now I have more sorrows than were ever seen in a man. By your courtesy, tell me how long it is since the time, sir, that I took that spear from here?'

Then the good man replied: 'My friend Taurian forgot it and left it here. He later bemoaned its loss to me. It's four and a half years and three days since you took it from him here. If you'd like to hear it, I'll tell you the reckoning.' By the psalter* he read to him all the years, and the full count of the weeks that had passed in the meantime.

461 'Only now do I realize how long I have been travelling, without guidance, and ignored by joy's help,' said Parzival. 'To me joy is a dream. I carry grief's heavy pack. Lord, I shall tell you yet more: wherever churches or minsters stood, where God's honour was pronounced, no eye has ever seen me since that same time. I've sought nothing but battle. And I bear God much enmity, for He is my sorrows' godfather. Those he has lifted all too high above the font. My joy is buried alive. If God's power could afford help, what an anchor my joy would be! Yet it sinks through grief's ground. If my manly heart is wounded—and can it indeed remain whole, since grief sets its thorny crown upon such honour as the shield's office has won for me against valorous hands?—then I count it as a disgrace

on the part of Him who has power over all help—if His help is quick
to help, that He does not then help me, when such great help is
avowed of Him.'

The host sighed and looked at him. Then he said: 'Sir, if you are
sensible, then you ought to trust well in God. He will help you, for
help He must. May God help us both. Sir, you must inform me—but   462
first be so kind as to sit down—tell me in sober mind how that anger
arose by which God won your enmity. By your courtesy's patience,
hear from me of His innocence, before you accuse Him of anything
before me. His help has ever been undaunted.

'Although I was a layman, I could read and write the true books'
tidings—how man must persist in His service, hoping for great help
from Him who has never wearied of constant help to prevent the
soul's sinking. Be faithful without any deviation, for God Himself is
faithfulness. False cunning never found favour with Him. We must
let Him profit from having done much for us, for His noble, high
lineage took on man's image for our sake. God means and is the
Truth. False conduct has always grieved Him. You must ponder
deeply upon this. He's incapable of deserting anyone. Now teach
your thoughts this lesson: be on your guard against deserting Him!

'You can win nothing from Him by defiance. If anyone sees you   463
in enmity towards Him, he will think you weak of wit. Consider now
the fate that befell Lucifer and his companions. They were, after
all, without gall.* So where, lord, did they derive such malice that
their endless battle receives bitter reward in Hell? Ashtaroth and
Belcimon, Belet and Radamant,* and others known to me there—that
bright heavenly host took on Hell's colour because of their malice.

'When Lucifer had travelled Hell's road with his host, a man suc-
ceeded him.* God wrought noble Adam out of the earth. From
Adam's flesh he plucked Eve, who delivered us to hardship by ignor-
ing her Creator's command and destroying our joy. Of these two
came birth's fruit. One man was prompted by his insatiety to deprive
his grandmother of her maidenhead in his greedy pursuit of fame.
Now many are inclined, before they have heard this tale out, to ask
how that might be—nevertheless, by sin it became manifest.'

Parzival said to him in reply: 'Lord, I cannot believe that ever   464
happened. Of whom was that man born by whom his grandmother
lost her maidenhead, as you tell me? You ought to have refrained
from uttering those words!'

The host replied to him in turn: 'From that doubt I shall remove you. If I do not truly tell the truth, then may my deception offend you! The earth was Adam's mother. Adam nourished himself by the earth's fruit.* At that time the earth was as yet a maiden. Nor have I yet told you who took her maidenhead from her. Adam was Cain's father. Cain slew Abel for paltry possessions.* When the blood fell upon the pure earth, her maidenhood was forfeit. It was Adam's child took it from her. Then, for the first time, man's malice arose; it has so persisted ever since.

'Yet nothing in this world is as pure as a maiden without false wiles. See for yourself how pure maidens are! God Himself was the Maiden's child. From maidens two men are descended. God Himself took on countenance after the first maiden's fruit. That was good breeding on the part of His high lineage. From Adam's kin arose both grief and delight. Since He who is seen as superior by every angel does not deny us kinship, and since kinship is sins' cart, so that we must carry sin,* may the might of Him with whom mercy keeps company have mercy, for His faithful humanity has fought with faith against unfaith.

'You must make peace with Him, if you do not desire to lose salvation. Let penance be with you to prevail against sin. Do not be so free of speech and deeds, for if a man so avenges his wrongs that he speaks unchastely—I'll acquaint you with his reward—his own mouth condemns him. Take old tidings in preference to new, if they teach you good faith. The dialogist Plato said in his time, as did Sibyl the prophetess, without missing the mark—they said many years ago that there would undeniably come to us a pledge against the greatest debt. The Highest Hand would take us out of Hell by Divine Love. The unchaste He would leave therein.

'Of the True Lover these sweet tidings tell that He is a translucent light, and does not deviate from His love. That man to whom He makes love manifest will be well content with His love. These matters are divided: to all the world He offers for purchase both His love and His hatred. Judge now which of the two helps more. The guilty man, lacking contrition, flees divine faith, but he who atones for his sins' guilt serves to earn noble grace.

'That grace is borne by Him who passes through thoughts. Thought resists the sun's glance. Thought is barred without a lock, protected against all Creation. Thought is darkness without radiance. The

Godhead is capable of such purity that it shines through darkness's wall, and has run that concealing leap which neither makes din nor sounds out when it leaps from the heart.* There is no thought so fleet that before it emerges from the heart, beyond the skin, it has not been tested. God is well-disposed towards the chaste. Since God sees through thoughts so well, alas for His sufferance of frail deeds! When a man's deeds so forfeit His greeting that the Godhead must 467 needs be ashamed, to whom does human breeding then abandon him? Where can that wretched soul find refuge? If you now desire to offend God, who is prepared for both, for love and anger, then you are a lost man. Now alter your thoughts, so that He may thank you for your goodness.'

Parzival then said to him: 'Lord, I am eternally grateful that you have informed me about Him who leaves nothing unrewarded, neither misdeed nor virtue. I have brought my youth, amid troubles, to this day, suffering hardship out of loyalty.'

The host replied in turn: 'If you've no cause to conceal it, I'll gladly learn what troubles and sins you have. If you let me judge of them, perhaps I can give you counsel which you yourself lack.'

Parzival replied: 'My highest anxiety concerns the Grail. Next comes my own wife. Never on earth did a more beautiful person suck at any mother's breast. For both these my desire pines.'

The host said: 'Lord, you speak well. You are in rightful sorrow's 468 endurance, since it is because of your own wife that you give yourself anxiety's fostering. If you are found in true marriage, then even if you suffer in Hell, that extremity will soon be at an end, and you will be freed of those bonds by God's help, without any delay. You say you long for the Grail. You foolish youth, that I must deplore, for no-one, indeed, can gain the Grail except he who is known in Heaven to be appointed to the Grail. So much I may say of the Grail. I know it and have seen it in all truth.'

Parzival said: 'Were you there?'

The host replied to him: 'Yes, lord.'

Parzival uttered no word to him of his having also been there. He asked him for knowledge about the nature of the Grail.

The host said: 'It is well known to me that many a valorous hand resides by the Grail at Munsalvæsche. In search of adventure they constantly ride many a journey. Those same templars—wherever they meet with grief or fame, they count it against their sins. A 469 combative company dwells there. I will tell you of their food: they live by a stone whose nature is most pure. If you know nothing of it, it shall be named to you here: it is called *lapsit exillis*.* By that stone's power the phoenix burns away, turning to ashes, yet those ashes bring it back to life. Thus the phoenix sheds its moulting plumage and thereafter gives off so much bright radiance that it becomes as beautiful as before. Moreover, never was a man in such pain but from that day he beholds the stone, he cannot die in the week that follows immediately after. Nor will his complexion ever decline. He will be averred to have such colour as he possessed when he saw the stone—whether it be maid or man—as when his best season commenced. If that person saw the stone for two hundred years, his hair would never turn grey. Such power does the stone bestow upon man that his flesh and bone immediately acquire youth. That stone is also called the Grail.

'Today a message will appear upon it, for therein lies its highest
470 power. Today is Good Friday, and therefore they can confidently expect a dove to wing its way from Heaven. To that stone it will take a small white wafer. On that stone it will leave it. The dove is translucently white. It will make its retreat back to Heaven. Always, every Good Friday, it takes the wafer to that stone, as I tell you; by this the stone receives everything good that bears scent on this earth by way of drink and food, as if it were the perfection of Paradise—I mean, all that this earth is capable of bringing forth. Furthermore, the stone is to grant them whatever game lives beneath the sky, whether it flies or runs or swims. To that knightly brotherhood the Grail's power gives such provender.

'As for those who are summoned to the Grail, hear how they are made known. At one end of the stone an epitaph* of characters around it tells the name and lineage of whoever is to make the blissful journey to that place. Whether it relates to maidens or boys, no-one has any need to erase that script. As soon as they have read the name, it
471 disappears before their eyes. As children they arrived in its presence, all those who are now full-grown there. Hail to the mother who bore the child that is destined to serve there! Poor and rich alike rejoice if their child is summoned there, if they are to send him to that host. They are fetched from many lands. Against sinful disgrace they are guarded for evermore, and their reward will be good in Heaven. When life perishes for them here, perfection will be granted them there.

'Those who stood on neither side when Lucifer and the Trinity began to contend, all such angels, noble and worthy, had to descend to the earth, to this same stone. The stone is forever pure. I do not know if God forgave them or whether he condemned them from that time forth. If He deemed it right, He took them back. The stone has been tended ever since by those appointed by God to the task, and to whom He sent His angel.* Sir, this is the nature of the Grail.'

Then Parzival replied: 'If chivalry can win the body's fame and, 472 nevertheless, the soul's Paradise, with shield and also with spear, then chivalry was always my desire. I fought wherever I found fighting, so that my combative hand might draw nigh fame. If God knows how to assess fighting, He ought to summon me there, so that they may acknowledge me. My hand will not forbear from battle there!'

His chaste host answered: 'You would have to be guarded against arrogance there by a humble will. Perhaps your youth has misled you into breaking with chastity's virtue. Arrogance has always sunk and fallen,' said the host. Both his eyes welled over, as he thought upon the matter he had put into words there.

Then he said: 'Lord, there was a king there who was and is still called Anfortas. You and I, poor wretch that I am, ought forever to pity his heartfelt distress, which arrogance offered him as its reward. His youth and his wealth brought sorrow to the world by him, as did his desire for love beyond chastity's intent. Such ways are not right 473 for the Grail. There knight and squire must both be guarded against haughtiness. Humility has always outfought arrogance. A noble brotherhood resides there. By their combative hands they have kept people from all lands in ignorance of Grail, except for those who are summoned there, to Munsalvæsche, to the Grail's company.

'One only arrived there unsummoned. That was a foolish youth, and he took sin away with him, too, for not speaking to the host about the anguish in which he saw him. I ought not to deride anyone, but he must pay for the sin of not asking about the host's affliction. He was so burdened with troubles that never was such great torment known. Before that *roys* Lähelin came riding to the lake at Brumbane. Intending to joust against him, Lybbeals, that noble warrior, had awaited him there. His death was determined by that joust. He was born of Prienlascors. Lähelin's hand led away that warrior's charger.* There corpse-robbery was made manifest.

474   'Lord, are you Lähelin? For in my stable stands a charger of similar
       appearance to those chargers which belong to the Grail's company;
       a turtle-dove stands on its saddle. That charger comes from
       Munsalvæsche. Those arms were given them by Anfortas when he
       was still joy's lord. Their shields have had these arms from ages past.
       Titurel bequeathed them then to his son, *rois* Frimutel. Beneath that
       device that bold warrior also lost his life by a joust. He loved his own
       wife so much that never was woman loved so intensely by man—I
       mean with true loyalty. You must renew his ways and love your
       spouse from your heart. You must hold to his ways. Your appearance
       bears the same marks as his. He was, indeed, lord over the Grail.
       Alas, sir, from where have you travelled? Be so kind, now, as to give
       me an account of your lineage.'

       Each looked hard at the other. Parzival said to his host: 'I am born
       of a man who lost his life by the joust, and because of his chivalrous
475   disposition. Sir, by your kindness, you should include him in your
       prayers. My father was called Gahmuret. He was an Angevin by
       lineage. Lord, I'm not Lähelin. If I ever resorted to corpse-robbery, I
       was weak of wit. And yet it did befall me—I must admit to that same
       sin. Ither of Kukumerlant was slain by my sin-laden hand. I laid him
       dead upon the grass, and took all that was to be taken there.'

       'Alas, world, why do you act thus?' said the host. He was unhappy
       at these tidings. 'You give people heart's wounds, and more grievous
       sorrow than joy. What reward do you offer? Thus your tale's melody
       ends!'

       Then he said: 'Dear sister-son, what advice can I give you* now?
       You have slain your own flesh and blood.* If you intend to bear this
       guilt before God—you being both of one blood—if God does right-
       ful justice there, then your life must pay for his. What compensation
       will you give Him there for Ither of Gaheviez? God made manifest in
       him true honour's usufruct, by which this world was ennobled.
476   Wrong-doing was a grief to him, he who was a balm* above loyalty.
       All wordly disgrace fled from him. Nobility made its home in his
       heart. Noble women ought to hate you for the sake of his charming
       person. His service to them was so entire that it made any woman's
       eyes shine to see him, because of his gentility. May God take pity
       that you ever brought about such a calamity! My sister also lay dead
       on your account—Herzeloyde, your mother!'

       'Oh no, good sir! What are you saying now?' said Parzival. 'Even if

I were lord over the Grail it could not compensate me for the tidings
that your mouth proclaims. If I am your sister's child, then act as
those who keep company with loyalty, and tell me, without devious
intent, are these tidings both true?'

Then the good man replied: 'I'm not one capable of deception.
Your mother's loyalty brought about, when you parted from her, her
immediate death. You were the beast that she suckled there, and the
dragon* that flew away from her. It all occurred to her in her sleep,
before that gentle lady gave birth to you.

'I have two other sisters. My sister Schoysiane gave birth to a child; 477
by that fruit she lay dead. Duke Kyot of Katelangen was her hus-
band. Nor would he have any truck with joy thereafter. Sigune, his
little daughter, was commended to your mother's care.* Schoysiane's
death must needs hurt me to the very heart. Her womanly heart was
so good, an ark against unchastity's flood. One maiden, my sister,
still practises such ways that chastity follows in her train: Repanse de
Schoye tends the Grail, which is of such heavy weight that false
humanity can never carry it from its place. Her brother and mine is
Anfortas, who both is and was, by lineage, the Grail's lord. Sadly, joy
is far removed from him, except that he retains the hope that his
troubles may take him to everlasting rest. It was by wondrous mat-
ters that it came to this grievous pass, as I shall tell you, nephew. If
you practise loyalty, then his grief will move you to pity.

'When Frimutel, my father, lost his life, his eldest son was chosen 478
after him as king, to be steward of the Grail and the Grail's company.
That was my brother Anfortas, who was worthy of that crown and
power. We were only small as yet. When my brother approached the
years of downy beard-growth—Love wages war with such youths,
she presses her lovers so hard that it may be reckoned to her dis-
honour—whichever Grail's lord, however, desires love other than
that which the inscription grants him must suffer for it, and enter
sigh-laden heart's sorrow—my lord and my brother chose himself a
lady-love who seemed to him of goodly ways. As to who she was, let
that be. He entered her service, cowardice fleeing from him. Con-
sequently, by his radiant hand many a rim was riddled with holes.
That gentle and comely king won such renown by adventure that, if
ever higher fame was known in all knightly lands, he was spared such
tidings. "Amor!" was his battle-cry. Such a call is, however, not 479
entirely compatible with humility.

'One day the king was out riding alone—that was greatly to the grief of his people—in search of adventure, seeking joy with Love's guidance, compelled to it by Love's desire. He was wounded in the joust by a poisoned spear, so that he has never regained his health, your gentle uncle—pierced through his genitals. It was a heathen who fought there and who rode that joust against him—born in Ethnise, where the Tigris* flows forth from Paradise. That same heathen was convinced that his courage would win the Grail. Its name was engraved in the spear. He sought chivalry far afield. It was solely for the sake of the Grail's power that he traversed water and land. By his battle joy vanished from us.

'Your uncle's fighting must be praised. He bore the spear's iron tip away with him in his body. When the noble young king came
480 home to his people, there misery was seen to shine. That heathen he had slain there, nor should we mourn overmuch for him.

'When the king came back to us, so pale, and all his strength gone from him, a doctor's hand delved into the wound until he found the spearhead. The splinter was of cane, part of it remaining in his wounds. The doctor took out both these. I fell down in genuflection, vowing to God's might that I would never more enact any knightly deeds, if God, for His own honour's sake, would help my brother in his need. I also forswore meat, wine and bread, and then everything that bears blood, never having any appetite for it again. That was a second sorrow for the company, dear nephew, I tell you—that I parted from my sword. They said: "Who is to be the protector of the Grail's mysteries?" Then bright eyes wept.

'They carried the king without delay before the Grail, seeking God's help. When the king beheld the Grail, that was *his* second sorrow—that he could not die, for death did not then become him,
481 since I had devoted myself to such an impoverished way of life, and the noble lineage's lordship had sunk to such a low ebb. The king's wound had festered. No matter what medical books were consulted, none gave any help's reward. Against the asp, the ecidemon, the ehcontius and the lisis, the jecis and the meatris*—those evil snakes bear hot venom—whatever anyone knows by way of an antidote to these and other serpents that bear venom—all that wise doctors can procure against them by way of physic's skills in herbs—let me shorten the tale for you—none of these could help. God Himself begrudged us such aid.

'We sought help from the Gihon and the Pishon, the Euphrates and the Tigris, the four rivers* that flow out of Paradise, so close to the source that their sweet scent cannot yet have faded, to see if there was any herb floating therein which might relieve us of sadness. It was lost labour. Then our heart's sorrow renewed itself.

'Still, we kept trying various methods. We obtained that very twig to which Sibyl referred Æneas as an antidote to Hellish pains and 482 Phlegethon's fumes, and against other rivers that flow in Hell.* We took pains to obtain that twig as a cure, in case the monstrous spear that kills our joy had been poisoned or leaded in Hellish fire. The spear was not of that nature.

'There is a bird called the pelican. When it gives birth to fruit it loves them overmuch. Its loyalty's desire compels it to bite through its own breast and let its blood flow into the mouths of the young. It dies at once.* We obtained that bird's blood, to see if its loyalty might avail us, and anointed the wound with it as best we knew how. That could not help us either.

'There is a beast called the monicirus.* It has such great respect for a maiden's purity that it sleeps in a maiden's lap. We obtained that animal's heart to help with the king's pain. We took the carbuncle-stone from that same beast's brow-bone, where it grows 483 below its horn. We anointed the wound's surface with it, then steeped the stone in it entirely. The wound looked to be simply full of venom. That hurt us, as it did the king.

'We obtained a herb called dragonwort*—we hear tell of this herb that whenever a dragon is slain, it grows out of the blood; this herb is of such a disposition that it has all the nature of air*—to see whether the dragon's orbit* might be of any avail to us against the stars' return and the day of the changing moon, on which the wound was painful. That herb's noble, high lineage was of no real avail to us.

'We fell in genuflection before the Grail. There we once saw written that a knight was destined to arrive. If his question was heard on that occasion, then our anguish would be at an end. Whether it be child, maid or man, if anyone gave him warning at all about the question, then the question would be of no help, but the affliction would remain as before, and hurt even more intensely. The inscription said: "Have you understood this? Your warning him may lead to disaster. If he does not ask on that first night, then his question's 484 power will disappear. If his question is put at the right time, then he

shall possess the kingdom, and the duress will be at an end, by the
authority of the Highest Hand. Anfortas will be cured thereby,
though he shall never more be king." Thus we read on the Grail
that Anfortas's torment would come to an end if the question were
put to him.

'We anointed the wound with everything we knew that might
alleviate pain—the good salve nard,* and everything theriacled,* and
the smoke of *lignum aloe,* but pain afflicted him at all times.

'It was then that I withdrew to this place. Feeble bliss is my years'
yield. Afterwards a knight came riding to the Grail. He might as well
have left it alone! He of whom I told you before won infamy there, as
he saw the true anguish, but did not say to the host: "Lord, what is
the nature of your distress?" Since his folly commanded him not to
ask the question there, in his slowness at that time he fell short of
great bliss.'

485   They were both sad at heart. By then it was nearing midday. The
host said: 'Let us go and look for nourishment. Your charger is
entirely unprovided for. I cannot supply food for ourselves, unless
God deigns to direct us. My kitchen rarely reeks. You must pay for
that today and all the time you stay with me. I ought to teach you
herb-lore today, if the snow would permit us. God grant that it soon
melts. Let us in the meantime pick yew-shoots. I believe your char-
ger often ate better at Munsalvæsche than here, yet you never came
to a host who would more willingly see to your wants, if there were
ready supply here.'

They walked out to forage for food. Parzival saw to the fodder. His
host dug up little herbs. That had to be their best food. The host did
not forget his rule. No matter how many he dug up, he ate none of
the herbs before nones.* He hung them carefully on the bushes, then
looked for more. To honour God he went unfed many a day, when he
forgot where his food hung.

486   The two companions did not think it too much trouble to walk to
where the spring flowed, to wash their roots and herbs. Their
mouths were seldom loud with laughter. Each washed his hands. In a
bundle Parzival carried yew-leaves, which he laid before the charger.
Then they went back to lie on their purple moorgrass, by their coals.
There was no need for anyone to fetch them further food. There
was neither braising nor roasting there, and their kitchen was ill-
supplied. To the thoughtful Parzival, because of the loyal love he

bore his host, it seemed he had even greater sufficiency than when Gurnemanz entertained him, and when so many a lady's bright complexion walked before him at Munsalvæsche, when he received hospitality from the Grail.

The host, wise in loyalty, said: 'Nephew, you must not disdain this food. You wouldn't find any host in a hurry who would willingly grant you better hospitality, without any hostility.'

Parzival said: 'Lord, may God's greeting be far from me if I was ever better suited by what I received from a host.'

Whatever food was brought forth there, if they remained 487 unwashed* afterwards, it did not hurt their eyes, as is said of fishy hands. As for me, I assure you that if anyone were to go hunting with me—if I were held to be a falcon—I would fly away most greedily from *that* falconer's hand! Given such morsels as those, I would show how I could fly!

Why do I make fun of those loyal folk? My old uncouthness counselled me to do so. You have heard, clearly enough, what has deprived them of luxury, why they were poor in joy, often cold and seldom warm. They suffered heart's grief for no reason other than true loyalty, without any blemish. From the Highest Hand they accepted it as their sorrows' reward. God was—and was yet to be—gracious to them both.

They arose and walked out, Parzival and the good man, to where the charger was stabled. With scant mirth's clamour the host said to the charger: 'I am sorry for your hunger-laden trouble because of the saddle that lies upon you, which bears Anfortas's arms.'

When they had attended to the charger, they took up a new lam- 488 ent. Parzival said to his host: 'Lord and dear uncle of mine, if I dared, despite my shame, to tell you of it, I would bemoan my misfortune. By your own courtesy, pardon it, for my loyalty finds refuge with you. I have done such great wrong. Unless you'll let me atone for it, then I shall part from solace and shall be forever unredeemed by contrition. You must bemoan my folly, by your counsel's loyalty. That man who rode up to Munsalvæsche and who saw that true anguish, and who spoke no question—I am he, child of misfortune that I am! Thus, lord, I have trespassed.'

The host said: 'Nephew, what are you saying now? We must, both together, grasp hold on heartfelt grief and let joy slip, since your wits have thus renounced bliss. When God conferred five senses upon you, they barred you their counsel. How was your loyalty protected by them, at that time when you saw Anfortas's wounds?

489 'Yet I will not despair of counsel. Nor must you lament too much. You must lament and refrain from lamenting in the right measure.* Mankind is of wild stock. Sometimes youth resolves on wisdom's path. If old age then resolves to practise youthful folly and sully clear ways, then the white becomes besmirched and that green* virtue fades by which what would befit honour might have taken root. If I could engreen things for you and so embolden your heart that you might pursue fame and not despair of God, then your aspiration might still strive towards such a noble end as might well be called atonement. God Himself would not abandon you. I am your counsel's guarantor, by God's grace.

'Now tell me, did you see the spear, up in the castle of Munsalvæsche? When the star Saturn stood at its station again, we were informed of it by the wound, and by the summerly snow. Never had the frost hurt him so much, your gentle uncle. The spear had to
490 go into his wound. There one extremity helped against the other—at that the spear turned bloody red.

'Certain stars' approaching days teach that company there grief's lament—those that stand so high above one another and return irregularly—and the moon's waxing and waning also hurts the wound sorely. At those times I have named here the king has to abandon rest. Great frost hurts him so much that his flesh becomes colder than snow. Ever since we have known the poison on the spearhead to be hot, at these times it is placed upon the wound. It conducts the frost out of the body, all around the spear, glass-coloured, like ice. No-one could, by any means, remove that ice from the spear, except Trebuchet, the wise smith, who wrought two knives of silver which cut it—they did not fail. That cunning he was taught by a charm inscribed upon the king's sword. There are many who would maintain that the wood asbestos does not burn. When any of this glass fell upon it, fire's flame leapt after it! Asbestos was burned by it! What wonders this poison can work!

491 'He can neither ride nor walk, the king, nor lie nor stand. He leans, not sitting, in sigh-laden mood. Come the moon's change he is in pain. Brumbane is the name of a certain lake. They carry him there, out onto its surface, for the sake of its sweet air, because of his bitter wound's cavity. He calls that his hunting-day. No matter how much

he can catch there, with such a painful wound, he has need of more at home. Because of this a tale emerged that he is a fisherman. That tale he has to bear with. Salmon, lampreys—he has little surfeit for sale, however—that sad fisherman, far from merry.'

Parzival said at once: 'It was on that lake I found the king, anchored on the waves. I believe he was on the lookout for fish, or in pursuit of some other pastime. I had travelled many a mile that day, before I reached that lake. I had departed from Pelrapeire precisely at mid-morning. That evening I grew anxious as to where my lodgings might be. My uncle supplied me with them.'

'You rode a perilous path,' said the host, 'well guarded by watch- 492 towers. Each is so manned by a troop that rarely does anyone's cunning help him on that journey. Everyone who has ridden that road towards them has always headed into peril. They accept no-one's oath of surrender. They risk their lives against their antagonists. That has been assigned to them as atonement for sin.'

'Well, without doing battle, on that occasion I came riding to where the king was,' said Parzival. 'I saw his great hall that evening, full of woe. How could they then so delight in woe? A squire leapt in at the door, at which the hall resounded with woe. He carried in his hands a shaft, which he took to all four walls—in it a spearhead, bloody red, by which the company entered grief's extremity.'

His host said: 'Nephew, never since nor before has the king been in such pain, for then the star Saturn had just manifested its approach. It is capable of bringing great frost with it. Just placing the spear on the wound, as it was seen to lie on it before, could be of no avail to us—they thrust the spear into the wound. Saturn races so 493 high aloft that the wound knew of it in advance, before the second frost followed. The snow was in no such haste. It fell only on the next night, in summer's reign. When we thus warded off the king's frost, it robbed the company of joy.' Chaste Trevrizent continued: 'They received sorrow's remuneration. The spear that so touched their heart's life and soul deprived them of joy. Then their grief's loyalty fully renewed baptism's doctrine.'

Parzival said to his host: 'Twenty-five maidens I saw there standing before the king, well versed in courtesy.'

The host replied: 'Maidens must tend it—so God has determined for it—the Grail, before which they served there. The Grail is select in its choosing. Thus it must be guarded by knights of chaste virtue.

The high stars' approaching season brings great grief to the company there, to young and old alike. God has held to his wrath against them all too long there. When are they to assent to joy?

494   'Nephew, now I shall tell you something you may readily believe. One turn of the dice often faces them, by which they give and take profit. They receive little children there, of high lineage and well-favoured. If a land somewhere becomes lordless, if its people recognize God's hand there, desiring a lord from the Grail's company, they shall be granted one. In return they must treat him with courtesy. God's blessing guards him there.

'God sends the men out secretly; maidens are presented openly. You can rest assured that King Castis* requested Herzeloyde, who was granted to him in splendour. Your mother was given him as a spouse, but he was not to learn to know her love—death laid him in the grave before. Before dying he gave to your mother Waleis and Norgals, Kanvoleis and Kingrivals, gifted to her by deed. The king was to live no longer. It befell on his journey back: the king took to his deathbed. She then wore the crown over two countries. There Gahmuret's hand won her.

495   'Thus maidens are given away openly from the Grail, the men secretly, for their fruit to serve there in turn, if their children come to add to the Grail's company by their service. God can well instruct them in this.

'Whoever undertakes to serve the Grail must renounce the love of women. The king alone is to have, lawfully, a pure spouse—and those others whom God has sent into lordless lands to be lords. I transgressed that commandment by practising love-service. My comely youthfulness and a noble woman's virtue persuaded me to ride in her service, in which I often fought hard. Wild adventures seemed so pleasing to me that I rarely engaged in tourneys. Her love conducted joy into my heart. For her sake I made much show of battle, compelled by the power of my love for her to face wild, far-off chivalry. Thus I purchased her love. Heathen and Christian were all alike to me in battle. She seemed to me rich in reward.

496   'I engaged in such activities for that noble lady's sake in the three parts of the earth: in Europe and in Asia, and far-off in Africa. When I wished to deliver splendid jousts, I rode beyond Gauriuon. I also delivered many a joust at the foot of Mount Famorgan. I put on a rich show of jousting at the foot of Mount Agremontin.* If a man

seeks a joust against those who dwell there, on one side of that mountain men of fire emerge; on the other side, they do not burn, no matter how many jousters are seen there. And when I had ridden beyond the Rohas in pursuit of adventure, a noble Wendish company came out to offer jousting's counter-challenge.

'From Seville I sailed all round the sea towards Cilli, through Friuli, out beyond Aquileia. Alack and alas that I ever beheld your father, whom I happened to see there! When I made my entry into Seville, the noble Angevin had taken lodgings there before me. I shall ever regret the journey he made to Baldac. By jousting he lay dead there. So you told me of him before. It will be my heart's 497 lament forever.

'My brother is rich in possessions. He often sent me away secretly on knightly journeys. When I departed from Munsalvæsche I took his seal with me and brought it to Karchobra, where the Plimizœl forms a lake, in the bishopric of Barbigœl. The burgrave there supplied me on the authority of the seal, before I parted from him, with squires and other expenses, to meet the wild jousts and other knightly journeys. He spared very little expense. I had to make my way there alone. On the return journey I left with him all I had kept by way of retinue. I was riding to where Munsalvæsche stood.

'Listen, now, my dear nephew: when your noble father first saw me in Seville, he soon claimed that I was brother to Herzeloyde, his wife, although he had never beheld my countenance before. At that time, indeed, it might truly be said of me that no man's form was ever more fair. I was as yet beardless. He rode into my lodgings. 498 Against his assertion I swore many an unstaved oath.* When he disputed what I said so strongly, I told him in secret that it was indeed so. By that he won much joy.

'He gave me his jewellery. I gave him whatever he wished for. My reliquary, which you saw before—it is greener even than clover—I had wrought out of a stone which pure Gahmuret gave me. He commended his kinsman to me as a squire—Ither, whose heart commanded all falsity to vanish from him—the King of Kukumerlant. Our journey could no longer be delayed; we had to part from one another. He headed for the Baruch's lands, and I rode beyond the Rohas.

'From Cilli I rode beyond the Rohas, where I fought much on three Mondays.* It seemed to me I had fought well there. After that, with all speed, I came riding to the broad Gandine, after which your grandfather was named Gandin. There Ither became well-known. That town lies where the Grajena runs into the Drau, a river containing gold. There Ither came to be loved. He found your aunt there—she was lady over that land. Gandin of Anjou commanded that she rule there. She is called Lammire, and the land is named Styria. If a man wishes to practise the shield's office, he must traverse many lands.

'Now I grieve for my red squire, for whose sake Lammire afforded me great hospitality. You are born of Ither's stock. Your hand has renounced that kinship, but God has not forgotten it; He is still well capable of assessing it. If you would live in good faith with God, then you must do penance to Him for this. It is with sadness that I tell you this: you bear two great sins. You have slain Ither; you must also mourn for your mother. Her great loyalty urged it upon her—your departure parted her from life, when you left her last. Now follow my counsel, accept penance for misdeed, and take heed now concerning your end, so that your toil here may win rest for your soul there.'

Without making an issue of it at all, his host began to question him further: 'Nephew, I have not yet heard how this charger came to be yours.'

'Lord, I won the charger in battle, when I rode away from Sigune. Outside a cell I spoke to her. After that I thrust a knight into flight, down from this charger, and led it away. The man was of Munsalvæsche.'

His host said: 'Did he survive, though—the man to whom the charger rightly belongs?'

'Lord, I saw him walk on ahead of me, and found the charger standing by me.'

'If you will rob the Grail's folk thus, and yet believe you may win their love, then your thoughts are going asunder.'

'Lord, I took it in combat. If anyone accounts this a sin on my part, let him first examine the circumstances. I had lost my own charger before.'

Then Parzival spoke again: 'Who was that maiden who carried the Grail? They lent me her cloak.'

His host replied: 'Nephew, if it was hers—that lady is your aunt—she did not lend it you to boast of. She thought you were to be lord of the Grail there, and her lord, and mine, as well. Your uncle gave you a sword, too, by which you have been granted sin, since your eloquent mouth unfortunately voiced no question there. Let this sin stand alongside the others. We must go and rest for this day, now.'

Few were the beds and cushions brought for them. They went and lay down upon sweepings. That bedding was no kind of match for their high lineage.

Thus he spent a fortnight there, the host tending him as I tell you. Herbs and little roots had to be the best of their food. Parzival bore this burden for the sake of sweet tidings, for his host parted him from sin, and yet gave him knightly counsel.

One day Parzival asked him: 'Who was that man who lay before the Grail? He was quite grey, yet had bright skin.'

His host replied: 'That was Titurel. He is your mother's grandfather. To him the Grail's banner was first entrusted for custody's purpose. There is a disease called podagra* from which he suffers, which cripples past help. Yet he has never lost his colour, for he sees the Grail so often. Because of that he cannot die. They support the bedridden king because of his counsel. In his youth he rode through many fords and meadows in pursuit of jousting. 502

'If you would adorn* your life and ride a truly worthy road, then you must be sparing of enmity towards women. Women and priests are known to bear defenceless hands, while God's blessing extends over the clergy. Your service must tend them with loyalty, if your end is to be a good one. You must be well-disposed towards priests. Whatever your eyes see on this earth, there is nothing equal to a priest. His mouth speaks of the Passion which destroys our doom, and his consecrated hand grasps the highest pledge* that was ever placed against guilt. If any priest has so conducted himself that he can bring chastity to his office, how might he live in more hallowed fashion?'

That was the day of their parting. Trevrizent, having made his decision, spoke: 'Give your sin over to me. Before God I am your atonement's guarantor. And act as I have told you—remain undaunted in that resolve!'

They parted from one another. If you wish, contemplate how.

BOOK X

503 WILD tales draw nigh now, which can dispel joys and yet bring high
spirits—with both these they wrestle.

By now more than a year's time had elapsed. The duel by combat,
which the landgrave had secured by the banks of the Plimizœl, had
been settled. It had been pronounced as transferred from Schamp-
fanzun to Barbigœl. There King Kingrisin remained unavenged.
Vergulaht, his son, came to meet Gawan there. Then the world
marked their kinship, and their kinship's potency averted the com-
bat.* Moreover, it was Count Ehkunaht who bore on his shoulders
the great guilt of which Gawan had been widely accused. Therefore
Kingrimursel renounced his quarrel with Gawan the bold warrior.

The two then went their separate ways, Vergulaht and Gawan, in
search of the Grail. In that pursuit their hands were to deliver many
a joust, for whoever aspired to the Grail had to approach fame with
the sword.* This is how a man ought, indeed, to hasten after fame.

504 How Gawan has fared, he who was ever free of misdeed, since he
departed from Schampfanzun, whether his journey has met with
fighting—let those tell of that who saw it for themselves—now he
has no choice but to draw near battle!

One morning Sir Gawan came riding across a green plain. There
he saw a shield glinting, through which a joust had been aimed, and a
horse that wore a lady's harness. Its bridle and saddle were costly
enough! It was tethered firmly to a branch, together with the shield.
Then he thought: 'Who may this woman be who possesses such a
warlike person that she wields a shield? If she engages in battle
against me, how am I then to defend myself against her? On foot I
am quite confident I can protect myself. If she wants to wrestle long
enough she may throw me, whether I win her enmity or her greeting*
by it, if a joust is to take place on foot here. Even if it were Lady
Kamille* herself, who won fame by her knightly prowess before
Laurente—if she were in her bloom as when she rode there, I would
still try my luck against her, if she were to offer me battle here!'

505 The shield had, moreover, been hacked to pieces. Gawan took a
look at it, as he came riding up. A joust's window had been cut
through it by a broad spearhead. Thus it is that battle paints shields.

Who would pay the shield-painters if *their* paints were of this nature?

The lime-tree's trunk was thick. Moreover, a lady, lame of joy, sat behind it on the green clover. Great misery hurt her so hard that she had entirely forgotten joy. He rode around the tree, closer to her. In her lap lay a knight, which was why her grief was so great.

Gawan did not deny her his greeting. The lady thanked him and bowed her head. He found her voice hoarse from the shrieks her peril had provoked. Then my lord Gawan dismounted. A man lay there, pierced by a lance, his blood flowing backwards into his body. Then he asked the warrior's lady if the knight was still alive, or was wrestling with death. She replied: 'Lord, he is still alive, but not for long, I believe. God has sent you here to comfort me. Advise me now according to your loyalty's desire. You have seen more troubles than 506 I. Let your solace befall me, so that I may behold your help!'

'I shall do so,' he said. 'Lady, I would prevent this knight from dying. I'd be quite confident of saving him if I had a tube. You may see and hear him healthy often yet, for he is not mortally wounded. It is the blood which is his heart's burden.'

He seized a branch of the lime-tree. He peeled the bark off it, forming a tube—he was no fool when it came to that wound—and pressed it in where the joust had entered the knight's body. Then he asked the woman to suck until the blood flowed towards her. The warrior's strength resurged, to the point where he was well capable of speech. Then, seeing Gawan above him, he thanked him profusely, averring that it was to his honour that he had parted him from weakness, and asking him if it was in pursuit of chivalry that he had come there, to Logroys: 'I too have wandered far, from Punturtoys, and desired to pursue adventure here. I must ever lament from my heart that I have ridden so close. You ought also to shun this land, if you are sensible. I did not believe that this would come to pass. 507 Lischoys Gwelljus has sorely wounded me, and dumped me behind my charger by a mighty joust. It passed with such a charge through my shield and my body! Then this good woman helped me onto her horse, as far as this place.'

He pressed Gawan to stay. Gawan said that he wanted to see the place where such harm had befallen him: 'If Logroys lies so close, if I can catch up with him before he gets there, he'll have to answer to me! I'll ask him what wrong he has avenged upon you.'

'Do not do so,' said the wounded man. 'I can tell you the truth of the story. It is no child's journey that leads there. It may rightly be called peril!'

Gawan bound up the wound with the lady's headdress. He spoke a wound-blessing upon the wound,* asking God to take care of both man and woman. He found their trail all bloody, as if a stag had been shot down there. There was no mistaking his road. It was not long before he saw the famed city of Logroys, honoured by many people's praise.

508　　Praiseworthy craftmanship had been invested in the citadel. Its hill resembled a spinning-top. Seeing it from afar, a foolish man might have imagined the citadel spun all round it. Even today it is said of that citadel that it is futile to attack it. It had little fear of such extremity, no matter where enmity assailed it. All around the hill lay a hedge, planted with noble trees: fig-trees, pomegranates, olive-trees, vines, and other crops, growing there in great profusion. Gawan rode all the way up the road to it. There he espied, down below him, his joy and his heart's torment.

A spring shot forth from the rock. There he found—not that it irked him—so lustrous a lady that he had no choice but to look gladly upon her—a *bêâ flûrs** of all womanly complexion. Except for Condwiramurs, no more beautiful person was ever born. That woman was sweet and lustrous, well proportioned and courteous. She was called Orgeluse de Logroys.* Moreover, the adventure tells us of her that she was a bait of love's desire, eyes' sweetness without pain, and a stretching-string of the heart.*

509　　Gawan offered her his greeting, saying: 'If I may dismount, by your favour, lady, and if I behold you disposed to be willing to accept my company, great grief will desert me, leaving me in joy's company. Never would a knight have been so happy! May I die if ever any woman pleased me better!'

'Fair enough. Now I have been apprised of that, too.' Such was her discourse, once she had taken a look at him. Her sweet mouth spoke still more: 'Now do not praise me overmuch. You may easily win dishonour by it. I do not wish that every man's mouth should make his assessment of me public. If my reputation were common knowledge, that would amount to small honour—if it were shared among the wise and the foolish, the straight and the crooked. How might it then excel to match honour's discernment? I must so preserve my reputation that the wise rule over it. I do not know, lord, who you are. It is high time you rode away from me! Yet *my* assessment will not let *you* off scot-free. You are in the presence of my heart, but far outside it, not within. If you desire my love, how have 510 you earned love from me? Many a man hurls his eyes in such a way that he might project them with a gentler trajectory on a catapult, if he were to avoid such looking as cuts his heart. Let your feeble desire roll* in search of other love than mine. If your hand serves for love, if adventure has sent you out after chivalrous deeds in pursuit of love, you will obtain no such reward from me! Indeed, you may well win disgrace here, if I am to tell you the truth.'

He replied: 'Lady, you do tell me the truth. My eyes are my heart's peril. They have so looked upon your person that I must in truth admit that I am your captive. Turn a womanly mind towards me. Although it may irk you, you hold me locked within. Now loose me or bind me. You find me so inclined that if I had you where I wanted, I would willingly endure such a Paradise!'

She said: 'Now take me along with you, if you wish to share such profit as you may win from me by love. In disgrace you will afterwards bemoan it. I would willingly know whether you are such a man 511 as would dare suffer battle for my sake. Refrain, if it is honour you require! If I were to advise you further, if you were then to follow my advice, you would seek love elsewhere. If you desire my love, you will be denied love and joy. If you *do* take me along with you, great sorrow will touch you in time to come.'

Then my lord Gawan replied: 'Who can have love unearned? If I may say as much to you, such a man carries it off amid sin. If a man hastens after worthy love, service is necessary, both before and after.'

She said: 'If you desire to give me service, then you must live valiantly, and yet you may well win disgrace. My service has no need of any coward. Take that path there—it's no road!—over that high bridge into that orchard. There you must tend to my horse. You will hear and see many people there, dancing and singing songs, playing the tabor and the flute. No matter where they try to escort you, walk through them to where my palfrey stands, and untie it. It will follow you.'

Gawan leapt down from his charger. Many thoughts passed 512 through his mind as to how the charger was to wait for him.* There was nothing in the vicinity of the spring to which he might tether it.

He wondered whether it might become him if she should take hold of it—whether such a request was seemly.

'I see clearly what you are worried about,' she said. 'Leave this charger standing here with me. I shall hold it until you return. But serving me will bring you very little profit!'

Then my lord Gawan lifted the reins from the charger, saying: 'Now hold them for me, lady.'

'I see you are in folly's company,' said she, 'for your hand lay there! That grip shall not make my acquaintance!'

The ardent knight replied: 'Lady, I never touched the front part!'

'Well, in that case I'll take hold of them there!' she said. 'Now you must hurry and bring me my palfrey quickly. You have my permission to accompany me on my journey.'

That seemed to him a joyous gain. Quickly he hastened away from her, over the bridge and in at the gate. There he saw many a lady's bright sheen, and many a young knight, dancing and singing.

513   Now my lord Gawan was so well accoutred a man that it taught them grief, for they held to loyalty, those who tended the orchard. Whether they were standing up or lying down, or sitting in pavilions, they most seldom neglected to bemoan his great troubles. Man and woman alike were not slow to speak, but enough of them said, saddened at this: 'My lady's treachery is intent on leading this man astray, into great hardship. Alas that he desires to follow her towards such grief-laden goals!'

Many a noble man walked towards him there, putting his arms about him in friendly welcome. Then he drew near an olive-tree. There stood the horse. Moreover, its bridle and harness were worth many a mark. Next to it there stood a knight with a broad beard, well braided and grey, leaning upon a crutch. He wept when Gawan walked towards the palfrey, yet he received him with gentle speech,

514   saying: 'If you will heed advice, you ought to let that palfrey be, though no-one here will prevent you from taking it. But if you were ever to act for the best, then you ought to leave the palfrey here. A curse upon my lady that she can part so many a noble man from his life!'

Gawan said that he would not relinquish it.

'Alas for what will happen hereafter!' said the noble grey knight. He loosed the halter from the palfrey, saying: 'You must stand here no longer. Let this palfrey walk after you. May He whose hand salted the sea advise you in your troubles. Be on your guard that my lady's beauty does not put you to scorn at all, for she is all too sour in her sweetness, just like a sunshiny shower.'

'Now let God prevail!' said Gawan. He took leave of the grey man, as he did of the people here and there. They all spoke words of lamentation. The palfrey walked along a narrow path out of the gate, following him onto the bridge. His heart's custodian he found there—she was lady over that land. Although his heart fled towards her, she reared* much anguish for him in it.

With one hand she had untied the ribbons of her headdress under 515 her chin, and placed them on top of her head. A woman found so attired bears belligerent limbs; she may well delight in mockery. What other clothes was she wearing? If I were even to think of examining her clothing now, her bright glance would spare me the task.

When Gawan walked up to the lady, her sweet mouth received him thus: 'Welcome, you goose!* No man ever lugged such great folly around with him, if you wish to grant me your service. Oh, how willingly you ought to forbear from it!'

He said: 'If you are quick to anger now, then favour ought by rights to follow. Since you scold me so harshly, yours shall be the honour of making amends. My hand will do you service until such time as you are of a mind to reward me. If you wish, I'll lift you up onto this palfrey.'

She said: 'I have expressed no such desire. Your untried hand may grasp after a meaner pledge!' She swept away from him and leapt from the flowers up onto the palfrey. She asked him to ride ahead: 'It would be a pity, indeed, if I were to lose such an estimable 516 companion!' said she. 'May God fell you!'

If anyone were to follow my advice now, he would avoid directing false words at her. Let no-one speak out of turn unless he knows what wrong he is avenging, until he gains knowledge of how it stood with her heart. I would be perfectly capable myself of wreaking vengeance upon that well-favoured lady. Yet no matter how ill she has treated Gawan in her anger, or may yet come to treat him, I exempt her from all such vengeance.

Orgeluse, that mighty duchess, was travelling an uncompanion-able road. She came riding up to Gawan's side so wrathfully that I'd have little hope of her freeing *me* from sorrow! Together they rode off, across a bright heath. There Gawan saw a plant growing, whose root he claimed could help against wounds. The noble knight then dismounted. He dug it up; he remounted. The lady was not slow to speak, saying: 'If this companion of mine knows how to be both 517 doctor and knight, he may well make an excellent living, provided he learns how to sell ointment-boxes!'

Gawan's mouth replied to the lady: 'I rode past a wounded knight, whose shelter is a lime-tree. If I find him again, this root will serve to heal him and cure him of all his weakness.'

She said: 'That I would like to see! Perhaps *I* may learn such skill!'

Soon a squire came riding after them, in a hurry to deliver an errand on which he had been sent. Gawan decided to wait for him. Then he thought him an uncomely sight! Malcreatiure* was that proud squire's name. Cundrie la Surziere was his well-favoured sister. He would have been identical with her facially, except that he was a man. Like hers, both of his teeth stuck out like a wild boar's, unlike human form. His hair, however, was not as long as that which had hung down from Cundrie onto her mule. Short, prickly as a hedgehog's hide it was. By the river Ganges in the land of Tribalibot people grow like that, not having any choice in the matter.

518 Our father Adam acquired from God the skill of giving names to all things, both wild and tame.* He knew each one's nature, too, and the cycle of the stars, of the seven planets, what forces they have. He knew also the powers of all herbs and each one's nature.* When his daughters had reached such years' number that they were capable of giving birth to human fruit, he counselled them against immoderation. When any of his daughters was with child, he would impress this upon them time and again, seldom omitting to advise them to avoid many herbs that disfigure man's fruit and dishonour his lineage—'other than those God prescribed for us when He went to work to create me,' said Adam. 'My dear daughters, do not now be blind to bliss.'

The women, however, acted as women do. Several amongst them were advised by their frailty to do such deeds as their heart's desire 519 suggested. Thus mankind was deformed. That grieved Adam, yet his will never despaired.*

Queen Secundille,* whom Feirefiz won by his knightly hand, both her person and her land, had had living in her realm since bygone times—most undeniably—many people with deformed

facial features. They bore strange, wild marks. Then she was told
about the Grail, that there was nothing on earth so wealthy, and that
its custodian was a king called Anfortas. That seemed wondrous
enough to her, for into her own land many rivers carried precious
gems rather than gravel—huge, by no means small—mountains
of gold she possessed. The noble queen pondered: 'How can I gain
knowledge of this man to whom the Grail is subject?' She sent to
him as tokens two human beings of wondrous appearance, Cundrie
and her radiant brother. She indeed sent him more besides, beyond
anyone's price—it would seldom be found for sale. Then gentle
Anfortas, being always most generous, sent that courteous squire
to Orgeluse de Logroys. A difference, brought about by woman's 520
craving, parted him from mankind.

This kinsman of the herbs and the stars raised loud quarrel
against Gawan, who had waited for him on the road. Malcreatiure
came riding up on a feeble nag that limped in all four legs with
lameness, often stumbling to the ground. Noble Lady Jeschute rode
a better horse that day when Parzival, by his fighting, won favour for
her from Orilus, favour she had lost through no fault of her own.

The squire stared at Gawan. Malcreatiure spoke angrily: 'Sir, if
you are of knight's order, you ought to have refrained from this. You
seem to me a foolish man, taking my lady away with you, and you'll
be taught such a lesson that you'll be praised for it if your
hand succeeds in defending you. If, on the other hand, you are a
man-at-arms, then you'll be tanned so hard by staves that you'll wish
you were well out of it!'

Gawan replied: 'My chivalry has never suffered such chastise-
ment. It is riff-raff who ought to be whipped thus, those who lack
valiant defence. I have as yet been spared such torment. If, however, 521
you and my lady wish to offer me scornful words, you alone will have
to bear the brunt of what you may well take for anger. No matter how
fearsome your aspect, I'll easily dispense with *your* threats!'

Then Gawan grabbed him by the hair and swung him under his
nag. The wise and worthy squire looked back up at him in some
anxiety. His hedgehog-like hair avenged itself, lacerating Gawan's
hand, so that it was seen to be all red with blood. The lady laughed at
this, saying: 'I am delighted to see you two in such fury!'

They rode on, the nag running alongside them. They came to
where they found the wounded knight lying. Loyally Gawan's hand

bound the herb about the wound. The wounded man said: 'How've you fared since you parted from me here? You have brought a lady with you who is bent upon your destruction. It is she who is the cause of my great suffering. In Av'estroit Mavoie* she helped me into

522 a fierce joust, to the cost of my body and property. If you would preserve your life, then let this treacherous woman ride, and turn away from her. See for yourself where her advice has led me. Yet I might readily recover if I were to get some rest. Help me in that, loyal friend!'

My lord Gawan replied: 'Take your choice of all help I can offer!'

'Close by here stands a hospice,' said the wounded knight. 'If I reach it soon, I could rest there for a long time. We still have my lady-love's palfrey standing here, a most sturdy horse. Now lift her up onto it, and me behind her!'

Then the well-born stranger untied the lady's palfrey from the branch, intending to lead it closer to her. The wounded man exclaimed: 'Away from me there! Why are you in such a hurry to trample upon me?' Gawan led the palfrey further away from the lady, who walked after him, gently, in no rush, all as her lover advised. Gawan hoisted her onto the horse. In the meantime the wounded knight leapt onto Gawan's Castilian. That was a foul deed, I believe! The knight and his lady rode off. That was a sinful profit!

523 Gawan complained greatly at this. The duchess laughed at it, finding more mirth in the matter than he thought at all seemly. Now that his charger had been taken from him, her sweet mouth said to him: 'At first sight I took you for a knight. Then it was not long before you became a doctor, curing wounds. Now you must be a page!* If any man is to survive by his skill, then your wits may console you! Do you *still* desire my love?'

'Yes, lady,' said Sir Gawan. 'If I might have your love that would be dearer to me than anything. There is no-one whatever who dwells upon this earth—whether without a crown—and all that wear the crown—and all who pursue joyous fame—if all their gains were on offer in exchange for you, still my heart's inclination would advise me to let them keep their own.* I would still wish to have your love. If I cannot win it, then I may soon be seen to die a bitter death. You are laying waste to your own property. No matter whether I ever won freedom, you must have me for your bondsman.* That seems to me your inalienable right. Now call me knight or squire, page or peasant,

whatever scorn you have heaped upon me, you incur sin thereby if   524
you disdain my service. If I were to benefit by my service, you might
spare me scorn. Even if it never hurts me, it still impinges upon your
honour.'

Back to them rode the wounded man, saying: 'It's you, is it,
Gawan? If you ever lent me anything, it's now repaid to you in full!
When your valorous strength took me captive in fierce knightly
combat, and you took me to the castle of your uncle Arthur, for four
weeks he made sure that I ate along with the dogs,* the whole time!'

Gawan replied: 'It's you, is it, Urjans? If you wish harm upon me
now, I bear no guilt in the matter. I won you the King's favour. It was
a base mind helped and counselled you. They parted you from the
shield's office and pronounced you entirely without rights, because a
maiden lost her rights by you, and the land's protection as well. King
Arthur would gladly have avenged it by the noose, if I had not
pleaded you off!'

'Whatever happened there, now you stand here. You've heard the   525
old saying, I dare say: he who helps another to survive will find he
will be his enemy thereafter. I act like those who have their wits
about them. It becomes a child to weep, better than a bearded man.
I'll keep this charger for myself!'

Applying his spurs, he rapidly rode it away. That grieved Gawan
greatly. He said to the lady: 'It happened like this: King Arthur was
at that time in the city of Dianazdrun, many a Briton there with him.
A lady had been sent there on an embassy into his land. That mon-
ster, too, had set out in pursuit of adventure. He was a stranger in
that land, as was she. Then his low mind counselled him to wrestle
with the lady, according to his desire, but against her will. Right into
the court came her screams. The King yelled out the hue and cry.
This happened at the edge of a wood. We all hastened to the spot.
I rode far ahead of the others and picked up the guilty man's trail.
I led him back, as a captive, to stand before the King.

'The damsel rode along with us. Her demeanour was grief-   526
stricken, because a man who had never entered her service had taken
her chaste maidenhead from her. For his part, he won precious little
glory there against her defenceless hand. She found my lord, loyal
Arthur, in anger's company. He said: "The whole world must rue
this accursed misdeed! Alas that that day ever dawned, by whose
light this calamity occurred! And in a place where my jurisdiction is

acknowledged, and I am today the judge!" He said to the lady: "If you are wise, appoint an advocate and bring your case." The lady was undaunted, and acted as the King advised her. A great company of knights stood there.

'Urjans, the prince from Punturtoys, stood there before the Briton, all his honour and his life at stake. The woman who was plaintiff stepped forward to where rich and poor could hear her. With accusing words she entreated the King, for all womankind's sake, to take her disgrace to heart—and in the cause of maidenly honour. She 527 entreated him further, for the sake of the Table Round's order, and because of the embassy's journey on which she had been sent to him there,* if he was acknowledged as judge, to adjudge then her complaint, by judgement's proclamation. She entreated all the Table Round's company to take heed of her rightful cause, as she had been robbed of what could never be returned to her, her chaste, pure maidenhead—urging them all as one to beseech the King for judgement and support her cause.

'The guilty man took as an advocate one whom I now grant small honour. He defended him as best he could, but that defence was of no avail to him. His life and reputation were condemned, and a noose was to be wound whereby death would make his acquaintance, without hands being bloodied.* He appealed to me, his extremity compelling him to it, and reminded me that he had offered me his surrender in order to save his life. I feared I might forfeit all my honour if he lost his life there. I entreated the woman who was plaintiff, as she had seen with her own eyes that I had avenged her 528 valorously, that she should, out of womanly grace, mollify her mind, since she had to attribute what had happened to her at Urjans's hands to love of her, and to her lustrous person, and if ever a man entered heart's distress through service to a woman, if she offered him her help thereafter—"do it in honour of such help, allow yourself to be averted from anger!"

'I entreated the King and his men that, if I had done him any service, he should bear it in mind—that he might shield me from disgrace's persecution by a single act, namely, by saving that knight. I implored his wife the Queen to help me, out of kinship's love, for the King had brought me up from childhood, and my loyalty had always sought refuge with her. That happened. She spoke privately with the damsel. He survived then, because of the Queen, but he had

to suffer great torment. Thus he was purged—such was the atone-
ment he was seen to suffer—whether they were leaders of the pack
or lymers,* for four weeks he ate out of the same trough as the
hounds. Thus the lady was avenged. Lady, this is *his* revenge 529
upon me!'

She said: 'His vengeance will turn awry. I shall, in all likelihood,
never look favourably on *you*, but *he* shall receive such a reward for
this, before he departs from my land, that even he will acknowledge
it as a disgrace. Since the King did not avenge it in the place where it
befell the lady and it has come within my jurisdiction, then you are
both now subject to my authority, even though I do not know who
you both are. He will be on the receiving end of battle because of
this—for the sake of the lady alone—precious little for your sake!
Gross impropriety must be avenged by blows and thrusts!'

Gawan walked over to the palfrey. With a light leap he managed to
catch hold of it. The squire had followed them. The lady gave him a
message to take back up to the castle, speaking to him entirely in the
heathen tongue.

Now Gawan's hour of need draws nigh. Malcreatiure went back
on foot. Then my lord Gawan took a look at the young lord's nag. It
was too feeble for a battle. The squire had taken it from a peasant,
before he had come down the slope. Now it fell to Gawan to keep it 530
instead of his charger. He had no choice but to accept the barter.

Orgeluse said to him—out of malice, I believe—'Tell me, do you
want to go any further?'

My lord Gawan replied: 'My journey from here shall be made
entirely in accordance with your counsel.' Orgeluse: 'That will be
slow to reach you.' Gawan: 'Well, I shall still serve you to that end.'
Orgeluse: 'I think you a fool for it. If you do not relent, you will have
to turn away from mirth's company and towards grief. Your troubles
will begin afresh.'

Then the ardent knight replied: 'I shall continue to serve you,
whether I meet with joy or distress by it, as love of you has com-
manded me to be at your command, whether I ride or walk.'

Still standing by the lady's side, he took a look at his war-horse.
For a speedy joust it would fetch a pretty feeble price, its stirrup-
leathers being of bast. That noble, worthy stranger had in time past
been better saddled. He avoided mounting it, as he feared he might
trample the saddle-gear to bits. The palfrey's back was crooked. If 531

his leap had landed upon it, its back would have been quite shattered. He had to bear all this in mind.

Another time this might have overwhelmed him. He led the palfrey after him, carrying the shield and a lance. At his severe difficulties the lady laughed a lot—she who was causing him so much distress. He tied his shield upon the palfrey. She said: 'Are you carrying pedlar's wares to sell in my land? Who has bestowed upon me a doctor and a pedlar's stall? Watch out for tolls on the road!* One or other of my toll-keepers will deprive you of joy!'

Her cutting sally seemed to him so comely that he didn't care what she said, for every time he looked at her, his debt to grief was quits. She was truly May-time to him, a *flôrî* * above all other radiance, eyes' sweetness, yet bitter company to the heart. Since both loss and gain combined in her, and that by which sick joy made good recovery, Gawan was rendered at all times free, and yet tightly bonded.*

532   Many a master* of mine says that Amor and Cupid, and Venus, the mother of those two,* confer love upon people thus: by shot and fire. Such love is monstrous. If a man is in heartfelt loyalty's company, he will never be free of love, along with joy, sometimes with grief. Real love is true loyalty. Cupid, your arrow misses me every time, as does Sir Amor's dart. If you two reign over love, and Venus with her hot torch, I know nothing of such troubles. If I am to speak of *true* love, it must befall me out of loyalty.

If my wits were to help anyone faced with Love at all, I am so well disposed to Sir Gawan that I would help him without remuneration. He is free of disgrace, even if he lies in Love's bonds. Even if Love moves him, Love which scatters strong defences, he was always so defiant, so like what noble defence should be, that no woman ought to oppress his defiant person.

533   Trot closer, Sir Press of Love. You give such a hard tug at joy that joy's place is riddled with holes, and heads off along grief's path. Thus grief's trail broadens. If its journey led elsewhere than into the heart's high spirits, that would seem to me to be to joy's benefit. If Love is quick to impropriety, I think she is too old for that! Or does she attribute it to her childhood, if she brings heart's sorrow to anyone? I would rather ascribe her impropriety to her youth than that she should break with the virtue of her old age. Many things have happened because of her. To which of the two ought I to ascribe

them? If she desires, because of youthful counsel, to make her old age inconstant, then she will soon be slow to fame. These distinctions ought to be spelled out to her better. Pure love I praise, as do all who are wise, be they women or men—I have their entire assent in this. Where affection encounters affection, pure without mirk, there neither is dismayed if Love locks their hearts with that love from which inconstancy ever fled. Such love is high above all other.

Gladly as I would absent him from it, my lord Gawan cannot 534 escape such love as desires to diminish his joy. What use would my intervening blow* be, whatever I am capable of saying about it? A worthy man ought not to resist love, for love may help preserve him. Gawan accepted hardship out of love. His lady rode; he walked on foot.

Orgeluse and the bold warrior entered a great forest. Still Gawan had no choice but to grow used to walking. He led the palfrey to a fallen tree-trunk. His shield, which had lain upon its back till then, which he carried for the sake of the shield's office, he now placed about his neck. He mounted the horse. It could barely carry him onwards out of the wood, into the cultivated land beyond. With his eyes he found a castle. His heart and his eyes averred that they had never known nor beheld any castle like it. It was of knightly aspect all around. High up in the citadel were many towers and great halls. Moreover, he could see many ladies in the windows. There were four hundred of them or more, four amongst them of proud lineage.

A great expanse of unpathed land, rutted by fords, led to where a 535 river flowed, shippable, fast and wide. He and the lady rode towards it. At the mooring-place lay a meadow, upon which much jousting was practised. The citadel stood high above the river. Gawan the bold warrior saw a knight riding after him, one who could spare neither shield nor spear.

Mighty Orgeluse said haughtily: 'If your mouth will concede to me as much, then I am not breaking faith. I told you before in so many words that you will win much disgrace here. Defend youself, now, if you are capable of defence. Nothing else can save you here. He who is approaching there—his hand shall so fell you that if your breeches are split in any part, you will be embarrassed because of the ladies sitting up above you and looking on. What if they catch sight of your shame!'

At Orgeluse's request the boat's captain came across. She stepped

from the land into the boat, which taught Gawan sadness. Turning
536 back, the wealthy and well-born duchess said angrily: 'You shall not
come on board here with me! You must stay out there, a hostage to
fortune!'

Sorrowfully he called after her: 'Lady, why are you hastening away
from me like this? Shall I ever see you again?'

She said: 'Such fame may befall you that I grant you further sight
of me, but not, I believe, for some considerable time!'

Thus the lady parted from him. Along came Lischoys Gwelljus.
If I were to tell you now that he was flying, I would be deceiving you
by my words. That said, he made such great haste that his charger
was honoured by it, for it made show of swiftness, across the wide,
green meadow.

Then my lord Gawan thought: 'How am I to await this man?
Which may be better? On foot, or on this little palfrey? If he intends
to attack me outright, not sparing the full charge, he will certainly
ride me down. What cause can his charger have to hesitate there,
unless it were to trip over my nag? If he then wishes to offer me
battle, both of us on foot, even if I never win the greeting of her who
has granted me this battle, I'll give him a fight, if he desires it!'

537 Well, there was no avoiding it. The approaching knight was cour-
ageous, as was he who waited there. Gawan made himself ready for
the joust, placing his lance at the front, upon the saddle's little piece
of felt,* as he had determined before. Thus their two jousts were
delivered: the joust broke both of their spears, so that the warriors
were seen to lie upon the ground. The better mounted man took
such a tumble then that he and my lord Gawan both lay upon the
flowers. What did the pair indulge in then? Up they leapt with their
swords, both avid for battle. Their shields were unspared—they were
so hewn at that little of them remained in front of their hands, for
the shield is always battle's forfeit.

Flashes and helmet's fire were seen there. You may account that
man fortunate in adventure whom God permits to carry away the
victory. He must win much fame first. Thus they held out, battling
on the meadow's breadth. Two smiths would have grown weary, even
if they were sturdier of limb, from striking so many a great blow.
538 Thus they strove in fame's pursuit. Who would praise them for it,
those unwise men, fighting without cause, only for fame's favour?
They had no issue to decide; they were selling their lives without

necessity. Each reproached the other that he had never seen any such cause.

Gawan knew how to wrestle and pin down his man by the throw. If he slipped through a swordsman's guard and grasped him to him with his arms, he could force him to do whatever he wished. Combat being required of him, he then acted in combative fashion. Noble Gawan, rich in courage, seized the bold youth, who also possessed manly strength. Soon he had thrown him. Sitting upon him, he said: 'Warrior, yield surrender now, if you wish to live!' Lischoys, lying beneath him, was unready to accede to the request, for he had never been in the habit of surrendering before. It seemed to him wondrous enough that any man should ever possess such hands as might overcome him, and exact from him what had never been taken from him—compulsory surrender, much of which his own hand had won in battle before. No matter how things had turned out there, he had 539 accepted so many surrenders that he was unwilling to pass them on. Instead of surrender he offered his life, and said that, whatever might happen to him, he would never concede surrender under duress. He desired to barter with death.

The man lying below said: 'Is it you who's the victor now? I indulged in the like myself, as long as God willed and I was destined to enjoy fame. Now my fame is at an end, vanquished by your noble hand. If men or women anywhere hear that I have been vanquished—I whose praise formerly hovered so high—then death is my preference, rather than that these tidings should deprive my friends of joy.'

Gawan sought his surrender, but Lischoys' desire and all his intent were bent solely on his life's perishing, or a quick death. Then my lord Gawan thought: 'Why should I kill this man? If he would subject himself to my command, as things stand I would let him walk away in good health.' He sought to persuade him by that argument, but surrender was not yielded in full as yet.

Nevertheless, he allowed the warrior to rise, without his having 540 sworn surrender. Both sat down upon the flowers. Gawan had not forgotten his difficulty—that his palfrey was so feeble. His thoughts instructed that wise knight that he might ride Lischoys's charger with spurs, until he had tried its mettle. It was well armed for battle; over the iron caparison it had a second covering of phellel-silk and samite. Since he had won it by adventure, why shouldn't he ride it now, since it befalls him to ride it? He mounted upon it; then it moved in such a manner that he was delighted by its wide leaps. He said: 'Is it you, Gringuljete? The horse that Urjans won from me by perfidious pleading, as he well knows how! Yet his fame has perished in consequence. Who has caparisoned you like this in the meantime? If it's you, then God, who often averts troubles, has sent you back to me in fine fettle!'

He dismounted. He found a mark—the Grail's device, a turtle-dove, was branded on its hock. Lähelin, mounted on that horse, had slain in the joust the knight of Prienlascors.* The charger had then 541 become Orilus's property. He had given it to Gawan on Plimizœl's plain.

Now his despondent kindness returned again to high spirits, except that he was oppressed by the one sorrow, the loyal servitude he bore his lady, although she had offered him ample disdain. It was in pursuit of her that his thoughts hunted him. Meanwhile, haughty Lischoys leapt to where he saw his own sword lying, which Gawan, that noble warrior, had wrenched from his hand in battle. Many a lady watched their second battle. Their shields had suffered such usage that they both left them lying there and hastened to the fight without them. Each arrived promptly, with a hearty man's defiance. Above them a host of ladies sat at the windows high up in the great hall, watching the battle fought below them. Each knight was so high-born that his fame would ungently suffer being outfought by the other. Their helmets and swords suffered distress. Those were now their shields against death. Whoever saw those warriors' battle there would, I believe, admit it brought hardship upon them.

542   Lischoys Gwelljus, that young, gentle knight, acted as follows: boldness and courageous deeds were his high heart's counsel. He dealt many a swift blow. Often he leapt away from Gawan, then back towards him with a vengeance. Gawan was constant in his purpose, thinking: 'If I grasp you to me, I'll reward you for this in full!'

Fire's flashes were seen there, and swords often flung high from courageous hands. They took to turning each other sideways, for-wards and backwards. They sought to wreak vengeance for no cause—they could have forborn from battle. Then my lord Gawan seized him, throwing him to the ground by his strength. May intimacy with such necking shun me! I couldn't bear it!

Gawan asked for surrender. Lischoys, lying beneath him, was still as unready to yield as when he had first done battle. He said: 'There is no need for you to delay. Rather than surrender I offer death. Let your noble hand put an end to whatever fame I was renowned for. I am accursed before God. He will never favour my fame again. For 543 love of Orgeluse, the noble duchess, many a worthy man has had to yield his fame to my hands. You may inherit much fame if you can put me to death.'

Then King Lot's son thought: 'Indeed, I must not do so, for I would forfeit fame's favour if I slew without cause this bold, undaunted warrior. It was love of her that chased him after me—she whose love oppresses me, too, and brings much trouble upon me. Why don't I let him live for her sake? If I am to possess her, he cannot avert it, if Fortune sends me that fate. If our battle had been seen by her, I believe even she would have to concede that I know how to serve for love.' Then my lord Gawan said: 'I will leave you alive for the duchess's sake.'

Great weariness was not far from their minds. Gawan let Lischoys rise. They sat down, at some distance from one another. Then the boat's master arrived, stepping from the river onto the land, carrying 544 on his hand a young moulted merlin, grey all over. It was his lawful due there that, whoever jousted on the plain, he should retain the charger of him who succumbed there—and as for him who carried off the victory, he was to bow to his hand and not be silent concerning his fame. Thus he was paid interest on his flowery fields; that was his best yield from those lands, unless his moulted merlin taught torment to a crested lark. He put his hand to no other plough. It seemed to him income enough. He was born of knight's lineage, well guarded by good breeding.

He walked over to Gawan and courteously asked him for the interest on the plain. Gawan, rich in valour, said: 'Lord, I was never a merchant!* You may as well let me off the toll.'

The boat's master replied: 'Sir, so many a lady has seen that fame has befallen you here. You must allow me my rights. Lord, acknowledge my rights to me. In formal joust, your hand has won me this 545 charger, along with unimpaired fame, for your hand has thrust to the ground one to whom the whole world, until this day, had always—and rightly—accorded praise. Your fame, and God's blow falling on him, has deprived him of joy. Great good fortune has touched you.'

Gawan said: '*He* thrust *me* down; I recovered later. If interest is to be paid to you on the joust, *he* can readily pay you interest. Sir, there is a nag standing there—his fighting won that from me. Take that, if you will. As for who is to dispose of this charger here, I shall do that myself. It must carry me away from here, even if you never acquire any charger. You talk of your rights. Claim them as you will, it would never become you if I were to walk away from here on foot, for it would be too great an injury to me if this charger were to be yours— it was so indisputably mine this very morning. If you're looking for easy prey, you would be better off riding a hobby-horse. This char- ger was given to me, beyond dispute, by Orilus the Burgundian.*

546 Urjans, the prince from Punturtoys, had stolen it from me, for a time. You'd find it easier to obtain a she-mule's foal* from me! Otherwise, I bear you no ill-will. Since he seems so noble to you, rather than the charger you desire here, keep the man who rode it against me. It matters little to me whether it brings him joy or sorrow.'

At that the boatman was delighted. With a smiling mouth he said: 'I never saw such a rich gift as this, if it were right and fitting for a man to accept it. Indeed, lord, if you will be my guarantor of this gift, then my demand has been overpaid. Truly, his fame was always so resounding that I would be unwilling to accept five hundred strong and swift chargers in his stead, for it would not become me. If you would make me rich, then act in knightly fashion. If you have the power to do so, deliver him into my cog, for that would indeed be a noble act.'

King Lot's son replied: 'Both into the boat and out the other side, as far as the inside of your door, I'll deliver him to you as a captive.'

547 'Then you will be warmly welcomed,' said the boatman with a bow; his great gratitude did not stint from bowing. Then he said: 'My dear lord, one thing more: be so kind as to rest with me yourself tonight. No greater honour ever befell any fellow ferryman of mine. My good fortune will be judged great if I put up such a worthy man.'

My lord Gawan replied: 'What you desire, I ought to request. Great weariness has conquered me and put me in need of rest. She who has commanded this hardship of me knows well how to turn sweetness sour* and make a man's heart rare in joy and rich in sor- rows. She rewards disproportionately. Alas, you find of a loss, you lower this one breast of mine, which aspired to the heights before, when God granted me joy. A heart once lay beneath it—I believe it has vanished. Where am I now to fetch solace? Must I endure without help such grief on love's account? If she practises womanly loyalty, she who knows how to injure me thus ought to magnify my joy.'

The boatman heard that he was wrestling with sorrow and that 548 Love oppressed him. He replied: 'Lord, that is the custom here, on the plain and in the greenwood, and everywhere where Clinschor is lord.* Neither cowardice nor manly cunning can shape it otherwise: sad today, happy tomorrow. It is perhaps unknown to you: all this land is but one single adventure. Thus it persists night and day. Good fortune can help, if courage is present. The sun knows how to stand so low. Lord, you must come aboard!'—the boatman entreated him. Gawan led Lischoys with him onto the waves. Patiently, picking no quarrel whatever, the warrior was seen to obey. The ferryman led the charger after them. Thus they crossed over to the far bank.

The ferryman entreated Gawan: 'Be host yourself in my house!' His home was such that Arthur, in Nantes, where he often resided, would have had no need to build a better. He led Lischoys in. The host and his household attended to him, while the host said to his 549 daughter: 'You must provide good comfort for my lord who stands here. You two go along together. Now serve him ungrudgingly. We have profited greatly by him.'

To his son he commended Gringuljete. What had been requested of the maiden was carried out with great courtesy. Gawan went up with the maiden into a chamber. Its stone floor was covered all over with fresh rushes, and pretty flowers had been cut and strewn upon it. Then the sweet maiden took off his armour.

'May God thank you for that!' said Gawan. 'Lady, I had need of it, but if it had not been commanded of you at court,* then you would be rendering me too great service.'

She said: 'I serve you more, sir, for your favour than for any other reason.'

The host's son, a squire, brought in ample soft bedding, placing it by the wall facing the door; a carpet was laid before it. There Gawan was to sit. The squire skilfully spread a quilt upon the bed, of red sendal-silk. A bed was also laid for the host. Then another squire 550 carries in and places before them table-linen and bread. Both acted on the host's orders. The lady of the house followed after them. When she saw Gawan, she welcomed him heartily, saying: 'Now you have made us rich at last! Sir, our good fortune wakes!'

The host came, the water was brought in. When Gawan had washed, there was one request he did not omit to make. He asked the host for company: 'Let this maiden eat with me.'

'Lord, no word has ever been uttered to her of her eating with lords or sitting so close to them. She might put on too many airs for my liking. Still, we have profited greatly by you. Daughter, do all that he wishes. I guarantee you have my full assent.'

The sweet maiden blushed for shame, but she did as the host commanded. Next to Gawan Lady Bene* sat down. The host had reared two strong sons besides. Now, that evening the merlin had caught three crested larks on the wing. The boatman ordered that all 551 three be brought before Gawan, with a sauce to accompany them. The damsel did not neglect to cut, with gracious courtesy, sweet morsels for Gawan, laying them with her lustrous hands on a white roll. Then she said: 'You ought to send one of these roasted birds over to my mother, lord, for she has none.' He said to the well-favoured maid that he would gladly do as she wished, be it this or any other request. One crested lark was sent to the hostess. She bowed courteously and copiously to Gawan's hand, nor were the host's thanks left unuttered.

Then one of the host's sons brought in purslane and lettuce, cut up and dipped in vinegar. Such nourishment is disadvantageous in supplying great strength in the long run, nor is it good for the complexion. Such colour as is slipped into the mouth tells the truth. Colour painted upon the skin has rarely found resounding praise. She whose womanly heart is constant through and through bears, I believe, the best sheen.

552   If Gawan could live off goodwill alone, he could have found fine sustenance there. Never did a mother wish better upon her child than that host whose bread he ate wished him. When the table had been carried away and the hostess had gone out, much bedding was then carried up. It was laid on the ground for Gawan. One was of down, its coverlet of green samite—not of the noble kind; it was a bastard samite. A quilt served as bed-covering, solely for Gawan's comfort, with a phellel-silk, without gold, fetched from far-off heathendom, quilted on palmat-silk.* Over this soft bed-clothes were drawn, two sheets of snow-white linen. A pillow was placed for him, and one of the maiden's cloaks, of new, pure ermine.

The host intervened to take leave of him, before he went to his rest. Gawan remained all alone there, I am told, along with the maiden. If he'd asked anything of her, I believe she'd have granted it him. He must indeed sleep, if he can. God guard him, once day comes!

BOOK XI

GREAT weariness dragged his eyelids down. Thus he slept till early 553 morning. Then the warrior awoke. On the one side the chamber's wall had many windows, with glass in front of them.* One of the windows was open, facing the orchard, into which he walked to take a look about him, and because of the air and the birdsong. His sitting there had not lasted long when he perceived a citadel—the same he'd seen that evening, when the adventure had befallen him—many ladies up in the great hall, not a few among them of great beauty. It seemed to him a great wonder that the ladies did not tire of waking, that they were not asleep. As yet the day was none too bright.

He thought: 'In their honour I shall devote myself to sleeping.' Back to his bed he went. The maiden's cloak embraced him; that was his covering. Did they wake him at all there? No, that would have grieved his host. In order to be sociable, the maiden, who was lying there at her mother's feet, broke off the sleep in which she was indulging and went up to her guest. He was still fast asleep. The 554 maiden did not neglect her service. On the carpet before his bed that lustrous damsel sat down. For my part, I seldom see such an adventure creeping to my side, neither in the evening nor early in the morning.

After a while Gawan awoke. He looked at her and smiled, saying: 'God preserve you, little lady, for thus breaking off your sleep on my account, and punishing yourself in a cause in which I have been entirely undeserving.'

The well-favoured maiden replied: 'I want none of *your* service. It is not for me to desire anything but your favour. Lord, command me. Whatever you command, I'll carry out. All those in my father's household, both my mother and her children, must hold you for their lord forever—you have done us so much kindness!'

He said: 'Have you been here long? If I had heard you arrive

before, I would have been glad, because I have some questions,* if it is
no trouble to you to be so kind as to answer them. In these last two
555 days I have seen many ladies high above me. Tell me about them, by
your kindness—who may they be?'

At that the little damsel was startled. She said: 'Sir, now do not
ask! I for one will never tell you. I can tell you nothing about them.
Even if I knew anything, I ought to keep quiet. Do not take offence,
but ask for other tidings. That is my advice, if you will heed me.'

Gawan replied to her, however, by pursuing with further ques-
tions concerning all the ladies he saw sitting up there in the great
hall. The maiden was, I believe, so loyal that she wept from her
heart, and made great lament manifest.

It was still very early as yet. Meanwhile her father entered. He
would not have been at all annoyed if the well-favoured maiden had
been forced to anything there, or if any wrestling had taken place
there. She acted as if something of the like had happened, that
maiden rich in courtesy, for she was sitting close to the bed. Her
father had no objection, saying: 'Daughter, don't you weep. If
something happens in jest like this, if at first it provokes anger, it is
soon forgiven afterwards.'

556   Gawan said: 'Nothing's happened here except what we would
gladly acknowledge before you. I put a few questions to this maiden.
She thought that boded ill for me and asked me to desist. If it does
not annoy you, then let my service prevail upon you, host, and be so
kind as to tell me about the ladies high above us here. Never in all
lands did I hear of a place where so many lustrous ladies might be
seen, with such bright headdresses.'

The host wrung his hands. Then he said: 'For God's sake, do not
ask! Sir, peril above all other peril is there!'

'Then I must indeed pity their misfortune,' said Gawan. 'Host,
you must tell me why my questioning grieves you.'

'Sir, because of your valour. If you cannot forbear from question-
ing, then you will perhaps desire to venture further. That will teach
you heart's sorrow and deprive us of joy, myself and all my children,
who are born to serve you.'

Gawan said: 'You must tell me about it. If you wish, however, to
keep it from me entirely and your account eludes me, I shall no
doubt hear, I expect, how things stand there.'

557   The host replied loyally: 'Sir, then I must regret that you will not

refrain from asking. I will lend you a shield. Arm yourself, now, for a battle. You are in Terre Marveile. Lit Marveile is here. Sir, that peril up in Schastel Marveile has never yet been tried. Your life desires to venture into death. If you know anything of adventure, all that your hand has ever won by battle was but child's play. Grievous goals draw near you now.'

Gawan said: 'I should be sorry if my comfort* were to ride away from these ladies without any hardship, without my looking further into their ways. Indeed, I have heard about them before. Now that I have come so close, nothing shall daunt me from desiring to venture further for their sake.'

The host loyally voiced his sadness. He replied to his guest: 'All anguish is as nothing to what will befall him who endures this adventure. It is unsparing and uncanny, in all truth. That is no lie, lord—I am incapable of deception.'

Gawan, he of renowned fame, ignored the ferryman's fears. He 558 said: 'Now give me advice for this battle. By your leave, I shall accomplish a knight's deeds here, if God wills. I shall forever be glad of your advice and instruction. Sir host, it would be ill done if I were simply to ride away. Friend and foe alike would take me for a coward.'

Only now did the host begin to lament, for such sorrow had never befallen him. Turning to his guest, he said: 'If God makes manifest that you are not doomed to die, then you will become lord of this land. All the ladies who are held hostage here, compelled to come here by a mighty marvel, which no knight's fame has ever yet matched—many a man-at-arms, a noble company of knights—if your prowess releases them here, then you will be adorned by fame, and God will have shown you great honour! You may be lord, amid joys, over many a bright sheen, ladies from many lands. Who would count it a disgrace on your part if you were simply to ride away, now that Lischoys Gwelljus has bequeathed his fame to you here—he 559 who has done many a knightly deed, that gentle youth! Rightly do I greet him so! Courage accompanies his chivalry. God's might never grafted so many a virtue onto any man's heart, with the exception of Ither of Gaheviez.

'He who slew Ither before Nantes—my boat carried him over the river yesterday. He gave me five chargers—may God let him live in bliss!—which dukes and kings had ridden. All that he has won from them by fighting will be told at Pelrapeire. He won their surrender. His shield bears many a joust's mark. He rode here searching for the Grail.'

Gawan said: 'Where has he gone? Tell me, host, did he hear, being so close by, what the nature of this adventure is?'

'Sir, he discovered nothing about it. I knew well how to guard against mentioning it to him. I would have been guilty of impropriety if I had. If you yourself had not thought to ask, you would never have been informed of these tidings here by me—harsh cunning
560 amid dread perils! If you will not desist, I and my children have never met with such great grief as if you were to lose your life here! If, however, you retain fame and come to rule over this land, then my poverty is at an end. I trust to your hand to raise me with riches. Your fame may acquire happiness here, joy without sorrow, if you are not to die. Now arm yourself to meet great troubles!'

As yet Gawan was entirely unarmed. He said: 'Bring me my equipment here.' The host was the guarantor that his request was carried out. From cap-à-pie the gentle, well-favoured maiden then armed him. The host went to fetch his charger. A shield hung on his wall, which was so thick and stout that afterwards, indeed, it saved Gawan's life. The shield and charger were brought to him.

The host deliberated, then stood before him again. He said: 'Lord, I will tell you how you must act in the face of your deadly dangers. You must carry my shield. It is neither pierced through nor
561 hacked to pieces, for I seldom do battle. How might it then suffer damage? Lord, when you arrive up there, one thing will help you concerning your charger. A pedlar sits before the gate. Leave the charger with him, outside. Buy something from him, it doesn't matter what. He'll be the more willing to keep your charger for you, if you leave it with him as a pledge. If you are not prevented, you'll be glad to have the charger back.'

Then my lord Gawan said: 'Am I not to ride in on my charger?'

'No, lord. All the ladies' bright sheen will be hidden from you. Then troubles will draw nigh. You will find the great hall empty; you will find nothing alive there, neither great nor small. May God's grace prevail when you enter the chamber in which Lit Marveile stands! That bed and its bedposts—even if the Mahmumelin of Morocco's* crown and all his wealth were weighed against them, they would not meet their price. What it befalls you to suffer on the bed

will be as God intends for you. May he make a joyous outcome
manifest! Remember, lord, if you are worthy, never let this shield and 562
your sword leave your side. Only when you believe that your great
troubles have come to an end will they take on battle's true
semblance!'

When Gawan mounted his charger, the maiden was bereft of joys.
All who were there lamented, little suppressing their grief. He said
to his host: 'If God permits me, I shall not be slow to repay your
faithful hospitality and the care that you have taken of me.' He took
leave of the maiden, whose great grief well became her. He rode off;
they were left behind lamenting. If you would like to hear now what
happened to Gawan there, I'll be all the more willing to tell you
about it!

I'll tell the story as I heard it: when he had reached the gate he
found the pedlar, whose booth was by no means empty. So much lay
for sale inside it that I'd be a happy man to have such rich posses-
sions! Gawan dismounted in front of him. He had never seen such
rich wares as it befell him to see there. The booth was of samite, 563
square, high and wide. What lay for sale within? If its value were to
be matched in money, even the Baruch of Baldac could not pay for
what lay within there, nor the Katholikos of Ranculat.* When Greece
so stood that treasure was found there,* its Emperor's hand there
could not have paid for it, even with assistance from the other two.
Those pedlar's garments were costly indeed!

Gawan spoke his greeting to the pedlar. When he saw what won-
ders lay for sale there, Gawan asked to be shown belts or brooches, to
match his modest means.

The pedlar said: 'Truly, I have been sitting here for many a year,
without any man—only noble ladies—daring to look at what lies in
my booth. If your heart commands courage, then you will be lord of
it all. It has been brought from far afield. If you seek to gain such
fame, if you have come here in pursuit of adventure, then if you
succeed, you may strike an easy bargain with me. Whatever I have 564
for sale will be entirely at your disposal. Proceed, and may God
prevail! Was it Plippalinot* the ferryman who directed you here?
Many a lady will praise your arrival in this land, if your hand releases
her here. If you would go in search of adventure, then leave the
charger standing quietly here. I shall guard it, if you'll leave it
with me.'

Then my lord Gawan replied: 'If it befitted your station, I'd gladly leave it with you, but I am daunted by your wealth. It has never suffered such a rich groom since I mounted it.'

The pedlar replied, without any animosity: 'Lord, I myself and all my possessions—what more might I say now?—will be yours, if you are to survive here. To whom might I more rightfully belong?'

Gawan's courage instructed him to proceed on foot, valorous and undaunted. As I told you before, he found the citadel's vastness such that on all sides it was structurally well-defended. No matter how
565 many attacks befell it, it wouldn't care a straw, not if it were assailed for thirty years. In the middle of the walls there was a meadow—the Lechfeld is longer! Many towers rose above the battlements. The adventure tells us that when Gawan saw the great hall, its roof, all around, was just as if it were entirely of peacocks' plumage, brightly marked and of such colours that neither rain nor snow might harm the roof's radiance.

Inside, the great hall was splendidly adorned and ornamented, the window-shafts well engraved, with vaulting rising high above them. In the window-niches lay a wondrous number of couches here and there, each on its own. Quilts of many kinds lay upon them, of costly nature. There the ladies had sat. They had not forgotten to withdraw. No welcome was given by them to their joys' advent, their day of bliss, which depended entirely on Gawan. If only they could have seen him, what dearer fate might have befallen them? None of them
566 was to do so, no matter how willing he was to serve them. Yet no blame attached to them for that.

Then my lord Gawan walked backwards and forwards, taking a look at the great hall. In one wall—I don't know on which side—he saw a door standing wide open. Once inside that, it would befall him to win high fame, or to die in fame's pursuit.

He walked into the chamber. Its floor's sheen was pure, smooth as glass—there where Lit Marveile was, the Bed of Wonder. Four discs ran below it, of round, bright rubies, racing faster than any wind! Forked bedposts were fixed upon these. I must praise the floor to you, fashioned from jasper, chrysolyte and sardine, as intended by Clinschor, who had devised it. From many a land his cunning wisdom had brought the artifice that was invested here.

The floor was so very slippy that Gawan could scarcely get a grip
567 with his feet's assistance. It was an adventurous path he trod. Every

time, no matter how often he took a step, the bed sped away from the
position where it had stood before. Gawan was encumbered by the
heavy shield he carried, which his host had commended so warmly
to him. He thought: 'How am I to get at you, if you will dart away
from me like this? I'd teach you a lesson if I could leap onto you!'

Then the bed came to a halt before him. He raised himself for the
leap, then leapt right up onto the middle of it. With unheard-of
speed the bed propelled itself in this direction and that! It ignored
none of the four walls, but charged at each at full tilt, so that the
whole castle echoed with the sound.

Thus he rode many a great charge. All the noise that thunder has
ever made, and all trumpeters combined, if the first were in there
together with the last, blowing for profit, there might be no greater
clamour there! Gawan had no choice but to stay awake, although he
lay on the bed. What did the warrior do then? He was so overcome
by the din that he pulled the shield up over him. He lay there, and let 568
Him prevail who has held help in His hands, and who has never
wearied of help, if anyone in his great trouble knows how to try His
help. A man who is wise and sound of heart, when troubles make his
acquaintance, calls upon the Highest Hand, for that bears help in
abundance and will help him helpfully. The same befell Gawan
there. He to whom he always attributed his fame, to His potent
Grace he appealed to protect him.

Now the din died down, the four walls acquiring equal dimensions
again, the splendid bed standing there in the middle of the floor.
Greater peril now made his acquaintance. Five hundred sling-staffs*
were cunningly poised, ready to hurl missiles. The hurling gave
them escort down onto the bed where he lay. The shield maintained
such stoutness that he felt very little of the impact. They were
pebble-stones, round and hard. Here and there even that shield was
holed, however!

Now the stones had all been hurled. Seldom before had he suf- 569
fered such fierce missiles flying at him. Now five hundred crossbows
or more were drawn, ready to shoot. They were all aimed at the same
place, straight at the bed on which he lay. If anyone has braved such
perils, he may know the nature of bolts! It lasted only a short while
until they had all whirred by. If anyone is looking for comfort, let
him not approach such a bed as this! No-one will promise him
comfort there! Youth might turn grey at such comfort as Gawan

found there on that bed. Yet still his heart, and his hand, too, lay
untouched by cowardice. Neither the bolts nor the stones had missed
him entirely. He was both bruised and cut through his chain-mail.

Now he had hopes that his troubles were at an end, but he still had
to fight to win fame by his hands. At that moment a door opened
570 opposite him. A sturdy churl walked in through it. He was of fear-
some appearance. He wore a surcoat and a bonnet of fishskin, and a
pair of broad breeches of the same. He carried a cudgel in his hand,
its clubhead bigger than a jug. He walked over towards Gawan. This
was by no means the latter's wish, for he took little pleasure in his
arrival. Gawan thought: 'This man is unarmed. His defence against
me is very slight.' He sat up on the bed, as if none of his limbs hurt
him at all. The churl took a step backwards, as if intending to retreat,
but he spoke out angrily: 'You have no need to be afraid of me! All
the same, I dare say I shall see to it that something happens to you by
which you will forfeit your life! It is the Devil's doing that you are
still alive! Even if it is he who has saved you here, you shall still not
be denied death. I shall show you what I mean now, the moment
I leave!' The peasant stepped back through the door.

With his sword Gawan knocked the crossbow shafts off his shield.
The arrowheads had all pierced it right through, rattling in his
571 chain-mail. Then he heard a roar, as if a man were beating some
twenty drums for a dance there. His firm, intact resolve, which true
cowardice never notched nor cut, thought: 'What is to happen to me?
I would have good reason to complain of troubles already. If my
troubles are to increase, I must look to my defences!'

Looking in the direction of the churl's door, he saw a mighty lion
leap out. It was as high as a charger. Gawan, who was ever unwilling
to flee, took hold of the shield by its buckles. Acting as befitted
defence, he leapt down onto the stone floor. Hunger had made a
monster of this huge, mighty lion, little though it profited by it there.
Angrily it ran at the man. Sir Gawan stood his ground.

The lion had almost succeeded in taking the shield from him. Its
first lunge had gone through the shield, along with all its claws.
Seldom before has a beast clawed with such force! Gawan prevented
it from snatching his shield. He hewed one leg off it! The lion leapt
572 about on three feet, the fourth foot stuck in the shield. It gave off
such a gush of blood that Gawan could now stand firm.* Backwards
and forwards the battle began to rage. The lion sprang at the

stranger time and again, with much snorting through its nose and baring of its fangs. If they took it into their heads to train it on such food that it devoured good folk, I for one wouldn't like to reside nearby! Nor did it afford Gawan any pleasure to fight for his life against the lion there!

He had wounded it so grievously that the whole chamber was wet with blood. Angrily the lion leapt at him, intending to pull him under itself.* Gawan dealt it a blow through the breast, burying the sword up to his hand. At that the lion's wrath vanished, for it tumbled down dead. Gawan had overcome the great peril by his fighting. His immediate thought was: 'What would it be best for me to do now? I don't like sitting down in this blood. I must be on my guard, too—this bed knows how to spin around in such fashion that I ought not to sit or lie upon it, if I have my wits about me!'

Now his head was so stunned by the missiles, and his wounds 573 began to bleed, causing his bold strength to desert his company entirely—he took to stumbling because he was so dizzy. His head lay upon the lion. His shield fell to the ground beneath him. If he ever possessed strength or senses, they had both been taken from him. He had been ungently assailed.

All his senses deserted him. His pillow was unlike that which Gymele of Monte Rybele, that gentle and discerning lady, placed for Kahenis, on which he slept away his fame.* Fame was running to meet this man, for you have heard clearly enough how he had come to lose his wits and lay there unconscious—how that had come about.

Covertly it was observed that the chamber's floor was bedewed with blood. They both had death's semblance, the lion and Gawan. A fair damsel peeped anxiously into the chamber from above. At the 574 sight her bright sheen grew most pale. The young girl was so dismayed that the aged lady broke into a lament—Arnive the wise. I still praise her today for saving the knight and averting his death then.

She too walked over to see. Then the lady looked down from the window into the chamber, but she could say neither one thing nor the other—whether it was the day of their joy's advent, or of everlasting, heartfelt sorrow. She feared the knight was dead. Her thoughts necessarily taught her that distress, for he simply lay there on top of the lion, and kept no other bed. She said: 'I shall grieve from my heart if your loyal valour has lost you your noble life. If you have met with death here for the sake of our most wretched company, since it was your loyalty prompted you to it, then your virtue will always move me to pity, whether you possess age or youth.'*

Turning to all the ladies, she then said, seeing the hero lying there like that: 'You ladies who practise baptism, appeal, all of you, to God for His blessing!' She sent two damsels to the chamber, entreating them to take proper care to creep in quietly and, even before they left the room, to give her tidings as to whether he was alive or if he had passed away. That order she gave to both of them. Those gentle, pure maidens—is either of them weeping? Indeed, both of them, copiously, on true grief's instruction, when they found him lying there like that, the shield floating in the blood from his wounds. They looked to see if he was alive.

One of them, with her lustrous hand, untied the helmet from his head, and his ventail, too. There a tiny bubble of foam lay on his red lips. She looked intently to see if he was drawing in breath at all, or if he were deceiving them into thinking he was alive. It was as yet in dispute. On his surcoat were two gampiluns of sable, such arms as Ilinot the Briton had worn with great fame. He took ample worth with him, in his youth, unto his end. The maiden tore off some of the sable with her hand and held it in front of his nose, to see whether his breath so stirred the hair that it moved at all.

Breath was found there! At once she ordered that clear water be brought at the bound. Her well-favoured playmate fetched it for her speedily. The maiden pressed her little finger between his teeth— this happened in all propriety! Then she poured the water into the gap, gently, and then some more. She did not pour too much, though, until he opened his eyes. He offered them his service, and spoke his thanks to the two gentle girls: 'That you should find me lying here in such ill-bred fashion! If you were to keep silent about this, I would think it a kindness on your part. May your courtesy guard you against telling!'

They said: 'You lay and lie as one who fosters the highest fame. You have won such fame here as you will joyfully cherish in old age. The victory is yours today! Now console us poor folk with the hope that your wounds may be of such a nature that we may rejoice along with you.'

He said: 'If you would like to see me live, then you must give me help.' He entreated the ladies: 'Let my wounds be seen to by someone skilled in such matters. Yet if I am to do further battle, then buckle my helmet on me and go. I am willing to defend myself!'

They said: 'You shall be spared battle now. Sir, let us stay with you—except one of us must win the messenger's bread from four queens, for the tidings that you are still alive! Moreover, comfort and pure medicaments must be prepared for you, and you will be tended loyally, with such a goodly salve as will ease your bruises and cure the wounds, helping you gently.'

One of the maidens leapt off, so nimbly that there was no hint of a hobble. She took to the court the tidings that he lived, 'and is so alive that he may joyfully make us rich in joy, God willing. Yet he is 578 in need of good help.'

They all said: '*Die merzis!*'* The wise old queen ordered a bed to be prepared, a carpet to be spread out before it, by a good fire. Salves of great value, well and wisely prepared, were obtained by the queen for the bruises and wounds. Then she gave immediate order that four ladies should go and remove his armour, taking it off him gently, and taking pains that he had no reason to feel at all ashamed. 'You must take a phellel-silk between you, and disarm him in its shade. If he is in a fit state to walk, permit him to do so, or carry him in to me here, by the bed. I shall see to the place where the hero is to lie. If his combat has so thriven that he is not mortally wounded, I shall soon restore him to full health. If any of his wounds were fatal, that would hew through our joys. We too would be slain thereby and would have to bear a living death!'

Well, these instructions were carried out. Sir Gawan was dis- 579 armed and led away, and help prepared by those who knew how to help. There were fifty or more of his wounds, but the bolts had not pressed too grievously through the chain-mail. The shield had been held up against them. Then the aged queen took dittany, and warm wine, and blue sendal-silk.* Next she wiped the bloodstains off the wounds, every single one, and bandaged him so that he would recover. Where the helmet had bent inwards his head was swollen, showing where the missiles had struck. She removed that bruising by the salve's power, and by her skill.

She said: 'I shall soon bring you comfort. Cundrie la Surziere is so kind as to visit me often. Whatever medicine can achieve she places at my disposal. Ever since Anfortas entered grief's endurance and they have sought help for him, this salve has helped prevent him 580 from dying. It has come from Munsalvæsche.'

When Gawan heard Munsalvæsche named, he began to sight joy. He thought it must be close by. Then he who was ever free of falsity, Gawan, said to the queen: 'Lady, my senses, which had run away from me, you have restored to my heart, and my pain is easing. Whatever I have by way of strength or senses, your servitor has entirely by your doing.'

She replied: 'Sir, to your favour we must all draw near, hastening there with loyalty. Now obey me, and do not talk much. There is a herb I'll give you which will make you sleep. That'll be good for you. You must not think of eating or drinking at all before nightfall. That way your strength will return to you. Then I'll step in with enough food to last you till tomorrow morning.'

She put the herb into his mouth, at which he immediately fell asleep. She saw to it that he was well bedded. Thus he slept beyond 581 daybreak, that knight rich in honour and poor in disgrace, lying quite comfortably, and he was warm, though sometimes in his sleep he shivered, gulping and sneezing—all brought about by the salve's power. A great company of ladies walked out, others entered in. They bore a bright, noble sheen. The aged Arnive gave order by her authority that none of them should call out for as long as the hero slept there. She requested, moreover, that the great hall be locked. All the knights there, the men-at-arms, the townsfolk—none of those heard those tidings until the next day. Then fresh sorrow came to the ladies.

Thus the warrior slept until nightfall. The queen then thought to take the herb out of his mouth. He awoke. It became him to drink. Then the wise queen ordered that drink and good food be brought in. He raised himself into a seated position and ate with relish. A great number of ladies stood before him. Never did nobler service make his acquaintance. Courteously they carried out their service. 582 Then my lord Gawan scrutinized first this one, then that, and then another. He was, to put it plainly, full of his old longing for the lustrous Orgeluse, for no woman in all his years had ever touched him so closely, no matter where he had received love, or love had been refused him.

Then the undaunted warrior said to his nurse, the aged queen:

'Lady, it goes against my good breeding—you may think it importunate of me—if these ladies are to stand before me. Command them to go and be seated, or have them eat along with me.'

'There will be no sitting down here by anybody except me. Sir, they would have good cause to be ashamed if they were not to give you great service, for you are our joys' compass. Yet, sir, whatever you command them, they must carry out, if we are of sound mind.'

Those noble ladies of high lineage were prevented by their courtesy from sitting, for they acted thus of their own free will. Their sweet mouths entreated him for permission to stand there until he had finished eating, none of them sitting down. When that had ensued, they withdrew. Gawan laid himself down to sleep.

BOOK XII

IF anyone were to deprive him of rest now—if resting became him— 583 I believe it would be a sin on that man's part. According to the adventure's record he had toiled hard, exalting and broadening his fame in great extremity. All that noble Lancelot suffered on the Sword Bridge, and afterwards, when he did battle against Meljacanz,* was nothing compared with this extremity—nor what is told of Garel, that proud, mighty king who threw the lion out of the great hall at Nantes in such knightly fashion. Garel also fetched the knife, on account of which he suffered hardship in the marble pillar.*

If a mule were to carry those bolts, it would be too heavily burdened by them—those that Gawan, with his accustomed courage, had allowed to whirr towards his body, as his valorous heart commanded him. The ford of Li Gweiz Prelljus,* and Erec, who won Schoydelacurt from Mabonagrin* in combat—neither of these caused such great anguish—nor when proud Iwan would not desist from pouring water upon the adventure's stone.* Even if all these troubles were to 584 be combined, Gawan's troubles would tip the balance, if any one were to weigh hardship's pick.

What troubles do I mean, now? If it did not seem to you too early, I would name them to you in full: Orgeluse entered right into Gawan's heart's thoughts—he who was ever weak in cowardice and strong when it came to true courage. How did it come about that such a big woman hid herself in such a small place? She came along a narrow path into Gawan's heart, causing all his pain to vanish in the face of these troubles. Those were, however, low walls, within which such a tall woman sat, one whom in his loyalty his wakeful servitude never forgot. No-one ought to laugh at a woman being capable of vanquishing such a valiant man. Alas and alack! What is the meaning of this? Here Lady Love is displaying her wrath against him who has won fame. Yet she has found him to be valiant and undaunted. Against that sick, wounded man she ought to have disdained to use force. He ought, after all, to benefit from her having overcome him against his will, when he was still in full health.

Lady Love, if you would win fame, you might perhaps permit yourself to be told that this battle does you no honour. Gawan lived all his days as your favour commanded him, as did also his father Lot. On his mother's side all his lineage observed your rule entirely, ever since the times of Mazadan, whom Terdelaschoye took to Famurgan,* moved then by your might. Of Mazadan's heirs it has often been heard since that none of them ever abandoned you. Ither of Gaheviez bore your seal. Whenever he was mentioned before women, none of them would ever feel ashamed—whenever his name was named—if she acknowledged Love's power. Now judge by her who saw him with her own eyes—to her the true tidings had come!* By his death, Lady Love, you were deprived of service.

Now put Gawan to death, too, as you did his kinsman Ilinot, that young, gentle knight whom your power compelled to strive to win a noble *âmîe*, Florie of Kanadic.* As a child he fled from his father's land. That same queen brought him up; he was a stranger in Brittany. Florie burdened him with Love's load, chasing him beyond that land's boundaries. In her service he was found dead, as you have indeed heard. Gawan's kin has often met with heartfelt wounds because of Love. I shall name to you more of his kinsmen, who have also been hurt by Love's pangs. Why was it that the blood-hued snow afflicted Parzival's loyal person? It was the queen, his wife, who brought that about. Galoes and Gahmuret, both those you trampled underfoot, consigning them to the bier. The young, noble Itonje loyally bore constant, unimpaired love for *roys* Gramoflanz.* She was Gawan's lustrous sister. Lady Love, you also bestowed your malice upon Soredamor, for Alixandre's sake.* She and all the others—all the kindred Gawan ever gained—Lady Love, you would not exempt

them from rendering you service. Now you wish to win fame by 587
Gawan himself.

You ought to pit strength against strength, and let Gawan live,
sick as he is with his wounds, and oppress instead those in good
health. Many a man has songs of love whom Love never afflicted so
sorely. I ought, I suppose, to be silent now.* Lovers, instead, ought to
lament what troubled him of Norway, when he had survived the
adventure, only to be assailed all too harshly, bereft of help, by
Love's storm.

He said: 'Alas that I ever beheld these restless beds! The one has
sorely wounded me, and the other increased my thoughts of love.
Orgeluse the duchess must show me mercy, if I am to remain in joy's
company.'

Out of impatience he so tossed and turned that several of his
wounds' bandages broke. In such distress he lay there. Now, behold,
the day shone in upon him! He had had an ungentle wait for its
coming. Often in the past he had endured many a fierce sword-fight
more comfortably than that time of rest.

If anyone's troubles resemble these, if any lover boasts of the 588
like, let him first recover full health after being so sorely wounded
by bolts—that may easily cause him as much pain as his love-pangs
did before!* Gawan bore love's burden, and had other cause for
complaint, too.

Then day began to shine so bright that his tall candles' glow could
stretch nowhere near as far. The warrior arose. His linen clothes
were stained by wounds and armour-rust. A shirt and breeches of
buckram had been laid out for him there—he was glad to accept that
exchange!—and a sleeveless marten-fur robe, a jerkin of the same,
over those two a woollen cloak, sent there from Arras. Two light
summer boots lay there too, which indulged in no great narrowness.
He put on these new clothes.

Then my lord Gawan went out by the chamber door. He walked
backwards and forwards until he found the sumptuous great hall.
His eyes had never become acquainted with wealth capable of equal-
ling it. Up through the hall on the one side rose a vault, none too 589
wide, with steps mounting high above the hall; the vault wound
round in a circle.* On top of it stood a lustrous pillar. It was not made
of rotten wood, but was bright and sturdy, so huge that Lady
Kamille's sarcophagus* could easily have stood on top of it. From

Feirefiz's lands wise Clinschor had brought the edifice that rose there. Round as a pavilion it was. If the hand of Master Geometras* had had to design it, such artistry would have been beyond him. It was wrought with cunning: diamond and amethyst—so the adventure informs us—topaz and garnet, chrysolite, ruby, emerald, sardine—such were its sumptuous windows. Wide and visibly matching in height the windows' columns—such was the whole roof above.

590   No column that stood amongst them could compare with the great pillar in the middle. The adventure tells us what wonders it could command. To view it, Sir Gawan went, alone, up into the watchtower, where he saw many a precious stone. There he found such a great marvel that he could never weary of watching. It seemed to him that in the great pillar all countries were made known to him, and that the lands were going round and round, and that the great mountains were on the receiving end of one another's joust. In the pillar he found people riding and walking, some running, some standing.* He sat down at one of the windows; he wanted to investigate the marvel further.

Then the aged Arnive entered, and her daughter Sangive, and two of her daughter's daughters. All four of them approached. Gawan leapt to his feet on seeing them. Queen Arnive said: 'Lord, you ought to be still indulging in sleep. Have you abandoned resting? You are too sorely wounded to do so, if fresh hardship is to make your acquaintance.'

He replied: 'Lady and mistress nurse, your help has given me such strength of body and mind that I shall serve to repay you, if I live.'

591   The queen said: 'If, as I perceive, you acknowledge me, lord, as your mistress, then kiss these ladies, all three. You will be spared disgrace in this. They are born of king's lineage.'

He was delighted at that request. He kissed the lustrous ladies then: Sangive and Itonje, and gentle Cundrie. Gawan sat down, making a fifth. Then he looked to and fro at the lustrous maidens' persons. Nevertheless, the one woman who lay in his heart so afflicted him that those maidens' radiance was nothing but a misty day compared with Orgeluse. She seemed to him, quite simply, so very fair— the duchess of Logroys—that was where his heart hunted him.

Well, it had come to pass that Gawan had been welcomed by all three ladies. They bore such bright sheen that a heart that had not suffered previous pangs might easily have been pierced thereby. He spoke to his mistress about the pillar he saw there, asking her for tidings as to its nature.

She replied: 'Lord, this stone has shone by day and every night 592 since I first became acquainted with it, for a radius of six miles into the surrounding country. Whatever happens within that compass, in the water and in the fields, can be seen in this column—it gives a true report. Be it bird or beast, stranger or forester, foreigner or familiar, they have been found therein. Its beam ranges over six miles. It is so solid and so intact that even with powerful cunning, neither hammer nor smith could ever harm it. It was stolen in Tabronit from Queen Secundille—against her will, as I believe!'

Gawan saw in the pillar at that moment a knight and a lady riding, both clearly visible. The lady seemed to him lustrous, the knight and charger fully armed, and the helmet adorned. They came hasting through the ford onto the plain. Gawan was the object of their journey. They were coming along the road through the moor that 593 had been taken by haughty Lischoys, whom Gawan had defeated. The lady was leading the knight by the bridle. Jousting was his intent. Gawan turned round, only to increase his sorrow. He had thought that the pillar had deceived him, but then he saw, beyond denial, Orgeluse de Logroys and a courteous knight on the turf, approaching the mooring-place. If white hellebore* is rapid and powerful in the nose—through his narrow heart the duchess entered in like fashion, in at the top and down through his eyes. A man helpless in the face of love, alas, is Sir Gawan! To his mistress nurse he said, seeing the knight approach: 'Lady, there comes a knight, riding with raised spear. He will not desist from searching, and his search shall find what it seeks. Since he desires to do knightly deeds, he will be granted battle by me. Tell me, who may the lady be?'

She said: 'That is the Duchess of Logroys, that lustrous lady. 594 Whom does she come to endanger in this fashion? The Turkoyt has come with her, he of whom it has so often been heard that his heart is undaunted. He has won such fame by spears that three lands would be honoured by it. You must avoid doing battle now against his valiant hand. It is far too early for you to fight. You are too sorely wounded to do battle. Even if you were in full health, you ought to desist from doing battle against him.'

My lord Gawan replied: 'You say I am to be lord here. If, then, anyone seeks knightly combat so close by, challenging all my honour, since he desires battle, lady, I must have my armour.'

At that much weeping ensued on the part of all four ladies. They said: 'If you would adorn your good fortune and your fame, then do not on any account do battle! If you lay dead before him, our extremity would grow afresh. Even if you were to survive—if you now wish to don armour—your earlier wounds will take your life. Then we shall be surrendered to death.'

595   Thus Gawan wrestled with troubles. You may hear, if you will, what oppressed him. He held the noble Turkoyt's approach to be an affront to his honour. Wounds troubled him greatly, too, and Love a great deal more, and the four ladies' grief, for he beheld loyalty in them. He entreated them to forbear from weeping. His mouth, furthermore, requested his armour, charger, and sword. The lustrous and noble ladies led Gawan back into the hall. He entreated them to walk down ahead of him to where the other ladies were, those gentle and lustrous women.

Gawan was soon armed for his battle's journey there, amid bright, weeping eyes. They did this so secretly that no-one heard the tidings, except the chamberlain who ordered his charger to be groomed. Gawan crept out to where Gringuljete stood, but he was so sorely wounded that he could scarcely carry the shield that far—and that, too, was amply riddled with holes.

Sir Gawan mounted the charger, then rode away from the castle, 596 heading for his loyal host, who denied him very little of all that his will desired. He furnished him with a spear, which was stout and untrimmed. Plippalinot had picked up many of these over there on the far bank, on his plain. Then my lord Gawan asked him to ferry him across quickly. In a punt he took him across to the far bank, where he found the noble and haughty Turkoyt. He was so guarded against disgrace that misdeed had vanished from him. His fame was of such high repute that whoever had indulged in jousting against him had been left lying behind his charger, felled by his joust. Thus he had vanquished in jousting all who had ever ridden against him in pursuit of fame. Moreover, that noble warrior boasted that he desired to inherit high fame by spears, without sword,* or else let his fame perish. If anyone gained such fame that he felled him in the joust, he would be seen to offer no defence and would concede surrender to that man.

Gawan heard these tidings from the jousts' stake-holder. Plip- 597
palinot took forfeits as follows: whatever joust took place in public
there, one falling, the other keeping his seat, he would receive, with-
out incurring either's enmity, the former's loss and the latter's
gain—I mean the charger, which he would lead away. He did not care
how long they fought. Which of them incurred fame or disgrace he
left to the ladies to pronounce upon—they had frequent occasion to
observe jousting there.

He entreated Gawan to sit firmly in the saddle. He led his charger
out onto the bank, proffering him shield and spear. Along came
the Turkoyt, galloping like a man who knows how to direct his
joust, neither too high nor too low. Gawan went riding towards him.
Gringuljete of Munsalvæsche did as Gawan asked, as the reins
instructed. Gawan headed onto the plain.

Charge on! Let the joust be done! Along came King Lot's son,
valorous, no tremor in his heart. Where are the helmet's cords tied?
At that very spot the Turkoyt's joust struck him. Gawan hit him
elsewhere, through the face-guard. Soon it was clearly perceived 598
who was the guarantor of the other's fall there. With his short,
sturdy spear Sir Gawan caught the Turkoyt's helmet—away rode the
helmet, here lay the man—he who had ever been a flower of honour
until he thus bedecked the grass with his fall by the joust. His
accoutrements' costly sheen vied with the flowers in the dew. Gawan
came riding at him, until the Turkoyt vowed surrender to him. The
ferryman spoke his claim to the charger. That was his right—who
would deny it?

'You would willingly rejoice, if only you knew why!' said lustrous
Orgeluse, again directing her malice against Gawan. 'Because the
mighty lion's paw is obliged to follow you about in your shield, you
now imagine that fame has befallen you. Since these ladies have seen
such jousting on your part, we must concede joy to you, if you are
content at Lit Marveile taking such small vengeance. Even so, your
shield is shattered, as if you had made battle's acquaintance. No
doubt you are now too sorely wounded to meet with battle's rough 599
and tumble. That might cause you more pain, to go along with being
called a goose!* Perhaps, so that you can boast about it, you are glad
that your shield is riddled with holes like a sieve, shattered by so
many a bolt. For the present you would doubtless like to flee hard-
ship. I tweak your nose! Ride back up to the ladies. How might you

dare behold such battle as I would procure for you, if your heart desired to serve me in pursuit of love?'

He said to the duchess: 'Lady, if I have wounds, they have found help here. If it can befit your help to deign to accept my service, then never was such harsh peril known that I shall not be summoned to face it, in order to serve you.'

She said: 'I shall permit you to ride, to fight for further fame, in my company.'

At that proud, noble Gawan became rich in joys. He sent the Turkoyt away, along with his host, Plippalinot. Up to the castle he sent a message that all the well-favoured ladies were to treat him with honour.

600   Gawan's spear had remained intact, even though both chargers had been driven by spurs into the joust's clash. In his hand he bore it away from the bright meadow. Many a lady wept that his journey parted him from them there.

Queen Arnive said: 'Our solace has chosen for himself one who is his eyes' ease, his heart's thorn. Alas that now he thus follows Orgeluse the duchess towards Li Gweiz Prelljus! That'll be of no profit to his wounds!'

Four hundred ladies were in mourning. He rode away from them, in fame's pursuit. No matter how much his wounds hurt him, all that pain had been averted by Orgeluse's radiant complexion. She said: 'You must procure for me a garland from a certain tree's branch. In return I shall praise your deed, if you will procure it for me. Thus you may seek to win my love.'

He replied: 'Lady, wherever that twig grows which can procure for me such high fame and bring me such bliss that I may lament to you, lady, my distress, hoping to gain your favour—I shall pluck it, if death does not prevent me!'

601   All the bright flowers that grew there were as nothing compared with the complexion brought there by Orgeluse. Gawan thought of her so intensely that his former hardship caused him no further distress. Thus she rode with her guest, a good few miles from the castle, along a road both broad and straight, until they came to a shimmering greenwood. The trees may have been of these species: tamarisk and brazil. This was Clinschor's forest. Gawan the bold warrior said: 'Lady, where I am to pluck the garland by which my hole-riddled joy may be made entire?' He should have just thrust

her to the ground, as has often happened to many a lustrous lady since!

She said: 'I shall show you the place where you may win fame.'

Across fields towards a ravine they rode, until they came so close that they could see the garland's tree. Then she said: 'Sir, that tree-trunk was planted by him who deprived me of joy. If you bring me a twig from it, never did a knight win such high fame by love-service'—so spoke the duchess—'Here I shall spare myself further 602 riding. God prevail, if you will ride further! If so, there is no need for you to prolong matters, but you must leap courageously, mounted thus upon your charger, across Li Gweiz Prelljus!'

She came to a dead halt upon the plain. Sir Gawan rode onwards. He could hear a rapid waterfall. It had riven a valley—broad, deep, impassable. Gawan, rich in courage, spurred his charger forward. The high-born warrior drove it on, so that with two feet it trod upon the further bank, but that leap had to be accompanied by a fall. Even the duchess wept at that. The current was fast and powerful. Gawan profited by his strength, even though he bore armour's burden. One branch of a tree had grown out into the river's flow. The strong knight grasped it, for he had as yet no wish to die. His spear was floating nearby. The warrior seized it. He climbed out onto the land.

Gringuljete was swimming, now above, now below the surface. Now he made to help his horse. The charger had floated so far 603 downriver that he was reluctant to run after it, for he wore heavy armour—he had wounds in plenty, too. Now an eddy drove it towards him, so that he could reach it with his spear, at a place where the rain and its downpour had broken through, bringing about a broad flow, by a steep slope. The bank was split—that saved Gringuljete. Using his spear, Gawan guided the charger so close to the land that he could grasp the bridle with his hand.

Thus my lord Gawan hauled the charger out onto the plain. It shook itself. Not only had the charger survived, but the shield, too, had not been left behind.* He girthed the charger and took hold of the shield. If anyone is not troubled by his sorrow, I'll let that pass! He was in some distress, however, for Love commanded it of him. Resplendent Orgeluse had hunted him in pursuit of the garland. That was a brave ride! The tree was so guarded that even if there had been two Gawans, they might have yielded their lives in the cause of

the garland. It was in the custody of King Gramoflanz. Nonetheless,
Gawan plucked the garland.

604   The river was called the Sabins. Gawan collected ungentle interest
when he and his charger paddled in it. No matter how brightly
Orgeluse shone, *I* wouldn't accept her love on such terms. I know
well enough what is meet for the likes of me.

When Gawan had plucked the twig, and the garland had become
his helmet's cover, a shining knight rode towards him, whose sea-
sons' years were neither too short nor too long. His mind compelled
him, out of arrogance, no matter how much a man injured him, not
to do battle with him, unless two or more opposed him. His high
heart was so haughty that no matter what any one man did to him, he
would leave him without battle.

Fil li roy Irot offered Gawan good morning—King Gramoflanz,
that is. He said: 'Lord, I have not entirely renounced my claim to this
garland. My greeting would have been entirely withheld as yet, if
there had been two of you who had not forborne, in pursuit of high
fame, thus to fetch a twig from my tree—they would have had to
accept battle. As it is, however, I must disdain to fight.'

605   Nor was Gawan, for his part, willing to do battle with him. The
king was riding without armour. Yet the famed warrior carried a
yearling sparrowhawk, which perched upon his radiant hand.
Itonje, Gawan's gentle sister, had sent it to him. Of peacock-feathers
from Sinzester* was the hat on his head. Of samite, green as grass,
was the cloak that the king wore, its edges almost touching the
ground on either side of him. Its down was of bright ermine. None
too big, yet sturdy enough was the horse that carried the king,
undeceived of equine beauty, led there from Denmark, or brought by
sea. The king rode entirely unarmed, for he had no sword about him.

'Your shield tells that you have been in battle,' said King Gramo-
flanz, 'so little of your shield is intact. Lit Marveile has fallen to your
lot! You have endured the adventure which ought to have awaited
606   me, except that wise Clinschor has always treated me peacefully, and
I am in a state of feud with her who has won true Love's victory by
her lustre. She can still wield anger against me. Indeed, extremity
compels her to it. I slew Cidegast, her noble husband, together with
three others. I abducted Orgeluse, offering her my crown and all my
land. No matter what service my hand offered her, she turned her
heart's hostility against it. I besought her with pleading for a whole

year. I could never win her love. I have every right to complain to you from my heart. I know full well that she has offered you love, since you seek my death here. If you had come here now in company with another, you might have taken my life from me, or you might both have been killed—that is the reward you would have won.

'My heart goes in search of other love, from one where help depends upon your favour, since you have become lord of Terre Marveile. Your fighting has won you such fame—if you will now wield kindness, then help me with regard to a maiden for whom my heart makes moan. She is King Lot's daughter. No woman on earth ever afflicted me so greatly. I have her tokens here.* Now convey my 607 service to that well-favoured maiden there. I am, moreover, confident that she is fond of me, for I have endured duress for her sake.

'Ever since mighty Orgeluse, with heartfelt words, denied me her love—if I have won fame since then—whether I have been happy or sad—all that was brought about by noble Itonje. Unfortunately I have seen nothing of her. If your solace is willing to promise me help, then take this elegant ring to my lustrous, gentle lady. You are spared fighting here entirely. Unless your company were greater in number, two or more, who would account it honourable on my part if I were to slay you or enforce your surrender? Such combat my hand has ever shunned.'

Then my lord Gawan replied: 'I may be only one man, but I can defend myself. If you have no wish to win fame by slaying me, then nor shall I gain any fame from having plucked this twig. Who would account it great honour on my part if I were to slay you, unarmed as you are? I am willing to be your messenger. Hand me that ring, and 608 let me tell her of your service, nor will I be silent concerning your sorrow.'

The king thanked him warmly. Gawan went on to ask him: 'Since you disdain to do battle against me, tell me now, lord, who you are.'

'You must not take it as a disgrace,'* said the king. 'My name is unconcealed. My father was called Irot. He was slain by King Lot. I am King Gramoflanz. My high heart has ever been of such integrity that never will I, at any time, do battle with one man, no matter how much he injures me—except for one called Gawan, of whom I have heard such fame that I would gladly meet him in battle, because of the grief I bear. His father broke faith, slaying my father in the act of greeting. I have ample cause for complaint against him! Now Lot has died, and Gawan has won such fame, excelling all others, that no-one who sits at the Table Round can compare with him in fame. I'll live to see battle's day against him yet!'

609　　　Noble Lot's son replied: 'If it is out of a desire to endear yourself to your lady-love—if such she be—that you are capable of attributing such treacherous cunning to her father, and would, moreover, gladly have slain her brother, then she is an evil-hearted maiden if she does not complain of such behaviour on your part. If she were capable of being a true daughter and sister, she would be an advocate for both of them, and you would renounce your enmity. How might it become your father-in-law if he had broken faith? Have you not exacted vengeance for proclaiming him false, now he is dead?* His son will not be daunted by this; nothing shall deter him, even if he cannot benefit by his well-favoured sister—he offers himself as a pledge. Sir, I am called Gawan. Whatever my father has done to you, avenge upon me—he is dead. I must give myself as hostage in his stead, to do combat against his disgrace's duress, if my life is honourable.'

The king replied: 'If it is you towards whom I bear irreconciled
610　enmity, then your noble worth brings me both joy and sorrow. One thing brings me pleasure where you are concerned—that I am to do battle with you. Moreover, high fame has fallen to your lot, since I have conceded to you alone that I shall meet you in single combat. It will profit our fame if we have noble ladies behold the battle. I shall bring fifteen hundred to it. You also have a lustrous company, up in Schastel Marveile. Your uncle Arthur will add to your share, from a land that is named Löver. Are you acquainted with the city of Bems on the Korcha? All that household is there. In a week's time from today Arthur should arrive, amid great *joye*. Sixteen days from today I shall arrive, to avenge my old wrong, upon the plain of Joflanze, to pay back the plucking of this garland.'

The king entreated Gawan to ride with him into the city of Rosche Sabbins: 'You won't be able to find any other bridge.'

My lord Gawan replied: 'I shall go back the way I came. Otherwise,
611　I shall meet your wishes.' They exchanged oaths that they would both arrive at Joflanze, along with a host of knights and ladies, to defend themselves on the day appointed, the two to meet alone in the rink.

Thus my lord Gawan parted from the noble king. Joyously he galloped along, the garland adorning his helmet. He had no desire to hold his charger in check, but drove it on with the spurs to the ravine. Gringuljete measured its leap, wide though it was, in good time, so that Gawan entirely avoided falling.

The duchess rode up to him, to where the warrior had alighted from his charger onto the grass, and was adjusting the horse's girth. Once in his presence, the mighty duchess rapidly dismounted. She threw herself at his feet, saying: 'Lord, such duress as I have desired of you went beyond what my worth ever merited. Truly, your toil brings such heart's sorrow upon me as a loyal woman should feel for her dear beloved's sake.'

He replied: 'Lady, if it is true that you are greeting me without 612 malice, then you are nearing honour. After all, I am wise enough to know that that if the shield is to have its due, you have acted badly by it. The shield's office is of such high degree that any man who has properly practised chivalry has always withdrawn himself from mockery. Lady, if I may say as much, whoever has seen me wielding the shield must concede chivalry to me. There have been times when you have spoken differently, since you first saw me. I'll let that be. Accept this garland. You must never again offer such dishonour to any knight inspired by your radiant complexion. If your scorn were to be my lot, I'd rather do without love.'

The lustrous and mighty duchess said, weeping from her heart: 'Lord, when I have told you of the distress I bear in my heart, then you will grant I have won profit in sorrow. Let all those who are slighted by my intent pardon me, by their courtesy. Never can I lose more joy than I lost by peerless Cidegast. My radiant, gentle *beâs âmîs**—so luminous 613 was his fame and so desirous of true honour that all men, whoever they be, born of mothers in his time's years, must concede him such honour as was never outfought by others' fame. He was a living well of virtue, guarded in his fertile youth against false practice. Out of the darkness toward the light he had grown, propping his fame so high that it was beyond the reach of anyone whom falsity could weaken. His fame knew how to grow so high out of his heart's seeds that all others were beneath it. How does swift Saturn race high above all the planets? A monicirus of fidelity—since I can speak the truth—such was my perfect husband. On that beast maidens should take pity, for it is slain on account of its purity.* I was his heart, he was my body—I lost him, loss-laden woman that I am. He was slain by King Gramoflanz, from whom you have taken this garland.

614 'Lord, if my words offended you, the reason was that I wanted to test whether I ought to offer you love on account of your noble worth. Indeed I know, lord, that my words offended you—it was done as a test.* Now you must be so kind as to forfeit your anger and forgive me entirely. You it is who are rich in courage. I compare you to the gold that is refined in the fire—so your spirit is refined. That man I brought you here to harm—as I think, and as I then thought—has inflicted heart's grief upon me.'

Then my lord Gawan replied: 'Lady, unless death prevents me, I shall teach the king such duress as shall check his arrogance. I have pledged my loyalty to ride to meet him in combat in a short time. There we are to collect interest on valour. Lady, I have forgiven you. If, by your courtesy, you will not disdain my foolish advice, I would
615 advise you about womanly honour and nobility's counsel. Now there is no-one here except us. Lady, grant me your favour!'

She said: 'In iron-clad arms I have seldom grown warm. Yet I will not contest your winning service's reward by me on other occasions. I shall bemoan your toil until you are fully recovered to health from all your wounds, until the damage is healed. I shall return with you to Schastel Marveile.'

'What you wish will increase my joy,' replied the ardent man. He hoisted the fair lady, pressing her to him, up onto her horse. She had not thought him worthy of that before, when he had seen her above the spring and she had spoken with such a crooked tongue.

Gawan rode on in joyous fashion, yet her weeping was not avoided until he lamented along with her. He told her to tell him why she was weeping, and to forbear, in God's name. She said: 'Lord, I must complain to you of him who slew my noble Cidegast. Because of this,
616 sorrow can do no other but grope into my heart, where joy lay when I tended Cidegast's love. I am not so reduced that I have not since then striven to bring harm upon the king, cost what it might, and have had many a fierce joust directed at his life. Perhaps help will come to me by you, avenging me and making me amends for the sorrow that whets my heart.

'Seeking Gramoflanz's death, I accepted the service offered me by a king who was perfection's lord. Sir, he is called Anfortas. For love's sake I accepted from his hand the pedlar's wares from Tabronit that still stand before your gate, which fetch a high price. The king, in my service, won such reward as caused all my joy to perish. Just as I was to grant him love, I had to wish new grief upon myself. In my service he procured injury. Equal sorrow—or more— than Cidegast could give me, was given to me by Anfortas's wound. Now tell me, how was I, poor woman, faithful as I am, to keep my wits in such extremity? Indeed, at times my mind weakens, since he 617 lies so helpless, he whom I chose to make amends for Cidegast and wreak vengeance. Sir, hear now how Clinschor acquired the rich merchandise before your gate.

'When radiant Anfortas was deprived of love and joy—he who had sent me the gift—I feared disgrace. Clinschor keeps constant company with the lore of necromancy, so that he is capable of overpowering by magic both women and men. Wherever he espies noble folk, he will not leave them without troubles. To be at peace, I gave over to Clinschor my merchandise, rich of aspect. If the adventure were ever withstood, if anyone ever won that prize, I was to seek that man's love. If he had no inclination towards love, then the merchandise would again be mine. Thus it is now to be ours. Those there present swore it. It was my desire to endanger Gramoflanz by that stratagem, but, unfortunately, that is still unfulfilled. If he had sought the adventure, he would have had to suffer death.

'Clinschor is courtly and wise. To enhance his fame, he permits 618 my renowned retinue to engage in chivalry all over his land, with many a thrust and cut. Throughout the weeks, all their days, all the weeks in the year, I have special forces on the alert, some by day, others by night. I have spared no expense in my intent to harm haughty Gramoflanz. He fights many a battle with them. What is it that has always protected him? I knew how to plot against his life. Those who were too wealthy to take my pay—if any of them were not otherwise well disposed towards me, I had many serve for love, but I did not promise them any reward.

'There was no man who ever beheld my person who was not willing to serve me, except for one, who wore red armour. He put my household in peril. He came riding up to Logroys. There he disposed of them, his hand scattering them upon the ground in a manner that gave me little pleasure. Between Logroys and your landing-stage five of my knights pursued him. He defeated them upon the plain and gave their chargers to the ferryman.

'When he had vanquished my men, I myself rode after that warrior. 619 I offered him my land and person. He said he had a more beautiful

wife, and that she was dearer to him. Those words weighed heavy
with me. I asked who she might be. "The Queen of Pelrapeire—so
that fair lady is named, and I myself am called Parzival. I want
nothing of your love. The Grail vouchsafes me other sorrow." Thus
spoke the warrior, in anger. Then that peerless knight rode off. Did
I act wrongly in this—would you inform me—if, in my heart's dis-
tress, I offered love to that noble knight? If so, my love has sold itself
cheaply.'

Gawan said to the duchess: 'Lady, I know him of whom you
requested love to be so deserving that if he *had* chosen you as his
beloved, your fame would have remained undiminished by him.'

Courteous Gawan and the Duchess of Logroys looked intently at
one another. They had now ridden so near that they could be seen
620 from the castle where the adventure had befallen him. Then he said:
'Lady, be so kind, if I may ask it of you, as to let my name go
unrecognized—the name given me by the knight who rode off with
my Gringuljete. Do as I have entreated you. If anyone should ask you
about it, then say: "My companion is unknown to me, in that he has
never been named to me." '

She said: 'I am most willing to keep it from them, since you do not
wish me to tell them.'

He and the well-favoured lady turned towards the castle. The
knights had heard there that that very knight had arrived who had
withstood the adventure and overcome the lion, and afterwards
felled the Turkoyte in formal joust. Meanwhile Gawan was riding
towards the landing-place on the plain, so that they could see him
from the turrets. They began to ride in all haste out of the castle,
amid great clamour, all carrying splendid banners. Mounted on swift
Arab chargers, they were riding up fast. Gawan thought they were
621 intent on battle. Seeing them approaching from the distance, he
turned to the duchess and said: 'Is that host coming to attack us?'

She said: 'It is Clinschor's company, which could scarcely wait for
your arrival. Joyfully they now come riding towards you, desiring to
welcome you. You have no need to disdain their welcome, since joy
has commanded it of them.'

Now Plippalinot had also arrived in a punt, together with his
proud and lustrous daughter. She walked towards Gawan, far across
the plain. The maiden welcomed him joyfully.

Gawan offered her his greeting. She kissed his stirrup and his foot, and welcomed the duchess, too. She took hold of his bridle, and entreated him to dismount. The lady and Gawan went to the prow of the boat, where a carpet and a quilt lay. At Gawan's entreaty the duchess sat down beside him there. The ferryman's daughter did not neglect to disarm him. As I heard tell, she had brought with her the cloak which had lain over him that night when he had lodged with her. Now he had fresh need of it. Sir Gawan put on her cloak and his 622 surcoat. She carried the armour away.

For the first time the lustrous duchess now looked upon his face, when they sat down next to one another there. Two roasted crested larks, a carafe of wine, and two white rolls were brought over to them by the sweet maiden, on a cloth sufficiently white. Their food had been caught in flight by a sparrowhawk. Gawan and the duchess could fetch the water themselves if they thought that washing became them, and indeed they both did so. Gawan had good supply of joy, for he was to eat with her for whose sake he desired to suffer both joy and duress. When she offered to him the carafe that her mouth had touched, fresh joy made his acquaintance—that he was to drink out of it after her! His grief took to hobbling and his high spirits sped. Her sweet mouth, her bright skin so chased troubles away from him that he complained of no wound.

Looking down from the castle, the ladies were able to observe 623 this hospitality. On the other side of the river, many a noble knight came riding up to the landing-stage. Their bohort was performed with skill. On this side, Sir Gawan thanked the ferryman and his daughter—as also did the duchess—for their kindly offered food.

The discerning duchess said: 'Where has the knight gone who delivered the joust yesterday, when I rode away from here? If anyone vanquished him, did life or death determine the issue?'

Plippalinot replied: 'Lady, I saw him alive today. He was given me in exchange for a charger. If you would set that man free, in return I must have Swallow, which belonged to Queen Secundille and which Anfortas sent to you. If that harp may be mine, the *duc de* Gowerzin is free.'

'That harp and the rest of the pedlar's merchandise,' she said, 'are in the hands of him who sits here, to give away or keep, as he wishes. Let him dispose of them. If I ever grew dear to him, he will ransom Lischoys, the Duke of Gowerzin, for me here, and also my 624 other prince, Florant of Itolac, who had command of my watch at night. He was my Turkoyt, so true that I shall never rejoice at his sorrow.'

Gawan said to the lady: 'You may see them both set free before night comes upon us.'

Then they decided to cross over onto the land. Gawan lifted the duchess, renowned for her radiance, up onto her horse again. Many a noble, worthy knight welcomed him and the duchess. They headed up to the castle. Joyfully they rode then, nor did the knights omit such skill as honoured the bohort. What more can I say?—except that noble Gawan and the fair duchess were welcomed by ladies in such a manner that they both had reason to rejoice, up in Schastel Marveile. You may count it a blessing upon Gawan that such good fortune ever befell him. Then Arnive led him to his rest, and those skilled in such matters saw to his wounds.

625   To Arnive Gawan said: 'Lady, I must have a messenger.' A damsel was dispatched; she brought a man-at-arms, valorous, discreet in courtesy, of high repute among men-at-arms. That squire swore an oath, whether he was to take good news or bad, that he would mention nothing of it to anyone there, nor elsewhere, but only where he was to deliver the message. Gawan asked for ink and parchment to be fetched. King Lot's son wrote with a skilled hand. He sent a message to the land of Löver, commending his service to Arthur and his wife with unimpaired loyalty, and saying that if he had won hard-earned fame, that would be dead to honour unless they would help him in his exigency—that they should both bear loyalty in mind and take the household to Joflanze, with its company of ladies—and that, he for his part, would also go to meet them there, in order to do combat, all his honour being at stake. Moreover, he impressed upon them that the combat was of such a nature that Arthur ought to arrive in

626   all pomp. Sir Gawan furthermore directed that all Arthur's retinue, be they ladies or men, should be minded of their loyalty and advise the King to come—that would be to the profit of their honour. To all the noble folk he commended his service, and urged upon them the exigency of his combat.

The letter bore no seal. He wrote it in a manner sufficiently recognizable, with unfalsified insignia. 'Now you mustn't delay any longer,' said Gawan to his squire. 'The King and the Queen are at Bems on the Korca. There, early one morning, you must speak to the Queen. Whatever she advises you, do. And mark one thing: conceal that I am lord here. On no account tell them that you belong to this household here.'

The squire was in haste to be off. Arnive stole softly after him. She asked where he intended to go and what his errand was. He replied: 'Lady, I'll tell you nothing, if my oath is to bind me. God keep you, I wish to depart.' He rode in pursuit of noble companies.

BOOK XIII

ARNIVE was hot on anger's trail, because the squire had not told her 627 the nature and destination of his errand. She asked the man in charge of the gate, 'Whether it be night or day, as soon as that squire rides back here, arrange that he waits for me until I have spoken to him. See to it to the best of your ability!'

Still she bore the squire ill-will. To question further she went back in, to the duchess. The latter, however, practised such discretion that her mouth would make no mention of what name Gawan bore. His entreaty had prevented her from divulging his name and his lineage.

Trumpets and other clamour rang out high up in the great hall, for joyous cause. Many a tapestry was hung at the back of the hall. No-one trod there except upon well-wrought carpets. A poor host would have been daunted by the expense. On all sides, all around, many seats were placed with soft cushions of down, upon which costly quilts are spread.

Gawan, after his labours, was indulging in sleep at midday. His 628 wounds were so skilfully bandaged that if a lady-love had lain with him, if he had then made love, it would have been soothing and good for him. He was better disposed for sleep than that night when the duchess had granted him gains in hardship. He awoke towards vespers' time. Nevertheless, he had, in his sleep, done battle with love once more against the duchess!

One of his chamberlains carried in—heavy with costly gold— clothes for him of bright phellel-silk, I heard tell. Then my lord Gawan said: 'We must have still more of these clothes, all to be equally costly, for the Duke of Gowerzin and radiant Florant, who has earned honour in many a land. See to it now that they are prepared.'

He sent a message by a squire to his host, Plippalinot, telling him

to send Lischoys to him. Attended by the ferryman's well-favoured
629 daughter, Lischoys was sent up to the castle. Lady Bene brought
him, leading him by the hand, because of the good will she bore
Gawan, and also for the following reason: Gawan had promised
much to her father, when he had left her weeping grievously—that
day when he rode away from her, when his valour won fame.

The Turkoyt had also arrived. Gawan's words of welcome were
heard without hostility by the two knights. Both sat down by him,
until clothes had been brought for them. Those were costly enough—
they could not possibly have been better! They brought them in for
all three.

There was a master called Sarant, from whom Seres* took its
name. He came from Triande. In Secundille's land there stands a
city called Thasme. It is bigger than Nineveh or than vast Acraton.
There Sarant, for fame's reward, devised a silken material—his work
brought great art to bear—which is called saranthasme. Does it
perhaps look sumptuous? You have no need to ask, for it must cost a
great deal!

630 The two knights and Gawan put on those clothes. They walked up
into the great hall, where on the one side there was many a knight,
on the other the lustrous ladies. To a discerning observer's eye the
Duchess of Logroys' bright sheen outdid them all. The host and
his guests stood before her who glittered there, she who was called
Orgeluse. The Turkoyt Florant and the radiant Lischoys were set
free without jeopardy—those two courteous princes—for the sake of
the Duchess of Logroys. She thanked Gawan for it, she who was
ignorant of falsity, and wise, from her heart, in womanly renown.

When this matter had been settled, Gawan saw four queens stand-
ing by the duchess. Out of courtesy, he entreated the two knights to
walk over to them. He commanded the three younger ones to kiss
those two. Now Lady Bene had also walked over with Gawan. She
was warmly welcomed there.

631 The host was no longer inclined to stand. He asked the two knights
to go and sit with the ladies, wherever they wished. Even though
they were obliged to do so, they did not find the request too irksome.

'Which is Itonje?' asked noble Gawan. 'She must let me sit by her.'
This question he put quietly to Bene. Since this was his wish, she
pointed out to him the lustrous maiden: 'She over there who has the
red mouth, the brown hair, and bright eyes to go with them. If you

wish to speak to her in secret, then do so discreetly,' said Lady Bene, rich in courtesy. She knew of Itonje's love-pangs, and that noble King Gramoflanz had offered his service to her heart with unimpaired knightly loyalty.

Gawan sat down by the maiden—I'm telling you what I was told—beginning by phrasing his words with discretion, for he was well capable of doing so. She, for her part, knew how to behave—for one of such short years as young Itonje had behind her—with such courtesy as sufficiently befitted them. He had determined upon questioning her as to whether she was, as yet, capable of harbouring love.

Then the maiden said, shrewdly: 'Sir, whom ought I to love? 632 Since my first day dawned there has never been a knight to whom I might ever have spoken a word, except what you have heard today.'

'Yet some tidings might have come to you whereby you might have heard of fame won by valour and chivalry, and of someone who, with all his heart, knows how to offer service for love,' said my lord Gawan.

The lustrous maiden answered him: 'No word of service for love has been uttered to me, but many a courteous knight serves the Duchess of Logroys, both for love and for her pay. Many of them have met with jousting here, where we have watched it. None of them ever came so close to us as you have. Your combat exalts fame.'

He said to the well-favoured maiden: 'Against whom does the duchess's company wage war—so many a peerless knight? Who has forfeited her favour?'

She said: 'It is *roys* Gramoflanz, who wears honour's garland, as is generally acknowledged. Sir, I know nothing more of the matter.'

Then my lord Gawan said: 'You are to have better acquaintance 633 with him, since he is approaching fame and hastening towards it with a will. From his own mouth I have heard that he has come to serve you, with all his heart, if you are so inclined, seeking help through solace from your love. It is fair for a king to meet with anguish for a queen. Lady, if your father was called Lot, then it's you he means, for whom his heart weeps. And if you are called Itonje, then it is you who gives him heartfelt pain.

'If you are capable of bearing loyalty, then you must avert his distress. I desire to be a messenger in both camps in this matter. Lady, take this ring. The radiant king sent it to you. I shall see to this in all sincerity. Lady, be bold and leave it all to me.'

She began to redden all over. The same colour that her mouth was before now made acquaintance with her whole countenance. The next moment she took on a different colour again. She held out her hand, full of embarrassment. The ring was quickly recognized. She took it into her lustrous hand.

634   Then she said: 'Lord, I see clearly now, if I may so speak before you, that you have ridden from him towards whom my heart strives. If you will do courtesy its justice now, sir, it will teach you a conceal-ing mind. This gift, indeed, has been sent to me before by the noble king's hand. This ring is a true token from him. He received it from my hand. I am entirely guiltless of any distress that he has ever suffered, for I have granted him in my thoughts all that he desires of me. He would soon have heard as much, if I had ever been able to go out of this castle.

'I have kissed Orgeluse, who so contrives to bring about his death. That was the kiss that Judas bore, of which enough is still spoken today. All loyalty vanished from me when the Turkoyt Florant and the Duke of Gowerzin had to be kissed by me. My peace with them will, however, never be entire—those who are capable of cherishing constant enmity against King Gramoflanz. You must not utter a word of this to my mother, nor to my sister Cundrie,' Itonje entreated Gawan.

635   'Lord, you entreated me to receive their kiss, though unforgiven, on my mouth. My heart is sick at this. If joy is ever to acquaint itself with us two, then the help for it is in your hands. Truly, the king loves me above all women. I wish to let him benefit by that. He is dear to me above all men. May God teach you help and counsel, so that you may deliver us into joy's company!'

He replied: 'Lady, now teach me how! He holds you there, you hold him here, and yet you are separated.* If only I could give you both such loyal counsel as would be of profit to your noble selves, I would gladly go about it. I would not let you perish for lack of it.'

She said: 'You must prevail over both the noble king and me. May your help and God's blessing so cherish our mutual love that I, wretched exile that I am, may avert sorrow from him. Since all his joy depends upon me, if I lack disloyalty, it will always be my heart's desire to grant him my love.'

636   Gawan heard from the little lady's words that she desired to be in love's company. Nor was she at all slow to hate the duchess. Thus she

bore love and hatred together. Moreover, he had sinned further against the innocent maiden who had lamented her sorrow to him, for he had not mentioned to her that one mother had carried both him and her in her womb, and that Lot was father to them both. He offered his help to the maiden. In return she bowed secretly, thanking him for not denying her comfort.

Now it was time for them to bring in tablecloths, white enough, many of them, and for the bread to be taken up to the great hall, where many a lustrous lady was present. A division was recognized whereby the knights had one wall to themselves, apart. Sir Gawan saw to the seating. The Turkoyt sat by him; Lischoys ate with Gawan's mother, the lustrous Sangive. With Queen Arnive ate the lustrous duchess. Gawan had both his well-favoured sisters sit by him. Each did as he commanded her.

My skill will not halfway suffice—I am no such master-cook—to 637 name the dishes which were, with courtesy, brought before them there. The lord and all the ladies were served by well-favoured maidens. On the other side many a man-at-arms served the knights by their wall. Respectful courtesy prevented any of the squires jostling the damsels. They were to be seen serving separately, whether it was food or wine they carried—such was the decorum they were obliged to observe.

They had good reason to speak of a hospitable feast then. It had seldom befallen them before, those ladies and that company of knights, since Clinschor's power had overcome them by his cunning. They were so unacquainted, even though one gate enclosed them, that they had never come to converse with one another, those ladies and men. Now my lord Gawan saw to it that the members of this company beheld one another; much pleasure came to them from that. To Gawan, too, pleasure had accrued, although he was obliged to look in secret at the lustrous duchess—she afflicted his heart's senses.

Now the day began to totter, its shine almost taking a fall, so that 638 through the clouds could be seen what are called night's messengers, many a star that passed rapidly by, claiming lodging for the night. Following her banners, night herself soon arrived. Many a costly chandelier was hung in splendour, all about the great hall, which was quickly well becandled. On each of the tables candles were placed in wondrous numbers. Moreover, the adventure says that the duchess was so bright that even if none of those candles had been brought in, there would be no night in her presence. Her very glance knew how to break day—so I heard tell of that sweet lady.

If no injustice is to be reported of him, then seldom have you seen before any host so rich in joy. It was as if joy itself were present there. With joyous desire the knights looked one way, the ladies the other, frequently meeting each other's eyes. Those who shrank back out of shyness—if they ever become more intimate, I ought not to begrudge it them.

639   Unless there was an absolute glutton there, they have eaten enough, if you will. The tables were all carried away. Then my lord Gawan asked about good fiddlers, whether there were any present there. There were many noble squires present, well skilled in stringed instruments. Yet none had such great skill that he could dispense with scraping old dances. Little was heard there of new dances, so many of which have come to us from Thuringia!

Now give thanks to the host—he did not thwart their joy! Many a well-favoured lady stepped up to dance before him. Their dance was adorned as follows: the knights were well intermingled among the ladies' company. Against grief they joined forces. Indeed, between every pair of ladies a radiant knight could be seen to walk there. Joy could readily be detected amongst them. If any knight was minded to offer service for love, such a request was permissible. Poor in sorrow and rich in joy, they passed the time in converse with many a sweet mouth.

640   Gawan and Sangive, and Queen Arnive sat quietly by the dancing throng. The well-favoured duchess walked round to sit by Gawan. He took her hand in his. They spoke of this and that. He was pleased she had walked over to him. His grief grew slender, his joy broad then; thus all his suffering vanished. Great as was the dancers' joy, Gawan had even less to irk him there.

Queen Arnive said: 'Sir, see now to your comfort. You must rest at this time, to heal your wounds. If the duchess has decided to see to your covering herself this very night, companionably, she is rich in help and counsel.'

Gawan said: 'Ask her about that. Here I am entirely at the command of you both.'

The duchess spoke as follows: 'He shall be in my care. Let this company go to their beds. Tonight I must take such care of him that no lady-love ever tended him better before. Let Florant of Itolac and the Duke of Gowerzin be attended to by the knights.'

All of a sudden the dancing came to an end. Damsels with shining 641 complexions sat down there and here; the knights sat down among them. If anyone spoke up in hope of noble love there, his joy avenged itself on sorrow, provided he found sweet words of response. The host was heard to command that drinks be brought before them. Wooers had reason to bemoan this. The host was wooing, along with his guests. Love knew how to emburden him, too. He thought they had been sitting there far too long. His heart, too, was afflicted by noble love. The drinking gave them leave to go. Many a bundle of candles was brought by the squires and placed before the knights. Then my lord Gawan commended those two guests to the care of them all. That must have delighted them. Lischoys and Florant went to their beds at once. The duchess was so considerate as to wish them goodnight. Then all the host of ladies also went to where they might find rest. They bowed with all the courtesy at their command. Sangive and Itonje departed, as also did Cundrie.

Bene and Arnive then saw to it that matters so stood that the host 642 endured comfort. The duchess did not fail to be near at hand with her help. Those three led Gawan away with them, so that he might rest. In a chamber he saw two beds lying apart. Now you will hear no word at all from me as to how they were adorned. Other tales draw nigh.

Arnive said to the duchess: 'Now you must provide good comfort for this knight whom you have brought here. If he desires help of you, you will be honoured by granting help. I'll say nothing more to you now, except that his wounds are bandaged with such skill that he could easily bear arms now. Yet you must take pity on his troubles. If you can ease them for him, so much the better. If you teach him high spirits, we may all benefit by that. Now don't let yourself be deterred!'

Queen Arnive left, having received leave from the court's lord. Bene carried a light before her as she walked away. Sir Gawan closed the door.

If these two know how to steal love now, I can with difficulty 643 conceal it. I shall tell you, perhaps, what happened there—except that uncouthness has always been averred of a man who makes hidden tales broadspread. Even today it grieves the courtly—indeed, a man damns himself thereby. Let good breeding be the lock upon love's ways.

Now, harsh Love and the lustrous duchess had caused Gawan's joy to be quite consumed. He would forever have been unhealed without an *âmîe*. The philosophers, and all who ever resided where mighty cunning was pondered upon—Kancor and Thebit*—and Trebuchet the smith, who engraved Frimutel's sword, in consequence of which mighty marvels ensued—and add to that the skill of all doctors— even if they had favoured him with concoctions made from potent herbs—without womanly companionship he would have had to carry his dire distress with him to the point of bitter death.

I will shorten the tale for you. He found the true hart's-eye,* which helped him recover, so that nothing evil hurt him. That herb was brown next to the white.* On his mother's side a Briton, Gawan *fil li roy* Lot practised sweet gentleness against bitter distress, with noble help, helpfully, until day. His help, however, took such a turn that it was concealed from all the people. Afterwards he attended with joy to all the knights and ladies, so that their sadness all but perished.

Hear now also how the squire fared on his errand, he whom Gawan had sent to the land of Löver, to Bems by the Korca. King Arthur was present there, and his wife the Queen, and many a bright lady's sheen, and a deluge of retinue. Now hear also how the squire acts.

It was early one morning—he took his errand in hand. The Queen had gone to the chapel, reading the psalter as she made her genuflection. The squire knelt down before her. He offered her joy's gift. A letter she took from his hand, in which she found written a script that she knew, even before the squire she saw kneeling there named his lord. The Queen said to the letter: 'Blessed be the hand that wrote you! I have never remained without sorrow since the day that I last saw the hand by which this script took shape.' She wept copiously and yet was happy. Turning to the squire, she said: 'You are Gawan's page?'

'Yes, lady. He sends you his dutiful greeting, loyal service without any deviation, and at the same time reports that his joy is slight, unless you wish to exalt his joy. Never did things stand so wretchedly with regard to all his honour. Lady, he informs you further that he will live amid noble joys if he hears of your solace's gift. Indeed, you may see more in the letter than I can tell you in words.'

She said: 'I see clearly why you have been sent to me. I shall do him noble service, taking there a company of lovely ladies, who truly win the contest in repute over all others in my time. Except for Parzival's wife, and Orgeluse's person, I know none upon this earth, baptized, who are so noble. Ever since Gawan rode away from 646 Arthur, sorrow and grief have assiduously assailed me with their clamour. Meljanz of Liz told me that he had afterwards seen him at Barbigœl. Alas,' she said, 'Plimizœl, that my eyes ever beheld you! What sorrow befell me there! Cunneware de Lalant, my sweet, noble companion, has never met my acquaintance again. The Table Round's law was much transgressed against there by accusations. Four and a half years and six weeks it is since noble Parzival rode from the Plimizœl in pursuit of the Grail. At the same time Gawan, that noble knight, headed for Ascalun. Jeschute and Ekuba parted from me there. Great grief on account of that noble company has since parted me from constant joys.'

The Queen spoke of much sadness. Turning to the squire, she said: 'Now follow my instructions. Go from me in secret now, and wait until the day has risen so high that the people may be present at court—knights, men-at-arms, the great menage. Then trot briskly 647 into the courtyard. Never mind whether anyone takes hold of your palfrey. You must walk quickly away from it over to where the noble knights are standing. They will ask you about adventure. Act with your words and ways as if you have come rushing away from a fire. They will scarcely be able to wait to hear what tidings you bring, but what does it matter, provided you press your way forward through the people to the true lord, who will not refuse you his greeting! Give this letter into his hand. He will soon have gleaned from it your tidings and your lord's desire. He will be the guarantor that it is carried out.

'I have further instructions for you yet. You must speak to me in public, where I and other ladies can hear and see you. There carry out your errand to us to the best of your ability, if you wish your lord well. And tell me, where is Gawan?'

The squire said: 'Lady, that will not be revealed. I shall not say where my lord is. If you so desire, he will remain in joy's company.'

The squire was glad of her counsel. He then parted from the Queen in the way you have heard described, and also returned as he had been told to return.

648   Promptly, about mid-morning, publicly and unconcealed, the squire rode into the courtyard. The courtly company mustered his garments, which satisfied squirely requirements. On both flanks his horse was badly scarred by spurs. Following the Queen's instructions he leapt briskly down from his horse. A great throng formed about him. Cape, sword and spurs, and the horse, too—if they were lost, he cared little. The squire walked off rapidly to where the noble knights were standing, who began asking him for tidings of adventure. They say that it was their custom there that neither woman nor man should eat at court before the court won its due—adventure of such a noble kind that it had adventure's semblance.

The squire said: 'I'll tell you nothing. My business imposes this upon me. By your courtesy bear with me, and be so kind as to tell me of the King! I would gladly speak to him first. My business presses upon me. You shall, I imagine, hear what tidings I have to tell. May God teach you to help and bemoan distress!'

649   His embassy impelled the page not to mind who jostled him until the King himself saw him and spoke his greeting to him. The squire gave him a letter which appealed to Arthur's heart. When he had read it two things were of necessity present with him—the one was joy and the other sorrow. He said: 'A blessing on this sweet day, by whose light I have heard that true tidings have reached me concerning my noble nephew! If I can perform manly service for the sake of kinship and companionship, if loyalty ever won power over me, then I'll do what Gawan has asked of me by this message, if I can.'

Turning to the squire, he said: 'Now tell me, is Gawan happy?'

'Yes, lord—if you desire it, he shall become joy's companion,' said the discerning squire. 'He would part from fame entirely if you were to leave him in the lurch. Who indeed could then harbour joy? Your solace will pluck his joy up high, chasing distress from his heart, out beyond grief's gate, when he knows that you will not let him down.*

650 His heart commended his service to the Queen over there. Moreover, it is his desire that all the Table Round's company bear in mind his service and think on their loyalty, and do not diminish his joy, but advise you to go to his aid.'

All the nobles present there entreated Arthur to do so.

Arthur said: 'My dear companion, take this letter to the Queen. Let her read its contents and say what we rejoice over and what we bemoan. That King Gramoflanz can proffer such arrogance and absolute irresponsibility towards my kindred! He imagines my nephew Gawan to be Cidegast, whom he slew. He has enough troubles on that count! I must magnify his troubles and teach him new manners!'

The squire came walking over to where he met with a good reception. He gave the Queen the letter, at which many an eye welled over, when her sweet mouth had read out all that was written in it, Gawan's lament and his plea. Then the squire did not omit to take his errand to all the ladies, in doing which his skill did not fail him.

Gawan's kinsman, mighty Arthur, heartily recommended this 651 journey to his retinue. Courteous Guinevere also guarded herself against any hesitation in commending this proud journey to the ladies. Kay in his anger said: 'Was ever such a noble man born, if I dared believe it, as Gawan of Norway! Tally ho! Seek him out there! Yet perhaps he is somewhere else altogether! If he takes to darting about like a squirrel, you may soon have lost him!'

The squire said to the Queen: 'Lady, I must return quickly to my lord. Exert yourself in his cause as befits your honour.'

To one of her chamberlains she said: 'Provide this squire with every comfort. You must take a look at his horse. If it is slashed by spurs, give him the best that is for sale here. If he has any other troubles, whether it be money to redeem a pawned horse or clothing, let it all be at his disposal.'

She said: 'Now tell Gawan that my service is subject to him. I shall take leave of the King for you. Say to your lord that he too is at his service.'

Now the King planned his journey. Thus the Table Round's order 652 had been observed there that day. It had awoken joy amongst them to hear that noble Gawan still retained his life, as they had learned. The Table Round's custom was followed there, without any dispute. The King ate at the Table Round, as did those who had the right to sit there, who had won fame by hardship. All the Table-Rounders rejoiced at these tidings.

Now give the squire leave to return, his message having been heard. Promptly he set off on his way. The Queen's chamberlain gives him pawn-money, a charger, and fresh clothing. Joyfully the squire rode off, for his embassy to Arthur had put to death his lord's distress. He arrived back, taking as many days as I cannot in truth tell, up at Schastel Marveile. Arnive was delighted, for the porter

sent her a message that the squire, with some hardship to his charger,
653 had quickly made his way back. She crept out to meet him, immedi-
ately he was admitted. She asked him about his journey and to what
end he had ridden out. The squire said: 'That cannot be, lady,
I daren't tell you. I must keep silent about it because of my oath. It
would not please my lord, either, if I were to break my oath by giving
information away. He would think me a fool. Lady, ask him about it
yourself.'

She plied her questions this way and that. The squire would only
say: 'Lady, you are delaying me unnecessarily. I'll carry out what my
oath has commanded of me.'

He went to where he found his lord. The Turkoyt Florant and the
Duke of Gowerzin, and the Duchess of Logroys were sitting there,
along with a great company of ladies. The squire walked into their
presence. My lord Gawan rose to his feet. He took the squire apart,
bidding him be welcome. He said: 'Tell me, my companion, tidings
either of joy or of extremity, or what message they have sent me from
court. Did you find the King there?'

The squire said: 'Yes, lord. I found the King and his wife, and
654 many a noble personage. They send to you their service and promise
to come. Your message was so nobly received by them that both poor
and rich rejoiced, for I informed them that you were still in good
health. I found a wondrous number of people there. Moreover, seats
were placed at the Table Round because of your embassy. If a
knight's fame ever won power—I mean over honour—then your
fame wears the crown the length and breadth of the lands, high in
splendour above others' fame!'

He told him also how it came about that he spoke with the Queen,
and what she had advised him, in her loyalty. He told him, too, about
all the company of knights and ladies—that he could expect to see
them at Joflanze, before the time came for his duel's combat.
Gawan's anxiety vanished entirely. He found nothing but joy in his
heart. Gawan stepped out of anxiety into joy. He entreated the squire
to keep it secret. All his anxiety he entirely forgot. He walked back
and sat down, and resided joyfully in the castle there, until King
655 Arthur came riding with his retinue to help him.

Hear now of both joy and sorrow! Gawan was happy at all times.
One morning it happened that many a knight and lady were present
in the sumptuous great hall. At a window facing the watercourse he

took a seat apart, sitting with Arnive, who had not forgotten wondrous tales.

Gawan said to the queen: 'Ah, my dear lady, if you were not to be offended, I would gladly ask you about such tidings as have been hidden from me! For it is only by your help's bestowal that I live among such noble delights. If my heart ever bore a man's mind, the noble duchess has held it locked in her power. Now I have so bene-fited by you that my distress has been alleviated. I would be dead of love and wounds, if your helpful solace had not freed me from my bonds. It is because of you that I am still alive. Now tell me, blessed lady, about the wonders that were and are still here, and why wise 656 Clinschor resorted to such relentless cunning. Were it not for you, I'd have lost my life by it.'

She who was wise from the heart—youth never advanced into age with such womanly renown—said: 'Lord, his marvels here are noth-ing but small and minor marvels compared with the potent marvels he has in many lands. If anyone says these put us to shame, he wins nothing but sin by his words. Lord, I shall tell you of his ways. Many a people has suffered bitterly because of them. His land is called Terre de Labur.* He is born of the descendants of one who also devised many marvels, Virgil of Naples.*

'Clinschor, his kinsman, acted thus—Capua was his capital—he trod such a high path of praise that he was undeceived of fame. Women and men alike spoke of Clinschor the Duke, until he met with affliction as follows: Sicily was ruled by a noble king. He was called Ibert. His wife was named Iblis.* She possessed the loveliest person that was ever weaned of breast. Clinschor had entered into her service, until she rewarded it with love. For that the king put him 657 to shame.

'If I must tell you his secrets, I must have your leave to do so, but these tales are unseemly for me to tell—how he came by magic's ways. By a single cut Clinschor was made into a capon!' At that Gawan laughed heartily.

She told him still more: 'In Caltabellotta* he won the world's scorn. That is a fortress of renowned strength. The king found him lying with his wife—Clinschor lay asleep in her arms. If he lay warm there at all, he had to pay the following forfeit for it: by the king's hands he was trimmed between his legs. To his host it seemed it was his due. He cut him about his person in such fashion that he cannot make any woman merry. As a result many people have met with sorrow.

'It was not in the land of Persia, but in a city called Persida,* that magic was first invented. There he went, and brought back with him 658 the means to carry out whatever he desires, magic goals achieved by cunning. Because of the shame to his person, he has never again been well disposed to man or woman—I mean those who bear nobility. Whatever joys he can take from them suits him to the heart.

'A king called Irot feared such extremity at his hands—the King of Rosche Sabbins. He offered to give him whatever of his property he desired, provided he should have a truce. Clinschor received from his hand this mountain, famed for its impregnability, and the land in its compass, eight miles all round. Clinschor then wrought upon this mountain, as you can clearly see, this mysterious edifice! Mighty marvels of wealth, of all kinds, are up here. If anyone wanted to attack this citadel, there would be food enough up here, of many kinds, to last for thirty years. Moreover, he wields power over all those, whether *mal* or *bêâ schent*,* who dwell between the firmament and the earth's compass—except for those whom God wishes to protect.

659 'Sir, now that your extreme peril has been averted without your death, his gift stands in your hands—this citadel and this demarcated land. He'll take no further interest in it now. That man was also to be granted a truce by him—so he averred publicly, being a man of his word—who withstood this adventure, and his gift would reside with him. Whatever noble people he beheld on Christian soil—maid, woman, or man—many of those are subject to you here. Many a pagan and paganess have also had to reside with us up here. Now let these people return to where anxiety has been heard voiced about us. Exile makes my heart cold. He who has counted the stars, let Him teach you help and turn us towards joy.

'A mother gives birth to her fruit. That fruit becomes its mother's mother. From the water comes the ice.* That by no means prevents the water issuing forth from it again. When I reflect to myself that 660 I am born of joy, if joy is to be perceived in me again, there one fruit will yield a second fruit. This you must bring about, if you possess breeding. It is a long time since joy fell off me.

'By the sail the keel-boat speeds fast. The man who walks on board is quicker yet. If you understand this image, then your fame will grow high and fast. You may make us loud with joy, so that we shall take joy with us into many lands where anxiety has been voiced on our account.

'There was a time when I practised joy enough. I was a woman who wore a crown. My daughter also wore a crown in splendour before her land's princes. We were both held in high honour. Sir, I never contrived any man's injury. I knew how to treat both women and men well, as was their due. I was duly acknowledged and beheld as a true lady over her people, please God, for I never treated any man ill. Let every blessed woman still, if she wishes to behave nobly, treat good people well. She may easily enter such sorrow's dole that an ill-bred page will give a wide berth to her narrow joy. Sir, I have waited a long time here. Never, either on foot or on horseback, has anyone arrived who recognized me and averted sorrow from me.' 661

Then my lord Gawan said: 'Lady, if I live long enough, joy shall yet be heard from your lips.'

On that same day Arthur the Briton, the son of the lamenting Arnive, was to arrive with his army, impelled by kinship and loyalty. Many a new banner Gawan saw drawing towards him, the field being covered by troops, along the road leading to Logroys, with many a brightly painted spear. Gawan delighted at their arrival. If a man has to wait in expectation of a muster, delay teaches him this thought: he fears that his help will fail him. Arthur confounded Gawan's doubt. *Ávoy*, what a sight his coming made!

Gawan secretly concealed that his bright eyes had to learn weeping. As a cistern, they were both useless then, for they couldn't hold any water! It was out of joy that those tears were shed that Arthur knew how to evoke. He had raised him from childhood. The unbelied loyalty of them both stood free of deviation, the one from the other, never undercut by perfidy. 662

Arnive perceived that he was weeping. She said: 'Lord, you must now begin to rejoice with a joyful sound! Sir, that will comfort us all. Against grief you must be on guard. Here comes the duchess's army. That will soon comfort you more.'

Tents and many banners Arnive and Gawan saw being borne onto the plain—amongst them all only one shield whose arms had a device Arnive could recognize. She named Isajes, Uther Pendragon's marshal. Another Briton carried that shield now, Maurin of the Handsome Thighs, the marshal of the Queen. Arnive knew little of

this—Uther Pendragon and Isajes had both died. Maurin had won his father's office, as was right. Towards the mooring-place, onto the flat meadow, the great menage rode. The Queen's men-at-arms took
663 such lodgings as well became ladies, by a clear, fast-flowing brook, where soon many a splendid pavilion was seen pitched. For the King many a broad tent-ring was established separately, further off, and for the knights who had arrived there with him. No question about it, their cavalcade had made a great trail of hoofprints!

Gawan sent a message by Bene down to his host, Plippalinot: the cogs and the punts he was to chain up, quickly, to prevent the army from making its crossing that day. Lady Bene received from Gawan's hands the first gift from his rich pedlar's store—Swallow, which even today is renowned in England as a precious harp.

Bene set off joyfully. Then my lord Gawan commanded the outer gate to be barred. Old and young alike heard what he courteously requested of them: 'Over there by the bank such a great army is encamped that neither on land nor at sea have I ever seen a company under way with such mighty hosts. If they seek to attack us here with their forces, help me, and I'll show them chivalry!'

664 That they all vowed as one. They asked the mighty duchess if the army were hers. She said: 'You must believe me—I recognize neither shield nor man there. He who has done me injury before has perhaps ridden into my land and fought before Logroys. I believe, though, that he found it well defended. This army must have met with some fighting at their redoubts and barbicans. If the angry King Gramoflanz did acts of knighthood there, then he was seeking compensation for his garland. Or, whoever they are, they must have seen spears raised, desirous of the joust.'

Her mouth lied little to them in this. Arthur had won much harm before he passed Logroys, many a Briton being felled in formal joust. Yet Arthur's army had paid back the wares they were offered there. Both sides had met with hardship.

The battle-weary were seen approaching, those of whom it has so often been heard that they sold their shirts dearly—they were those who were hardy in battle. Both sides have suffered losses. Garel and
665 Gaherjet,* and *rois* Meljanz *de* Barbigœl, and Jofreit *fiz* Idœl had been captured and sent up to the castle before the bohort was over. For their part, the Britons had captured from Logroys *duc* Friam *de* Vermendoys and *kuns* Ritschart *de* Navers. The latter only broke one

lance—all against whom his hand offered it fell before him in the joust's extremity. Arthur, by his own hand, had captured that warrior of noble renown. The full tilts were so uninhibitedly interlocked there that a whole forest might have been laid waste. Jousts uncounted shed splinters. The noble Britons also fought valiantly against the duchess's army. Arthur's rearguard was obliged to be in battle mood. They were pressed that day to where the flood of the army lay.

Indeed, my lord Gawan ought to have informed the duchess that a helper of his was in her land! Then no fighting would have taken place. However, he didn't want to tell her or anyone else about it as yet, until she could see it for herself. He acted as became him, and 666 saw to it that his own cavalcade to meet Arthur the Briton was accompanied by costly pavilions. No-one was to be disadvantaged there if he was unknown to him. Generous Gawan's hand began to give with such a will as if he had no desire to live any longer! Men-at-arms, knights, ladies—all were obliged to accept and behold his lavish gifts, so that they said, all as one, that true help had come to them. Now they, too, were heard to rejoice!

Then the noble warrior called for sturdy packhorses, handsome ladies' palfreys, and armour for all the company of knights. Great numbers of men-at-arms, clad in iron, were at hand there. Then he behaved as follows: my lord Gawan took four noble knights aside—one was to be chamberlain, the second cupbearer, the third steward, and the fourth was not to forget that he was marshal.* Thus he arranged matters. Those four carried out his bidding.

Now let Arthur lie still in his camp! Gawan's greeting was denied 667 him that whole day long. With difficulty he held it back. Early next morning, amid clamour, Arthur's army rode towards Joflanze. His rearguard he put in defensive position. When they found no fighting there, they followed in his tracks.

Then my lord Gawan took his officers aside. He wanted to wait no longer. He commanded the marshal to ride out onto the plain at Joflanze. 'I wish to have a separate camp. You see the great army encamped there. It has now come to the point where I must name their lord to you, so that you may know him. It is my uncle Arthur, in whose court and castle I was brought up from childhood. Now arrange my cavalcade with such unmistakably lavish expenditure that wealth may be clearly observed, but let it be unrevealed up here in the castle that Arthur's army has come here for my sake.'

They did all that he commanded them. As a result Plippalinot was
668 soon far from idle. Cogs, punts, skiffs, and ferries, with bands of
bold warriors, both on horseback and on foot, had to cross with the
marshal—men-at-arms, squires. Following the Briton's course, they
turned this way and that, along with Gawan's marshal, pursuing
the trail.

They carried with them, too—rest assured of that!—a pavilion
that Iblis had sent Clinschor as a love-gift, which is how that couple's
secret had first become public. They were dear to one another. No
expense had been spared on that pavilion. No scissors had ever cut
better cloth, except for a certain tent that had belonged to Isenhart.*
Near Arthur, but apart, on a meadow, the pavilion was erected. Many
a tent, I heard tell, was pitched in a wide ring around it. That was
thought a sumptuous show!

In Arthur's presence it was heard that Gawan's marshal had
arrived; he had encamped on the plain, and noble Gawan was also to
arrive during the day. This became the common talk of all the
669 household. Gawan, free of falsity, assembled his troops back in the
castle. He embellished his cavalcade in such fashion that I could
tell you marvels about it. Many a packhorse had to carry chapels*
and chamber-apparel. Many a pack loaded with renowned armour
walked amongst them too, helmet tied on top, alongside many a fair
shield. Many a handsome Castilian was seen to be led among the
packs. Knights and ladies rode in the rear, close by one another. The
train must have measured a good journey-stage in length. Nothing
was neglected there, Gawan assigning in every case a well-favoured
knight to a lustrous lady. They were weak of wit if they spoke noth-
ing of love. The Turkoyt Florant was chosen as a companion to
Sangive of Norway. Lischoys the wholly unlaggardly rode alongside
sweet Cundrie. Gawan's sister, Itonje, was to ride with her brother.
Arnive and the duchess had also determined to be companions on
that occasion.

670　　Well, this was how it had turned out: Gawan's tent-ring made its
way right through Arthur's army, where the King lay encamped.
What staring they indulged in there! Before that host had ridden
through them, Gawan, following courtly custom and in pursuit of
honour, bade the foremost lady* halt at Arthur's tent-ring. His
marshal had to see to it that a second lady rode up close by her. None
of the other ladies omitted to halt there thus, in a circle—here the

sage, there the youthful—at each lady's side a knight in attendance on her and busying himself in her service. Arthur's wide ring was seen to be surrounded on all sides by ladies. Only then was Gawan, rich in blessings, welcomed—affectionately, as I believe.

Arnive, her daughter, and the latter's child, have dismounted along with Gawan, as have the Duchess of Logroys and the Duke of Gowerzin, and the Turkoyt Florant. To meet these people of noble renown Arthur walked out of his pavilion, giving them a friendly welcome there, as did the Queen, his wife. She welcomed Gawan and 671 the rest of his company with loyal affection's fervency. Many a kiss was bestowed by many a comely lady there.

Arthur said to his nephew: 'Who are these companions of yours?'

Gawan said: 'I must see my lady the Queen kiss them. It would be harsh to spare them that. They are both of high enough lineage.' The Turkoyt Florant was kissed at once there, as was the Duke of Gowerzin, by Guinevere the Queen.

They retired into the pavilion. Many a man thought that the broad field was full of ladies. Then Arthur, acting like no laggard, leapt upon a Castilian.* All those comely ladies, and all the knights at their side—he rode all round that ring. Courteously Arthur's mouth welcomed them on that occasion. It had been Gawan's intention that they should all halt there until he rode off together with them—that was a courtly way to behave!

Arthur dismounted and went into the tent. He sat down next to his 672 nephew, pressing him for tidings as to who the five ladies might be. Then my lord Gawan began with the eldest first, saying to the Briton: 'If you recall Uther Pendragon, this is Arnive, his wife. You yourself were born of that couple. Then this is my mother, the Queen of Norway. These two are my sisters. See what pretty girls they are!'

A second bout of kissing ensued. Joy and grief were to be seen by all who had an eye for it. It was affection that caused them to suffer. Their mouths knew full well how to manifest both laughter and tears. Great affection was the cause.

Arthur said to Gawan: 'Nephew, I am still without information as to who this lustrous fifth lady may be.'

Courteous Gawan replied: 'It is the Duchess of Logroys, whose favour I enjoy. I'm told you have attacked her. Show me, without hesitation, what profit you have made by that! You ought to act 673 kindly towards a widow.'

Arthur said: 'She holds Gaherjet, your aunt's son, captive over there, and Garel, who has wrought a knight's deeds in many a charge. That dauntless warrior was taken captive at my side. One charge of ours, at full tilt, had reached as far as their barbican. Up and at them! What deeds were done there by noble Meljanz of Liz! He was taken captive under a white banner, and led up to the castle. That banner had been accorded a black arrow of sable, with heart's blood's marks depicting a man's sorrow. "Lirivoyn!" was the cry of all the band that rode into battle beneath it. They won the prize in battle, taking it up to the castle. My nephew Jofreit has also been taken up there as a prisoner—that troubles me. I had charge of the rearguard yesterday,* which is why this anguish of mine throve.'

The King spoke much of his losses. Courteously the duchess said: 'Lord, I pronounce you free of any disgrace. You had received no greeting from me.* You might have done me damage which I have 674 not, after all, deserved. Since it was you who attacked me, let God now teach you how to make amends. He whom you have ridden to help, if he ever did battle with me, I was acknowledged to be defenceless and charged at on my exposed side. If he still desires battle against me, I dare say it will be settled without swords.'

Gawan then said to Arthur: 'What would you advise if we were to bedeck this plain with even more knights, since we're well capable of it? I trust I may obtain from the duchess permission for your men to be set free, and that her company of knights may make its way over here, with many a new spear.'

'I assent to that,' said Arthur.

The duchess then sent to her castle for the noble knights. Never, I believe, was there a more splendid assembly on earth.

Gawan asked leave to make his way to his lodgings, which the King granted him. Those who had been seen to arrive with him rode away with him to their quarters. His sumptuous camp had such a knightly appearance that it was costly and devoid of poverty.

675 Into Gawan's camp rode many a man who had grieved from his heart over his long absence. By now Kay had recovered from the joust by the Plimizœl. He scrutinized Gawan's expenditure, saying: 'My lord's brother-in-law Lot—from him we had no need to fear rivalry, nor a separate tent-ring!' He was still thinking of the affair of Gawan not having avenged him there, when his right arm had been shattered. 'God wreaks wonders among men! Who gave Gawan this

load of ladies?'—thus spoke Kay in his mockery. That was no fit way
to treat a friend. The loyal man rejoices at his friend's honours. The
disloyal man raises the hue and cry when a happy event befalls his
friend and he sees it. Gawan enjoyed good fortune and honour. If
anyone desires still more, where is he heading with his thoughts? Yet
the small-minded are full of envy and enmity, while it delights a
courageous man if his friend's fame stands fast, so that disgrace
retreats before him. Gawan, free of false hostility, never forgot manly
loyalty. It was no injustice if it ever befell him to be seen in Fortune's 676
company.

How did he of Norway entertain his people, those knights and
ladies? There Arthur and his household might behold lavish hospi-
tality bestowed by noble Lot's son. Let them sleep, now that they
have eaten! Rarely would I begrudge them their rest!

In the morning, before daybreak, a host came riding up, of warlike
aspect—all the duchess's knights. Their crests were fully visible in
the moonlight from where Arthur and his men lay encamped. The
army made its way through them to where, on the other side, Gawan
lay encamped with his broad ring. Whoever can command such help
by his courageous hand may truly be accorded fame! Gawan asked
his marshal to show them to their lodging-place. As the duchess's
marshal advised them, the noble company of Logroys graced many a
separate tent-ring. Before they had encamped it was well into the
mid-morning. Now new sorrows draw nigh.

Arthur of famed renown sent his messengers into the city of 677
Rosche Sabins, entreating King Gramoflanz: 'Since it would seem
that it is now inevitable that he will not renounce his combat against
my nephew, then my nephew must grant it him. Ask him to come to
meet us soon, since we hear such ill-will of him that he will not
relent. On any other man's part, it would be excessive!'

Arthur's messengers set off. Then my lord Gawan took Lischoys
and Florant aside. Those who had come from many lands, Love's
paid soldiers, he asked to be shown at once—those who had been in
such devoted service to the duchess, hoping for high reward. He
rode over to them and welcomed them in such fashion that they said,
all as one, that noble Gawan was a valorous, courteous man.

With that he left them and went back. In secret, he now acted as
follows: he went into his wardrobe and straight away bedecked his
body with armour, to see whether his wounds had healed to the point 678

that the scars no longer hurt him. He was intent on exercise, since so many men and women were to see his duel, at a place where discerning knights would be able to observe whether his undaunted hand was to be accorded fame that day. He had asked a squire to bring him Gringuljete. He gave the horse free rein, wanting to practise manoeuvres which would test whether he and the charger were ready. Never was I so sad at his departure. Alone, my lord Gawan rode away from the army, far off onto the plain. May good fortune decide the issue!

He saw a knight halting by the river Sabins, one whom we may well call a flintstone of manly strength. He was a storm of chivalry! Falsity never struck below his heart's guard. He was in his person so entirely feeble in all that is called infamy that he bore not even half an inch's length nor breadth of it about him. You may well have heard of this same noble knight before. This tale has returned to the tree's true trunk.

BOOK XIV

679 IF a joust is to be delivered valiantly there by noble Gawan, then never did I fear so much for his honour in battle! I ought also to be anxious on the other's behalf, but I will set that worry aside! He was, in battle, a whole army against any one man! From far-off heathendom, across the sea, his accoutrements had been brought. Redder even than a ruby were his surcoat and his charger's caparison. That warrior rode in pursuit of adventure. His shield was entirely pierced through. He too had plucked from the tree guarded by Gramoflanz such a bright garland that Gawan recognized the twig. Then he feared disgrace, thinking that the king might have been waiting for him there. If he had ridden towards him to do battle, then battle had to befall there, even if no lady ever beheld it.

From Munsalvæsche they had come, both the chargers which they thus let gallop towards one another here, charging into the full tilt, admonished by the spurs. Nothing but green clover, no dusty sand,* grew dewy where that joust took place. I grieve for the distress they
680 must both suffer. They did justice to their charge—both were born of the joust's lineage. Little gain, much loss will accrue to whoever

wins the prize there. He'll bemoan it forever, if he is wise. The
loyalty they bore one another was steadfast, never notched by holes,
neither old nor new.

Hear now how the joust passed—with a fierce charge, and yet in
such fashion that they both had good reason to be unhappy!
Acknowledged kinship and exalted companionship collided there
with hostile force, in fierce combat. Whoever wins the prize there,
his joy is pledged to sorrow for it. Each hand delivered such a joust
that those kinsman and companions were obliged to fell one another
to the ground, together with their chargers. This is how they acted
next: a wedge was nailed there, hammered home by swords. Shields'
splinters and the green grass were mixed in equal measure, once they
began to do battle. They had to wait all too long to be parted—they
started early in the morning. Indeed, no-one intervened to part
them. No-one was there as yet except those two.   681

Would you like to hear more, now—how at that very time
Arthur's messengers found King Gramoflanz with his army on a
plain, by the sea? On the one side flowed the Sabins, and on the other
the Poynzaclins—there the two rivers flowed into the sea. The plain
was firmer elsewhere—Rosche Sabins, the capital, encompassed the
fourth side there,* with walls and moats, and many a tower raised
high. The army's encampment stretched for a good mile in length
over the plain, and a good half a mile in breadth, too. Towards
Arthur's messengers rode many a knight quite unknown to them,
turcopoles, many a man-at-arms, iron-clad and with lances. After
them there strutted briskly, under various banners, many a great
troop. The clamour of trumpets rang out there. The entire army was
visibly astir. They were about to ride to Joflanze. Ladies' bridles
jingle-jangled. King Gramoflanz's tent-ring was surrounded by   682
ladies.

If I can now wield a tale, I shall tell you who was encamped there
on the grass on his behalf, who had come to his muster. If you have
not heard about this before, let me acquaint you with it: from the
water-guarded city of Punt his noble uncle, King Brandelidelin, had
brought him six hundred lustrous ladies, each of which could behold
her *âmîs* there, armed and intent on chivalry and fame. The noble
Punturteis were in good heart on this journey.

Also present, if you'll believe me, was the radiant Bernout *de*
Riviers, whose wealthy father Narant* had bequeathed Ukerlant to

him. He had brought, in cogs upon the sea, such a lustrous host of ladies that people spoke of their bright complexions there, none contradicting the report. Two hundred of these formed a separate company of maidens; two hundred had their husbands there. If I've counted correctly, Bernout *fiz cons* Narant had five hundred knights
683 of noble renown accompanying him there, men who knew how to endanger enemies.

Thus King Gramoflanz intended to avenge in combat the loss of his garland, so that many people might see to whom fame was to be accorded there. The princes from his kingdom were there with their knights, fully armed, also with a company of ladies. There were some well-favoured people on view there!

Arthur's messengers arrived. They found the king—now hear how! A thick mattress of palmat-silk lay beneath the king where he sat; over it, quilted, a broad phellel-silk. Damsels, lustrous and merry, were buckling iron greaves onto the proud king's legs. A phellel-silk conferred costly renown, woven in Ecidemonis,* both broad and long, fluttering high above him to give shade, supported by twelve shafts. Arthur's messengers had arrived. To him who bore haughtiness's hoard they spoke these words:

'Lord, we have been sent here by Arthur, who was reputed erstwhile to have enjoyed fame. Indeed, he possessed honour enough.
684 This you desire to diminish for him. How could it enter your head to wish to inflict such disgrace upon his sister's son? Even if noble Gawan had caused you greater heart's distress, he might have benefited by each and every member of the Table Round, for he is granted companionship by all who crave the right to sit at it.'

The king said: 'My undaunted hand will grant the sworn combat, so that this day I shall chase Gawan either towards fame or into disgrace. I have, in all truth, heard that Arthur has arrived with a warlike band, and his wife, the Queen. She shall be welcome. If the malicious duchess advises him to bear me ill-will, you pages, you must prevent that. There is nothing else for it, but I must carry out this combat. I have, I think, so many knights here that I fear no force. Whatever befalls me at one man's hand—such duress I will willingly endure. If I were now to shirk what I have resolved upon,
685 then I would abandon love-service. She to whose favour I have devoted all my joy and my life—God well knows that Gawan has benefited by her, for I was always reluctant before to do battle

against one man alone. Yet noble Gawan has so taxed himself that I am glad to meet him in combat. Thus my valour demeans itself—never did I fight such a feeble battle! I have fought, so they say of me—if you wish, ask about it—against people who conceded to my hand that it was of famed renown. Never did I oppose one man alone. Nor should women praise it if I win the victory today. My heart rejoices, for I'm told she has been released from bonds, she for whose sake this duel will now be fought. Arthur the far-famed—so many a foreign *terre** is heard to be subject to him—she's perhaps come here with him, she for whose sake I am to take joy and duress, serving at her command, to the point of death. How might I fare better than if such good fortune were to befall me that she deigns to see my service?'

Bene sat with the king's arms about her.* She had no objection 686 whatever to the combat. She had seen so much of the king's valour in battle that she had set all anxiety aside. If she knew, however, that Gawan was her lady's brother and that these arduous affairs related to her lord, she would be disillusioned of joy there. She had brought to the king that very ring which Itonje, the young queen, had sent him out of love—that which her brother of noble renown had brought across the Sabins. Bene had come in a skiff on the Poynzaclins. She did not omit these tidings: 'From Schastel Marveile my lady has departed, with hosts of other ladies.' She bade Gramoflanz be mindful of loyalty and honour on her lady's part, more than any girl had ever sent by a messenger to a man, and that he should think of her duress, since she offered service for his love, in preference to all other gains. That raised the king's spirits. Nevertheless, he is doing Gawan an injustice. If *I* were to suffer thus for my sister, I would rather have no sister at all!

Accoutrements were brought in for him, of such evidently lavish 687 expense that all whom Love ever compelled to strive for women's reward—were it Gahmuret or Galoes, or King Kyllicrates*—none of them could ever have adorned his person better for women's sake. Neither from Ipopotiticon, nor from vast Acraton, nor from Kalomidente, nor from Agatyrsjente had better phellel-silk ever been brought than had been designed for his accoutrements there. Then he kissed the ring which Itonje, the young queen, had sent him out of love. He knew her loyalty to be such that whenever he was daunted by distress, her love would be a shield against it.

Now the king was armed. Twelve damsels took a hand, mounted on pretty palfreys. They were not to be negligent—that lustrous company—but each was to carry by a shaft the costly phellel-silk beneath which the king wished to arrive. They bore it to give shade

688 to the belligerent warrior. Two little ladies, none too feeble—indeed they bore the brightest sheen there—rode with the king's stout arms about them. Then there was no more waiting. Arthur's messengers rode away and came, on their return journey, to where Gawan was doing battle. Never had the pages been so distressed. They cried out loudly at his peril, for their loyalty commanded it of them.

It had very nearly come to the point where Gawan's battle-companion might have carried off the victory there. His strength so overpowered Gawan that the noble warrior had almost renounced victory, were it not that the pages, who recognized him, named him as they lamented. At that, he who had before been his battle's guarantor forbore desire to do battle against him. He flung his sword far from his hand: 'Accursed and unworthy am I!' said the weeping stranger. 'All fortune failed me when this battle made acquaintance with my dishonoured hand! It was gross impropriety on my hand's part. I willingly admit my guilt. Here my ill-fortune stepped for-

689 ward, parting me from fortune's choosing. Thus my old arms have manifested themselves all too often in the past—and now again! That I should have done battle against noble Gawan here! I have outfought my own self and awaited ill-fortune here. When this battle was begun, Fortune had fled me.'

Gawan heard and saw this lament. He said to his battle-companion: 'Alas, lord, who are you? You speak graciously to me. If only such words had passed before, when I could still lay claim to strength, then I might not have parted from fame! You have won the prize here. I would gladly learn from you where I might find my fame hereafter, if I were to seek it. As long as Fortune favoured me, I had always fought well against any one man's hand.'

'Kinsman, I make myself known to you, at your service now and at all times. It's me, your kinsman, Parzival.'

Gawan said: 'This was only just. Here crooked folly has been straightened. Here two hearts that are one have shown their strength in hostility. Your hand has outfought us both. Now may you grieve

690 for both our sakes. You have conquered your own self, if your heart practises loyalty.'

When these words had been spoken, my lord Gawan was indeed so lacking in strength that he could no longer stand. He started to totter, quite dazed, for his head had been made to resound. He tumbled down onto the grass. One of Arthur's young lordlings leapt to support his head. Then that gentle youth untied his helmet and fanned the air beneath his eyes with a hat of bright peacock feathers. That page's diligence taught Gawan new strength.

From both armies companies of warriors were arriving here and there, each army going to its allotted place, where their positions were marked out by mighty tree-trunks, polished bright as mirrors. Gramoflanz had met this expenditure to mark the occasion of his combat. There were a hundred such trees, of bright, radiant appearance. No-one was to step between them. They stood—so I've heard—at a distance of forty horse-charge lengths from one another, shimmering with coloured brightness, fifty on each side. Between these the battle was to befall. The army was to halt outside, as if 691 separated by walls or deep moats. Gramoflanz and Gawan had clasped hands on that truce.

To meet that unvowed battle many a troop arrived in time, from both armies, to see to whom they were to accord fame there. They wondered, indeed, who was fighting there in such bellicose fashion, or against whom that battle was intended there. Neither army had escorted its champion into the rink. These seemed wondrous matters to them.

When that battle on the flower-bright plain was over, King Gramoflanz arrived, intent on avenging the loss of his garland. He heard a full account of what had happened there—a combat so fierce that no harder sword-fight had ever been seen. Those who granted each other that battle had done so without any cause at all. Gramoflanz rode out of his host, over to the battle-weary knights. He heartily lamented their hardship.

Gawan had leapt to his feet. His limbs were spent. Here those two stood. Now Lady Bene had also ridden with the king into the rink 692 where the battle had been endured. She saw Gawan devoid of strength—he whom above all the world she had chosen as her joy's highest crown. With heart's sorrow's sound, she leapt shrieking from her horse—she flung her arms about him. She said: 'Cursed among all men be the hand which has acquainted your radiant person with this hardship! Truly, your complexion was a mirror of manliness.'

She sat him down upon the grass. Of her weeping little was omitted. Then the gentle maiden wiped the blood and sweat away from his eyes. He was hot in his armour.

King Gramoflanz then said: 'Gawan, I'm sorry for your hardship, as it wasn't my hand that inflicted it. If you'll come to the plain again tomorrow, to meet me in battle, I will gladly await you. I would rather attack a woman now, than you in this exhausted state. What fame might I win by you, unless I heard you reported to be in better strength? Now rest tonight. You will have need of it, if you desire to stand in for King Lot.'

693   Sturdy Parzival, for his part, had not a single weary limb, nor any mark of pallor. He had untied his helmet in the meantime. When the noble king looked at him, Parzival spoke courteously to him: 'Sir, whatever my kinsman Gawan has done to offend you, let me stand surety for him. My hands are still capable of combat. If you desire to direct anger against him, I must prevent you by the sword.'

The Lord of Rosche Sabbins said: 'Lord, he shall pay me interest tomorrow—that is owed for my garland—so that either his fame will stand high and entire, or he will pursue me to such a place where I shall set foot on disgrace's path. Granted, you may well be a doughty warrior, but this duel is not destined for you.'

Then Bene's gentle mouth spoke to the king: 'You faithless dog! Your heart lies in the hand of that man towards whom your heart fosters hatred. To whom have you devoted yourself out of love? It is she who has to live by his favour! You pronounce your own self vanquished. Love has lost her due by you. If you ever bore love, it was with false intent.'

694   Meeting with so much anger, the king spoke to Bene in private. He entreated her: 'Lady, do not be angry at my fighting this duel. Remain here with your lord. Tell Itonje, his sister, that I am her true servitor, and I desire to serve her in all that I can.'

When Bene heard in no uncertain words that her lord was her lady's brother—he who was to do battle on the grass there—then sorrow's oars pulled a full boatload of heartfelt grief into her heart, for she practised heart's loyalty. She said: 'Be off with you, accursed man! You are one who never won loyalty!'

The king rode away, as did all his company. Arthur's young lordlings caught the chargers of the two combatants. The chargers looked to have fought their own, separate battle. Gawan and Parzival and the fair Bene rode off towards their army. Parzival, with manly valour, had won such fame that they rejoiced at his coming. Those who saw his approach there all acknowledged his high fame.

I shall tell you more, if I can. Concerning that one man, those of 695 discernment in both armies spoke up in praise of his knightly deeds—he who has won the prize there. If you'll admit as much, it's Parzival. He was, moreover, of such fair features that no knight was ever better favoured, as women and men alike averred when Gawan escorted him there; his intention was to order fresh clothes for Parzival. Then identical clothing of great cost was brought in there for them both. Everywhere the tidings spread that Parzival had arrived, he of whom it had so often been heard that he pursued high fame. Truly, there was many a one who said as much.

Gawan said: 'If you'd like to see four ladies of your kin, and other well-favoured ladies too, then I will gladly walk over with you to them.'

Gahmuret's son replied: 'If there are noble ladies here, you must not let me offend them by my presence. Any lady who has heard false words spoken of me by the Plimizœl is unwilling to see me. May God 696 look on their womanly honour! I will always wish women good fortune, but I am as yet so very ashamed that I am unwilling to enter their company.'

'Yet it must be,' said Gawan. He led Parzival off to where four queens kissed him. It taught pain to the duchess that she had to kiss the man who had declined her greeting when she offered him love and her land—on that count she was in anguish out of shame there—when he had fought before Logroys, and she had ridden so far in pursuit of him. The radiant Parzival was talked over by their sincerity, so that all shame was then conducted out of his heart. Free of embarrassment, he grew content.

Gawan, for good reason, commanded of Lady Bene, if she wished to retain his favour, that her gentle mouth should not inform Itonje 'that King Gramoflanz bears me such enmity because of his garland, and that we are to give one another battle tomorrow, at the proper time agreed for combat. You mustn't say anything of this to my sister, and must suppress your tears entirely.'

She said: 'I have good reason to weep and show unceasing grief, 697 for whichever of you succumbs there, my lady will foster grief on his account. She will be slain on both sides. I have every reason to mourn for my lady and myself. How does it help her that you are her brother? It is with her heart that you desire to fight a battle.'

The whole army had filed in. The meal was now ready for Gawan and his companions. Parzival was to eat with the vivacious duchess. Nor did Gawan forget to commend him to her. She said: 'Would you commend to me a man who can scorn ladies? How am I to entertain this man? Yet I shall serve him, as you command it. I do not care if he makes mock of me.'

Then Gahmuret's son said: 'Lady, you would do me an injustice. I know myself to be wise enough to avoid making mock of any woman.'

If it was there, it was supplied in ample quantity; with great courtesy it was brought before them. Maidens, women and men ate with pleasure. Itonje, however, did not neglect to look at Bene's eyes, 698 and saw that they were weeping secretly. Then she too took on grief's appearance. Her sweet mouth shunned eating altogether. She thought: 'What is Bene doing here? I had, after all, sent her to him who bears my heart there, that heart which stirs me most ungently here. What punishment have I merited? Has the king renounced my service and my love? His loyal, manly mind can gain nothing more here, except that the wretched body that I bear here must die out of heartfelt grief for him.'*

When they had finished eating there, it was already past midday. Arthur and his wife, Lady Guinevere the Queen, with a band of knights and ladies, rode over to where the well-favoured warrior sat in noble ladies' company. Parzival's welcome then took such a turn that he had to see himself kissed by many lustrous ladies. Arthur did him honour and thanked him profusely that his high fame ranged so far and wide that he ought by rights to enjoy praise above all men.

699 The Waleis said to Arthur: 'Lord, when I last saw you, a charge had been run through my honour. I gave away such a high pledge of fame that I almost lost fame altogether. Now I have heard from you, sir, if your words are sincere, that fame is in part justified where I am concerned. However ungently I have learned that lesson, I'd be glad to believe it of you, if the rest of that company from which I then parted in shame would also believe it.'

Those sitting there assured him that his hand had won fame in many lands, with such high fame that his fame was unimpaired.

All the duchess's knights had also come to where well-favoured Parzival was sitting next to Arthur. The noble King did not neglect to welcome them in the host's lodging.* Courtly, wise Arthur, no matter how broad Gawan's pavilion was, sat outside upon the plain. They sat around him in the tent-ring. Unfamiliar tidings assembled—who this man or that man was—the tales would stretch far if both Christians and Saracens were to be named in full there. Who was in Clinschor's army? Who were those who had ridden out 700 so valiantly time and again from Logroys, where they had fought in Orgeluse's cause? Who were those whom Arthur had brought with him? If anyone were to name all their lands and castles in full, it would be a hard task to identify them all! They all averred as one that Parzival alone excelled, being so radiant of person that women might love him with a will, and as for what related to high fame, honour had cheated him of nothing.

Gahmuret's son stood up. He said: 'All those present here, let them remain seated and help me towards one thing whose lack I feel most urgently. It was a mysterious marvel that parted me from the Table Round. Those who granted me companionship before, let them help me now to sit at it once more in companionship!' What he desired Arthur granted him handsomely.

He then entreated a second entreaty—with a few people he stepped aside—that Gawan should grant him the battle which he was to fight at the appointed time for the combat the following morning: 'I will gladly await him there—he who is called *rois* 701 Gramoflanz. From his tree I plucked a garland early this morning, intending that it should bring me battle. I came into his country in order to do battle, solely for the purpose of fighting against his hand. Kinsman, I little trusted to find you here. Never did such great grief befall me. I thought it was the king, who would not forbear to fight against me. Kinsman, let me take him on now. If ever dishonour is to befall him, my hand shall cause him such affliction as will truly suffice for him. My rights have been restored to me here. Now I can act companionably, dear kinsman, towards you. Think of the acknowledged kinship between us, and let this battle be mine. I will display manly courage there!'

My lord Gawan replied: 'Kinsmen and brothers I have here in plenty, among the King of Britain's company. I will permit none of you to fight in my place. I trust to my good cause, if Fortune prevails, that I may retain fame. God reward you for offering to fight in my stead, but that time has not yet come.'

702   Arthur heard that entreaty. He interrupted the conversation, sitting down with them again at the ring. Gawan's cup-bearer did not neglect to have young lordlings carry over many a costly golden goblet, adorned with precious stones. Nor did the cup-bearer walk alone. When the drinks had been poured, the people all went to their rest.

Night now began to draw nigh. Parzival was intent on inspecting all his armour, to see if any strap were missing. He commanded it should be put in good order and splendidly decked out, and that a new shield be procured. His own had been battered, both outside and inside, by the charge, and hewn to pieces, too. A new, stout shield had to be brought in. That was seen to by men-at-arms with whom he was very little acquainted—one or two of them were Frenchmen. His charger, which the templar had brought into the joust against him, was seen to by a squire. Never afterwards was it better groomed. By then it was night and time for sleep. Parzival, too, indulged in sleep. All his armour lay there before him.

703   For his part, King Gramoflanz regretted that another man had fought for his garland that day. His men had neither dared nor been able to intervene there. He began to be bitterly sorry that he had delayed. What did the warrior do then? Because he had always pursued fame, at the very moment day broke his charger was armed, as was he himself. Had realmless women contributed to the cost of his accoutrements? They were, in any case, lavish enough. He adorned himself for the sake of a maiden—in her service he was undaunted. He rode out alone to spy out the land. It troubled the king greatly that noble Gawan did not soon arrive on the plain.

Now Parzival, too, all in secret, had stolen out. Out of a banner he took a sturdy spear* from Angram; he was also in full armour. The warrior rode off alone towards the mirror-bright tree-trunks where the combat was to be. He saw the king halting there. Before either

704 had spoken a single word to the other, they say that each of them thrust through the other's shield's rim, causing the splinters to fly up from their hands, twisting up through the air. They were both well versed in jousting, and in other fighting, too. All over the meadow's width the dew was dispersed, and the helmets felt the touch of sharp blades that cut deep. Both fought undauntedly.

The meadow was trampled upon there, the dew waded through in many places. I grieve for the red flowers, and still more for the warriors who endured extremity there, devoid of cowardice. What man whom they had not offended would feel joy without sorrow at this?

Meanwhile Sir Gawan, too, was preparing himself to meet his combat's anxieties. It must have been about mid-morning before the tidings were heard that bold Parzival was missing. Was he intending to bring about a reconciliation? He certainly wasn't acting like it, fighting so manfully against one also versed in battle. By now the sun stood high.

A bishop sang mass for Gawan. There was a great press of armed   705
men there. Mounted knights and ladies could be seen at Arthur's tent-ring, before mass had been sung to its end. King Arthur himself stood where the priests are performing their office. When the benediction had been spoken, Sir Gawan armed himself. Before that the proud knight had already been seen to be wearing his iron greaves on his well-shaped legs. Then ladies began to weep. The army filed out on all sides, to where they heard the clash of swords, and fire flying from helmets, and blows dealt with might and main.

It was King Gramoflanz's custom to entertain great disdain to do battle with one man—now it seemed to him that six were taking up the fight there. Yet it was Parzival alone who was showing him defiance. He had given him a lesson in courtesy such as is still praised today—never again did he boast of such prestige that he would offer combat to two men, for one is granting him too much of it there!

The armies from both sides had arrived on the broad, green   706
meadow, each at its assigned post. They appraised these hostilities. The bold warriors' chargers had been left standing. Now the noble knights were fighting on foot on the ground—a hard, fierce, famous battle. High in the air the heroes threw their swords from their hands, time and again, turning the blade's edge.*

Thus King Gramoflanz paid bitter interest on his garland. His lady-love's kin* also endured scant delight at his hands. Thus noble Parzival suffered on account of Itonje the fair, by whom he ought to have benefited, if right were to side with right. Those who had journeyed much in pursuit of fame had to reap the harvest of battle, the one fighting to keep friend from peril, the other commanded by Love to be Love's subject. Then my lord Gawan also arrived, by

which time it had almost reached the point that the proud, bold
Waleis had won the victory there. Brandelidelin of Punturteis, and
707 Bernout de Riviers, and Affinamus of Clitiers—bare-headed, those
three rode closer to the combat.* Arthur and Gawan, from the other
side, rode across the plain towards the battle-weary pair. Those five
agreed that they wished to part the battle. It seemed high time to
intervene to Gramoflanz, who by his words conceded victory to the
man seen opposing him there. Others still were to make the same
admission.

Then King Lot's son said: 'Sir King, I shall do by you today as
you did by me yesterday, when you entreated me to rest. Rest, now,
tonight. You will have need of it. Whoever has offered you this battle
has accorded you scant strength to meet my warlike hand. Right now
I could easily take you on singly, but you only ever fight against two.
I'll risk it tomorrow, alone. May God make a just issue manifest!'

The king rode away to his men, having first sworn an oath that
next morning he would come to meet Gawan to do battle on the
plain.

708 Arthur said to Parzival: 'Kinsman, since it so befell you that you
requested the combat and acted valorously, and Gawan refused it
you, your mouth lamenting it so grievously then—well, now you've
fought the battle, after all, against his opponent who had awaited him
there—whether we liked it or not. You sneaked away from us like a
thief. Otherwise we might well have denied your hand this battle.
Now Gawan has no need to be angry, no matter how much fame is
spoken of you on this account.'

Gawan said: 'I am not grieved at my kinsman's high honour.
Tomorrow morning is all too early for me, if I am to grasp at battle.
If the king would release me from it, I would acknowledge his
moderation.'

The army rode back in, with many a company. Well-favoured
ladies were to be seen there, and many a man so accoutred that no
army ever again acquired such a marvel of accoutrements. Those of
the Table Round and the household of the duchess—their surcoats
shone with phellel-silk from Cynidunte,* and brought from Pelpiunte.
709 Bright were their caparisons.

Comely Parzival was so praised in both armies that his friends had
good reason to be delighted. In Gramoflanz's army they averred that
never had the sun shone upon a knight so bold in battle. Of all that

had been done on both sides there, he alone had to have the prize. As yet they did not know the identity of him to whom every mouth accords praise there.

They advised Gramoflanz that it would be well to send a message to Arthur to the effect that he should guard against any other man of his company emerging to meet him in battle—that he should send to him the right man, Gawan, King Lot's son, with whom he desired to do combat. The messengers were sent forth, two discerning youths, known to be courteous. The king said: 'Now you must be on the lookout for one to whom you would accord the prize among all those lustrous ladies there. You must also observe, in particular, at whose side Bene is sitting. Mark well how she behaves, whether joy or sadness resides with her. Take note of that, secretly. You will see 710 clearly by her eyes whether she feels sorrow on a beloved's behalf. See that you do not neglect this—give to Bene, my friend, this letter and this ring. She knows full well to whom it is to be furthered. Act discreetly, and you will have done well.'

Now in the other camp it had reached the point where Itonje had heard that her brother and the dearest man a maiden ever took to her heart were to fight with one another, and would not desist. Then her wretchedness broke through her modesty. If anyone finds her sorrow fitting now, he does so contrary to my counsel, for she has not deserved it!

Both her mother and her grandmother led the maiden apart, into a small silk pavilion. Arnive reproached her for her pangs, scolding her for her misdeed. Then there was simply no other option—she admitted unreservedly there what she had long concealed from them. The maiden of noble renown then said: 'If my brother's hand is now to cut through my heart's life-blood—he ought willingly to avoid such behaviour!'

Arnive said to a young lordling: 'Now tell my son to come and 711 speak with me soon, and see to it in private.' The squire brought Arthur in. Arnive's intention was to let him hear—perhaps he might put a stop to it?—for whose sake lustrous Itonje was so sore at heart.

King Gramoflanz's pages have arrived, in search of Arthur. They dismounted on the field. Before the small pavilion one of them saw Bene sitting next to a lady who was saying to Arthur: 'Does the duchess consider it praiseworthy if my brother is to slay my *âmîs* at her haughty prompting? My brother ought to admit it would be a

misdeed. How has the king* injured him? He ought to let him benefit
by me. If my brother is sensible, he knows our mutual love to be so
pure, so unsullied, that if he practises loyalty, he will regret this. If
his hand is to procure me a bitter death on account of the king, lord,
let this complaint be laid at your door!'—said that gentle maiden to
712 Arthur—'Now remember you are my uncle. Out of loyalty, part this
battle.'

Arthur spoke out of a wise mouth then: 'Alas, my dear niece, that
your youth displays such lofty love! It may turn sour on you. Your
sister Surdamur behaved in the same way for the sake of *Lampruore**
of the Greeks. Gentle, comely maiden, I might well prove capable of
averting this combat, if I knew, with regard to both of you, whether
his heart and yours are united. Gramoflanz, Irot's son, has such
valiant ways about him that the battle will be fought unless love for
you prevents it. Has he ever seen your bright sheen in joy's company
at any time, and your sweet, red mouth?'

She said: 'That has not happened. We love without having seen
one another. He has, however, sent me, inspired by his affection and
out of true companionship, many love-tokens. He has also received
from my hand something belonging to true love, which destroyed
doubt in both of us. The king is constant towards me, devoid of false
heart's counsels.'

713 Then Lady Bene recognized those two squires, King Gramo-
flanz's pages, who had come in search of Arthur. She said: 'No-one
ought to be standing here. If you wish, I shall order the people to
step back, beyond the guy-ropes. If such unhappiness is to move my
lady on account of her beloved, the tidings may soon spread too far.'

Lady Bene was sent out. One of the pages smuggled the letter and
the ring into her hand. They had indeed clearly heard the intense
anguish of her lady, and said they had come with the intention of
speaking to Arthur, if she would deign to arrange it. She said: 'Stand
there, over in the distance, until I beckon you to walk over to me.'

Then Bene the sweet maiden told those in the pavilion that
Gramoflanz's messengers were there, asking where King Arthur
was. 'It seemed to me unfitting if I were to direct them towards this
discussion. Look, what wrong would I then be avenging upon my
lady, if they were to see her weeping like this here?'

714 Arthur said: 'Are those the boys I saw trotting after me to the tent-
ring? They are two pages of high lineage. What if they are so discreet,

so entirely guarded against misdeed, that they may well be admitted
to this counsel? One or other of them will be sufficiently discerning
to see clearly my niece's love for his lord.'

Bene said: 'I don't know about that. Lord, if it please you, the king
has sent this ring here, and this letter. Just now, when I ran out of the
pavilion, one of the pages gave it to me. Lady, look, you take it.'

Then the letter was much kissed. Itonje pressed it to her breast.
Then she said: 'Sir, see from this whether the king bids me bear love
in mind.'

Arthur took the letter into his hand; in it he found written what
he who was versed in love, Gramoflanz the constant, had to say, in
the words of his own mouth. Arthur saw in the letter matter that
convinced him that never in his times had he, to his knowledge,
perceived such sincere love. Words stood there that well became
love:

'I greet her whom I must needs greet, from whom I fetch greeting 715
by service. Little lady, it is you I mean, for you it is who consoles me
with solace. Our loves bear each other company. That is the root of
my joy's abundance. Your solace outweighs all other solace, for your
heart cherishes loyalty towards me. You are the lock upon my loyalty,
and the loss of my heart's grief. Your love gives me help's counsel, so
that I shall never be seen to do any kind of misdeed. Indeed, I may
ascribe to your benevolence such undeviating constancy as Polus
Artanticus has in relation to the Tremuntane.* Neither of these
departs from its spot. Our love must stand in loyalty, nor must we
part from one another. Think now of me, noble maiden, of what
sorrow I have lamented to you. Do not be slow to help me. If ever
any man, because of the enmity he bears me, desires to part you from
me, then bear in mind that Love is well capable of rewarding us both.
You must protect ladies' honour and let me be your servitor. I shall
serve you in all I can.'

Arthur said: 'Niece, you are right. The king greets you without 716
guile. This letter acquaints me with such tidings that I have never
seen such a wondrous invention addressed to love.* You must avert
his distress, as must he yours. Leave it, both of you, to me. I shall
prevent the combat. Meanwhile, you must spare your tears. Now,
you were held captive, weren't you? Tell me, how did it happen that
you became dear to one another? You must allot to him your love's
reward—that is what he desires to earn by his service.'

Itonje, Arthur's niece, said: 'She's present here, she who brought this about. Neither of us has ever said a word about it. If you wish, she may well arrange that I see him to whom I accord my heart.'

Arthur said: 'Show her to me. If I can, I shall arrange matters for him and you, so that your desire is fulfilled and the happiness of you both comes to pass.'

Itonje said: 'It is Bene. There are two of his squires here, too. Can you determine—if you care for my life—whether the king to whom I must owe my joy wishes to see me?'

717   Arthur, that wise and courtly man, walked out at once to the pages, greeting them immediately he saw them. One of the pages then replied: 'Lord, King Gramoflanz entreats you to observe in full the vows that have been made between him and Gawan, for your own honour's sake. Lord, he further asks of you that no other man should go to do battle with him. Your host is so great that if he had to outfight them all, that would bear no resemblance to justice. You must have Gawan come to meet him against whom the combat has been arranged there.'

The King said to the pages: 'I shall free us from that reproach. No greater grief ever befell my nephew than when he did not fight there himself. He who fought with your lord was a goodly heir to the victory. He is Gahmuret's son. All those who in three armies* have arrived here from all sides—never did they hear of a warrior so valorously meeting battle. His deeds match his fame entirely. He is my kinsman, Parzival. You must see him, this knight of fair appear-
718 ance. Because of Gawan's loyalty's extremity I shall accomplish what the king's embassy requests of me.'

Arthur and Bene and those two squires rode back and forth. He pointed out to the pages the bright glance of many a lady. They could also observe the rustling of many a crest on the helmets there.* Even today it would do a man of might little harm to behave so sociably. They did not dismount from their horses. Arthur showed the pages the noble personages everywhere in the army, where they were able to observe perfection—knights, maidens and women—many a comely person.

There were three parts to the army, with two gaps in between. Arthur rode off with the pages, away from the army onto the plain. He said: 'Bene, gentle maiden, you've heard, I'm sure, what Itonje, my sister's child, has lamented to me. She can little spare her tears.

My companions halting here may believe it, if they will: Gramoflanz has almost quenched Itonje's bright radiance. Now help me, you 719 two, and you also, friend Bene, to ensure that the king rides over to me here, and fights the battle tomorrow, nevertheless. I shall bring my nephew Gawan to meet him on the plain. If the king rides into my army today, he will be all the better equipped to defend himself tomorrow. Here Love shall give him a shield by which his battle-companion will be daunted. I mean high spirits bent on love, which wreak havoc among the enemy. Let him bring courtly people with him. I will mediate here between him and the duchess. See to this discreetly, now, my dear companions—it will be to your honour. I must lodge another complaint with you: in what way have I, wretched man, injured King Gramoflanz, since he bears towards my kindred—apparently weighing it lightly—such great love and unlove? Any fellow king of mine ought to be glad to spare me such treatment. If he now desires to reward Itonje's brother, whom she loves, with enmity—if he thinks it over, his heart is deviating from love if it teaches him such thoughts.'

One of the pages said to the King: 'Sir, my lord ought to desist 720 from imposing all the hardship of which you complain, if he desires to hold to true propriety. You know, I imagine, about the old grudge. It suits my lord better to remain where he is than to ride over here to you. It is still the duchess's custom to refuse him her favour, and she has complained of him to many a man.'

'Let him come with a small company,' said Arthur. 'In the meantime I shall have obtained a truce from the well-born duchess as regards that grudge. I shall give him a good escort. Beacurs, my sister's son, will escort him from the halfway point. Let him ride in my escort's safe-keeping. There is no need for him to regard that as a disgrace. I shall show him some noble personages!'

Given leave, they departed. Arthur halted alone on the plain. Bene and the two little pages rode into Rosche Sabbins, and out on the other side, where the army lay. Never had Gramoflanz experienced such a dear day as when Bene and the pages spoke to him. His heart averred that such tidings had been brought to him as Fortune herself had devised for him.

He said that he would gladly go. A group of companions was 721 formed there. Three princes from his land rode off from there, alongside the king, as did his uncle, King Brandelidelin. Bernout de

Riviers and Affinamus of Clitiers each took a companion well befitting the cavalcade. There were twelve of them in all. Countless numbers of squires and many sturdy men-at-arms were also appointed to the cavalcade.

What might those knights' clothes have been? Phellel-silk, which gave off most bright sheen from the gold's weight. The king's falconers rode with him, intent on hawking. Arthur, for his part, had not failed to send Beacurs of the bright complexion halfway towards them, to be the king's escort. Over the fields' breadth, whether through ponds or brooks, wherever he saw fords, the king rode along, hawking, and, keener still, bent on love's desire. Beacurs welcomed him there, in such a way that joy ensued.

722   Together with Beacurs have come more than fifty radiant youths, emitting the bright sheen of their lineage—dukes and countlets. Along with them rode several kings' sons, too. Then a great show of welcome was seen from the youths on both sides. They welcomed one another without rancour.

Beacurs had a bright complexion. The king was not slow to ask about him. Bene informed him who the radiant knight was: 'It is Beacurs, Lot's son.'

Then he thought: 'Heart, now find her who resembles him who rides so charmingly here. She is his sister, indeed, who sent me this hat, wrought in Sinzester, together with her sparrowhawk. If she grants me more favour—all earthly wealth, even if the earth were twice as broad again—I would prefer her alone to it all. Her love must be loyally meant. It is in search of her favour that I have come here. She has always so consoled me that I am fully confident that she will treat me in such a way that my spirits will rise still higher.' Her radiant brother's hand took his hand in his. That too was acknowledged to be fair.

723   Meanwhile, in the other army, it had come about over there that Arthur had obtained a truce from the duchess. Compensation's gain had come to her for Cidegast, whose death she had mourned so grievously before. Her anger was almost covered over,* for several embraces from Gawan had awakened her, which was why her wrath was so enfeebled.

Arthur the Briton took to one side the lustrous, courteous ladies, both the maidens and women, those who were comely of person. He had assembled a hundred of the noble ladies in a separate pavilion.

Nothing could have pleased her better but that she should see the king—Itonje, that is, who was also sitting there. She was not oblivious of constant joy. Yet it could be perceived by her eyes' sheen that Love was teaching her torment.

Many a knight of fair appearance sat there, but noble Parzival carried off the prize above all other lustre. Gramoflanz rode up to the tent-ropes. The fearless king was wearing a phellel-silk, stiff with gold, wrought in Gampfassasche,* which glittered far and wide.

They dismounted, those who have arrived there. Many of King 724 Gramoflanz's pages leapt ahead of him, pressing their way into the pavilion. The chamberlains vied with one another to clear a broad path leading to the Queen of the Britons. His uncle, Brandelidelin, preceded the king into the pavilion. Guinevere welcomed him with a kiss. The king was welcomed in the same way. Bernout and Affinamus were also seen to be kissed by the Queen. Arthur said to Gramoflanz: 'Before you sit down, see whether you love any of these ladies, and kiss her. Let permission be granted to both of you here.'

He was told which was his lady-love by a letter he had read out in the fields—I mean that he had seen the brother of her who had avowed to him, before all others in the world, her noble, secret love. Gramoflanz's eyes recognized her who bore love for him. His joy had reached ample heights. Since Arthur had granted permission that they might, without dispute, bid each other welcome by a greeting, he kissed Itonje on the mouth.

King Brandelidelin sat down next to Guinevere the Queen. And 725 King Gramoflanz sat down next to her who had soaked her bright radiance with tears. That was the profit she had won by him. Unless he wishes to punish innocence, he must talk to her in such fashion that he offers his service for love. She, for her part, knew how to busy herself in thanking him for having come. Their converse was heard by no-one. They were glad to see one another. If I ever come to learn such converse, then I'll determine what they spoke there—whether no or yes.

Arthur said to Brandelidelin: 'You have told my wife enough of your tidings now.' He led the undaunted warrior into a lesser pavilion, a short way across the field. Gramoflanz remained seated—that was what Arthur intended—along with other companions of his. There ladies cast a lustrous sheen, causing the knights there little dismay. The pastime they enjoyed was so great that even now a man desirous of winning joy after sorrow would willingly put up with the like.

726   Drink was then brought before the Queen. If they drank enough, all the knights and ladies, then they were all the rosier of hue. Drink was also taken in to Arthur and Brandelidelin. The cup-bearer withdrew. Arthur began his speech as follows: 'Sir King, now supposing they act as follows: if the king, *your* sister's son, were to slay *my* sister's son—if he were then to desire to bear love towards my niece, that maiden who is now lamenting her troubles to him where we left them sitting—if she were then to act sensibly, she would never become fond of him on that count, but would dole out to him such enmity's payment as might prove wearisome to the king, if he desired to profit by her at all. Where hostility crosses love, it denies joy to the constant heart.'

Then the King of Punturtoys said to Arthur the Briton: 'Sir, these are our sisters' children who act as enemies to one another. We must prevent this duel. The only possible outcome is that they should love 727 one another from the heart. Your niece Itonje must first command my nephew to relinquish the duel for her sake, if he desires her love. Then, indeed, the duel and all its bellicose practices will be avoided. And help my nephew, too, to obtain favour with the duchess.'

Arthur said: 'That I will do. Gawan, my sister's son, has, I imagine, such power over her that she will yield the cause both to him and to myself, out of her courtesy. For your part, put a stop to the battle on your side.'

'I shall do so,' said Brandelidelin. They both went back into the great pavilion.

Then the King of Punturtoys sat down next to Guinevere. She was courteous. On her other side sat Parzival. He was so fair of appearance that no eye ever beheld such a handsome man. Arthur the King set off to find his nephew Gawan, who had been informed that *rois* Gramoflanz had arrived. Soon it was heard in his presence that Arthur had dismounted before the pavilion. Gawan leapt out into the field to meet him. They arranged it between them there that 728 the duchess should assent to a reconciliation, but only on condition that Gawan, her *âmîs*, would relinquish the duel for her sake—then she would be willing to grant a truce. This truce would be granted by her, provided the king would withdraw the accusation levelled at her father-in-law, Lot. She sent this message off with Arthur.

Arthur, that wise and courtly man, conveyed these tidings. Then King Gramoflanz was obliged to renounce his garland, and all the enmity he bore Lot of Norway vanished like snow in the sun, for the sake of lustrous Itonje, cleanly, without any rancour. This happened while he was sitting at her side; he spoke assent to all she requested.

Gawan was seen to approach with a resplendent company. I couldn't spell out all their names to you, or of what lineage they were born. There, for affection's sake, offence was forgiven. Proud Orgeluse and her noble soldiers, and Clinschor's company, too—part of it; not all of them were there—were seen to arrive with Gawan. From Arthur's pavilion the side-flaps had been removed from the covering.* 729 The goodly Arnive, Sangive, and Cundrie—those Arthur had requested earlier to take part in the truce negotiations. If anyone thinks these are small matters, let him aggrandize whatever he wishes. Jofreit, Gawan's companion, led by his hand the duchess of renowned beauty into the pavilion. Out of courtesy, she thoughtfully let the three queens enter before her. Brandelidelin kissed them. Orgeluse also welcomed him with a kiss. Gramoflanz, desiring reconciliation and her favour, walked up to her. Her sweet red mouth kissed the king in reconciliation, although she longed to weep, thinking of Cidegast's death. Womanly distress still imposed grief for him upon her. Concede, if you will, that this is loyalty!

Gawan and Gramoflanz also made their reconciliation entire by a kiss. Arthur gave Itonje to Gramoflanz in formal marriage. To that end he had performed great service. Bene was delighted when this took place. Furthermore, to him whom love for her had taught 730 pangs, to the Duke of Gowerzin, Lischoys, Cundrie was given. His life had been bereft of joy until he experienced noble love for her. To the Turkoyt Florant Arthur offered Sangive as a wife; before she had been King Lot's wife. The prince, for his part, was delighted to accept her; that was a gift that well became Love.

Arthur was lavish with ladies; concerning such gifts he had no compunction. This had been thought through previously in counsel. When these matters had been dispatched, the duchess announced that Gawan had earned her love by his highly renowned fame, so that he was by law lord over her person and her land. This announcement weighed heavy with her soldiers, who had broken many a spear in their desire for her love.

Gawan and his companions, Arnive and the duchess, and many a radiant lady, and also noble Parzival, Sangive, and Cundrie took their leave; Itonje remained there with Arthur. Now no-one can tell where 731 a more splendid wedding ever took place. Guinevere welcomed into her care Itonje and her *âmîs*, that noble king who had often won many a prize in the past by chivalry, compelled to it by love of Itonje. Many a man rode to his lodgings to whom lofty love brought grief. As for their meal that night, we may as well forget that tale. Whoever practised noble love there desired night in place of day.

King Gramoflanz sent word, compelled by his pride's extremity, to Rosche Sabbins, to his men, that they should take pains to break camp by the sea, and, before daybreak, arrive with his army, and that his marshal should take such lodgings as befitted an army: 'See to it that my own quarters are magnificent, and that each prince has a separate tent-ring.' This was intended as lavish expenditure. The messengers departed. Then it was night.

Many a man was seen to be sorrowful there, taught such a lesson by women, for if a man's service fades without his finding any reward, he has no choice but to hasten towards sorrow, unless women's help stretches out a hand.

732 Now Parzival thought once more of his fair wife and of her chaste gentleness. Did he greet no other, offering service in pursuit of love, indulging in inconstancy? In such love as that he is sparing. Great loyalty had so guarded his manly heart, and body too, that, truly, no other woman ever held sway over his love—only Queen Condwiramurs, that flourishing *bêâ flûrs*. He thought: 'Ever since I have been capable of love, how has Love acted by me? And yet I am born of love. How have I thus lost love? If I am to strive for the Grail, then I must ever be compelled by her chaste embrace—that of her from whom I parted, too long ago. If I am to see joy with these eyes of mine, and yet my heart must admit to sorrow—these two are out of joint. No-one with such cares will be rich in high spirits. May Fortune guide me as to what it is best for me to do about it.' His armour lay close by him.

733 He thought: 'Since I lack what is subject to those blessed by Fortune—I mean Love, which cheers many a man's sad mind with joy's help—since this is not allotted me, I care not what happens to me now. God wants none of my joy. She who compels me to Love's desire—if our love were such, mine and hers, that severance belonged to it, such that doubt troubled us, I might, I suppose, have

found another love. But love of her has deprived me of other love and joy-bearing solace. I am unredeemed of sadness. May Fortune grant joy to those who desire true joy! May God grant joy to all these companies! I will depart from these joys now.'

He reached over to where his armour lay, to which he often attended alone so that he could arm himself quickly in it. Now he desires to seek new torment. When that fugitive from joy had donned all his armour, he saddled his charger with his own hand. He found shield and spear at the ready. Next morning they were heard to bemoan his journey. When he departed, dawn was beginning to break.

BOOK XV

It has irked many people that this tale has been kept locked away 734 from them. Plenty have never been able to find out what happened. Now I shall hold back no longer, but I'll acquaint you with it by a true account, for I carry in my mouth the lock of this adventure:* how gentle and comely Anfortas was restored to full health. The adventure acquaints us with how the Queen of Pelrapeire retained her chaste, womanly disposition until she arrived at her reward's destination, where she stepped into high bliss. Parzival will bring this about, if my art does not fail me.

First, though, I shall tell of his toil. All that his hand has ever yet won in battle has been mere child's play. If I could reverse this story, I'd be unwilling to risk him, for it affords me no pleasure, I assure you. Now I commend his fate, his bliss's portion, to his heart, where boldness lay with chastity, for it never practised cowardice. Let that fortify him, so that he may now keep his hold on life, since it has fallen to his lot to be assailed by one who is a lord of all battle, on his 735 undaunted journey. That same courteous man was a heathen, who had never made baptism's acquaintance.

Parzival was riding rapidly towards a great forest, across a bright clearing, where he met with a wealthy stranger. It will be a marvel if I, poor man that I am, prove capable of telling you of the wealth the heathen wore by way of accoutrements. At the risk of saying too much on the subject, I may, however, tell you more, being unwilling to be altogether silent concerning his wealth. All that served Arthur's hand in Britain and in England would not pay for the stones, which, with their noble, pure nature, studded the warrior's surcoat. It was costly beyond all deception: rubies and chalcedony would fetch a poor price there. The surcoat gave off a dazzling sheen. In the mountain of Agremontin the salamander worms had woven it together in the hot fire.* The true precious stones lay upon it, dark and bright—I cannot name their nature.

736   His desire was directed towards love and fame's gain. Indeed, it was for the most part women with whose gifts the heathen had sumptuously accoutred his person. Love conducted high spirits into his manly heart, as it still does to the ardent lover today. In addition, he wore, for the sake of fame's reward, an ecidemon upon his helmet. All snakes possessed of venom, such is that beastie's power, have no time left to live if it is once scented by them. Thopedissimonte and Assigarzionte, Thasme and Araby are devoid of such phellel-silk as his charger wore as caparison. That comely infidel strove for women's reward; that was why he accoutred himself so splendidly. His high heart compelled him to strive for noble love.

    That same valiant stripling had laid anchor at sea in a wild harbour, at the edge of the woodland. He had twenty-five hosts with him, none of which understood the others' speech. As well became 737 his wealth, so many different lands served his noble hand—Moors and other Saracens, of dissimilar aspect. In his army, assembled from far afield, was many a wondrous armament.

    It was in search of adventure that this man had ridden off alone, away from his army, into the woodland to exercise his limbs. Since they themselves have claimed this right, I shall let these kings ride alone to fight for fame. Yet Parzival did not ride alone. Together with him there were his own self and his high spirits, too, which render such valorous defence there as women ought to praise, unless they were to take to raving out of sheer folly.

    Here two desire to imperil one another who were lambs of chastity and lions in boldness. Alas, the earth being so broad, that they did not avoid one another, those who fought for no good reason there! I would be anxious on account of the man I have brought here, were it not that I have thought of the solace that the Grail's power must protect him. Love, too, must defend him. Both these he served without deviation, with a servitor's strength.

My art does not grant me sufficient wit to tell in full detail the 738
course of this battle. Each man's eyes flashed as he saw the other
approach. If either's heart promised him joy at this, sadness stood
close by. Those pure knights, free of flaw, both bore the other's heart.
Theirs was an amply intimate estrangement!

Now I cannot part this heathen from the Christian, if they wish to
make show of enmity. That ought to bow down the joy of those
acknowledged as goodly women. Each of them, for his lady-love's
sake, offered his life to meet harsh battle. May Fortune decide the
outcome without death ensuing!

The lioness gives birth to a lion, dead; by his father's roar he is
brought to life.* These two were born of the clash, chosen for fame by
many a joust. And they were well versed in jousting, in the lavish
consumption of spears. At the gallop, they shortened the reins and
took aim each time they charged, intent on not missing the target.
They neglected no skill, but sat firmly there, shaping for the joust, 739
their chargers pricked by their spurs.

Here the joust was ridden in such fashion that both their gorgets*
were cut open by stout spears that did not bend. Splinters flew up
from the joust! The heathen took it very ill that this man retained his
seat against him, for never before had any antagonist of his done so
in battle. Did they carry swords as they closed in on one another?
Those were there, sharp and at the ready! Their skill and valour was
soon shown there. Against the beast ecidemon several wounds were
struck, giving the helmet beneath it good cause to complain. The
chargers grew hot from fatigue. They tried out many a new circle.
They both leapt down from their chargers. Now at last the swords
rang out!

The heathen hurt the Christian hard. His battle-cry was 'Thasme!'
and whenever he shouted 'Thabronit!' he took a step forwards. The
Christian defended himself valiantly as they made many a swift
run at one another. Their battle has taken such a turn that I cannot 740
keep my peace, but must bemoan their battle, by my loyalty, since
one flesh and one blood is wreaking such hardship upon itself.
They were both, after all, one man's sons, a fundament of purified
fidelity.

The heathen never wearied of love, which was why his heart was
great in battle. He was intent on fame because of Queen Secundille,
who had given him the land of Tribalibot—it was she who was his

shield in extremity. The heathen was gaining the upper hand in the battle. What am I to do with the Christian now? Unless *his* thoughts turn to love, he cannot prevent this battle procuring him death at the heathen's hand. Avert this, potent Grail—Condwiramurs, fair of feature—here the servitor of you both stands in the greatest peril he ever confronted!

The heathen threw his sword up high. Many a blow of his brought Parzival to his knees. It is easy for anyone to say: 'thus *they* fought', if he wants to call them two, but they were both but one person. My brother and I are but one, as is a good man and his good wife.

741   The heathen hurt the Christian hard. His shield was of a wood called asbestos, which neither rots nor burns. He was loved by her who gave it him, rest assured of that! Turquoise, chrysoprase, emerald, and ruby, many gems with their own peculiar sheen were set, for the sake of sumptuous fame, all about the boss's branches.* On the boss-point itself was a gem with whose name I will acquaint you: 'antrax'* it was called yonder; here it is known as 'carbuncle'. To be love's conducement the ecidemon, that pure beast, had been given to him as his device by her in whose favour he desired to live, Queen Secundille. That device was her wish.

There loyalty's purity did battle. Great loyalty fought with loyalty there. Out of love both had set their lives at stake, to do combat, awaiting the verdict; to this each had pledged his hand. The Christian has trusted confidently in God since he parted from Trevrizent, who had advised him so wholeheartedly to request help from Him who is capable of granting joy in sorrow.

742   The heathen was strong-limbed, no doubt about it! Whenever he shouted 'Thabronit!'—where Queen Secundille resided, by the Caucasus mountain—he won fresh high spirits to face that man who had ever been guarded against the burden of such battle's supremacy. He was a stranger to defeat, never having suffered it, although many a man had fetched it from him.

Skilfully they swung their arms. Fire's sparks leapt from helmets. A bitter wind blew from their swords. God protect Gahmuret's sons there! This wish is made for both of them, the Christian and the heathen. I called them one and the same before. They too would start to think the same if they were better acquainted with one another. They would not wager such high stakes! The price of their battle was no more than joy, fortune, and honour. Whoever wins the prize there, if he loves loyalty, has lost worldly joy, and opted for heart's grief forever.

Why are you slow, Parzival, to think of that chaste and fair one—I mean your wife—if you would keep your life here? The heathen had two companions, in which, indeed, lay the greatest part of his power. First, he practised love, which lay with constancy in his heart. Secondly, there were the gems which by their noble, pure nature taught him high spirits and increased his strength. It troubles me that the Christian is becoming so wearied by the battle and the running, and those mighty blows. If neither Condwiramurs nor the Grail can help him now—valiant Parzival, you must, nonetheless, cling to the one hope—that those radiant, sweet boys, Kardeiz and Loherangrin,* should not be orphaned so early. Both were carried, living, by his wife, when he last embraced her body. Children won with true chastity are, I believe, man's bliss.

The Christian was gaining in strength. He thought—it was none too early for that!—of his wife the queen, and her noble love, which he had won by merry swordplay, there where fire had sprung from helmets as blows were struck, before Pelrapeire, from Clamide. 'Thabronit!' and 'Thasme!'—to those a counter-cry was weighed here—Parzival, for his part, took to shouting 'Pelrapeire!' Condwiramurs, at that moment, across four kingdoms,* took him into her protection there, by love's powers. Then splinters sprang—so I believe—from the heathen's shield, one or two worth a hundred marks! The sturdy sword from Gaheviez broke by a blow upon the heathen's helmet, so that the bold, wealthy stranger, stumbling, sought his genuflection. God no longer deigned that what Parzival had taken from the corpse should fittingly be in his hand—the sword he had taken from Ither, as then well befitted his folly. He who had never before sunk at the sword's swing, the heathen, leapt quickly to his feet then. It is undecided as yet. It is for the Highest Hand to judge over them both. May He avert their deaths!

The heathen was magnanimous. He spoke courteously then—in French, which he knew—out of his pagan mouth: 'I see clearly, valiant man, that you would fight on without a sword. What fame might I win by you then? Stand still, and tell me, valiant warrior, who you are. Truly, you would have won my fame, which has long been granted me, if your sword had not shattered. Let there now be a truce between us both, until our limbs have rested somewhat.'

They sat down upon the grass. Valour, alongside courtesy, resided with them both, and both their years were of such a season that they were both neither too old nor too young for battle. The heathen said to the Christian: 'Believe me, now, warrior, I have never seen in my time any man who better deserved such fame as a man must pursue in battle. Now be so kind, warrior, as to tell me both your name and your lineage. Then my journey here will have been well wended.'

Herzeloyde's son replied: 'If I am to do so out of fear, then no-one need trouble to request it of me. Am I to grant it under compulsion?'

The heathen of Thasme said: 'I shall name myself first, and let the disgrace be mine. I am Feirefiz Angevin, so mighty, I may say, that many a land serves my hand with tribute.'

746   Hearing those words, Parzival said to the heathen: 'How comes it that you are an Angevin? Anjou is mine by inheritance—castles, land and cities. Sir, you must, at my request, choose another name. If I were to lose my land and the noble city of Bealzenan, you would be doing me great wrong. If either of us is an Angevin, then it is I who must be so by lineage. Still, I have been told in all truth that an undaunted warrior lives in heathendom, who has won by knightly strength such love and fame that he may lay rightful claim to both. He has been named as my brother. They have acknowledged his fame there.'

Parzival continued: 'Sir, your countenance's features—if I might familiarize myself with them, then you would soon be told how he has been described to me. Lord, if you'll trust me, then bare your head. If you'll believe me, my hand will refrain from all battle against you until your head is armed once again.'

747   The heathen replied: 'I've little fear of your fighting. Even if I stood entirely unarmed, as I have a sword you would in any case be granted defeat, since your sword is shattered. All your valiant skill cannot protect you from death, unless I decide of my own will to spare you. Before you were to start wrestling, I would have my sword ring out, piercing both your iron and your skin.' The strong, bold heathen showed manly courage: 'This sword shall belong to neither of us!' The brave, courageous warrior flung it far from him into the forest, saying: 'If battle is to take place here now, the odds must be even.'

Then mighty Feirefiz said: 'Warrior, as you practise courtesy, since you may have a brother, then tell me, what is he like? Acquaint me with his countenance—how his complexion has been described to you.'

Herzeloyde's son replied: 'Like a written-on leaf of parchment, black and white here and there—thus Ekuba described him to me.'

The heathen said: 'I am he!' Then both hesitated little, but each 748 quickly bared his head of helmet and coif, simultaneously. Parzival found an exalted find, and the dearest that he ever found. The heathen was soon recognized, for he bore the magpie's marks. Feirefiz and Parzival put an end to enmity by a kiss. Indeed, amity became them both better than heart's hatred towards one another. Loyalty and affection parted their battle.

Then the heathen joyfully exclaimed: 'A blessing upon me that I ever beheld noble Gahmuret's son! All my gods are honoured by this! My goddess Juno has good reason to rejoice at this honour! My mighty god Jupiter was my guarantor of this blessing. Gods and goddesses,* I shall love your power forever! Honoured be that planet's beam beneath which this journey of mine in search of adventure was undertaken, to meet with you, dreadly gentle man, whose hand has brought me to grief! Honoured be the air and dew that descended upon me this morning! Love's courteous key!* Blessed are the women 749 who are to behold you! What bliss will have befallen them!'

'You speak well. I would speak better, if I were capable, and with no hostility whatever. Now, unfortunately, I am not so wise that your noble fame may be enhanced by my words, yet God is fully aware of my intention. Whatever skills my heart and eyes possess, none will be spared by your fame, which will dictate, and they will obey. Never did greater extremity befall me at a knight's hand, I know that to be the truth, than at yours,' said he of Kanvoleiz.

Mighty Feirefiz replied: 'Jupiter has invested his industry in you, noble warrior. You must call me "thou" now—we both had, after all, one and the same father.' With brotherly loyalty he entreated that he should relinquish calling him 'you' and address him in 'thou'-fashion.*

These words grieved Parzival. He said: 'Brother, your wealth presumably equals that of the Baruch, and you are also older than I. My youth and my poverty ought to be on their guard against such arrogance as my offering to address you as "thou", if I am to cultivate courtesy.'

He of Tribalibot honoured his god Jupiter in words in many ways. 750

He also accorded most high praise to his goddess Juno for so arranging the weather that he and all his army, approaching the land from the sea, had found that firm ground where they had encountered one another.

For a second time they sat down, neither forgetting to offer the other honour. Then the heathen spoke on: 'I will cede to you two rich lands, forever subservient to your hand, which my father and yours won when King Isenhart died: Zazamanc and Azagouc. His valour betrayed no-one there, but he left me orphaned. The wrong done to my father there is as yet unavenged by me. His wife, of whom I was born, met with death for love of him, when she lost love by him. I would gladly see that same man! I have been informed that there was never a better knight. This costly journey of mine is made in search of him.'

751   Parzival replied to him: 'I never beheld him either. They tell me of his goodly deeds—in many a place I hear of those—that he knew well how to broaden his fame in battles and raise his honour high. All misconduct fled him. He was women's servitor. If they could possess loyalty, they rewarded him for it without false deceit. He practised that which by baptism is still honoured, loyalty without deviation. He knew well, too, how to hold all treacherous deeds in low esteem; heart's constancy gave him that counsel. They deigned to tell me this who were acquainted with him in person—he whom you would so gladly see. I believe you would have accorded him fame if he were still alive, for he strove for fame himself. His service compelled that Reward of Women* to meet King Ipomidon in the joust. That joust befell before Baldac. There his noble life, in love's cause, was consigned to the bier. We lost him in formal joust, he of whom we are both born.'

752   'Alas for this unavenged calamity!' said the heathen. 'Is my father dead? I may indeed speak of joy's loss, and espy joy's find, in all truth! At this moment I have both lost joy and found joy! If I would reach out for the truth, then both my father, and you also, and I—we were all one entirely, although it was made manifest in three parts.* Wherever a wise man is beheld, he does not count any kinship as separating the father and his children, if he seeks the truth. It is with your own self that you have fought here. It was to do battle against myself that I came riding here. My own self I would gladly have slain, but you were incapable then of being daunted and defended

my own self against me. Jupiter, write down this wonder! Your power made us acquainted with help, intervening to prevent our dying.'*

He laughed and wept, secretly. His heathen eyes started to shed water, all in accordance with baptism's honours. Baptism's intent is to teach loyalty, since our covenant, the new order, was named after Christ. By Christ loyalty is made manifest.

The heathen spoke on, as I shall tell you: 'We must sit here no longer. Ride with me, not too far off, to encamp upon the *terre*. For you to behold, I'll summon from the sea the mightiest army to which Juno ever gave sail's air. In truth, without deception's boast, I shall show you many a noble man who serves me as subject. You must ride there with me.' 753

Parzival said to him: 'Have you such power over your people that they await you today, and all the time you are away from them?'

The heathen said: 'Indisputably. Even if I were away from them for six months, rich and poor alike would await me—they would not dare go anywhere else. Their ships in the harbour are well provided with provender, as is fitting; neither horse nor man need disembark, unless it were to find a spring for fresh water, or onto the plain for the sake of fresh air.'

Parzival said to his brother: 'For your part, you shall see ladies' sheen and great delight, and many a courteous knight of your noble kin. Arthur the Briton lies encamped close by here with a noble host, from which I parted today, a numerous and charming company. We shall see well-favoured ladies there.' 754

When the heathen heard women mentioned—they were as dear to him as life itself!—he said: 'Lead me there with you! Moreover, you must tell me tidings I would ask of you. Shall we see our kinsmen when we come to Arthur? I have heard of his high bearing—that he is rich in fame and also acts nobly.'

Parzival replied: 'We shall see ladies of fair appearance there. Our journey will not miss its mark—we shall find our true lineage, people of whose blood we are born, several heads chosen to wear crowns.'

Then neither remained seated any longer. Parzival did not forget to fetch his brother's sword, thrusting it back into the noble warrior's sheath. Wrathful enmity was shunned by both of them then, and companionably they rode off.

Before they had reached Arthur, tidings about them had been heard there. That same day there was general lament throughout the 755 host that noble Parzival had parted from them in such fashion. Arthur had determined in counsel that he would await Parzival there for a week, not riding away from that place. Gramoflanz's host had also arrived; for them many a broad ring had been marked out, with lavishly embellished tents. Lodging had been provided there for those proud, noble people. The four brides could not have been more delightfully treated.

A man came riding from Schastel Marveile at that time, who related that in the pillar, up on the watch-tower, such a battle had been seen that whatever sword-play had taken place hitherto—'It is as nothing compared with that battle!' He tells these tidings in Gawan's presence, where he sat at Arthur's side.

Many a knight spoke up then, guessing by whom that battle had been fought there. Arthur the King said at once: 'I am sure I know who one of the combatants was! The battle was fought by my kinsman of Kanvoleiz, who parted from us this morning.'

756 Just then that pair came riding up. As well befitted battle's honour, their helmets and shields had been much charged at by swords. They both bore well-skilled hands, those who had mapped out those battle-marks. In battle, too, art is needed. They rode past Arthur's tent-ring. Many glances were cast in their direction as the heathen rode by—he bore such wealth about him!

The field was well lodged with tents. They headed past the high pavilion to Gawan's ring. Was it brought to their attention that people were glad to see them? I believe that did indeed happen there! Gawan came in hot pursuit, for he had seen, sitting in Arthur's presence, that they were riding towards his pavilion. He welcomed them there in joyous fashion. They were still wearing their armour. Courtly Gawan commanded that they be quickly disarmed. The beast ecidemon had had its share of the battle. The heathen wore a surcoat which had also been hurt by blows. It was a saranthasme, studded with many a precious stone. Beneath it shone a tabard,

757 rough of texture, figured, snowy-white, on both sides of which precious stones faced one another. The salamander worms had wrought it in the fire. She abandoned to adventure her love, her land and her person—a woman gave him these accoutrements—he, for his part, gladly carried out her command, both in joy and in sorrow—that of Queen Secundille. It was her heart's desire to grant him her wealth. His high fame fought for and won her love.

Gawan urged that care be taken that these handsome accoutrements should not be at all mislaid, nor anything broken off—the surcoat, helmet, or shield. A poor woman would have been overwhelmed by the cost of the tabard alone, so precious were the stones on all four items. Lofty love can adorn splendidly where wealth combines with good will, and noble skill besides. Proud, wealthy Feirefiz served with great zeal to earn women's favour—in return one in particular did not neglect to reward him.

Their armour had been removed. Then all those who knew how to speak of marvels gazed at that colourful man. They could see in all truth there that Feirefiz bore strange markings! Gawan said to Parzival: 'Kinsman, acquaint me with your companion. He has such a dazzling sheen that I never saw the like!' 758

Parzival said to his host: 'If I am your kinsman, then so is he. Let Gahmuret be your guarantor of that! This is the King of Zazamanc. It was there that my father won with fame Belacane, who gave birth to this knight.' Then Gawan kissed the heathen often enough. Rich Feirefiz was both black and white all over his skin, except that his mouth evinced redness, in half measure.

Velvet apparel was brought for both of them. It was recognizably of great cost, brought there from Gawan's wardrobe. Then ladies bright of hue arrived. The duchess had Cundrie and Sangive kiss him first; then she herself and Arnive kissed him. Feirefiz was happy to see such lustrous ladies. I believe he found pleasure in it.

Gawan said to Parzival: 'Kinsman, your helmet, and your shield, too, tell of new hardship on your part. You have both been playthings of battle, you and your brother. From whom did you fetch this torment?' 759

'Never was a fiercer battle known,' said Parzival. 'My brother's hand exacted defence from me in great duress. Defence is a charm against death. My stout sword shattered by the blow it struck on this intimate stranger. Then he made little show of fear. He threw his own sword far from his hand! He feared to sin against me, even before we worked out that we were kin. Now I possess his favour proudly, and shall gladly serve to earn it.'

Gawan said: 'I was told of an undaunted battle. Up in Schastel Marveil they see all that happens within a compass of six miles, in the pillar up on my watchtower. Then my uncle Arthur said that he who was fighting on that occasion there was you, kinsman of

Kingrivals. You have brought the true tidings with you, though we already suspected it was you in that battle. Now believe me when I
760 tell you: we would have waited a week for you here, amid a great, lavish festivity. The battle you two have fought troubles me. Now you must rest after it, as my guests. Now that you have fought one another, you know one another all the better. Now choose friendship in preference to enmity.'

Gawan ate all the earlier that evening because his kinsman from Thasme, Feirefiz Angevin, had fasted as yet, as had his brother. Mattresses thick and long were spread out in a broad circle. Quilts of many a kind, of palmat-silk, none too thin, then became the mattresses' covering. Costly furs were seen piled upon them, both long and broad. Clinschor's wealth was brought forth for display there. Then they hung up—so I heard tell—four tapestries of lavish design at the back, facing one another on four sides; beneath them soft beds of down, covered with quilts, with back-cloths placed at their rear.

The ring took up such a wide compass that six pavilions might have stood there without any jostling of their ropes—I would be
761 acting indiscreetly if I were to let the adventure continue in this fashion. Then my lord Gawan sent tidings to Arthur's court of who had arrived there: that wealthy heathen was there whom the heathen Queen Ekuba had praised so highly by the Plimizœl. Jofreit *fiz* Ydœl told the tidings to Arthur, winning much joy by it. Jofreiz entreated him to eat early, and then to play his part, in all splendour, with a company of knights and ladies, and go over there, in courtly fashion, and see to it that they gave a noble welcome to proud Gahmuret's son.

'I shall bring all such noble people as are present,' said the Briton.

Jofreit said: 'He's so courteous that you will all be glad to see him, for you shall see marvels about his person. He is backed by great wealth. No-one could ever pay the price of his battle garments—no man's wealth could match it. Löver, Britain, England—from Paris as far as Wissant—even if a man placed all those *terres* in the balance, they would be far from meeting the cost.'

762 Jofreit had returned. From him Arthur had heard how he was to act if he desired to welcome his kinsman, the heathen. The seating was arranged in courtly fashion at Gawan's ring. The household of the duchess and the companions sat down amongst themselves at

Gawan's right. On the other side dined, with delight, the knights, Clinschor's company. The ladies' seating was so arranged that Clinschor's ladies sat facing Gawan at one end there—many of them were fair of feature. Feirefiz and Parzival sat in the middle between the ladies. Beauty might be beheld there!

Florant the Turkoyt, and Sangive of noble renown, and the Duke of Gowerzin, and Cundrie, his wife, sat opposite one another. Nor, I believe, did Gawan and Jofreit forget their old companionship, but dined together. The duchess with her dazzling glances ate together 763 with Queen Arnive, neither of them neglecting to be most ready to offer one another companionship. By Gawan sat his grandmother, with Orgeluse on the other side. From that circle true discourtesy was seen to take rapid flight. In proper form and with due decorum the food was brought in for all the knights and ladies.

Wealthy Feirefiz said to Parzival his brother: 'Jupiter has devised this journey to my good fortune, his help having brought me here where I see my noble kinsmen. It is only fitting that I should acknowledge the fame of my father, whom I have lost; he was born of true fame.'

The Waleis said: 'You have yet to see people whose fame you must acknowledge, in the company of Arthur, their captain—many a knight of valour. As soon as this meal is over it won't be long before you see those noble people arrive, of whom much fame is heard. Of the numbers of the Table Round there are only three knights sitting here: the host and Jofreit; there was a time when I also fought and 764 won such fame that I was requested to sit at it, which request I then granted them.'

They took away the tablecloths which had lain before all the ladies and the men. It was time to do so, now that they had eaten. Gawan the host no longer remained seated. He began to entreat and urge the duchess, and his grandmother, too, to take first Sangive and gentle Cundrie, and go over to where the heathen of colourful complexion sat and entertain him. Feirefiz Angevin saw these ladies walking towards him. At once he rose to his feet to welcome them, as did his brother Parzival. The duchess of radiant hue took Feirefiz by the hand. All the ladies and knights she found standing there, she entreated to be seated.

Then, amid clamour, Arthur rode up with his host; trumpets, tabors, fluting, and piping were heard there. Arnive's son rode over

with a racket! This merry business was pronounced by the heathen
765 to be a noble affair! Thus Arthur rode up to Gawan's tent-ring, with
his wife and many a lustrous personage, with knights and ladies.
The heathen could observe that there were also people there who
were of such young years that they kept radiant complexions. King
Gramoflanz was still being entertained by Arthur at that time; along
that same path there also rode Itonje, his *âmîe*, that gentle maiden
free of falsity.

Then the company of the Table Round dismounted, together with
many a well-favoured lady. Guinevere had Itonje kiss her kinsman
the heathen first.* Then she herself approached, welcoming Feirefiz
with a kiss. Arthur and Gramoflanz, replete with loyal affection,
welcomed the heathen. They both offered him honour and homage,
and others of his kin showed him their goodwill. Feirefiz Angevin
had arrived among good friends there, as he quickly heard by their
talk.

766 Women and men, and many a comely maiden took their seats. If
he took the trouble, some knight or other might find there sweet
words issuing from a sweet mouth, if he knew how to pursue love.
Such a request was permitted entirely without any offence being
taken by many a lustrous lady seated there. Good women have never
been seen to wax wrath, if a worthy man applied for their help; they
hold denial and consent in reserve. If joy is said to yield any profit,
then true love can pay such interest. Thus I have always seen noble
people live. There service sat next to reward. It is a helpful melody
when a lady-love's discourse is heard which can come to a lover's aid.

Arthur sat down by Feirefiz. Neither of them neglected to do his
questioning justice, in gentle and straightforward converse. Arthur
said: 'Now I praise God that He has offered us this honour of seeing
you here. No man ever travelled from heathendom through baptism-
practising lands to whom I would more willingly do homage by my
service, in whatever way your will might desire.'

767 Feirefiz said to Arthur: 'All my ill-fortune foundered when the
goddess Juno steered my sail-wind to these Western realms. You act
most like a man whose honour is proclaimed by stories far and wide.
If you're called Arthur, then your name is renowned afar.'

Arthur said: 'That man did himself honour who praised me to you
and before other people. His own courtesy gave him that counsel,
more than my deserts. He did it out of courteousness. I am indeed

named Arthur, and would gladly know how you came to this land. If a lady-love sent you forth, she must be most comely, if it was in search of adventure that you have travelled so far. If she is unfailing of reward, that will exalt women's service still further. Let every woman incur enmity from her service-offerer, if you go unrewarded!'

'A very different tale is to be told,' said the heathen. 'Hear now of my journey. I bring with me such a mighty army that Troy's defence, 768 and those who besieged her, would have to make way for me if both sides were still alive and strove to do battle against me—they would not be able to win the victory, but would have to suffer defeat at the hands of me and my men. In many perils I have achieved such success by knightly deeds that Queen Secundille now looks on me with favour. Whatever she desires is my wish. She has mapped out my life for me. She commanded me to give generously and gather good knights about me—that would become me for her sake. This has come to pass. Many a noble, renowned knight, hung with shield, is counted among my household. In return, her love is my reward. I wear an ecidemon on my shield, as she commanded me. Whenever I have since met with peril, immediately I thought of her—her love brought help. She has been a better guarantor of hope to me than my god Jupiter!'

Arthur said: 'You have inherited this in entirety from your father 769 Gahmuret, my kinsman—your distant journeying in women's service. I shall tell you of such service that seldom has greater ever been rendered on this earth to any woman than to her lovely person—I mean the duchess sitting here. For her love much woodland has been laid waste. Her love has cost many a goodly knight his happiness and deprived him of high spirits.'

He told Feirefiz all about her feud, and of Clinschor's company, who were sitting there on all sides, and of the two battles which Parzival, his brother, had fought at Joflanze on the broad meadow, 'and all the other things he has experienced, not knowing how to spare his person, he must acquaint you with himself. He is in search of a high find; his quest is for the Grail. It is my request that both of you tell me the people and lands which are known to you from your battles.'

The heathen said: 'I shall name those who have brought their knights with them here in my cause:

770
    King Papiris of Trogodjente,
    and Count Behantins of Kalomidente,
    Duke Farjelastis of Affricke,
    and King Liddamus of Agrippe,
    King Tridanz of Tinodonte,
    and King Amaspartins of Schipelpjonte,
    Duke Lippidins of Agremuntin,
    and King Milon of Nomadjentesin,
    of Assigarzionte Count Gabarins,
    and of Rivigitas King Translapins,
    of Hiberborticon Count Filones,
    and of Centriun King Killicrates,
    Count Lysander of Ipopotiticon,
    and Duke Tiride of Elixodjon,
    of Oraste Gentesin King Thoaris,
    and of Satarchjonte Duke Alamis,
    King Amincas of Sotofeititon,
    and the Duke of Duscontemedon,
    of Araby King Zaroaster,
    and Count Possizonjus of Thiler,
    Duke Sennes of Narjoclin,
    and Count Edisson of Lanzesardin,
    of Janfuse Count Fristines,
    and of Atropfagente Duke Meiones,
    of Nourjente Duke Archeinor,
    and of Panfatis Count Astor,
    the men of Azagouc and Zazamanc,
    and of Gampfassasche King Jetakranc,
    Count Jurans of Blemunzin,
    and Duke Affinamus of Amantasin.*

771 One thing I thought a disgrace: they said in my land that there could be no better knight who ever bestrode a charger than Gahmuret Angevin. It was my desire and also my custom to travel until I might find him. Subsequently I gained battle's acquaintance. From my two lands I brought an army across the sea—a mighty one. My intent was set on chivalry. All lands that were valiant and worthy I forced to surrender to my hand, ranging far into foreign lands. There two powerful queens granted me their love, Olimpia and Clauditte.

Secundille is now the third. I have done much for women's sake.
Today I have at last learned that my father Gahmuret is dead. Let
my brother, too, tell of his perils.'

Then noble Parzival said: 'Since I departed from the Grail, my
hand has displayed much chivalry, fighting in close quarters and in
the open, lowering the fame of a few who had been unused to it ever
before. I shall name them to you now:

> Of Lirivoyn King Schirniel, 772
> and of Avendroyn his brother Mirabel,
> King Serabil of Rozokarz,
> and King Piblesun of Lorneparz,
> of Sirnegunz King Senilgorz,
> and of Villegarunz Strangedorz,
> of Mirnetalle Count Rogedal,
> and of Pleyedunze Laudunal,
> King Onipriz of Itolac,
> and King Zyrolan of Semblidac,
> of Jeroplis Duke Jerneganz,
> and of Zambron Count Plineschanz,
> of Tuteleunz Count Longefiez,
> and of Privegarz Duke Marangliez,
> of Pictacon Duke Strennolas,
> and of Lampregun Count Parfoyas,
> of Ascalun King Vergulaht,
> and of Pranzile Count Bogudaht,
> Postefar of Laudundrehte,
> and Duke Leidebron of Redunzehte,
> of Leterbe Colleval,
> and Jovedast of Arles, a Provençal,
> of Tripparun Count Karfodyas.*

This happened where tournaments were held, while I was riding in
search of the Grail. If I were to name all those I have done battle
against, those would be unknown numbers.* I needs must keep silent
about much of my fighting. All those that are known to me, I believe
I have named.'

The heathen was heartily glad that his brother's fame was such 773
that his hand had won so many a high honour in battle. He thanked
him fervently for it; he himself had honour by it.

Meanwhile Gawan ordered—as though it were done without his knowledge—that the heathen's accoutrements be brought into the ring. They thought highly of them there. Knights and ladies all took a look at the tabard, the shield, the surcoat. The helmet was neither too close-fitting nor too loose. All as one they praised the costly precious stones which were worked into it. No-one need ask me about their nature, what kind they were, the light and the heavy stones. You would have been given a better account by Eraclius, or Hercules, or Alexander the Greek*—or another still, wise Pythagoras, who was an astronomer and so wise, beyond dispute, that no-one since Adam's time could equal him in intellect. He knew well how to tell of stones.

774 The ladies whispered among themselves, saying that whatever woman had adorned his person with these accoutrements, if he deviated from her, his fame would be injured. Nevertheless, several were so well inclined towards him that they would gladly have endured his service—because of his strange markings, I imagine. Gramoflanz, Arthur and Parzival, and the host Gawan—those four walked off to one side. The wealthy heathen was committed to the ladies' care.

Arthur was organizing a festivity, to take place on the meadow the following morning, without fail, to give a welcome there to his kinsman Feirefiz: 'Apply your diligence to these arrangements, and your best ideas, so that he may sit with us at the Table Round.' They all vowed individually to bring it about, if Feirefiz had no objection.

Then wealthy Feirefiz vowed companionship to them. All the people went in unison, when the parting-cup had been poured, to their rest. That following morning joy befell many, if I may be permitted to say so, when the sweet, famed day appeared.

775 Uther Pendragon's son Arthur was seen to act as follows: he had prepared a lavish and sumptuous Table Round, constructed from a drianthasme.* You have, I imagine, heard before how on Plimizœl's plain a Table Round had been fashioned. This new one was carved on the same model, circular, of such a kind that it displayed lavish expense. Around it a circle was formed on a dewy, green meadow, so that there was a good horse-charge's length from the seats to the Table Round. That stood, isolated, in the middle there, not for use's sake, but just for the name. An ignoble man would have good reason to be ashamed if he sat among the noble company there—it would be a sin if his mouth were to eat such food!

The circle was measured out that fine night and well arranged in advance to meet wealth's mark. A poor king might have been overwhelmed by the way in which the circle was found to be adorned, when mid-morning was espied. Gramoflanz and Gawan—by those this expense was borne. Arthur was a stranger in that land, but his wealth was not found wanting there.

Seldom has night come without it being the sun's nature ever to 776 bring the day thereafter—all that happened there, too. Day shone upon them, sweet, clear, lustrous. Then many a knight combed his hair well, placing upon it a flowery garland. Many an unfalsified lady's complexion was seen there, next to red mouths. If Kyot told the truth, knights and ladies wore apparel not tailored in one single country—women's headdresses, low, high, as called for by their land's fashion. That company had been assembled from afar, which was why their customs differed. Any lady lacking an *âmîs* dared on no account approach the Table Round. If she had accepted service for her reward and given reward's surety, she rode up to the Table Round's ring. The others could take no part—they sat in their lodgings.

When Arthur had heard mass, Gramoflanz was seen to arrive, and the Duke of Gowerzin, and Florant his companion. Those three requested, one by one, membership of the Table Round. Arthur 777 granted it them at once. If a woman or man asks you who had the wealthiest hand of all who ever, from any land, sat at the Table Round, you could not give them a better answer than this: it was Feirefiz Angevin! Let that be the last word.

They proceeded towards the ring in noble fashion. One or two ladies were jostled. If their horses had not been well girthed they would soon have fallen off. Many a costly banner was seen to approach on all sides. Then the bohort was ridden in a broad circle around the Table Round. It was a matter of courtly propriety that none of them rode into the ring. The field outside it was so broad that they could spur their chargers on and intermingle in the charges, and they rode, indeed, with such artistry that the women were delighted to observe it.

They came in time to where the ladies sat, where those noble personages were dining. Chamberlains, stewards, cupbearers had the task of devising how the food be brought before them with decorum. I believe they were all given sufficient there. Each lady sitting there 778

by her *âmîs* was of repute; many a one of them had been served by
high deeds, prompted by an ardent heart's counsel. Feirefiz and
Parzival had a sweet dilemma as to whether to feast their eyes upon
this lady or that. Never in ploughed field nor in meadow were seen
brighter complexions nor rosier mouths in such profusion as were
found at that ring. Joy made the heathen's acquaintance at the sight!

Hail to the adventitious day! Honoured be the sweet tidings' tale
that was heard from her mouth! A damsel was seen to approach, her
garments costly and well tailored, expensive in the French fashion,
her cape a rich samite, blacker even than a civet-cat. Arab gold shone
from its surface, many a turtle-dovelet, well woven after the device of
the Grail. She was much stared at on that occasion by those avid for
marvels. Now let her hasten over here! Her headdress was high and
white; her countenance was hidden by many a thick veil, not exposed
779 to view. In leisurely fashion, and yet at brisk amble-gait,* she came
riding across the field. Her bridle, her saddle, her palfrey were rich
and costly beyond all dispute. They permitted her to ride directly
into the ring. That wise woman, no fool, rode all round the ring.
They showed her where Arthur was seated. She did not neglect to
greet him. It was *en franzoys* that she spoke. She besought them to
forfeit vengeance upon her and listen to her tidings. She entreated
the King and the Queen for help, and to assist her cause.

Immediately she turned from them to where she found Parzival
sitting, close by Arthur. Hastily she leapt down from the horse onto
the grass. She fell with the courtesy she possessed at Parzival's feet,
beseeching him, all in tears, for his greeting, and that he might
abandon anger towards her and pardon her, without a kiss. Arthur
and Feirefiz applied their diligence to her suit. Parzival bore resent-
780 ment towards her—at his friends' entreaty he relented, sincerely,
without malice. That noble, though not lustrous lady rapidly leapt to
her feet again. She bowed to them and spoke her thanks to those who
had helped her to favour, after the great wrong she had committed.

With her hand she unwound her headdress, both hood and ties,
slinging them from her down into the ring. Cundrie la Surziere was
quickly recognized then, and the Grail's device that she bore was
then amply gazed upon. She was still physically the same person
whom so many a man and woman had seen approach the Plimizœl.
You have heard about her countenance: her eyes were still the
same, yellow as a topaz, her teeth long. Her mouth shone like a

woad-coloured violet. Were it not that she was concerned about her repute, she would have had no need to wear that costly hat she had worn on Plimizœl's plain. The sun had not harmed her at all. It could not penetrate her hair, nor sully her skin, for all its rays' malice.

Courteously she stood there and spoke what they avowed to be exalted tidings. Thus she then commenced her speech: 'Praise be to 781 you, Gahmuret's son! God desires to grant you grace now! I mean him whom Herzeloyde bore. Feirefiz of the dappled hue must be welcome to me for the sake of Secundille, my lady, and because of many a high honour his fame has won by fighting since his boyhood!'

To Parzival she then said: 'Now be at once chaste and joyful! Hail to you for the high lot that has befallen you, you crown of mankind's salvation! The epitaph has been read: you are to be the Grail's lord. Condwiramurs, your wife, and your son, Loherangrin, have both been summoned there with you. When you left the land of Brobarz, she was carrying two sons, living. Kardeiz, for his part, has ample possessions there. If no more good fortune were to make your acquaintance than that your truthful mouth shall now greet in speech that noble and gentle man—now your mouth's question will cure King Anfortas, fending away from him great sigh-laden grief. Where was there ever your equal in bliss?'

Seven stars she then named in the heathen tongue. Those names 782 were recognized by wealthy, noble Feirefiz, who sat before her, black and white. She said: 'Now take note, Parzival: the highest planet Zval, and swift Almustri, Almaret, and bright-shining Samsi, manifest good fortune for you. The fifth is called Alligafir, and the sixth Alkiter, and the nearest to us Alkamer.* I do not speak this out of any dream. These are the firmament's bridle, which rein in its race. Their dispute has ever contested its course. Sorrow is an orphan now for your part. All that the planets' journey encompasses and that their radiance covers are goals staked out for you to attain and win. Your grief must perish—except for insatiety alone*—the Grail and the Grail's power forbid you fellowship with such false company. In your youth you reared sorrow. Coming joy has deceived you of that. You have fought and won the soul's rest, and awaited in anxiety the body's joy.'

Parzival was not displeased at her tidings. For joy water flowed 783 from his eyes, the heart's outpouring. Then he said: 'Lady, such matters as you have named here—if I am so acknowledged before God that my sinful body—and if I have children, and my wife, too, that they are to share in this—then God has acted well towards me. Any amends that you may make me show your loyalty at work. Yet if I had not done wrong, you would once have spared me anger. It was simply not yet time for my salvation. Now you grant me so high a portion that my sadness is at an end. It is your clothing tells me the truth. When I was at Munsalvæsche with sorrowful Anfortas, all the shields I found hanging there had the same device as your apparel. You wear many turtle-doves here. Lady, now tell me when or how I am to travel towards my joys, and let me not delay it long.'

She replied: 'My dear lord, one man is to be your companion. Choose him. Look to me for escort. Do not delay long to bring help.'

784   All around the ring it was heard: 'Cundrie la Surziere has arrived!'—and what her tidings purported. Orgeluse wept for joy that Parzival's question was to avert Anfortas's torment. Arthur, bold of fame, said to Cundrie, courteously: 'Lady, ride to your rest. Have yourself tended to, as you yourself instruct.'

She said: 'If Arnive is here, whatever comfort she accords me I will live with until such time as my lord departs from here. If she has been freed from imprisonment, then permit me to see her, and those other ladies to whom Clinschor dealt out his malice, holding them captive this many a year now.' Two knights lifted her onto her horse. The noble maiden rode to Arnive.

By now it was time for them to have finished eating there. Parzival was sitting by his brother. He asked him to bear him company. Feirefiz was fully willing to ride to Munsalvæsche with him. Then, all at once,
785 they stood up, all around the ring. Feirefiz had high aims in mind. He asked King Gramoflanz, if the affection between him and his kins-woman* were entire, that he should make it manifest by him: 'Help, Gramoflanz, and my kinsman Gawan—all those kings and princes we have here, all the barons and poor knights—see to it that none of them depart from here before they behold my treasures. Disgrace would befall me here if I were to depart without dispensing gifts. All the travelling people* here look to me for gifts. Arthur, now I will entreat you—do not let the nobles disdain this. Hurry to them on this errand and be the pledge against them incurring any disgrace by it—never did they know such a lavish hand! And give me messengers, to send to my harbour, where the presents are to be brought from my boats.'

Then they vowed to the heathen that they would not depart from the field for four days. The heathen was delighted—so I heard tell. Arthur gave him discerning messengers, for him to send to the harbour. Feirefiz, Gahmuret's son, took ink and parchment in hand. His script was not short on marks of identification—I believe no letter ever accomplished so much.

The messengers departed with zeal. Parzival commenced his 786 speech thus: *en franzoys* he told them all, as Trevrizent had pronounced previously, that no-one might ever win the Grail by battle, except he who is summoned there by God. Those tidings spread over all lands—that no battle could procure it. Many people then abandoned their plans to procure the Grail, which is why it is still hidden.

Parzival and Feirefiz taught the women grief's practice. They would have been reluctant to omit it—into all four parts of the army they rode, taking leave of all the company. Each departed joyfully, well armed to resist combat. On the third day, such great gifts were brought to Joflanze from the heathen's army as had never before been imagined. If any king met with his gifts there, that helped his land for evermore. Never was such costly show of gifts manifested to each man, according to his degree—to all the ladies lavish presents from Triande and from Noriente. I don't know how the company divided here. Cundrie, and those two men, rode off.

BOOK XVI

ANFORTAS and his people were still suffering sorrow's throes. It was 787 their loyalty that left him in this extremity. Often he sought death from them; it would, indeed, soon have befallen him, except that they often had him see the Grail and the Grail's power.

He said to his company of knights: 'I know for sure that if you practised loyalty you would take pity on my grief. How long is this to last for me? If you desire justice for yourselves, then you will have to atone before God for your treatment of me. I was always willing to serve you, ever since I first bore arms. I have paid dearly enough for it if infamy ever befell me,* and if any of you saw it. If you are free of disloyalty, then release me for the sake of the helmet's lineage and

the shield's order. You have often perceived, if you did not disdain
to do so, that I applied both these, undauntedly, to knightly deeds. I
have traversed dale and hill with many a joust, and made such play
with the sword that my enemies wearied of me, little benefit though
788 it has brought me from you. Exile from joy that I am, at the Judge-
mental End I alone shall accuse you all. Then your fall will draw
nigh, unless you let me part from you. My anguish ought to grieve
you. You have both seen and heard how this misfortune came upon
me. What use am I to you as your lord now? It will be all too early an
hour for you, alas, if you are to lose your souls by me! What way is
this you have chosen to treat me?'

They would have released him from his anguish, were it not for
the consolatory solace which Trevrizent had previously pronounced,*
having seen it written on the Grail. They were awaiting for a second
time the man whose joy had all fled from him there, and the helpful
hour when his mouth should voice the question.

The king often took to blinking constantly, sometimes for four
days at a time. Then he was carried to the Grail, whether he liked it
or not, and the illness forced him to lift up his eyes. Then, against his
789 will, he had to live, and not perish. Thus they treated him until that
day when Parzival and Feirefiz of the dappled hue rode joyously up
to Munsalvæsche. Now time had waited for Mars or Jupiter to
return in their course, full of ire—then Anfortas was bought and
sold*—to where they had leapt forth from before. That brought pain
to his wound, Anfortas being in such torment that maidens and
knights heard the frequent sound of his screaming and met with
wretched glances from his eyes. He was wounded past help—they
could not help him. The adventure tells, however, that true help is
coming to him now. They held heart's grief in their grip.

Whenever the sharp, bitter anguish imposed upon him that acute
distress, the air was sweetened and the wound's stench alleviated.
Before him on the carpet lay piment* and terebinth's* scent, musk,
and aromatics. To sweeten the air theriac and costly amber also lay
790 there; the scent was comely. Wherever people trod upon the carpet,
cardamom, cloves, and nutmeg lay crushed beneath their feet, to
sweeten the air. Whenever footsteps ground the spices, the sour
stench was repelled. His fire was *lignum aloe*, as I told you before.

The posts of his camp-bed were of viper-horn. To bring him ease
against the poison the powder of many spices was strewn upon his

pillows. Piled, not sewn, was what he leaned upon there—phellel-silk of Noriente, and his mattress was of palmat-silk. His camp-bed was adorned still further by gems, none of them anything other than precious. The camp-bed was pulled together by strands of salamander—such were the tie-ropes beneath him. He had small share in pleasure. His bedding was sumptuous on all sides. No-one need contend that he ever saw better. It was costly and ornate, by virtue of the precious stones' nature. Hear now their true names:

> Carbuncle and moonstone, 791
> balas and gagathromeus,
> onyx and chalcedony,
> coral and bestion,
> union and ophthalmite,
> ceraunite and epistites,
> hierachite and heliotrope,
> pantherus and androdragma,
> prasine and sagda,
> hæmatite and dionise,
> agate and celidony,
> sardonyx and chalcophonite,
> cornelian and jasper,
> aetites and iris,
> gagate and ligurite,
> asbestos and cegolite,
> galactite and hyacinth,
> orites and enhydrite,
> absist and alabandine,
> chrysolectrus and hyæna,
> emerald and loadstone,
> sapphire and pyrites.
> Here and there stood also
> turquoise and liparite,
> chrysolite, ruby,
> paleise and sardine,
> diamond and chrysoprase,
> malachite and diadochite,
> peanites and medusite,
> beryl and topaz.*

792 Several of these taught high spirits. There was many a stone there whose peculiar nature was conducive towards bliss and healing. Great power could be found in them, if a skilled man applied them. With these they had to preserve Anfortas, who held all their hearts. To his people he gave grief enough. Yet now we are to hear of joy for him. Into Terre de Salvæsche, having travelled from Joflanze, has come he whose sorrow had deserted him, Parzival, with his brother and a maiden. I have not been told in truth how great the distance was between the places.* They would now have met with battle's tidings, were it not that Cundrie, their escort, parted them from hardship.

They were riding towards a lookout-post when there came hastening at great speed towards them many a well-mounted templar, armed. They were so courteous as to discern by the escort that joy was to draw near them. That troop's captain, on seeing many turtledoves glittering on Cundrie's apparel, said: 'Our sorrow is at an end. With the Grail's seal here, there comes to us what we have desired,

793 ever since sorrow's snare enlocked us. Halt! Great joy draws near us!'

Feirefiz Angevin was urging on Parzival, his brother, at that very moment, and hastening towards battle. Cundrie caught hold of his bridle to prevent any joust of his taking place there. Then the harsh-featured maiden said, quickly turning to her lord, Parzival: 'Those shields and banners you will soon be able to recognize! Those halting there are none other than the Grail's company. They are all bent on giving you great service.'

Then the noble heathen said: 'In that case, let the battle be abandoned!'

Parzival asked Cundrie to ride along the track towards them. She rode over and told them tidings of what joys had come to them. All the templars there alighted onto the grass. Immediately many a helmet was unbuckled. They welcomed Parzival on foot—his greeting seemed to them a blessing. They also welcomed the black-and-white Feirefiz. Up to Munsalvæsche they rode, all in tears, yet with joyous demeanour.

794 They found innumerable people, many a charming elderly knight, noble pages, many men-at-arms. That sad menage had good reason to rejoice at their arrival. Feirefiz Angevin and Parzival, both of them, were given a splendid welcome before the great hall, at the steps. They walked into the great hall.

According to their custom, a hundred broad, circular carpets lay there, upon each a bed of down and a long quilt of samite. If those two had their wits about them, they could find somewhere to sit there until their armour was taken off them. A chamberlain came up, bringing them costly garments, identical for both. They sat down, all the knights present there. They brought before them many a costly goblet of gold—it was not glass! Feirefiz and Parzival drank, and then walked over to Anfortas, that sad man.

You have heard before, I imagine, that he leaned and that he seldom sat, and how his bed was embellished. Anfortas then welcomed those two, joyfully, and yet with sorrowful demeanour. He 795 said: 'Mine has been an ungentle wait, if I am ever to be brought joy by you. You parted from me not long ago in such a way that, if you practise helpful loyalty, you will be seen to regret it. If fame was ever spoken of you, if there be knights or maidens present here, then seek from them my death and let my duress end. If you are named Parzival, then prevent me from seeing the Grail for seven nights and eight days—by that all my anguish will be averted. I daren't prompt you in any other way. A blessing upon you, if help is reported of you!

'Your companion is a stranger here. I do not permit him to stand before me. Why don't you let him go to his rest?'

All in tears, Parzival replied: 'Tell me where the Grail lies here. If God's grace triumphs by me, this company will witness it.' He fell in genuflection in the direction of the Grail, three times, in honour of the Trinity. He sought to cure the sad king's heart's sorrow. He rose to his feet, and then he said: 'Uncle, what troubles you?'

He who for Saint Silvester's sake bade a bull walk alive away from 796 death,* and who bade Lazarus arise—He Himself helped Anfortas to recover and regain full health. What the Frenchman calls *flôrî*—that sheen came to his skin. Parzival's beauty was but a breath of air now, and that of Absalom, David's son, and that of Vergulaht of Ascalon, and of all those who inherited beauty, and what was averred of Gahmuret when he was seen to file into Kanvoleiz in such splendour—the beauty of none of them could compare with that which Anfortas carried forth from his sickness. God still has great skills at his command!

Then no other election occurred there, for the inscription on the Grail had named him as their lord. Parzival was soon recognized as king and lord there. I doubt if anyone might find elsewhere two such wealthy men—if I am capable of assessing wealth—as Parzival and Feirefiz. Much assiduous service was offered to the host and his guest.*

797 I don't know how many journey-stages Condwiramurs had by then ridden towards Munsalvæsche, with joyous demeanour. She had already heard the truth. The message sent to fetch her was such that her lamenting distress was averted. Duke Kyot, with many another noble knight, had escorted her to Terre de Salvæsche, into the forest where Segramors had been felled by the joust, and where the snow, with the blood, had once taken on her semblance. There Parzival was to go and fetch her. That was a journey he might willingly endure!

These tidings were told him by a templar: 'Many a courteous knight has escorted the queen, with all due courtesy.'

Parzival decided to take a part of the Grail's company and ride out to Trevrizent. The latter's heart rejoiced at the tidings that Anfortas's fate was not to be to die of the joust, and that the question had procured him ease. He said: 'God has many mysteries. Who has ever sat at His council,* or knows the limits of His power? All the angels, together with their hosts, can never determine its boundaries. God is Man and His Father's Word. God is Father and Son. His Spirit is capable of great help.'

798 Trevrizent said to Parzival: 'Greater miracle has seldom happened, since your defiance has caused God's endless Trinity to be acquiescent to your will.* I lied to you about the Grail—a stratagem to deter you—about how things stand regarding it. Grant me atonement for that sin. I must now be obedient to you, sister's son and lord of mine. The tale that I told you was that the expelled spirits, with God's support, were present by the Grail, waiting there until they won favour. God is so constant in His ways that He contends forever against those I named to you as being in His favour. Whoever wishes for any reward from Him must renounce the same. For all eternity they are doomed. That doom they have chosen for themselves.* It was only that I was troubled by your suffering. It has ever been uncustomary that anyone, at any time, might gain the Grail by fighting. I would gladly have deflected you from that purpose. Now it has come about otherwise in your case. The prize you have won is all the higher. Now turn your thoughts to humility.'

799 Parzival said to his uncle: 'I wish to see her whom I have never

seen in the last five years. When we were together, she was dear to me—as she is still. Yet I will gladly have your counsel for as long as death does not part us. You advised me before, in great need. I wish to ride to meet my wife, who, I have heard, is coming to meet me at a certain place by the Plimizœl.' He asked Trevrizent to give him leave. Then the good man commended him to God.

Parzival set off that night. The wood was well-known to his companions. When dawn came, he found a happy find, many a pavilion pitched. From the land of Brobarz, I heard tell, many pennants had been planted there, many a shield having marched in their train. His land's princes lay encamped there. Parzival asked where the queen herself lay, whether she kept a separate tent-ring. They showed him where she lay, encamped in a well-adorned ring, surrounded by pavilions.

Now Duke Kyot of Katelangen had risen early that morning. Those men came riding towards the ring. The day's gleam was grey 800 as yet, but Kyot recognized the Grail's device among that company there—they all wore turtle-doves. Then the old man sighed, for Schoysiane, his chaste wife, had won him bliss at Munsalvæsche, she who died by Sigune's birth. Kyot walked to meet Parzival, heartily welcoming him and his men. He sent a young lordling in search of the queen's marshal, asking him to provide good comfort for all the knights he saw halting there. He himself led Parzival by the hand to where he found the queen's chamber, an elegant pavilion of buckram. All his armour was taken off him there. The queen knows nothing of this yet.

Parzival found Loherangrin and Kardeiz lying by her—then joy must have vanquished him!—in a pavilion, high and broad, where here and there, on all sides, lustrous ladies lay in plenty. Kyot slapped the coverlet, asking the queen to wake and laugh for joy. She looked up and saw her husband. She was wearing nothing but her shift. She 801 threw the coverlet about her. Condwiramurs of the fair features leapt onto the carpet by the bed. Then Parzival embraced her. They tell me they kissed one another.

She said: 'Good fortune has sent you to me, my heart's joy!' She bade him be welcome: 'Now I ought to be angry—I can't! Honoured be the hour and this day which have brought me this embrace, by which my sadness is enfeebled. I have now what my heart desires. Sorrow is granted little reward by me!'

Now the little children awoke, too, Kardeiz and Loherangrin. They lay upon the bed, quite naked. Parzival showed no reluctance to kiss them lovingly. Kyot, rich in courtesy, asked that the boys be carried away. He went about telling all the ladies, too, to go out of the pavilion. They did so, once they had welcomed their lord back from his long journey. Kyot the courteous commended her husband to the queen; he led all the damsels away. It was still very early as yet. Chamberlains hastily closed the flaps.

802   If blood and snow had ever plucked the companionship of his wits from him before—it was on the same meadow he found them lying—Condwiramurs now repaid that debt of sorrow—she held the pledge there. He never received love's help against love's distress elsewhere, although many a noble woman offered him love. I believe he practised pleasure until that day's mid-morning.

The whole army rode over to see—they gazed at the templars. They were accoutred, and had been much charged at, their shields much ridden through by jousts, and slashed by swords, too. Each wore a surcoat of phellel-silk or samite. They still had on iron greaves. The rest of their armour had been taken off them.

There can be no more sleeping there now! The king and the queen arose. A priest sang mass. In the ring great jostling arose on the part of the courageous army, who had once defended themselves against Clamide. When the benediction had been spoken, Parzival's subjects welcomed him with loyalty, in noble fashion—many a knight rich in courage.

803   The pavilion's flaps were taken off. The king said: 'Which of these two is the boy who is to be king over your lands?' To all the princes he proclaimed: 'Waleis and Norgals, Kanvoleis and Kingrivals this boy is to have by right—Anjou and Bealzenan.* If he ever comes to man's stature, bear him company into those lands. My father was called Gahmuret, he who bequeathed me these by rightful inheritance. With God's blessing I have inherited the Grail. Now accept on this occasion your fiefs from my child, if I find loyalty in you.'

That took place with a good will. Many pennants were seen to be brought forward. There two little hands enfeoffed many a stretch of broad lands. Then Kardeiz was crowned. Afterwards he did indeed conquer Kanvoleiz, and much that had been Gahmuret's. By the Plimizœl, on a meadow, seating and a broad ring were established, where they were to come and break bread. Hastily the meal was eaten there. The army headed off on the journey home. All the pavilions were taken down. They returned with the young king.

Many a damsel and the rest of her people parted from the queen, 804 showing their sorrow. Then the templars took Loherangrin and his fair mother and rode rapidly away to Munsalvæsche. 'Once, in this forest,' said Parzival, 'I saw a cell standing, through which ran rapidly a fast-flowing, lucent spring. If you know it, then lead me there.'

His companions told him that they knew one: 'There a maiden lives, all in mourning over her beloved's tomb. She is an ark of true grace. Our journey passes close by her. She is seldom found free of grief.'

The king said: 'We must see her.' They voiced their assent. They rode straight on, rapidly, and late that evening found Sigune, dead at her genuflection. There the queen saw grief's extremity. They broke into her cell. Parzival, for his cousin's sake, asked that the tombstone be raised. Schionatulander appeared, unrotted, handsome, balsam-hued. They laid her in there next to him, she who had given 805 maidenly love to him when she lived, and closed the grave. Cond-wiramurs broke into lament for her uncle's daughter, I heard tell, and lost much joy, for Schoysiane, the dead maiden's mother, had reared her as a child, which was why joy fled her—Schoysiane was Parzival's aunt, if the Provençal read the truth of the matter. Duke Kyot knew little of his daughter's death—King Kardeiz's tutor. It is not crooked like the bow—this tale is true and straight.*

Then they did their journey its due, riding by night to Mun-salvæsche. There Feirefiz had been waiting for them, whiling the time pleasantly away. Many candles were then lit, just as if the whole forest were on fire. A templar of Patrigalt, armed, rode at the queen's side. The courtyard was wide and broad; in it stood many distinct companies. They all welcomed the queen, and the host and his son. Then they carried Loherangrin to his uncle Feirefiz. He being black and white, the boy did not want to kiss him. Even today, fear is 806 reported of noble children. At that the heathen laughed. Then those in the courtyard began to disperse, the queen having dismounted. Profit had come to them by her, with the arrival of joy there. They took her to where she found a noble band of many lustrous ladies. Feirefiz and Anfortas both stood courteously on the steps beside the lady. Repanse de Schoye, and Garschiloye of Greenland, Florie of

Lunel—bright eyes and lustrous complexions they bore, and maidenly fame. Also standing there, pliant as a sapling, not lacking in beauty and grace, was she who was said to be his daughter, that of Jernis of Ril—that maiden was called Ampflise. From Tenabroc— I am told—Clarischanze* stood there, a gentle maiden, of bright hue, all unblemished, waisted like an ant.

Feirefiz stepped towards the hostess.* The queen asked him to kiss her. She then also kissed Anfortas and rejoiced at his redemption. 807 Feirefiz led her by the hand to where she found the host's aunt, Repanse de Schoye, standing. There much kissing had to ensue. Even before, her mouth had been so red—now it suffered such duress from kissing that it troubles me, and I am sorry that I do not have such hardship in her stead, for she was weary when she came to them. Damsels led their lady away.

The knights remained in the great hall, which was well candled— they burned very brightly. Then, with decorum, they began to make preparations for the Grail. On every occasion it was brought forth, it was not as a spectacle for the company, but only when a festivity required it. Because they had hoped for solace on that evening when they were deprived of joy by the bloody spear, the Grail had been brought forth in hope of help on that occasion. Parzival afterwards abandoned them to sorrow. Now it is with joy that it is to be brought forth. All their sorrow has been struck down.

When the queen had taken off her travelling clothes and tied up her hair, she entered in a manner that well became her. Feirefiz, at 808 one of the doors, took her by the hand. Now, it was simply beyond dispute that no-one ever heard or spoke at any time of a more beautiful woman. She wore on her person, moreover, phellel-silk which a skilled hand had wrought in the fashion once devised with great cunning by Sarant, in the city of Thasme. Feirefiz Angevin escorted her—she who shed a bright radiance—down the middle of the great hall. Three huge fires had been made, *lignum aloe* being the fire's scent. Forty carpets lay there, and more seating than at that time when Parzival had previously seen the Grail brought forth there. One seat was adorned above all others, where Feirefiz and Anfortas were to sit by the host. Then they acted with courtesy's wits, all those who wished to serve there when the Grail was to arrive.

You have heard enough before of how it was carried before Anfortas; they are seen to do the same now, bringing it before noble

Gahmuret's son, and also Tampenteire's child. The damsels delay
no longer now. In orderly fashion they entered on all sides, twenty-
five in number. The glance of the first seemed lustrous to the 809
heathen and their hair wavy—those that followed more beautiful still
when he saw them enter immediately afterwards, and all their clothes
costly. Sweet, charming, comely were all the maidens' faces, without
exception. Behind them all came the fair-featured Repanse de
Schoye, a maiden. The Grail permitted itself, I am told, to be carried
by her alone, and no other. Much chastity resided in her heart; her
complexion was *flôrî* to the eye.

If I were to tell you of the ceremony's commencement, how many
chamberlains proffered water there and what tables were carried
before them—more than I mentioned to you before—how vulgarity
fled the great hall—what carts were drawn in with costly vessels of
gold, and how the knights were seated—that would be too long a
yarn by far. I will be quick in brevity. With courtesy they took from
before the Grail dishes wild and tame, this man his mead, that man
his wine, as his custom would have it—mulberry juice, sinopel, clary.
Fil li roy Gahmuret found Pelrapeire quite different when it first 810
made his acquaintance.*

The heathen inquired as to how the empty gold vessels became
full before the table. That was a marvel it delighted him to see. Then
radiant Anfortas, who had been assigned him as a companion, said:
'Sir, do you see the Grail lying before you?'

The heathen of dappled hue replied: 'I see nothing but an achmardi
which my lady the damsel carried past us—she with the crown
standing there before us. Her glance penetrates my heart. I believed
my body to be so strong that no maiden nor woman might ever
deprive me of joy's strength. Now it has become repugnant to me if
I ever received noble love before. Discourtesy has forestalled my
courtesy if I tell you of my distress, since I have never offered you
service. How can all my wealth help me, and all the battles I have
ever fought in women's cause, and if my hand has ever bestowed any
gifts, if I am to live in such pangs? Jupiter, you mighty god, why did
you wish me here to meet with such harshness?'

Love's strength, combined with joy's weakness, rendered him pale
in his white parts. Condwiramurs, famed for her fairness, now very 811
nearly found a rival in that lustrous maiden's complexion's sheen.
Then Feirefiz, the noble stranger, trapped himself in her love's

snare. His former amour failed him because of his oblivious desire. What help was her love to Secundille then, and her land of Tribalibot? It was a maiden that granted him such harsh anguish. Clauditte and Olimpia, Secundille—and other remote regions where women had rewarded him for service and fostered his fame—that of Gahmuret of Zazamanc's son—to him the love of all these seemed a mere trifle.

Then radiant Anfortas saw that his companion was in torment, his white marks all grown pale, high spirits deserting him. He said: 'Sir—my sister—I'm sorry if she teaches you such anguish as no man ever suffered before on her account. No knight has ever ridden in her service, nor has anyone obtained any reward from her. She has been here with me, amid great grief. That has, indeed, impaired her complexion somewhat—that she has so seldom been seen to be merry. Your brother is her sister's son—he may well be able to help you there.'

812 'If that maiden is your sister,' said Feirefiz Angevin, 'she who wears the crown upon her loose-flowing hair there, then give me advice about how to win her love. All my heart's desire is bent upon her. If ever I won fame by the spear—oh, if only that had happened entirely for her sake, and she would then grant me her reward! Tourneying knows of five thrusts*—these have been delivered by my hand. One is the head-on charge. The second I know as the side-charge. The third is to await the opponent's attack. I have ridden the good formal joust at the full tilt. Nor have I avoided the charge in pursuit of the opponent. Since the shield first became my covering, today is the greatest hardship I have felt. Before Agremuntin I thrust at a fiery knight; if my surcoat had not been of salamander and my second shield of asbestos, I would have been consumed by fire in that joust. Wherever I won fame at physical cost—oh, if only it had been your sister of the lovely hue who had sent me there! I would gladly be her messenger yet, to meet battle. I shall always cherish hatred towards Jupiter, my god, unless he averts this mighty grief from me!'

813 The father of them both was called Frimutel. Anfortas possessed the same countenance and the same complexion as his sister. The heathen looked at her long enough, and then back, time and again, at him. No matter how many dishes were carried back or forth, his mouth ate none of them—yet he sat there like a man eating!

Anfortas said to Parzival: 'Sir, your brother has not yet, I believe, seen the Grail.'

Feirefiz acknowledged to the host that he could see nothing of the Grail. This seemed wondrous to all the knights. These tidings were also heard by Titurel, the aged, bedridden cripple. He said: 'If he is a heathen, then he need have no desire that his eyes—without baptism's power—may join the company and behold the Grail. A fence has been hewn before it.'*

He sent that message into the great hall. Then the host and Anfortas told Feirefiz to mark what all that people lived upon entirely—it was cut off from any heathen's sight. They sought that he should accept baptism, and endless gain's purchase.

'If I, for your sakes, come to be baptized, will baptism avail me 814 in love?' asked the heathen, Gahmuret's son. 'It has never been anything but a mere breath of air till now, all that to which battle or love compelled me. Whether the time be short or long since my first shield covered me, never have I received greater duress. Out of courtesy I ought to hide love, but now this heart can conceal none of it.'

'Whom d'you mean?'* asked Parzival.

'Only that maiden bright of hue, my companion's sister here. If you'll help me win her, I shall acquaint her with such wealth that broad lands will serve her.'

'If you'll let yourself be given baptism,' said the host, 'then you may aspire to her love. I may indeed now call you "thou". Our wealth is almost equal, mine coming from the Grail's power.'

'Help me, brother,' said Feirefiz Angevin, 'to make your aunt's acquaintance. If baptism is won by battle, have me taken there at once and let me serve for her reward! I have always been glad to hear that melody when splinters leap from the joust and where swords ring out upon helmets!'

The host laughed much at that, and Anfortas still more. 'If you 815 can receive baptism thus,' said the host, 'I shall bring her close, by means of true baptism, to your command. Jupiter, your god, you must forfeit for her sake, and renounce Secundille. Tomorrow morning I shall give you such counsel as befits your wooing.'

Anfortas, before his sickness's time, had spread his fame far through chivalry undertaken for love. In his heart's mind were kindness and friendliness. His hand, too, had won many a prize in battle.

There by the Grail sat three of the best knights of all who then wielded shields, for they were not afraid to run the gauntlet.

If you will, they have eaten enough there. Courteously they carried away from them all the tables and tablecloths. Humbly, all the little damsels bowed. Feirefiz Angevin saw them turning away from him—that caused his sadness to increase. His heart's lock carried away the Grail. Parzival gave them leave to go.

816 How the hostess herself withdrew, and what arrangements were afterwards made to ensure that he was well bedded—he who, nevertheless, lay uneasy because of love—how all the templars' company parted them from unease by ease—that would make for a long yarn. I will tell you of the next day.

When that shone brightly the next morning, Parzival decided, in agreement with good Anfortas, that they should entreat him of Zazamanc, whom Love oppressed, to enter the temple, into the Grail's presence. At the same time he commanded that the wise templars be present. Men-at-arms, knights, a great company stood there. Then the heathen walked in. The baptism-bowl was a ruby, mounted upon a circular step of jasper. Titurel had had it thus constructed, at great expense. Parzival then said to his brother: 'If you would have my aunt, you must renounce all your gods for her sake, and always be willing to wreak vengeance upon the opposition of the Highest God, and must loyally protect His commandment.'

817 'All that I must do to have the maiden,' said the heathen, 'will be done, and faithfully observed by me.' The baptism-bowl was lowered a little towards the Grail. At once it became full of water, neither too hot nor too cold. An aged, grey priest stood there, who in that font had thrust many a baby away from heathendom.*

He said: 'You must believe, to rob the Devil of your soul, in the Highest God alone, whose Trinity is universal and everywhere of equal yield. God is Man and His Father's Word. Since He is Father and Son, who are all honoured alike, of equal stature to His Spirit, by the authority of these Three this water fends heathendom from you, by the Trinity's power. In the water He walked to baptism, He from whom Adam received countenance. By water trees are sapped. Water fruits all those creatures acknowledged as Creation. By water man has sight.* Water gives many a soul such sheen that the angels need be no brighter.'

818 Feirefiz said to the priest: 'If it helps me against distress, I'll

believe all that you command. If her love rewards me, then I'll gladly carry out his command. Brother, if your aunt has a god, I believe in him and in her—I never met with such great extremity! All *my* gods are renounced! Let Secundille, too, lose all that she ever honoured herself by giving me. For the sake of your aunt's god have me be baptized!'

They began to treat him in Christian fashion and pronounced baptism's blessing upon him. When the heathen had received baptism, and the baptismal clothing had been laid upon him—which he uneasily awaited—they delivered the maiden to him. They gave him Frimutel's daughter. He had been blind when it came to seeing the Grail, until baptism had covered him. Thereafter the Grail was revealed to his vision.

After this baptism's eventuality, they found written on the Grail that whichever templar God's hand appointed to be lord over a foreign people should advise against any questioning of his name or his lineage, and that he should help them to justice. Once that question is put to him, they can no longer keep him. Because gentle Anfortas had been so long in bitter anguish and the question had avoided him for a long time, questioning is now forever painful to them. All the fellow-custodians of the Grail want no questions asked of them.

The baptized Feirefiz pressed his brother-in-law with entreaties to depart with him, and never to be sparing in his presence in sharing all his wealthy possessions. Then Anfortas courteously diverted him from that purpose: 'I don't want my humble intent towards God to fail. The Grail's crown is of equal worth—it was arrogance deprived me of it. Now I have chosen humility for myself. Wealth and love of women distance themselves from my mind. You take from here a noble woman. She gives to your service a chaste person, with good womanly ways. My order will not be neglected here—I will ride many jousts, fighting in the Grail's service. I will fight no more for the sake of women. There was one woman who gave me heart's sorrow. Yet any hostility of mine shall be forever most slow to confront women. High manly joy comes from them, however small my profit by them has been.'

Feirefiz then urged Anfortas fervently, in his sister's honour, to accompany him on his departure. He persisted in declining. Feirefiz Angevin sought that Loherangrin should depart with him.* His mother was adept at preventing that. Moreover, King Parzival said: 'My son is destined for the Grail. To that end he must devote a humble heart, if God permits him to acquire the right spirit.' Feirefiz indulged in pleasure and pastime there until the eleventh day. On the twelfth he departed. The wealthy king wished to take his wife to his army. At that sadness began to stir in Parzival, because of his loyalty. The matter taught him grief. He took counsel with his men, concluding that he would send a great company of knights with Feirefiz, out beyond the forest. Anfortas, that gentle, bold warrior, rode with him as escort. Many a maiden there did not shun tears.

821 They had to make a new trail, out towards Karchobra. Gentle Anfortas sent a message to the man who was burgrave there, admonishing him that, if he had ever received rich gifts from Anfortas's hand, he should now honour his loyalty to him by serving him and guiding his brother-in-law and his wife, Anfortas's sister, through the greenwood of Læprisin to the wild, wide harbour. And now it was time for leave-taking. The templars were to go no further then. Cundrie la Surziere was chosen to take that message there. All the templars took leave of the wealthy king. Courteous Feirefiz rode off.

The burgrave did not fail to carry out all that Cundrie commanded him to do. Wealthy Feirefiz was received in knightly fashion, with great ceremony. There was no need for him to be bored there. Soon he was led further, with a noble escort. I don't know how many lands he rode through until he reached Joflanze on the broad meadow.

822 They found only some of the people there. Feirefiz asked at once for tidings as to where the army had gone. Each had gone to his own land, on the journey known to him. Arthur had headed for Camelot.* He of Tribalibot then rode in splendour, as he well knew how, to meet his army. They lay encamped at the harbour, quite despondent at their lord's having parted from them. His coming brought fresh high spirits to many a good knight there. There the burgrave of Karchobra and all his men were sent home with rich gifts. Cundrie found tidings of great import there—messengers had come in search of the army—death had taken Secundille.

Only then could Repanse de Schoye rejoice at her journey. She gave birth afterwards, in India, to a son, who was called Johan. Prester John they called him; forever after they retained that name for the kings there. Feirefiz had letters sent all over the land of India,

telling them about the Christian way of life. It had not been so strong 823
there before. We call that land India here; there it is called Tribalibot.
Feirefiz sent a message by Cundrie back to his brother, up in Mun-
salvæsche, telling him what had happened to him since, and that
Secundille had departed this life. Anfortas rejoiced then that his
sister was undisputed lady over many such broad lands.

The true tidings have come to you concerning Frimutel's five
children,* how virtuously they acted, and how two of them died. The
first was Schoysiane, free of falsity before God; the second was called
Herzeloyde, who thrust falseness from her heart. Trevrizent had
devoted his sword and knightly life to the sweet love of God, and in
pursuit of endless gain. Noble, radiant Anfortas was valorous and
chaste of heart. In accordance with his order he rode many a joust,
fighting for the Grail's sake, not for women.

Loherangrin grew manly and strong; cowardice concealed itself
from him. When his thoughts turned to chivalry, he won fame in the
Grail's service.

Would you like to hear more now? In later times, in a far-off land 824
there resided a lady, free of all falsity. Wealth and high lineage had
both been bequeathed to her. She knew how to act well, with true
chastity. All human lust perished in her. There were noble people in
plenty who sought her hand, several of whom wore a crown, and
many a prince, her peer. Her humility was so great that she paid
them no heed. Many counts from her own country grew hostile
towards her because of this—why was she so reluctant to take a
husband who might fittingly be her lord?

She had devoted herself entirely to God, no matter what anger
was directed at her. Many a man did her wrong, innocent though she
was. She called an assembly of her land's lords. Many a messenger
from a far-off land made his way to her. She abjured all men except
him whom God might direct towards her. His love she would gladly
honour.

She was princess in Brabant. The man whom the swan brought
and whom God intended for her was sent from Munsalvæsche. At 825
Antwerp he was hauled ashore. She was entirely undeceived in him.
He knew how to act well. He was perforce held to be handsome and
valorous in all the realms where he ever came to be known. Courtly, a
man wise and decorous, generous and loyal in his every vein, he was
bare of blemish.

That land's lady gave him a splendid welcome. Now hear what words he spoke. Rich and poor alike heard them, standing at all corners there. He said: 'Lady Duchess, if I am to be lord of this land, I am leaving behind me just as much. Hear now what I would request of you: never ask who I am. Then I may remain with you. If you choose to question me, then you shall have lost my love. If you do not heed this warning, then God will give *me* warning—He knows the reason well.'

She pledged a woman's oath which afterwards, out of affection, suffered deviation: that she would heed his command and never transgress against whatever he ordered her to do, if God left her in her senses.

826   That night he knew her love. Then he became prince in Brabant. The wedding passed off sumptuously. Many a lord received his fief from his hand, as was his due. That same prince became a good judge. Moreover, he often did knightly deeds, retaining fame by his prowess.*

They had handsome children together. There are many people still alive in Brabant who know all about that couple—her welcome, his departure—that her question drove him away—and how long he remained there. He did indeed depart unwillingly. Then his friend the swan again brought him a small, pliant skiff. Of his treasures he left behind there a sword, a horn, a ring. Away sailed Loherangrin. If we would do justice to the tale, he was Parzival's son. He travelled the waves and ways until he was back in the Grail's tending.

How did it come about that the good woman lost her noble beloved's charming presence? He had previously advised her against questioning, when he came before her, from the sea. Here Erec ought now to speak—he knew how to avenge himself through words.*

827   If master Chrétien of Troyes has done this tale an injustice, Kyot, who sent us the true tidings, has good reason to wax wrath. Definitively, the Provençal tells how Herzeloyde's son won the Grail, as was decreed for him, when Anfortas forfeited it. From Provence into German lands the true tidings have been sent to us, and this adventure's end's limit. No more will I speak of it now, I, Wolfram von Eschenbach—only what the master said before. His children, his high lineage, I have correctly named to you, those of Parzival, whom I have brought to where Fortune had, despite all, intended him to go. If any man's life ends in such a way that God is not robbed of his

soul because of the body's guilt, and he yet can retain, with honour, this world's favour, that is a useful labour. Good women, if they are of sound mind—I shall be all the worthier in their estimation if any one of them wishes me well, now that I have told this tale to its end. If it is for a woman's sake that this has happened, she may concede that I have spoken sweet words.

TITUREL

FRAGMENT I

[The first fragment describes the parallel childhoods of Sigune
and Schionatulander. Sigune is the daughter of Kyot of Katelangen
and Schoysiane, daughter of Frimutel and granddaughter of the
bedridden Grail King, Titurel. After Schoysiane's death in child-
birth, Sigune is brought up first by her uncle, Tampenteire, and
then by her aunt, Herzeloyde. Schionatulander, the Dauphin of
Graswaldan and grandson of Gurnemanz, is assigned by Queen
Amphlise to Gahmuret, to be his squire.]

While strong Titurel could still bestir himself, he ventured willingly
into the attack, leading his men with him. Afterwards, in old age, he
said: 'I learn that I must relinquish the shaft. Once I wielded it well
and willingly.   (1)
'If I could still bear arms,' the bold king said, 'the air would be
honoured by the spear's crack from my hand. Splinters would give
shade from the sun. Many ornaments on top of helmets have been
set on fire by my sword's blade.   (2)
'If I ever received solace from lofty love, and if love's sweetness
ever exerted its blissful power over me, if I ever received a lovely
woman's greeting—all this has now flown wild* from my languish-
ing, lamenting body.   (3)
'My bliss, my chastity, my constancy of mind—and if my hand ever
won high fame by giving gifts or in attacks—my young kinsfolk are
ensured against decline by this. Indeed, all my lineage must forever
inherit true love, together with loyalty.   (4)
'I know well that if a man is welcomed by womanly smiles, chastity
and constancy will forever draw near his heart. Those two can never
estrange themselves from him, except at death alone. Otherwise,
no-one can prevent their proximity.   (5)
'When I received the Grail by the message which the exalted angel
sent me, by his high authority, there I found written all my order.
That gift had never been given, before me, to human hand.*   (6)

'The Lord of the Grail must be chaste and pure. Alas, my gentle son Frimutel, I have retained only you, of my children, here by the Grail. Now receive the Grail's crown and the Grail, my fair son! (7)

'Son, in your time you practised the shield's office, earning good interest by your charge. There your wheel was stuck fast:* I had to draw you away from chivalry. Now, son, defend yourself alone! My strength is intent on fleeing from us both.   (8)

'God has provided you, son, with five noble children. They are a most blessed, noble household for the Grail here. Anfortas and Trevrizent the swift—I may yet live to hear their fame resound above all other fame!   (9)

'Your daughter Schoysiane holds so many virtues locked within her heart that the world's bliss will profit by them. Herzeloyde is of the same will. Urrepanse de Schoye's praise cannot be silenced by other praise.'   (10)

These words were heard by knights and ladies. Among the templars, many a man's heart's sorrow could be beheld—those whom he had often rescued from many a hard pass, when he defended the Grail by his own hand and with their help.   (11)

Thus strong Titurel was grown weak, both by great age and sickness's hardship. In Munsalvæsche Frimutel nobly took charge of the Grail, which was perfection surpassing all earthly realms.   (12)

Of his daughters, there were two of such years that they were full-grown enough to meet lofty love in a lover's arms. Schoysiane's love was sought with splendour by many kings from diverse lands. She granted it, however, to one prince alone.   (13)

Kyot of Katelangen won Schoysiane. No fairer maiden was ever seen, before nor since, by sun nor by moon. He, too, could boast of many virtues. His heart was ever unabashed in pursuit of high fame, heedless of expense and deeds.   (14)

In splendour she was brought to him, and lavishly welcomed. King Tampenteire, his brother, came to Katelangen. Countless wealthy princes were present there. No-one had seen such a costly wedding for many years.   (15)

Kyot, that land's lord, had won fame by his generosity and his courage. His deeds were unfailing, wherever men had to charge into battle and ride, accoutred, into the joust in pursuit of womens' reward.   (16)

If ever a prince won dearer wife, what heartfelt delight he endured.

That was what Love wished upon that couple! Alas, now his sorrow nears him! Thus the world ends: all our sweetness must, in the end, ever turn sour. (17)

In due time his wife granted him a child. May God spare me such company in my own household, if I have to pay for it so dearly! As long as I am in my right mind, I would seldom wish for the like! (18)

Sweet Schoysiane, lustrous and constant, gave birth, as she died, to a daughter who possessed many blessings. From her all maidenly honour emanated. She practised such great loyalty as is still spoken of in many lands. (19)

Thus the prince's sorrow was undercut by joy. His young daughter lived—her mother dead—that was the reward he had by them both. Schoysiane's death helped him borrow the loss of true joys, and never-ending profit in sorrows. (20)

Then, amid sorrow, the lady was commended to the earth. First she had to be aromatized and balsamed in splendour,* because they had to wait a long time. Many kings and princes came from far and wide for the corpse-laying. (21)

The prince held his land in fief from Tampenteire, from his brother, the king, who was called sovereign of Pelrapeire. He urged that the land be given in fief to his little daughter. He then abjured the sword, the helmet and the shield. (22)

Duke Manfilot observed great suffering in his noble brother; it was a bitter feast for the eye. He also parted, out of grief, from his sword, neither of them any longer desirous of lofty love or jousting. (23)

At baptism the child was named Sigune, she whom her father Kyot had purchased at such a high price, for he lost her mother by her. She whom the Grail first permitted itself to be carried by was Schoysiane. (24)

King Tampenteire took little Sigune to his daughter. When Kyot kissed her at parting, many tears were seen to be shed. Condwiramurs was still a suckling then. The two playmates grew up without any word ever being spoken of their fame's diminishment. (25)

In those days Castis had also died. He had won the hand of the lustrous Herzeloyde at Munsalvæsche. Kanvoleiz he gave to the beautiful queen, and Kingrivals. In both his head had worn the crown before princes. (26)

Castis never took Herzeloyde to wife; she lay a virgin in Gahmuret's arms. Yet she became lady over two lands, gentle Frimutel's daughter, who had been sent there from Munsalvæsche. (27)

When Tampenteire died, and radiant Kardeiz—in Brobarz he wore the crown—that was in the fifth year that Sigune had been in their care there. Then they had to separate, the two young playmates, by no means old. (28)

Queen Herzeloyde's thoughts turned to Sigune; with all her intent she sought to have her brought to her from Brobarz. Condwiramurs began to weep at the thought that she was to be bereft of Sigune's companionship and constant affection. (29)

The girl said: 'Dear daddy, have my chest filled with dolls when I leave here to go to my aunt. Then I shall be well equipped for the journey. There is many a knight now alive who may yet commit himself to my service.' (30)

'Blessed am I to have such a worthy child, who is so sensible! May God long grant Katelangen such a noble lady as yourself! My anxiety sleeps as long as your good fortune is awake. If the Black Forest were hereabouts, it would be all turned into spear-shafts for you!' (31)

Kyot's child, Sigune, thus grew up in her aunt's home. Whoever saw her looked more fondly on her than on May's sunshine among dew-wet flowers. Bliss and honour blossomed forth from her heart. Let her grow into the years of her full fame, and I shall say more in her praise! (32)

Of that measure which is due to a pure woman if she is to have her fill of virtues, not a whit was neglected in her most gentle person. A pure fruit was she, perfectly unsullied, devoid of falsity, noble Schoysiane's daughter, of the same lineage, that chaste, pure young maiden! (33)

Now we ought also to think of Herzeloyde the pure. Nothing could injure her reputation. In truth I will turn my thoughts to that dear lady, she who was the fountain of all womanly honour. She well deserved to have her fame spread throughout the lands, (34)

That virgin widow, Frimutel's daughter—wherever in her youth the talk was of ladies' praise, none resounded as loud as hers. Her repute travelled far into many realms, until her love was earned by the spears' clash before Kanvoleiz. (35)

Hear now strange wonders of the maiden Sigune: when her little breasts rounded and her curly, fair hair began to turn brown, then high spirits rose in her heart. She began to act with pride and speak freely, and yet did so with womanly grace. (36)

How Gahmuret parted from Belacane, and how he nobly won Schoysiane's sister, and how he broke with the French queen—of that I shall be silent here, and tell you instead of maidenly love. (37)

To the French queen, Ampflise, a child was entrusted, born of princes' kin and lineage, capable of restraint in all matters whereby fame perishes. When all princes shall have been born, not one of them shall ever strive better for fame. (38)

When Gahmuret received the shield from Ampflise, the noble queen assigned this boy to him. We may yet have cause to praise him, as his true child's sweetness demanded. He will be this adventure's lord. I am right to salute all youths for his sake. (39)

This same child also travelled with the Angevin* across the sea to heathendom, to the Baruch Ahkarin. He brought him back again to Waleis. Wherever boys espy boldness, it must help them, if they are ever to grow to manhood. (40)

A little I will tell you of the boy's lineage. His grandfather was called Gurnemanz of Graharz, who knew how to cleave iron. He did so by many a charge in the joust. His father was called Gurzgri; he lay dead because of Schoydelacurt.* (41)

Mahaute was his mother's name, sister of Ehkunat, the mighty Count Palatine, who was named after the stronghold of Berbester.* He himself was called Schionatulander. Such high fame was never won in his time by any other. (42)

That I did not name noble Gurzgri's son before the maiden Sigune was because her mother had been sent out from the custody of the pure Grail. Her high birth and her fair kinfolk also wrest her into precedence. (43)

All the Grail's company are chosen ones, ever blessed in this world and counted of constant fame in the next. Now Sigune was of the same seed, which was sown forth from Munsalvæsche into this world, and received by those blessed by salvation. (44)

Wherever this same seed was taken from that land, it was bound to be fertile and a veritable storm directed against disgrace for them. For this reason Kanvoleiz is renowned far and wide. In many a tongue it has been called loyalty's capital. (45)

Hail Kanvoleiz, how your constancy is spoken of, and the heartfelt affection which was not slow to grow in you! Love arose early there in two children. Its course was so pure that the whole world could find none of its mirk there. (46)

Proud Gahmuret reared these children together, in his chamber. When Schionatulander was as yet not strong of resolve, he was already locked in heart's distress for love of Sigune. (47)

Alas, they are still too young and foolish for such anguish, for when Love is grasped in youth, it lasts longest of all. While old age may renounce Love, youth still resides in Love's bonds, Love is unrobbed of its power. (48)

Alas, Love, what avails your power amongst children!—for a man who has no eyes could espy you, though he were blind. Love, you are too diverse. All scribes combined could never wholly describe your lineage or character, (49)

Since the monk himself, and even the true hermit, are hard pressed by Love, their minds are so obedient that there are many things they can barely accomplish. Love oppresses the knight beneath the helmet. Love allows little room for leeway. (50)

Love has narrowness and width in its grasp. Love has its house here on earth, and is in Heaven a pure escort to God. Love is everywhere, except in Hell. Strong Love is crippled in its power, if doubt and deviation become its companions. (51)

Devoid of both deviation and doubt were the maiden Sigune and Schionatulander. With suffering great affection was intermingled there. I would tell you many wonders of their youthful love, except it would prolong the tale. (52)

Their modest good breeding and their inherited lineage—they were born of pure love—imposed upon them the custom of concealing their love externally, in their fair features, although their hearts were inwardly tormented. (53)

Schionatulander had no doubt acquired discretion from many a sweet message which the French Queen Ampflise sent in secret to the Angevin. These he delivered, time and again averting their distress. Now avert his, too! (54)

Schionatulander very often observed how his aunt's son* Gahmuret knew how to speak with manly sentiments and how he could part himself from pangs. Many baptized people acknowledged this of him here, as did the noble heathens in their lands. (55)

All you who have practised love and laid love upon yourselves, hear now of maidenly sorrow and manliness amid hardship. I will tell adventures of this to such righteous people as may have ever felt languishing sorrow because of heartfelt love.   (56)

Gentle Schionatulander grew bold, although barely encouraged by intimacy, amid much anxiety. He said: 'Sigune, rich in help, help me now, noble maiden, out of my sorrows—that would be a helpful deed!   (57)

'*Duzisse* of Katelangen, let me prosper! I hear tell you are born of such lineage as could never weary of being helpful with their reward to all who received sorrowful anguish on their behalf. Preserve your salvation by your dealings with me!'   (58)

'*Bêâs âmîs*,* now say, fair friend, what you mean. Let me hear if you are resolved in what you would wish of me, if your lamenting request is to be of any avail! Unless you know the full truth of your feelings, you oughtn't to be too hasty!'   (59)

'Where favour resides it must be sought. Lady, I desire favour. By your favour, you must grant it me. Noble companionship well befits the young. Where true favour never won fame, who can find it?'   (60)

She said: 'You must proclaim your sadness, if you seek solace, somewhere where you may be better helped than by me. Otherwise you are sinning if you desire that I should avert your sorrow, for I am truly an orphan, exiled from my kinfolk, land and people.'   (61)

'I know full well that you are a great lady possessed of land and people. I desire nothing of all that, only that your heart look through your eyes upon me, and ponder on my sorrow. Now help me speedily, before my love for you destroys my heart and happiness.'   (62)

'If someone has such love that his love is perilous to such a dear friend as you are to me, that unseemly word "love" will never be named to him by me. As God is my witness, I never knew love's loss nor love's gains.   (63)

'Love—is that a he? Can you interpret Love to me? Is it a she? If Love comes to me, how am I to cherish Love? Must I keep it among my dolls? Or does Love fly unwillingly on a falconer's hand through the wilderness? Can I perhaps lure Love?'   (64)

'Lady, I have heard concerning both women and men that Love knows how to stretch, so shot-like, old and young alike, that its shots inflict wounds through thoughts. It hits—never missing—all that walks, creeps, flies, or floats.*   (65)

'Indeed, sweet maiden, I was well acquainted with love before from tales. Love is in thoughts—that I can now prove by my own case. Constant affection compels thoughts to it. Love steals joy out of my heart—it would be beneath the dignity of a thief!' (66)

'Schionatulander, thoughts so oppress me, when you go out of my sight, that I have no choice but to be bereft of joy, until I come to gaze at you in secret. Because of this I am sad not just once a week—it happens all too often!' (67)

'In that case, sweet maiden, you have no need to ask me about Love. Without your asking, Love's loss and her gains will become familiar to you. See now how Love turns from joy to sorrow! Give Love her due, before Love destroys us both in our hearts.' (68)

She said: 'If Love can so sneak into hearts that neither man nor woman nor maiden is fleet enough to escape her, does anyone know, however, what wrong Love is avenging upon people who never sought to harm her, by destroying their joy?' (69)

'Indeed she wields power over both the young fool and the greybeard. No-one alive is so skilful that he can praise her worth and wonders to the full! Now let us both battle for her help. With unimpaired affection, Love with her wiles can deceive no-one.' (70)

'Alas, if only Love could show other help than that I should surrender to your command my free person as your bondswoman! Your youth has not yet properly earned me. You must first serve to earn me under shieldly cover—be warned beforehand!' (71)

'Lady, when once I can direct arms with force—between now and then, and thereafter too, I shall be seen in sweet, bitter labours, my service striving for your help. I was born to be helped by you. Help now, so that I may succeed with you!' (72)

This was the beginning of their companionship in words, at that time when Pompey had proclaimed his campaign before Baldac, with his forces, together with noble Ipomidon.* By their army many new spears were shattered. (73)

Gahmuret, all in secret, headed off in that direction, with his own shield alone, although he indisputably possessed great power, for he held, in splendour, three lands' crowns. Thus Love hunted him to his deathbed. Death he received at Ipomidon's hands. (74)

Schionatulander was loath to embark on the journey, for love of Sigune denied him entirely high spirits and joy. Nevertheless, he departed along with his kinsman. That brought heart's anguish

upon Sigune, and upon him. Love rode in ambush of them
both.   (75)
The young prince took leave of the maiden in secret, saying: 'Alas,
how am I to live to see Love make me rich in joys, speedily, and
divide me from death? Wish me good fortune, sweet maiden! I must
away from you, to the heathens!'   (76)
'You are dear to me, loyal lover. Tell me now, is this Love? In that
case, I shall be forever wishing for such profit as will win us both
great joy. All rivers will burn before affection on my part
perishes.'   (77)
Much love remained there, love departed that place. Never did you
hear tell of maidens, of women, of manly men, who could love one
another more heartily. Parzival marked that well thereafter, when he
saw Sigune at the lime-tree.   (78)
King Gahmuret of Kingrivals parted secretly from his kinsmen and
subjects, hiding his departure from them entirely. For the journey he
had chosen only twenty courteous youths of high lineage and eighty
squires in armour, without shields.   (79)
Five handsome chargers and much gold, precious stones from
Azagouc, followed him on his journey, his shield all alone, without
any other shields. The reason why one shield ought to choose a
companion is so that the second shield might say 'Bless you!' if the
first shield should happen to sneeze.   (80)
His panther was inverted.* A precious anchor of sable was fastened to
his shield, as the comely knight was travelling in warrior's fashion.
Thus that knight rich in praise was accoutred. Beneath that shield he
will meet his end before Baldac, in headlong joust.   (80a)
Noble Gahmuret took his leave of Herzeloyde. Such a true
loyalty-bearing tree-trunk will never be born anywhere on this
earth, nor a more faithful woman, as she made manifest. Out of
that couple's parting grew grief, over which many an eye wept
thereafter.   (80b)
His heartfelt affection and her love had never yet grown at all distant
through force of habit. The queen gave him her shift, of white silk,
as when it had touched her own whiteness. (It had also touched
something brown at her hip.)* He wore it into the charge before
Baldac.   (81)
From Norgals to Spain he headed, as far as Seville, bold Gandin's
son, who would shed much water from eyes when they heard how

his journey met its end. His high fame will never be exiled from
baptized people, nor from the heathen. (82)

They have no choice but to acknowledge it; it cannot grow old.
Hermann of Thuringia* once enjoyed honour, he who always had
perfection at his command. Wherever we hear tell of his peers, who
passed away before him—how his renown could so outshine
them! (82a)

That I say with certainty, by no means as a surmise. Now we must
also turn our thoughts to the young prince from Graswaldan, to
what Sigune compelled him to do, his chaste *âmie*. She drew the
joy forth from his heart, as the bee does sweetness from the
flowers. (83)

The lovely sickness he bore because of Love, the loss of his high
spirits, the gains in sorrow, imposed full many a pang upon the
Graharzois. He would have found death gentler, as Gurzgri did at
the hands of Mabonagrin.* (84)

If ever a joust, in the charge, with spear-breaking's crack, is
delivered by his hand through a shield—yet he is too slight for
such hardship! Mighty Love enfeebles him, his thoughts thinking
so unforgettingly of loving affection. (85)

Whenever other young lords were riding to the attack in teams or
wrestling, in the fields or on the roads, he had to refrain because of
languishing distress. Love taught him to languish, where constant
joys were concerned. When children learn to stand with the aid of
chairs, they first have to crawl over to them. (86)

If he is now to love loftily, then he must think how he may raise
himself to the heights, and how his lasting fame, in youth and in age,
may destroy all falseness in him. I know some princes—if *they* had to
learn that lesson, it would be easier to teach a bear the psalter! (87)

Schionatulander bore much anguish in secret, before noble Gahmuret
became aware, through constant observation, of his covert sor-
rows—that his dearest kinsman thus struggled with troubles. He
was, indeed, in torment throughout the months, whatever season
came, winter or summer. (88)

His so perfect form, inherited by lineage, his complexion, his bright
eyes, all that could be seen there of his countenance's radiance,
parted, because of his anguish, from their pure brilliance. It was no
hole-riddled inconstancy impelled him to this, but mighty Love, all
unimpaired. (89)

Gahmuret's heart, too, had been oppressed by Love's heat, and her singeing had at times scorched his pure skin, acquainting it with mirk. He had in some part received Love's help, but he also knew her oppressive hours. (90)

No matter how cunning Love may be, she must expose herself. If a man turns observant and skilled eyes to bear on Love, then her power cannot conceal itself. She is also a T-square—I hear that accusation levelled against her—she designs and weaves most cunningly, better even than any weaving-frame or embroidery. (91)

Gahmuret became aware of the covert sorrow—that the young Dauphin of Graswaldan* was so bereft of joy. He took him aside, in the field, off the road: 'Why does Ampflise's page fare thus? Your sadness does not suit me. (92)

'I carry true concern, equal to your torment—the Roman Emperor and the Admirat* of all the Saracens could not avert it with their wealth—whatever has brought you sigh-laden pangs must also pawn away my joy.' (93)

Now you may readily believe that the Angevin would gladly help, if he could, the young, languishing Dauphin. He said: 'Alas, for what reason has your countenance abandoned its pure radiance? Love is robbing herself by her treatment of you. (94)

'I trace Love in you—all too broad is her trail. You must not conceal your secrets from me, as we are such close kin, and both one flesh by rightful lineage. I trace that closer than descent from that mother who grew out of a larcenous rib.* (95)

'You fountain of love, you fertile sap of Love's blossom! Now I must take pity on Ampflise, who assigned you to me out of womanly kindness. She brought you up as if she herself had given birth to you, treating you as if you were her own child, so dear you are to her still and always have been. (96)

'If you conceal your secrets from me, that will wound my heart, which has ever been *your* heart, and your loyalty will have dishonoured itself, if you estrange* such great distress from me. I cannot believe it of your constancy that you should act against your nature so fickly.' (97)

The youth replied, sorrowfully: 'Then let my hope be for your protection and your favour, and that your anger may oppress me no more. It was out of good breeding that I concealed all my pain from you. Now I must name Sigune to you, she who has conquered my heart. (98)

'You can, if you will, alleviate the disproportionate burden. Now let me remind you of the Frenchwoman—if ever I carried any of your cares, remove me from the weakness she has caused me! A sleeping lion was never so burdened as my waking thoughts.* (99)

'Bear in mind, moreover, what seas and lands I have traversed out of affection for you—not because of poverty! I have deserted kinsmen and subjects, and Ampflise, my noble lady. I ought to benefit by you from all that. Make your help manifest! (100)

'You can readily untie me from lock-like bonds. If I ever become master of the shield beneath the helmet, fighting for pay in foreign lands—if my helpful hand is to win fame there—be my guardian for such time, so that your protection may save me in the face of Sigune's oppression!' (101)

'Ah, frail lad, what woods must first be laid waste by your hand in the joust if you are to experience the *duzisse*'s love! Noble Love is dealt according to degree. It is won more readily by the fortunate man of courage than the wealthy coward. (102)

'Yet I am pleased at the tidings that your heart climbs so high. Where was a tree's trunk ever so laudably twigged about the branches? A shining flower she is, on the heath, in the forest, in the field! If my little niece has oppressed you, a blessing upon you for this delightful news! (103)

'Schoysiane, her mother, was renowned for God Himself and His skill having purposefully created her lustre. Schoysiane's sun-graced brightness—that Sigune, Kyot's child, has from her, as familiar stories tell of her. (104)

'Kyot, that pursuer of fame in fierce hardship, the prince from Katelangen, before Schoysiane's death denied him joy—the child of those two I thus greet in all truth—Sigune, victorious in that election where maidens' chastity and sweetness are chosen. (105)

'She who has conquered you—you must strive for victory by serving loyally for her love. Nor am I inclined to delay any longer now in bringing in her noble aunt* to help you. Sigune's radiance shall cause your complexion to blossom like the dazzling flowers.' (106)

Schionatulander replied as follows: 'Now your solace and your loyalty will break entirely all my sorrows' fetters, since it is with your permission that I love Sigune, who for a long time now has robbed me of joy and joyful spirits.' (107)

He could, if he wished, count upon help, Schionatulander. Nor

should we forget the great distress that Kyot's child and Schoy-
siane's seed bore. Before she received solace, she had to dispense
with joy. (108)

How the Princess of Katelangen had been oppressed by harsh Love!
Thus for too long her thoughts had struggled ungently, because she
desired to conceal it from her aunt. The queen perceived with a
tremble of the heart what Sigune was enduring. (109)

Just like a dewy rose, and all wet with redness her eyes became. Her
mouth, all her countenance fully felt her anguish. Then her chastity
could not conceal the loving affection in her heart, which was so
tormented on account of her youthful warrior. (110)

Then the queen spoke out of affection and loyalty: 'Alas, Schoysiane's
fruit, I bore already far too much grief of a different kind, which I
suffered on account of the Angevin. Now a new thorn grows in my
sorrow, since I perceive such pangs in you. (111)

'Tell me what ails you with regard to your land and people! Or is my
solace and that of my other kinsmen so distant from you that their
help cannot reach you? Where has your sun-like sheen gone? Alas,
who has stolen it from your cheeks? (112)

'Wretched maiden, your exile can do no other but move me to pity
now. I must be accounted poor forever, despite my crown over three
lands,* unless I live to see your troubles fade and I find out the true
tidings of all your sorrow.' (113)

'In that case I must, amid anxiety, tell you all my anguish. If you think
any the less of me for it, then your good breeding is capable of sinning
against me, since I cannot part from my unhappiness. Let me remain
in your favour, sweet love! That becomes us both well. (114)

'May God reward you! All that a mother ever offered her child with
loving tenderness—that same loyalty I find here most constantly in
you, I who am bereft of joy. You have freed me of an exile's misery.
I thank your womanly kindness for it. (115)

'Your counsel, your solace, your favour, all these I need, now that,
keening for my beloved, I suffer sorrow, much tormenting distress. It
is unavoidable. He tortures my wild thoughts and fetters them. All
my mind is bound to him.* (116)

'I have entirely wasted all my gazing, many evenings, looking out of
the windows over the heath, onto the road and towards the bright
meadows. He comes to me too seldom. For this my eyes must pay
dearly with weeping for love of my lover. (117)

'Then I walk away from the window to the turret. There I look east and west, to see if I can catch sight of him who has long oppressed my heart. I may well be numbered with the old languishers, not the young. (118)

'I sail a while upon a wave. There I peer far, thirty miles and more, to hear such tidings as might rid me of anxiety on behalf of my young, radiant beloved. (119)

'Where has my gambolling joy gone, or how have high spirits thus departed from my heart? An "Alas!" must follow us both now, which I alone would gladly suffer in his stead. I know well that languishing sorrow will hunt him back to me, though he knows how to shun me. (120)

'Alas, his arrival is all too rare for me, he for whom I often grow cold—and then it is as if I lay in a sparkling fire, so Schionatulander beglows me! His love gives me heat, as Agremuntin does the serpent salamander.'* (121)

'Alas,' said the queen. 'You speak as do the wise. Who has led my Sigune astray? Now I fear the Frenchmen's Queen Ampflise has avenged her anger upon me.* All your words of wisdom are spoken out of her mouth. (122)

'Schionatulander is a high and powerful prince. His nobility, his chastity would never dare such hazards as that his youth should ask for your love, if proud Ampflise's hatred were not avenging itself upon me, in its hostility. (123)

'She reared that child after it was taken from the breast. If it was not with deceptive intent that she gave the advice which has moved you so ungently, then you may procure much joy for him, and he for you. If you're fond of him, then do not let your perfect beauty perish! (124)

'Do him this honour, let your eyes, your cheeks, your chin regain their lustre! How does it become such youthful years, if such a bright complexion is extinguished? You have mixed far too much sorrow with fleeting joys. (125)

'If it is the young Dauphin who has deprived you of joys, he may well enrich you in joys yet. Many blessings and love have been bequeathed to him by his father and the Dauphinette, Mahaute, who was his mother, and the queen, his aunt, Schoette. (126)

'I only lament that you are his *âmie* all too early. You would inherit the sorrow that Mahaute suffered because of the Dauphin Gurzgri.

Often her eyes found him winning fame in many lands beneath
buckled helmet. (127)

'Schionatulander is bound to rise in fame. He is born of such people
as do not let their fame sink down. For them it grew broad and
stretched out long. Now hold hopeful joy out to him, and may he
cast no cares upon you! (128)

'No matter how much your heart smiles in your breast on his
account, I do not wonder at it! How becomingly he can move
beneath shieldly cover! Down on him many tears shall be shed, of
sparks leaping from helmets as sword-blades strike, where fiery rain
gathers thick. (129)

'He is designed for the joust. Who could have thus measured him?
In a man's countenance, to find womanly favour, never was less
neglected in a mother's fruit, as I judge. His radiance shall sweeten
your eyes. In the hope of reward, I shall tell him of your love for
him.' (130)

There and then love was permitted, locked by love. Intent on love
without deviation, both their hearts were unstinting of love. 'Happy
am I, aunt,' said the duchess, 'that I thus love the Graharzois now,
with consent, before all the world!' (131)

FRAGMENT II

[Sigune and Schionatulander, with attendants, are encamped in the
forest. They have, perhaps, been awakened from a siesta.]

They did not lie thus encamped there long. Suddenly they heard, in
a high sweet voice, in red-hued pursuit of a wounded beast, a berce-
let barking,* coming on the hunt towards them. It was detained for a
while. For my friends' sake I still grieve over this.* (132)

When they heard the forest resounding with such clamour—
Schionatulander had been known since childhood to excel the
swift—except for Trevrizent the pure he outran and outleapt all who
exercised knights' legs— (133)

Now he thought: 'If anyone can catch up with that hound, let him
have knightly legs!' He desires to sell his joy and receive constant
sorrow in return. Up he leapt in pursuit of the bark, intent on
outpacing the bercelet. (134)

Since the fleeing game could not turn into the wide wood, but could
only run past the Dauphin, his hardship will be increased, bringing
future sadness to his share. Now he hid himself in a thick bush.
Along there came, hunting, dragging the leash,   (135)
the bercelet of the prince, from whose hand it had escaped, down
after the arrow-cut traces. May she never again send forth a hound,
she who sent it to that great-spirited knight, from whom it raced
until it reached the proud Graharzois, afterwards depriving him of
many joys!   (136)
When the hound thus broke through the thicket, pursuing the trail,
its collar was of Arabian braid, very tightly woven by the loom; on it
could be seen precious and bright gems, which glittered through the
forest like the sun. There he caught not only the bercelet—   (137)
What he seized along with the bercelet, let it be told to you: grief
lined with hardship he had to learn, undaunted, and forever more
great striving in pursuit of battle. The bercelet's leash was truly a
source of joy-losing times for him.   (138)
He carried the hound in his arms to the lustrous Sigune. The leash
was a good twelve fathoms long, the braid-silk of four colours:
yellow, green, red—brown the fourth—wherever one span ceased,
ornamentally wrought together.   (139)
Over these joins lay rings brightened by pearls; between the rings in
each space, a good span's length, not diminished by gems, four
leaves, in four colours, perhaps a finger's breadth. If I ever catch a
hound on such a leash, the leash will stay with me, even if I let
the hound go!   (140)
When this was unfolded from between the rings, script could be
perceived on it, on the outside and the inside, of precious material.
Hear adventure now, if you command it! By golden nails the gems
were riveted to the cord.   (141)
The letters were of emerald, mingled with rubies. There were
diamonds, chrysolites, and garnets. Never was a leash better
hounded, and indeed the hound was very well leashed. You may well
guess which I would choose, if the hound were the alternative
choice!   (142)
Upon samite, green as in the May-time wood, the collar was a
stitched braid, many gems of various kinds fixed upon it. The script
was as a lady had instructed. Gardeviaz was the hound's name. That
means in German: 'Keep on the trail!'*   (143)

Duchess Sigu.ne read the beginning of the tales: 'Although this is a bercelet's name, these words befit noble people. Men and women alike, may they keep fairly to the trail! They will enjoy favour in this world here, and in the next bliss will be their reward.' (144)

She read more on the collar, not as yet what was on the leash: 'If a man can keep well to the trail, his fame will never be sold cheap. It will live so strengthened in a pure heart that no eye will ever ignore it in the inconstant, fluctuating market-place.' (145)

The bercelet and the leash had been sent to a prince out of love. She was of lineage a young queen beneath a crown. Sigu.ne read the account on the leash of who the queen was, and also the prince. The identity of both was proclaimed there. (146)

She was born of Kanadic, the sister of Florie, who gave to Ilinot the Briton her heart, her thoughts and her person as an *âmîe*, all that she had, except for lying together. She reared him from childhood until he went on a shieldly journey, and chose him above all gains. (147)

In pursuit of her love he, for his part, met his end beneath the helmet. If I were not to break with courtesy, I would still curse the hand that delivered the joust which caused his death! Florie died by the same joust, although she never neared a spear's tip. (148)

She left behind one sister, who inherited her crown. Clauditte was that maiden's name. Chastity and her grace earned her the stranger's praise, as well as that of him who knew her. Thus her fame was acclaimed in many lands, no-one hindering it. (149)

The duchess read about this maiden on the leash: the princes of her realm desired a lord for her, to be appointed by tribunal. She summoned a court at Beaufremont.* To it came rich and poor unnumbered. They decreed that she should make her choice at once. (150)

She had borne *duc* Ehkunat de Salvasch Florie in her heart before then. She had, indeed, chosen him as her *âmîs*. At that his heart stood higher than her crown. Ehkunat aspired to the goal of all princes, for he kept to his trail most splendidly! (151)

She was compelled by his youth, as by the law of her realm. Since she had been assigned the choice, the maiden did now choose worthily. Would you like to know her beloved's name in German? Duke Ehcunaver of the Wild Bloom—thus I heard him named. (152)

Since he took his name from the wilderness, into the wilderness she sent him this wildish letter, the bercelet, who kept to the trail in

forest and field, as he ought to by nature. Moreover, the leash's script
averred that she herself desired to keep to the womanly trail.   (153)
Schionatulander, with a feathered bait, was catching perch and gray-
ling, while she was reading—and catching, also, such loss of joy that
he was very seldom merry thereafter. The duchess loosed the knot,
in order to read the rest of the inscription on the leash.   (154)
It was firmly tied to the tent-pole. It troubles me that she loosened
the knot. Oh, if she had only desisted! Gardeviaz strained and strug-
gled before the duchess could speak and order food for him. It was
her intention to give him something to eat.   (155)
Two damsels leapt out past the tent-ropes. I grieve for the duchess's
white, soft hands, if the leash is to lacerate them! What can I do
about it? It was rough with jewels. Gardeviaz tugged and leapt to
hasten after the hound-game's trail.   (156)
It had run away from Ehkunat in the same way that day. She called
out to the damsels. They had found food for the bercelet. They
scampered quickly back into the pavilion, but the hound had
slipped out through the tent-wall. Soon he could be heard in the
forest.   (157)
He had simply torn some of the pegs out of the tent-wall. When he
got back on to the fresh, red trail he made no secret of it, but hunted
quite openly, without stealth. In consequence, it befell noble
Gurzgri's son to suffer much extremity thereafter.   (158)
Schionatulander was catching large and small fish with his rod,
standing there on his bare, white legs to enjoy the coolness in the
clear-swift brook. Now he heard Gardeviaz's bark, resounding to
bring him hardship.   (159)
He threw the rod from his hand. With speed he hastened over fallen
tree-trunks, and through briars too, but despite this could not get
anywhere near the bercelet. Unpathed ground had so far removed
the hound that he could find no trace anywhere of the game, nor of
the hound, and his hearing was misled by the wind.   (160)
His bare legs were scratched all over by the brambles. His white feet
met with their share of wounds, too, from running through the
thorns. His wounds were more apparent than those of the speared
beast. He ordered that they be washed before he entered the tent.
Thus he found Sigune there: (161)
The palms of her hands were grey, as if hoar-frosted, like a jouster's
hands whose shaft slips in the counter-charge, scraping, grazing the

bare skin. In just that way the leash had run through the duchess's
hands.   (162)

She marked the many wounds on his legs and feet. She grieved for
him; he also grieved for her. Now this tale will turn sour, as the
duchess began to lay her claim to the inscription on the leash. That
loss must break many lances now.   (163)

He said: 'I have never heard much about superscribed leashes. I am
well acquainted with letter-books *en franzoys*.* Such skill I do not
lack—I can read all that may be written in those. Sigune, sweet
maiden, pay no heed at all to the inscription on the leash!'   (164)

She said: 'There was adventure written on the rope. If I am not to
read that to its end, then I care nothing for my land of Katelangen.
All the wealth anyone might offer me—even if I were worthy of
accepting it—I would rather possess that writing.   (165)

'In saying this, noble beloved, I do not seek to harm you, nor anyone
else. If we two, young as we are, were to live into the time of our
future years, your service still desiring my love, then you would first
have to procure for me the leash to which Gardeviaz stood tethered
here.'   (166)

He said: 'Then I shall willingly seek the leash on those terms. If it is
to be won by battle, then either I and my fame must perish, or I shall
bring it back to your hands. Be gracious, sweet maiden, and do not
hold my heart so long in your fetters!'   (167)

'Favour and all that a maiden ever ought to fulfil for her noble,
radiant beloved, I shall grant, and no-one can avert me from this
intent, if your intent strives for the rope that the hound which you
brought captive to me dragged on the trail.'   (168)

'To that end my service shall ever constantly strive. You offer rich
reward. How am I to live until such time as when my hand may bring
about the securing of your favour? That will be attempted, near and
far! May Fortune and your love rule over me!'   (169)

Thus they had recompensed one another with words, and with good
will. The beginning of many troubles—how was it ended? That the
young fool, and the greybeard too, will hear from the daunted
pledge-bearer*—whether he swims or sinks in fame.   (170)

EXPLANATORY NOTES

4 *adventure*: 'adventure' has three meanings in *Parzival*: 'adventure' in the sense of 'story, tale', as here and in Book IX, personified as 'Lady Adventure'; 'adventure' in the more common English sense, as in 'to ride in pursuit of adventure'; it can also mean 'chance' or 'hazard'.

5 *chaste*: a keyword in *Parzival*, applied particularly to the Grail family. Its meaning extends to monogamous fidelity.

6 *Gylstram . . . Ranculat*: *Gylstram* has not conclusively been identified, but it must refer to somewhere in the extreme West. In the Middle High German (MHG) epic *Kudrun* 'the sun's shine set, hidden behind the clouds, far off in Gustrate'; the places are presumably identical. *Ranculat* is Hromgla on the Euphrates, in the extreme East.

Fil li roy Gandin: Old French (O.Fr.): 'son of king Gandin'.

7 *samite*: a rich silk fabric, sometimes interwoven with gold, or a garment of the same.

8 *Baldac*: Baghdad, the seat of the Caliph.

Baruch: a Hebrew word in origin, meaning 'the Blessed One'.

caparison: the horse's (generally ornamental) covering.

achmardi: a green, silk fabric of Arab origin. The etymology has not been satisfactorily explained.

10 *burgrave*: the governor of a city or castle.

11 *messenger's reward*: it is a commonplace in medieval literature that the messenger is given 'messenger's bread'. In the *Nibelungenlied* this practice extends even to personages of high rank, such as Siegfried on his return from Iceland to Worms.

15 *tokens*: these are favours that have been presented to Hiuteger by ladies; they may have taken the form of precious stones.

heron: the stuffed (hence erect) heron was a delicacy in the Middle Ages. The heron and the fish refer both to the food at the table, and to the incipient relationship between Gahmuret and Belacane.

16 *knelt down*: the meal is being served at a low trestle table. Belacane, out of courtesy, is taking on a servant's part.

18 *into the city*: Hiuteger and Gaschier, the two leaders of the Scottish party, are now hostages, so Gahmuret is, in effect, ordering their men to cease attacking.

aunt's son: Kaylet is the son of an (unnamed) sister of Gahmuret's mother Schoette.

bells made music: knights often had small bells sewn to their clothes, the noise lending emphasis to their movements.

Beacurs: modern French *beau corps*. Beacurs is brother to Gawan and nephew of King Arthur. In Malory's *Le Morte Darthur* Gareth, son of King Lot, is called Beaumains by Kay.

19 *by the sea*: the white, Christian armies have been defeated, so Gahmuret now tackles the heathens.

ostrich: the ostrich was famed for its digestion: 'whose greedy stomach steely gads digests' (Guillaume de Saluste du Bartas, trans. Joshua Sylvester (1592–1609)).

20 *Lachfilirost*: the belated naming of the burgrave is typical of the medieval romance.

Schahtelacunt: O.Fr.: 'the count of the castle'.

ventail: (O.Fr. *ventaille*) a mail flap attached to the coif or hood, which could be fastened across the mouth.

21 *who holds him captive here*: Gahmuret is jokingly referring to himself.

bêâ kunt: O.Fr.: 'handsome count'.

22 *Morholt . . . strength and cunning*: in Gottfried's *Tristan*, Morolt of Ireland, Isolde's uncle, fights with and is slain by Tristan; 'strength and cunning' is a word-for-word quotation from *Tristan*.

deal with you differently now: these words might have been accompanied by a gesture, such as a clap on the back.

sarapandratest: probably from O.Fr. *teste de serpent*, 'serpent's head'.

23 *fold my hands in his*: the legal gesture of subservience, which would be accompanied by kneeling.

25 *Famurgan . . . Terdelaschoye*: Wolfram mischievously inverts place name and personal name here. Famurgan is Morgan the Fay, Terdelaschoye the land of joy. Both were familiar to him from Hartmann von Aue's *Erec*.

turtle-dove: Cf. the English folk song: 'Oh don't you see yon little turtle-dove, | Sitting over the mulberry tree, | And a-making mourn for his true love, | As I do mourn for thee, my dear, | As I do mourn for thee.'

26 *the adamant . . . leg-guards*: Hiuteger had vowed to send Isenhart's equipment to Gahmuret.

Waleis: Wales, or Gaul, or Valois. Wolfram's Arthurian geography defies definition.

28 *Leoplan*: perhaps from O.Fr. *lee plaine*, 'broad meadow'.

29 *Lot of Norway*: in Geoffrey of Monmouth's *History of the Kings of Britain*, Loth of Lodonesia becomes king of Norway. He marries King Uther Pendragon's daughter Anna, and has by her two children, Gawain and Mordred.

quartered out in the field: the opposing camp, the outer army, is composed of the older generation, the fathers and uncles of knights who will play a prominent role later in the romance.

29 *Morholt of Ireland*: in Gottfried's *Tristan*, Morolt is similarly renowned
    for taking hostages.

30 *Gurnemanz de Graharz*: uncle of Condwiramurs, Gurnemanz instructs
    Parzival in knighthood in Book III.

    vesper tournament: the unofficial fighting on the eve of the tournament
    proper.

31 *desired other pledges*: these are probably knights errant with mercenary
    intent.

    Caucasus mountain: like much of Wolfram's geography, this probably
    derives from the *Collectanea Rerum Memorabilium* or *Polyhistor* of the
    third-century geographer Caius Julius Solinus.

    wore the cross: literally: 'crossed knights'. Templars had worn the cross
    since 1119.

32 *Riwalin*: father of Tristan in Gottfried von Strassburg's romance.

    Lohneis: in *Tristan* Gottfried refers to an erroneous tradition whereby
    Riwalin is king of Lohnois. The name may derive from Lothian in
    Scotland, or Léon in north-west Brittany. Characteristically, Wolfram
    sides with the tradition rejected by Gottfried. In later sources, this
    becomes the legendary land of Lyonesse.

    stole a knight from them: i.e. from the inner party, that of the city.

    Lac: father of Erec in the romances of Chrétien de Troyes and Hartmann
    von Aue. He is also the father of Jeschute, who will figure in Book III.

    Duke of Brabant: presumably an ancestor of the duchess in the Lohengrin
    story in Book XVI.

    Britain: Brittany may be meant, as Arthurian geography does not
    acknowledge the Channel.

    King of Punturteis: i.e. Brandelidelin, uncle of Gramoflanz.

33 *Bien sei venûs, bêâs sir*: O.Fr.: 'Greetings, handsome sir'.

    rêgîn de Franze: O.Fr.: 'Queen of France'.

35 *A noble woman has sent you . . . into this land*: the queen is addressing
    Gahmuret's surcoat.

36 *The tablecloths had been taken away*: Gahmuret and his company have just
    concluded their meal.

38 *Carolingia*: i.e. France.

    sitting under the edge of the queen's robe: this position indicates that
    Herzeloyde is extending special protection to Kaylet, in a similar way,
    perhaps, to that in which suppliants to the Madonna sit under the folds
    of her dress. If Gahmuret accepts Ampflise's offer, Kaylet's position, his
    hope of liberty, will be endangered.

39 *overlooking the injury out of fear*: Hardiz's lines are obscure, as is the
    situation underlying the antagonism.

tethered me down: the image is that of a horse whose head is tethered back to prevent it eating.

40 *fole*: O.Fr.: 'mad, foolish'. The reference may be to Queen Annore, although conceivably Fole is a proper name, and Galoes died for the love of two different queens. There is a family tradition of adultery here.

41 *good breeding*: it was customary for a knight to be educated at a foreign court, often by a lady of high rank.

42 *faërie lineage*: Gahmuret's great-great-grandmother is Terdelaschoye of Famurgan (Morgan the Fay).

44 *travelling people*: these would include minstrels, customary recipients of generosity in medieval literature.

45 *he-goat's blood*: in T. H. White's translation of *The Book of Beasts*, a twelfth-century bestiary, we read: 'The nature of goats is so extremely hot that a stone of adamant, which neither fire nor iron implement can alter, is dissolved merely by the blood of one of these creatures.'

46 *âvoy*: O.Fr.: 'oh!' or 'ah!'.

ruby, through which he shone: the ruby is presumably a stone through which Gahmuret's corpse can be seen.

47 *eighteen weeks*: the eighteenth week of pregnancy was regarded as the beginning of a child's life.

48 *pizzle*: this noun, like those denoting parts of the body in the following breast-feeding scene, is unique to Wolfram.

'Bon fîz, scher fîz, bêâ fîz': O.Fr.: 'Good son, dear son, handsome son'.

49 *Wolfram's Self-Defence*: this excursus between Books II and III is primarily concerned with Wolfram's role as lyric poet, and the conduct of courtly love. It is rich in literary allusions.

spavin: a tumour in a horse's leg.

for the sake of his own lady alone: praise of one lady to the exclusion of all others is a common topos in the medieval German lyric (*Minnesang*). The chess imagery here echoes a song by Reinmar der Alte, and a riposte by Walther von der Vogelweide, both contemporaries of Wolfram.

50 *I don't know a single letter of the alphabet*: this passage has given rise to much debate concerning Wolfram's literacy.

bundle of twigs: such bundles serve as fig-leaves in medieval illustrations of bathing scenes.

poverty serves no useful function: these deliberations may have been influenced by religious movements such as the Franciscans, which embraced poverty. There is an echo of the Sermon on the Mount (Luke 6: 20).

Waste of Soltane: derived from Chrétien's *gaste forest*. *Soltane* may be modelled on O.Fr. *soltain*, 'solitary'.

looking for flowers on the meadow: Wolfram is referring to the plucking of the flower, *deflorare*, the central motif of the *pastourelle*, a lyric genre depicting an amorous encounter in a rural setting.

50 *garland*: in a *pastourelle* by Wolfram's contemporary, Walther von der Vogelweide, the lover offers a garland to his beloved.

51 *doubt's deviation*: the key word 'doubt', announced in the first line of *Parzival*, recurs here.

52 *javelin*: a short hunting-spear is meant; several fit into a quiver.

uncut-up: an allusion to Gottfried's *Tristan*. The young Tristan, in contrast to Parzival, is an expert in the dissection of game.

Ieh cons Ulterlec: O.Fr.: 'the count Ulterlec' (beyond the lake). The name Karnahkarnanz may be a conflation of the Celtic place names Carnac (Morbihan) and Karnant, familiar from Hartmann's *Erec*.

53 *knight God*: the manuscripts diverge here. The Munich (G) branch have 'good knight', but the more blasphemous reading of the D (St Gall) branch, 'ritter got', seems preferable.

54 *Meljahkanz*: the arch-rapist in Arthurian romance. He occurs in Chrétien's *Lancelot*, and also in Hartmann's *Iwein*, as the abductor of Guinevere.

Imane . . . Beafontane: variants on the name Imane occur in the families of Brabant Loos, and Chiny. In the vicinity of Chiny (in the Belgian department of Luxembourg) there are two places called Bellefontaine. Wolfram shows interest in Brabant in Book XVI, in the Lohengrin story.

55 *high spirits*: a central, but problematic concept in the ethos of courtly love. The meaning ranges from 'exaltation' to the moral quality of 'an elevated mind'.

Waleis and Norgals: if *Waleis* is Wales, then *Norgals* is presumably North Wales. The Welsh connection suggests strongly that Lähelin derives from Llywelyn. It is uncertain whether Wolfram has in mind Llywelyn ap Seisyll, the eleventh-century king of South Wales, or Llywelyn ab Iorweth (Llywelyn the Great), Welsh antagonist of the Angevins in the late twelfth and early thirteenth centuries, but the latter seems more likely.

Broceliande: the forest in Brittany associated with Merlin, familiar to Wolfram's audience from Hartmann von Aue's *Iwein*. It occurs in Chrétien's *Yvain*, though not in his *Perceval*.

57 *where his hostess sat*: medieval etiquette required the hostess to determine where her guest sat.

Her shame started to sweat: MHG *scham* means 'sense of shame, modesty', but Wolfram is here punning on its other meaning, 'pudendum'. Cf. James Joyce, *Ulysses*: 'And with loving pencil you shaded my eyes, my bosom and my shame.'

âmîs: a loan word from O.Fr., meaning 'lover, suitor', frequently used by Wolfram.

Erec . . . fil li roy Lac: Wolfram here borrows the name and by-name of the hero of Hartmann von Aue's *Erec*, creating a whole new nexus of relationships.

Prurin: in Hartmann's *Erec*, to celebrate the marriage of Erec and Enite, a tournament is held 'between Tarebron and Prurin' in Brittany. Orilus's name, reflecting his pride, derives from Hartmann's source, Chrétien de Troyes, where *li orgueuillus de la lande* ('the proud man of the land') is unhorsed by Erec. Typically, Wolfram coins a proper name from the O.Fr. epithet.

58 *Plihopliheri*: the name probably derives from Hartmann's *Erec*. A knight called Bliobleherin sits at the Round Table there.

Table Round: the motif of the Round Table enters the Arthurian tradition in Wace's Anglo–Norman *Roman de Brut* (*c.*1155).

the sparrowhawk at Kanedic: Wolfram here combines a major motif in Hartmann's *Erec*, the tournament whose prize is a sparrowhawk, with another name taken from the list of knights seated at the Round Table in the same romance: 'the king's son of Ganedic'.

Cunneware: an etymological interpretation would suggest that the meaning is something like 'knowledge true'.

by my joust he lay dead: the slain knight is Schionatulander, the betrothed of Parzival's cousin, Sigune.

59 *Sigune*: an anagrammatic formation from O.Fr. *cosine*.

Schionatulander: probably also anagrammatic in origin. The first element is based on O.Fr. *juene* (young); *atulander* is a loose anagram of *tavulander* (table round).

60 *Bon fîz, scher fîz, bêâ fîz*: see note to p. 48.

straight down the middle: the etymology is obscure. Perhaps from O.Fr. *perce a val*, 'traverse'.

your mother is my aunt: Sigune's mother is Schoysiane, sister of Herzeloyde. In *Titurel* Sigune's upbringing in Herzeloyde's country is described, which would explain her knowledge of Parzival's nicknames.

your father's brother: i.e. Galoes.

bercelet: a small hound, probably of the spaniel family. The pursuit of the hound is the subject of the second *Titurel* fragment.

61 *Hartmann von Aue*: the allusions which follow are to Hartmann's *Erec*. Enite is the heroine of the romance.

62 *Curvenal*: the tutor of Tristan in Gottfried von Strassburg's romance.

reddened . . . leaded: technical terms of the swordsmith's trade. 'Leading' may refer to tempering steel in a lead bath; 'reddening' may be the hardening process generally termed 'browning'.

63 *goblet . . . upturned torches*: the seizing of a goblet and the upturning of torches are both acts symbolizing territorial claims.

64 *bustard*: the Little Bustard (*tetrax tetrax*), in an antagonistic display, beats

its feet on the ground 7–10 times in 2.5 seconds. Its chief breeding ground until the early twentieth century was in the area around Erfurt, the seat of Wolfram's probable patron, Hermann of Thuringia.

65 *without a bar*: the bar stretched across all the planks of the medieval door, holding them together.

staff: in medieval law a judge's staff is held up and hands are laid upon it to take the oath.

captive net: perhaps a hairnet is meant.

Antanor: Wolfram borrows the name from Heinrich von Veldeke's *Eneide*, but it is an ironic borrowing, for Veldeke's character is dubbed 'the wise Anthenor'.

66 *My greeting shall be refused you*: this amounts to a formal declaration of enmity, as in war.

turned his shaft round: Ither is deliberately using the blunt end of his spear to avoid killing Parzival.

68 *monstrance*: the vessel containing the consecrated Host.

scraped from his parchment: scraping with a knife was a common way of erasing writing.

69 *Gurnemanz de Graharz*: the name derives from the list of knights in Hartmann's *Erec*.

70 *knight*: etymologically, MHG *ritter* means 'rider'; in the twelfth century it came to mean 'knight'. English 'cavalier' has gone through a similar semantic change. Parzival takes the word literally—he has to remain a rider.

72 *scarlet*: a fine woollen material, which may be dyed red, but also other colours.

74 *rink*: the area of ground designated for combat.

75 *four nails*: the four nails holding the opponent's shield-boss are the ideal target of the jouster.

76 *Schenteflurs*: the name derives from O.Fr. *gent flurs*, 'gentle blossom'.

Condwiramurs: another name derived from O.Fr., combining the verb meaning 'to guide, lead' with the word for 'love'. In the manuscripts the name is often written as two words: *Cundwir amurs*.

Ehkunat: the brother of Schoette, wife to Gandin, and therefore Parzival's maternal great-uncle.

Schoydelakurt: a reference to Erec's final adventure in Hartmann von Aue's romance.

fallen sadly on the four: one of the dice-playing metaphors so beloved of Wolfram.

78 *vile archers*: knights entertained a prejudice against wielders of long-distance weapons.

79 *Trühendingen . . . doughnuts*: the castle of Hohentrüdingen lies about twenty miles south of Wolframs-Eschenbach. Doughnuts can still be bought in nearby Wassertrüdingen. Friedrich von Truhendingen appears as a witness in documents dating from 1192 and 1213, together with Graf Poppo von Wertheim, who may have been one of Wolfram's patrons.

80 *Kyot of Katelangen*: father of Sigune, brother-in-law to Herzeloyde.

Enite: the heroine of Hartmann's *Erec*.

Isaldes: the spelling is that employed by Eilhart von Oberge in the earliest German version of the Tristan legend, but there can be no doubt that Wolfram is again cocking a snook at Gottfried von Strassburg's *Tristan*, in which the two Isoldes are Isolde the Fair (of Ireland) and Isolde White Hands (of Arundel).

82 *overstuffed*: falcons whose crops are too full have no desire to hunt.

84 *Iserterre*: Clamide is later described as king of this obscure country.

86 *put up her hair*: Condwiramurs is donning the headdress of the married woman.

87 *Galogandres . . . Gippones*: Galogandres derives from the list of knights in Hartmann's *Erec*; the place name is obscure.

Ukerlant: the land on the banks of the river Uecker, which flows into the Baltic at Ueckermünde.

heathen wild fire: Greek fire, the most effective combustible in siege warfare, its ingredients kept a close secret.

hedgehogs . . . cats: hedgehogs are iron-studded battering rams; cats are protective roofs on wheels to cover mining or battering operations.

88 *gussets*: projecting, wedge-shaped pieces of armour.

89 *Grigorz*: the name is perhaps derived from Grigoras in Hartmann's *Erec*.

90 *uncut*: the spear may be 'uncut' in the sense that it is made from an intact branch, or because it has not yet been cut by an opposing weapon.

92 *Löver*: in French sources King Arthur's land is called Logres. The word may be of Celtic origin, 'Lloegr' being the Welsh word for England.

Dianazdrun: in Chrétien *Dinasdaron*. The first element, *Dinas*, is common in Welsh place names, and means 'hill-fort'.

Spessart: the central forest of Germany, etymologically 'the woodpecker's forest'.

special devices: presumably these are knights or princes independent of Arthur.

93 *Pilate of Poncia*: Pontius is thought to indicate Pilate's descent from the family of the Pontii, but in the Middle Ages the name was sometimes interpreted as a place name.

Mabonagrin: Erec's adversary in the final battle in Hartmann's *Erec*.

95 *in this fashion either*: i.e. without a book's guidance. Wolfram is again stressing his independence of book-learning.

96 *bowed to his hand*: the gesture is ambivalent. Parzival is insisting that he expressed his thanks, and denying any suggestion that he adopted an attitude of surrender.

bohorts: mounted charges carried out in teams.

Abenberg: the fortress of Abenberg, east of Wolframs-Eschenbach, still preserves a tilting-yard.

97 *lignum aloe*: Latin *lignum* combined with Greek *aloe*, 'wood of the aloe', a fragrant plant thought to possess healing powers. Wolfram playfully confuses the fire and the firewood.

Wildenberg: an exact German equivalent of 'Munsalvæsche', this is the name of a number of castles, among them a picturesque ruin with a medieval fireplace, on top of a high hill near Wolframs-Eschenbach.

98 *headdress*: being virgins, they have not yet tied up their hair (like Condwiramurs on her marriage).

99 *four-times-two*: Wolfram is playing with numbers, as he later makes clear.

100 *took water*: it was the practice to wash hands before a meal, and often afterwards, too.

101 *verjuice*: verjuice is made from green or unripe grapes, or other sour fruit, reduced by boiling. It descends from the Roman sauce *defrutum*.

sinople: a rare word for a rare drink, a red-coloured wine named after the dye sinopis.

103 *bright hue*: i.e. Parzival's skin, of which they manage to catch a glimpse.

clary: a mixture of wine, clarified honey, and spices.

of Paradise's kind: in Paradise, located in the Orient, figs and pomegranates grow.

105 *eyes*: Wolfram here puns on the eyes of the man and the 'eyes' of the dice.

lime-tree: traditionally the tree of love because of its heart-shaped leaves. Sigune's lime-tree is commemorated by the huge 'Wolframslinde' near Burg Haidstein (Kötzting), which claims to be the oldest lime-tree in Germany. It was given its name *c.*1880.

106 *Munsalvæsche*: 'Mount of Salvation', or perhaps 'wild mountain'. Wolfram is aware of both possible meanings, having already referred to the fires at Wildenberg, a German equivalent.

royâm: O.Fr. *roiame*, 'realm', a borrowing only attested here.

Titurel: the name occurs in Hartmann's *Erec*, in the list of the knights of the Round Table.

neither ride nor walk: Anfortas has been stricken in the member with which he has sinned.

107 *Lady Lunete's counsel*: in Hartmann's *Iwein*, as in Chrétien's *Yvain*, the maid Lunete persuades her mistress, Laudine, to marry her husband's killer.

Trebuchet: the name of the smith in Chrétien, and in two continuations of *Perceval*.

Lac: the father of Erec in Chrétien's and Hartmann's romances.

109 *exposed side*: the exposed side of a knight in the joust is the side unprotected by his shield, but the word *blôz* also means 'naked'.

common . . . come off: Wolfram's worst (or best) bilingual pun. The word translated as *common* is MHG *vilan* (from O.Fr. *vilain*), meaning a peasant, but Wolfram also expects of his audience the word-division *vil-an* ('much on'). A more literal translation: 'If anyone were to call her *vilan*, he would be doing her an injustice, for she had little on her.'

breastlets: Wolfram's use of the erotic diminutive suffix so offended one medieval scribe that he erased this word throughout the manuscript.

110 *Tenabroc . . . Bealzenan*: perhaps Wolfram is drawing here upon Hartmann's *Erec*, in which there is a king 'Beals von Gomoret'. If 'Gomoret' suggested Gahmuret, then the king's name may have inspired the name for Gahmuret's capital. Moreover, 'Tenabroc' may derive from *Erec*. Wolfram may well have had a manuscript of *Erec* before him.

Brumbane de Salvâsche ah muntâne: Brumbane is the lake in which Anfortas angles; an O.Fr. paraphrase of Munsalvæsche follows.

free of loyalty's claims: Parzival and Orilus attack without any declaration of hostilities, but there is no breach of faith. Wolfram here deviates from Chrétien, whose Haughty Knight explains the reasons for his attack before the joust.

111 *not on foot*: Wolfram is emphasizing the skill with which the knights employ their swords on horseback. More commonly, the initial stage of the joust was followed by swordplay on foot.

greeting: ambiguous here, referring both to the greeting that Orilus denies his wife, and the more erotic greeting which Parzival had given her.

112 *two lands*: the irony is that the two lands, Waleis and Norgals, are Parzival's inheritance.

114 *herald's cry*: heralds were given torn, discarded clothing as rewards in tournaments.

Lämbekin: he occurs twice in Book II as the Duke of Brabant, married to Alize, sister of Hardiz. Otherwise, the allusion is obscure.

jûven poys: O.Fr.: 'young wood'. Orilus appears to be admitting by metaphor that his punishment of his wife was an act of youthful folly.

Troyes: twice this spear is traced to Troyes. The motif is absent in Chrétien. Wolfram only names *von Troys meister Cristjân* in the epilogue. Perhaps this is an oblique reference to his source.

Taurian: in Book IX Trevrizent refers to Taurian as his friend. Otherwise, he is unknown.

114 *Dodines*: a knight of the Round Table who occurs elsewhere in Arthurian romance, for example in Hartmann's *Iwein*, as one who is unhorsed.

115 *scales . . . dice*: Wolfram characteristically mixes two favourite sources of metaphor here.

117 *apple*: the apple is a round knob on the top of the tent.

118 *Karidœl*: an Arthurian residence in Hartmann and Chrétien. The name may derive from Caer-Luel (Carlisle).

119 *stood that night*: falcons, like most land birds, sleep in the standing position.

With a charge: a phrase generally associated with the joust.

bêâ curs: O.Fr.: 'beautiful body'.

two red drops . . . chin: the three red dots occur frequently in medieval book illustration.

120 *His lady, too, was loose*: this unexpected criticism of Cunneware has puzzled all commentators. It seems unlikely that this is an obscene, punning allusion to her name, though this has been suggested.

121 *ulter juven poys*: O.Fr: 'through the young wood'. In Book V, Orilus similarly rode astray.

flee from her solace: the threat to desert the lady who denies her lover hope is a topos in *Minnesang*, particularly in the lyrics of Walther von der Vogelweide.

123 *riddled with holes*: the allusion is to a shield pierced by spears.

eyes' edges: a reference to the 'eyes' of the dice.

Heinrich von Veldeke: in Veldeke's *Eneide*, a twelfth-century version of Virgil's *Aeneid* commissioned by Hermann von Thüringen, a tree is substituted for the cave in which Dido and Aeneas consummate their love. Wolfram's love discourse belongs to a tradition of which Veldeke was the first German exponent, as was pointed out by Gottfried von Strassburg in the 'literary excursus' in *Tristan*, which employs the same tree imagery.

124 *Kardeiz*: named here and in *Titurel* as Condwiramurs's brother; the name derives from the list of knights in Hartmann's *Erec*.

lopping: another echo of Veldeke's tree-imagery.

bercelet's leash: this may refer to a medieval form of legal punishment, similar to that meted out to Urjans the rapist in Book X. The phrase also points forward to the central motif of the second *Titurel* fragment.

idleness: presumably a periphrastic reference to a lazy donkey.

125 *put up with himself*: i.e. the blow Kay struck before the joust.

watcher: these spies figure frequently in love lyrics, denouncing and impeding love relationships.

Hermann of Thuringia: Landgrave Hermann I (d. 1217) was probably at some point Wolfram's patron. Walther von der Vogelweide also performed at his court.

'*Good day, base and worthy alike!*': this is generally thought to refer to a lost song by Walther von der Vogelweide. However, medieval quotation was not an exact science, and the reference may be to a song that begins: 'If a man is sick of the earache', in which Walther criticizes the noisy, drunken crowds at the Thuringian court, and refers, like Wolfram, to the jostling crowds there.

126 *Heinrich of Rispach*: Heinrich von Rispach has not been identified. *Rispach* may be Reisbach an der Vils (Lower Bavaria, east of Landshut), which has the remains of a Romanesque church.

127 *Uncounted kinship*: immediate descent, not counted by degrees—i.e. Parzival's parents.

pierced his hand with the knife: the episode outlined here is not attested elsewhere.

128 *It's you*: at this key moment Parzival switches from the formal *ir* ('you') to the more informal *du* ('thou'). This may be in recognition of the kinship tie between the two, Parzival being Gawan's mother's father's father's brother's son's son's son's son.

forest splintered: Parzival uses a jousting image, that of wooden spears shattered by jousting, to describe the severity of the beating.

130 *Antanor*: the silent knight at Arthur's court in Book III.

131 *Acraton*: Wolfram probably derived the name from Solinus: 'On the toppe of [Mount Athos] was sometime ye Towne acrothon, wherin the Inhabiters liued halfe so long againe as the inhabiters of other places'.

old wife: this pleasantry is lacking in the Munich (G) branch of manuscripts. In Chrétien Arthur is over 60 years old, while Guinevere's age is unspecified.

scrape away: see note to p. 68.

132 *nose-slit and branded*: nostril-slitting and branding were medical procedures intended to cure unhealthy horses.

heathen: presumably Arabic.

dialectic . . . geometry . . . astronomy: three of the seven liberal arts, the medieval curriculum derived from the education of the ancient world.

Surziere: O.Fr.: 'sorceress, magician'.

bêâ schent: O.Fr.: 'beautiful people'.

137 *ohteiz!*: O.Fr.: 'aha!'

141 *Clias the Greek*: the hero of Chrétien's romance *Cligés*.

The Turkoyt: later identified as Florant of Itolac (Book XII). An obscure name, though presumably of Turkish origin.

Itonje . . . Cundrie: these are sisters of Gawan; this Cundrie is not to be confused with Cundrie la Surziere. Perhaps Wolfram would have welcomed such confusion.

141 *Arnive . . . Sangive*: Arthur's mother and sister.

Oraste Gentesin: Oraste possibly derives from Orestae in Solinus. Gentesin may be a corruption of Latin *gentes*, 'peoples'.

Ekuba: wife of Priam, the name probably derived from Veldeke's *Eneide*.

142 *aimed at one woman in particular*: no lyric in which Wolfram is critical of women has survived. Like the 'Self-Defence', this allusion presumes knowledge of his lyric corpus.

linking and breaking them: linking rhymes is the art of creating couplets. Breaking them means splitting them syntactically, so that a new sentence starts midway through a rhyme-pair.

143 *false, deceitful tale*: this obscure opening passage is probably an attack upon other, unnamed authors.

144 *the Sea*: the Mediterranean, 'Outremer'.

146 *lost him by a joust*: this is perhaps meant ironically, as Annore, the beloved of Galoes, lived on to die a natural death.

147 *schahteliur*: O.Fr. *Chasteleur*, 'burgrave'.

fore-flight: a Wolframian image and neologism, from the field of falconry.

doubt: the keyword which links Gawan's fortunes with those of Parzival.

148 *'Byen sey venûz!' . . . 'Gramerzîs!'*: O.Fr.: 'Welcome!' . . . 'Many thanks!'

turcoples: lightly armed soldiers, predominantly archers, known from the crusades.

pillager: a lightly armed youth, below knightly rank, a forager for booty at tournaments.

150 *win a pledge*: taking hostages is what the advisers have in mind.

Scottish and Welsh: 'Scottish' may mean Irish; 'Welsh' may mean French, or even Italian.

151 *trespassing on their sown fields*: an allusion to the custom, recorded in the thirteenth-century *Sachsenspiegel*, whereby any stranger riding across a cultivated field had to pay a forfeit.

never earned a jewelled token from a woman: this probably refers to the discourteous Meljacanz.

hanging from a branch: Kay's discomfiture is described in Hartmann's *Iwein*.

155 *no son*: Wolfram puns on the rhyme-word here. The normal word for 'son' would be *sun*, but *suon* is a short form of *suone* ('reconciliation, appeasement').

tossing rings: a child's game. Mor(r)a, the Italian game in which the number of fingers held up has to be guessed, is one possibility, but rolling rings to predict the future seems more likely, especially in view of

Obilot's preoccupation with her love life: 'Finding a ring of any kind means someone you know very well is going to get married, though I know an old lady who keeps all the rings she finds and she is still a spinster' (Girl, *c*.13, Forfar)—Iona and Peter Opie, *The Lore and Language of Schoolchildren* (Oxford, 1959, repr. 1967).

157 *only the host is left alive*: the expression may be proverbial: 'to the last ditch' would be an alternative translation.

a scant seeding for you two: Gawan's joke implies that many wooden spears will be broken for love of Obilot and Clauditte.

158 *Ethnise*: an Oriental land or town on the banks of the Tigris, near Paradise.

160 *chestnuts*: incisions were made into sweet chestnuts to prevent them bursting when roasted.

Erfurt's vineyard: in the summer of 1203 Hermann of Thuringia besieged the Hohenstaufen king, Philip of Swabia, in Erfurt. Hermann at this point was siding with the Welfs, under Otto IV of Brunswick and Poitou, Richard the Lionheart's favourite nephew.

161 *Leh kuns de Muntane*: O. Fr.: 'the count of the mountain'.

Muntane Cluse: the French-based place name is obscure; MHG *klôse* denotes 'a pass', so the sense may be 'at a mountain pass'.

162 *gampilun*: a winged lizard or 'dragonlet'. The word is probably cognate with 'chameleon'. In Wace's *Brut* Arthur wears the helm of his father, Uther Pendragun, which has a dragon on its crest.

163 *Brevigariez*: the duchy of Lyppaut's brother, Marangliez.

sarjande ad piet: O.Fr.: foot-soldiers, men-at-arms.

Sword Bridge: the Sword Bridge, consisting of a single 'sharp and gleaming sword' across cold waters, is a motif in Chrétien's *Lancelot*. It is beautifully illustrated on the capitals of St-Pierre in Caen.

165 *Ingliart of the Short Ears*: in counterpoint to Gawan's other horse, Gringuljete of the Red Ears.

rims: the 'rim' is *pars pro toto* for the shield.

My lord: i.e. the absent Prince Lyppaut.

166 *both*: i.e. Gawan and Lyppaut.

king's hall: presumably the hall in which Meljanz has taken up residence. The geography and sequence of events is confusing here, and the manuscripts diverge considerably.

167 *two other beardless kings*: the King of Avendroyn and Schirniel of Lyrivoyn.

168 *obtained a gift*: an allusion to gifts presented to travelling minstrels at weddings or other festivities.

169 *Carthage*: in Heinrich von Veldeke's *Eneide*, Carthage possesses seven hundred towers.

169 *Vergulaht . . . Mazadan*: Vergulaht is the son of Kingrisin and Flurda-murs, Gahmuret's sister; he is, therefore, nephew to Gahmuret (and first cousin to Parzival). Mazadan is Gahmuret's great-great-grandfather.

Falcons' charges: the falcons are anthromorphized as jousters.

to the falcons' aid: according to the Emperor Frederick II's manual of falconry, falcons are afraid of water.

170 *Ider fil Noyt*: these highly condensed allusions are to the first cycle of adventures in Hartmann's *Erec*.

grown-up ladies: an allusion to the treatment of Gawan by Obie, rather than little Obilot.

171 *broadly . . . Haidstein*: perhaps an allusion to the girth of the Margravine. The castle of Haidstein lies east of Cham, in Lower Bavaria, off Wolfram's customary track. The Margravine may be Elisabeth von Vohburg, wife of Berthold II, thought to have died before 1199. Her sister Sophie had been married to Landgrave Hermann of Thuringia since 1196.

Antikonie: in Chrétien, typically, the corresponding character has no name. The name derives from the classical Antigone, known to Wolfram perhaps through the O.Fr. *Roman de Thebes* (*c.*1150).

died so early: this is the earliest record of the death of Heinrich von Veldeke.

172 *hiplet*: another instance of Wolfram's delight in the erotic diminutive.

174 *My uncle's son*: Kingrimursel's father was brother to the slain King Kingrisin.

175 *when he was accompanying Gawan*: this obscure episode is only alluded to here. Ehkunat is brother to Mahaute, who married Gurzgri, one of the ill-fated sons of Gurnemanz. Jofreit is a kinsman of Arthur.

176 *Kyot*: this first mention of Wolfram's probably fictitious source antici-pates his role in Book IX.

la schantiure: O.Fr.: 'the singer', or possibly 'the enchanter'.

singing and speaking: the customary description of the narrative poet's art.

en franzoys: O.Fr.: 'in French'.

177 *Turnus . . . Tranzes*: in Veldeke's *Eneide*, Turnus is the adversary of Eneas, while Drances is reluctant to fight.

Vedrun: perhaps Pontevedra on the west coast of Spain.

any Briton: an allusion to Gawan.

hearing tales about it: an echo of the prologue of Hartmann's *Iwein* (writ-ten *c.*1205), where Hartmann says of Arthur's knights: 'I wouldn't like to have lived then at the expense of existing now, as we still derive such great pleasure from their tales—then it was the deeds that gave them pleasure.'

Wolfhart: the hot-headed nephew of Hildebrant in the *Nibelungenlied*, who, against the advice of Dietrich von Bern, provokes the final catastrophe.

178 *barred by ditches ... hooded over*: the first image is from siege warfare. The second is from falconry: a hood covers the bird to restrain it.

Rumolt: in the *Nibelungenlied*, Rumolt, King Gunther's kitchen-master, advises the Burgundians not to accept Kriemhilt's invitation to Hungary. In the C version of the text Rumolt refers to the pleasures of basting in oil.

Segramors: the hasty knight. See Book VI, 284.

Sibeche ... Ermenrich: Sibeche is the evil and cowardly adviser of King Ermenrich in the Dietrich epics; these heroic epics survive in manuscripts of later date than *Parzival*, but must by *c.*1200 already have been circulating in (presumably) oral form. Ermenrich is in origin the Ostrogothic king Ermanaric (d. *c.*375).

179 *moulted*: falcons were held to be in their prime after their first moult.

Læhtamris: perhaps derived from O.Fr. *les tamaris*, 'the tamarisks'.

180 *cleft stick*: the image is from bird-catching.

181 *flown beneath*: the image may be from falconry, referring to the falcon cutting off another bird's means of escape.

to prevent any of them being wounded: this retrospective motif is obscure. It may be an allusion to the wholesale slaughter of unarmed pages in Etzel's hall in the *Nibelungenlied*.

Liaz ... Gandiluz ... Schoydelacurt: the names Liaz and Gandiluz may derive from the list of knights in Hartmann's *Erec*, in which Schoydelacurt is the last adventure.

moulted merlin: a sparrowhawk that is at least 1 year old.

183 *sloth*: an allusion to Hartmann's *Erec*, whose hero devotes himself to lying in bed, in preference to knightly pursuits.

184 *Lady Lunete*: see note to p. 107.

garland ... in pursuit of joy: these lines are directed against Laudine's overhasty second marriage; the garland may refer both to that worn to a dance and to a widow's wreath.

to his regret: Parzival is sorry for intruding upon a hermit or hermitess.

185 *headdress*: presumably Sigune wears no decoration in her hair, or possibly a widow's wreath.

186 *no hiding-place ... fly between*: a mixed metaphor, based upon *geberc*, 'place of refuge', and *underswingen*, 'to fly between', from falconry.

187 *rode over this man's seed*: a man riding over cultivated land had to pay a small fine or ransom. Trespassers were bound with straw.

188 *templar*: Wolfram probably drew the term from the order of the Knights Templar, founded in 1119.

189 *slavin*: O.Fr. *esclavine*, coarse woollen pilgrims' clothing.

190 *on foot*: in Thomasin von Circlaria's *Der Wälsche Gast* (*c.*1225), it is declared unfitting to ride if a lady is walking. Walking in armour was, however, a cumbersome undertaking.

191 *Fontane la Salvatsche*: O.Fr.: 'the wild spring'.

Toledo: an important meeting-point of Christian, Arab, and Jewish learning.

193 *pied . . . adorned*: echoes of the prologue.

194 *quite bare*: in the Catholic church the altar is bare between Maundy Thursday and Easter Saturday.

By the psalter: the psalter evidently had a calendar bound with it.

195 *without gall*: the gall is the source of all evil feelings, from which angels, being incorporeal, are exempt.

Ashtaroth . . . Belcimon . . . Belet . . . Radamant: As(h)taroth is in origin a Phoenician goddess, the plural form of Ashtarte. It was a common medieval name for a demon. Belcimon may be an attempt to render the Phoenician 'Lord of the Skies', 'Bel' meaning 'lord', 'samain' meaning 'skies'. Bêlet, a Phoenician word for 'lady', is sometimes used for the consort of Bêl. Radamant, a Greek god by origin, is Lord of Hell in Veldeke's *Eneide*.

a man succeeded him: man was frequently seen in the Middle Ages as the successor of the fallen angels, to replace the tenth choir.

196 *the earth's fruit*: it was only after Noah's Flood that man began to eat meat.

for paltry possessions: this unscriptural interpretation of Cain's slaying of Abel emphasizes the link with Parzival's slaying of Ither.

we must carry sin: a reference to the doctrine of original sin. The image of the cart has not been satisfactorily explained, but may derive from Isaiah 5: 18: 'Woe to those who draw down punishment on themselves | with an ox's halter, | and sin | as with a chariot's traces.'

197 *leaps from the heart*: God as the leaping lover is an image from the Song of Songs (2: 8).

198 *lapsit exillis*: these corrupt Latin words are rendered variously by the manuscripts, and interpreted even more variously by critics. The sense would seem to be 'it (or: a stone) fell from the heavens'.

epitaph: the word *epitafum* is used in the general sense of an inscription, with no apparent association with a tomb.

199 *He sent His angel*: this subject is treated in the *Titurel* and in its continuation, Albrecht's *Jüngerer Titurel*. The status of the neutral angels has been the matter of much debate. Wolfram is the first to make them custodians of the Grail.

that warrior's charger: the charger is Gringuljete, which passes from Lähelin to his brother Orilus, and then to Gawan. See Book V, 261 and Book VIII, 339.

200 *you*: here Trevrizent, acknowledging the kinship between himself and Parzival, employs the familiar *dû* ('thou') form for the first time.

your own flesh and blood: Ither is the child of Uther Pendragon's sister. The link between Gahmuret and Uther Pendragon is explained in Gahmuret's letter to Belacane (Book I, 56).

balm: the oily liquid derived from balm or balsam rises to the top during cooking.

201 *the dragon*: this refers to Herzeloyde's dream at the end of Book II. Trevrizent cannot, logically, know of the dream, but at times Wolfram defies logic.

your mother's care: see *Titurel*, strophes 29 ff.

202 *Tigris*: the Tigris is named as one of the four rivers that flow from Eden in Genesis 2.

asp . . . meatris: with the exception of the ecidemon, perhaps influenced by Latin *echidna*, 'viper', the names of these snakes occur in twelfth- and thirteenth-century manuals. The closeness to alphabetical order suggests that Wolfram used a glossary.

203 *four rivers*: the names of the rivers are found in the Vulgate Bible; Wolfram may also have drawn upon the *Straßburg Alexander*, which tells of beautiful flowers floating down the Euphrates.

that flow in Hell: Wolfram is drawing on the account of the Underworld in Veldeke's *Eneide*.

It dies at once: Wolfram's account resembles that of the *Physiologus* and other medieval bestiaries.

monicirus: one of the many names for the unicorn. It also occurs in the *Straßburg Alexander*, which tells of the unicorn's carbuncle-stone.

dragonwort: the legend is attested in late antique writings.

the nature of air: it is dry and cold, and therefore effective against inflamed wounds.

the dragon's orbit: probably a reference to the progression of the Dragon's Head (or Dragon's Tail) through the zodiac.

204 *nard*: an aromatic balsam, applied by Mary Magdalen to the feet of Jesus (John 12: 3).

theriacled: derived from theriac, an antidote to poison.

nones: the ninth hour of the day, usually about 3 p.m.; by tradition, the time of Christ's death.

205 *unwashed*: in the absence of cutlery, it was customary to wash hands both before and after meals.

206 *lament and refrain from lamenting in the right measure*: Wolfram is paraphrasing Ecclesiastes 3: 4–5.

white . . . green: in this enigmatic image, white is associated with old age, and green with youth.

208 *Castis*: the name may derive from Lat. *castus*, 'pure, chaste'. See *Titurel*, strophes 26–7.

Mount Agremontin: presumably Acremonte in Sicily, near Mount Etna.

209 *unstaved oaths*: an oath not sworn by placing the hands upon a staff was not regarded as legally binding.

Mondays: Monday was the customary day for tournaments.

211 *podagra*: gout of the feet.

adorn: an echo of the prologue: 'scorned and adorned'.

the highest pledge: i.e. the Host of the sacrament.

212 *their kinship's potency averted the combat*: here the greatest red herring in medieval romance is finally left to sink. Ehkunaht had been revealed as the killer of Kingrisin in Book VIII, 413. Vergulaht and Gawan are distantly related through their common ancestor, Mazadan.

approach fame with the sword: Wolfram's assertion of belief in martial prowess echoes what he says of himself in the 'Self-Defence', although it is at variance with Trevrizent's advice on how to approach the Grail.

wrestle . . . greeting: Gawan's humour is reliant upon the double meaning of *ringen*, 'to wrestle', and 'to strive for love's favours'; 'greeting' is a keyword in courtly love.

Lady Kamille: Kamille (Camilla) fights against the Trojans in the *Aeneid*. In Veldeke's *Eneide*, this battle takes place outside the walls of Laurente. The forms of the names and the vocabulary suggest that Wolfram is drawing on Veldeke's version.

214 *spoke a wound-blessing upon the wound*: many medieval German charms serving to staunch bleeding have survived.

bêâ flûrs: O.Fr.: 'fair flower'.

Orgeluse de Logroys: in Chrétien she is *l'Orguelleuse de Logres*, 'the proud one of Logres'. As with Orilus and Sigune, an appellative is converted into a proper name.

a stretching-string of the heart: what kind of string or rope is meant here has been disputed: a bow, a crossbow, a siege-machine, or even, perhaps, a windlass.

215 *catapult . . . roll*: terms from siege warfare. A catapult is a siege-machine; 'roll' refers to the rolling of such siege-machines.

how the charger was to wait for him: Chrétien makes it clear that the bridge, being nothing more than a plank, is too narrow for the charger.

217 *fled . . . reared*: both these terms probably refer to the field of falconry.

you goose!: an echo of the insult shouted at Parzival on leaving Munsalvæsche (Book V, 247).

218 *Malcreatiure*: O.Fr. *male creature*, 'evil creature'. Chrétien gives him no proper name.

giving names to all things, wild and tame: cf. Genesis 2: 20.

the powers of all herbs and each one's nature: the source for Adam's herb-lore and advice to his daughters was perhaps the *Lucidarius*, commissioned by Henry the Lion, Duke of Bavaria and Saxony, in the late twelfth century.

despaired: the motif of 'doubt' or 'despair', voiced in the romance's first line, is here traced back to the first of men.

Secundille: the name Secundilla occurs in the *Polyhistor* of Solinus.

220 *Av'estroit Mavoie*: presumably from O.Fr. *eave estroite malvoiée*, 'narrow water (on an) evil road'.

be a page: etymologically, a *rîter*, a knight, is mounted, whereas a page might not be.

let them keep their own: the topos of the lover who renounces worldly wealth for his beloved is common, as in the *Carmina Burana* lyric, contemporary with Wolfram: 'If all the world were mine, | from the Elbe to the Rhine, | I would renounce it | if only the King of England | lay in my arms.'

your bondsman: the imagery of feudal subservience is common in the medieval love lyric.

221 *ate along with the dogs*: a common punishment for sexual misdemeanours.

222 *the embassy's journey on which she had been sent to him there*: emissaries, often female in courtly romance, were regarded as inviolable.

a noose . . . bloodied: execution by the sword was a more customary and less demeaning punishment for rape.

223 *lymers*: tracking hounds used to find the trail of the quarry before a stag-hunt.

224 *tolls on the road*: knights were normally exempt from tolls.

flôrî: O.Fr.: 'bloom'.

free . . . tightly bonded: again the imagery derives from what C. S. Lewis termed 'the feudalisation of love'.

master: a master of arts, an author, here referring specifically to Heinrich von Veldeke.

Amor and Cupid, and Venus, the mother of those two: Cupid and Amor are distinct brother gods in Veldeke's *Eneide*.

225 *intervening blow*: the expression may derive from fencing, referring to an umpire's or second's blow separating the duellists.

226 *little piece of felt*: the piece of felt on the saddlebow on which the lance is balanced, common in O.Fr. literature, but this is the only German instance of it.

228 *the knight of Prienlascors*: Lybbeals, a Grail knight. See Book IX, 473.

229 *never a merchant*: a reference back to events in Book VII.

230 *Orilus the Burgundian*: Orilus may be called a Burgundian because in the *Titurel* (strophe 92) he is conqueror of the Dauphin Schionatulander of Graswaldan, whose lands were part of Burgundy in Wolfram's time.

she-mule's foal: mules are, of course, barren.

turn sweetness sour: a quotation from the first line of a strophe by Walther von der Vogelweide: 'Can my lady turn sweetness sour?'

231 *where Clinschor is lord*: Clinschor's actions have already been referred to in Book II, 664, although he was not then given a name, nor is he named in Chrétien.

at court: the idiom may suggest polite flattery on Gawan's part.

232 *Bene*: the name, not in Chrétien, may be an abbreviated form of Benedicta.

palmat-silk: a soft silk material, first attested here.

233 *windows, with glass in front of them*: glass windows were a luxury in the early thirteenth century.

234 *I have some questions*: the motif of questioning links the Gawan adventures to those of Parzival.

235 *my comfort*: Gawan's comfort is here personified as a knight errant.

236 *the Mahmumelin of Morocco*: the Caliph or Commander of the Faithful, from the Arabic *Amī ru ʿl-muʾminīn*.

237 *the Katholikos of Ranculat*: the Katholikos is the Patriarch of the Armenian Church.

When Greece so stood that treasure was found there: this probably refers to the sacking of Constantinople by the crusaders in the spring of 1204.

Plippalinot: a typical example of the delayed naming of characters favoured by Wolfram. Plippalinot combines an onomatopoeic first element, suggestive of waves, with *nôt*, 'distress, extremity'.

239 *sling-staffs*: the nature of these sling-staffs or slingstaves is not clear from the context. A Latin gloss tells us they were small machines with a base and hanging staff. They may be an early form of the siege-engine known as the trebuchet.

240 *Gawan could now stand firm*: either the congealing blood gives Gawan a firm footing on the slippery floor, or the sense might be 'that he could barely stand'.

241 *to pull him under itself*: the fight with the lion is described in terms of a wrestling-match.

pillow . . . on which he slept away his fame: the allusion is probably to the twelfth-century *Tristrant* poem of Eilhart von Oberge. Kahenis intends to bed Gymele, but Queen Isalde's pillow is placed beneath his head: 'this pillow was of such a kind that whoever's head lay upon it would sleep day and night'.

242 *whether you possess age or youth*: Gawan's helmet prevents her seeing his face.

243 *'Die merzis!'*: O.Fr.: 'Thank God!'

dittany ... blue sendal-silk: dittany, a herb of the marjoram family, had been used since ancient times as a painkiller and wound-healer. It was thought to enable stags to shake off arrows that had pierced them. Blue is sacred, being the colour associated with the Virgin Mary.

245 *Sword Bridge ... Meljacanz*: the allusions are to Chrétien's *Lancelot*. See Book VII, 387.

Garel ... the marble pillar: the allusions are to narratives which are now lost.

Li Gweiz Prelljus: O.Fr.: 'the perilous ford'. This anticipates Gawan's adventure later in Book XII.

Erec ... Schoydelacurt ... Mabonagrin: an allusion to the final adventure in Hartmann's *Erec*.

the adventure's stone: an allusion to the first adventure in Hartmann's *Iwein*, or his source, Chrétien's *Yvain*.

246 *Mazadan ... Terdelsachoye ... Famurgan*: see Book I, 56.

to her the true tidings had come!: perhaps a reference back to Guinevere's lament for Ither in Book III, 160.

Florie of Kanadic: see *Titurel*, strophes 147–8.

roys Gramoflanz: this anticipates events later in *Parzival*.

upon Soredamor, for Alixandre's sake: an allusion to Chrétien de Troyes' *Cligés*, or its lost German translation.

247 *to be silent now*: the gulf between rhetoric and experience, and the singer falling silent, are commonplaces in the medieval German love lyric.

wounded by bolts ... his love pangs did before: Wolfram is alluding to the professed love pangs of the Minnesingers; 'bolts' refers both to the crossbow bolts shot at Gawan, and to Cupid's darts.

wound round in a circle: the spiral staircase is an innovation of Romanesque architecture.

Lady Kamille's sarcophagus: in Veldeke's *Eneide*, Kamille's coffin rests upon a pillar which rises above a vault with jewelled windows.

248 *Master Geometras*: the designer of Kamille's sarcophagus in Veldeke's *Eneide*.

In the pillar ... some standing: this is loosely based on Veldeke's *Eneide*, in which a mirror is fitted to Kamille's mausoleum, enabling anyone arriving from a mile's distance to be seen.

249 *white hellebore*: Wolfram's word is *nieswurz*, 'sneeze-herb'.

250 *inherit high fame ... without sword*: the victor 'inherits' the fame of the vanquished. Often a knight who is unhorsed has recourse to sword-fighting.

251 *being called a goose*: see Book X, 515.

253 *the shield, too, had not been left behind*: presumably the shield was tied to the horse.

254 *Sinzester*: perhaps Silchester, where in Geoffrey of Monmouth's *History of the Kings of Britain* a council elects Constantine, father of Uther Pendragun, to the kingship. Winchester and Chichester have also been suggested.

255 *I have her tokens here*: i.e. the sparrowhawk and the peacock-feather hat.

take it as a disgrace: normally, revealing one's name was an admission of defeat and surrender.

256 *exacted vengeance . . . now he is dead*: i.e., vengeance upon yourself, in your capacity as future son-in-law to Lot.

257 *beâs âmîs*: O.Fr.: 'handsome lover'.

maidens . . . on account of its purity: the only way to catch a unicorn is to use a virgin's lap as a snare.

258 *as a test*: these words, and the biblical image of refined gold that follows, are a free quotation, with reversal of the gender roles, from Hartmann's *Erec*, whose hero ultimately apologizes to the heroine, Enite, for having tested her.

264 *Seres*: the Chinese city of Ser(es) was renowned for its silk. Most of the names that follow appear to be Wolfram's own invention. The material *saranthasme* is found in Veldeke's *Eneide*. Here it forms the basis for the names Sarant and Thasme.

266 *He holds you . . . yet you are separated*: Wolfram is playing with the topos of lovers exchanging their hearts.

270 *Kancor and Thebit*: Thebit is an Arabian naturalist of the tenth century, Thabit ibn Qurra. Perhaps Kancor is a corruption of Qurra, who is named in Latin sources as Bencore.

hart's-eye: perhaps a species of wild dittany, a herb of the marjoram and oregano family. The herb-lore probably derives from Solinus.

brown next to the white: a proverbial expression referring to the female genitalia. See *Titurel*, strophe 81.

272 *pluck his joy up high . . . let him down*: the source or sources of the imagery are uncertain. One of Wolfram's favourite images, weighing, is probably present here, but perhaps joy is in grief's prison, and is hoisted up by solace through a trapdoor. In all probability, Wolfram is mixing metaphors.

275 *Terre de Labur*: Terra di Lavoro, in central Italy.

Virgil of Naples: Virgil's 'Messianic' Fourth Eclogue, taken by the medieval Church to prefigure the birth of Christ, led to his reputation as a prophet and magician. Virgil studied at Naples and is buried near there.

Iblis: Iblis is an anagram of Sibil. Sibylla, wife of King Tancred of Sicily, fled to Caltabellotta to escape the Hohenstaufen Emperor Henry VI in 1194, and she may have inspired the name.

Caltabellotta: from the Arabic *Qalat-al-ballūṭ*, 'Castle of the Oak', near Sciacca in Sicily.

276 *Persia . . . Persida*: The MHG *Lucidarius* (*c.* 1190) describes Persida as the city in which magic was first invented. Most sources hold that magic was invented by Zoroaster of Persia.

mal . . . bêâ schent: O.Fr.: 'evil . . . good people', meaning, presumably, spirits.

From the water comes the ice: this widespread riddle dates back to late antiquity. A version in the Exeter Book (*c.* 1000 AD) tells of a monster on the waves which stove in the ship's sides. The monster describes its own nature thus: 'My mother is of the dearest race of maidens; she is my daughter grown to greatness.' The solution is: an iceberg.

278 *Garel . . . Gaherjet*: Garel is a common name in Arthurian romance. He occurs in Hartmann's *Erec*. Gaherjet is one of Gauvain's brothers in Chrétien's *Perceval*.

279 *chamberlain . . . cupbearer . . . steward . . . marshal*: these are the four highest offices at court, established in Ottonian times, in the tenth century.

280 *a certain tent that had belonged to Isenhart*: see Book I, 27 and 52.

chapels: portable chapels to be set up in tents.

the foremost lady: i.e. Sangive, Arthur's sister.

281 *Arthur . . . leapt upon a Castilian*: the ambivalent treatment of Arthur in *Parzival* (and in much Arthurian literature) is epitomized here. Wolfram is aware of how in Arthurian romance Arthur becomes a weak king (*roi fainéant*).

282 *had charge of the rearguard yesterday*: Jofreit and the other prisoners were in the vanguard, at some distance from Arthur.

received no greeting from me: the refusal of a greeting, or failure to give it, was tantamount to a declaration of hostilities.

284 *no dusty sand*: the sand customarily found in the tournament rink where a formal duel took place.

285 *the fourth side there*: three sides are formed by the two rivers and the sea.

Narant: Narant had died in Clamide's cause (Book IV, 205).

286 *Ecidemonis*: the place name is presumably based upon the ecidemon, a fabulous reptile akin to the ermine or stoat, whose scent is deadly to snakes.

287 *terre*: O.Fr. 'land'.

with the king's arms about her: probably this is a gesture of special affection and protection towards Bene as the messenger of Itonje.

Kyllicrates: King Killicrates of Centriun is listed in Feirefiz's retinue in Book XV. Wolfram derives the name from Solinus; the place names that follow probably also come from Solinus.

292 *die out of heartfelt grief for him*: Itonje is playing with the conceit of the exchange of hearts. Her heart resides with Gramoflanz, while his mind is visiting her body.

293 *the host's lodging*: i.e., Gawan's.

294 *Out of a banner he took a sturdy spear*: presumably a bundle of spears was wrapped in a banner.

295 *turning the blade's edge*: this skilled manoeuvre occurs in both the heroic epic and the Arthurian romance, as for example in Hartmann's *Erec*.

his lady-love's kin: Itonje is related to Parzival through their ancestors, Mazadan and Terdelaschoye.

296 *those three rode closer to the combat*: this trio belongs to Gramoflanz's army; their bare heads demonstrate that they have no warlike intent.

Cynidunte: presumably the name derives from *cyondontœ*, 'the dog-toothed one', which occurs in Solinus.

298 *the duchess . . . the king*: in Itonje's speech 'the king' refers to Gramoflanz, while 'the duchess' is Orgeluse.

Surdamur . . . Lampruore: O.Fr. 'the emperor'. The reference is to Alexander and Sordamors in Chrétien's *Cligés*. Cf. Book XII, 586.

299 *Polus Artanticus . . . Tremuntane*: the former is corrupt Latin for 'the Antarctic Pole', a star posited by medieval astronomy; the latter a borrowing from O.Fr. *tresmontane*, 'North Star, Polar Star', or perhaps Italian *tramontana*. In a crusading lyric of Wolfram's contemporary, Der Tannhäuser, it denotes the North Wind. The two stars, the Antarctic Pole and the Polar Star, form the axis of the firmament.

a wondrous invention addressed to love: the genre of the love letter was well established in medieval Latin, but this, and the letter from Ampflise to Gahmuret in Book II, 76 are among the earliest German examples. There are some German lines in the predominantly Latin Tegernsee love letters, purportedly exchanged between a nun and a monk, of *c.*1170.

300 *in three armies*: those of Arthur, Gawan (and Orgeluse), and Gramoflanz.

rustling . . . on the helmets there: Wolfram is placing emphasis on the new fashion for elaborately ornamented helms.

302 *covered over*: a play on words, as when Mak's wife in *The Second Shepherd's Play* says: 'Come cover me'; 'awakened' continues the double entendre.

303 *Gampfassasche*: perhaps derived from the African people, Gamphasantes, who occur in Solinus.

305 *the side-flaps had been removed from the covering*: presumably to accommodate the increased numbers; possibly, however, the flaps have been removed in order to make the events visible to the general public.

307 *the lock of this adventure*: the opening of Book XV refers to Chrétien de

Troyes' incomplete work, which also inspired several French continuations. Wolfram is asserting his exclusive claim as continuator.

308 *salamander worms . . . hot fire*: as Swift puts it: 'Further, we are by Pliny told | This serpent is extremely cold.' The salamander was reputed to live in fire, and supplied Prester John with an incombustible cloak.

309 *a lion . . . brought to life*: in the *Physiologus* and the bestiaries, the lion-cub is brought to life by his father's breath. His roar has this function in Isidore of Seville's *Etymologies*.

   gorget: a piece of armour covering the neck. A borrowing from O.Fr.

310 *the boss's branches*: bars that fix the boss in place.

   antrax: the Greek word for the Latin *carbunculus*.

311 *Kardeiz and Loherangrin*: Kardeiz is named after Condwiramurs's brother; Loherangrin may derive from O.Fr. *Loherain Garin*, 'Garin the Lotharingian'. Loth(a)ringia (Lorraine) is the home of the Swan Knight legend.

   across four kingdoms: a proverbial expression denoting a great distance.

313 *Gods and goddesses*: Wolfram attributes to the Moslems the polytheism of classical beliefs.

   Love's courteous key!: the key and lock of love, an image found in classical poetry, is present in the Tegernsee love letters, in one of the oldest German love lyrics in the female voice: 'You are locked in my heart. The little key is lost. May you remain inside forever!'

   in 'thou'-fashion: medieval German distinguishes between a formal *ir*, 'you' and an informal *dû*, 'thou' (as in Modern French *vous* and *tu*). The translator's embarrassment echoes that of Chancellor Kohl, who is rumoured to have said to President Reagan: 'You know, Ronald, we have known one another for so long that I think we can call each other "you".' Parzival does not address Feirefiz as *dû* until he is acknowledged as Grail King.

314 *that Reward of Woman*: this echoes the appellation given to Gahmuret in Book I, 23: 'Love's Requitement's Reward'.

   in three parts: the irony, anticipating the events of Book XVI, is that this image of a trinity is in the mouth of a heathen.

315 *intervening to prevent our dying*: Feirefiz attributes the same helpful powers to Jupiter as Parzival has learned to attribute to God.

320 *kiss her kinsman the heathen first*: Itonje and Feirefiz are related through Mazadan, Arthur's great-grandfather, who is great-great-great-grandfather to Feirefiz.

322 *King Papiris . . . Affinamus of Amantasin*: the fashion for exotic name-lists in German literature was formed by Hartmann's *Erec*. Feirefiz's list takes up exactly thirty lines, one manuscript column (as does the list of gems in section 791). One source that has been identified is Solinus.

323 *Lirivoyn King Schirniel . . . Count Karfodyas*: Parzival's list has no obvious

single source. Schirniel of Lirivoyn, the King of Avendroyn, and Marangliez, Duke of Brevigariez, occur in Book VII, and Vergulaht in Book VIII.

323 *unknown numbers*: Parzival's distinction between opponents defeated in tournaments and in open battle does not seem valid, as there was no tourney at Bearosche, and Vergulaht was defeated in open battle. Perhaps his memory, or Wolfram's, is at fault.

324 *Eraclius ... Hercules ... Alexander the Greek*: the Byzantine Emperor Eraclius was known as a connoisseur of gems to Wolfram either through the O.Fr. romance of *Eracle* by Gautier d'Arras, or its adaptation into MHG by Meister Otte. Here Wolfram would appear to be confusing names; the Greek demigod Hercules has nothing to do with the Latin Eraclius. Alexander the Great is said to have been taught knowledge of precious stones by Aristotele. In Lamprecht's *Alexander*, a twelfth-century text known to Wolfram, the Emperor is sent a stone from Paradise.

drianthasme: a coinage perhaps modelled upon the name of the city Triande (Book XIII, 629) and the costly fabric *saranthasme*.

326 *amble-gait*: the horse alternates its right and left legs as it paces forwards.

327 *Zval ... Alkamer*: the names of the planets are thought to derive from a Latin translation from the Arabic; such translations were common in the twelfth century. Zval (Arabic zuḥal) = Saturn; Almustri (al-muštarī) = Jupiter; Almaret (al-mirrīch) = Mars; Samsi (aš-šams) = the Sun; Alligafir (az-zuhara) = Venus; Alkiter (al-kātīb) = Mercury; Alkamer (al-quamar) = the Moon.

except for insatiety alone: amorous insatiety is meant here, such as that of Anfortas.

328 *his kinswoman*: i.e. Itonje.

travelling people: a term that might include Wolfram himself.

329 *if infamy ever befell me*: this must refer to Anfortas's unsanctioned relationship with Orgeluse.

330 *the consolatory solace ... previously pronounced*: the hope of which Trevrizent is said to have spoken here does not appear earlier in the work; this has led to much scholarly speculation.

bought and sold: probably an allusion to Judas Iscariot's selling of Christ.

piment: a perfumed salve.

terebinth: a resinous tree, the source of turpentine. Terebinth, musk, aromatics, and theriac, an antidote for wounds, all occur in Veldeke's *Eneide*. Many of these spices, such as amber, cardamom, and cloves, occur for the first time in German in *Parzival*.

331 *Carbuncle ... topaz*: the list of gems is exactly thirty lines long, the length of a manuscript page. Wolfram's major source was Marbod of Rennes' *De Lapidibus* (c.1090), which contains fifty-three of the fifty-eight names.

Names which have not been satisfactorily explained have been left in their original form.

332 *the distance . . . between the places*: Wolfram affects ignorance of both the time-scale and the geography of his narrative.

333 *for Saint Silvester's sake . . . walk alive away from death*: St Silvester called a bull back to life by whispering Christ's name in its ear.

334 *the host and his guest*: Parzival is now lord and host of Munsalvæsche.

sat at His council: an echo of Jeremiah 23: 18.

since your defiance . . . acquiesced to your will: this passage, problematic in syntax and theology, is known as 'Trevrizent's Retraction'. It raises several questions: has God changed His mind? What precisely is the role of the neutral angels? Has Parzival won the Grail by defiance or fighting? Trevrizent is clearly contradicting what he said earlier (Book IX, 463). The simplest answer is that Trevrizent is wrong, for, as he himself admits, not even the angels can read God's mind. It could be the case that Wolfram is here adopting a more orthodox position as a result of criticism of Book IX.

That doom they have chosen for themselves: this is the orthodox theological position, as echoed by Dante:

> The dismal company
> Of wretched spirits thus find their guerdon due
> Whose lives knew neither praise nor infamy;
>
> They're mingled with that caitiff angel-crew
> Who against God rebelled not, nor to Him
> Were faithful, but to self alone were true;
>
> Heaven cast them forth—their presence there would dim
> the light; deep Hell rejects so base a herd,
> Lest sin should boast itself because of them . . .

(*The Divine Comedy: Hell*, iii. 34–42, trans. Dorothy L. Sayers (Penguin: Harmondsworth, 1949).)

336 *Waleis . . . Bealzenan*: the lands are named first, then their capitals.

337 *this tale is true and straight*: Wolfram is relishing the complexities of kinship. In *Titurel* Sigune and Condwiramurs are companions as suckling-babes, contradicting this account. The bow image harks back to Book V, 241.

338 *Clarischanze*: in Chrétien's *Conte del Graal*, Clarissanz is the name of Gawan's sister.

the hostess: Condwiramurs, in accordance with Parzival's new role, is lady and hostess of Munsalvæsche.

339 *Pelrapeire . . . when it first made his acquaintance*: the allusion is to the short rations imposed on Pelrapeire by Clamide's siege (Book IV). An

identical comparison is made on Parzival's first visit to the Grail castle (Book V, 228).

340 *five thrusts*: the precise meaning of some of the jousting terms is unclear; manuscript variants suggest that they were not widespread.

341 *A fence has been hewn before it*: a metaphor expressing an invisible barrier. The invisibility of the Grail to pagans is a motif present in the O.Fr. Grail poem of Robert de Boron.

   'Whom d'you mean?': from this point onwards Parzival addresses Feirefiz as *dû*, 'thou'. See Book XV, 749.

342 *thrust . . . away from heathendom*: in the Middle Ages baptism by total immersion was the norm. The miraculous filling of the font occurs in the legend of Prester John, widespread in Germany in the twelfth century.

   By water man has sight: according to Hildegard von Bingen, water is the source of sight.

343 *that Loherangrin should depart with him*: the uncle–son link is so strong in the Germanic tradition that this would not be an unusual request.

344 *Camelot*: Camelot is rare in early sources. The first mention is in Chrétien's Lancelot romance, *La Charrette*, which may have been Wolfram's source. Ultimately the name derives in all probability from *Camlan*, a battle site in the *Annales Cambriae*, which record events of the early sixth century.

345 *Frimutel's five children*: Wolfram is playing with numbers (and with his audience) here. There are only four in the list that follows, as Repanse de Schoye, Frimutel's fifth child, was the subject of the preceding lines.

346 *retaining fame by his prowess*: there is an implicit contrast with Hartmann's *Erec* here, in which the hero neglects chivalry after his marriage.

   Erec . . . knew how to avenge himself through words: in the second section of Book I there is an allusion to Hartmann's *Erec*; another, symmetrically, ends the penultimate section of the last book. Erec reproved his wife, Enite, for questioning his inertia, and forbade her to speak. Hartmann's source was Chrétien's *Erec et Enide*, which leads Wolfram into the final discussion of authorship.

349 *flown wild*: David Dalby in the *Lexicon of the Mediaeval German Hunt* suggests this unique phrase means 'to return to a wild state, of a hawk'.

   human hand: previously the Grail had been in the custody of the 'neutral angels'.

350 *your wheel was stuck fast*: probably the Wheel of Fortune is meant.

351 *aromatized and balsamed in splendour*: the long journey of the foreign dignitaries meant that the corpse had to be carefully preserved.

353 *the Angevin*: i.e. Gahmuret.

   Gurzgri . . . Schoydelacurt: Gurzgri had fallen at Schoydelacurt, the final challenge in Hartmann's *Erec*.

Berbester: the city of Barbastro in Northern Spain, which figures in Wolfram's *Willehalm*.

354 *his aunt's son*: the relationship is unclear. Schionatulander's mother, Mahaute, may have been a sister of Schoette, Gahmuret's mother.

355 *Bêâs âmîs*: O.Fr.: 'fair friend'.

all that walks, creeps, flies, or floats: the four kinds of beast, i.e. the whole of creation.

356 *Pompey . . . Baldac . . . Ipomidon*: cf. the end of Book II of *Parzival*.

357 *His panther was inverted*: see *Parzival*, Book II, 91.

something brown at her hips: cf. *Parzival*, Book XIII, 644.

358 *Hermann of Thuringia*: Landgrave Hermann of Thuringia, probably Wolfram's patron, died on 25 April 1217.

Gurzgri . . . Mabonagrin: Gurzgri fell at Schoydelacurt, killed by Mabonagrin, in Hartmann's *Erec*.

359 *Dauphin of Graswaldan*: from the twelfth century the lords of Viennois and Graisivaudan were called 'dauphin'.

Admirat: from the Arabic *amīr*: the Caliph of Baldac (Baghdad), ruler of the Saracens.

out of a larcenous rib: the implication is that Gahmuret and Schionatulander are more closely related than by their descent from Eve.

estrange: this refers to a falcon that returns to its wild state.

360 *sleeping lion . . . my waking thoughts*: in the *Physiologus* and in other bestiaries (medieval books of beasts) the lion sleeps with his eyes open.

her noble aunt: i.e. Herzeloyde.

361 *three lands*: Waleis, Norgals, and Anjou.

keening . . . bound to him: *keening* is a falconry term describing the keenness of hawks for their prey; *bound* is a term from hunting with hounds.

362 *Agremuntin . . . salamander*: cf. *Parzival*, Book IX, 496; Book XV, 735.

Ampflise . . . avenged her anger upon me: Ampflise's anger was incurred by Gahmuret's rejection of her in favour of Herzeloyde. (*Parzival*, Book II, 87).

363 *a bercelet barking*: see *Parzival*, Book IX, 446.

I still grieve over this: the lament appears to be expressed by a female persona. An unidentified female narrator has been suggested, or the personified 'Lady Adventure'; perhaps there is a scribal error here.

364 *'Keep on the trail!'*: either from Old Provençal *garda vias* or Latin *garde vias;* probably a hunting term.

365 *Beaufremont*: a town and castle south of Neufchâteau (Dép. Vosges), near the Meuse; in Wolfram's time part of the duchy of Upper Lorraine, within the German Empire.

367 *letter-books en franzoys*: presumably a reference to the correspondence between Ampflise and Gahmuret.

the daunted pledge-bearer: this last strophe is characteristically ambiguous. It is not clear whether the 'daunted pledge-bearer' refers to Schionatulander, or to Wolfram himself as the guarantor of the story.

LIST OF PEOPLE AND PLACES

IN this list names are followed (except where they do not differ) by the normalized MHG forms, as they occur in Lachmann's editions of *Parzival* and *Titurel*, e.g. **Arthur** (Artûs). The major variants in these editions are adduced in brackets. Lachmann only normalizes to a limited extent; the manuscripts offer a scarcely finite variety of spellings. Self-explanatory names, such as Adam and Antwerp, have been omitted. Possible derivations of the names are discussed in the Explanatory Notes (with the exception of those derived directly from Chrétien de Troyes' *Conte del Graal*); in the many instances where the origin of a name has not been satisfactorily traced, no comment has been supplied.

Abenberg (Abenberc) Fortress near Schwabach, east of Wolframs-Eschenbach.

Acraton (Acratôn) Oriental place name.

Addanz Son of Lazaliez, grandson of Mazadan, great-grandfather of Parzival.

Admirat (Admirât) Ruler of the Saracens.

Affinamus Duke of Amantasin, in the retinue of Feirefiz.

Affinamus Ruler of Clitiers, in the retinue of Gramoflanz.

Africa (Afrike, Affricâ) Land of Duke Farjelastis.

Agatyrsjente Oriental place name.

Agremont(in) (Agremont(în), Agremuntîn) Volcanic mountain, duchy of Duke Lippidins.

Agrippe Land of King Liddamus.

Ahkarin (Ahkarîn) The name of the Baruch in *Titurel*.

Alamis (Alamîs) Duke of Satarchjonte, in the retinue of Feirefiz.

Aleman(s) (Alemane) Germans < Lat. *Alemanni*.

Aleppo (Hâlap) City in Syria.

Alexander Alexander the Great.

Alixandre (Alexander) Byzantine emperor, married to Soredamor, in Chrétien's *Cligés*.

Alize (Alîze) Sister of King Hardiz of Gascony, wife of Duke Lambekin of Brabant.

Alkamer (Alkamêr) The Moon.

Alkiter (Alkitêr) A planet, perhaps Mercury.

Alligafir Venus.

Almaret Mars.

Almustri (Almustrî) Jupiter.

Amantasin (Amantasîn) Duchy of Duke Affinamus.

Amaspartins (Amaspartîns) King of Schipelpjonte, in Feirefiz's retinue.

Amincas King of Sotofeititon, in Feirefiz's retinue.

Ampflise (Ampflîse, Amphlîse, Anphlîse) Queen of France, Gahmuret's first amour.

Ampflise (Ampflîse, Anphlîse) Grail maiden, daughter of Jernis of Ril.

Anfortas (also Amfortas) Grail King, the Fisher King, son of Frimutel, uncle of Parzival.

Angevin (Anschevîn) Family name of Gandin and his heirs; byname of Gahmuret, Parzival, and Feirefiz.

Angram Obscure place name, source of stout spears.

Anjou (Anschouwe) Land of Gandin and his heirs (Gahmuret, Herzeloyde, Parzival).

Annore (Annôre) Queen of Navarre, beloved of Galoes.

Antanor Silent knight at Arthur's court.

Antikonie (Antikonîe) Daughter of King Kingrisin of Ascalun, sister of Vergulaht.

Aquileia (Aglei) Seat of the Patriarch in Northern Italy.

Arabia (Arabîe) Oriental country.

Araby (Arabî) Oriental city.

Aragon (Arragûn) Land of King Schafillor.

Archeinor Duke of Nourjente, in Feirefiz's retinue.

Arles (Arl) Seat of the Provençal Jovedast, defeated by Parzival.

Arnive (Arnîve) Wife of Uther Pendragon, mother of Arthur.

Arras (Arraz) Flemish city, famous for textiles.

Arthur (Artûs, der Bertenoys) King of Britain, son of Uther Pendragon, husband of Guinevere.

Ascalun (Ascalôn) Land of King Kingrisin.

Assigarzionte (Assigarzîonte) City of Count Gabarin.

Astaroth (Astiroth) Fallen angel.

Astor Duke of Lanverunz.

Astor Count of Panfatis, in Feirefiz's retinue.

Atropfagente Land of Duke Meiones.

Aue (Ouwe) Hartmann von Aue, adaptor of Chrétien's romances, *Erec* and *Yvain*.

Avendroyn Land of King Mirabel.

Av'estroit Mavoie (Âv'estroit mâvoiê) Place where Urjans is wounded.

Azagouc Oriental country of King Isenhart, won by Gahmuret.

Baldac Seat of the Baruch, Baghdad on the Tigris.

Barbigœl (also Barbygœl) Capital of Liz, the land of King Meljanz.

Baruch (Bâruc) Lord of the Saracens.

Beacurs (Bêâcurs, Bêâkurs) Son of King Lot, brother to Gawan.

Beaflurs (Bêâflûrs) Wife of Pansamurs, mother of Liahturteltart, page of Ampflise.

Beafontane (Bêâfontâne) Home of Imane, abducted by Meljahkanz = possibly Bellefontaine near Chiny in Belgium.

Bealzenan (Bêâlzenân, Bêalzenân) Capital of Anjou.

Bearosche (Bêârosche) Fortress of Lyppaut.

Beauffremont (Beuframunt) Town, south of Neufchâteau (*Département* Vosges).

Beauvais (Bêâveys) City of the Burgrave Lisavander.

Behantins (Behantîns) Count of Kalomidente, in Feirefiz's retinue.

Belacane (Belacâne, Belakâne) Queen of Zazamanc, wife of Gahmuret, mother of Feirefiz.

Belcimon (Belcimôn) Fallen angel.

Belet Fallen angel.

Bems Town on the Korcha in the land of Löver.

Bene (Bêne, Bên) Daughter of the ferryman Plippalinot.

Berbester Fortress of the Count Palatine Ehkunaht = (?) Barbastro in northern Spain.

Bernout de Riviers Son of Count Narant, ruler of Ukerlant, in Gramoflanz's retinue.

Blemunzin (Blemunzîn) Land of Count Jurans, in Feirefiz's retinue.

Bloom *See* **Wild Bloom**

Bogudaht Count of Pranzile, conquered by Parzival.

Brabant (Brâbant) Land of Duke Lambekin and Princess Alize.

Brandelidelin (Brandelidelîn) King of Punturtoys, uncle of Gramoflanz.

Brandigan (Brandigân) Capital of Iserterre, Clamide's country.

Brevigariez (also Privegarz) Land of Duke Marangliez.

Brickus Son of Mazadan and Terdelaschoye, brother of Lazaliez.

Britain (Bertâne, Bretâne, Britâne) Realm of King Arthur, encompassing Britain and Brittany.

Briton (Bertûn) Inhabitant of Britain.

Brobarz (Brôbarz, Brûbarz) Land of Tampenteire, Kardeiz, and Condwiramurs.

Broceliande (Brizjlân) Forest in Brittany.

Brumbane (Brumbâne) Lake in the Grail country.

Caltabellotta (Kalot enbolot) City of King Ibert of Sicily.

Camelot (Schamilôt) Town of King Arthur. In the MSS Scamylot, Schambilot.

Camille *See under* K.

Capua (Câps) Capital of Clinschor's land, Terre de Labur.

Carolingia (Kärlingen) France.

Castis (also Kastis) King of Waleis and Norgals, first husband of Herzeloyde.

Caucasus (Kaukasas) Thought to mean the mountain(s) of the Hindu Kush (*Caucasus Indicus*).

Centriun (Centriûn) Kingdom of Killicrates, in Feirefiz's retinue.

Chrétien de Troyes (von Troys meister Cristjân) Author of the *Conte du Graal*.

Cidegast Duke of Logroys, lover of Orgeluse.

Cilli (Zilje) Cilli, or Celje, in Slovenia, formerly in Styria.

Clamide (Clâmidê) King of Iserterre, suitor of Condwiramurs.

Clarischanze (Clârischanze) Countess of Tenabroc, Grail maiden.

Clauditte Queen, beloved of Feirefiz.

Clauditte Sister of Florie of Kanadic, beloved of Ehcunaht in *Titurel*.

Clauditte Daughter of the burgrave Scherules of Bearosche, playmate of Obilot.

Clias (Clîas) The Greek, Knight of the Table Round, hero of Chrétien's romance *Cligés*.

Clinschor Duke of Terre de Labur, kinsman of Virgil of Naples, sorcerer.

Clitiers Land of Prince Affinamus.

Colleval (Collevâl) Of Leterbe, knight defeated by Parzival.

Condwiramurs (Cundwîr, Condwîr(e)n, Condwier âmûrs) Queen of Brobarz, daughter of Tampenteire.

Cundrie (Cundrîe, *la surziere, surzier*) Grail messenger, sister of Malcreatiure.

Cundrie (Cundrîe) Daughter of Lot, King of Norway and Sangive; sister to Gawan.

Cunneware (Cunnewâre de Lâlant) Duchess of Lalant, sister to Lähelin and Orilus.

Curvenal (Curvenâl) Tutor of Tristan.

Cynidunte Place name, source of phellel-silk.

Destrigleiz Land of King Erec.

Dianazdrun (Dîanazdrûn) Town in the land of Löver.

Dido (Dîdô) Queen of Carthage.

Dodines (Dôdînes) Knight of the Table Round, brother of Taurian the Wild.

Dollnstein (Tolenstein) Dollnstein an der Altmühl, south-east of Wolframs-Eschenbach.

Drau (Trâ) The river Drau or Drave, in Slovenia and Austria.

Duscontemedon (Duscontemêdon) Duchy.

Ecidemonis (Ecidemonîs) Place name, source of silk.

Edisson (Edissôn) Count of Lanzesardin, in Feirefiz's retinue.

Ehkuna(h)t (Ehkunat, Ehcunaht, Ehcunaver) Ehkunaht, Duke of

Salvasche Florien = Ehcunaver of the Wild Bloom (*Bluome diu wilde*). Son of Gurzgri, brother of Mahaute and Schoette, Palgrave of Berbester.

Ekuba (E(c)kubâ) Heathen queen of Janfuse, related to Feirefiz.

Elixodjon (Elixodjôn) Land of Duke Tiride.

Enite (Enîde) Daughter of Karsnafide, wife of King Erec.

Eraclius Greek Emperor.

Erec Son of Lac, King of Destrigleiz.

Ermenrich (Ermenrîch) Ermanaric, King of the Goths (d. *c.*375).

Ethnise (Ethnîse) Land from which samite comes, source of the Tigris.

Euphrates (Eufrâtes) River flowing out of Paradise.

Famurgan (Fâmurgân, Fâmorgân, Feimurgân) Fairy land of Terdelaschoye.

Farjelastis Duke of Africa, in the retinue of Feirefiz.

Feirefiz (also Feirafîz) Son of Gahmuret and Belacane, King of Zazamanc and Azagouc.

Filones Count of Hiberborticon, in the retinue of Feirefiz.

Flegetanis (Flegetânîs) Heathen scholar, learned in the lore of the Grail.

Florant (Flôrant) der Turkoyte Prince of Itolac, suitor of Orgeluse.

Florie (Flôrîe) of Kanadic Sister of Clauditte, beloved of Arthur's son, Ilinot.

Florie (Flôrîe) *de* Lunel Grail maiden.

Flurdamurs (Flûrdâmûrs) Daughter of Gandin and Schoette, wife of Kingrisin.

Fole (Fôle) Perhaps the name of the Queen of Navarre, beloved of Galoes.

Fontane la Salvatsche (Fontân(e) la salvâtsche) Spring near Trevrizent's cell.

Friam (Frîam) Duke of Vermendoys.

Fridebrant (Vridebrant) King of Scotland, married to the daughter of Schiltunc.

Frimutel Grail King, son of Titurel, father of Anfortas, grandfather of Parzival.

Fristines Count of Janfuse, subject of Queen Ekuba, in the retinue of Feirefiz.

Gabarins (Gabarîns) Count of Assigarzionte, in Feirefiz's retinue.

Gaherjet (Gaharjet, Gaherjêt) Cousin of Gawan.

Gaheviez Seat of Ither, King of Kukumerlant.

Gahmuret (also Gamuret) Son of Gandin of Anjou and Schoette, father of Feirefiz and Parzival.

Galoes (Gâlôes) Son of King Gandin of Anjou, elder brother of Gahmuret.

Galogandres Duke of Gippones, standard-bearer of Clamide.

Gampfassasche (Gampfassâsche) Land of King Jetakranc, perhaps an African country.

Gandiluz (Gandilûz) Duke, son of Gurzgri and Mahaute, brother of Schionatulander.

Gandin (Gandîn) King of Anjou, son of Addanz, father of Gahmuret, Galoes, and Flurdamurs.

Gandine (Gandîne) Styrian city, seat of Lammire, Ither's beloved. Probably modern-day Haidin.

Ganges (Ganjas) River in Tribalibot (= India).

Gardeviaz (Gardevîaz) Name of the hound in *Titurel*.

Garel (Gârel) A king, cousin to Gawan, knight of the Table Round.

Garschiloye Grail maiden from Greenland.

Gaschier (der Oriman) Count of Normandy, nephew of Kaylet.

Gauriuon (Gaurîuon) Site of jousts executed by Trevrizent.

Gawan (Gâwân) Gawain, son of King Lot of Norway and Queen Sangive, nephew of Arthur.

Geometras (Jêometras) A sage, designer of Kamille's sarcophagus in Veldeke's *Eneide*.

Gihon (Gêôn) One of the four rivers flowing out of Paradise.

Gippones Duchy of Galogandres.

Gors Land of King Poydiconjunz.

Gowerzin (Gowerzîn) Duchy of Lischoys Gwelljus. Possibly Cahors, in the South of France.

Graharz (Grâharz) Seat of Gurnemanz.

Graharzoys (Grâharzoys, Grâharzois, Grahardeiz) Inhabitant of Graharz, used in particular of Schionatulander.

Grajena (Greian) River in Styria, which flows into the Drave.

Gramoflanz King of Rosche Sabbins, son of Irot, nephew of Brandelidelin.

Graswaldan (Grâswaldân) Seat of Schionatulander = Graisivaudan, north-east of Grenoble.

Greenland (Gruonlant) Land of Garschiloye and Lanzidant.

Grigorz (Grîgorz) King of Ipotente, kinsman of Clamide.

Gringuljete (also Gringuljet) 'of the Red Ears', warhorse of Lähelin, Orilus, and Gawan.

Guinevere (Ginover, Ginovêr) Wife of King Arthur.

Gunther Gundaharius (d. 437), King of the Burgundians, a character in the *Nibelungenlied*.

Gurnemanz (also Gurnamanz) Prince of Graharz, father of Schenteflurs, Lascoyt, Gurzgri, and Liaze.

Gurzgri (Gurzgrî, Kurzkrî) Son of Gurnemanz of Graharz, husband of Mahaute.

Guverjorz Castilian warhorse of King Clamide.

Gweiz Prelljus, Li (Li gweiz prelljûs) The Perilous Ford, over which Gawan must leap.

Gybert King of Sicily, married to Iblis.

Gylstram Unidentified Western country.

Gymele (Gymêle) Of Monte Rybele, a friend of Queen Isalde in Eilhart von Oberge's *Tristan*.

Hardiz (Hardîz) King of Gascony, brother of Alize.

Hartmann von Aue (Hartmann von Ôuwe) Author of *Êrec* and *Îwein*.

Heinrich von Rispach (Heinrîch von Rîspach) Perhaps a patron of Wolfram.

Heinrich von Veldeke (Heinrîch von Veldeke) Author of the *Eneide*.

Heitstein Haidstein, castle near Cham, Eastern Bavaria.

Herlinde Beloved of Fridebrant.

Hermann (Herman) Hermann, Landgrave of Thuringia (d. 1217), Wolfram's patron.

Hernant A king slain by Fridebrant, enamoured of Herlinde.

Herzeloyde (Herzeloyd(e), Herzelöude) Queen of Waleis, Norgals, and Anjou, daughter of Frimutel.

Hiberborticon (Hiberborticôn) Seat of Count Filones.

Hiuteger Scottish duke in Fridebrant's retinue.

Hoskurast Seat of Kaylet.

Ibert King of Sicily, husband of Iblis.

Iblis Wife of Ibert, King of Sicily.

Ider (Idêr) Son of Noyt.

Idœl (also Ydœl) Father of Jofreit.

Ilinot (Ilinôt, Ilynôt) Prince, son of Arthur and Guinevere, enamoured of Florie of Kanadic.

Imane (Imâne von der Bêâfontâne) Maiden abducted by Meljahcanz.

Ingliart (Ingliârt) 'of the Short Ears', warhorse of Parzival and Gawan.

Inguse (Ingûse) Queen of Pahtarliez, beloved of Gawan.

Ipomidon (Ipomidôn, Ipomedôn) King of Babylon and Nineveh, brother of Pompey.

Ipopotiticon (Hippipotiticûn, Ipopotiticôn) Land of Count Lysander.

Ipotente Land of King Grigorz, Clamide's kinsman.

Irot (Irôt) King, father of Gramoflanz, brother-in-law of Brandelidelin.

Isaies (Isâies, Isâjes) Marshal of Uther Pendragon, father of Maurin.

Isalde Name of the two women beloved of Tristan.

Isenhart King of Azagouc, son of Tankanis, suitor of Belacane.

Iserterre Land of King Clamide.

Ither (Ithêr) Of Gaheviez, King of Kukumerlant, the Red Knight, nephew of Uther Pendragon.

Itolac Land of King Onipriz and Florant the Turkoyte.

Itonje (Itonjê) Daughter of King Lac of Norway and Sangive, sister of Gawan.

Iwan (Iwân) Knight of the Table Round, Chrétien's Yvain, Hartmann's Iwein.

Iwan (Iwân) Count of Nonel, father of a Grail maiden.

Iwanet (Iwânet, Ywânet) Squire and kinsman of Guinevere.

Jamor (Jâmor) Land of Kardefablet, brother-in-law of Lyppaut.

Janfuse (Janfûse) Land of Queen Ekuba and Count Fristines.

Jerneganz Duke of Jeroplis, defeated by Parzival.

Jernis (Jernîs) Count of Ril, father of the Grail maiden Ampflise.

Jeroplis (Jeroplîs) Land of Duke Jerneganz.

Jeschute (Jeschûte) Daughter of King Erec of Karnant, wife of Duke Orilus de Lalander.

Jetacranc King of Gampfassasche, in Feireiz's retinue.

Joflanze (Jôflanze) Site near which tournaments take place on a plain.

Jofreit (Jôfreit) Son of Idœl, kinsman of King Arthur, companion of Gawan.

Johan (Jôhan) Prester John, son of Feirefiz and Repanse de Schoye, priest-king of India.

John, Prester *See* Johan.

Jovedast A Provençal, of Arles, defeated by Parzival.

Jurans (Jûrâns) Count of Blemunzin, subject of Feirefiz.

Kahenis (Kahenîs) Brother of Isolde White-Hands, Tristan's beloved.

Kahenis (Kahenîs) Punturteis prince, the Grey Knight, brother-in-law of the King of Kareis.

Kaheti (Kahetî) Homeland of the turcoples who besiege Bearosche.

Kahetine (Kahetîne) Inhabitants of Kaheti.

Kalomidente Land of Count Behantins.

Kamille Camilla, virgin queen of the Volsci in Veldeke's *Eneide*.

Kanadic Land of Florie and Clauditte.

Kancor A sage.

Kanvoleiz Capital of Waleis, land inherited by Herzeloyde.

Karchobra (Karc(h)obrâ, Carcobrâ) Town at the mouth of the Plimizœl.

Kardefablet (Kardefablêt) Duke of Jamor, brother-in-law of Lyppaut.

Kardeiz King of Brobarz, son of Tampenteire, brother of Condwiramurs.

Kardeiz King, son of Parzival and Condwiramurs, brother of Loherangrin.

Kareis (Kâreis) Land of a king married to a sister of Kahenis, the Punturteis prince.

Karfodyas Count of Tripparun, defeated by Parzival.

Karidœl Citadel of Arthur.

Karminal (Karminâl) Hunting-lodge of Arthur in Broceliande.

Karnahkarnanz Count of Ulterlec.

Karnant Land of King Lac, father of Erec and Jeschute.

Karsnafite (Karsnafîde) Mother of Enite.

Katelangen Catalonia, in the kingdom of Aragon, duchy of Kyot, Manpfilyot, and Sigune.

Katholikos (Katolicô) Title of the Armenian Patriarch, whose seat is Ranculat.

Kay (Keie, Keye, Kai) Steward of King Arthur.

Kaylet Of Hoskurast, King of Spain, husband of Rischoyde, cousin to Gahmuret.

Killirjacac (also Kyllirjacac) Count from Champagne, nephew of Kaylet.

Kingrimursel (also Kyngrimursel) Landgrave and burgrave of Schampfanzun, brother of Kingrisin.

Kingrisin (Kingrisîn) King of Ascalun, husband of Gahmuret's sister Flurdamurs, brother of Kingrimursel.

Kingrivals (Kingrivâls, Kyngrivâls) Capital of Norgals, inherited from Castis by Herzeloyde.

Kingrun (Kingrûn) Seneschal of King Clamide.

Korcha (Korchâ) River in the land of Löver.

Kukumerlant (Kukûmerlant, Cucûmerlant) Land of King Ither, presumably Cumberland.

Kyllicrates (also Killicrates) King of Centriun, in Feirefiz's retinue.

Kyot (Kyôt) Duke of Katelangen (Catalonia), husband of Schoysiane, father of Sigune.

Kyot (Kyôt) Sage, Wolfram's alleged source, known as *la schantiure*, or the Provençal.

Lac King of Karnant, father of Erec and Jeschute.

Lac Magic spring in Karnant.

Lachfilirost (Lahfilirost) Burgrave and marshal of Belacane in Patelamunt.

Lähelin (Lähelîn) King, brother of Orilus and Cunneware de Lalant.

Læhtamris (Læhtamrîs) A forest.

Lämbekin (Lämbekîn) Squire of Orilus.

Læprisin (Læprisîn) A forest.

Laheduman (Lahedumân) Count of Muntane, in Poydiconjunz's army.

Lalander (Lâlander) Land of Duke Orilus.

Lalant (Lâlant) Duchy of Orilus, homeland of Cunneware.

Lambekin (also Lämbekîn) Duke of Brabant and Hainaut, husband of Alize, Hardiz's sister.

Lammire (Lammîre) Queen of Gandine in Styria, daughter of Gandin and Schoette, beloved of Ither.

Lampregun (Lampregûn) Land of Count Parfoyas, defeated by Parzival.

Lancelot (Lanzilôt) Knight of the Table Round.

Lanverunz Land of Duke Astor.

Lanzesardin (Lanzesardîn) Land of Count Edisson, in Feirefiz's retinue.

Lanzidant Prince of Greenland, messenger of Ampflise.

Lascoyt Count, son of Gurnemanz.

Laudunal (Laudûnal) Of Pleyedunze, defeated by Parzival.

Laudundrehte Seat of Postefar, defeated by Parzival.

Laurente Town in the Campagna di Roma.

Lazaliez Son of Mazadan and Terdelaschoye, brother of Brickus, father of Addanz.

Lechfeld (Lechvelt) A sandy plain near Augsburg in Swabia.

Leidebron (Leidebrôn) Duke of Redunzehte, defeated by Parzival.

Leoplane (Lêôplâne) Plain outside Kanvoleiz.

Leterbe Seat of Colleval, defeated by Parzival.

Liahturteltart (Lîahturteltart) Son of Pansamurs and Beaflurs, one of Ampflise's pages.

Liaz (Lîâz) Count of Cornwall, son of Tinas.

Liaze (Lîâze) Daughter of Gurnemanz, cousin of Condwiramurs.

Liddamus Duke in Galicia, subject of King Vergulaht.

Liddamus King of Agrippe, in Feirefiz's retinue.

Liedarz (Lîedarz) Prince, son of of Count Schiolarz, one of Ampflise's messengers.

Li Gweiz Prelljus Ford crossed by Gawan.

Lippidins (Lippidîns) Duke of Agremuntin, in Feirefiz's retinue.

Lirivoyn Land of King Schirniel.

Lisavander (also Lysavander) Burgrave of Beauvais, in the service of Meljanz.

Lischoys Gwelljus (also Lishoys) Duke of Gowerzin, suitor of Orgeluse.

Lit Marveile (Lît marveile) The Bed of Marvels in Schastel Marveile.

Liz (Lîz) Kingdom of Meljanz.

Löver A land belonging to King Arthur.

Logroys (Lôgroys, Logrois) Land and castle of Cidegast and Orgeluse.

Loherangrin (Loherangrîn) Son of Parzival and Condwiramurs, the Swan Knight.

Lohneis Land of King Riwalin.

Longefiez Count of Tuteleunz, defeated by Parzival.

Lorneparz Land of King Piblesun, defeated by Parzival.

Lot (Lôt) King of Norway, husband of Sangive, father of Gawan.

Lunel Home of the Grail maiden Florie.

Lunete (Lûnete) Maidservant of Queen Laudine in Hartmann's *Iwein*.

Lybbeals (Lybbêâls von Prienlascors) Grail knight.

Lyppaut (also Lippaut) Prince of Bearosche, subject of King Schaut and King Meljanz, father of Obie and Obilot, brother of Duke Marangliez, brother-in-law of Kardefablet.

Lysander Count of Ipopotiticon, in Feirefiz's retinue.

Mabonagrin (Mabonagrîn) Of Schoydelacurt (in Hartmann's *Erec*), kinsman of Clamide.

Mahaute Wife of Gurzgri, sister of Schoette and the palgrave Ehkunat, mother of Schionatulander and Gandiluz.

Mahmumelin (Mahmumelîn) Moroccan potentate, Prince of the Believers.

Malcreatiure (Malcrêâtiure) Dwarf, brother of the Grail messenger Cundrie, sent by Queen Secundille of Tribalibot to Anfortas.

Maliclisier Dwarf who figures in Hartmann's *Erec*.

Manpfilyot (Manpfilyôt, Manfilôt) Duke of Katelangen, uncle of Condwiramurs.

Marangliez Duke of Brevigariez, brother of Lyppaut.

Maurin (Maurîn) Marshal of Queen Guinevere, son of Isaies.

Mazadan (Mazadân) Father of Lazaliez and Brickus, ancestor of Arthur and the Angevins.

Meiones Duke of Atropfagente, in Feirefiz's retinue.

Meljahkanz (also Meljacanz) Son of King Poydiconjunz of Gors, arch-abductor.

Meljanz King of Liz, son of Schaut, nephew of Poydiconjunz.

Milon (Milôn) King of Nomadjentesin, in Feirefiz's retinue.

Mirabel King of Avendroyn, brother of Schirniel, defeated by Parzival.

Mirnetalle Land of Count Rogedal, defeated by Parzival.

Monte Rybele (Monte Rybêle) Homeland of Gymele.

Morholt (Môrholt) Of Ireland (antagonist of Tristan, uncle of Isolde in Gottfried's *Tristan*).

Munsalvæsche (Munsalvæsche, Muntsalvâsch(e)) Grail castle and land.

Muntane (Muntâne) Homeland of Count Laheduman.

Muntane Cluse (Muntâne Clûse) Where Poydiconjunz captures a company of Britons.

Muntori (Muntôrî) Site of the death of Galoes.

Nantes Capital of Arthur's Breton/British kingdom.

Narant (Nârant) Count of Uckerlant, father of Bernout de Riviers.

Narjoclin (Narjoclîn) Land of Duke Sennes, in Feirefiz's retinue.

Navarre (Averre) Land of Queen Annore.

Navers (Nâvers) Land of Count Ritschart.

Nebuchadnezzar (Nabchodonosor) King of Babylon.

Nibelungs (Nibelungen) Warrior-race in the *Nibelungenlied*.

Nineveh (Ninivê, Ninnivê) Oriental city founded by Ninus.

Ninus (Nînus) Ancestor of Pompey and Ipomidon, founder of Nineveh.

Nomadjentesin (Nomadjentesîn) Land of King Milon, in Feirefiz's retinue.

Nonel (Nônel) Land of Count Iwan.

Norgals (Norgâls) Land inherited by Herzeloyde from Castis. North Wales, or North Gaul?

Noriente (Neurîente, Oriente, Orjente, Nourjente, No(u)rîent(e), etc.) Oriental land of Duke Archeinor, source of silks.

Norman (Oriman, Orman) Byname of Duke Gaschier.

Noyt Father of Ider.

Obie (Obîe) Elder daughter of Lyppaut, wooed by Meljanz.

Obilot (Obilôt, Obylôt) Younger daughter of Lyppaut.

Olimpia (Olimpîâ, Olimpîe) Heathen queen, beloved of Feirefiz.

Onipriz (Oniprîz) King of Itolac, defeated by Parzival.

Oraste Gentesin (Oraste Gentesîn, Orastegentesîn) Heathen marshland of King Thoaris.

Orgeluse (Orgelûs(e)) Much-courted Duchess of Logroys.

Orilus Duke of Lalander, brother of Lähelin and Cunneware, husband of Jeschute.

Oriman Byname of Gaschier the Norman.

Orman Byname of Gaschier the Norman.

Pahtarliez Land of Queen Inguse.

Panfatis (Panfatîs) Homeland of Count Astor, in Feirefiz's retinue.

Pansamurs (Pansâmûrs) Wife of Beaflurs, father of Liahturteltart.

Papiris (Papirîs) King of Trogodjente, in Feirefiz's retinue.

Parfoyas Count of Lampregun, defeated by Parzival.

Parzival (Parzivâl) Son of Gahmuret and Herzeloyde.

Patelamunt (Pâtelamunt) Capital of Zazamanc, residence of Belacane.

Patrigalt Kingdom, and home of a Templar.

Pelpiunte (Pelpîunte) City, source of silks.

Pelrapeire Capital of the kingdom of Brobarz, residence of Condwiramurs.

Persida (Persidâ) Oriental city where magic was invented.

Phlegethon (Flegetône) River in Hell.

Piblesun (Piblesûn) King of Lorneparz, defeated by Parzival.

Pictacon (Pictacôn) Land of Duke Strennolas, defeated by Parzival.

Pishon (Fîsôn) One of the four rivers flowing out of Paradise.

Pleyedunze Homeland of Laudunal, defeated by Parzival.

Plihopliheri (Plihopliherî) Knight defeated by Orilus.

Plimizœl (also Plymizœl) River that flows through Liz.

Plineschanz Count of Zambron, defeated by Parzival.

Plippalinot (Plippalinôt) Ferryman of Schastel Marveile, Bene's father.

Pompey (Pompeius) King of Nineveh, brother of Ipomidon, nephew of Nebuchadnezzar.

Poncia (Ponciâ) Homeland of Pontius Pilate (Pilâtus von Ponciâ).

Possizonjus Count of Thiler, in Feirefiz's retinue.

Postefar Of Laudunrehte, defeated by Parzival.

Poydiconjunz King of Gors, brother of Schaut, father of Meljacanz, uncle of Meljanz.

Poynzaclins (Poynzaclîns) River, near the river Sabins.

Poytwin de Prienlascors (Poytwîn) Knight defeated by Gahmuret.

Pranzile (Pranzîle) Land of Count Bogudaht, defeated by Parzival.

Prienlascors Homeland of Poytwin and Lybbeals.

Prothizilas (Prôthizilas) Prince in Azagouc, subject of Belacane.

Prurin (Prurîn) Town outside which Erec fells Orilus.

Punt A port.

Punturteis Inhabitants of Punturtoys.

Punturtoys (also Punturteis, Punturteys, Punturtois) Land of King Brandelidelin, Kahenis, and Urjans.

Pythagoras (Pi(c)tagoras) Greek astronomer.

Radamant Fallen angel.

Ranculat Hromgla on the Euphrates, seat of the Katholikos, Patriarch of Armenia.

Razalic (Razalîc) Moorish prince in Azagouc.

Redunzehte Land of Duke Leidebron, defeated by Parzival.

Repanse de Schoye (Ur)Repanse de schoy(e) Grail-bearer, daughter of Frimutel.

Ril (Rîl) Land of Count Jernis = (?) Rhyl in North Wales.

Rischoyde Daughter of Titurel, sister of Frimutel, wife of Kaylet of Hoskurast.

Risbach (Rîspach) Seat of Sir Heinrich of Risbach = (?) Reisbach an der Vils.

Ritschart Count of Navers.

Riviers Land of Count Bernout.

Rivigitas Kingdom of Translapins, in Feirefiz's retinue.

Riwalin (Riwalîn) King of Lohneis, father of Tristan.

Rogedal (Rogedâl) Count of Mirnetalle, defeated by Parzival.

Rohas (Rôhas) The Rohitscher Berg, or Donatiberg, a mountain in Styria, now Rogaška gora near Cilli (Celje) in Slovenia.

Rosche Sabbins (Rosche Sa(b)bîn(e)s) Capital and residence of Gramoflanz.

Rozokarz Land of King Serabil, defeated by Parzival.

Rumolt (Rûmolt) Master of the kitchens at the court of Worms, in the *Nibelungenlied*.

Sabins (Sa(b)bîns) River in the land of King Gramoflanz (= (?) the Severn).

Salvasche ah Muntane (Salvâsche ah muntâne) = Munsalvæsche.

Salvasch Florie (Salvâsch flôrîe) Home of Duke Ehkunaht in *Titurel*.

Samsi (Samsî) Bright-shining planet.

Sangive (Sangîve) Wife of King Lot of Norway, daughter of Uther Pendragon and Arnive.

Sarant (Sârant) Master tailor of Triande.

Satarchjonte Duchy of Alamis, in Feirefiz's retinue.

Schafillor (Schaf(f)illôr) King of Aragon.

Schamilot *See* Camelot.

Schampfanzun (also Schan(p)fanzûn, Tschanfanzûn) Capital of Ascalun, land of King Vergulaht.

Schastel Marveile (Schastel marveil) Castle of Clinschor.

Schaut King of Liz, brother of Poydiconjunz, father of Meljanz.

Schenteflurs (Schenteflûrs, Schentaflûrs) Son of Gurnemanz, brother of Liaze and Gurzgri.

Scherules Burgrave of Bearosche, father of Clauditte.

Schiltunc Cousin of Kaylet, father-in-law of Fridebrant.

Schiolarz (Schîolarz) Count of Poitou, father of Liadarz.

Schionatulander (Schîânatulander, Schîanatulander, Schîonatulander, Schoynatulander) Dauphin of Graswaldan, son of Gurzgri and Mahaute, grandson of Gurnemanz of Grâhârz.

Schipelpjonte Land of King Amaspartins, in Feirefiz's retinue.

Schirniel (Schirnîel) King of Lirivoyn, brother of Mirabel of Avendroyn.

Schoette (Schôette) Wife of Gandin, mother of Gahmuret, sister of Mahaute and Ehkunaht.

Schoydelacurt (Schoye de la kurte, Schoydelakurt) Garden of Mabona-grin in Hartmann's *Erec*.

Schoysiane (Schoysîane, Schoysîân, Tschoysîâne) Daughter of Frimutel, wife of Kyot of Katelangen.

Secundille (Secundill(e)) Queen of Tribalibot.

Segramors King, knight of the Table Round, kinsman of Guinevere.

Semblidac Land of King Zyrolan, defeated by Parzival.

Senilgorz King of Sirnegunz, defeated by Parzival.

Sennes Duke of Narjoclin, in Feirefiz's retinue.

Serabil King of Rozokarz, defeated by Parzival.

Seres (Sêres) Chinese city, renowned for its silk.

Sibeche Evil counsellor of Ermenrich in the Dietrich epics.

Sibyl (Sibille) Prophetess in Veldeke's *Eneide*.

Siegfried (Sîvrit) Hero of the *Nibelungenlied*.

Sigune (Sigûn(e)) Daughter of Kyot of Katelangen and Schoysiane, niece of Anfortas.

Silvester Saint, Pope, d. 335.

Sinzester English town (= ? Silchester).

Sirnegunz Land of King Senilgorz, defeated by Parzival.

Soissons (Sessûn) City in Picardy.

Soltane (Soltâne) Waste land, forest subject to Herzeloyde.

Soredamor (Sûrdamûr) Daughter of Lot of Norway and Sangive, wife of Alixandre in Chrétien's *Cligés*.

Sotofeititon (Sotofeititôn) Land of King Amincas, defeated by Feirefiz.

Spessart (Spehteshart) Forest in central Germany.

Strangedorz Of Villegarunz, defeated by Parzival.

Strennolas Duke of Pictacon, defeated by Parzival.

Styria (Stîre) Land of Lammire = the Steiermark, in Austria and Slovenia.

Surin (Surîn) Oriental land = (?) Syria.

Tampanis (Tampanîs) Chief page of Gahmuret.

Tampenteire (also Tampunteire) Husband of Gurnemanz's sister, father of Condwiramurs.

Tankanis (Tankanîs) King, father of Isenhart.

Taurian (Taurîan) The Wild, brother of Dodines, friend of Trevrizent.

Tenabroc Homeland of the Grail maiden Clarischanze; site where chain-mail is made.

Terdelaschoye A fairy in Famorgan, by whom Mazadan sired Brickus and Lazaliez.

Terre de Labur (Terre de Labûr) Land of Clinschor.

Terre Marveile (Terre marveile) Land of Clinschor.

Terre de Salvæsche The Grail kingdom.

Thabronit Capital of the Oriental land of Tribalibot, ruled by Secundille.

Thasme (Thasmê) City in Tribalibot, ruled by Secundille.

Thebit (Thêbit) An Arab sage, Tānit ibn Qurra (d. 901).

Thiler (Thilêr) Land of Count Possizonjus, in Feirefiz's retinue.

Thoaris (Thôarîs) King of Oraste Gentesin, in Feirefiz's retinue.

Thopedissimonte Oriental city.

Thuringia (Dür(n)gen) Province of Margrave Hermann I, Wolfram's patron.

Tigris (Tîgrîs) One of the four rivers flowing out of Paradise.

Tinas (Tînas) Father of Count Liaz of Cornwall.

Tinodonte Land of King Tridanz, in Feirefiz's retinue.

Tiride (Tiridê) Duke of Elixodjon, in Feirefiz's retinue.

Titurel (also Tyturel) Grail King, father of Frimutel, grandfather of Anfortas.

Toledo (Dôlêt) Land of King Kaylet.

Translapins (Translapîns) King of Rivigitas, in Feirefiz's retinue.

Tranzes Character from Veldeke's *Eneide* (Drances).

Trebuchet Smith who engraved Frimutel's sword and made Anfortas's sword.

Trevrizent Son of Frimutel, brother of Anfortas, Herzeloyde, Repanse de Schoye, and Schoysiane.

Triande (Trîande) Homeland of Sarant, the master tailor.

Tribalibot (Tribalibôt) Oriental kingdom of Secundille (= India).

Tridanz King of Tinodonte, in Feirefiz's retinue.

Tripparun (Tripparûn) Land of Count Karfodyas, defeated by Parzival.

Trogodjente Land of King Papiris, in Feirefiz's retinue.

Troyes (Troys) Home of Chrétien de Troyes, author of *Le Conte del Graal*.

Trühendingen Bavarian town famous for doughnuts (= Hohentrüdingen or Wassertrüdingen).

Tulmeyn Site of a battle, castle of Duke Imain in Hartmann's *Erec*.

Turkentals (Turkentâls) Prince in Waleis and Norgals, subject of Herzeloyde.

Turkoyte (also Turkoite) Byname of Florant, Prince of Itolac.

Turnus Prince, rival of Eneas in Veldeke's *Eneide*.

Tuteleunz (Tutelêunz) Land of Count Longefiez, defeated by Parzival.

Ukerlant (U(c)kerlant) Land of Count Narant and his son, Bernout de Riviers.

Ukersee (Ukersê) Northern lake.

Ulterlec Land of Count Karnahkarnanz.

Urjans (Urjâns, Urîans) Prince of Punturtoys, rapist.

Uther Pendragon (Utepandragûn) King of Britain, son of Brickus, father of Arthur.

Vedrun (Vedrûn) Place in Galicia, perhaps Pontevedra on the west coast of Spain.

Veldeke Heinrich von Veldeke, poet, author of the *Eneide*, a MHG version of the *Ænead*.

Vergulaht King of Ascalun, son of Kingrisin and Flurdamurs, brother of Antikonie.

Vermendoys Land of Duke Friam (= Vermendois, north-east of Paris).

Villegarunz Homeland of Strangedorz, defeated by Parzival.

Virgil (Virgilîus) Of Naples, ancestor of Clinschor.

Waleis (Wâleis, Wâls) Land bequeathed to Herzeloyde by Castis = South Wales, or Valois?

Waleis (Wâleis) Inhabitant of Waleis; byname of Parzival.

Waleisinne (Wâleisinne) Byname of Herzeloyde.

Walther (hêr Walther) Walther von der Vogelweide, Minnesinger (*fl.* c.1190–1230).

Wertheim Bavarian town, home of a count who may have been one of Wolfram's patrons.

Wild Bloom (Bluome diu wilde, Salvasch florie) Home of Duke Ehcunaver in *Titurel*.

Wildenberg (Wildenberc) Castle. Possibly Burg Wildenberg near Wolframs-Eschenbach.

Wissant (Wîzsant) Channel port between Boulogne and Calais.

Wolfhart Reckless warrior in the *Nibelungenlied*.

Zambron (Zambrôn) Land of Count Plineschanz, defeated by Parzival.

Zaroaster (Zarôastêr) King of Araby, in Feirefiz's retinue.

Zazamanc Kingdom of Belacane.

Zval (Zvâl) Highest of the planets.

Zyrolan King of Semblidac, defeated by Parzival.

The Grail and Arthurian Dynasties

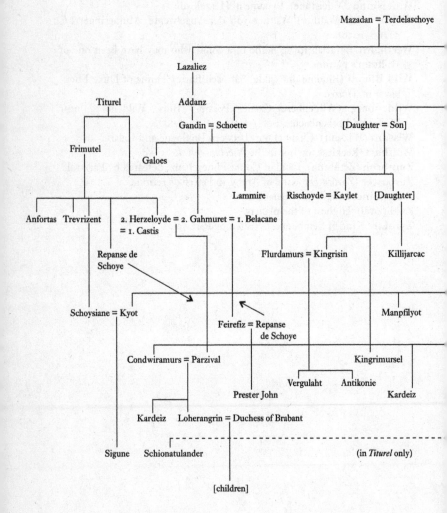

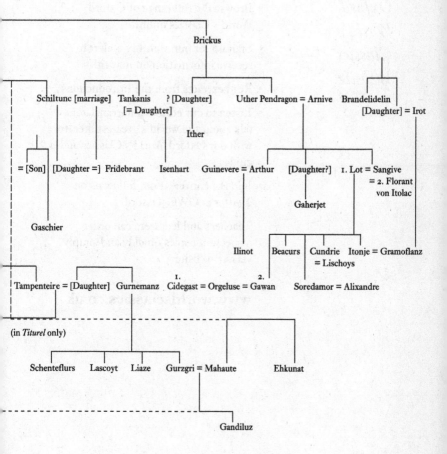

American Literature

British and Irish Literature

Children's Literature

Classics and Ancient Literature

Colonial Literature

Eastern Literature

European Literature

Gothic Literature

History

Medieval Literature

Oxford English Drama

Poetry

Philosophy

Politics

Religion

The Oxford Shakespeare

A complete list of Oxford World's Classics, including Authors in Context, Oxford English Drama, and the Oxford Shakespeare, is available in the UK from the Marketing Services Department, Oxford University Press, Great Clarendon Street, Oxford OX2 6DP, or visit the website at www.oup.com/uk/worldsclassics.

In the USA, visit www.oup.com/us/owc for a complete title list.

Oxford World's Classics are available from all good bookshops. In case of difficulty, customers in the UK should contact Oxford University Press Bookshop, 116 High Street, Oxford OX1 4BR.

Travel Writing 1700–1830

Women's Writing 1778–1838

JAMES BOSWELL   Life of Johnson

FRANCES BURNEY   Cecilia
                       Evelina

JOHN CLELAND   Memoirs of a Woman of Pleasure

DANIEL DEFOE   A Journal of the Plague Year
                       Moll Flanders
                       Robinson Crusoe

HENRY FIELDING   Jonathan Wild
                       Joseph Andrews and Shamela
                       Tom Jones

WILLIAM GODWIN   Caleb Williams

OLIVER GOLDSMITH   The Vicar of Wakefield

ELIZABETH INCHBALD   A Simple Story

SAMUEL JOHNSON   The History of Rasselas

ANN RADCLIFFE   The Italian
                       The Mysteries of Udolpho

SAMUEL RICHARDSON   Pamela

TOBIAS SMOLLETT   The Adventures of Roderick Random
                       The Expedition of Humphry Clinker

LAURENCE STERNE   The Life and Opinions of Tristram
                           Shandy, Gentleman
                       A Sentimental Journey

JONATHAN SWIFT   Gulliver's Travels
                       A Tale of a Tub and Other Works

HORACE WALPOLE   The Castle of Otranto

MARY WOLLSTONECRAFT   Mary and The Wrongs of Woman
                       A Vindication of the Rights of Woman